"A nifty comb... ...tasy. Not too ...basement for ...erage law enfo...

...ooselling author

"Rowland's world of arcane magic and demons is fresh and original . . . [and her] characters are well-developed and distinct. . . . Dark, fast-paced, and gripping.   —SciFiChick

"A fascinating mixture of a hard-boiled police procedural and gritty yet other-worldly urban fantasy. Diana Rowland's professional background as both a street cop and forensic assistant not only shows through but gives the book a realism sadly lacking in all too many urban fantasy 'crime' novels."
        —L. E. Modesitt, Jr., author of the *Saga of Recluse*

"Diana Rowland has built a fascinating and compelling urban fantasy series, with main character Kara as tough as she needs to be yet vulnerable enough to be realistic."
        —Fresh Fiction

"Rowland once again writes the perfect blend of police procedural and paranormal fantasy."
        —Night Owl Paranormal

"Phenomenal world building, a tough yet vulnerable heroine, a captivating love triangle, and an increasingly compelling metanarrative that just gets juicier with each book. . . . Blows most other urban fantasies out of the park."
        —All Things Urban Fantasy

"Yet again, Diana Rowland has knocked my socks off with a stellar book that left me positively desperate for more."
        —A Book Obsession

"*Mark of the Demon* crosses police procedure with weird magic. Diana Rowland's background makes her an expert in the former, and her writing convinces me she's also an expert in the latter in this fast-paced story that ends with a bang."
        —Carrie Vaughn, *New York Times* bestselling author

FURY OF THE
DEMON

DIANA ROWLAND

DAW BOOKS, INC.

DONALD A. WOLLHEIM, FOUNDER

375 Hudson Street, New York, NY 10014

ELIZABETH R. WOLLHEIM
SHEILA E. GILBERT
PUBLISHERS

www.dawbooks.com

First Printing, January 2014
1 2 3 4 5 6 7 8 9

DAW TRADEMARK REGISTERED
U.S. PAT. AND TM. OFF. AND FOREIGN COUNTRIES
—MARCA REGISTRADA
HECHO EN U.S.A.

PRINTED IN THE U.S.A.

To Jack and Anna.

Chapter 1

I clung to the pain like a badge of honor. Blood dripped in a slow splatter from a deep gash in my forearm, and my left knee throbbed from a vicious twist, but I couldn't suppress my grin. I dragged my sleeve across my face to clear some of the sweat and grime, and squinted at the massive demon who crouched beside the white trunks of grove trees a dozen feet across the clearing. Two blue-white splodges of arcane potency writhed on his chest like knots of electrified worms where my rounds had struck. That had to sting.

"Well played," Gestamar rumbled as he stretched his leathery wings wide then folded them close. He bared wicked fangs, bright white against the rich bronze of his heavy-featured bestial face. "You have been practicing."

"Every single day," I replied. It was the first time I'd won in nearly four months of games, and it felt damn good. "Games" with Gestamar—the demonic lord Mzatal's essence-bound *reyza*—were like a combination of hide and seek, tackle football without pads, and hunting, all while trying to reach and defuse a bomb that happened to be on the other side of a kick-your-ass obstacle course from hell.

Not that we were in hell or anything remotely like it. This world, known simply as the "demon realm," was about as far from the Earth concept of hell as a rain forest was from an oil refinery.

And as much as it sucked to get battered, bloodied, and knocked on my ass, I remained grateful for every scenario he ran with me. Whether here or back on Earth, I needed all the training and conditioning I could get—physical, mental, and arcane. My background as a cop and demon summoner would only get me so far with the kind of enemies I had: Rhyzkahl, Jesral, Amkir, and Kadir—four demonic lords dubbed by Lord Seretis as the *Mraztur*, which loosely translated as "motherfucking asshole dickwad defilers."

The designation fit perfectly.

Those four were bound and determined to either forge me into their tool or kill me trying. Too bad I had other ideas.

I wiped blood from the Glock with a relatively clean corner of my shirt and jammed it into its holster at the small of my back. Technically it wasn't a Glock at all, but a masterfully wrought demon knock-off with weight and action near indistinguishable from the real deal—invaluable for training since my gun was an integral part of both offense and defense on Earth. Ammunition made of resin casings, gunpowder, and potency pellets—an ingenious creation of Mzatal's—turned the thing into what I lovingly called my potency paintball gun. The option to include my cop weapon-training in live fire scenarios rocked.

"You endure much for Idris," Gestamar said and swept a clawed hand over his chest several times to clear the residue of the potency strikes.

"He'd do the same for me." My jaw clenched. Like me, Idris Palatino was a summoner—a human with the ability to open a portal between Earth and this world, the demon realm. Moreover, he was Mzatal's protégé, utterly brilliant, and a damn nice guy who I was proud to call friend.

But four months ago, I'd inadvertently almost destroyed the demon realm during a ritual to retrieve Vsuhl—one of the three essence blades. And, when the dust cleared, Idris was gone—kidnapped by the fucking asshole Mraztur.

"We'll be going after him soon, and I intend to be ready." I straightened my shoulders. "But it's not just for Idris. When I get back to Earth, I have family and friends to protect."

Gestamar grunted and dropped his eyes to my arm. "Your wound requires care. Do you wish me to bind it?"

I looked down and grimaced. A shallow jagged gash from one of Gestamar's claws ran from elbow to wrist on the outside of my forearm. "The bleeding has pretty much stopped," I said. "I'll get Mzatal to fix it, but you have my thanks for the offer."

Gestamar stood, towering over me by several feet. He bared his teeth in the scary demon equivalent of a smile. "Again, well played," he said, then bounded toward me and leapt into flight at the last instant.

I ducked and covered my head, instinctively shielding myself from the strong downdraft of his wings. "Thanks!" I called after him. The windblast carried the bold musky spice scent of a reyza after exertion, much more pleasant than the human equivalent. I sniffed my pits and gave a disgusted shudder. First, find Mzatal for a little damage repair, then a long soak in the bath.

Fortunately, we'd ended the action in the grove, which was only a few minutes walk from the palace. A couple of hours earlier, we were far afield in the eastern hills, and it would've been a long limp home.

Sunlight filtered through the brilliant purple and green leaves of the canopy, danced over the white trunks and onto the short, soft grass of the clearing. Ahead of me, two parallel lines of trees formed a tunnel that led out of the clearing and toward the palace. I released a soft sigh of ease and allowed myself a moment of serenity as the grove's presence wrapped around me like a comforting hug. The groves formed a network of organic teleportation nodes, with one in each realm of the eleven demonic lords and about a dozen or so more scattered across the planet. My intuitive connection to the special trees baffled the lords, and though it felt perfectly natural to me, I had no logical explanation for it either.

Not that I was complaining. It was a damn powerful connection to have.

As I limped toward the tunnel, a tailless flash of orange, white, and black darted past me and disappeared into the trees. Fuzzykins, Eilahn's cat. Her presence meant that my awesome *syraza* bodyguard was somewhere nearby. Not that she was ever far.

As if in response to my thought, Eilahn approached through the trees. Here in the demon realm, she kept her syraza form—long-limbed with graceful bird-like fragility, gorgeous pearly iridescent skin and delicate wings that looked too flimsy to be of use. The perfect example of how looks could be deceiving. There wasn't a damn thing fragile about her. On Earth she took the form of a human woman

in order to blend in, though the form she chose was *smokin'
hot chick*. She drew a fair amount of attention with her
looks, though admittedly less than wings and three-fingered
hands would.

"You are victorious," she said, her large violet eyes shining with pride.

I beamed, still basking in the warm glow of triumph. "I
am! I was done, exhausted, and then faked a face plant—
which must've been convincing, because Gestamar swooped
down for the kill. I twisted around and nailed him twice,
point blank. It was *sweeeet*."

"Sweet, yes, for the victory," she said in the beautifully
musical syraza tones that brought birdsong and meditation
chimes to mind. She eyed me critically, touched my
wounded arm then dipped her head toward my knee. "Injured nearly to immobility." Displeasure touched her elegant, humanoid features. "Not good."

"Got my foot wedged between some roots," I told her,
looking down at the swelling. "I turned, my foot didn't, and
my knee paid the price. It wasn't pretty." It actually hurt like
blazes, but if I'd been back on Earth my big worry would
have been whether the damage was repairable and if it
would need surgery and how long I'd have to do physical
therapy in order to walk properly again and how much it
would end up costing me. I smiled to myself. Pain was easier
to handle when a bit of time with a favorably disposed demonic lord would make it good as new. Best healthcare plan
ever.

I flashed a grin. "Even with the bum knee, I still managed to make it through the tree tunnel, drop Gestamar,
and unweave the wards before they blew."

All jubilation drained away as a cold presence like an
exhalation from a tomb washed over me. I recognized the
feel, sought its source, and hoped I was wrong.

But I wasn't. Lord Kadir glided toward us from the tree
tunnel entrance. Androgynous golden-haired beauty and
violet eyes were wasted on the lord I'd mentally dubbed
Creepshow. An icy half-smile played on his lips as his gaze
slid over Eilahn then fixed on me with predatory intensity.
I'd only been this close to him once, at Rhyzkahl's palace,
before the betrayal. Once in a lifetime was more than
enough.

Like a phantom, Eilahn melted into the forest. I hoped it was to go warn Mzatal that one of the Mraztur was here unchallenged.

Kadir's aura saturated me, like a dozen psychopaths all merged into one. Instinctively I summoned grove power, cloaked myself in it and shielded my thoughts from the innate mind reading ability of the lords. "What are you doing here?" I managed, thoroughly pissed that his feel alone set me shaking.

He stopped two paces from me. "Whatever I choose, Kara Gillian," he purred.

That sure as hell wasn't an answer to ease my mind. I mentally reached for Mzatal. We shared a deep connection beyond words—like an emotional telepathy—but right now I felt him in the plexus chamber, deeply absorbed in his work with the planetary arcane flows. Damn it.

"Get the hell out of here," I snarled. Kadir was a demonic lord with firepower beyond my normal ability to counter, but right now we were in the grove, and this was *my* turf.

He leaned closer, spoke with slow, deliberate menace. "I depart because I choose to do so, not at your mandate, little morsel."

"I'm not stopping you." I stepped aside, swept my arm in a *Don't let the door hit you in the ass on the way out* gesture.

Fuzzykins chose that moment to stalk out of the trees beside Kadir, tail straight up in the air and pregnant belly making her look as if she'd swallowed a Chihuahua. I silently willed the silly animal to get the hell away from here before Something Bad happened, but to my dismay she wound around his ankles and rubbed against his boots. "Mrrrrow?"

I gaped. Seriously? *Seriously?* The cat hated me but liked *him?*

Kadir let out a laugh that sent splinters of unease through me, then crouched and ran his hand over Fuzzykins back. She responded with loud purring and a head butt as he slid his hand around her neck, rubbed.

Blood pounded in my ears. *If you hurt that stupid cat . . .* I called to the grove, pulled more of its potency to me. I'd nearly killed Rhyzkahl with grove energy once. I knew its potential.

Kadir went still, then lifted eyes that shone with focused intensity to mine. "Do it," he murmured, and the challenge cut as clearly as if he'd screamed it. His lips parted with anticipation, and he closed his hand around the cat's neck, though not yet hard enough to cause her alarm.

"Kara, no," Eilahn said with force as she stepped from the trees. "He cannot—will not—harm Fuzzykins."

Kadir's mouth pinched together in annoyance as though his day had just been ruined. He released the cat and stood smoothly. His gaze swept over Eilahn then returned to me. "This borders upon a breach."

Eilahn kept her eyes on mine while I struggled to figure out what the weird lord was talking about. "A breach would only occur if I were to speak with one to whom it is not permitted," she said. Though her smile was tight and dangerous, her tone remained utterly conversational, as if describing the puffiness of cumulus clouds. "As I have spoken only to you," she informed me, "no breach has occurred."

Comprehension dawned. Okay, so apparently the two weren't allowed to speak to each other? Were we in third grade?

Whatever the deal was, the moment of tension seemed to be past. "I'm not playing into your bullshit this time, Kadir," I sneered. "You said you were going, now go."

He ran his thumb slowly over his lips as he regarded me, though there was absolutely nothing sexual in the gesture. It was more as though he contemplated sinking his teeth into my flesh, and not in any cool-romantic vampire way either. Like Hannibal Lecter with an extra helping of psycho-sinister.

To my relief and surprise, he dropped his hand and gave a light shrug, inclined his head slightly to me then sauntered past toward the center of the clearing with Fuzzykins trailing him. I watched as he crouched to make the potency offering to the grove and chucked the stupid cat under the chin while she rubbed and purred up against him. Kadir set the pregnant cat aside with an oddly careful gentleness, then straightened, met my eyes, and was gone.

The grove rippled with his departure. I exhaled in relief, then extended into the connection and followed his signature to his realm. "Good fucking riddance," I said to the empty air when I felt him arrive in and then leave his own grove.

Fuzzykins sat where Kadir had placed her and fastidiously cleaned her right front paw in a position that sure as hell looked like she was giving me the finger. "Traitor," I muttered.

"She simply follows her instincts," Eilahn said from behind me.

"Crappy instincts!" I turned on her, annoyed—admittedly, a bit unfairly—to see her relaxed stance. "Why did you leave when he came into the grove? I could have used backup from the beginning."

"I did not wish to risk violating agreements," she stated, "and so I stepped away. I did not intervene until you were close to engaging in a dangerous action." She gave me a faintly reproachful look, and I knew she meant my readiness to use grove power against the skeevy lord.

Eilahn scooped Fuzzykins into her arms and murmured to her in demon as the foul beast hissed at me. "In any event, it seems you did not need backup," she continued calmly. "You are unscathed."

I gave an involuntary shudder. "That's a matter of opinion. I *despise* him. I feel like I've been slimed." I scowled at her. "What was he doing here? Why didn't anyone tell Mzatal?"

Eilahn cocked her head. "Mzatal knew."

"Knew?" I stared at her. "Wait, you mean he knew and was too involved in his work to come out and kick Kadir's ass?"

"No, that is not what I mean," she said. "Do you believe that Fuzzykins will require the services of a veterinary obstetric specialist when it is time to expel her spawn?"

"A veterinary . . . what? No! Jeez, she's just having kittens." I narrowed my eyes. "And stop changing the subject. What *did* you mean?" I suspected she enjoyed messing with me.

"Simply that Kadir was here under agreement, and therefore Mzatal knew."

"What kind of agreement would he have with that—" I stuttered to a stop as I focused on the tingle of distant grove activation. "I need Mzatal. *Now*." My voice trembled with urgency. "Rhyzkahl and Jesral just used the grove network. They have Idris and someone I couldn't identify with them."

Eilahn shifted from casual to hyperalert-no-nonsense in a heartbeat. She grabbed my wrist and hauled me toward the tree tunnel. "We will find Mzatal."

"No! Wait!" I hop-limped in her grasp, failing every attempt to stop. "I'm staying here. I need to know if they move."

"If they choose to move *here*, you are vulnerable," she stated.

"I can't leave!" I struggled to dig my heels in, but the injured knee didn't want any part of it. "Look, we'll wait at the tunnel entrance," I said, damn near pleading. "I'll still be able to feel if they move, but I won't be right in front of them if they come here. *And* I have the grove potency."

She looked over her shoulder at me, slowed as we neared the arch of trees that marked the boundary to open ground. "Agreed," she said, though her eyes remained narrowed.

"Okay. Good. Thanks." It wasn't often I won an argument with Eilahn. Though this was more of a draw than an actual win.

We finally stopped on the broad step of basalt just past the entrance. Ahead, beyond a grassy ravine, the glass-walled palace hugged the cliff that dropped five hundred feet to the sea. I *reached* for Mzatal again, this time with the mental equivalent of a shoulder shake to get his attention. "C'mon, Boss," I murmured as I repeated the touch, then exhaled in relief as I felt his acknowledgement like a wave of warmth through me.

The air shimmered a few feet in front of me, and Ilana, Mzatal's ptarl—*demahnk* advisor—appeared. Though similar in appearance to Eilahn, Ilana was larger, with definitive characteristics of the demahnk: ridges in the hide of her torso and a subtle vertical ridge on her forehead.

"Mzatal is deeply engaged in the plexus chamber and asks what your need is," she informed me in a chiming voice much like Eilahn's, but with greater complexity of tone.

"Tell him he needs to get *un*engaged," I told her flatly. "Rhyzkahl, Jesral, Idris and someone else just made a grove transfer, and I'm not moving from here in case they go to another location."

Her large, near-luminous violet eyes went distant, and I

knew she was in telepathic communion with Mzatal. After a few seconds she refocused on me. "Which groves?"

"From Jesral's grove to the one on the coast of the southern continent," I said, "then immediately to the one where Mzatal brought me when he was going to remove Rhyzkahl's mark."

She inclined her head in acknowledgment and silently relayed my message while I fidgeted and waited impatiently for the reply.

It had only been a little over six months since Mzatal had succeeded in summoning me against my will from Earth, but the time before then seemed like a completely different life. And in a lot of ways it was. Back then I thought I had some sort of real agreement with Rhyzkahl, believed he had honor, even if self-serving. My eyes were forced open by his treachery—the evidence of which covered my torso in hideously beautiful scars, sigils Rhyzkahl had carved onto me with Xhan, his own essence blade.

Everything changed that day. I wasn't the same person anymore. Couldn't be. Not and survive to protect those around me.

Ilana laid a gentle three-fingered hand on my shoulder. "He is anchoring the strands in the plexus now. I will bring him." She vanished before I could thank her.

The itch to *do* something intensified with the waiting, but I ruthlessly shoved down the impulse to make the transfer to the distant grove and do some preliminary recon. Instead, I pygahed—mentally tracing the soothing *pygah* sigil in an effort to gain calm and aid concentration.

Nope, still antsy. The purely mental version of the pygah was a great way to quickly chill, but I wanted and needed every scrap of focus I could muster. With fluid motion, I traced the glowing sigil in the air before me and breathed in the energy. Instantly, I felt my tension ease. Yeah, that was the good stuff.

Echoes of the four recent travelers remained, but attempts to sense beyond the boundaries of the other grove failed. Like reaching an island and being able to walk every inch of it, yet unable to see anything beyond its shores but foggy sea.

My scars tingled as I felt Xhan, and a shudder ran through me. I knew without a doubt that Rhyzkahl held the *rakkuhr*-tainted essence blade even now. Millennia ago, Mzatal created the three blades—Khatur, Xhan, and Vsuhl—for himself, Rhyzkahl, and Szerain. For ages the triumvirate held unshakable dominion over the demon realm.

Something happened to break up their little power bloc, but I had yet to put the pieces of that puzzle together.

Ilana appeared before me with Mzatal. Elegant and broad-shouldered, he had lustrous black hair woven into a thick complex braid that hung to the small of his back. His eyes—piercing silver-grey set in a face with an oriental cast—met mine, while both his expression and his aura radiated dark intensity.

"We have to go *now*," I urged as he moved to me, but instead of agreeing he dropped to a crouch and wrapped his hands around my knee.

"Some repair first, *zharkat*," he said, and I felt his focus like a flow of warmth over me as he assessed my injuries. "I have sent word to Elofir and await his confirmation that he has readied his plexus chamber for monitoring our activities and those of the Mraztur." Elofir, another of the eleven demonic lords, was a frequent visitor and one with whom Mzatal was damn near friendly.

"I'm okay," I insisted. "I can walk. We don't want to lose them." Though even as I said it, I had to admit that being mobile was way smarter.

Unruffled, he lifted his head, fixed his eyes on mine. "Precisely. With your information, Elofir may well be able to isolate Idris's strand and lock onto it. Invaluable in the event we do not recover him now," he explained.

It was what we'd been seeking for months, yet every time we grew close, the Mraztur used the vile potency *rakkuhr* to thwart our efforts, and moved Idris—much like how I'd used the arcane-nullifying cuff on Earth to avoid being summoned to the demon realm. For Mzatal to leave such an important task to Elofir spoke volumes of the trust he placed in the other demonic lord. Trust, or an airtight agreement.

Searing heat blossomed in my knee and thigh as Mzatal worked an intense and rapid healing. I sucked in a breath, bit down on a curse as he shifted his hands to my arm and eased the pain of the gash.

A syraza passed overhead, made a tight circle then

swooped down to land gracefully. Steeev, whose name—
with the drawn out *eee* sound—had quite amused me the
first time I heard it. Slightly larger than Eilahn, he crouched
beside her and waited silently for Mzatal to finish his work
on me. A few seconds later Gestamar swept down and settled behind Mzatal. Our strike team, ready to go.

A message sigil of glowing gold and amber appeared beside us, and I recognized a twist of potency at the bottom as
Elofir's signature. Mzatal lifted one hand from my arm and
touched the sigil, but a heartbeat later his implacable intensity degraded into a dark scowl. He dissipated the sigil with
a violent sweep of his arm. "He has isolated Idris, but there
is interference again, and he cannot get a lock."

"What does that mean?" I asked, flexing my knee exper-
imentally. "We go as is?"

Mzatal stroked his hand over my arm in a final gesture of
healing, then stood, traced out a message and sent it off. "We
have no other option. If we can determine the source of the
interference and eliminate it, Elofir may still be successful."

"But if we get Idris back now, it's a moot point, right?"

He took my hand, strode toward the center of the grove
with long strides that made me thankful my knee only muttered now rather than screamed. "You are correct," he said.
"Having a link to him through a strand lock is valuable
should he slip from us. Best to assure he does not." He released my hand and prepared to make the potency offering
to the grove, then stopped and looked to me. "It is more
expedient if you make the transfer."

Right. Other than myself, only the lords and the
demahnk could activate the grove transportation. However,
the grove required no offering from me—yet another part
of my lord-confounding grove connection.

I gripped his hand again, found the destination we
sought, then asked the grove to take our group there.

The trees around us shifted subtly in position. Different
trees, different grove. Soft light of an overcast sky filtered
through the purple and green leaves, and warm, humid air
carried an acrid tinge.

Mzatal lifted his chin, assessing the area nearby for signs
of activity. A heartbeat later his grip tightened on my hand,
and he strode toward the tree tunnel, anger flashing in his
eyes.

"What's going on?" I asked as I tried to keep up.

Vehemence laced the word as he spoke it. "Ritual."

"Wait!" I tugged him to a stop halfway down the tunnel while Eilahn, Steeev, and Gestamar continued on. "We need a plan," I told him. "Or at least *I* need a plan since I can't go in throwing potency spikes."

Mzatal laid his free hand against my cheek. "Forgive me, beloved," he said. "You are correct. Steeev has gone to gather what information he can, but while we wait for his return I can share what I have assessed of this." He caressed my grimy cheek with his thumb. "Rhyzkahl and Jesral are with Idris, approximately ten miles from here, and are stationary. The other you sensed but could not identify is Katashi."

Isumo Katashi. Once Mzatal's marked summoner, and now a traitorous ally of the Mraztur. And no way had they walked ten miles in the few minutes since they arrived, which meant either Jesral's ptarl agreed to provide transport or they had syraza with them. The demahnk could teleport multiple people long distances, while a mature syraza had the ability to make short teleportation hops with a single person. Now I understood why Mzatal had asked Steeev to come with us. "What kind of ritual?"

He took my hand again and continued down the tree tunnel. "It is odd. I sense a nexus that should not be here, and therefore suspect they have located a natural potency confluence and created a rudimentary nexus." A nexus was a focal point of power—like a massive arcane generator that could supercharge a ritual laid atop it. Mzatal's eyes went briefly distant as he continued to monitor. "A dual ritual." His mouth tightened. "Possibly to conduct an Earth transfer."

To send Idris to Earth. Far easier to hide him there. "And they developed a nexus out here to keep you from finding out what they were up to," I noted.

We stepped out of the tree tunnel, and the source of the acrid tang became apparent. The grove stood in the center of a charred area the size of a football field. Though verdant rainforest hugged the perimeter, not a single blade of grass or touch of color broke the blacks and grays of the sea of ash. Remnants of potency writhed on its surface like dying worms, and a graceful pavilion of pale stone columns glimmered at the fringe, as if uncovered by whatever had nuked the forest.

Could this be a remnant of the cataclysm? A few hundred years earlier, a summoner by the name of Elinor had performed a ritual with the demonic lord Szerain. For reasons still unknown, the ritual collapsed and global catastrophic destruction ensued—earthquakes, volcanoes, rains of fiery acid, tsunamis, you name it. Moreover, the ways between the demon realm and Earth slammed shut and had remained so until early in Earth's twentieth century.

But I had a personal stake in all that ancient history. During the ritual, Szerain stabbed Elinor with the essence blade Vsuhl, killed her, and trapped her essence in the blade—again, for reasons still unknown. Yet somehow, a chunk of her memories and emotions latched on to my own essence, and during my first months in the demon realm I experienced a number of odd dreams and weird *déjà vu* experiences, all of which stopped when I retrieved Vsuhl. Perhaps coincidence, but still, another mystery amongst so many others.

I'd been around remnants of the cataclysm before. At Szerain's palace a crater the size of a small city lay not far to the northeast, and a rift still spewed gouts of arcane flame. In Rhyzkahl's realm, part of a mountain range looked as if a planet-devouring monster had taken a ragged bite. But the devastation before me now felt newer . . . and disquietingly familiar.

I licked dry lips. "What happened here?"

Mzatal's grip tightened almost imperceptibly on my hand, but he remained silent.

I searched his face. "Mzatal? What is it?"

"It is a flash burn," he said quietly, focus remaining straight ahead.

I swept my gaze around again. Freshly disturbed ash nearby marked where Rhyzkahl and those with him had passed. Centuries-old char would surely have settled more. "This didn't happen all that long ago," I observed.

"No. Not long. Months." Mzatal's gaze followed Gestamar as the reyza leapt into flight.

I took in the magnitude of the destruction, felt the ripples of arcane residue, unable to deny that it felt like . . . "Mzatal?" My voice quavered for an instant before I controlled it. "Tell me what happened here."

He continued to watch Gestamar. "I caused it. I unleashed flash potency."

I stared at him, shocked and baffled. "Why?"

Mzatal's eyes dropped to mine. "Because when you escaped me and used the grove to flee to Rhyzkahl, I . . ." He paused, jaw tightening. "Rather than taking you by force from the reyza Pyrenth, I retreated. I lost you not only due to your cleverness, but because of my adherence to agreements subsequently ignored by Rhyzkahl." Remembered pain flashed silver in his eyes. "I vented my rage."

I shifted close and rested my cheek against his chest. "I'm sorry," I murmured.

Mzatal wrapped his arms around me. "I cannot allow myself to lose control thus again."

I sensed the turmoil within him, held him close. "I will try very hard not to be so unspeakably clever again."

A quick laugh escaped him, and I felt some of the tension ease away. "Impossible," he said, then cradled my face between his hands and kissed me.

I returned the kiss and did my best to conceal how gobsmacked I was at the amount of power it must have required to wreak this much devastation, pushed down the quick flare of *Holy shit, I'm dating a demigod, what the hell?*

"Well, if this demonic lord gig doesn't work out for you," I said with a smile, "I can hire you out to clear cropland."

Amusement touched his mouth. "An interesting proposition, zharkat."

"Just something to keep in mind."

Chapter 2

A touch like a brush of leaves caressed me as the grove activated. "Someone's coming," I told Mzatal, then scowled. "Amkir." One of the Mraztur. King of the assholes.

Mzatal growled a curse. "He will be a thorn in our side if we do not turn him away now."

"Then we'd best kick his ass quickly so we can get on with our business," I advised with a tight smile.

"Agreed." His expression darkened with annoyance over the distraction. With me at his side, he strode toward the stand of white-trunked trees. Ten yards from the grove he stopped, took a wide stance and coalesced a glowing ball of potency in his right palm.

I prepared to trace the sigils and direct the flows that would augment his attack, should it come to that. I no longer traced a standard summoner support diagram to feed him potency. We'd become a team, unique, communicating without words or even direct thought, in more of a unified awareness. All of the *qaztahl*—demonic lords—lacked the ability to create portals, and so I was able to supply those aspects, along with touches of grove energy. As he formed either attack or defense, I wove in flows, added my tweaks, and together we created pure awesomeness.

Amkir emerged from the tree tunnel trailed by a syraza and a venerable-looking reyza. I knew—or at least was pretty sure—we didn't have to worry about the two demons since they all tended to stay out of any direct conflict with the demonic lords. Sometimes the demons would fight amongst themselves for their "side," though I had yet to figure out the dynamics, and their explanations of the rules left me baffled. It was easiest to let them do their thing and not try to make sense of it.

Hard-faced, with dark eyes and a slightly olive complexion, Amkir came to a sharp halt at the sight of Mzatal. His confident smirk slipped into a scowl, but then he lifted his chin and squared his shoulders. "I have no business with you, Mzatal."

Mzatal's aura flared with menace. He swept his hand up to send potency in a scintillating veil to block the entrance to the tree tunnel. "If you travel with your syraza to your *allies*," he snarled the word, "I will hunt you, and I *will* hurt you."

The native potency flowed around us, appearing in my othersight as rivulets of varicolored light that spiderwebbed through a faintly luminescent mist. I chose the strands I needed and called them to me, then wove them into enhancements for our shield, smiling in fierce satisfaction as the arcane barrier settled solidly into place. Mzatal wasn't about to let Amkir retreat only to return once we'd gone for Idris.

Amkir glowered and clenched his fists at his sides. He knew Mzatal could and would carry out his threat. "Why block the grove then? Do you wish to entertain yourself and your slut by attacking me with no provocation?" His disdainful gaze slid to me, then back to Mzatal. "Or does she revel in carnage? Do the screams of others make her wet?"

Mzatal slowly opened his right hand. I felt the power build. "You will agree to depart and not return to this hemisphere for half a day," he stated.

Amkir dropped his eyes to Mzatal's hand and he took a step back, fear marring his expression for an instant before Totally Pissed Off took its place. "No," he said through gritted teeth. "I will depart for half a day *if* you agree to stay any attack on me."

"You will depart via the grove within fifty-five heartbeats," Mzatal pronounced as he continued to draw power. "You will not return to this hemisphere for half a day. Unless you take aggressive action, I will stay any attack on you for fifty-five heartbeats, beginning . . . now."

"Agreed," Amkir snapped, clearly not happy that the

countdown had already begun. "I will depart and pass my time imagining myself deeply buried in your *chikdah*."

Oh, dude, did you ever say the wrong thing. Mzatal was already in a pissy mood, plus he had a few minutes to kill while we waited for Steeev.

Looked like he was going to kill more than time. Okay, maybe just damage. A lot.

"Well worth imagining," Mzatal said, "and a pleasure you will never have."

Amkir didn't seem to notice that Mzatal had yet to drop the shield, and I allowed myself a silent chortle. I knew damn well Mzatal had fully intended to allow Amkir to leave—right up until the point the scowly-faced lord made his *chikdah* comment, a word which translated best as "cunt."

Feeling safe for the remainder of the countdown, Amkir turned his gaze on me and licked his lips. "When you are with Rhyzkahl again, I will have my time with you, little whore." I gave him a bored look, which served nicely to rile him up more. "You will beg for the mercy of my cock in your throat rather than all else I have planned for you," he sneered. With a final smirk, Amkir turned to depart then froze as he realized the shield still blocked the grove entrance. He glanced over his shoulder, a hint of panic in his eyes. "Drop the barrier, Mzatal, and I will depart as agreed."

"As it is not an attack, it is not included in our agreement," Mzatal informed him, then narrowed his eyes. "For utter clarity, that which you speak to my zharkat, you speak to me, Amkir." He uttered the name with dark menace. "Kara Gillian does not beg. *Nor do I.*" He shaped the potency already gathered, drew in more. "Two heartbeats."

Amkir spun to face us again and hastily traced protections, but the *Oh Fuck* look on his face told me he knew they'd be woefully inadequate.

Moving faster than thought, Mzatal swept his hands in a complicated pattern that stripped Amkir's weak shielding, then followed it with a dazzling blue net of potency that blanketed the hapless lord in crackling arcane bindings.

The syraza stepped back and the old reyza pulled his wings in close as Amkir gave a strangled cry and dropped to his knees. Face contorted in pain, he collapsed to his back, jerking in the glowing net. It was meant to simply hurt him and not damage him, I knew. Well, not *long term* damage at least. Dumbass. If he'd kept his mouth shut, he could've left unscathed.

Mzatal dissipated the shield over the tree tunnel. "Have you more to say to us?" he asked the downed lord. After a moment of no answer except labored gasps and choked whimpers, Mzatal released the net and inclined his head to the reyza. "Honored one, please depart with Amkir in accordance with our agreement, as you witnessed."

The reyza rumbled assent and moved forward to scoop up the lolling Amkir. Mzatal turned away, took my hand and strode toward Steeev, who'd returned from his reconnaissance while we were occupied with Amkir.

Eilahn joined us as Steeev gave his brief report: Rhyzkahl and Jesral were already engaged in the ritual process, and Idris wasn't the only human they were sending back to Earth. Katashi was in the ritual as well.

"We are out of time," Mzatal said. "As soon as Amkir recovers enough, he will warn Rhyzkahl that we are coming. We must go now and stop the process."

Steeev laid his hand on Mzatal's shoulder even as Eilahn laid hers on mine.

"With you, Boss," I murmured.

Mzatal brushed my cheek with his fingertips, then gave a nod to Steeev. In the next heartbeat the world dropped away, then surged back up again in a different location.

It took me a few seconds to get my bearings as we arrived, but Mzatal already had his essence blade, Khatur, in one hand as he traced glowing strike enhancements with the other. The nexus was little more than a cleared and well-trampled circle in the rainforest with eleven stones, of about my height, evenly spaced around its perimeter. Idris and Katashi crouched in the center, and filling the space between the two men and the stones were more than a dozen concentric rings of ignited, floating sigils. Like strands of colored light woven into intricate patterns, the sigils drifted from ground-level to chest height, some pulsing light to dark, and others simply shimmering. By the degree of activation, I knew the ritual was well underway.

Idris had his back to us, and though I couldn't see any ropes or bindings, I knew there were more subtle ways in which he might be restrained. Katashi faced our way and fixed his gaze on Mzatal. The old summoner had two hands again, I noted. Mzatal had sliced one off during Katashi's failed attempt to snatch me for the Mraztur, but obviously one of the lords had decided to grow it back. Bully for him.

On the far side of the nexus, Rhyzkahl, tall, blond, and angelically beautiful, traced completion sigils with hurried, though precise, gestures. Jesral worked feverishly beside him to direct the energies toward the center of the ritual and initiate the transfer. Jesral's keen eyes flicked our way once, sharp features betraying only confidence. Slim and dark-haired, he reminded me of a male model, though not the hunky kind. He'd be the model wearing the purple velvet suit and slouching oh-so-perfectly in a wingback chair while an unlit cigarette dangled from between two fingers.

I sank into my connection with Mzatal, felt his purpose then captured and wove elusive strands from the flows to enhance his tracings with my personal touches. But my eyes were on Idris. As though feeling our presence, he glanced back over his shoulder, and my heart lurched at the haunted look on his face as he met my eyes.

A translucent silver-blue cylinder of power snapped into existence around Idris and Katashi—Mzatal's creation, designed to delay the ritual for as long as possible. Without his intervention it would finalize in a matter of seconds, sending both Idris and Katashi to who-the-hell-knew-where on Earth.

Mzatal's intention flowed clearly through our connection. *Disrupt the ritual without damaging Idris.* I quickly traced sigils to augment his containment cylinder as I searched for weak spots in the sigil patterns.

There. Between the second and third rings, a link wavered as though its bounding sigils had been hastily set. I "showed" Mzatal the weakness, but to my dismay I realized he couldn't exploit it. He needed all of his focus and power to hold the shield that slowed the ritual, and had nothing to spare to make a strike.

I felt his frustration mingle with mine as the ritual built to a throbbing crescendo. "Five heartbeats, zharkat," he said through gritted teeth. Cursing, I desperately sought a solution. *Four.* I had my not-a-Glock, but that wouldn't be enough to even put a ripple in it. It would be like using paintballs to try and stop a charging crack addict.

Three. Beside me Mzatal trembled with the stress of holding the shield. Beyond the diagram Rhyzkahl bared his teeth in a triumphant smile, lifted his blade and gave Mzatal a mocking salute.

That was it. I *knew* a way to exploit the weakness.

Two. The rings flared, and there was no time left to consult with Mzatal. With his attention so intensely focused on holding Idris, he'd never be able to read my intention in time to respond.

I slammed closed my connection to the grove, jerked my hand into the air and called Szerain's essence blade to me.

Vsuhl coalesced in my hand for the first time since I'd nearly caused a second cataclysm during its retrieval. During that ritual my grove power had melded with the blade's with no ill effect, but the addition of *rakkuhr*—the foul potency utilized by the Mraztur—had catalyzed the other two powers into an uncontrollable force that had nearly ripped the world apart.

I really didn't want to repeat that experience, hence the decision to cut myself off from the grove before calling the blade. Safety first, and all that.

The blade's potency flooded me, sharp and fierce, but I had no time to revel in it. I tightened my grip on the hilt and united its power with that of Mzatal's blade.

Mzatal faltered in shocked surprise, entire body jerking as if he'd brushed a live wire. Yet his loss of focus lasted only an instant, and he quickly recovered to weave the combined blade potencies into the strike. I focused on the weak spot in the rings, but instead of sending potency directly toward the ritual, he simply thrust his hand palm down toward the ground.

Nothing happened.

One.

Even Jesral shot us a look of *What the fuck?* His eyes came to rest on Vsuhl, and his hands ceased to work the potency. Hunger and desire and avarice flowed from him. Holy shit did he ever want this blade.

Zero. I sucked in a breath as I felt it, and in the next instant Mzatal's strike burst from the ground in a blinding flash beneath the weak spot of the rings.

The cylinder turned into a seething vortex of potency. Katashi screamed as a surge threw him from the center to land in a crumpled heap almost twenty feet left of the perimeter. Idris cried out in pain, then hunched in on himself as if clinging to the center.

I held Vsuhl, focused the power as I sought a way to extract him from the still active ritual. As soon as the vortex dropped, anyone still in that center would go to Earth. And with the ritual damaged, I had a feeling it wouldn't be a fun experience.

"Idris," I breathed, and in that moment I was right beside him—part of the vortex, yet untouched by it. "Idris."

He looked up at the vortex—at me—tortured desperation in his eyes as he clutched the ritual strands together, repaired them. "Kara . . . no," he choked out. "I need to go. *Have* to let them send me. Please. Stop."

He's been manipulated, I thought with sick rage. An extension of the mind reading ability of the lords, manipulation involved altering memories, attitudes, motivations, or damn near anything else an inventive lord could dream up. In a summoner, such tampering drastically decreased their effectiveness, yet I couldn't come up with any other explanation for why he resisted our help. Mzatal continued his efforts to unwind the diagram, but with Idris holding the ritual from the center, I didn't see how we could extract him without damaging him profoundly.

"It's going to be all right," I told Idris.

Closing his eyes, he shook his head, then pulled the strands and was gone.

I yelled a curse and dove forward, both physically and arcanely, to catch a portal strand. I closed my grip around one right before it slithered through.

Idris, crumpled on his side on a cement floor. A man's hand on his shoulder. A ring on the middle finger—dual stones, dark red and onyx, set in intricate gold filigree.

Mzatal's frustration and anger filled our connection, and the strand flashed and disintegrated as he sent a seething blast of power into the ritual. The sigil rings shattered, and I felt Mzatal direct the backlash toward Rhyzkahl and Jesral.

Rhyzkahl staggered back a step but managed to deflect most of it. Jesral wasn't so fortunate and took a direct hit that cast him back hard into the trunk of a tree. Eyes locked on Mzatal, Rhyzkahl stalked into the center of the nexus, likely to replenish potency.

Breathing hard, Jesral shoved away from the tree. His gaze dropped to the blade in my hand, and his face hardened, then in a move like a striking viper he cast an attack at Mzatal.

Mzatal shifted his weight and deflected the strike with an angry flick of his hand. "Send Vsuhl away," he gritted out.

I hesitated, tempted to argue the need for both blades, yet Mzatal's insistence remained firm. Reluctantly, I sent the blade away, even as Mzatal hurled a return volley of jagged potency like stylized lightning. With a determined sweep of both arms, Jesral deflected all but one, staggered and spun as it struck him in the hip.

Mzatal's aura washed over me and tumbled like a raging river of acid toward Jesral, pressing his advantage. His attack followed, in a barrage that knocked the already off-balance Jesral back several feet. Jesral shot a quick look at Rhyzkahl, face shifting to a mixture of anger and outrage as he seemed to realize that Rhyzkahl wasn't planning to help him in his duel with Mzatal. The Mraztur had broken the age old "lords only fight one-on-one" agreement when they sought to prevent me from recovering Vsuhl but, for whatever reason, Rhyzkahl didn't seem willing to do so again.

Continuing to trace and enhance Mzatal's attacks, I glanced at Rhyzkahl. His attention remained fixed on Mzatal, eyes narrowed in what looked like calculated interest. As I watched, he shifted his scrutiny to me and began to trace an odd compact construct with both hands.

Dread coursed through me, and I gave Mzatal a mental nudge. *Rhyzkahl's doing something, Boss,* but to my dismay his response was sluggish, distracted. Snarling, he sent another strike toward Jesral, while I tried harder to get his attention. *Mzatal. Stop attacking Jesral for a second!*

Rhyzkahl's mouth spread in a vulpine smile as whatever he'd formed coalesced into a golf ball-sized creation that seethed orange and red. My dread shifted to full-blown alarm. *Rakkuhr.* Mzatal swiped aside a valiant effort from Jesral and drew power for a blow that would take Jesral down. Rhyzkahl glanced to the fully occupied Mzatal, smirked, then lobbed the tightly wound ball toward me in an underhand throw.

"Boss!" I yelled, eyes widening. Frantically, I tried to pull power from Mzatal's strike to deflect the thing as it expanded and arced toward me like a softball from hell. My alarm finally cut through Mzatal's haze of anger even as he loosed the attack on Jesral. He snapped his focus to me and then to the *rakkuhr*-laced sigil ball as it struck his shields. Its outer layers burned away like a meteor entering the atmosphere, the sigil emerging as a glowing red speck that arrowed toward the center of my chest.

In a fraction of a blink of an eye, Mzatal slammed a wave of power at the speck to deflect it.

Almost deflect it. The thing struck my left deltoid and drove in with a wave of agony utterly at odds with its size. I choked out a cry of pain as the sigil scars on that side of my body erupted in fiery pins and needles.

I felt Mzatal call Eilahn and Steeev to us, then he seized my head in his hands, eyes boring into mine in assessment. Breath hissing, I clutched my shoulder, though the fire in the sigils seemed to be fading. Cursing low, Mzatal released me and turned to focus on Rhyzkahl, who stood with his hands held out in imitation of a non-threatening position, although his expression was positively gleeful and full of satisfaction. Jesral lay sprawled behind him, taken down by Mzatal's last strike.

Rhyzkahl lowered his head. "Rowan." The name dragged razored claws through my mind.

Rowan. The name he'd used when he sought to enthrall me. I shook my head to clear a brief wave of dizziness, then bared my teeth at him. "Kara," I told him. "I'm *Kara.*"

Rhyzkahl ignored my response and moved to Katashi, crouched and laid a hand on the old man. Jesral groaned and tried to roll over, but couldn't manage even that.

Mzatal wrapped an arm around me. "You are Kara," he said firmly.

I dragged my attention back to Mzatal, surprised to see distress in his eyes. "Huh? Oh." I frowned. That sounded right. "Yeah, Kara. I'm Kara." Of course I was Kara. Grimacing, I continued to hold my shoulder. "Shit, that stung."

The two syraza swooped in to land beside us. Rhyzkahl

effortlessly swung Katashi's limp form over his shoulder and stood, then gave an ugly laugh. "She will be your downfall, Mzatal," he called out.

A muscle twitched in Mzatal's jaw, but he swiveled his head to look at Eilahn. "Take her to the grove."

Eilahn hissed in Rhyzkahl's direction as she set her hand on my arm. The world dropped away and reformed, and then we were at the entrance to the tree tunnel. I took a deeper breath as we entered, relieved that the *not quite right* sensation was far less now that I was in the grove.

"What did Rhyzkahl mean by that?" I asked Eilahn, troubled. "How would I be Mzatal's downfall?"

"I do not know," she replied, eyes dark with worry. "Perhaps he believes you distract Mzatal."

Could that be it? I rubbed my shoulder, unsettled, but the arrival of Mzatal and Steeev halted any further musing. Mzatal's face was an unreadable mask as he strode toward us, but to my shock it melted into full-blown concern as he saw me. He gripped my shoulders. "Zharkat," he said, once again giving me an assessing look.

"Let's get out of here," I said, and didn't wait for a reply before asking the grove to take us back to Mzatal's realm.

"Mzatal, I saw Idris after he went through to Earth," I said as soon as we were within the familiar trunks of his grove. "I didn't see much. Cement floor, and there was a man there with a funky ring—gold, with a red stone and a black stone."

He released my shoulders, and I watched him visibly shift his focus from what happened to me and onto Idris. "The summoner who received him?" He lifted a hand, traced a quick message sigil and sent it.

"It had to have been." I rolled my shoulder, grimacing slightly at the residual ache. "Boss, I need to go to Earth to look for him."

To my surprise he shook his head. "No," he said almost absently, eyes focused elsewhere.

"No? Why not?" I frowned at him. "He's on Earth. We sure as hell won't find him from here."

His attention steadied on me, and he took my hand. "Forgive me, zharkat," he said as he headed out of the grove. "I meant not you alone."

I peered up at him as we walked. What the hell was going on with him? I'd never seen him this distracted.

"Right," I said. "Of course. You send me, and then I summon you." I searched his face. "Are you all right?"

"I have asked Elofir to come here," he told me as we exited the tree tunnel. Ilana was there, and beyond her the glass of Mzatal's palace glittered in the afternoon sun. I gazed at the waterfall that tumbled from the cliff beneath the palace to join the sea far below. How had I never noticed the way the spray transformed the light into wavering rainbows?

"To help you prepare a ritual to send me to Earth," I said with a slight nod. "That makes sense." I gazed at the palace. *Those are some seriously nice digs*, I thought in admiration, then blinked as the view shifted to the interior of Mzatal's solarium. Ilana had transported us. I hadn't expected that, but I didn't mind at all that she'd saved us the walk.

Mzatal murmured thanks to his ptarl, then turned to me as she departed. The worry was back in his eyes. "No," he said. "I have asked him to come assess you."

My brow furrowed. "Me? Why?" I moved to an elegant settee, ran my hand over the lustrous wood and marveled at its sheen and the rich depth of the finish. "I hardly feel that zap anymore," I told Mzatal.

"It missed its mark," he said, eyes going to the center of my chest before lifting to my face again, "but it is still quite active. I need perspective, and so I have called for Elofir."

I looked at him sharply. "Active?" All thoughts of wood and polish fled. "What is it doing?"

He moved to me, very lightly touched my sternum. "That is what I will determine with Elofir," he said. "You feel it in the scars, yes?"

Anxiety began to tie clever knots in my stomach. "Well, they burned at first, but that's mostly faded." I felt the tingle of the grove activating. "Elofir's here."

I startled a heartbeat later as he arrived in the room accompanied by Greeyer, his ptarl. Not that there was anything about Elofir I feared. Lithe like a dancer and with a gentle demeanor backed by quiet strength, he carried no hint of threat in his aura, and was the only true pacifist among the lords. Yet the situation had to be pretty serious if it couldn't even wait the five minutes or so it took to walk from the grove.

My heart began to pound unevenly as Mzatal turned to him. "It was an unknown implant wrought with *rakkuhr*," he said without preamble.

A grave expression settled on Elofir's face. "Where did it strike?"

"Her left shoulder," Mzatal replied, "though it was intended for center chest. You will find it easily on assessment." He tugged his hand over his hair in a *very* uncharacteristic show of anxiety.

Elofir looked to me. "With your permission?"

Throat tight, I nodded. "Yes. Yes, of course," I said, eased ever so slightly by the courtesy.

He gestured for me to sit, then dropped to one knee before me when I did so. Immediately I had the hyper-awareness of every single ache or pain or twinge or tickle or itch now that I knew *something* was wrong. Nose itches? Yep, definitely a brain tumor.

He lightly touched my shoulder, then went still. To my surprise—and dismay—Mzatal began to pace.

"How have you felt since it happened?" Elofir asked, voice mild.

I gave Mzatal a worried glance. His obvious distress was starting to seriously freak me out. "I feel fine," I told Elofir, looking back to him. "If anything, I seem to be more aware of stuff around me."

Mzatal stopped pacing abruptly and traced the pygah sigil to calm and center himself, apparently realizing he wasn't exactly helping me chill.

Elofir pulled his hand back and stood. He looked over at Mzatal and gave a small nod, confirming some suspicion to judge by the pain that flashed through Mzatal's eyes.

"Y'all need to tell me what's going on before I lose it," I said with a tight smile.

Mzatal crouched before me and took my hands in his, ran his thumb over the cracked gem of my ring. It had been his Christmas present to me, though the rich blue stone in its intricate gold and silver setting had been whole at the time. The damage had happened when I threw the ring against the wall during a heated argument—a confrontation that had proven to be necessary to clear the air and establish trust in our relationship. I now cherished the ring with its crack as a reminder of the obstacles we'd overcome.

He drew a breath. "Rhyzkahl used the *rakkuhr* to create an implant that can not only self-replicate but also adapt to accomplish its purpose," Mzatal said, voice low. "Within minutes of the initial contact, it had diffused its outer layer throughout your physical body as well as in your aura."

I forced myself to not react, not speak, until I could process that a few times. "Like some sort of arcane virus?" I asked, a bit surprised that my voice actually sounded mostly normal.

"That is a close analogy."

"And what is this virus meant to do?" I asked, very carefully maintaining my it's-all-cool voice as much as possible.

Mzatal's hands spasmed briefly on mine, betraying the depth of his wrath, though it didn't show in any other way. "Rhyzkahl activated it with a word," he said, eyes on mine.

I gulped. "Oh." *Rowan.* He'd called me Rowan. In the horrific torture ritual, Rhyzkahl had sought—and failed—to strip my identity and create Rowan, a thrall unswervingly dedicated to his service, his tool. Looked like he hadn't given up on his desire to own me. "That fucking son of a bitch." I scowled to bury the sick fear. "My asshole ex-boyfriend gave me an *infection.*"

"Elofir and I will contain it," Mzatal assured me. "The implant missed its intended target." He laid his fingers on my sternum, over the scar of the first sigil Rhyzkahl had carved. "Had it struck here, it would have activated my sign, then those of the other ten lords. Once complete, you, beloved, would be gone and Rowan birthed."

I shook my head in denial. "But I thought he couldn't do shit with the scars after you crashed the ritual."

He moved his hand to rest on the small of my back over the twelfth scar, the one Rhyzkahl had failed to ignite during the ritual. "The unifier sigil is inert," he said. "It is true that he cannot use it to conjoin the others and create that which he sought, a Rowan thrall to focus the unified potency of all eleven lords."

The place under his hand felt . . . normal. Though the other scars burned or tingled or crawled or itched at times, the twelfth seemed nothing more than grotesquely beautiful body art. "If he can't turn me into a weaponized super Rowan, what the hell is he trying to do then?"

"Adapt and use the other sigils to create a lesser thrall," he told me. "One dedicated to his cause. I cannot determine the full purpose, but if nothing else it serves them to destroy you and strip my zharkat from me."

"Great. A budget Rowan." The sick fear twisted. High tech or low end, either way I lost my identity and ceased to exist. "Can you get rid of it?" I asked tightly. "Some arcane antiviral?"

"As it is crafted of *rakkuhr*, I do not know a means at this time." His aura went very dangerous and dark. "The implant must first be contained so that it cannot migrate to your chest, and then we will wring the means of its deactivation from Rhyzkahl."

I lifted a hand to his cheek. "First contain it, then we get Idris, and *then* we wring it out of Rhyzkahl."

"First you, then Idris. Yes," he said softy, and I felt him pygah and calm. "It is best if you sleep deeply while we create the containment. Will you acquiesce?"

"I'll never argue with naptime," I told him lightly.

A faint smile brushed his lips, then he leaned in, kissed me, and sent me to sleep.

Chapter 3

I woke in bed to the sight of morning sunlight playing on the shimmering leaves of the grove beyond the southern window wall. A couple of feet away, Jekki crouched on his two hind legs and, with his other four paws, carefully held a hot mug of coffee ready and waiting for me. Damn, but I was spoiled.

"Jekki, you're amazing," I said with a sleepy smile.

The little blue *faas* chittered, purple iridescence shimmering over his pelt as his long and sinuous tail twisted. "Hell-o, how . . . arrrrre you. I am fine! Have a niiiiiice day. Earth!"

It took a lot of effort, but I managed to contain my laughter. I sat up and took the mug from him. "That was excellent," I told him. "You can also use 'What's up?' and 'Have a good one!'" I resisted the urge to teach him *Hasta la vista, baby.*

He peered at me, blinking his large bright golden eyes. "One of what?"

"Er, a day or moment or encounter," I said, then shrugged. "It's fairly vague."

"Okie dokie!" he burbled. "Have a goooood one! Buh-bye!" And with that he zipped out.

Remarkably cheered by the exchange with the clever demon, I sipped my coffee and conducted a quick personal assessment. I felt great, to my immense relief. I didn't know exactly what Mzatal and Elofir had done, but not only did I no longer feel weird-tingly-odd, my twisted knee and various other dings and scratches were as good as new.

Yep. Definitely spoiled. I finished my coffee, quickly

bathed and dressed, then sat like a good girl so that the faas
Faruk could braid my hair into something that looked a tad
nicer than Unkempt Mop. As soon as she burbled her satisfaction with the result, I gave her a thanks and a head pat,
then headed to the plexus.

I was two steps past the entrance to the solarium when
it registered that someone was asleep on the broad sofa.
Mzatal? I jerked to a stop and wheeled back, then exhaled
softly in relief as I realized it was Elofir. He lay spooned up
against a sleeping dark-haired woman, his arm draped over
her. I couldn't help but smile at the tender sight. The woman
was Michelle Cleland—a former drug addict who'd ended
up in the demon realm as a "sacrifice" from the Symbol
Man serial killer to Rhyzkahl.

. Ironically, it had probably saved her life. No longer a
strung-out crack whore, Michelle had bloomed into a lovely
young woman, clever and quick-witted. Moreover, she and
Elofir had formed a deep attachment to rival the one I
shared with Mzatal. She'd been sent to the demonic lord
Vahl when she first arrived but had found her home with
Elofir.

The two looked utterly adorable curled up together like
that, but as I continued down the hall, it clicked that the
containment of the arcane virus must have been exceedingly difficult. The lords only needed sleep for a night every
eight to ten days or after great exertion, and I highly
doubted Elofir's current slumber was simply from normal
fatigue.

With that unsettling thought, I continued on and successfully located Mzatal in the plexus chamber, relieved to
find him awake and aware. He stood before the pedestal
and basin in the center of the room adroitly working planet-
stabilizing potency with practiced precision. Each of the
lords maintained his own plexus, and if any shirked in their
responsibilities, the entire world suffered. Every lord did his
share. It was the *one* thing they all agreed on.

Two *ilius*—Wuki and Dakdak—lay curled in the cush-
ions like shifting multicolored smoke with hints of fangs,
eyes, and sinuous bodies. A third, Tata, ceaselessly coiled
and uncoiled beside Mzatal, waist-high, its eyes steadily visible and focused on the plexus flows. They were three of the
dozen or so third-level demons that made their home in and

around the palace. In the demon realm, ilius fit into the niche of arcane vultures, feeding on stray essence from dead or dying creatures. When I'd summoned them to Earth, I'd paid them with nutria which seemed to work well for all concerned except perhaps the nutria. I'd also thought of them as being fairly low in sentience and intelligence, little more than arcane bloodhounds I used to help me occasionally on cases. However, even though I still couldn't communicate with them worth a damn, Mzatal had deep affinity with the creatures and actually consulted with them.

Mzatal's eyes remained on the blue-green strands and the pair of glowing orbs before him, but I felt his awareness of me as well as his assessment of my well-being. After I patiently waited a few minutes, he anchored the strands then moved to me, touched my cheek with the back of his fingers. He looked much better today, I noted. The stress and dismay no longer vibrated through him, which served to relieve the last traces of my own anxiety.

I gave him a light kiss. "I feel fine now. It's all going to be okay," I said, reassuring us both.

A surprisingly gentle smile touched his mouth. He rested a hand against my cheek, caressed it with his thumb. "Yes, the containment was successful."

"Perfect. Because in about five minutes I'm going outside. I'm going to nail down the seventh ring today, and then you can culminate it." I referred to the seventh ring of the shikvihr—a powerful ritual consisting of eleven rings of eleven sigils each. Mastery of each ring significantly augmented a summoner's focus and mastery of potency. Moreover, the completion of all eleven rings gave the ability to create and use floating sigils, or "floaters," on Earth rather than only in the demon realm. The ability to use floaters meant a huge advantage in speed and effectiveness over chalk and blood drawings. Mastering all eleven rings was a rare accomplishment, but I intended to beat the odds and take home the This Summoner Kicks All the Ass Award.

"You will have it by midday," he said with utter confidence.

I grinned. "Damn straight."

He glanced to the strands to make sure they still held, then slipped an arm around my waist. "If all agreements are made satisfactorily today," he said as we exited the plexus, "it is my intention to set the ritual to send you to Earth for mid-afternoon today. Kadir arrives soon to begin preparations."

I stopped dead and stared at him. "Whoa. Hang on." I held up a hand. "You want *him* to assist you in the ritual? You expect me to get inside a diagram with him at the controls?"

Mzatal gave me a small frown. "Under agreement, there is no better choice."

"I don't understand." I shook my head. "He's one of *them*. And, for that matter, why was he here yesterday?"

He put his hands on my shoulders. "He was here yesterday under a long-standing agreement allowing him access to the Little Waterfall. It helps him maintain stability." He paused, gathering thoughts to explain. "Kadir and I have a history that extends far beyond his association with the Mraztur. His skill with the flows is unparalleled and, because of the implanted *rakkuhr* virus—even contained as it is—the sending ritual must be flawless."

I struggled to put aside my emotional reaction to Kadir. "I trust *you*, but how do you know he won't break the agreement?" I gave him a sour smile. "The Mraztur haven't exactly been bound by their ethics lately."

"No, they have not," he agreed. He looked off into the distance even though we were still in the corridor. "But Kadir is meticulous with agreements. I have never known him to break even the smallest point." He met my eyes again. "However, if what I require conflicts in any way with terms he has with the Mraztur, he will not come to agreement with me, and I will find another to assist."

His eyes held a flicker of worry. It was clear he preferred to have Kadir do the ritual with him, and I forced myself to remember that his worry for me mattered as well. It was unfair not to take that into consideration.

"All right." I gave a grudging nod. "It's obviously a complicated relationship, but I'll trust you to trust him for me." I angled my head. "Speaking of complicated things, are you going to give me some sort of training or FAQ on how to use Vsuhl properly?"

Mzatal went still, and I felt the connection between us thin slightly as if it had grown distant. "Beloved, Vsuhl was not recovered for your use," he said in a quiet, grave voice. "It is Szerain's blade."

The odd change in his mood had me baffled, but I forged on anyway. "I know that," I said. "But I'm its bearer now. Wouldn't it be safer if I knew how to actually use it while I have it?"

"No," he said firmly, brows drawn together. "You are safe when it is away. You are *not* Vsuhl's bearer. You are its custodian. It is Szerain's blade." His aura flared with each sentence, as if to punctuate it. "Too much for a human."

I'd taken a step back without realizing it. "Right," I said. "Okay." My throat felt tight, and I took another step back, feeling the sting of the rebuke. Had I said or done something wrong? Maybe I'd messed up when I used the blade the day before, and he was mad about it? "I . . . I'd better go work on the shikvihr," I said and turned to go, bewildered and hurt.

He reached out and caught my shoulder, pulled me to him. I didn't resist and let him hold me close. Tension kept his body rigid, and though he said nothing, I felt his pain and regret that he'd upset me.

I sighed against him, did my best to not be a ninny. There was obviously a lot more he wasn't telling me, but now wasn't the time to push the issue.

"Yaghir tahn," he finally said, voice soft. *Forgive me.* "The matter is complex and fraught."

"Yeah, it's cool." I looked up at him and forced a smile. "I'd better get started on the seventh ring."

He hesitated briefly, then released me and stepped back. "I will be there to culminate it when you are ready."

I nodded, turned and departed, smile slipping as I headed outside and to the column. The connection Mzatal and I shared was incredibly intimate, amazing and profound, yet it did nothing to balance the massive difference in the power dynamic between us. It wasn't an issue of one of us being more "in control" of the relationship than the other. This was a flat and simple: "He's super powerful and can read my every thought, and I'm . . . really good at feeling what he needs and helping him be super powerful."

I reached the column, began some basic warm-up movements. No, it wasn't a flat and simple anything, I realized. Our partnership benefited us both, and the shikvihr was a perfect example of it. Learning it from him with the added input I gained through our bond, I understood nuances of the creation process that would be impossible to grasp from words and demonstration alone. I *knew* it on a deeper level, which ultimately enhanced it. Yes, I still had to create it and weave the sigils in their rings completely on my own, but what I ended up with was simply *awesome*.

With my psyche thus soothed, I began to dance the shik-vihr. The first six rings flowed out of me without hesitation, igniting perfectly and carrying the deeper resonance that showed they'd been culminated by a demonic lord—like hitting the enter key on a computer. They drifted in slow rotation around me, a foot above the ground, colors shifting and sparkling.

The seventh ring poured from me effortlessly as well, each sigil joining harmoniously with the next as I traced and danced. I felt the grove activate with Kadir's arrival, but I ignored it, utterly focused. Nine sigils, ten. I'd never played sports, but I knew now what it meant to be "in the zone," because I was dead center. Even the awareness that Mzatal watched from beyond the outer ring didn't faze me. I had this shit.

I traced the eleventh and last sigil in the ring, ignited the series, then looked over at Mzatal with a proud and silly grin on my face. "Pretty, ain't it?"

He moved carefully through the rings, hands behind his back as he assessed. "Well done, zharkat," he said with a warm smile.

"Thanks," I said, exultant. I wiped sweat from my face with my sleeve. "Now hook 'em up so you can send me to Earth."

He chuckled low. "We must work on your lack of assertiveness, beloved." He kissed me lightly then moved behind me, draped his arm over my shoulder and pulled me against him. I leaned back and carefully followed his method as he wove the rings together. Without this step, the seventh ring was little more than a pretty circle of sigils.

"Now ignite the whole," he murmured.

I took a moment to savor the accomplishment I'd worked toward for months, then ignited the unified rings in a flare of potency that left me dizzy even as it infused me. Mzatal held me to his chest and rewarded me with a rare delighted laugh that echoed through our connection.

"That's even prettier," I said with a grin as I shifted to face him.

"So it is." He held me close and gave me a toe-curling victory kiss, then broke it reluctantly, and nuzzled my cheek. "The ritual will be ready in less than two hours. Ilana will bring you to the nexus at that time."

Still smiling, I kissed him soundly then dispelled the rings. "I'd better go bathe and pack."

Chapter 4

I returned to the rooms I shared with Mzatal to find that Faruk had already carefully packed my duffel. To my delight and relief, the sweet faas had not only included my Earth clothing, but she had also selected a variety of the lovely garments made for me here in the demon realm by the clever little demons called *zrila*. After thanking Faruk effusively for saving me the trouble, I tossed in one or two little keepsakes, then made a quick trip to Idris's room.

The faas had straightened up, made the bed, and put clothing away, but otherwise everything in the room was the same as Idris had left it four months ago. I found his hairbrush in the bathing chamber and pulled a few dozen blond and curling hairs from it, then put them and his toothbrush in a small cloth bag. Arcane power was cool and awesome, but DNA testing was pretty damn neat as well, and I intended to find out once and for all if Idris was my cousin.

I put the cloth bag in my duffel, then had nothing to do but wait with zero patience for the ritual. At long last all was prepared, and Ilana transported me down to the black sand beach near the nexus, saving me the walk down the bajillion stairs that hugged the cliff face. Running up them had become an *almost* enjoyable mind and body clearing ritual. However, it also cleared the pores with gallons of sweat, and since I didn't really want to arrive back home a sodden mess, I expressed my deep gratitude to Ilana once we arrived on the beach. Though I didn't see her, I knew Eilahn was somewhere close by, watching.

To the right the waterfall ended its five hundred foot plummet into a deep sea pool. To the left stood a large

raised circle of basalt surrounded by eleven dark columns—
Mzatal's nexus. Unlike the utilitarian nexus Rhyzkahl and
Jesral had created in the rainforest, this structure had stood
for millennia as an augmented arcane hotspot that capital-
ized on a convergence of power flows. Eleven was the
"magic" number for arcane work in the demon realm, based
on the eleven lords, the qaztahl, who kept it all flowing.
Above the surface of the nexus a hundred or more floaters
of brilliant colors twisted and drifted, while Mzatal and
Kadir stood on the far side, deep in a debate over the best
means to finalize the section of sigils before them.

I felt the readiness of the ritual, the thrum of potency.
Cold fear threatened to pry its way in, warning me of the
perils of entering a ritual, especially one that had been
formed by one of the Mraztur. *I trust Mzatal*, I reminded
myself. Besides, there was no fucking way I was going to
show fear in front of Lord Creepshow.

By the time I reached them, the debate between the two
lords had been settled. Kadir stood back, his eyes on me,
saying nothing, which was fine with me. Mzatal took my
hand, and together we stepped onto the basalt and into the
vortex energy of the nexus. I paused a moment, clung to his
hand while I recovered my equilibrium, then moved carefully with him through the floaters to the center.

Mzatal laid his hand against the side of my face, caressed
my cheek with his thumb. "I have much to do to prepare for
my own departure," he told me, "but I will be here, awaiting
your summons, in twenty-four Earth hours."

"You'd better be," I said, smiling. "I don't want to have
to hunt you down."

Kadir moved in my peripheral vision, and I riveted my
focus on Mzatal's face to help me avoid all thoughts of
Creepshow's involvement. After a lovely moment of saying
goodbye, Mzatal released me and retreated to the perimeter of the diagram. Together, he and Kadir walked the full
circle, then ignited the floaters with a dizzying rush of upward spiraling energy.

When I felt the ritual set, I slung the strap of my duffel
over my shoulder, smiled and blew Mzatal an exaggerated
kiss. "See you soon, Boss."

The ritual coalesced around me like viscous slime, icy
cold and smothering. My smile disappeared as alarm shot

through me. This wasn't right. I'd been summoned twice before and both times it felt like being dragged through shards of glass. Hideously unpleasant, yet this was far different. Worse, even though it didn't have the same flaying pain.

The energy wrapped around me like the coils of a snake, squeezing the air from my lungs. I fought to suck in a breath, to move, to twitch, abruptly reminded far too much of the confining potency that had bound me during Rhyzkahl's torture.

Mzatal and Kadir continued to work the flows side by side, focused and calm as though everything was going exactly as planned. *But whose plan?* I wondered as I fought against the rising panic. Suffocation sure as hell wasn't in mine. Had Kadir found a loophole in Mzatal's careful agreement? The potencies held me fast, pressed me inward upon myself, squeezed the breath from me. I struggled, consumed now with the need to get the hell out of the center of the nexus, to move, to do *anything* to stop this.

I felt Mzatal's intimate touch flow through me, urging me to peace. Felt him. Felt the calm assurance.

It wasn't enough to overcome the stab of primal terror, the memories of Rhyzkahl's vile blade parting my flesh as I was held bound, immobile, far too similar to how the slime held me now. I tried to scream, to plead with Mzatal, but had no breath to do so.

Still Mzatal persisted, suffusing me with his steady presence, flooding me with reassurance and calm. He spoke, and though I couldn't hear the words, I read them upon his lips, felt them in my core.

I am here, zharkat. Peace, beloved. Here, Kara. Here.

The panic slipped away, and I extended, met his eyes.

He lifted his hands and thrust them downward in a final gesture. The world twisted and, with a wrenching pull, the constricting slime and sunlight above gave way to weightlessness in silent, icy darkness. Cold seared through my bones, froze even the concept of movement. No sound, no scent, nothing but the void.

Warmth touched me, bringing a rippling discomfort like circulation returning to a limb. A moment later, I felt something solid beneath my feet, sensed my legs buckling. Pain shot through my knees and palms as I caught myself and gasped in precious air.

I heard a man's voice. A shocked curse. Ryan. Still breathing hard, I looked up in time to see him leap to his feet from where he'd been sitting on a futon in my basement. His laptop nearly dumped onto the floor as he did so, but he managed a lightning fast save, then slung it without further regard to the futon. "Kara!?"

Finally catching my breath, I sat back on my heels, gave Ryan a grin, and put aside evil thoughts of how I was going to kill Mzatal for putting me through that. "Miss me, sweetie?"

He rushed over and crouched beside me. "You okay?" he asked, eyes searching me for any indication I wasn't. "I had no idea you were coming."

"I'm good," I said. "It was a rough and weird ride, but I'm good." I gave him a grateful smile as he helped me to my feet. "Nice to see you again."

His face lit with a smile and he pulled me into a hug. "Missed you around here."

Smiling, I wrapped my arms around him, took in his familiar scent. "I missed you too. It's good to be back."

He released me then hooked a thumb over his shoulder toward the futon and other furnishings at the far end of the room. "And yes, I'm living in your basement," he said, his tone colored with apology.

"You certainly are," I said with a wry smile. Ryan and Zack had moved in when I was captive in the demon realm to help keep the place up, as well to be immediately on hand in the event of any new developments. Both were FBI agents, my friends, and so much more. Ryan was the exiled demonic lord Szerain, forced to live submerged as an unaware human, and named *kiraknikahl*—oathbreaker—by the demons. Zack was his demon guard and guardian, as well as my best friend Jill's boyfriend and baby-daddy. I had no idea if Zack and Jill had discussed cohabitation, but considering that Jill was a pretty damn private person and that Zack *needed* to be living with or very near Ryan, I doubted they were shopping for a new house.

I swept my gaze around the basement, noting the evidence of manly habitation. Stacks of work files on the table, a pair of socks under the edge of the futon, a new small dresser and wardrobe against the far wall, an open bag of chips on the side table, trousers draped over the chair. I had a sudden hysterical image of Zack telling Ryan to take his mess downstairs where no one else had to see it. Not that it was really *messy*. But it was definitely lived in. "So. The temporary arrangement became more permanent?"

Chagrin flickered across his face. "Well, we thought that with everything going on with you and the demons, it'd be good to have a solid base of operations." He drew a breath and released it in a rush, looking like a man desperately hoping to sell a wild idea. "Somewhere secure for you to come home to and for us to work from when you're gone." He tugged a hand through his hair in a familiar gesture. "And yeah, I know we didn't ask. Hope you're not mad."

It hit me. Hard. These people were my friends, put their own lives aside and gave a shit about me, *for real*. Sure, I'd already known that in an intellectual way, but something about having it demonstrated so clearly hit me right in the warm-fuzzy-feely parts. And, damn it, I liked the idea of having Ryan around.

"Mad? Hell no," I said with a broad smile. "That's one of the coolest things anyone's ever done for me." I thumped him in the chest. "But don't think I'm changing my morning groggy-sometimes-bitchy, pre-coffee routine just because you're here."

Ryan laughed. "I hope not. You wouldn't be you without it."

I looked him over. He wore navy blue sweats and running shoes, and the hair around his ears was damp, leading me to think he'd recently showered. Four months, and still much the same. Short wavy brown hair with a hint of red, rugged yet handsome face, and green eyes flecked with gold. But there were also new lines of strain around his eyes. "You resting okay?" I asked.

"It's been a rough few months, but I'm all right." He made a dismissive gesture and focused on me with earnest intensity. "What's next on your agenda?"

Nice change of subject, Ryan. I let it slide for now. "You know that Idris got taken by Rhyzkahl's gang, right?" At his nod I continued, "Well, yesterday, they sent him back to Earth, I'm assuming to better hide him and probably for some other as-yet-unknown purpose as well." I scowled.

"I'm here now to do what I can to track him down and stop whatever the hell else is going on." He frowned and opened his mouth to comment, but I held up a hand. "And, as soon as I have my storage diagram charged up, I'm summoning Eilahn. Then tomorrow night, Mzatal." The storage diagram was basically an arcane "battery" that helped me stockpile potency. Damn handy since that meant I wasn't restricted to summoning only on the high potency days of the full moon.

"You have a pretty full plate," he said with a sympathetic smile. "And you still look a little shaky. Maybe you should sit down for a few." He glanced at his watch. "It's a little after eight p.m. You hoping to summon tonight?"

He had the shaky part right. I headed for the futon and let out a sigh of relief as I plopped down. "As soon I can get the diagram charged and my head clear."

Ryan sat beside me and shifted half-sideways. Closer than friend distance and not as close as a lover. It was comfortable and right—for now. There was too much hidden. Ryan didn't know he was Szerain, and I hadn't known it until relatively recently, well after we'd already developed a rapport and even a relationship, albeit a rocky one. Now, I knew Szerain existed, fully aware, beneath the overlay façade of Ryan, even if Ryan didn't. It made things *interesting* between us.

"When I was here before, I told you about Katashi going over to the Mraztur." I said.

He nodded. "Right. He betrayed Mzatal, was his sworn summoner, had his Mark and all that."

"Well, I'm pretty sure his people here on Earth are the ones who have Idris." I gave him a hopeful smile. "Anything you and Zack could dig up with your FBI resources would be a huge help."

"Sure, no problem," he said without hesitation. "We can do info-scrounging."

"Thanks. Mzatal made a list of his known associates. It's in my bag somewhere. I'll dig it out for you later." I abruptly frowned as my gaze rested on a diagonal wall and door nestled in the far corner. "Ryan. There's a door in my basement."

"Yeah. Basic bathroom and shower. Figured it couldn't

hurt anything." He cleared his throat. "We've made a few, uh . . . other additions too." He gave me a wide smile. "By the way, you look pretty damn good."

Change of subject number two. Noted. My mouth twitched in amusement. "Thanks. I work out. A *lot*," I said, then grinned. "Me. Working out and actually *wanting* to." It sure wasn't that way before I went to the demon realm. Jill used to have to drag me kicking and screaming to go for a run.

"Inconceivable," he said with a laugh. His eyes travelled over me. "And your *hair* is different."

Puzzled, I reached up and touched my hair. "Oh! The faas—blue furry demons that look like dog-sized lizards—won't let me style it myself anymore. Possibly because my idea of style is to stuff it into a ponytail."

His face softened. "You're really okay. And the lord . . . Mzatal. He's treating you right?"

"He treats me very well," I reassured him. "And I'm learning *so* much. It's amazing."

"Good. I'm glad." He even sounded like he meant it, despite the jealousy Ryan had displayed in the past concerning both Rhyzkahl and Mzatal. Tension rose in his face, the muscle of his jaw working. "And what about Asshole?"

I didn't need to ask. He meant Rhyzkahl. My mouth twisted in a scowl. "He's alive and well, working closely with Jesral."

Ryan froze, face reflecting angry darkness. "Jesral," he said through clenched teeth. Ryan didn't know Jesral but Szerain did. From the vehemence that laced the name, I had no doubt Szerain had punched his way through the overlay to express his animosity. Then Ryan sucked in a breath, shook his head as though to clear it, gave me a flicker of a smile. "Sorry. Things have been weird since you left."

I covered his hand with mine, squeezed lightly in reassurance. "I bet they have." And I knew the starting point for the weird times even if Ryan didn't. When my aunt Tessa summoned me home from the demon realm four months ago, Ryan was in the basement with her. I arrived with Vsuhl, Szerain's essence blade in my hand, and its presence triggered Szerain to try and recover the blade; empowered him enough to fight his way out of the submersion. For a few heart-pounding minutes, he'd been free, a hundred percent Szerain, until Zack submerged him again. But Zack didn't seal Szerain's prison as tightly as before and intentionally left the "lug nuts" loose, as he put it, on the mental grate that held him down. That meant Szerain was able to surface more in small ways, where the previous standard had been for the Ryan-overlay to eclipse Szerain on all levels. That had to be shaking up Ryan's world. My heart ached for him.

"It's going to be all right," I continued. "I know it is."

He turned his hand over and closed his fingers around mine. "Sometimes I'm not so sure. It feels like I'm going crazy."

"You're not. Promise." Since I couldn't tell him why I knew that, I decided it was my turn to change the subject. "Is there any food in the house? I could use a bite."

Ryan managed a smile. "Yeah. Sure. I think there's some leftover meatloaf in the fridge from last night. Zack keeps us in groceries, and he's pretty much claimed your guest room." His grimness slid away into amusement. "See what happens when you abandon us?"

"Hey, at least there's food!"

Ryan stood and tugged me to my feet. "Yes, there's actually something in your fridge besides a block of mild cheddar cheese and expired milk. C'mon."

I laughed as we headed for the stairs. "As long as the cheddar's still in there."

"Oh, it's there," he told me. "No guarantees on its condition though. It'll be underneath the Real Cheese."

I noted changes in the house as we walked through. A game system by the TV in the living room. About twice as many DVDs on the shelf as before. A new cushy-looking recliner. Uncluttered kitchen counters, and the sink completely devoid of dishes. Could this even be my kitchen? Okay. So, Zack and Ryan were kitchen elves. No way was I going to complain about that.

And the fridge. I stopped in my tracks. An enormous gleaming stainless steel French door fridge stood where my dinky, noisy white one used to be.

My shock must have been obvious. Ryan nudged me with his arm as he headed to the gorgeous monstrosity. "The old one gave out about a month ago, so Zack replaced it." He pulled the right door open to display a colorful variety of fresh fruit and vegetables, containers with food, and a noticeable lack of mold—all a rare sight in my fridge.

I closed my mouth. "Ryan, I can't possibly afford this." Not only was I without a job, but my meager savings were, well, meager.

He pulled meatloaf and sandwich fixings from the fridge and set them on the counter. "No worries, really. We're living in the house, so we took care of this." He glanced back. "And anyway, you have a job."

I stared at him stupidly.

"You're a special consultant assigned to our task force." He grinned, obviously enjoying my bewilderment. "I have *no* idea how Zack got that approved without you being here, but it's official. Oh, and Zack also got you set up with a concealed carry permit so you can continue to pack heat." He chuckled. "Again, *no* idea how he managed it, but I've stopped asking questions."

"Hot damn!" I had a strong suspicion he'd accomplished all this by using his demonhood somehow. "And does the job come with a paycheck?"

"Absolutely," Ryan said as he threw sandwiches together. "Gotta love government spending."

I exhaled in deep relief. "Very cool. I was worried about how I'd pay for silly things like property taxes and utilities and food and stuff."

"We've been keeping up the utilities," he told me, "and we'll pitch in for other stuff for as long as we're here." He set plates with sandwiches on the table. "If you're back for a while, you'll probably boot us out. And I wouldn't blame you." He grinned. "I'm easy to get along with, but Zack's another matter."

"Right, he's *so* difficult and moody, unlike you." I rolled my eyes as I sat at the table and pulled one of the plates to me. I was definitely getting used to the idea of housemates. Hell, after seeing that fridge, I'd be okay if the two suddenly decided they wanted to learn the bagpipes.

Suddenly *starving,* I tucked into my sandwich, then stopped chewing as I tried to figure out why there was a control panel with a little video screen on the wall. I finished the bite, stood and moved over to the panel.

"It's the gate system," Ryan volunteered with a hint of hesitancy. "New fence on the whole perimeter and a keyed gate."

I peered at the screen that showed the end of my drive and the highway beyond, and forced my mind past the sheer magnitude and expense of fencing the full ten acres. I'd entertained a "fence fantasy" for ages, but hadn't ever thought of it as a real possibility. I had good protective wards around the property, but so much more could now be done with the additional vertical surface, not to mention the benefits of the mundane physical barrier. "That is so cool!"

Ryan grinned, obviously relieved at my reaction. "Yeah. That was all Zack's idea. Speaking of which," he said as he pulled out his phone, "I'm calling him to let him know the good news. Anyone else you want me to call?"

"Jill," I said. "I'll call Tessa when I finish eating."

"Will do." After a brief conversation with Zack, he shook his head and hung up. "Did he say to give you a hug or anything? Hell no. He said to tell you he has a stash of chocolate in the utility room, upper shelf, right cabinet."

I let out delighted laughter. "He knows me!"

After I finished the sandwich, I called my aunt to let her know I was okay and would see her soon. The conversation was unexpectedly a little teary on both sides. Damn, it felt good to be home.

Ryan hung up with Jill at about the same time I said goodbye to Tessa. "She's coming over tomorrow as soon as she can get a break at work," he told me, mouth curving in a smile. "Her exact words were, 'Don't you let that crazy woman disappear again before I get there!'"

I grinned. "That sounds like the Jill I know and love!" Jill was, hands down, my best friend. Ryan was a damn good friend as well, but that relationship had certain significant quirks, to say the least.

I picked up my plate from the table and put it in the sink. That was almost like doing dishes, right? "I'm going to head downstairs and get started on the prep to summon Eilahn," I said to Ryan.

"I have to run some errands. Need anything while I'm out?"

"As long as we have coffee, I'm good until tomorrow."

"Okay. I'm going to clean up here, then head out."

I have a kitchen elf! Chuckling to myself, I headed down to get to work.

Down in the basement, I crouched beside the storage diagram, assessed it, frowned. It was nearly fully charged though I'd drained it when I last used it to summon Mzatal four months earlier. Had Tessa stopped by and done it? Not that I was going to complain. It meant I could summon Eilahn an hour from now rather than waiting the six it would take me to charge an empty storage diagram.

I spent the next ten minutes doing arcane hygiene to clear residual energies from the summoning area. It wasn't absolutely necessary, but I'd learned from experience that the tedious task saved hassle later. During the actual summoning stray energy could cause unforeseen problems, the arcane equivalent of a rock hitting a fan blade or sand in a car engine.

Once I was satisfied the space was clear, I rummaged through my box of chalk and found what I needed, then moved to a spot on the concrete floor not far from the storage diagram. Kneeling, I sighed. In the demon realm, floating sigils traced in the air replaced the crude and boring scrawls of chalk. But until I mastered the full shikvihr, the speed and ease of floaters wasn't possible for me on Earth.

"Use what you have, Kara," I muttered to myself as I began to create the perimeter for a syraza summoning diagram. I continued to sketch on the concrete, delighted to find ways to incorporate new principles I'd learned from Mzatal. *Chalk's not so bad when you know what you're doing*, I decided.

I'd nearly completed the diagram when the basement door creaked opened. "Hey, gorgeous," Zack called out. "Okay if I come down."

I smiled, set the chalk on the floor, and stood. "Hey, sexy. You may enter my lair."

Zack quick-timed down the stairs, his movement smooth and athletic. Trim, with short blond hair, perpetual tan, and a ready smile, he looked more like a surfer dude than an FBI agent, despite the suit and haircut. Grinning, he swept me into a hug, lifted me off my feet and spun me around.

I let out a piercing half laugh, half shriek. "Put me down, you weirdo," I demanded as I hugged him fiercely.

After one more revolution, he set me on my feet. "Welcome home!"

I couldn't have suppressed my grin if I'd wanted to. "Good to be home."

"Ryan and I, we've sort of moved in. A little," he offered with a sidelong glance.

"Right," I said with a laugh. "Like Russia invaded Poland a little."

"Yeah. Something like that." His eyes sparkled with humor. "What do you have going on?" he asked.

"Eilahn told me she'd flay me alive if I left the property without her. You know how she is. I'm summoning her so that I'm not stuck here."

Zack forced his mouth into a mock frown. "She could have amended it to where she'd flay you alive if you left the property without her or *me*. I have some skills, y'know."

"Yes you do," I agreed. As a demahnk—an elder syraza—he had whatever innate skills Eilahn possessed, and more. "But you're not as scary as she is." I grinned. "I think it was really her way of making sure I got Fuzzykins back to Earth as soon as possible." At his questioning look, I explained, "When Tessa summoned Eilahn a couple of months ago, Eilahn brought Fuzzykins along, and the horrid thing proceeded to get knocked up. So now Eilahn wants her to," I rolled my eyes, "give birth on her home world.'"

Zack laughed. "Gotcha."

"By the way," I said, "Tessa sent me the newspaper article about Roman Hatch and how he confessed to the murder of Tracy Gordon and how he permanently disposed of the body." My mouth twitched in a smile. "Nicely done." Roman Hatch was an ex-boyfriend who'd teamed up with Tracy Gordon—a fellow cop who'd turned out to be a summoner—to create a gate between this world and the demon realm. Not so bad on the surface, except that they murdered several people in the process and intended to trap me in the gate to power it.

Amusement flashed in his eyes. "Well, Roman *did* murder Tracy when he threw him into the active gate," he said. "And since the gate shredded Tracy into teeny bits, he *did* permanently dispose of the body, too." Zack spread his hands and assumed an utterly innocent expression. "However, I suppose it's possible that someone *helped* him remember a version where he shot Tracy and then dumped his body in the river."

I snorted a laugh. Though it took a lot of effort, Ryan was able to shift memories—a mere shadow of true manipulation but still useful when circumstances were dire enough to require it.

Zack's gaze swept over the basement. "You need anything for the summoning?"

"I think I'm good. Almost done with the diagram." I mentally reviewed the preparation steps, then glanced at him. "Did Tessa charge my storage diagram? It was darn near full."

"She hasn't been here since you left." He cleared his throat. "I've kept it topped up for you," he said. "I didn't know when you'd be back, but I thought you might need it."

I angled my head and regarded him. Though he had great skills with wards, I'd never known he could do anything related to summoning diagrams. Eilahn had never indicated that she could do so. Maybe it had to do with his being an elder syraza? "That's awesome. Thanks." I crouched and sketched the final sigil. "I think that's about it. I'm almost ready to summon."

"You want me to stay or go?"

I looked up at him, smiled. "I don't mind if you stay."

"Sweet. I'll be over here." He moved to the wall, put his back to it and went demon still.

Smoothly drawing power from the storage diagram, I laid the foundation and created the anchor points for the strands that would form the portal. The arcane structures coalesced with smooth ease, and when the time came to make the call, the power slid through me in a continuous flow rather than coming in stops and starts—far easier than ever before. Apparently, having the seventh ring of the shik-vihr and a buttload more knowledge from training with Mzatal made a real difference. I could get used to this.

"Eilahn!"

Through the woven potency of the summoning, I felt the ritual find and take hold of the syraza. Had she been unwilling, this would have turned into a battle, like trying to land a big and powerful fish. But with Eilahn eager and ready to come, she slipped through the portal with minimal exertion on my part.

Not as easy for her. Summonings *hurt*. I knew that from experience. Eilahn stood in the center of the diagram with her head bowed and eyes closed, with only her shuddering breath betraying the stress of the summons. She was in her human form, and I breathed thanks to Mzatal for saving me the hassle and facilitating her shift from syraza to human. Dark skinned and tall, with sleek black hair that flowed past her shoulders, Eilahn had a multi-ethnic look that managed to combine the best of every continent. Her figure was long sleek muscles and curves, feminine and tough. Smokin' hot chick, no doubt about it.

An unearthly screeching yowl reverberated through the basement, and I almost fumbled the strands. I quickly recovered, grounded the power and dropped the protections, then scowled at the cat carrier that I now saw beside Eilahn's feet.

"You couldn't forget the cat in the demon realm?" I asked sourly.

Eilahn gave a lovely frown. "That is a silly notion," she stated. "I do not forget."

I turned my attention to the carrier. "Hello, Fuzzykins," I said with a sugary smile. "Why haven't you been playing with hungry reyza like I've asked you to do?"

Eilahn gave me a *look*, crouched, and murmured to the cat as she released her from the carrier. The evil feline dashed out as quickly as her turgid body allowed, then proceeded to rub up against Zack's legs, purring loudly. In the next heartbeat she turned, hissed at me, then waddle-ran up the stairs as I returned the hiss.

Zack met Eilahn's eyes, and I sensed the demon connection like a vibration on the farthest edge of hearing. She emitted an odd chirp-trill more suited to her demon form. He approached her fluidly, took both of her hands, interlaced their fingers and leaned in to touch his forehead to hers. The vibration shifted quality, intensified.

I busied myself to give them space to do their demony thing, closed out the summoning diagram, and directed residual potency into the storage diagram.

A moment later, they parted, and Eilahn turned a steely eye on me. "You have not left this property?"

"I haven't," I said as I held up my hand. "Scout's honor."

"Excellent! Flaying is so very messy," she observed as she turned and sauntered up the steps. "I do prefer to avoid it, though I would perhaps make an exception in the case of Ryan."

I smiled. It was good to be home.

Chapter 5

Some people had to deal with jet lag. Me, I got dimension lag. Four-thirty in the morning, and wide awake with zero hope of getting back to sleep. The house was quiet, which I was used to after living alone for so long. However, I felt obliged to creep about, since I figured Ryan probably didn't want to hear me thumping around this early in the morning.

I doubted Eilahn and Zack were asleep since the demon-kind seemed to need far less rest than puny humans, but I had no idea where they were. Eilahn's favorite place on the property was the roof and her second favorite was the woods on my nearly-ten acres of property. The roof, most likely, I decided, with the pair of them perched like beautiful human-shaped gargoyles by my satellite dish.

After making my silent-ish way to the kitchen, I plunked my laptop and notepad on the table, started a pot of coffee, then scrounged in the fridge while I pondered what needed to go on my Hunt for Idris to-do list. Even though I knew he was still in the demon realm, Katashi was definitely right there at the top, so I went ahead and scrawled his name on my pad before prepping my first cup of coffee with the appropriately massive amounts of sugar and cream.

Like me, Zack had a list of the known Katashi people and would do some digging there. Katashi's main base of operations was in Japan, but I wasn't going to make the assumption that his people had Idris there. Master Isumo Katashi had too damn many connections.

Over eighty years ago, he'd performed the first summoning since the mid-seventeenth century. Self-taught, he'd called Gestamar, a challenging as all hell high-level demon.

It still boggled my mind that he'd managed to do so and survive. I couldn't stand the man, but I had to give him mad respect for that feat.

As the first summoner of the twentieth century, he naturally became the root source of *all* modern summoning, which meant that every active summoner had either learned directly from Katashi or one of his students, myself included. Though I'd spent only a couple of useless months with him, my aunt Tessa—who'd taught me—was his student for almost a decade.

In other words, the old man surely had one hell of a network with students and associates all over the world, which meant a myriad of potential hiding places for Idris.

I sat, took a sip of coffee and noted *Follow up with Ryan and Zack* beneath Katashi's name. Better to wait for some solid info on the old bastard before tackling that mess. I tapped my pen on the paper and considered the events that occurred right before I was summoned to the demon realm six months ago, then wrote *TRACY GORDON* in all capital letters. Though not directly linked to Idris, Tracy had tried to sacrifice me to make a permanent gate between this world and the demon realm, which meant he surely had connections to *someone*. Most likely one of the Mraztur since Kehlirik, a reyza of Rhyzkahl, had guarded Tracy's focus diagram.

Ryan, Zack, and I had already done a pretty thorough search/tear-down of the house where Tracy Gordon had lived, helped by some nice sledgehammer-to-wall action. I was pretty damn confident nothing remained there that could be useful to us.

It was his other house that interested me, the one that he owned through a shell corporation, and the one where, in a room packed full of books and papers, Kehlirik had guarded the diagram. If Tracy had kept journals, I figured they'd be there, and I damn well intended to find and take them, along with anything else in his library that caught my eye.

Finders keepers, you son of a bitch.

With the sun now rising and my plans of library-pillaging firmly in mind, I finished my coffee, took a quick shower, dressed, then grabbed my bag and headed for the front door.

I made it out and onto the porch before I realized the

hitch in my plans. Two Chevy Impalas sat in the drive, along with a Toyota Camry I didn't recognize. The Impalas had government plates, which told me that my fed-boys had finally been issued new vehicles to replace their Crown Vics. And I didn't know who the Camry belonged to, except that it wasn't me.

I have no car. I'd resigned from the Beaulac police department, which meant I didn't have a department-issued vehicle anymore. *Well, shit.* Ride on the back of Eilahn's motorcycle? That would make pillaging the library a *lot* more challenging. I sighed and turned to head back inside, then paused. Something was different about my porch.

A *lot* was different, I realized with a start. The stairs had been rebuilt and the railing along the front replaced and painted. Moreover, a swing now graced the porch—a lovely wicker thing that hung from two solid eye-bolts in the ceiling.

I moved down off the porch and onto the gravel driveway, turned to get a better view of the front of my house. There were flowers—actual living plants—in neat beds on either side of the steps. A pretty little crystal and brass arrangement hung from a corner of the porch, catching the morning sunlight and casting it back out in shards of rainbow. There was even a birdfeeder hanging from the other corner, though I wondered whether any bird would come near the house while demons perched atop it.

I smiled with warm pleasure. My house looked . . . *nice.*

Eilahn leapt lightly from the roof and smiled at me. "You have your bag. Where are we going?" she asked with an enthusiastic lift in her voice.

"I was hoping to go to Tracy Gordon's summoning house to check out his library," I told her. Maybe I could borrow the Camry? That would be better than riding pillion on the motorcycle.

Her face grew hard and more than a little scary. "Tracy Gordon *baztakh unk kirlesk.*" She spat into the gravel.

I didn't know what that all meant, but it was simple enough to guess the sentiment, and I certainly couldn't blame her for it. He'd shot her twice, point blank, and killed her. Fortunately, because it happened on Earth, she made it through to the demon realm and recovered. Once through the void was usually successful. Twice, not so much.

I nodded toward the Camry. "Whose car is that?"

She followed my gaze, then looked back to me and beamed. "Yours!"

I gave her a blank look. "How can it be mine?"

Eilahn ducked through the front door and returned before I had time to process she'd gone. She dangled a set of keys in front of me, displayed the brass fob with *Kara's Kar* neatly engraved in script on it. "Because this proclaims that these keys match your vehicle, I have tested them in the ignition, and they fit. Therefore, that," she said with a nod toward the car, "is your vehicle by the process of a successful trial."

Kara's Kar? I rolled my eyes. My house elves were out of control, but right now I wasn't about to complain. I took the keys from her and smiled. "Well, let's try it out!"

A note on the dash in Zack's neat handwriting held clear, concise instructions for operating the automatic gate. Yet another point for the elves.

The house Tracy Gordon had used for summonings and other arcane practices was on the far side of Beaulac, but since it was so early in the morning, and there was little traffic, I went ahead and cut straight through town.

A garbage truck made noisy work of dumpster-emptying behind Beaulac Junior High, while across the street a man in nothing but shorts and sleep-tousled hair ignored his dog's yappy barking at the din. A few determined souls headed into Magnolia Fitness Center, clutching towels and water bottles. I was probably still a member there, I realized, since my dues were on auto-payment.

"Back when I was a street cop, this was right about the time I'd be heading to the station for shift change," I told Eilahn. "Whether I was coming on or going off duty, I always liked seeing the world wake up."

She slanted a disbelieving glance my way. "*Liked?* You who pulls your pillow over your head if any dares disturb you before mid-morning?" She let out a low snort. "I doubt you woke to your alarm and thought, 'Oh, what a pleasure it will be to see the world wake up!' You would have *liked* to have been in your bed."

"Okay, so maybe 'liked' is a relative term," I said with a laugh. "But since I had to be up anyway to keep my job, I figured I might as well dig for a silver lining."

"Ah, yes," she replied, "because you are always a model of good cheer before you have had your coffee."

"Are you crazy?" I asked with mock horror. "Who the hell said anything about going to work without coffee? Do you *know* how many people I'd have shot even before roll call?"

Eilahn gave a musical laugh, then nodded toward *Grounds For Arrest*, the coffee shop across the street from the PD. "I wonder how he has remained in business with you gone."

"Now *that's* a mystery."

My mood remained light as we continued on through town. We passed by the Garden Street Industrial Park, and I stuck my tongue out at it since it was from there that I'd finally been summoned to the demon realm. The industrial park had been developed a couple of decades ago with grandiose plans of bringing in high-tech industry. Too grandiose for Beaulac, it turned out. A gate in the chain link fence was closed and locked, and a large sign proclaimed it to be the future home of an "exciting new development in health care" by RiseHigh LLC.

I doubted the new development would be as exciting as promised, but at least something worthwhile would come of the place.

We made it to the house without any issues and, thanks to the early hour, we managed to avoid problems with nosy neighbors. To my relief and dismay, the wards on Tracy's house remained intact. Good because it meant the contents probably hadn't been vandalized, and bad because we'd have to get through some serious protections.

It took close to half an hour of us working together to unwind and temporarily neutralize protections, but finally Eilahn and I squeezed through and into the back of the house without causing an explosion or major blood spillage.

"You will acquire his library?" she asked as we gazed at the books and scrolls and papers.

"Yes. I'm claiming it under Article Five, subsection three, paragraph A of the Multidimensional and Interplanar My Goddamn Property Now statute, namely the section titled Right to Have All The Shit of The Guy Who Shot You and Tried to Fuck Me Up." I nodded firmly. "This is *all* mine now."

Her mouth twitched. "I do not argue your right to ownership," she said. "But I wonder *how* you will acquire it." She arched an eyebrow at me. "You recall our difficulty entering this dwelling? It will be similar on the egress."

My mood took a nose dive. "Well, shit." Double shit. Because of the complexity of the protections, we hadn't dismantled most of them, simply eased by. "Mzatal would be able to rip through them like a wet dog through tissue paper, right?"

"The analogy, while odd, seems apt."

"Fine," I said, scowling at being thwarted, even if only temporarily. "Then for now, we'll gather up as much as we can carry of stuff that looks personal to Tracy. Journals, notes, letters, whatever. That man was up to some weird-ass shit, and I don't think he came up with it on his own."

"Nor do I," she replied, expression grave. "Then let us begin."

Together, we moved toward the bookcases.

Chapter 6

We managed to remove two foot-high stacks of spiral note-books, loose papers, a few beaten up leather journals, and one raggedy Trapper Keeper without getting badly zapped by any of the wards as we left. Though we ended up leaving the majority of the library behind, what remained looked to be older volumes and reference materials, and I mollified myself with the reminder that the stuff was as safe there as it would be darn near anywhere else.

Both of the Impalas were gone when we returned home. An early morning for the two agents, I noted. Eilahn and I dumped our piles of plunder on the coffee table and then settled in for some nice light reading.

I picked up a battered red leather journal at random, flipped through it casually to see if anything stood out. Annoyingly, there didn't seem to be any sort of central theme. Accounts of specific summonings jumbled together with diagram sketches, miscellaneous notes, and mundane to-do lists. A dozen or so names filled the margin next to a half-way decent sketch of a zrila. I read through them one by one, murmuring each name to myself. *Sara Fillmore. Bryce Thatcher. Robert Finch. Henrietta Sloan. Jose Luis Hernandez. Carla Billings.* There were more, but none sparked even a sliver of familiarity. Eilahn denied knowledge of them as well, so I marked the page for future investigation and moved on. One folder, with a picture of a kitten on the cover, held several pages from a sketch book—all with odd drawings of leaf-less trees. Or at least I thought they were trees. In all of the drawings the tree-thing had a weirdly short central trunk with branches above that divided and spread and divided some more. Yet it also reminded me of pictures I'd seen of arteries and veins and capillaries, the way they all divided into smaller and smaller vessels.

A few of the sketches had snatches of alliterative phrases penciled along the outer edges of the pages, but with no meaning or central theme that I could grasp. *Boss-boy begets better brains. Masters make misery manually. Cancer clutched Claire's comfort. Good games give great gifts.* And many others just as bizarre.

I read through the odd phrases several times, turning the papers around as I did so to see if anything clicked from different angles, but finally admitted defeat, replaced all of the sketches in the folder, and moved on to the next item.

We pored through for another hour or so and found lots of interesting factoids and tidbits, such as how to determine the gender of a *savik*, and that a mature faas has seventy-two teeth, but nothing directly relevant. At around eight thirty a.m. we took a break, Eilahn to the roof for some morning sun, and me to scrounge breakfast and make another pot of coffee. I had a feeling it wouldn't be the last one I made this morning.

My phone buzzed with Zack's number as the pot began its gurgling. "Hey, Zack, what's up?"

"Beaulac PD just called Ryan and me out to a scene," he said. "Since you're a special consultant, it would be righteous if you could make it."

Special consultant. That still cracked me up. "I can do that," I said. "Text me the address. What kind of scene?"

His voice turned grim. "Murder."

"A murder that your team gets called out on," I said. Shit.

"We haven't seen pics yet, but they're saying Symbol Man."

My eyes narrowed even as a chill crept through me. "The real Symbol Man is long dead. Let's hope this is just a mundane copycat."

"I don't know. I'm not holding my breath on that one."

"I'm leaving in two minutes." Shit. The Symbol Man was a serial killer who'd terrorized the Beaulac area for four years around the time I became a cop. He was dubbed thus for the convoluted mark he'd carved into each tortured and murdered victim. After thirteen victims he stopped, and when three years went by with no sign of more victims, most people concluded he'd either died or left the area.

And then a little over a year ago, the marked and mutilated bodies started showing up again.

The Symbol Man case was the first one I worked with Ryan and Zack as part of a serial killer task force. It was also how I first encountered Rhyzkahl. The Symbol Man turned out to be a summoner who sought to call and bind the demonic lord to his will, and during the first attempt Rhyzkahl managed to escape by hijacking a completely un-related summoning I was performing at the same time. Instead of a fourth-level *luhrek*, the beautiful and powerful lord appeared instead. And, well, from there *events* pro-gressed that I still kicked myself over.

I slipped on a dress shirt and khaki trousers, pulled on a shoulder holster and tugged a jacket over it. I exited the front door, then looked up at the roof. "Eilahn," I called up. "The task force has been called to a murder. Supposedly looks like a Symbol Man victim."

She dropped to the ground with a leap graceful enough to make an Olympic gymnast weep in envy. Her face lit with exuberance. "A murder scene! This is exciting!" Then she quickly sobered, chagrined. "Perhaps not the choicest re-sponse."

I tried not to laugh, with only partial success. "Perhaps not." After giving her the details and location I climbed into the Camry and headed out with her following on the mo-torcycle. I really needed to learn how to ride one of the damn things. A woman on a motorcycle automatically got something like fifty "hot chick" points. Then again, there was no way in hell Eilahn would ever let me risk myself like that. *Hmmf.*

The Walmart parking lot appeared to be business as usual when we arrived, with no sign of a crime scene. It wasn't until I continued around to the back that I found the swarm of cops. The majority of the activity appeared to be centered around a parked eighteen-wheeler with an open back. Crime scene tape had been strung between cars to form a sizeable perimeter.

I found a convenient place to park, got out, and adjusted my jacket. Eilahn pulled up behind me and dismounted, removed her helmet, then went into scan-for-threats mode.

I walked up to the deputy who stood with a clipboard by the crime scene tape. "I'm a special consultant for the FBI," I told him, taking great pleasure in showing my pretty ID. To my annoyance, the deputy barely even glanced at it and failed to show even the slightest bit of awe at my status. Vaguely disgruntled, I signed the crime scene log then headed toward the open back end of the truck and the knot of law enforcement types there. I automatically looked for the familiar sight of Jill among the cops before remembering that the snarky-yet-awesome crime scene tech was eight months pregnant and working in the lab instead of the field.

A heavy set man with greasy black hair stood a few feet from the truck, phone pressed to his ear. Not far from him a much smaller, wiry man sucked on a cigarette as he tucked a notepad into his pocket. Vincent Pellini and Marcel Boudreaux, two of Beaulac PD's Violent Crimes detectives and all-around royal pains in the ass. Pellini did enough work to get by, but that was about it. He gave the impression of being perpetually miserable and didn't hesitate to ridicule or belittle anyone or anything whenever the opportunity arose. Boudreaux was cut from the same cloth and exacerbated the general unpleasantness.

Pellini gave me a nod and, to my surprise, sent what might have almost been something vaguely resembling a smile in my direction. He ended his call as I approached.

"Hey, Pellini," I said. I even gave him a smile in return. What the hell. I was feeling generous.

His gaze swept over me, easily noting the gun under my jacket to judge by the way his eyes stopped at the slight bulge before continuing on. "Damn, Gillian," he said with a little scowl that was oddly lacking in malice. "Never thought you'd go Fed on us."

"I didn't," I replied. "It's worse. I'm a *civilian consultant*."

Pellini shuddered. "Well, we'll get you started on a good case."

"What's the deal?" I looked over at the dark maw of the semi-trailer. "I heard it looked like a Symbol Man victim." My eyes went back to his. "But the Symbol Man's dead." I stopped short of saying, *I saw him die. I saw the demonic lord rip his head off for daring to attempt to summon and bind him.* Probably best not to go there.

"Looks like somebody doing a copycat but making it

their own," he replied, shrugging. "It's a lot cleaner, and there's no doubt they wanted us to find the body."

"You got an anonymous tip?"

Pellini's mouth twisted beneath his thick black moustache. "You could say that." He dug a photo out of the folder in his hand and passed it to me. It was an aerial shot of the parking lot with the semi in clear view. *Dead Body Inside* had been painted in huge letters on top of the truck.

"Yeah, that would be a Clue," I agreed.

"Hey, Pellini!" The crime scene tech called over. "Pics are done."

Pellini gave the tech a nod before returning his attention to me. "The Beaulac airport is just a couple miles that way," he continued as he hooked a thumb over his shoulder. "This is right under the approach. Anyone flying in or out would see the message."

Great. A killer who wanted to show off. I jerked my head toward the semi. "Mind if I go take a look?"

"Sure thing. Garner and Kristoff are already in," he told me. "Vic's female, young twenties, I'd say. No ID yet. And she wasn't killed here."

I thanked him and headed to the truck, more than a little weirded out that I'd had a normal and not unpleasant conversation with Pellini. As I climbed up into the truck, I shifted into othersight. Zack stood by the doors, phone to his ear, and gave me a smile.

"Ah, shit," I breathed as I took in the scene. This was no mundane copycat. Arcane residue flickered like pale blue fire over the body, clearly visible even though I was still a good twenty feet away.

Ryan looked back at me from where he stood, a few feet from the body. "Yeah, that about sums it up."

I approached and stopped beside him, swallowed back nausea. She lay naked on her back, arms stretched out to the sides and legs spread to shoulder width. A perfectly symmetrical red chalked circle surrounded her, but it was her skin that drew my gaze, held it. Her murderer had carved patterns into her flesh, sigils that, in any other scenario, would be beautiful, but on this canvas were horrors. The pale blue of the arcane flames shifted to red, flaring and subsiding in a rhythm eerily reminiscent of breathing. My own sigil scars itched, and I took a step back, cold sweat breaking. I dimly heard Ryan mutter a curse under his breath right before he turned and moved to me.

"You don't need to stay in here," he told me, voice low. I tore my gaze from the body, met his green-gold eyes.

"No." I breathed deeply, took a few seconds to find my way back to a reasonably calm center. "No, I can handle it." I released othersight and looked back at the body, this time focusing on the person and not the arcane trash suffusing her. Her face held a deceptively peaceful expression, though I knew there'd been nothing peaceful about her death. Her body had been thoroughly washed, her long black hair blow-dried and laid artistically over her shoulders with no trace of blood matting it. I saw now why Pellini had been so certain she hadn't been killed here.

"She's not someone off the streets," I noted. The Symbol Man's victims had been the sort of people who could disappear and wouldn't be missed. This woman was in good physical condition, nails neat and short with a coating of pale polish, brows waxed, and with faint tan lines from a bikini.

Even without othersight, the sheer magnitude of the arcane residue remained a constant distraction. I easily sensed the dance of the potency on her body, rhythmic, enthralling. I moved toward her again, welcoming the increasing tingle in my sigils as a reminder of what was done to me, and to her.

Ryan remained at my side as I advanced. "No, not a street person, for sure."

I glanced around to make absolutely sure no one else was in the trailer with us or within earshot. "The sigils aren't the same," I said, keeping my voice low.

Ryan knew what I meant. "I haven't had a good look at yours, but I'm inclined to agree." He gestured to where the sigils crept down her legs. "Hers are on more of her body, too."

His voice sounded oddly distorted through the rising whir coming from the dead woman. Couldn't he hear it? Like a piece of paper stuck in a fan, louder and louder. The rhythm of her sigil potency changed, strengthened, and I shifted to othersight to not miss a flicker of its fascinating, patterned beauty. I stepped over the curve of red chalk marking the circle, sucked in a breath as my scars, *my* sigils, began to pulse with fire, to match the cadence of hers.

Kara? A distant voice queried.

"Rowan," I murmured, correcting him.

Something in my mind snapped like a winter twig. Rowan? *No!* I summoned every shred of my will, focused. Everything crystallized into stark clarity. Potency coalesced in ruby coils between the woman's breasts, like a snake poised to strike. I gritted my teeth, tried to throw myself back and away from the trap. Pain like molten metal seared through my scars, but I couldn't budge.

"Kara!" Ryan's voice cut through the din like a chainsaw through cardboard. The whir crescendoed to a thunder-crack, and the world flashed red as something hit me hard from the side, drove me into the wall and knocked the wind out of me.

Ryan. His arms supported me, kept me from going down. Full understanding of what happened slammed through me, and I couldn't be sure if the fire that writhed through my scars came from the heat of my fury or the effects of the failed trap. Breathing heavily, I shoved away from the wall and Ryan. *Kara. Kara. I'm Kara*, I thought fiercely—and without a shred of doubt, to my utter relief.

"Everything okay in there?" a voice called out from beyond the open doors.

Zack stepped to the edge of the trailer and stood casually, silhouetted against the daylight beyond. "Yep!" he said, tone amused and buoyant. "Just us clumsy Feds tripping over our own feet."

"A fucking Kara-trap," I growled, jaw tight, eyes locked on the body. An attempt to activate Rhyzkahl's contained virus. "That poor woman suffered and died for what? So the Mraztur can get their way? Can get their tool?" My breath came in harsh rasps. "The assholes still want to use me. It's not happening." I finally pygahed, allowed the anger to dull a bit, though it did nothing to ease the pain in my scars. I dragged my eyes away from the body, looked up. Ryan stood in front of me, face set in determination and his eyes full of worry. "You saved my ass," I said. "You okay?"

"I feel like I touched a live wire, but I'm good," he said, concern easing somewhat.

I pygahed again so I could deal with people who didn't know about demons and lords and nefarious otherworldly plots. "Okay, let's finish this and get out of here." I willed myself to focus on the mundane aspects, moved to the open door of the semi. "Pellini," I called. "Can we turn her?"

"Let Baxter get his pics," Pellini said, giving a jerk of his head at the tech. "Boudreaux and I need to see too."

I stepped back as the lanky crime scene tech swung easily into the truck, followed by Pellini and scrawny Boudreaux.

"Already got my pics of all this," the tech said with an easy smile. "Just waitin' for y'all to finish your looksee."

"We've lookseed the front," I told him. "Now we want to looksee the rest of her."

His smile didn't flicker at my acerbic tone. "Not a prob! C'mon, detective," he said to Boudreaux. "Turn the princess here so I can do my shots."

Boudreaux and Zack turned the woman over and settled her onto her stomach. Zack gently pulled her hair aside, showing the sigils that spread over her upper arms, back and buttocks, and down her legs to her calves. Beautiful and horrible. And only the barest trace of arcane residue now. Everything had coalesced for the trap and then dissipated.

Zack gave me a nod, confirming that it was safe for me to approach. I hated to do it but I pulled on gloves, crouched and carefully eased her legs apart, then shone a flashlight at her vagina and anus. "God damn it," I breathed. The plastic of the flashlight creaked as my grip spasmed on it. It was hideously obvious she'd been raped and sodomized.

I closed her legs, stood. Pellini cursed under his breath, and when I glanced back at him I saw his eyes on the body, outrage and anger naked on his face.

"I will see these motherfuckers *fry*," he muttered to himself. I gave him a slight nod. That was one thing we could totally agree on.

Pellini's phone rang. He looked at the ID and headed out again.

My gaze skimmed over her as I looked beyond the sigils. No ligature marks. Bruising at her wrists, thighs, and breasts. Held down, not tied for the rape. Immobilized with either drugs or arcane power for the sigil cuts. No obvious sign of what killed her. Possibly blood loss, though I had a feeling the cause of death was arcane in nature.

Exhaling, I stepped back, tugged my gloves off. "Thanks for letting us have a look," I told Boudreaux.

"Sure thing," he said. "You'll tell me or Pellini if you get anything, right?" His voice held an almost desperate edge. I actually felt a little sorry for him. He knew in his gut that this was way out of their league.

"Damn straight I will," I replied with a firm nod as I lied through my teeth. *Sorry, Boudreaux, but I don't think you want most of what I might get.*

I stepped out into the sunlight and hopped down from the trailer bed, feeling as if darkness sloughed away from me as I left the confines of the semi. Ryan and Zack climbed down, each giving sighs of relief that echoed my sentiments.

I disposed of my gloves in a biohazard bag, then walked over to Pellini as he tucked his phone away. "Thought we had an ID, but it didn't pan out," he told me then nodded toward the trailer. "Related to the Symbol Man?"

"It *might* be a copycat," I told him honestly, "but I think you have a brand new flavor of sicko on your hands."

"Lovely," he muttered.

"Any other leads on the ID?" I asked.

He shook his head. "No match on prints. I'm checking missing persons and other channels. Still no clue where she was killed."

"All right, we'll work our angles as well. Thanks." I moved to leave but the expectant look on Pellini's face halted me.

"So, did you, uh, come up with . . . anything?" he asked, and I had the strangest impression he really did mean *anything.* That was a first. Pellini had never sought my input before. And especially not for anything with even a whiff of strange.

I gave him a guarded look. "Um. Well, we're going to follow up on the—" I stopped short of saying sigils, "—patterns carved into her skin. I think those are significant."

He surprised me by listening intently, giving a nod, and then *writing down what I said* in his notebook. No lie. I could read his oddly neat handwriting from where I stood. *Gillian: patterns of cuts may be significant, will follow up.*

Good grief. Had I come back to an alternate world version of Beaulac? I hid a smile at the thought.

"Doc will probably get right on this," he said, referring to Dr. Lanza, the coroner's office pathologist. "I'll let you know as soon as he does."

"I appreciate that." I paused, gathering my thoughts. "This is a weird one, that's for sure."

He remained quiet for several seconds, then nodded. "Yeah." For an instant it looked as if he wanted to ask me something. His face displayed an odd struggle as he grappled with some problem or issue, but then he shook his head and it was gone. "Yeah, weird," he simply said, apparently deciding that, whatever the question, it was best left unasked.

"I'll keep you posted on my end," I said in an effort to cover the slightly awkward moment.

"Sure," he said, then cleared his throat. "Thanks. You, uh, got the same cell number?"

"Yep, same number," I said.

He fidgeted with his pen. "Hell, maybe we can grab a beer or something . . . sometime."

I stared, stunned for a second before I managed to regain a semblance of composure. "Uh, my schedule's pretty tight right now with the task force," I lied. "But I'll definitely keep it in mind." I'd never grabbed a beer or done anything remotely resembling a casual-social-friendly thing with Pellini or Boudreaux. There'd been a shift of some sort in him, but with everything else going on, now wasn't the time to start exploring it.

I abruptly realized it might have been a set up line for some insulting joke, and mentally braced myself for him to laugh it off with a not-so-veiled nasty remark or snide comment.

"Okay. Good," he replied quickly, almost eagerly, which only increased my feeling of *what the hell?* "I'm always up for a beer," he added. Then he coughed, shuffled his feet a bit as if abruptly embarrassed. "Anyway, uh, keep in touch."

"Will do," I managed, then forced a smile, turned, and walked quickly away, weirded out by more than just the dead body and Kara-trap. *A friendly Pellini?*

The fire had faded from my scars, but an annoying itch remained that no amount of physical scratching would relieve. I headed to Ryan's car and waited for him and Zack to conclude whatever FBI stuff they needed to finish up. After a few minutes they joined me.

Ryan's demeanor was somber. "That shit," he jerked his head toward the truck trailer, "is so wrong."

"On too many levels," I agreed. The trap had been targeted at me, and it was a no-brainer to figure that the Mraztur knew I was back on Earth. After all, Kadir had been involved in sending me here. But how the hell had they sent word to Katashi's people in time to have a trap set so quickly? I hadn't left my property until this morning, so even surveillance on my house couldn't explain it. Maybe one of Katashi's people summoned a demon last night who told them? Certainly possible, though a lucky coincidence for them.

I scowled. Or not a lucky coincidence. While I was in the demon realm, Tessa and I had mailed letters back and forth via demon-messenger once a week or so. However, Katashi had lots of people working for him, including plenty of summoners, which meant the Mraztur could have a minor demon summoned every day to exchange messages. Anger rose again, but this time at myself. I should have anticipated something like this. Of course they'd have some means of frequent communication.

Score one for their team for setting the trap. Score one for me and my posse for foiling it. But score another for them for apparently having a better carrier-demon message system than us. Damn it.

"Game on, assholes" I muttered to myself. I gave Ryan a determined and humorless smile. "Thanks again for the save," I said. "I'm heading home. I have work to do."

Chapter 7

The drive home left me wrung out and bleak as both the nature of the murder and its purpose gnawed at me. And how the hell had the Mraztur managed to get an elaborate trap set for me so quickly? The body had most likely been planted in that semi-trailer mere hours after I arrived on Earth.

As I drove, I considered the possible explanations. Okay, so Katashi's people could easily summon a demon to pass messages on a daily basis. Perhaps they really were lucky enough to get a demon-memo about my trip to Earth immediately after my arrival? That was the only explanation I could come up with for how they had enough time to set a complex *rakkuhr* trap for me—one that required ritualistic murder and skills far beyond my own.

Not that it really mattered *how* they accomplished it. They'd damn near succeeded, and would have if not for Ryan. I missed Mzatal, wanted him here—not to tell me everything was okay when we both knew it wasn't, but to share this with him, get his perspective, his support, and simply feel his arms around me. This whole having a partner thing was damn nice, but I felt his absence keenly right now.

As I parked near the house, I glanced in the rear view mirror and caught sight of Ryan's car rounding the first curve of the driveway. I didn't wait for him but trudged into the house and then to the kitchen, determined to do whatever it took to shake the numb, sick horror that threatened to swamp me. I opened and closed cabinets, stared into the fridge looking for something besides fresh fruit or leftovers. Something . . . perfect.

Ryan came in and set his laptop bag on a chair by the

table. I didn't look over at him but I felt his eyes on me. "Isn't there any plain ordinary squidgy white bread in the house?" I demanded.

"Uh, no," Ryan said, a hint of apology his voice. "Zack gets a sprouted grain and a really good multigrain bread. On the top shelf of the fridge."

Sprouted grain? Why would any sane person want plants growing in their sandwich? Did nobody realize what happened when you swallowed a watermelon seed? I didn't want a friggin' bread garden growing in my gut.

My scowl deepened until it felt as if my face would break. I pulled out the multigrain, laid two slices on a paper towel and squirted liberal amounts of honey on each one. "It's a funny thing," I said tightly. "Seeing a girl who'd been horribly raped, tortured by cutting sigils into her body, then murdered so she could be a lure to trap and subvert me, kind of kills my mood."

"It sucks. I'm really sorry." He let out a heavy breath. "Is there anything I can help with to follow up on the arcane part?"

"I'm not sure, to be honest." I dumped a layer of brown sugar on the honey and pressed the two pieces of bread together. "I have no idea how to track that shit." I directed my scowl at the newly made honey and brown sugar sandwich, then flicked a burner on and set a skillet on it. I rummaged in the fridge, found the butter, dropped a quarter stick in the skillet.

"It needs bacon on it," Ryan offered.

I turned a scathing look on him. "That's a *completely* different unhealthy comfort food sandwich," I said with a curl of my lip. "It's like when you add olives instead of little onions to vodka. Totally different drink." I plopped the sandwich to fry in the butter.

"I'll have to take your word for it," he said, his voice laden with concern. "I'm going downstairs to get started on my report. Let me know if you need anything, okay?"

Smart boy to retreat. He knew me well enough to know I needed a little space but not abandonment. "I will."

He picked up his laptop case, turned to go.

"Hey, Ryan?" I looked over at him as he glanced back. "Thanks." A faint smile shifted my scowl. "This whole thing would be worse if I didn't have a friend like you."

He smiled and gave me a wink. "I'm one in a million, baby, and don't you forget it." And with that he left.

I finished frying my multigrain sugar fest, dismally aware that it would have been far better on good old reliable squidgy white bread. That was going at the top of the grocery list.

Still, even multigrain bread fried in butter and covered with honey and sugar wasn't bad at all, and while I felt a teensy bit ill upon finishing it, I didn't mind one bit, and my mood was somewhat improved.

After cleaning up my mess, I looked at the clock and exhaled. Over six hours before Mzatal would be ready to be summoned. I wanted him here *now*, wanted to feel his strong reassurance that we would get through this—*all* of this—together. I put the clean skillet away, then headed down to the basement to check the storage diagram. It brought him one step closer, plus Ryan was down there, and I was ready for the company of a friend.

Ryan glanced up from his laptop and gave me a smile which I managed to return.

"I'm going to check the storage diagram," I told him. "Nothing fancy, so it shouldn't disturb you."

"No problem," he said. "Do what you need to do."

I crouched beside the diagram, assessed it. Ryan sat with his laptop in a pretense of industry, but I felt his eyes on me. I gathered wisps of potency, funneled as much as I could into the diagram, then sealed it. It would take a while for more potency to be available for collection, sort of like water seeping slowly in through concrete. One more session would likely fill it enough for my needs.

I let out a long soft breath. The routine focus of the work had eased the trauma of the morning a bit more.

Ryan shifted and cleared his throat. I stood and turned to him, amused to see him looking a little guilty for watching me instead of working.

"All done?" he asked.

"For now," I said, keeping my humor well hidden. "I'll come back in a couple of hours and top it off."

Ryan nodded, his eyes still on me. "God, I've missed you."

I moved to the futon and sat beside him then leaned my head on his shoulder. "I've missed you too."

He set the laptop aside. "Like I said, it's been a weird few months. Sometimes when I think of you being off with *him*, I get so pissed I do stupid shit like hit the wall." He winced. "Or kick a concrete barricade. Not one of my brighter moments." He dropped his head back. "Most of the time it's not like that, though. I can think of you with him, and I'm . . . happy for you."

I had no doubt Szerain maintained the calm as best he could, which supported my suspicion that *he* didn't have a problem with my relationship with Mzatal even if Ryan did. And those times when Szerain couldn't resist the submersion enough to influence Ryan were the times when the Ryan aspect lashed out in jealous frustration.

Submersion. Revulsion shuddered through me at the reminder. A few months ago I'd talked Mzatal into submerging me so that I could understand Ryan/Szerain better. It was a nightmare—like being placed in a shoulder-width vertical tube with cold, viscous gel up to your chin, then having a grate pushed down until you had to press your face against it to keep from drowning. To add to the torment, you were forced to witness yourself living and interacting, but with little direct control over it. Never sleeping. Never knowing the relief of oblivion.

Szerain had existed thus for the past decade and a half. Horrific. I had no idea how he remained sane. I doubted I'd have lasted more than a week.

I slid my arm around him. "Mzatal's very good to me. And *for* me." I let out a low sigh. "I'm still a bit of a mess from what Rhyzkahl did to me, and I really believe Mzatal wants me to be, well, whole again."

Ryan continued to stare up at the ceiling. "Yeah. That's good. Can't deny you look and sound better."

"I'm getting there," I said, then winced. "Sure wish I'd listened to you earlier though. About Rhyzkahl."

He swiveled his head to look at me. "Yeah. What the hell is that all about?" he asked. "I know how I was, *am*, about you being around Rhyzkahl. But I don't get that with Mzatal." A perplexed look crossed his face. "Sure, I get my fits of jealousy, but it's not the same at all. Makes no sense. I don't know either one of the bastards."

Ryan didn't know them, but Szerain sure did since he'd spent millennia with them. Ryan was Szerain and Szerain was Ryan, but in an unhealthy, cruel imbalance. Unfortunately, I couldn't tell Ryan that was why he had fervent opinions he didn't understand. "I think it must be part of your talent or whatever," I said with a diffident shrug. "You've met them both, and maybe you got a shitty vibe from Rhyzkahl and a not so shitty one from Mzatal."

He didn't look convinced. "Maybe. But I'm pretty sure I had it in for Rhyzkahl long before I had the so-called pleasure of meeting him." He gave me a wry smile. "Must be my impeccable instinct. You'll listen to me from now on."

"I absolutely will," I said and snuggled up against him a bit. "It's nice to be back home."

Ryan went still for a second then shifted to drape his arm over my shoulders. "I wonder what I can think up to tell you."

I laughed. "Behave, or I won't believe you when it's important."

"The Fed who cried wolf?" he said with a smile, though I sensed something more brewed within him.

"Something like that," I said.

He went quiet. The smile faded and his body tensed as the *something more* revealed itself. "I saw you two when you left—you and Mzatal," he said. "I *felt* what there was between you. I know it doesn't make any sense, but I did. I know." With each word, his voice grew more strained, more intense. "What does that mean for you and me?"

What the hell was I supposed to say to *Ryan*? Szerain wouldn't have an issue with this, but Ryan was in control right now. Maybe something to pacify him without lying?

"The lords don't really do the monogamy-jealousy thing," I said carefully. "And I do care for Mzatal, love him even." There was zero use denying it. Ryan had felt it before, and if anything, it was stronger now. Besides, it sure wouldn't be hidden once I summoned Mzatal.

I twined my fingers through his. "Ryan, I *do* love you. And not just as a friend." Okay, maybe this wasn't as pacifying as I'd intended it to be, but a big part of me wanted *Ryan*, not Szerain, to accept me for me. And at the same time a part of me wondered what the hell I was doing. Ryan wasn't *real*. At the most he might be a distorted shadow of Szerain.

"You're more than just friends with Mzatal, too!" he retorted, voice sharp and tinged with frustration. "What do you want me to say? It's okay, I'll share? That's not happening."

"No, no! It's not that," I protested, aching for him and for me. Or maybe it was *exactly* that. Shit. Why the hell hadn't I kept my big mouth shut and played the I-don't-know-and-I'm-confused game to let this blow over? "Never mind," I said. "Forget everything I just said. You asked what my relationship with Mzatal means for you and me, and I don't *know* what it means."

Ryan pulled his hand from mine. "Yeah. Right. Forget what you said. Like that's going to happen." He shot to his feet, stalked several steps away and stood with his back to me, right hand opening and closing repeatedly. "*He* might not be into monogamy and all that, but what about *you*?" he demanded. "You're from here. Are you throwing all that away because *he* doesn't have the same values? Oh, wait. Maybe those aren't your values?"

The ache blossomed to agony with the vehemence in his tone. All perspective on the Ryan-Szerain quandary evaporated, and I stood. "Fuck you, Ryan," I said to his back, using my pain to fuel my anger. "Fuck you and your *values*. You think I'm some kind of slut now?" I took a shaking breath. "In the past year and a half, I've slept with exactly two men—Rhyzkahl and Mzatal. TWO," I repeated loudly. "And I've loved two: *you* and Mzatal. It's not like I fucked my way through the demon realm or jumped straight into Mzatal's bed! I was trying to tell you that I still had—*have*—you in my heart, that there was room for you there in whatever way you're willing to have me." I realized I was crying, realized that the pain was real and that this was fucked. "I went through HELL, and Mzatal put me back together," I continued, voice rising to a shout, "and I don't need you or anyone else judging me for the relationship that followed."

I didn't wait to hear what he came up with next. I turned, fled up the stairs and to my room, pursued by a stream of loud and mostly unintelligible curses. Channeling all the fury and pain that boiled through me, I slammed my door, threw myself on the bed and sobbed like a heartbroken teenager.

A few minutes later I heard a knock on the door. I sat up, snarled, "Go away, Ryan! I don't need more of your shit!"

Jill answered. "Nope, it's me."

Relief swept through me. Exactly who I needed. I wiped my eyes. "Come in."

She opened the door, and I did a double take. When I'd left, her pregnancy had been showing, but now, at about eight months along, it was *showing* and even more prominent due to her petite frame. "Damn. You're preggers."

"No shit, Sherlock," she said as she moved to sit beside me on the bed. "Glad to see you still have those awesome detective skills. I came over for a visit and walked in on a major throwdown. Now, tell me. What the hell did Ryan do to you?"

As though on cue, the basement door slammed with violent force.

I wiped my eyes again. "Shit. We were talking. It was nice. And then he said he knew Mzatal and I were *together* and asked what that meant for him and me." She offered a tissue, and I paused to blow my nose. "And shit," I continued, "I didn't even know what to say, so I said something dumb about how I loved Mzatal but loved Ryan too, and not just as a friend. As soon as I said it, I knew it was the wrong thing to say, but by then it was too late, y'know? He got all pissy and 'what, you expect me to share?'" I sighed, still feeling the sting of his response. "I told him that wasn't what I meant but later thought maybe it was. And I told him I didn't know what any of it meant for him and me." I looked over at her. "I was floundering, but doing okay up to that point. Then he got really assholeish and started going on about how I'd thrown away my values. Fucking shit! My goddamn *values*." I exhaled a shuddering breath as some of the tension melted. Simply being able to vent my frustration helped. "And that's about the time I told him, 'Fuck you and your values' and some other stuff and came up here."

"Oh jeez. What you said!" Jill put her arm around me and gave me a squeeze. "You've been away a while, and it sounds like you're used to talking pretty openly about stuff." She wrinkled her nose. "Ryan's a *guy* and, well, you know how he is."

I snorted. "Yeah, I do." Yet I knew what she didn't. Ryan wasn't just a *guy*. I knew the Ryan-Szerain struggle, had a better understanding of his moodiness and the challenges he faced. It was no wonder that, after Szerain tasted a sliver of freedom, he fought to reclaim it, even if it unbalanced his entire prison, Ryan included. I needed to remember that before doing or saying shit that would screw them both up. Away from the heat of the moment, that knowledge sparked a stab of guilt.

I should've been able to keep it together better for both of us. I sighed. Too late now to worry about it. "Jesus, woman," I said. "You're *really* pregnant."

She grinned and laid a hand on her belly. "A bit. She's feisty!"

"It's the tail," I said with as straight a face as I could manage. "I've heard they're usually twice as long in demon-human babies as—" I ducked and laughed as she grabbed a pillow and swung at me.

"You are EVIL!" she yelled, but laughter danced in her eyes. "You're damn lucky I asked Zack a *long* time ago if I was going to have to push out something with wings. Plus, I've seen the ultrasound. Bitch."

I grinned. "Yeah, I figured you'd had an ultrasound by now, and didn't think you'd be so calm if it had four arms."

"Two arms and two legs," she stated firmly. "No wings. And *no* tail."

I resisted the urge to tease her more. "Got any names picked out yet?"

"Nothing that's stuck. And Zack won't commit to anything." Her amusement slipped away. "He won't even talk about it anymore except to say it's too soon to name her."

"Too soon?" I gave her an incredulous look. "She'll be here in a month!"

"I know, but he won't budge," she said with a touch of resentment. "He's so *weird* sometimes." Then she gave a dismissive wave of her hand. "Enough of that. What's next for you?"

"I'm back on Earth to find Idris." I quickly filled her in on who he was and the search for him, and how special he was to both Mzatal and me. "So to really get the ball rolling, I have to summon Mzatal tonight." A scowl tugged at my mouth. "That's sure to set Ryan off again."

Jill shifted to face me more. "Yeah, about that." She narrowed her eyes in the way that told me she wasn't on board with something. "Did I hear you say you told Ryan you loved Mzatal? You do? Really?"

My scowl deepened. I didn't need anyone else judging my relationship. I took a deep breath and did a mental pygah. "He's really special to me. We worked closely for two months before we slept together. And it's been another four months since then. So, yes. We've grown really close."

"That's cool," she said unconvincingly. "I wanted to check and be sure. But he has to be a miracle worker to raise my opinion of these lords."

"Trust me, babe, he has the miracle worker part covered," I told her fervently. "I'm telling you, I was in *bad* shape after Rhyzkahl damn near destroyed me."

Her brow wrinkled. "That's about all you said when you came back last time. What did Rhyzkahl do to you?"

I hesitated, then stood and stripped off my shirt. "*This* is what he did to me."

Jill's hands flew to her mouth. "Oh my god."

I lifted my arms, turned a slow circle to give her a clear view of all twelve sigil scars that covered my torso, front and back. One for each demonic lord, and then one more whose purpose had been to harness and focus the power of the other eleven.

Naked horror filled her eyes. "Why? How?"

I lowered my arms. "It was a ritual meant to turn me into a thrall, a tool for him to use to further other plans. And, to lay the foundation to recover an arcane blade similar to the one he used to carve these into me." I pulled my shirt on again. "As for the how, he slugged me, bound me in strappado position, then took his knife to me. Both shoulders dislocated, fractured cheekbone, mental and emotional torment, and . . . the scars."

"Oh my *god*."

"Yep. That about sums it up." My mouth tightened. "Oh, and this was *after* he made love to me in the middle of the ritual circle." I sat heavily on the edge of the bed. "Stupid. Blind."

Jill pulled me into a hug. "I'm so sorry, babe. I want to kill him."

I returned the hug. "Mzatal got me out of there before Rhyzkahl could finish it." I said. "He healed me, but it was a lot longer before I could trust anyone, myself included." I sighed. "There were so many signs that I missed or ignored."

Jill echoed my sigh. "Probably because he was a hunk.

And I sure didn't help matters by telling you to ignore Ryan and enjoy the sex." Guilt flashed across her face.

I pulled back to look into her face. "No, don't do that," I said sharply. "Your advice was spot on with the knowledge you had. *I* had a lot more information, a lot more clues. Some were obvious in hindsight, though subtle at the time, while others were like glaring neon signs. He even went on my computer, for fuck's sake!" I blew my nose on a fresh tissue to get rid of the last gunk from my cry. "He knew how lonely and needy I was, and he used it, knew I'd be blind to his bullshit because of my stupid angst."

"He played you hard," she said, a scowl deeply etched on her face. "He needs to get taken down for sure. Mother-fucker."

"I'm with you there." I gave her hand a light squeeze. "Anyway, Mzatal's been really good for me," I said, smiling. "I'm stronger now. Not just physically." I chuckled. "I'm a forged-in-fire bitch."

"And you have muscles," she noted, leveling a proud smirk at me. "I thought you were allergic to exercise."

I let out a laugh. "Well, now I'm allergic to getting my ass kicked. Funny how the threat of serious bodily harm can change your attitude."

She wrinkled her nose. "Guess it's worse than the Beaulac bad guys."

I thought of the Mraztur. "Lots worse." I tilted my head. "If you stay late tonight, you can meet Mzatal when I summon him." Then I groaned. "Which reminds me, I have to go back down to *Ryan's* basement to charge the storage diagram some more. Shit."

"I confess, the thought of meeting Mzatal weirds me out," she said, "but I also want to see what the hell you're up to." Then she wrinkled her nose in sympathy. "I don't know what to say about the Ryan-in-the-basement situation."

"Fuck it." I shrugged. "Zack gave me the location of a chocolate stash. I think it's time to hit it."

She blinked at me. "*Zack* keeps a chocolate stash?"

"Well, he might have put it there in anticipation of my return." I dragged myself off the bed and out the bedroom.

Jill scramble-waddled to follow as I headed for the utility room. "That's probably true. Though I wouldn't be surprised if he had a secret chocolate addiction." There was a touch of resentment in her voice. Not the first time I'd heard it either.

I found the stash in the promised location, then set the big box of assorted goodies on the kitchen table. "Okay, chick. Spill. Is something going on with you and Zack?"

She fished out a miniature bar. "Nothing a little chocolate won't cure," she replied.

I could respect that. For now at least. We settled in to eat chocolate while she caught me up on the local gossip, and I shared fascinating, bizarre, and gross stories of my time away. As much as I'd grown to love my life in the demon realm, I'd really missed this sort of interaction.

"Don't you *love* the new fridge?" Jill asked with a covetous gaze.

"It rocks," I agreed. "What other so-called minor changes have those two made to my property?"

Gleefully, she proceeded to give me a rundown. Several projects I already knew. The fence and gate, porch railings and steps, basement bathroom. But there was more. A full obstacle course and running trail through the woods, new washer and dryer on order, plans to enclose the back porch, and a host of miscellaneous fixes and changes.

My mood declined as she spoke. I pinched the bridge of my nose, struggled against a bizarre sense of violation. Who the hell did they think they were? Who told them they could swoop in and take over the house my grandfather built and make so many changes *without* me?

I took a careful breath, told myself that this resentment hadn't come up when I saw the spruced up porch and steps. It was simply the stress of the murder victim and the fight with Ryan that had me out of sorts. The two men had done nothing I wouldn't have wanted on my own. Every bit of it had been undertaken in a spirit of friendship and caring while I'd been off learning how to save the world and myself. Plus, it had to have cost a *fortune*.

"It's awesome," I admitted truthfully, and was rewarded with a shimmer of relief in Jill's eyes. She'd been in on it too, I realized, and she knew me well enough to understand how I might feel about the many changes to my home. I gave her a smile. "Y'all are awesome. Thanks."

The front door creaked open, and I heard the jangle-clunk of keys dropping onto the table by the door.

"Honey, I'm home!" Zack called out.

"Don't you dare ask if dinner is ready," I hollered back.

The lanky blond agent sauntered into the kitchen. "I was thinking more along the lines of lunch." He leaned down and gave Jill a lingering kiss, laid his hand on her belly. "Or I could just have chocolate right here," he said, kissing a stray bit from the side of her mouth.

Jill beamed. "Chocolate *and* I can make a sammich for you."

"Mmmm," he said, then straightened. "That would be good, but I need to get with Ryan. He didn't answer his damn phone. Don't know why he has one if he isn't going to answer."

I winced. "We had a bit of an argument."

Jill's face tightened briefly at Zack's statement, and she gave a jerky nod. "Ryan. Sure. But you'll come back up when you're done, right? Feels like I haven't seen you in days."

"Yeah, sure, sweetie. You know this has been a crazy couple of months." He moved over to me, gave me a quick hug from behind. "Rough day, sunshine."

"No kidding," I said. "I'm ready for it to be over."

"Before you know it," Zack said and headed to the basement. He gave two sharp cop knocks, went on through, and closed the door behind him.

I narrowed my eyes. "I'm giving him five minutes, and then I need to get down there."

Jill snorted and shook her head. "I *guarantee* he won't be back up here in five minutes."

"He and Ryan have been busy?"

"Ever since you left for the demon realm again."

Crap. I knew it had to be the result of Zack easing Szerain's confinement. Sure, it was a good thing for Szerain since it relieved some of the tortuous pressure, but it also meant it was more challenging for Zack to maintain him.

I reached over and gave her hand a squeeze. "There's a lot of stuff on Earth that's been set in motion with Katashi and the Mraztur," I told her. "Zack and Ryan's task force focuses on weird stuff, so maybe they've been busy with some of the fallout." It was thin and lame, but it was the best I had since I couldn't tell her the truth.

And why was that? I suddenly wondered. Why the hell couldn't Zack save her some grief and tell her *something* about Ryan-Szerain? She already knew Zack was a demon, and even though there were all sorts of oaths surrounding the reasons for Szerain's imprisonment, they seemed to have loosened in the past several months. Surely Zack could drop a hint or three?

"You think that's what Ryan and Zack are doing?" she asked, dubious.

"I don't know. I just know everything's weird." I sighed and stood. "And I need to get into my damn basement. Be back in a few, babe."

"Okay. I'll be here babysitting the chocolate."

Chapter 8

I headed to the basement door, knocked twice. "Sorry, boys," I called out, "but I need to charge my diagram." I turned the knob and pulled, but the door didn't open. Locked. Annoyance curled through me. It was probably exacerbated by the general shitty nature of the day, but in that moment, I didn't care. *It's my goddamn house,* I fumed. *You can do all the repairs and cleanup and additions you want, but you don't fucking lock me out of any part of it.*

I went up on tiptoes to retrieve the key from the top of the doorframe, but even unlocked the door still refused to budge. Annoyance shifted to outright indignation as othersight revealed a clever little ward. Zack's work, I knew, and completely impervious to my attempt to unwind it.

Controlling the urge to pound on the door and yell, I once again knocked.

When Zack finally opened the door, I leveled a glare at him. "I need to get into *my* basement to start my summoning prep."

Zack regarded me, his face serious. "Will you do so quietly?"

The question didn't do anything to improve my mood. "Sure," I snarled. I pushed past him then headed *quietly* down the stairs, moved to the storage diagram and crouched. I deliberately didn't look in Ryan's direction, mostly out of pique though with a good measure of guilt. Sure, he'd been an ass to me, but I'd lost it when I should have walked away, considering his circumstances. Out of my peripheral vision I could see him supine on the futon, eyes closed. So much for making a statement by not looking at him.

Shifting to sit cross-legged, I started feeding potency into the diagram. Zack returned to kneel near Ryan's head, clasped his hand and spoke soothingly in demon. Ryan was certainly unaware, maybe sleeping, but Szerain never slept—part of the horrible nature of his imprisonment.

Another pang of guilt wound through me. Ryan wasn't playing a petty game of I'm-not-looking-at-you-because-I'm-pissed. Zack had him unconscious as he worked diligently to re-stabilize his world and Szerain's.

Damn it, I shouldn't have put him in that position in the first place. What was I thinking snuggling up to him? Talk about giving a confusing message. Too caught up in my own shit to think about the consequences, I couldn't have come up with a better way to send him into a tailspin if I'd tried. I wanted comfort. Comfort food. Comfort friend. But I'd crossed the friend line, used Ryan, and been a needy jerk.

The guilt retreated at the realization. It didn't change what had happened, but I now saw how I'd been stuck in an old pattern. I could beat myself up about today's situation, or I could take the lessons and move on. Screw it. I was *done* with being so damn needy.

I listened to Zack's fluent speech as I fed the diagram, let it soothe me like the murmur of a brook. Though I caught snatches of the demon words, I couldn't understand it. For all I knew Zack was telling him the story of Little Red Riding Hood. While in the demon realm I'd grown used to understanding meaning, even though I couldn't speak the language. The grove connection acted like a universal translator, and I missed it for that and so much more. I could live without it, but it sure was nice to live *with* it, kind of like indoor plumbing. I hadn't realized how much I was used to its comfort, its *presence*—one of those things where I didn't miss it until it was gone.

After about ten minutes I assessed the potency level of the diagram and found it nearly full. I sealed it and quietly retreated upstairs to check on Jill.

She still sat at the table. "I hate chocolate," she said as she shoved the container away.

"That's the hormones talking." I gave her a weak smile. "Looks like Ryan and Zack are deep in discussion about some case. They barely noticed me. Sorry." I hated lying to her. Zack needed to tell her *something*.

Disappointment flickered on her face, but she simply shrugged. "I guess it *is* the middle of a workday." She glanced at the clock. "Yikes! Speaking of which, I need to get back. I took a long lunch, but now I'm running late."

"I guess I'll catch you later," I said. "I won't be summoning Mzatal until about eight tonight. You want to put off scoping out my awesome new boyfriend until tomorrow?"

"That's probably a good idea. I need all the sleep I can get." She put her hand on her belly. "The bean kept me up half the night kicking, then my neighbor's dog started barking at about five. It didn't last long, but I couldn't get back to sleep."

"Bummer. I'll see you tomorrow then." I paused, frowned. "What day of the week is it?"

She rolled her eyes. "It's Tuesday." She stood, snatched a miniature chocolate almond bar from the container and slipped it into her pocket. "You okay on the year?"

"Yeah, sure." I grinned. "Got that part down."

Jill laughed. "Whew! Gotta run. Call me tomorrow."

"Will do. Take care, babe."

She gave me a quick hug, and I startled at the sudden jab in my midsection. I pulled back and stared at her belly.

"Holy shit," I said. "No wonder you can't sleep!"

Jill made a face. "She wants out. Now." Her phone dinged. "Shit. They're looking for me. I'll see you tomorrow." She snatched up her bag and dash-waddled to the door, leaving the house strangely quiet in her wake.

A long shower, real food, and a short nap worked wonders to recharge me and put some distance on the morning's murder scene and the Ryan fiasco.

I looked at the basement door and sighed. It had been several hours. Hopefully, Zack had Ryan stabilized. Time to make the donuts.

I hesitated, then knocked twice.

Zack called out, "It's open."

Relieved, I quick-stepped down the stairs, a lot calmer than I'd been the last time. Ryan appeared to be asleep on the futon, and Zack still sat in the chair beside him. I had a feeling Zack been there the whole time I was gone.

Zack cleared his throat. "Sorry about earlier."

"No problem," I said. "Ryan needed you." I quickly

checked the storage diagram to verify it was full, then returned my attention to him. "It was a short but nasty fight."

He exhaled softly. "He was pretty off balance."

My shoulders slumped. "I'm sorry," I said. "I got sucked in to reacting to the stupid overlay." Despite everything, it still grated at me that the "stupid overlay" constituted the majority of the Ryan I knew.

"I know it isn't easy for you," Zack said gently. "He's stable now, and Szerain has a better handle on it. There shouldn't be much fallout from Ryan on this, if any."

I smiled weakly. "I get a do-over?"

"Something like that."

"Thanks," I said, relieved. "I'll do my damndest not to let it happen again."

With my guilt somewhat assuaged, I gathered several colors of chalk from the supply table and paced the summoning area, prepared to clear it of arcane residuals in preparation for the new diagram. Yet to my surprise, not only was the area already clear it was impossibly spotless, arcanely speaking. No way should it have been so squeaky clean after my summoning of Eilahn.

I slanted a look at Zack. "Did you do the clearing?"

He gave me a wry smile. "Least I could do for taking up your basement."

"Thanks." Clearing wasn't hard, but it was a chore. I knelt and sketched out the central sigil then stopped and set the chalk down. My thoughts kept darting back and forth between the task at hand and the issues with Ryan, and only a foolish summoner laid a pattern with less than full focus.

Standing, I returned my gaze to Zack and gestured him over. Even with Ryan asleep, Szerain could hear everything. Zack stood and moved to me. I met his eyes and kept my voice low. "I fell in love with Ryan," I told him flatly, "but I don't even know if that person is real." I grimaced. "No. That's not true. I *know* he's not the real Ryan Kristoff." I struggled to find the words to express my persistent inner dread. "Is there anything of the Ryan I know in Szerain?"

"It isn't ever fully one or the other," Zack replied with gentle honesty. "It can't be. Most of what you've seen is the Ryan-overlay in domination. Though even that is a diluted extension of Szerain." He scrubbed a hand through his hair. "It's complicated. So very complicated."

I let out a sigh. "Yeah, I guess it is." I crouched again, examined the sigil I'd drawn and made a correction. "No matter whether he's Ryan or Szerain, I care about him, and I can't simply write him off. The problem is, he keeps being *Ryan* to me, so I have trouble seeing and remembering that Szerain's in there as well." I blew out my breath, watched chalk dust swirl in the air. "I think I understand us both—maybe *all* of us—a little better now."

"A benefit for everyone," Zack agreed.

"And speaking of you and Ryan," I said, "you haven't explained to Jill why you spend so much time with him, have you?" At his pained grimace, I went on, "She's hurting you know. Not badly enough for me to kick your ass, but enough that I think you should do something. She's my friend, and so are you."

His eyes grew distant, and for a fleeting moment it looked as if he carried the weight of the world on his shoulders. Being a 24/7 guard no doubt took its toll, demon or not.

"I'll do better with Jill," he said, then he flashed a smile and the crushing weariness was gone. No, not gone, I noted. Masked. "I promise," he added.

I nodded and let the subject go. For now. "How will Szerain handle Mzatal being here?"

Zack shrugged helplessly. "Damned if I know. I've never had anything like this come up before. It will likely be a challenge, to say the least."

"Move over, there's a new lord in town." I added a laugh to cover the flicker of worry.

He let out an answering chuckle. "Good grief. Did I sign up for this shit?"

"As much as any of us did."

"So basically, someone forged our signatures."

"Yeah, let's go with that."

Chapter 9

I spent the rest of the day readying the diagram and making some last minute non-arcane arrangements for Mzatal's arrival. By eight in the evening, I had plenty of power stored up, Zack and Ryan were off somewhere else, Eilahn was either in the woods or on the roof, and the house was nice and quiet and empty.

Most of my summoning superstitions had disintegrated after close to six months of training with Mzatal. I didn't have special summoning clothing any more, and I certainly no longer felt the need to strip in the hallway and then go down to my basement naked. I smothered a laugh at the thought of doing so with Ryan still here. *"Surprise!"*

I did, however, shower, shave my legs, and dress in a nice zrila-made shirt and soft pants in gorgeous shades of blue. Hey, I was having a torrid love affair with a hot and sexy demonic lord who I hadn't seen in a whole twenty-four hours. We were in the middle of a crappy, stress-laden situation. No way was I going to be less than my awesomest best to welcome him to Earth.

The summoning itself went smoothly and, while not exactly effortless, I again appreciated the value of the shikvihr and the intensity of my recent training.

I made the call to Mzatal, felt the strands coalesce through the portal, and pulled. A moment later he knelt on one knee in the center of the diagram, and I smiled as I saw he was wearing the charcoal grey Armani suit. My dude was ready to kick some Earth butt. Beside him, Jekki lay curled atop a small trunk with his tail tightly wrapped around a foot-high keg.

"Hello, Jekki," I said. The ball of blue fur unwound, and the faas burbled a greeting. Mzatal stood as I moved to him. "Hi, Boss."

"Zharkat," he murmured, face serious in his *I'm assessing everything* mode. But he wasn't so preoccupied that he ignored me. He slipped a hand behind my head and kissed me, then frowned. "You are troubled."

I slid my arms around him, rested my cheek on his chest. "Other than finally having you here, it's been a pretty crappy day." I proceeded to tell him about the murder victim and the trap on her body, and also the issues with Ryan and Zack.

He cradled me close as he listened. "I am deeply relieved you are safe and that Szerain intervened." He kissed me again. "Have you any information on Idris?"

"Nothing yet," I said, enjoying the lovely tingle left behind by the kiss. "But I've put out feelers."

He hesitated a split second before nodding, no doubt reading the meaning of the phrase from me. "I will begin adaptation to the flows here so that I am not as . . . crippled."

Crippled. That was how it felt to him. In the demon realm, he was connected to the arcane flows through his own lord-ability and time in his plexus, which allowed him to track and monitor damn near anything that touched or involved the arcane. Here, he had almost none of that. *Like losing the sense of touch.*

I took his hand and started toward the stairs. "Let's get out of the basement, and I'll give you the grand tour."

I watched Mzatal's face and enjoyed his reactions as he took in everything: the fascinating Earth scents, my table with summoning tools, Ryan's area with futon, table and dresser, and the very ordinary basement staircase. At the top of the stairs I stepped out into the hallway with him, then gestured around. "Welcome to my realm," I announced grandly.

His face remained impassive save for a very slight wrinkle between his eyebrows, likely undetectable by anyone who didn't know him fairly well. "It is very . . . compact," he finally said.

My lips twitched. "Try imagining it with the standard ceiling height of eight feet. These are fourteen. But it's not exactly a palace, that's for sure." I gave him a quick tour of the spacious living room, office, bedrooms, bathrooms, oh-so-cluttered dining room, kitchen, utility room, and all exits, while Jekki zipped from room to room in an excited blur of blue.

"You'll probably like it better outside," I told him as I led him through the kitchen and toward the back porch. In the kitchen Jekki happily explored, opening and closing cabinets and peering at items in drawers. He tugged the refrigerator open, made a quick assessment of the contents, then closed it and moved on to inspect under the sink.

I paused, though Mzatal continued moving to the back of the house, his brows drawn together in concentration. "Hey, Jekki," I said, "if you need any supplies for Mzatal, you have to let me know so we can buy them." Ahead of me, Mzatal strode across the porch and on into the yard.

"Have *tunjen* juice from home," Jekki announced, and now I realized what the small keg was for. Juice of the tunjen fruit served as quick replenishment for the body, mind and arcane, and was a staple of the demonic lord diet. "Earth fruit here. Enough today!"

I grinned and followed Mzatal. I could only aspire to the near-perpetual enthusiasm of the faas. Mzatal's steps slowed as he moved across the grass, both hands spread slightly in front of him, palms down and fingers slightly up. I hung back, watching with interest as he moved forward like a beachcomber with a metal detector, slowly sweeping his body back and forth in gentle, elegant arcs.

He paused, turned and backtracked, then shifted toward the right, shoulders tense with focus. Finally, he stopped, brought his hands to his sides, lowered his head and went still.

Goosebumps prickled over my skin as memory seared through me. Rhyzkahl had come out to the backyard and stood in precisely that spot, and for a bizarre instant the image of him overlaid that of Mzatal. Exact spot, exact stance. One light, one dark.

Vaguely unsettled, I walked out into the yard. He lifted his head as I reached him, and he inhaled deeply. "This will serve well," he said.

"What is this place?" I asked. "Rhyzkahl also seemed drawn to it. Stood right here."

He held his hand out to me, drew me to stand with my back to his chest. His hands slid down over mine, and he interlaced our fingers.

"Feel," he murmured.

I forced myself to relax, leaned my head back against him as I extended my senses. For a while there was nothing but the sturdy beat of his heart, the warmth and security of his hands on mine. Cicadas and crickets rasped and chirruped from the trees and brush. An owl hooted, answered a few seconds later by another farther away. A soft breeze carried the crisp scent of pines, much more subtle than the evergreens of Mzatal's realm, though perhaps still a vaguely familiar comfort for him.

And then I noted a warmth below me. No, that wasn't the right description. A subtle glow of power like the potency I worked with, but more concentrated than I was used to on Earth. "What is it?" I asked, voice barely above a whisper, as if certain the sensation would shatter if I spoke too loudly.

Keeping our fingers entwined, he wrapped his arms around me. "It is . . ." He paused, as if searching for a suitable English word. "It is a confluence, a convergence point of power flows, albeit different and of much lower intensity than in my own world. Such is the foundation of a nexus."

I processed that. "A mini-nexus."

"In a manner of speaking," he said. "It is raw now but with development, yes, potentially a . . . mini-nexus." I heard the smile in his voice.

"That's pretty darn nice," I said. "Why is it in my backyard?"

He gave me a light squeeze before releasing me. "The question is, why is your backyard here?"

I turned and gave him a puzzled look, but an instant later it hit me. "My grandparents had this house built here. And my grandmother was a summoner."

"She no doubt sensed it, even if subconsciously."

I looked down at the unassuming bit of grass. "Having this here should help, right?"

"It will help much in accessing and deciphering the flows," he agreed.

"And now it's OURS!" I threw my head back and did my

best Evil Laugh. Mzatal gave me an indulgent look, though amusement flashed in his eyes.

"Indeed, quite useful," he replied with deliberate understatement.

I laughed more normally, then gave him a quick kiss. "Hang on, I'll be right back." I ran to the porch, grabbed a battery-powered lantern, then returned and took his hand again. "I have to finish the tour. There's one more thing I want to show you."

He didn't resist as I led the way across the yard and down the hill. At the edge of the tree line was a path I'd attacked with the weed-whacker and pruning shears earlier in the day. The light from the lantern cast long shadows before us as we worked our way through the trees.

The path finally opened into a broad clearing. A pond took up most of the area, about sixty feet across at its widest point, with a perimeter of grassy bank that extended another twenty feet or so. I led him to the left, then lifted my lantern high to show him the rough pavilion I'd set up for him—a rug over a waterproof tarp on the ground, covered by a wide canopy tent with its walls rolled up despite the likelihood of rain. Mzatal loved open spaces and could easily ward for environmental control to suit his mood. A decent air mattress, simple chair, and a folding table completed the lavish furnishings.

"It's not much, I know," I said, suddenly nervous. Compared to anything in the demon realm, this was a lame, tacky ensemble. "But I didn't think you'd enjoy staying in the house all the time, and I know it's not an ocean view, but I've always liked the place." I clamped my lips shut as I realized I was babbling.

He gave my hand a squeeze, then pulled me close. "I deeply appreciate the consideration," he said, gratitude in his voice. "I would not care to abide the confines of the dwelling for extended periods."

Relieved, I put my arms around him. "There's a lot we can do to improve on this, too. I had to make do with what I could scrounge in limited time," I told him. "I sort of threw this together in about an hour after I looked around the house this afternoon and realized it wouldn't do at all."

"It is more than sufficient for my needs, beloved," he said as he lowered his head to kiss me.

I slid my arms around his neck, returned the kiss, and proceeded to welcome him to Earth in the best way I knew how.

Chapter 10

A raucous squawk from a blue jay woke me, and it took me several seconds of *Why the hell is a bird in my bedroom?* before I remembered where I was.

Sunlight filtered through leaves and pine needles to create shifting patterns on the tent canopy above me. A squirrel chattered in annoyance not far away, and a dragonfly buzzed near the canopy and then zipped past. Subtle wards designed to keep insects away shimmered by the tent poles. "Afterglow" had consisted of my polite and loving demand that Mzatal teach me that particular arcane protection.

I sat up and found Mzatal standing naked a few feet from the edge of the pond. With his back to me and his unbound hair pulled forward over one shoulder, I had a lovely view of his back, where well-formed lats swept down to a narrow waist above a perfectly muscled ass. Though he was the eldest of the demonic lords, I couldn't help but think that sort of thing was irrelevant considering they were all several millennia old. All had an ageless look about them of men in their prime, though I now knew that most trained diligently to maintain peak physical condition — Mzatal included.

Mzatal's hands worked potency strands in rhythmic patterns, but I had no idea what he was doing. I felt the caress of his mental touch as he turned his head to give me a smile. I returned both smile and mental caress, then scooped up my clothing. It would be lovely to while away the day watching him work in the nude, but the pile of stuff from Tracy Gordon's house awaited my attention.

"What are you doing?" I asked as I dressed.

"There is much potential in the confluence behind your house," he told me. "I am using this valve as an anchor point to stabilize the flows between here and there."

Frowning, I tugged shoes on. "Wait, there's a valve *here?*"

"Yes. I will adjust the concealments." He made a peculiar little twist of his hands. "Are you able to sense it now?"

I moved toward him, then felt it—a ripple in the arcane flows, as if a layer of thin silk waved over my skin. I'd experienced it before with the valve in my aunt's library and the one in the parking lot of the Beaulac PD. I hadn't understood the sensation at the time, but now I had some hardcore training under my belt, along with the seventh ring of the shikvihr.

"Oh wow," I breathed. "When I was a kid I came out here *all* the time, and I'd sit right where you are and read or do homework or just daydream." A smile spread across my face at the memory. "It always felt so . . ." I groped for a word to describe it, then shrugged. "Right. It felt *right.*"

Mzatal touched my cheek and gave me a fond smile. "You were drawn to it even then, beloved." But his eyes went back to the valve, and his smile faded.

"What's wrong?" I asked.

"It is very draining being on Earth," he said, frustration lacing his voice. "I do not know how long I can maintain. Perhaps two days."

Shit. The amount of native potency on Earth was vastly lower than in the demon realm. The lords depended on that energy source, like a plant depended on the sun, and right now Mzatal was a battery draining faster than it could recharge. Humans didn't have the same problem when in the demon realm—in fact they tended to thrive and only risked "overcharge" if the ways between the two worlds closed, such as what happened during the cataclysm.

Yet while I'd known he wouldn't be able to remain indefinitely, I hadn't expected the time frame to be so desperately short. *We don't even have a real lead yet,* I thought with worry.

"How are Zack and Szerain able to stay here for such an extended length of time?" I asked. "Can't you do whatever they do?"

He shook his head. "Zakaar is demahnk and thus not affected in the same manner as other demons," he said.

"And Szerain is diminished, much disconnected from potency, and living as a human. Neither means serves as a solution for me."

I sighed. So much for an easy fix. "Does it help for you to be around the valve?"

"It does," he reassured me. "And the confluence may also prove useful. I will work today to stabilize and integrate both, since I will need them to seek Idris as well as to maintain my potency."

"All right." I kissed him, slid my hands around to cup his delightfully firm ass. "I take all the credit for using up your power last night."

Chuckling low, he caught my head and returned the kiss with toe-curling fervor. "And *I* will give credit where credit is due."

I returned to the house with a spring in my step, and told myself I wasn't going to worry about Mzatal's limited time here. We'd simply have to work our butts off until he had to leave. Our current plan was for him to immerse in tracking Idris through the flows—which had the added bonus of allowing him to recharge at the same time, even if only a trickle. Meanwhile, I'd focus on the more conventional, though no less important, aspects.

Breakfast was a quick affair, consisting of coffee alongside bacon piled atop a cream-cheese covered bagel and smushed into a sandwich. I ate this with one hand while Eilahn and I retired to the living room to continue the Sisyphean task of working through Tracy's journals. I'd been fooled by the ordered condition of his library. Sure, everything was arranged all nice and neat, but within the actual journals and notebooks, disorder reigned on a scale to eclipse that of my aunt's library.

However, despite the pervasive random passages and enough stream of consciousness to make James Joyce cringe, I gradually found a rhythm to the entries, and after about half an hour of reading, I straightened.

"I think I have something. These look like some of his notes for that gate he made in the warehouse."

Eilahn shifted with uncanny smoothness from her kneel-sit to peer over my shoulder. "Yes, it does appear so." Numbers, notes, neatly sketched sigils, and a half dozen alternate ritual configurations covered several pages in a tattered and coverless spiral bound notebook. She reached and traced a slender finger down a column of numbers. "What are these?"

Frowning, I puzzled over them. "Oh! It's dates and times," I said after a moment. "Look, it's year month day hour minute, though it's only the ones that had passed before Tracy died that have the hour and minute." With that realization, I examined them more closely and looked for patterns. "See how these dates have a range of times by them, but crossed out? He'd narrowed them down to specific times. Then we have ones with the range only, and here, these later dates don't even have a range."

"Ah, yes." She angled her head. "It is as if he was tracking an event."

I peered at the numbers. "You mean like he knew the date of something but didn't know the time?" I drummed my fingers on the page as I considered that. "I think I get it. He knew the date of whatever it was, wrote down the time of it, and then managed to extrapolate a range of time for the next few dates."

Eilahn's finger paused on one line of numbers. "That is the date you were summoned by Mzatal."

"And the day Tracy died." A curse whispered out of me. "He didn't live to mark down the time of whatever it was." There were many more dates after that one. A year's worth, every few weeks. Including—

"Today!" I bounced in my seat. "Eilahn, look. Whatever it is, there's one happening today."

She lowered to a crouch, gaze skimming the column of dates and times. "Yes, between nine and noon." Her mouth twitched as she angled her head at me. "I assume you wish to go witness this event, whatever it is?"

I laughed. "Do you really need to ask?"

"No," she replied with a smile. "It was indeed a foolish query. But we will need to make haste as it is already after nine."

Standing, I grabbed for my bag. "Let's roll."

A sturdy padlock secured the chain link gate at the industrial park, but after Eilahn peered closely at the lock for nearly half a minute she announced that "someone" had very carelessly failed to clasp the lock shut.

I grinned and helped her pull the gate open. My demon bodyguard had some cool tricks up her sleeve.

We passed through the gate and closed it behind us, then continued down the main drive. An eerie ghost-town quality pervaded the complex as we passed empty storefronts—auto supply store, ceramic tile showroom, discount furniture outlet, and others of that general ilk. None of the high tech industry the developers had hoped for.

"No way all these places went out of business since I was last here," I said, a little shocked as I realized that was nearly six months ago. "The new owner must have cancelled all the leases as soon as he bought the buildings."

Eilahn's steady gaze tracked around us. "Perhaps the one who purchased this complex did not wish to wait for the end of the various lease periods before beginning work on the exciting new development in health care?"

After a few seconds of thought, I shook my head. "Still doesn't make sense. These places look like they've been closed several months. If there was a rush, all of this would be torn down by now."

"A mystery," she murmured, smile playing on her mouth. "We shall endeavor to solve it, yes?"

I laughed. "Sure. I'll put it on the to-do list."

The warehouse where Tracy Gordon had attempted the gate—and where he'd died—still looked much the same as it had several months ago: a faded industrial grey facade with grime-covered glass double doors and a dark foyer beyond. It had belonged to a corporation owned by Roman Hatch, my now-incarcerated ex-boyfriend who'd decided to help Tracy Gordon kill a bunch of people and lure me to my doom.

I scowled. Damn it, all of my exes were pieces of shit. Rhyzkahl headed the list, of course, even if he didn't count as a "boyfriend." Didn't matter. He was a steaming piece of shit. On the other hand, I couldn't discount that the common factor with all of the exes was *me*. With each one I'd ignored warning signs, too lonely and needy and desperate to listen to the little voice within me that questioned my actions.

Yet I'd changed a hell of a lot in the past six months, as

had my perspective. Mzatal and I shared a trust and connection beyond anything I'd ever thought possible, and I had every belief that I'd finally broken the self-destructive pattern.

I pushed away all thoughts of boyfriends and exes and pieces of shit as I noted the white SUV in the warehouse's parking lot. I continued past the building, frustrated that I couldn't personally run the tag without jumping through hoops and calling in favors. Compromising, I stopped long enough to grab a pen and scrawl the tag number on a gas receipt. I could always give it to Ryan and Zack to check it for me later if need be.

When I reached the end of the block, I turned and came back. Still no sign of people anywhere. A golf cart was parked in an alley two buildings down from the warehouse, but I didn't see anything else that struck me as out of the ordinary. I finally parked across the street, got out and swept an assessing gaze around while Eilahn did the same. Still no sign of people or obvious threats, so together we hurried across the street to the parking lot.

I placed my hand on the hood of the SUV. "Warm," I murmured to Eilahn. "Hasn't been parked here long." Whoever it belonged to either had permission to access the complex, or had gained entry by illicit means, much as we did. Either way, it bothered me that it was parked by this particular building.

Uneasy, I headed into the shadowy narrow street that ran along the side of the building. I knew we were going to have to break into the warehouse, but I had no desire to be obvious about it and go through the front.

We were nearly to the rear of the building when Eilahn placed a hand on my arm. "Voices." Her eyes narrowed, and now I heard them from around the corner of the warehouse.

A yelp of what sounded like shock.

Another voice, shrill with stress. *"Hands up!"*

A third, calmer voice. *"No trouble here, sir."*

"That can't be good," I murmured and broke into a jog. Within two strides Eilahn overtook me, peered around the corner quickly before motioning for me to continue. I did so, then followed as she made her way toward an open door on the back end of the warehouse.

"No sudden moves! Let me see some ID!"

And a quieter, *"It's no problem. I'm cooperating."*

Wary, I put my hand on my gun to reassure myself it was there. We peered around the doorway and suddenly found ourselves with a prime vantage as two men stood near the center of the large, empty warehouse, facing a third who leveled a large handgun at them.

None of the men seemed to notice us in their peripheral vision, and I quickly processed details as Eilahn and I crouched to avoid becoming targets ourselves. Tall and gangly and with freakishly long arms, the gunman wore a baggy Apex Security uniform along with an expression that hovered between panic and bravado. His finger rested on the trigger in a mockery of any sort of proper training or trigger discipline, and his aim jerked back and forth between the other two: a young man with Hispanic features and a slender build, and a tall, broad-shouldered man dressed in a dark suit.

The wide-eyed younger man clutched what looked like a tablet computer to his chest with one hand and held the other up, fingers splayed. In sharp contrast, the suited man modeled utter calm as he performed a slow and careful two-finger extraction of something from his inside jacket pocket, most likely the demanded ID. As he did so I caught the hint of a bulge beneath his left arm.

A shoulder holster? Not that it made a difference. Even if the guard had seen a weapon it was idiotic and reckless for him to confront possible intruders without backup. Still, the situation needed to be defused before this twitchy rent-a-cop shot someone. I opened my mouth to tell Eilahn to call nine-one-one, even as a series of beeps abruptly sounded from the young man's tablet. He jerked and gave a muffled cry, then fumbled and dropped the device.

The tense tableau shattered into chaos. The security guard startled, swung his gun toward the younger one. "Don't move!" the guard cried with an excited, cocky edge to his voice. I'd heard that tone before, usually from rookie cops who were too hyped up by the power of the badge and gun, and in desperate need of a solid kick in the ass.

"Paul! Get down!" the dark-suited man ordered. In a fluid move, he dropped his ID and shifted his weight, made a twisting dive to put himself in front of the young man and take him down. A flash burst from the muzzle, and the sound of a gunshot slammed through the warehouse as the two men tumbled in a heap.

For an instant I thought the takedown had succeeded and the guard had missed, then I heard a horrible wet cough and saw blood spatter.

"Eilahn, get the gun!" I snapped out as I ran forward. She bypassed me in a flash of demon speed then used a cool spin-twist move to easily wrench the gun from the idiot security guard and drop him to the floor.

I slid to a stop and fell to my knees by the two men. The suited man jerked and struggled for breath as he lay face down atop the one he'd called Paul. A small dark splodge glistened on the back of his navy suit jacket, but the blood splatter on Paul and the floor told me the bullet had blown through.

"Bryce! No!" Paul's eyes were wide with shock as he scrabbled beneath the man, trying to hold him and wiggle from beneath him at the same time. I siezed the injured man's shoulder, tugged and rolled him onto his back, then bit back a curse as I saw his blood-soaked shirt and the dark red pool on the concrete. Blood bubbled from his mouth as he fought for breath. Paul scrabbled up and to his knees, horror filling his face at the sight.

"Eilahn, a little help here!" I called over my shoulder only to find the syraza already beside me. She dropped into a crouch and set the gun down—a .45 I absently noted—then ripped the bloody shirt open and covered the terrible exit wound in his right center chest with both hands. I shifted away to give her room and pulled out my phone to call nine-one-one. There wasn't much else I could do for the guy at this point. *A .45*, I thought in disgust. *For a security guard. Compensating much?*

My eyes fell on the ID he'd dropped. *Bryce Thatcher. StarFire Security.* That was a top-notch personal security company with an excellent reputation. Was he Paul's bodyguard? He'd sure as hell acted like one. There'd been zero hesitation to leap and take a bullet that would have no doubt killed Paul. I winced. And probably *had* killed Thatcher.

Bryce Thatcher. How did I know that name?

An electric jolt of memory zapped through me. *The list of names in Tracy's red journal.* I jerked my eyes up to the young man. "His name is Bryce Thatcher?"

Eyes glazed in shock, he managed to focus on me and give a jerky nod.

"He does not have long," Eilahn murmured with a slight nod to me that indicated she remembered Thatcher's name from the list. Shit. This guy was named in a summoner's journal and happened to be in *this* warehouse at this particular time. Finally a possible lead, and that dumbfuck security guard had to go and blow a hole in him.

Eilahn shifted her attention to Paul. "Give me your shirt."

"Wh-what?" He gave her a baffled look, too rattled to understand her intent. She growled low in her throat as she stripped off her own shirt, packed the wound with it and held pressure.

"We need Mzatal," I said.

Eilahn's mouth tightened. "Yes, I cannot hold him long." I didn't need othersight to see her weave the potency strands for healing but I could tell it was rudimentary compared to a lord's. "Three minutes," she added. "Perhaps a minute more."

Even EMS can't help him at this point, I thought with grim certainty. I hit Zack's number on speed dial, then stood and moved a short distance away, far enough to be out of earshot of Paul and the dazed guard.

Thatcher coughed up blood and frantically struggled to breathe. Paul groped for his hand, clung to it. "No—no! You can't die."

I turned away from the scene as Zack answered.

"Garner here."

"Zack, I need Mzatal where I am—Tracy Gordon's warehouse—as soon as possible," I said, voice low and urgent. "There's a man here who might hold some answers to the Mraztur's plans, and he's been shot. He's close to death."

I expected an *I'll get right on it* or something like that. Instead there was only silence on the line. Dread curdled in my gut. While Eilahn's ability to arcanely travel was drastically compromised on Earth, Zack was demahnk and didn't have the same limitations. I *knew* he had the ability to get Mzatal here before Thatcher died. Why hesitate?

"Please," I said. "I know you can do this. It's important."
I glanced back at the trio. Eilahn's face remained clenched
in a rictus of concentration. Paul clutched at Thatcher's
hand as if holding him back from the jaws of death.

My dismay rose as Zack remained silent. "If he agrees,"
he finally said, voice oddly taut.

If he agrees? My annoyance flared at his hesitation. "If
Mzatal doesn't agree, let me talk to him. This is important!"

"If he doesn't agree, I'll call back," he replied, then disconnected.

I stared at the phone as shock and anger battled it out
for precedence in my skull then jammed the phone into my
pocket and returned to crouch beside Eilahn. "Zack was
hesitant about coming," I said in a low voice, "but he said
he'd bring Mzatal if he agreed." And if Mzatal didn't agree,
there would be some *words* between us. Oh, hell yeah.

She gave me a tight nod, then narrowed her eyes and
focused on Thatcher. "You must stay here," Eilahn told him.
"Do not go. *Stay here.*"

"Yes, god, Bryce," Paul wept openly. "You can't leave me.
Please. I . . . I can't take it there without you!"

Thatcher's hand spasmed in his. Blood bubbled in his
mouth as his eyes sought Paul's. The attachment between
the two was clear. Though Paul looked to be around twenty,
he radiated an innocence that made me think of him as
younger. Thatcher might have been Paul's bodyguard, but
there was something deeper as well.

"Please. Please," Paul continued, voice choked with
barely restrained sobs. "I can't stay there without you. I
can't do it. I'll die. You're all I have. You have to live!"

Out of the corner of my eye I saw the guard stagger to
his feet, then stumble toward the door. I briefly entertained the notion of chasing him down and securing him,
then discarded it. I doubted he was going to run and tell
anyone he'd just shot a guy. If charges needed to be
pressed later, I could track him down through the security
company.

Thatcher's hand clenched on the kid's again, then his
head lolled to the side. Dead, I thought in dismay, then saw
that blood still bubbled at his mouth. No. Not dead. *Yet.*

A ripple of arcane touched me. I turned to see Zack and
Mzatal by the front entrance.

I stood as Mzatal strode toward us. "Boss, he's in bad shape. Can you save him?"

The lord's gaze went to the dying man, eyes narrowing at the severity of the injury. "I do not know," he replied and went to one knee beside Thatcher as he said something in demon to Eilahn. He removed the blood-soaked shirt from the wound and laid his own hands over it, face hardening with intense focus.

Eilahn crouched nearby, naked to the waist, and obviously completely unconcerned by it. Zack remained at a distance, face expressionless and arms folded over his chest. Paul shifted back as Mzatal knelt, then looked up at him and went still, mouth dropping open. I had to control a smile. Yeah, Mzatal had that effect on people.

"I will need your assistance, zharkat," Mzatal told me, voice tight. "He is very nearly gone."

I'd never worked with him during a healing before, and I struggled for several precious seconds while I sought the best way to support. The lords didn't heal with sigils and wards. As far as I could tell from all I'd witnessed, they healed by drawing damaged flesh together with elegant sutures of potency and then "reminding" the body of its proper form in order to restore itself—encouraging the tissues to heal a thousand times faster than naturally.

But no matter the method, it still required potency, and I could at least help collect and prepare the patterned strands.

Mzatal drew from me and through me the instant I touched the pattern. I sucked in a sharp breath while I sought to maintain the balance of the flow of power. Through the support connection I felt his struggle to hold a spark of life in Thatcher's body. Sweat broke out on Mzatal's brow, though he remained motionless. The strands burned away as he tapped them, and I was hard pressed to keep up with the drain and help control the integrity of the structure.

Thatcher coughed up a gout of blood and drew a gurgling breath. Paul surged forward to seize his hand again. "Bryce, oh god, come on," he pleaded, eyes on his friend's face. "You can do it. Don't leave."

With the initial heavy drain past, I balanced the flow to Mzatal to fuel his effort. Like a shadow seen through a sheer curtain, I watched him locate critical bleeding and weave repairs, felt him urge Thatcher's body to remember its healthy state and form.

Again Thatcher coughed, but this time he followed it with a clearer breath. Through Mzatal, I felt his tenuous connection to life strengthen as the sense of drowning in his own blood decreased. Paul gripped Thatcher's hand, yet his gaze remained on Mzatal, an almost worshipful expression on his face. He *knew* Mzatal was doing something miraculous to save his friend.

Thatcher's face twisted in pain. "God . . . Oh, god," he rasped, breath noisy, but without the horrible death-rattle gurgle of before. "P-Paul . . . okay?"

Tears spilled down the young man's face as he gave his friend a tremulous smile. "I'm okay. You saved me."

Even my cynical ass could appreciate the poignancy of the moment, but I didn't have much chance to do so as a movement by the back door yanked my attention. At first I thought that perhaps it was emergency services, summoned by the damn security guard. It would be a bit of a pain to deal with cops or EMS right now, but—

I stared, mind in denial for several precious seconds as, impossibly, Katashi's senior summoner strode into a warehouse on the outskirts of a small town in south Louisiana. Tsuneo, the treacherous asshole who bore a tattoo of Jesral's mark on his hip, and who had performed a hostile summoning of Gestamar several months back. Beside him loomed another man I recognized from my brief time as Katashi's student: Tito, not a summoner, more of a thug type with a sensitivity to the arcane.

Anger flared. "You!" I shot to my feet and moved to get in front of Mzatal and the others. I drew my gun even as Tito pulled his to put us into a great little standoff.

Tsuneo's gaze hardened at the sight of me, but in the next instant his face went slack with shock as he not only saw Mzatal but *felt* his aura.

What the hell was Tsuneo doing here? For that matter, what were Thatcher and a computer nerd doing here? Was everyone here for a frickin' arcane flash mob?

Moreover, was Thatcher also a summoner? Was Paul? *Even more vital for Thatcher to live through this so we can question the hell out of him,* I thought grimly.

I heard a hiss-growl from behind me, and the hair on the back of my neck lifted as Mzatal's aura flared, dark with fury. He stood and stepped forward with hands still dripping blood, radiating Bad Mojo like a sun about to go supernova as he faced the traitorous summoner. His left fist remained clenched at his side as his right opened in a stance I recognized all too well. Lowering his head, he moved toward the interlopers.

Shit! I kept my gun leveled on Tito and risked a quick glance back at Thatcher. He still breathed, but I knew he was far from stable.

As Mzatal advanced, Tsuneo took a stumbling step back and looked around wildly as if trying to come up with a miraculous defense. He apparently concluded there was none because his next move was to run like hell for the exit.

Mzatal lifted his right hand and called scintillating blue-white potency to it even as Tsuneo darted through the door and out. Tito frowned, apparently balanced upon a razor's edge decision of whether to fire or run.

Mzatal rendered the decision moot. Face stone-hard and focused, he hurled the potency at Tito like a lightning strike. The man screamed and dropped the gun as the burst impacted his belly and spread over him in a rippling cascade of light. He jerked heavily for several seconds, then crumpled to lie twisted and utterly still.

The deadly potency flickered and died as Mzatal continued forward. Behind me I heard Thatcher's struggle for breath, and Paul's agonized entreaties for him to hold on, to stay.

"Boss!" I yelled, holstering my gun. "You're losing Thatcher. Let Tsuneo go! We'll track his ass down later."

Mzatal took two more steps then stopped, his hands clenched at his sides, violently seething potency boiling off of him. Yet he still didn't turn back toward me and the man dying on the floor. I knew he wanted to pursue Tsuneo, exact revenge for the injury to Gestamar and the insult of the summoner's betrayal and allegiance to the Mraztur.

"Boss," I urged. "Mzatal, please! We need Thatcher alive." Behind me, the wounded man's breath grew more labored.

Mzatal remained lord-still for several more agonizing seconds while I fought the urge to grab him and pull him back to finish the healing. Finally he turned, met my eyes for a powerful instant before striding back to Thatcher. I let out a ragged sigh of relief as he knelt and placed his hands back on the mess of the chest wound.

I quickly resumed balancing the pattern and the flows, then looked back at the crumpled body of Tito. No doubt he was dead.

Shit. This was a mess.

Welcome to Earth, Boss, I thought with a sigh.

Chapter 11

I'd have downed more coffee if I'd known the day was going to descend into chaos so thoroughly. Now I had to figure out a way to clean up this clusterfuck.

"Zack." I kept my voice low, but I knew he could hear me. "Maybe you should get hold of Ryan to help take care of—" I grimaced, lifted a chin toward the corpse. Under other circumstances Mzatal could have disposed of the body with a potency-fueled cremation. Yet I felt his reserves through our connection, and I knew he didn't have the strength to do so and still have a chance of saving Thatcher.

Zack remained silent and still for several heartbeats, but finally gave a slight nod and pulled out his phone. He thumbed in a text message, sent it, then moved over to the dead man, crouched and laid a hand on his chest, face filled with a look of such unbearable sadness that I had to turn away. I heard him murmuring something over the body, but I was too far away to make out the words. The rhythm and lilt of it led me to believe it wasn't English, though it didn't sound like demon either.

Thatcher drew a steadier breath. Paul still clung to his friend's hand, his eyes red and puffy in a face wracked with shock and desperation.

"What were you two doing here?" I asked.

It took a few seconds for Paul to realize I was talking to him, and another couple for him to focus on me. "It . . . it was my stupid idea," he said, voice cracking. "This is all my fault." His eyes dropped to Thatcher again. "I'm sorry,

Bryce. Oh god, I'm so sorry." His face twisted, and I reached out and seized his arm.

"Stop it," I ordered. "He's going to be all right." I filled my voice with as much absolute certainty as possible. It helped that I truly did believe Mzatal would save the man's life. "Why did you come here?" I pressed.

Paul's eyes flicked up to Mzatal, and a whisper of hope crept into them. He swallowed, visibly struggled to be strong. "It was going to be at ten-seventeen a.m.," he said and cast a worried look over to where his tablet lay where he'd dropped it. "There was going to be a wiggle in the feeds at ten-seventeen." His lower lip quivered for an instant before he firmed his mouth and regained a bit of control. "I told him I wanted to come check it out. Made him bring me."

I look at him in bafflement. "A what? A wiggle in the feeds? What the hell does that mean?"

"It's, uh . . ." The grief on his face melted away as he focused on finding words to describe whatever it was. He opened his mouth to speak, then shook his head. "I do stuff with computers," he explained, apparently giving up on providing details. "Lots of, er, deep level stuff. And I'd noted some, well, wiggles, shifts in the data patterns and streams. Always after the fact though. I figured out some of the parameters and extrapolated to predict one for today right here. I just wanted to be here to see what happened."

I struggled to parse his explanation. Data patterns? Streams? "You do stuff with computers?" I echoed. "That's it?"

A trace of insult crossed his face at the slight. "Yeah. That's it." His brow furrowed as he looked around, *really* looked around at us all for the first time. Zack and I probably looked normal enough, but Eilahn crouched shirtless near Thatcher's feet, and there was no mistaking Mzatal for ordinary. And, of course, there was that pesky dead body not all that far away.

His attention returned to me. "Who *are* you people?"

"We're . . . " Shit. Now I was the one at a loss for how to explain things. "We're the good guys, trust me," I finally said lamely. "So, you don't do any, er, arcane or 'magic' type stuff?" I even did the quotey marks with my fingers, which didn't at all help how silly I felt asking him if he did magic.

Paul turned wide eyes to Mzatal again, and it was clear he knew something "magical" was happening to save his friend. He shook his head slowly, voice dropping to a rough whisper. "No."

"What about him?" I asked, jerking my head toward Thatcher. "What's he do? Does he do anything arcane?"

Paul looked back over at me. "He's my bodyguard." The sudden look of stunned realization that swept over his face was almost comical in its unabashed extreme. "Oh my god. He saved my life."

I sat back on my heels and processed all he'd told me. According to Paul, neither of these two were arcane practitioners, though I knew he could easily be lying. Fortunately, I had a Mzatal-shaped lie detector, and as soon as he wasn't otherwise occupied in major tissue and organ repair, I'd ask him to assess Paul and find out for sure.

But if Paul was telling the truth, and Thatcher wasn't a summoner, then why on earth did Tracy have a bodyguard's name in his journal? Maybe he'd planned on hiring one? Maybe Thatcher had actually worked for him at one point? Only the man bleeding on the floor could answer those questions.

I abruptly noticed that the blood on Paul wasn't all Thatcher's. "Your arm is bleeding," I gently pointed out. Looked like the bullet had scored his left upper arm after exiting Thatcher's chest.

Paul blinked and looked down at the shallow wound. I fully expected him to freak a bit at being shot, especially after being so upset about Thatcher, but to my surprise he simply gave a somewhat distracted frown. "Oh. Yeah. Guess it is."

I took a closer look at him. Now I saw that his nose was slightly crooked, with a bump on one side that told me it had been broken. A thin scar ran along one cheekbone, and another one cut through an eyebrow. He'd taken damage before, I realized.

Falling silent, I continued to weave support while I wondered about this pair. Why did a computer nerd need a bodyguard? And how the hell had he used a computer to trace what he called a "wiggle" to this precise spot and time if he didn't know about the arcane? Sure, Tracy—and obviously Tsuneo—had tracked it, but they were summoners. More questions to be answered.

"Enough," Mzatal said after a while, voice drawn and lacking its usual resonance. He lifted his hands from Thatcher's chest. Raw, angry tissue sealed the ugly wound, and though Thatcher's skin still held a sickly pallor, he breathed slowly and with relative ease.

Blue-green potency flared on Mzatal's hands as he burned the blood cleanly away. I felt his profound exhaustion, but there was no more I could do for him at this point except worry. I reached for his hand. He took it, gave it a soft squeeze, conveying reassurance, affection, and gratitude in the simple gesture.

"Is he going to be okay?" Paul asked, face twisted with concern.

Mzatal met the young man's eyes, remained silent for several heartbeats before answering. "He will recover, Paul Ortiz," he told him. "Now breathe."

Paul drew in a ragged breath and gazed up at Mzatal in utter awe.

The side door creaked as Ryan entered. He swept his gaze around the warehouse, taking it all in. His eyes briefly met mine before moving on to rest on the corpse, and I watched the emotions crawl over his face as the implications hit home. Mzatal had killed a man, and now Ryan, a federal agent, was expected to help cover it up. Ryan had dealt with a lot of grey areas in the past year, including faking a story about the death of Tracy Gordon. But this crossed another line.

Yet when his eyes returned to mine, they offered reassurance. It reminded me of the old saw, "A friend will help you move. A best friend will help you move bodies." This was a horrible scenario fraught with all sorts of issues, but at the end of the day I knew he'd help me clean up the mess we were in.

I stood, legs a little shaky from managing the support for so long. "We need to get these two back to the house," I told Ryan with a nod toward Paul and Thatcher. "And take care of . . ." I gestured toward Tito.

He rubbed a hand over his jaw. "Right. Zack gave me a summary in his text. I'm thinking."

"Wait. House?" Paul scrambled to his feet to stare at me in horror. "What house? I can't go!" Terror suddenly flooded his face for no reason I could pinpoint. "We *can't* go," he gasped, then fumbled in his pocket and pulled out his phone. "We can't go! Oh, god. I need . . . I need to make a call!"

"No!" I lunged to grab his arm. "No. Paul, please, you have to trust me. Your friend needs more care." I searched his face. Sweat dotted his upper lip, and his breath came in short panicked gasps. "And you're somewhere you don't want to be," I said. I hadn't forgotten what he'd said to Thatcher when he thought the man was dying: *I can't take it there without you! I can't stay there without you. I can't do it. I'll die.*

"Let us help you," I urged.

All color drained from his face. "No. You don't understand." He shook his head and struggled to twist free of my grip. "Please," he said, voice breaking. "I need to call."

My skin prickled at the odd fervency in his voice. I glanced over at Mzatal to see him regarding the young man with narrow-eyed intensity. "Why?" I asked Paul. "Why do you need to call?"

"I j-just do," he said. I felt a tremble go through him. "It's where we need to be."

I stared at him in confusion. "What will happen if you don't call?"

He gulped and cast a panicked gaze around him. "They'll be looking for us soon if we don't call in. I can't just *go* with you. I have to get back. To work." Emotions warred on his face, and I didn't need to be a mind reader to know there was some serious turmoil going on in there.

"*Who* will be looking for you?" I asked.

He made an unintelligible response and pulled against my grasp. His eyes darted this way and that like a cornered animal seeking any possible escape, even if it meant off a cliff.

What the hell was his deal? "Paul, it's all right," I said as calmly as possible. Whoever "they" were, he had some heavy duty fear associated with them, and Mzatal would get farther by reading him than I would by pushing the question. "You don't have to answer me right now, but you do need to listen." I kept a firm grip on his arm and turned him to face me more. "Thatcher is still in bad shape. If he doesn't get more healing, he'll die. He needs to stay with us to get that healing." I let that sink in for a few seconds before continuing. "I won't keep you against your will, but do you really want to leave your friend? Or allow him to die?" Yeah, I was playing horribly dirty, but I only felt a little guilty about it. Okay, shit, I felt a *lot* guilty about it since it was like telling a kid that the bogeyman would take him away forever if he didn't eat his vegetables.

His mouth dropped open as a look of undisguised horror temporarily replaced the fear. "No. No! He can't die!"

"Then come with us," I said. "I promise you'll be able to leave whenever you want." Or rather, I'd let him leave *after* I found out why he wanted to go so badly.

He drew a breath and relaxed a bit, and for a shining moment I thought he'd accepted the pure genius of my argument. Yet in the next instant he yanked in wide-eyed desperation against my grip as the fear returned.

I bit back a curse. "Boss, I need some help here."

Mzatal moved to us and, without any preliminaries, gripped Paul's head between his hands. Paul's face abruptly went slack, eyes glassy as he succumbed to Mzatal's influence. I released Paul's arm and rested my hand on Mzatal's back as he worked, offering what support I could. The healing of Thatcher and the potency strike on Tito had drained him, and it showed in his pallor and the lines of tension on his face.

Mzatal's eyes narrowed. "He carries a pervasive influence that is not a direct manipulation," he said. "It is insidious, as though he has been steeped in an energy that has contaminated all parts. Very different from conscious manipulation and challenging to clear."

"Who did it? A lord?"

Mzatal shifted his grip on Paul. "No. His fear is of Big Mack."

"He's afraid of a burger?" I asked, baffled.

Mzatal's brows drew together as he deciphered the meaning from me. "No. Big Mack is a man." He returned his attention to Paul, and I held back further questions. Fortunately, Mzatal provided an explanation before I went too far into my vision of a scary hamburger clown wreaking havoc. "It is one named Farouche."

"He must mean James Macklin Farouche," I said. "These guys work for StarFire Security, which is owned by him." I frowned. J.M. Farouche was a prominent Louisiana businessman and philanthropist. The security company was only one of his many holdings. "*That's* who he's so afraid of?" I asked, unable to fully hide the note of disbelief in my voice. "Everything I've ever heard about him is that he's a great guy—gives tons to charity, treats his employees well. His family has lived around here for a couple hundred years. In fact he still lives on the Farouche plantation."

"It is truth. This Farouche held heavy influence over this one," Mzatal said. "A compulsion component wound tightly with primal fear. I have removed much of the influence and dispersed the residuals such that they will not obligate him to take action."

I had a tough time believing a respected—and seemingly ordinary—businessman like Farouche could do such a thing, but I also knew better than to doubt Mzatal. "All right. That's pretty, um, interesting." I took a few more seconds to process it all. "If it's not manipulation, then how does it work? And how is a *human* doing it?"

Mzatal frowned. "I have seen talent for such in three humans before," he said. "For two of them, it was an innate ability to influence the actions of others simply by being in their presence, though without lasting effect." His frown deepened. "The third, long ago, demonstrated not only the passive influence, but also a conscious and invasive ability to impose her will in more permanent fashion, much as Farouche has to Paul Ortiz."

A shiver ran over me. Bad enough that lords could mentally control people, but at least they were usually tucked safely away in the demon realm. I knew there were humans other than summoners who had more-than-normal abilities. In fact, it had been less than a year since I tracked down a killer who fed on the essences of her victims.

But I'd never heard of one who could control actions and behavior as Farouche supposedly did, and even the concept left me cold.

"I asked Paul if he or Thatcher ever used the arcane," I told Mzatal. "He denied it, but I wanted to check with you. Did you assess him?"

"I did," Mzatal said. "He speaks the truth of himself and what he knows of Bryce Thatcher."

"Can we trust them?" I asked. "I told Paul we'd help

them both, but at the same time I don't want to bring a potential enemy into our midst."

Mzatal withdrew his hands from Paul's head and stepped back. "In this moment, Paul Ortiz holds no intention of taking action against us," he assured me. "However, I will continue to monitor him for any indication of duplicity or threat."

"Thanks, Boss," I said, relieved. "I'd rather be over-paranoid, y'know?"

Paul blinked, focused on Mzatal. "What happened?"

Mzatal regarded the young man. "I have eased your unnatural fear of James Macklin Farouche."

Paul opened his mouth as though to protest but then closed it again. Bafflement swept across his face, followed quickly by amazement as he no doubt felt the difference in himself.

"Oh my god. Oh my god!" He gazed up at Mzatal as though looking into the face of a superhero. "Thank you." Tears glistened in his eyes.

Mzatal inclined his head. "You are most welcome."

"Paul, this is Lord Mzatal," I said. "We need to get Thatcher out of here and get the place cleaned up. You cool to go with us now?"

"Yeah," he replied, voice barely above a whisper, eyes still on Mzatal. "I'm okay now."

A sudden wave of disorienting vertigo hit me, as though I stood in the middle of an upward swirling vortex. I threw a hand out to steady myself, felt Mzatal gather me to him.

We both held onto each other and swayed for nearly a full minute until the sensation subsided.

"What the *hell* was that?" I gasped out.

"Ten-seventeen!" Paul exclaimed with unmistakable exuberance, though he looked just as shaky as I felt. "It's ten-seventeen. That was the wiggle!"

"This is a nodal point of the valve system," Mzatal said, face set in the familiar frown that told me he was deep in assessment of the area. "What we experienced was a type of valve emission, a release of—" He paused as though seeking the words. "—a release of pressure, like unto a geyser."

Comprehension dawned. "It's a place that regulates the pressure of multiple valves?" Mzatal nodded. *Like an arcane Old Faithful,* I thought. "And Tracy was trying to use that burst, that emission, to feed his gate creation," I added with satisfaction as a few more bits of the puzzle came together. It also explained why Tsuneo had shown up, though it didn't explain what he'd planned to do once he was here.

"It was unwise of him to attempt such," Mzatal said, expression darkening. "The balance of both worlds depends upon the integrity of the valves. They are not to be altered or misused. Tampering with a node risks damaging many valves." He swayed again, but this time I knew it was from potency depletion and not an aftereffect of the node geyser.

"Let's get out of here," I said. "I'll bring the car close to the door. Eilahn, can you carry Thatcher?"

"Wait!" Paul exclaimed, aghast. I paused mid-stride to give him a questioning look. "You can't just go *outside* like that!"

Frowning, I glanced down at myself and then at the others. "Oh, of course," I said with a low laugh. "Good catch. Boss, will you please loan Eilahn your jacket?"

Mzatal slipped off the Armani suit jacket and handed it to the still-topless Eilahn, but Paul shook his head. "No, no, no. Not *that,*" he said with a touch of exasperation. "There are *cameras* out there. My tablet. I need my tablet." He looked around, face twisting with a different kind of worry as he looked where he'd dropped it. "Shit."

I retrieved the tablet and handed it to him. It was in a rugged, shockproof case, and the screen wasn't cracked, so hopefully it was all right for whatever he needed it for. "You can do something about the cameras?" I asked doubtfully. I hadn't really been worried about surveillance when we arrived, but that was before we'd stumbled into a gigantic mess.

"If my tablet still works, sure," he said matter-of-factly as he pushed the power button. His shoulders slumped in relief when it turned on, and he proceeded to quickly tap away at it.

"You're serious." I stared at him. "You can hack into the security system here?" Was he so good with computers he warranted a bodyguard?

He shook his head. "There's no system in here. I mean, not in this building, and not one that's active anymore." Intense concentration suffused his features as he continued to tap, reminding me weirdly of Mzatal's super-focused expression.

"Streetlight cam that catches the entrance to the industrial park," he murmured to himself. "Two cameras covering the back of this section of the park. Knock the street cam out for a bit, loop the others to cover." He frowned, tapped some more. "Wipe our entry." He flicked a glance up then back down. "And yours." His frown deepened, but about a minute later his mouth spread into a grin. "There. All set!" He took a deep satisfied breath and released it, looking almost recharged by the quick bit of hacker work.

"Um, okay." I gave a mental shrug. With Mzatal monitoring him for anything treacherous, I had no reason not to trust him at this point.

I hurried out and brought the car closer. Eilahn carried Thatcher out, showing no more strain than if he were a child. Paul followed her, clearly impressed and amazed by what surely seemed like a superhuman feat.

Through the open door I saw a blue-green shimmer as Mzatal burned the rest of the blood from the floor of the warehouse. Ryan passed me with the body of Tito slung in a fireman's carry and gave me a tight nod as he headed to his own car. "See you back at the house," he said over his shoulder.

I didn't ask what he and Zack intended to do with the body. Some things were best left undiscussed.

Eilahn climbed into the back of my car and cradled the unconscious Thatcher to her, while Paul settled in beside her and took hold of the limp hand again. Eilahn's eyes closed, and I knew she would arcanely support the wounded man until we could get back to the house.

I turned to Mzatal as he exited the warehouse, his hands clasped behind his back. "Boss, you're going to have to ride with me since Ryan and Zack are . . . cleaning up the mess."

"With you is my desire, zharkat," he said, voice lacking its usual fullness which only served to increase my worry for him. He kissed me tenderly then slid a hand down to take mine.

I walked with him to the car, got him settled in the front passenger seat and prayed that Paul wasn't feeding us a line of bullshit about the cameras. "Everyone good?" I asked with a glance into the back before I slid into the driver's seat.

"What about Bryce's car?" Paul asked, brow furrowing with renewed concern as he looked over at the white SUV. "Oh man, they're gonna freak out no matter what."

"We'll deal with it," I said. Somehow. It was all too probable that we'd deal with the SUV by leaving it right where it was.

I started the car and headed home. I couldn't even be relieved that we were leaving a mess behind. I flicked a quick glance at the rear view mirror. No, we were bringing this mess home with us. All I could do was hope it would be worth it.

Chapter 12

We made it home without further incident. I parked and got out, opened the back door to let Eilahn carry Thatcher inside. I watched her go in, Paul trailing her, then took Mzatal's hand as he got out of the car.

"Boss," I said softly. "You're drained." I looked up at him with deep concern.

He gave a weary nod. "I will go to the confluence now," he said, starting to walk around the house. "It will help."

I tightened my hold on his hand as we walked. "It won't be enough. You need to return." I hated it, but I didn't want him to overextend or get hurt, either due to the drain itself or by being ambushed by a hostile lord upon his return to the demon realm more depleted than he already was.

"I will rest," he said again, shook his head. "It is too soon to leave."

"I don't want you to go," I said, turning to face him as we reached that spot in the backyard. "But I'd rather kick you off Earth than see you do yourself lasting damage."

Exhaling, he sank to his knees in the grass, then shifted to sit cross-legged. I crouched before him and kissed him. "What's the deal with Paul?" I asked, changing the subject. There was only so much arguing I could do with Mzatal. "You said he was coerced into working for Farouche by that fear. Is he a prisoner?"

"I do not know more of his status with Farouche," Mzatal told me, expression darkening. "He carried deep, pervasive fear of the man and of the consequences of betraying him."

My knees began to ache, so I plopped down cross-legged.

"Is his devotion to Thatcher also influenced or implanted by Farouche?"

"The attachment to Bryce Thatcher seems genuine, beloved," Mzatal said. "It continues even though I have unwound the compulsion." His brow creased. "Paul was at war with himself, both wanting and not wanting to return to this Farouche. He found a deep sense of security and fulfillment in Farouche's service, even though it carried with it a strong undercurrent of fear."

I carefully mulled all of this over, including the very selfish consideration that Paul and his apparent genius hacker computer skills could be *really* useful to us. "Thatcher needs a lot more healing, doesn't he?"

"He does. I will continue after I rest."

Seriously? Mzatal had to be the stubbornest lord *ever*. "No, Boss," I said. "I think that after you rest you should return to your realm and take those two with you." I took a deep breath, fixed him with a hard look. "That will allow you to recharge, Thatcher to get completely healed, and will keep Paul away from Farouche for a couple of days—hopefully long enough for us to figure out what the real deal is."

"I will rest," Mzatal replied, but before I could open my mouth to argue with him again he added, "and then I will reassess." He took my hand, stroked his thumb over the cracked stone of my ring. "We have no information on Idris," he said, the ache in his voice palpable.

I lifted my hand and kissed his fingers. "I know." I gave him a slight smile. "Why the hell do you think I want to get a hacker on our side?"

His eyes met mine, and I saw him read the implications from me. "Ah, I understand." He considered it, gave a slight nod. "Useful, yes."

"You'll do it? You'll go home and take them with you?"

"I will reassess after I rest. Soon."

I rolled my eyes. I'd *reassess* upside his head if he didn't get the hell home and recharge properly. "Of course, darling," I said with a sweet smile. I knew damn well he'd read those thoughts. "I'll go in and check on our guests now." I gave him a parting kiss, then stood and headed inside.

Eilahn had situated Thatcher on the bed in the guest room where Zack had been staying. She'd stripped and bagged his gear and bloody clothing and wrapped him in a sheet. Paul sat on a stool beside the bed, clutching Thatcher's hand. I stopped in the open doorway, leaned against the jamb.

"Lord Mzatal will take care of him," I said gently. "It's going to be okay."

"I don't get it," Paul said, voice carrying his fatigue and worry. He looked over at me. "How is this possible? Who *is* he? Who are you?"

"I'm Kara Gillian," I told him. This part, at least, was easy. "I used to be a homicide detective with the Beaulac Police Department." Now came the not so easy part. Then again, this kid had already seen some miracles, so maybe it would go over all right. "I'm also an arcane practitioner," I continued. "I have the ability to open a portal between this world and another and summon its denizens through it. Lord Mzatal is a qaztahl, one of eleven lords of that world." I stopped to let that sink in.

He stared at me. "Another *world*?"

I nodded. "It sounds pretty crazy, I know. But, then again, you've seen that arcane power truly exists." I lifted my chin toward his friend on the bed.

Paul gulped, looked down at his hand in Thatcher's. "Yeah. Miracle. He was almost . . ." His face paled as he choked on the word. *Dead.*

"He's going to be okay," I repeated. I wanted to emphasize the hell out of that. I tilted my head and regarded him. "How long have you worked for StarFire and Mr. Farouche?"

"Um," he darted his eyes around the room nervously, as if wishing someone else could answer the question for him. "About a year," he finally said.

"Cool." I gave him a friendly smile. This was nothing more than two people chatting, shooting the shit, getting to know each other. Nice and casual. "You like working for them?"

A variety of emotions crawled across his face, running the gamut from wonder to fear. "It's, um, good work for me."

Nice way to not answer the question. "How'd you get the job with them?"

His face paled, and he hunched his shoulders.

"Recruited," he said though it was almost more question than statement.

I took a step into the room, met his eyes. "Forcefully?"

Panic whispered through his eyes. He opened his mouth to speak, cleared his throat and tried again. "Force?" His voice shook on the word, but then he took a breath and eased as though a nightmare slipped away. Lingering echoes of the Farouche influence, perhaps.

"How did they get you, Paul?" I asked quietly as I moved farther into the room. "Did they coerce you by threatening someone else, someone close to you? Or did they simply grab you in the night and put you to work?"

He looked away, shoulders slumping and misery written into his face. "No threats," he said in a low voice. "They came and took me. No warning."

The poor guy looked so beaten down, bewildered and torn. "Paul, we can help you."

"I just need Bryce to get better."

"He's still in bad shape, Paul," I said. "He needs the kind of healing the lord can only do in his own world." I touched his shoulder. "Would you be willing to go with your friend to that other world for a day or two? He needs it, and it would also give you more time to decide how you want to live the rest of your life."

He stared at me in baffled shock, clearly trying to figure out if what he thought he heard me say was really what I'd said. "You mean not on Earth?"

"Right," I said. "Not Earth. The other world. You'd be safe there, under the lord's protection."

His eyes went distant. "That's the only place we'd be safe from Big Mack," he murmured.

"You need to be safe, Paul. Give yourself this time."

He focused on me again, confusion and hope and fear in his face. "I need Bryce to get better," he repeated, voice steadying as he seemed to come to a decision. "He's my best friend. He . . . saved me." His chin lifted as he straightened. "Okay. Yes."

Relieved, I gave him a smile. "It'll be about two hours," I told him. "Lord Mzatal is resting right now." I suddenly realized Paul was still wearing the same blood-soaked clothing. "Damn. You need a change of clothes and a bandage on that arm. Hang tight. I'll be right back." I left the room without waiting for a response, headed to my bedroom, and grabbed an old PD t-shirt and a pair of sweat pants that I had a feeling would fit him perfectly, as slim as he was. On the way back I detoured to the bathroom and grabbed the first aid kit, a towel, and a wet washcloth.

"Here you go," I said as I returned. I set the shirt and sweats on top of the dresser. "Go ahead and take that mess off," I gestured to his bloody shirt, "and I'll get your arm fixed up."

Paul looked oddly discomfited. "Um, maybe you can do it if I just pull the sleeve up?" He reached over and began to awkwardly roll up his sleeve above the shallow wound.

I gave him a withering look and cocked an eyebrow at him as I pointedly raked my gaze over his blood-soaked clothing. "It's a mess," I stated firmly. "I'd need to soak it for a week in meat tenderizer to get the blood out. Off with it."

He swallowed, but went ahead and pulled the shirt off to reveal a roadmap of scars on his torso. I pygahed to keep my face expressionless. Three surgical scars along his spine, and two abdominal, including one that started at his solar plexus and disappeared into the top of his pants. Another half dozen irregular scars were scattered randomly, perhaps a result of the injury or accident that had necessitated the surgeries.

"Let's get the dried blood off first," I said, very matter-of-factly. I folded the wet washcloth and began to carefully wipe where Thatcher's blood had soaked through Paul's shirt and crusted on his torso. He stood silently, not resisting and not looking at me. "Any of these areas still cause pain?" I asked, remaining as clinical as possible. "I don't want to hurt you."

"Um, my back does some," he said, eyes still averted, "but not you touching like this."

"Good to know." I did my best to get the blood cleaned off while I worked around the numerous scars. Some were still red and obviously tender, while a couple had the whiter shade of an older scar, with others falling along a spectrum in between. He'd obviously gone under the knife quite a few times. "Are you done with surgeries or do you still need more?"

"I'm done," he said quietly. "They said they can't do anything else until there's degeneration later." He exhaled a sigh.

I shifted my attention to the shallow wound on his left arm. It had pretty much stopped bleeding, but was a sticky mess. Didn't look like it needed stitches though. "Lord Mzatal can probably fix up any lingering issues," I said while I gently dabbed at clotted blood. "He fixed me up when I was a bloody mess."

Paul looked at me for the first time since taking his shirt off. "You were a bloody mess?" His brow furrowed, eyes skimming over me as if trying to find the signs of it. "What happened?"

Mouth tightening, I finished cleaning the wound and set the washcloth down, then stepped back and pulled my shirt up to right below my bra, revealing the sigil scars on my torso. Paul sucked in a gasp as his eyes went to the scars and their horrific beauty. Cold prickled over me as the memory of the unnatural pain shifted, fighting to rise up and wash over me from where I'd shoved it down.

"These were cut into me by an arcane blade while I hung from my wrists bound behind me," I said, voice flat and toneless. "Both shoulders dislocated, fractured cheekbone, and cuts like this all over my torso, front, back, and sides, from the nape of my neck to my tailbone."

He swallowed audibly. "Oh my god."

I let my shirt fall back in place and fixed my gaze on him. "Your turn. What's your story?"

Grief and shame clouded his eyes. "I . . . got beaten up. It was pretty bad."

Pretty bad? That was the understatement of the millennium judging by his scars. Had Farouche done this to him?

No, I decided after a bit of thought. He'd worked for Farouche only about a year, and some of those scars were obviously older than that. Yet I didn't think Paul was much more than twenty, which meant he'd likely been a teenager when it happened. Why the hell would anyone beat the everloving dogsnot out of a kid this mild and gentle?

"Who did this to you, Paul?" I asked quietly.

His hand trembled as he touched the scar on his cheekbone. "M-my dad," he whispered.

"I'm sorry." I let out a sigh. "It's even worse when it's someone you trust, isn't it?"

"Yes! Oh god, yes, so much worse!" He shook his head.

"I'm sorry. I never thought anyone else could understand. It's the worst." Breath shuddered out of him. "It *hurt*."

I knew he didn't mean the physical pain. My throat tightened without warning in a weird mix of grief and anger. I opened the first aid kit, busied myself with getting supplies out while I regained my composure. "I was betrayed by my lover," I said when I could control my voice again. "He made love to me, then strung me up and did all that shit to me." I began to clean the wound with betadine wipes. "It's the shattering of trust that hurts the most," I continued. "You trust this person. They're supposed to be the one protecting you, helping you, and instead they fuck you up." I found gauze in the first aid kit and carefully taped it over the wound. "And it's like something's broken, and you think you'll never be able to trust or love again." *But I did*, I thought fiercely. *I did trust, and I did love again. Fuck you, Rhyzkahl.*

"Yeah." His voice broke a bit, and he paused to clear his throat. "I've got Bryce. And I know that's screwy because . . . because I was a prisoner and he was my guard." He sighed. "But I've got Bryce."

"I have Mzatal," I said. "And it's not screwy. I get it. Bryce really cares about you." I knew damn well he didn't take that bullet for Paul simply because it was his job. I closed the first aid kit and handed Paul the clean t-shirt.

He pulled it on then looked down at the pale form of Thatcher on the bed. "He does." A smile touched his mouth. "He does really care. It's like having the best big brother ever sometimes." He took a deep breath, shifted his attention back to me and abruptly changed the subject. "Mzatal. From another world. Wow." A weak chuckle slipped out. "Sorry, still trying to get a handle on it. I mean, he used magic—"

"Arcane," I put in, then shrugged. "Doesn't sound quite as *weird* then."

Paul managed a crooked smile. "Right. Arcane. He used it to heal Bryce and," he paled, gulped, "kill that other guy. Oh my god. I've never felt anything like that before."

"He's got some mojo when he's worked up," I said with a nod.

"Mojo," he echoed. "That's putting it mildly, to say the

least. I mean, I felt it before, big time, when he was doing his thing to Bryce," he continued, growing more animated, "but when he stood up, whoa!"

"It's definitely palpable," I agreed, hiding a smile at the awe in Paul's expression.

"What was the deal?" he asked. "Who were those guys? He *killed* one, just like that. Blam!"

I had to bite the inside of my cheek to keep from bursting out laughing. *I wonder if Mzatal knows he has a fanboy now?* "They work for the lords who did this to me," I said, sobering a bit as I tapped my chest, indicating the scars. "Those lords want this world, and they don't intend to be nice about it."

His eyes widened. "Want this world?" He took a few seconds to process that. "This is big stuff," he stated, as if the fact that another world existed was old news now.

"It sure is," I said, doing my best to keep a serious expression. If not for Mzatal's assessment and assurance that Paul wasn't a threat to us, I might have worried that Paul's ingenuous nature was simply part of an act to gain my trust. But I trusted Mzatal, and I knew he'd pick up anything suspicious the instant it cropped up.

"My torture wasn't simply for torture's sake," I told him. "It was part of a ritual meant to make me a thrall, a powerful tool for them to construct a permanent arcane gate between their world and ours, and more."

"And you really want me and Bryce to go to the other world?" he asked, an eager edge in his voice now.

I managed to give him an appropriately serious nod. "It would only be for a day or two," I said, "but I truly believe it would be for the best."

"It would be," he agreed, then grimaced. "Big Mack will look for us. He'll find out we were brought here."

"You're pretty valuable to your boss," I said. "I'm sure they'll be hunting for you."

His brow creased. "How do you know that? I mean, that I'm valuable."

I lowered myself to sit on the ottoman. "Because your boss went to the trouble of kidnapping you."

He hunched in on himself. "Yeah. I guess that makes sense."

I eyed him, remembering what Mzatal had said about

residuals of the influence and compulsion from Farouche. "You're still afraid of him."

"It's better now," he said slowly. "Way better since Lord Mzatal did . . . whatever he did." He looked down at his hands, clenched and unclenched them as if making sure they worked. "Mr. Farouche never *hurt* me or anything. He made sure I had all the medical care and surgeries the doctors recommended. Gave me everything I needed. Hell, just about anything I wanted, too. He's just . . . " Paul shivered and rubbed his arms, then sighed. "Yeah. He still scares me."

"I think Lord Mzatal can help you more with that," I said, then stood. "I'm going to scrounge up some food. You sit tight here, and I'll bring something in for you."

He gave me a wavering smile. "Thanks, Kara, for everything."

I returned the smile. "Sure thing, Paul." I left the room and headed to the kitchen.

And hopefully you'll be able to repay the favor by using your valuable *computer skills to help us find Idris.*

Chapter 13

I found various snack fixings and piled them onto a TV tray that dated back to when I was a kid. The front door opened, and I turned to see Ryan come in. He dropped his keys on the table in the hall and continued my way.

"Don't you know how to have a *quiet* day?" he asked sourly.

I put on my best baffled look. "Kuh . . . kuh why-et dey? I do not know this phrase."

He laughed. "I agree. It is beyond your comprehension."

"No kidding!" I lifted my chin toward the hall door. "Thatcher and Ortiz are in there." I shuffled items around on the tray. "I told Mzatal he should go back to the demon realm soon, and that he should take those two with him. Thatcher needs a *lot* more healing, and it would be good to keep Ortiz off the radar for a while." I quickly filled him in on what I'd learned about Paul's forced recruitment and the injuries and beatings from his dad.

"He's been through a lot," Ryan agreed after I finished. "What's the deal? How'd someone like that end up at the intersection of you and Katashi's people?"

"Dunno, but Thatcher's name was in one of Tracy Gordon's notebooks, along with another dozen or so names."

Ryan let out a low whistle. "Maybe he knows more about this stuff than Ortiz thinks he does."

"That's possible," I said. "Paul seems innocent enough in all of this, but Thatcher could be in deep." I snorted. "Their time with Mzatal should be pretty enlightening." The demonic lord would pull every shred of information out of both men if it could increase our chances of finding Idris.

"Maybe *I* should take a vacation to the demon realm," Ryan said with a grin.

I managed to give a light laugh. "I think it would do you a world of good."

He snorted. "Yeah, I'm sure they'd looooooove me there." The demons called him kiraknikahl, oathbreaker. That meant most demons looked upon him with varying degrees of animosity. Eilahn had settled into tolerant-but-not-too-tolerant, only allowing that much latitude because we were around him all the time. I still didn't have the full story of what happened and what oath he broke, though it seemed that some of the bans against even speaking of it had been eased.

"Right now I'm just worried about Mzatal," I said, totally ducking having to make a reply to his comment.

"What's wrong with the fuc—I mean, what's wrong with him?"

I shot him a sour look. "He's away from his power base, he did a major healing, and he laid a huge smackdown on one of Katashi's men."

"He's fading," Ryan said with a slow nod, eyes growing distant. "Shows he shouldn't fucking be here." His breath quickened, and his face twisted in agitation. "He shouldn't be here!"

"Hey, where's Zack?" I asked a little too loudly as I recognized an agitated Szerain coming through.

The distraction worked. Ryan blinked and looked over at me. "Uh, he must still be out front. Jill called when we pulled up, and they sort of got into it." He winced, shook his head. "There've been some pretty rocky times in these last few months."

Dismay wound through me. "Shit. Why?" I asked. "They were so into each other."

He leaned back against the counter and tucked his thumbs into the front pockets of his pants. "He's not spending as much time with her as he used to," he explained. "She's not happy about it, and he doesn't want to talk about it." His face twisted in frustration. "I'm hoping he isn't done with her. In all the time I've known him, he's never been in a serious relationship." He snorted. "Or even a not-serious relationship. Just some short flings. Nothing stable. Nothing until Jill."

"He's about to be a baby-daddy," I muttered. "He'd better *not* be done with her." Yet I knew the situation was way more complicated than simply his losing interest. Not that I could share those complications with Ryan. *You see, your partner is actually a demon, and he's ditching his baby-mama to deal with your alter ego.* "The whole thing sucks," I said.

"It's weird," Ryan said. "It's not like he's afraid of having a kid. I could sort of get it if that was the problem. Doesn't seem to be, though."

"Maybe every now and then you could push him to spend time with her?" I suggested.

"I've tried that," he replied, mouth twisting sourly. "Sometimes it works. Usually not."

"I'll talk to Jill," I said with a sigh, then lifted the tray. "Lemme go feed our guest."

"Thatcher still unconscious?"

"Yeah, and I think he'll stay out until he gets to the demon realm with Mzatal," I said. "He's in pretty bad shape."

Ryan winced. "Zack told me he took a .45 in the back that pretty much blew out his chest."

I started to say something about how Thatcher would have been dead in minutes, but I clamped down on it in time. No way would I be able to explain how Mzatal got there so quickly without mentioning Zack's teleport ability. Best to let him assume Mzatal had gone to the warehouse with me. "The bullet nicked Paul's arm too," I said, glossing over the details of how Thatcher survived. "Speaking of, I'd better go feed him!" I hurried off down the hall before Ryan could ask any more questions.

Paul was still sitting on the stool by the bed. He looked up as I entered, and a faint smile touched his mouth as he saw the loaded tray.

"Thanks. I didn't realize how hungry I was." He tried for a smile and failed. "I'd made a deal with Bryce. If he took me to the warehouse, I'd *let* him stop at Hamburger Haven for a double bacon combo."

I set the tray on the dresser. "When y'all get back we'll see if we can make a Hamburger Haven run."

Desperate hope lit his eyes. "You think he'll really be able to eat one by then?"

"He won't come back until he's good as new," I promised. "And I *know* Mzatal will take excellent care of him." I paused as I heard Ryan call my name from the kitchen. "Eat up," I told Paul. "Holler if you need anything."

He nodded, and I returned to the kitchen. Ryan stood in front of the window, looking out at the back yard.

"You bellowed?" I asked cheerfully.

"You should probably check on him," he said, with a not-quite-Ryan undertone in his voice.

I didn't waste time with questions. I ran out to the back and slid to a stop, dropped to my knees beside Mzatal where he lay prone on the confluence point. "Boss?" I placed a hand on his back. He felt cold, and his aura was so faint I could barely detect it. "Mzatal?"

He drew a deep slow breath. "Here . . . zharkat."

"You doing all right?" I asked, even though I *felt* that he wasn't.

"No," he murmured. "The confluence is but slowing the drain. I am fading."

Fading. The same word Ryan used. "You're going back *now*," I ordered in a don't-you-even-think-about-arguing-with-me tone of voice. "I already talked to Paul, and he's okay with going with you. Let me get Eilahn to carry Thatcher out here."

Mzatal didn't argue and instead simply pushed himself to his side and then sat up. Even that small effort seemed to drain him. I ran inside, found Eilahn and asked her to get Thatcher, then hurried to the guest room.

"Paul, it's time to go," I told him.

Surprise flickered across his face. "Now?" At my nod he set the bunch of grapes he'd been nibbling back on the tray and moved aside as Eilahn entered to get Thatcher.

"Sorry for the rush," I said. "Come on out to the back yard, and we'll get this show on the road."

He grabbed his tablet, eyes bright with excitement and perhaps a bit of fear as he followed me. I thought briefly about telling him not to bother bringing the tablet since the demon realm had some majorly shitty broadband, but then realized the tablet was probably a comfort thing.

Mzatal had managed to stand and waited on the little worn patch of grass with a worried-looking Jekki leaning against his thigh. Paul's eyes went to Jekki and widened in pure astonishment. *Oh, right. Forgot to tell him we had a demon here with us.* Eilahn gently placed Thatcher at Mzatal's feet, and as soon as she stepped back, I moved to Mzatal and kissed him. "Two days," I told him. "I'll summon you in two days."

He wrapped his arms around me, gave me a deep and lingering kiss, then reluctantly broke it. "Two days. We will be on the nexus."

I stepped back, gave him a smile that did nothing to hide my worry. Mzatal gestured Paul to stand close to him and placed a hand on his shoulder. I gave the young hacker an encouraging wink and a thumbs-up.

And then they were gone.

Chapter 14

Prickles of arcane energy flickered over my skin as they departed. I stood for a moment, watched the grass slowly struggle back upright where seconds earlier it had been crushed beneath them. My own life felt that way at times, pushed and changed by forces beyond my control.

But there are plenty of forces that are *within my control*, I sternly reminded myself. My life—and what I knew to be possible—had certainly shifted dramatically in the past couple of years, but I was still tough enough to roll with the punches. So far at least. It helped that I had an awesome posse of friends to back me up.

Smiling wryly, I returned inside. Voices carried from the hallway—Zack's and Ryan's—and cut off as the basement door closed with a dull thud. The two would likely be occupied for the evening while Zack tended Szerain.

The place felt crushingly empty with Mzatal gone and everyone else busy. I'd lived so many years alone, it seemed this should be the norm. But it wasn't the norm. Not anymore. It was time for me to admit the truth: I liked living with others, both human and demon.

The bag with all of Bryce's stuff sat in a lump in the hallway. After tugging on latex gloves, I hauled it to the laundry room, tossed bloody clothing straight into the washer and set his shoes aside, since they didn't appear to have any blood on them. Also in the bag were his gear and weapons, all of it top quality. The nylon ankle holster and knife sheaths were unbloodied, but the leather shoulder holster that held his gun—a Glock 27, I noted with approval—had quite a bit on it. I carefully cleaned all traces of blood or other gunk from leather, gun, and knives, then tucked everything away in a cabinet and returned to the kitchen.

I scrounged in the fridge for a snack and laughed out loud when I found a plastic snap top container brimming with an Earth version of what I fondly called "cat turds"— Jekki's demon realm delicacy that tasted anything but turdlike. I put half a dozen on a plate and headed for the living room. I figured I'd peruse Tracy's journals for a bit then take a nice long hot bath, which I intended to follow with going the hell to bed.

It was tedious work, not at all helped by the fact that I didn't really know what I was looking for, and could only hope I'd know it if/when I saw it. After half an hour of munching cat turds and poring through notebooks, folders, and binders, I decided the best analogy was a shopping trip to an utterly disorganized thrift shop. You had to search through mountains of useless shit in the thin hopes of stumbling upon a treasure. Except that in this case, Idris's life depended on my finding that treasure.

I fought my way through a notebook with Farrah Fawcett on the cover that contained some excruciatingly bad poetry, and another plain yellow one with what looked like calculus homework interspersed with pages of basic summoning sigils. Tossing those aside in annoyance, I moved on to a journal with a faded blue leather cover.

My skin prickled as I paged through it. No lines of poetry or homework here. This one contained at least half a dozen date and time lists like the one I'd found for the warehouse node, except that these lists all began in handwriting far different from Tracy's. Two different styles—one an elegant cursive, and the other a cramped print. *His grandparents*, I realized. Both had been summoners, killed by Rhyzkahl over thirty years ago during a failed attempt to summon Szerain.

Slowly and carefully, I deciphered the handwriting. At the top of every list was a series of numbers—most likely a coded way to ID the list, I decided. However, my tired brain refused to derive any meaning or pattern in the various series, so I mentally tabled that aspect for now. Each list also contained dates, written in the lovely cursive, from when both summoners were alive. Tracy had added more recent and upcoming dates, as well as at least a dozen of the seemingly random alliterative phrases. "Boss-boy breaks boss's balls" and "Cowboy creek crevice creates confusion" and "Twin twilights twinkle," but not a damn thing I could easily decipher to give me a location.

Groaning in defeat, I set aside the notebook and its stupid "Mountains mean multiple mergers" list. Figuring that shit out could go on my to-do list for after we found Idris. Right now the going-the-hell-to-bed part of my personal to-do list looked awfully appealing.

My phone rang in the kitchen where it was charging, and I groaned. "Shit." It was so *far* to the kitchen. Twenty feet *at least*. Surely I didn't have to get up and answer it, did I? *But I should at least check the number*, my far more mature conscience pointed out.

Crap. My far more mature conscience was right. Too much shit going on to ignore calls. I heaved myself up and shuffled to the kitchen, then scowled as the phone stopped ringing the instant I picked it up. I peered at the caller ID and scowled some more. *Blocked*. Probably stupid telemarketers. I unplugged the phone, about to stuff it in my pocket when it rang again. *Blocked*.

I started to hit the ignore button, then hesitated. Telemarketers didn't usually call back. Could be a cop or something work-related.

I answered. "Kara Gillian."

"Hey, Kara," said a familiar voice.

It took a second for it to register. "Idris! Where are you? Are you all right?"

"I'm fine. And I intend to stay that way," he said, voice calm but carrying a tinge of stress.

"Where are you?" I demanded as I ran to the basement door. "We've been crazy worried."

"You know I can't tell you that, and anyway, I'm calling to tell you to lay off. Don't try to find me. It's better for everyone that way."

I yanked the basement door open, started down the stairs. "Idris. What's going on? Why shouldn't we try to find you?" I had zero doubt this call was being monitored by Katashi's people, but I clung to the hope that Idris could give me a clue I'd be able to decipher but wouldn't be significant to his captors.

"I don't want you to find me, and I know you. I know

you'll try," he said, a hint of desperation in his voice. "Don't. Just *don't*."

Zack and Ryan stood and looked at me as I descended to the basement. I gesticulated wildly with my free hand and mouthed "*Idris.*" Ryan gave a nod, pulled out his phone and started a call, likely to get the trace. Zack dug for something in his pocket as he moved toward me.

"Idris, how can you expect me to stop looking for you?" I asked as I switched the phone to speaker. "I can't believe you don't want to be back with us, with Mzatal."

"Yeah. I thought that too at first, thought I needed to get back. But my perspective has changed. I've had new training, seen more of the truth. Kara, you need to trust me. I'm dealing with things you can't even imagine."

My gut twisted with the horrible fear that Idris had been manipulated. "You might be surprised." I kept my voice steady. "I have a damn good imagination."

Zack put a digital recorder in my free hand, and I held it close to the phone.

Idris sighed. "I care about you, and I don't want to see you or Lord Mzatal hurt. But if you find me, the shit's going to hit the fan and people will get hurt."

"Idris, you know Mzatal won't give up on you and leave you to the Mraztur. He loves you. You know that, right?"

He went quiet for a second. "I know he won't give up. That's why it's up to you to convince him. We know he's here, and we'll be prepared for him next time. Tito died because Tsuneo hadn't anticipated Mzatal being at the warehouse. We won't be making that mistake again."

Nausea churned my stomach. Manipulated? Doubtful since manipulation decreased a summoner's ability. Or simply playing along with his captors? And obviously Katashi's people didn't know everything. They didn't know Mzatal *wasn't* here anymore. "We," I echoed. "You mean you and Katashi's flunkies? You and *Rhyzkahl*? How can you include yourself as part of that 'we' after all you and I have seen?"

"I've seen a lot more in the past month. At first I thought they were trying to plant a seed of doubt, wanting me to shun my old associations. But there's *far* more shit going on than I ever dreamed of. You think you have everything figured out, then *whoosh!* the game changes."

I paced. "Idris, we're spinning our wheels here. Why did they risk letting you call? Just to warn us off with some nebulous threat of dire consequences? I find that hard to believe."

"I'm calling because I told them I wanted to call. And yeah, part of it is to say please, *please* leave off searching for me. It's better for everyone that way." He said it all with utter conviction, as though he actually believed it. "But mainly, I called because I wanted to hear your voice, to talk to you." And now his voice carried an unmistakable echo of longing. And grief.

I had no way to unravel truth from bullshit, but that didn't stop the wrenching ache in my heart. "All right. Let's talk about something besides us not coming after you." I gave Ryan a desperate *Anything yet?* look, but he pressed his lips together and shook his head. "I locked down the seventh ring of the shikvihr a few days ago," I told Idris.

"Yeah? You're kicking ass," he said with a lightness that wasn't there before. "I bet you got hung up on the next to last sigil though. You never could balance inverse coils worth a damn."

I let out a weak laugh. "You're right about that, but I think I have the hang of it now. I'm a prodigy, remember?" I said with a snort of amusement. "I even shaved eight minutes off the stair climb. You still staying in shape? Running any?"

Ryan finally gave me a thumbs up which I hoped meant he had the trace, but he followed it with a *keep going* hand signal.

"I was until last week," he said. "Got the ninth right before I . . . came to Earth, but I haven't done any training in the past few days, even with Master Katashi here. There hasn't been time."

Fuck. The Mraztur had found a way to send the old bastard to Earth. "You've been busy with your new associates?"

I heard a shuffling on his end and muffled voices as though he'd lowered the phone and covered it. A second later he returned. "I have to go now," he said the tension of the earlier part of the call back in his voice. "Tell Mzatal I still have his ring, and I haven't forgotten *gheztak ru eehn*. So leave me be. You don't want to start a fire you can't put out."

My throat tightened. "I'll tell him. No promises on the fire though." I paused. "*Tah agahl lahn.*"

"Me too," he said, the words catching. "I'm sorry."

I was about to ask what for when a man's voice I didn't recognize spoke a single word.

"Rowan."

The line went dead. My heart thudded as I recoiled from the unexpected assault, yet other than the adrenaline response, I didn't feel any different. Was the asshole simply fucking with me? I wouldn't put it past an ally of the Mraztur, but my instinct told me they had a deeper purpose. Why else allow the phone call?

Zack took the recorder from me, switched it off and eyed me critically. "You okay?"

I lowered the phone, stared at it. "Shit." I drew a shaky breath, then looked up at Zack. "I think so. Fucking bastards." Anger threaded with fear coiled through me. "I'm pretty sure Kastashi's people attempted to Rowanize me with a command word." I frowned and fell silent while I did a quick personal assessment. Name? Kara Gillian. Age? Thirty. Love life? Pretty damn awesome. "I still feel like me," I told Zack. "I don't know if the attempt failed, or if it has a delayed effect, but either way, I intend to be hyper-vigilant until I summon Mzatal."

"You might not notice any difference in yourself," Zack warned. "We'll keep an eye on you as well, and I'll make sure Eilahn understands fully too. You all right for now?"

I did my best to push down the worry. "So far I feel peachy. Thanks for having my back."

"You got it, babe," he said with a reassuring smile. "However, my guess is they expected at least part of their trap on the murder victim to touch you. They didn't count on Ryan being such a badass and tackling you away from it in time."

Grinning, I looked over at Ryan who was still on his phone. "I'm a seriously lucky bitch." I returned my attention to Zack, caught his sleeve, and pulled him in close. "What does 'gheztak ru eehn' mean?" I murmured.

He answered softly, "Roughly, 'the devastating failure.'"

I frowned. What the hell was that supposed to mean?

Ryan hung up and came over to us. "Got something. Idris was on a cell phone registered to Russell Dobry of Austin, Texas. Best guess based on changing cell towers is that he's thirty to forty miles north of Austin on US 183 in a northwest-bound vehicle. I wanted you to talk as long as possible to see if the tower switched again. The phone is off now."

"Northwest of Austin." I tugged a hand through my hair. "Heading where? New Mexico? Utah? The local fucking diner?" I let out an unintelligible word in frustration.

Ryan grimaced in sympathy. "There are a lot of possible destinations. What did you get from the call?"

"He's either rolled over, been manipulated, or is playing a tight game with his captors," I said. "I can't see him going over willingly to them. However, he also said he's 'seen some stuff' in the past month and implied that it changed his perspective, so I'm putting turncoating on the back burner but not eliminating it. He also let slip that Katashi's on Earth now, but I don't know if he meant to do so."

"You got a recording?" Ryan asked.

"Most of the call," I said. "I'll go over it to see what I can pick up." I pressed my hands to my eyes, forced myself to think through it logically. "If his heart is still on our side, he'd have tried to get some info into the call that could help us. There were others there with him, so it'd be cryptic." I dropped my hands, inhaled a ragged breath. "Here's what I know. He's around Katashi's people for sure because he knew Katashi was here on Earth *and* knew about Tsuneo and Tito being at the warehouse. He said he cares about Mzatal and me and doesn't want to see us hurt, said we will be if we go after him. Claims that bad stuff will happen if we find him, but didn't elaborate."

Ryan frowned. "Why let Idris talk to you at all? Why not just call and say . . . that name?"

"I don't know. There has to be more to it." I started pacing again. "Whatever Katashi and his peeps are, stupid ain't one of them. Maybe a combination of small components." I shrugged. "Like, I'm pretty sure Idris really *did* want to talk to me. The captors placating their captive. And maybe they needed some time with me on the phone to build up to the whammy." I gave a helpless shrug. "I'm grasping at straws, but they *had* to know there was a chance we'd trace the call. So why weren't they concerned about that?"

"Either they want us to know where they are," Ryan said, "or it doesn't matter because they don't think we can find them, even with a trace."

I nodded, way too tired to get my brain to digest it properly. "That phone was most likely stolen. Can you find out when and where the last call was made on it? That might give us another clue."

"Sure thing," he said, then laid his hand on my arm. "There's not much we can do tonight. Why don't you go grab some sleep and get a fresh start in the morning."

I started to protest, to tell him Idris was out there somewhere right now in Texas and we had to *do* something. Ryan's hand tightened slightly on my arm as though anticipating my response, and it was enough to stop the resistance. I let out a long exhale, slumped a little. "Yeah, you're right. I'll be a lot more useful once I've slept." I rubbed my eyes. "I'm going to go curl up in bed, but I'll listen to the recording a few times before I go to sleep. I can do that much."

"Sounds reasonable."

Zack handed the recorder to me. "I made a copy and erased the command word part. You don't need to hear that again."

I gave him a grateful smile. "Thanks. Y'all try not to blow the house up or anything while I sleep."

Ryan gave a laugh. "Not making any promises on that one."

I gave him a smile, then headed upstairs. I stopped by the living room, picked up the empty turd plate along with my note pad from atop the stack of Tracy's journals, then stuck the plate in the dishwasher and trudged to the bedroom.

Fatigue held me firmly in its grip by the time I crawled into bed with the notepad and recorder. I wasn't sure I'd make it through one listen, but I had to at least try. I owed Idris that much. I settled back in the pillows and started the recording.

"I care about you," Idris said, *"and I don't want to see you or Lord Mzatal hurt."*

I squeezed my eyes shut against the fierce ache at the sound of his voice, familiar and dear.

"But if you find me, the shit's going to hit the fan and people will get hurt."

An image of him crystallized in my mind as I listened. Eager smile and keen blue-grey eyes beneath an unruly mop of blond curls. His words ran together like the distant rush of a river.

"You think you have everything figured out, then whoosh! *the game changes."*

His voice cleared as though right by my ear. *"You don't want to start a fire you can't put out."*

You don't want to start a fire you can't put out.

The room was cold. Achingly so. I needed a fire to counter the chill that knifed straight to my core. Shouldn't be so cold this time of year. *I could go turn up the heat,* I thought dimly, but when I got out of bed to do so the room was pitch dark and the floor ice cold glass.

I wandered barefoot through darkness on an endless plain of smooth glass. Cold and black. Nothing. Forever. Step after frigid step.

"Dear one." A voice. *His* voice. "Do not fret. It does not become you."

"Lord Rhyzkahl?" I whispered, felt the darkness swallow the words. "Where are you?"

"I am here. I am always here."

I looked down as a pale amber glow pierced the darkness. A beautiful filigree design of intricate fine lines glimmered on my upper chest with soft, breathtaking radiance. My throat tightened. "My lord? I do not understand."

"Do you not, precious one?"

The glassy plain began to tilt. A voice like the hiss of sand flowing over stones whispered in my ear.

Rowan.

I cried out in shock as I lost my footing. "My lord!" Heart pounding, I flattened myself on the glass, braced with hands and feet to keep from sliding.

"Elinor. Elinor!" A different voice. Distant and desperate.

"Giovanni!" I called into the darkness. "I am lost! Help me!"

"Count, Elinor. Uno. Due. Tre. Quattro. *Count.*"

Rowan.

"Uno," I said, then shrieked as the glass tilted more. Terror gripped me as I began to slide toward oblivion.

"Elinor!" he called. "Kara!"

Giovanni's face swam in the darkness. Square jaw set with worry. Teasing smile gone. "Kara. Count." His image distorted. Twisted. "Kara."

"Due. Tre," I said through gritted teeth. The glass leveled

enough to stop my descent. "I'm here. *Kara*. Quattro. Cinque."

Giovanni slipped away but other faces rose from the darkness to take his place.

Tessa. Jill. Zack. Mzatal. Ryan. Jekki. Eilahn.

People. My people.

My family.

I woke with a start, pulse stuttering as the fragments of the dream scattered. "People," I gasped. "Family." I scrabbled for the recorder, scanned through it, seeking the sentence. Found it, listened, then listened again.

"I care about you, and I don't want to see you or Lord Mzatal hurt. But you find me, and the shit's going to hit the fan and people will get hurt."

"Fucking shit." I played it one more time to hear the slight emphasis on "people." I threw the covers off and ran down the hall, yanked the basement door open and flew halfway down the stairs before realizing I couldn't see a goddamn thing. "Ryan!" I shouted as I ran back up the steps, flicked the switch at the top of the stairs then scrambled back down as fluorescent light filled the basement. "Ryan! Wake up!"

He jerked upright. "What? Shit!" He threw an arm over his eyes to shield them from the glare. "What's wrong?"

"I need you to look something up." I snatched his laptop from the end table and thrust it at him. "Idris said he didn't want to see me or Mzatal hurt. Then he said if we looked for him, the shit would hit the fan and people would get hurt. *People*. Not just Mzatal and me. The first people who come to mind are his family." I continued to hold the laptop out for him while I shifted impatiently from foot to foot like a pee-pee dance. "I need you to find out what you can about his family. Close members first. Then you need to do your FBI shit and get them into a safe house until this blows over." I made a frustrated noise. "Damn it! Why didn't I think of this earlier?"

"Whoa. Slow down." He rubbed a hand across his eyes, tucked the sheet around his waist then took the computer from me and settled it on his lap. "Gimme a sec to catch up."

I paced back and forth on the rug in front of the futon. "I know he has two older sisters. Both his parents are alive, and at least one grandmother. No idea about extended family." This was the family who'd adopted him when he was fourteen, after the parents who'd adopted him when he was a baby had been killed in a car accident. Even though Idris had been with the Palatinos for less than a decade, I knew he'd fully embraced them as family, as real as any he might've been born to.

"I'm working on it, hotshot." He flicked a glance up as he typed, then raked a more thorough gaze over me. "I like the new look." A smile twitched at the corners of his mouth.

I stopped my pacing, looked down, then rolled my eyes. I still had on what I'd worn to bed: pink tank top and blue panties. No bra. "Oh great. Nearly naked," I groaned, though I couldn't fully hide my own amusement.

"Yes, you are." The smile lingered on his mouth, then he dropped his eyes to his screen.

"It's not fair." I plopped onto the futon to watch him type. "I've never seen *you* nearly naked."

"I'm naked right now," he told me, eyes still on the screen, though the skin around them crinkled in amusement, "but *I* have the sense to keep the sheet over me. It might be too much for you."

"I can take anything you dish out," I shot back, grinning. If the view from the waist up was any indication, I had no doubt he'd look good naked.

"I do love a challenge," he murmured with a low chuckle, working the touch pad and clicking on stuff. "Here we go. Sister, Amber Palatino Gavin. Sister, Rose Palatino. Parents, Angela and Jerome Palatino. All in the Seattle area. Maternal grandmother, paternal grandfather living. Definitely extended family. Aunts, uncles, cousins."

I nodded. "Let's focus on the immediate family. Can you get them to a safe spot?"

He gave me a reassuring nod, then glanced at the clock on the end table. "Five-fifteen a.m. I need to connect with Zack. Is he up?"

"No clue," I lied. I had every confidence he was awake since the demahnk slept about as infrequently as the lords did, but Ryan only knew Zack as human. "He's usually up before me anyway. I'll go make coffee and see if I can find him."

Ryan gave an absent nod, already doing stuff on his laptop again.

I returned upstairs, looked out the back window and was unsurprised to see Zack nimbly climbing over the high wall of the new obstacle course, neck and neck with Eilahn in the predawn light. I turned back to the kitchen and got a pot of coffee going, and a few minutes later I heard a thump on the roof as Eilahn found her favorite spot, and the simultaneous creak of the back door as Zack entered.

"Hey, Zack." I held out a towel and gave him the rundown of my morning revelations and suspicions while he wiped off a sheen of sweat and mud. "And now Ryan needs your help to arrange a safe house."

"Good work," he said with an approving nod. "I'll go check with him."

"Thanks." I grimaced. "I want to be sure they're safe."

He gave me a reassuring smile. "We'll do everything we can. I promise." He tossed the towel neatly through the laundry room door and into the hamper, then headed down into the basement.

I set to work cleaning the kitchen in an effort to channel my angst and worry. Unfortunately, Zack and Ryan kept the kitchen fairly spotless, and the three minutes it took to empty the dishwasher and wipe down the counters didn't do much to ease my mood.

I pulled an egg carton from the fridge then fumbled it, barely hearing the squish-crunch of eggs meeting the floor as a truly horrible thought occurred to me. "Zack! Ryan!" Ignoring the mess, I ran for the steps and bounded down. "Check to see if any of his family are missing. One of his sisters? A cousin?"

Both Ryan and Zack turned to look at me, faces grim.

"Oh shit," I breathed. "Who?"

"His sister Amber and his mom," Ryan said. "They both went missing a few weeks ago."

It fit all too well. I sank to sit on the futon as dread clenched at my gut. "Pull a pic of Amber," I said dully. "I bet she's our vic from the trailer."

Chapter 15

Tears of fury stung my eyes as I mercilessly whisked the surviving eggs. A photo of a smiling Amber in her wedding dress confirmed her as the murder victim. Poor Idris. No wonder he was cooperating. Sister tortured and killed, and no telling what they threatened to do with his mom, if she was even still alive. And Idris was the kind of guy who'd do everything he could to protect anyone—even a perfect stranger. This surely ripped his heart out.

Ryan came upstairs but didn't wisecrack about the ferocity of my egg-murder, which told me his news wasn't particularly good. I dumped the eggs into a pan on the stove. "Anything?"

"Not really. They were abducted from a mall parking lot in broad daylight," he told me, voice flat. He pulled two mugs down from the cabinet, filled both with coffee. "They had lunch with some ladies from their church, left the restaurant, but never made it to their car." Impotent fury swept over his face. "Security cameras malfunctioned, so no vid, and no witnesses have come forward."

I jabbed at the congealing eggs and let out a number of curses.

"You asked about the last call made on the phone Idris used," Ryan said as he dumped cream and sugar into one of the mugs, left the other black, then brought them both to the table and sat. "It was from the Austin area about two hours earlier."

I scraped eggs as I did my best to cling to the sliver of hope that offered. "They stole a cell phone in Austin and headed northwest. Called, then turned off the phone and probably ditched it for good measure." I sighed. "Not much help. Thanks for checking though." But then I frowned. "I keep coming back to Tsuneo being in this area. That *means* something. Maybe Idris was here with him, and they're moving him somewhere else?"

Ryan grimaced. "'Northwest of Austin' covers a lot of ground. We need another lead."

He was right, damn it. The location clue had felt like a big victory but was virtually useless by itself.

I removed the eggs from the heat, clicked the burner off and mentally shifted gears. "Give me your opinion on something." I pulled two plates from the cabinet and divided the eggs onto them. "If you were holding Idris against his will and wanted his cooperation—having already killed his sister—would you also kill the mother?"

He remained silent for a moment then shook his head. "Makes more sense to keep her as insurance. A hostage."

Thin relief went through me. I placed the pan in the sink, nodded. "My thought as well. So, the good news is that she's probably not dead." I set one of the plates and a fork in front of Ryan. "The bad news is they almost certainly have Idris's cooperation." I grabbed my plate and a fork and thunked down into the chair across from him, mood suddenly bleak over our lack of progress. "Now I know why Idris told me to stop looking for him."

"You like him a lot," he observed.

I squirted ketchup onto my eggs, ignored Ryan's wince as I did so. "He's like a kid brother. A seriously talented and really great kid brother."

"I'm sorry. This must suck for you." He forked some eggs into his mouth, gave me an approving nod.

"It does." I offered him a slight smile. "You'd like him too." I paused to eat. "Mzatal loves him," I said after a few minutes. "Like a son."

Ryan leveled a deeply skeptical look at me. "Mzatal? Like a son?"

"Yeah." I started to dump sugar into my coffee, then remembered Ryan had already fixed it the way I liked it. "Crazy, I know, but he really does. Mzatal hasn't stopped looking for Idris since he was taken." I took a long sip of coffee, then lowered the mug and gave an evil smile. "And

Mzatal *slammed* Jesral after he and Asshole sent Idris to Earth. It was fucking beautiful."

Ryan let out a bark of laughter. "I bet." He scooped up the last of the eggs. "Thanks for breakfast."

"Anytime." I finished my own then stood and cleared the plates. "Should I call Pellini and let him know we have an ID?"

"Yes, and tell him we'll send over details shortly."

Ryan returned to the basement to finish his report. I retrieved my phone, thumbed through the address book to Pellini's name, and pressed call. It rang half a dozen times before he picked up.

"Pellini," he rasped in a sleep-clouded voice.

"Hey, it's Gillian. Wake up."

I heard some mumbling and scuffling, then, "Yeah. I'm here. You got something?"

"An ID on our vic," I told him. "Garner and Kristoff will be shooting the details your way shortly."

"This just come down? Who is she?"

"Found out in the last half hour. Her name's Amber Palatino Gavin from Seattle."

"It's a solid ID?"

"Unfortunately, yeah."

"Unfortunately?" he asked, puzzled.

"Turns out she's the sister of a friend of mine. A guy I'm trying to find."

He blew out his breath. "Coincidence?"

I hesitated, unsure how much to tell him or how to frame it in a way that didn't sound weird.

"Kara? You don't think it's a coincidence, do you?" He sounded tense, but his tone held none of its usual belligerence or mocking. "Look, anything you can tell me is more than I got now. Maybe we can meet to talk about it? I'll buy you a beer. Or lunch." His words tumbled over themselves. "There's this Italian place that's pretty good and not expensive. I mean, like a business lunch. Work." He spoke the last in a rush as if to be absolutely certain I knew it wasn't a date-type thing.

Good god, an offer of a *date* from Pellini would put me right over the edge.

"Um, my schedule's pretty packed right now," I

demurred. "Here's the info I have." I gave him a rundown of the basics with Idris, that he was missing, family name, vitals, told him we'd stumbled across the ID on Amber while researching Idris's family. Everything I told him was true, but guilt nagged. I knew a lot more that I wasn't telling him, but I couldn't do so without delving into demons and lords and general weirdness.

He listened, asked a few questions. When it was time to hang up, he didn't. "Maybe when your schedule clears up we can get a beer?"

"Uh," I said in a brilliant delaying tactic. "Sure. We'll talk about it then." I disengaged quickly and hung up, more than a little weirded out by his persistence. Was it because I was in better shape now, or was the reason more sinister? Then again, his desire to be friendly could just as easily be completely benign. Last year, after a particularly ugly incident, Ryan had influenced both Pellini and Boudreaux to lighten up and not be such assholes to me, and since then the two had been far less hostile. Perhaps Ryan's little tweak had started a chain reaction of don't-be-a-dick.

I was drying the last of the breakfast dishes when Ryan emerged from the basement, dressed for work, empty coffee cup in hand. "We've sent the info on to Pellini and Boudreaux."

"Thanks. Pellini will be glad to get it," I said then scrunched my face. "He wanted me to meet him for lunch."

Ryan let out a snort of laughter. "Lunch with *Pellini*? That's a first."

"He wanted to talk about the case, but I gave him the non-demon facts over the phone. There's not all that much." I shrugged, frowned. "He's acting a little weird, though he's not being a total asstard the way he used to."

"Maybe he's a pod person," he suggested as he poured more coffee into his cup. "Anyway, I'll be downstairs for a while if you need me. We're working on the safe house and the Farouche info, then have a meeting at nine."

I nodded. "I'm going to listen to Idris's call a few more times. He may have used that emphasis technique somewhere else. Right now it's our only source of clues."

"I'll let you know if we come up with anything else," he said and then departed down the basement stairs.

I grabbed the recorder and a set of headphones then

settled on the sofa, this time listening for nuances in emphasis and timing. On the third time through, I stopped it at the end, ran it back about ten seconds. Listened to it again. And again.

Tell Mzatal I still have his ring, and I haven't forgotten gheztak ru eehn. So leave me be. You don't want to start a fire you can't put out.

Start a fire.

Except he hesitated for the barest instant before and after "start," mumbled the "a" and hesitated again after "fire."

There were two options. Either my imagination was working overtime, or Idris had told me who had him: *Star-Fire*.

Ryan dashed up from the basement, laptop in hand, when I hollered. "You have something new?"

"I think so." I played the end of the recording, but to my disappointment he simply responded with a puzzled look. "*Listen* to it," I urged and played it again. "Start a fire. Star-Fire." I scowled at his dubious expression. "I know it's a little crazy but I hear it now. I can't *not* hear it."

To his credit, Ryan didn't shoot me down in flames. "Play it one more time." I did so, and this time he rewarded me with a slow nod. "It's possible," he admitted. "If that's for real, Idris is one clever guy. That's a hard thing to pull off."

"He's super smart," I said. "And that's why I believe it's a real clue."

"StarFire, huh?" He opened his laptop on the kitchen table and sat. "I was actually on my way to show you what I came up with on Farouche. Basically, he's a fucking saint. Gives tons to charity, bought new computers for every public school in St. Long Parish, even arranged for bulletproof vests for the Sheriff's department K-9 units."

"He got vests for the dogs?" I blinked in disbelief. "Are you serious?"

"As a heart attack," he said as he scrolled to another page. "Married twice. Two kids, boy and a girl, with the first wife. They divorced seventeen years ago," he winced, "two years after their five-year-old daughter was abducted in broad daylight from in front of her school. Never found."

"Shit," I breathed. "I remember that. It was a couple of years after my dad died, and all the schools and parents were freaking out about security." I gave a wry grimace. "A few days later I missed the bus home because I was out behind the gym trying pot for the first time. Tessa thought I'd been kidnapped too, and ripped me up one side and down the other. Grounded me for a month."

Ryan snorted. "Once a troublemaker, always a trouble-maker."

I punched him lightly on his shoulder. "I've upgraded to a higher class of troublemaking. What else do you have on Farouche?"

He continued to skim the page. "He remarried about a year later, had two more kids." He blew out a breath. "And the second wife, Claire, passed away from ovarian cancer about three years back."

I fought down a shiver. My mother had died of that same cancer when I was eight. But to lose a child *and* a wife? This guy had been through hell twice.

"The feds have sniffed around a time or two with regards to some vaguely questionable dealings," Ryan continued, "but it's never reached the level of a full-blown investigation. And nothing's ever turned up that was unusual for a businessman with multiple holdings. His employees love him. He's generous with benefits, pays fairly. No one has ever filed a complaint against him." He clicked on another screen. "Big supporter of the arts, too. Paid for a new roof for Beaulac Little Theater, and even invested in some zombie movie over in St. Edwards Parish."

I peered at the image on the screen: A sharply dressed man with steely grey hair, a hard and steady gaze, and an air of confidence that remained palpable even in a still photo. "Mzatal *insisted* that this guy fucked with Paul's head," I said. "What's the deal?"

Ryan lifted his shoulders in a helpless shrug. "No idea," he confessed. "StarFire's the company he's most known for, but he's CEO of a number of corporations. I checked them all: The Child Find League, Farouche Technologies, Rise-High, Esoteric Enhancement Enterprises, Sapphire Star Resorts, and several others. By all accounts, clean as a whistle, with a polished halo as well."

"Wait." I held up my hand while I forced my brain into overdrive. "RiseHigh LLC." My pulse quickened. "That's who bought the Garden Street industrial park."

He gave me a long look, then swung his attention back to his laptop, started clicking and typing away. "Huh. That's damn interesting."

"Spill it, fed-boy," I ordered.

"Looks like RiseHigh LLC began inquiries about the purchase of the complex about a week after you were first summoned to the demon realm. The sale was finalized about three weeks later."

"It's all connected," I murmured. "I'm betting he bought the whole place to keep that warehouse—and that node—safe and secure."

Ryan's brow creased as his eyes skimmed the info on his screen. "I agree it's one hell of a coincidence, but it looks like he really does intend to build the Claire Farouche Cancer Center there once the permits and paperwork and plans are in order."

"It's a big place," I said, considering. "Wouldn't be hard at all to have a cancer center there and still keep the node protected." I felt an almost physical jolt as a puzzle piece snapped into place. "Cancer. Claire," I breathed. "Fucking shitballs. Not only is Thatcher's name in one of Tracy's journals, but there's also a page in there with all sorts of sketches of tree-things and random stuff written in the margins—and 'Claire's cancer' is one of them."

Ryan pushed back from the table, peered at me. "You think Tracy was working with Farouche in some way?" he asked. "Or maybe stalking him? Farouche is a big enough public figure to attract a whack-job, and Tracy was definitely that."

"I don't know," I said slowly, trying to see the whole picture. "On the one hand I have every indication that Farouche is a saint who's been through some horrible shit." Ryan nodded agreement, and I went on, "Then on the other hand I have Mzatal and Paul who tell me that Farouche is an evil dude who kidnaps people and uses fear to gain their compliance. And on *another* hand, I have whack-job Tracy with some sort of interest in him, and on yet another hand I have the intriguing fact that Farouche bought an industrial park that happens to contain a valve node."

"You do know that's four hands," Ryan pointed out.

"Yeah, well, we can pretend I'm a faas for now."

His mouth twitched. "Will you wear a furry blue suit?"

I smacked him lightly on the back of the head, though I couldn't help but laugh. "Focus!"

He grinned and made a show of rubbing where I'd hit him. "Okay, okay. I doubt the industrial park—or any of it, for that matter—is a coincidence." He sobered and shook his head. "Too many links. However, I can do some more digging to see if there were any dealings between Farouche's holdings and the companies Tracy owned with Roman Hatch."

"That would be great," I said. "Thanks."

"I bet Thatcher can shed some light on all this," Ryan said, then winced. "If he survives, that is."

"He'll be fine," I said with confidence. "Mzatal knows healing." I had far too much experience on that end. "Speaking of, did y'all ever run info on Thatcher? I know it's been crazy busy, but maybe we can get a hint of why Tracy had his name."

Ryan stood and moved to the counter to pour more coffee for himself. "Sure did. The guy has a spotless record. Security expert, licensed to carry for the past fifteen years, all of which have been with StarFire." He returned to the table, fiddled with the laptop's touchpad. "Only one hitch in his past turned up," he continued. "It's a doozy, though. Shot and killed this guy about a year before he got his concealed-carry permit." He took a sip of coffee, gestured to the pic on the screen with his other hand. "Pete Nelson. His friend and housemate, a graduate student. Thatcher was never charged, and the case was closed, ruled an accidental shooting."

And, with no felony conviction on his record, he could still get the gun permit, I mused as I peered at the photo of a smiling man in his early twenties. He was kneeling in a grass lawn, one arm draped over the neck of a rottweiler with a head bigger than his. "You come up with anything that makes you think it wasn't accidental?"

"No, but afterward things got odd," he said. "The deceased's family made a scene, and it looks like Thatcher was going to be charged with manslaughter or at least negligent homicide, but less than a month after the shooting the entire investigation was dropped."

"It's possible they didn't find any evidence to suggest it was anything other than a tragic fuckup," I said. "Still, it's a data point. How long was this before Thatcher signed on with StarFire?"

"Gimme a sec." He scrolled through a few pages. "About a week after the potential charges evaporated, he was on the StarFire payroll."

"One more data point in the no-way-is-this-a-coincidence file," I mused. "If Farouche really did have Paul kidnapped, I doubt he'd bat an eye at finagling the charges so he could take on Thatcher. Did Thatcher have any skills of note that might have interested Farouche?"

"Not unless he's an animal lover," Ryan replied. He pulled up a photo of a much younger Thatcher, grinning beside a baby elephant that had its trunk wrapped playfully around him. "Thatcher was in his third year of veterinary medicine at LSU, and though he owned a gun he wasn't an enthusiast. He didn't have any sort of martial arts training, and no combat or police experience either."

"Let me make sure I have this right," I said, narrowing my eyes. "He shot and killed his buddy, then went from vet school to security in the span of a few weeks? You'd think he'd want to stay the hell away from anything to do with possibly shooting people."

"You'd think," he agreed.

"This whole thing stinks," I said. "Why would Farouche recruit him?" I frowned, picked up my mug to take a sip then made a face as I realized it was Ryan's. "Yech. What the hell's in this?"

"Coffee," he replied mildly. "No milk, no sugar."

"You're so weird," I said with a shudder, then found my own mug and took a long gulp to chase away the taste of coffee done wrong. "Anyway, I suspect the reason why Farouche recruited Thatcher is somehow tied to why his name is listed in Tracy's journal."

"Looks like we'll have a lot of questions for the man when he returns."

"And not until tomorrow," I said with a sigh. "Thanks for the info. I'm going to head over to Tessa's. We've been so busy that I haven't seen her since I got back. Keep me posted."

"Absolutely," he said and closed the laptop. "Zack and I will be out and about. Work, ya know."

"Don't forget, you can check in with your special consultant any time," I reminded him with a smile. "I need those billable hours."

"You're on salary."

"Hot damn. In that case, don't call me unless the world's about to end."

Chapter 16

After going through my usual get-clean-and-dressed routine, Eilahn and I headed to my aunt's house. On the way there, I listened to the recording of my phone conversation with Idris, played it over and over while I fought to catch any new reference or hint, any meaningful cough or hesitation. By the time we reached my aunt's neighborhood of old, quality, lakefront houses, I'd been through it at least a dozen times, with no new revelations.

I saw Carl's white minivan parked at the curb in front of my aunt's house. Carl was her boyfriend, though I also knew him as the morgue tech at the coroner's office.

It wasn't until I pulled into Aunt Tessa's driveway that I realized the last time I'd visited her was the day I was abducted to the demon realm. Everything about her century-old two-story house was the same—white with blue gingerbread trim, carefully maintained landscaping, rocking chairs on the porch—yet it was impossible to quantify how much I'd changed since then. Then again, my aunt probably knew a little something about major life changes. After a decade of living in Japan as Katashi's student, she'd given up her life there and returned to Louisiana to raise me after my dad died. Not that leaving Katashi was a bad thing, in light of recent events.

I slipped through my aunt's aversion wards with ease and smiled at the *Welcome!* sign on her door. It stood in sharp contrast to the arcane protections around her house that would keep any unwelcome visitors from actually making it to the porch, much less gain entry, unless they were exceedingly determined *and* arcanely skilled.

As I climbed the steps, Carl stepped out of the front door, keys in hand. Tall and thin with close-cropped pale hair, he offered me a ghost of a smile which I took as a huge welcome home greeting from him. "Morning, Kara," he said. "Doc and I miss seeing you at the morgue."

"I bet you do. Who else can you torment with the whole needles-in-dead-eyes thing?" From the very first time I'd gone to an autopsy, Carl had attempted to get me to collect the vitreous—a process that involved sticking a needle into the eyeball to draw out the fluid. *Hugely* squicky.

He gave a dry chuckle. "At least you finally called my bluff."

"Damn straight. Are you on your way to the morgue now?"

"I am. Running late."

"I won't keep you. Good to see you, and tell Doc I said Hi."

"Will do."

I watched him for a moment as he continued to his minivan, then I turned to the door, still baffled at the odd-couple match between my diminutive, whacky aunt and the lanky, taciturn—though seemingly devoted—Carl. After knocking once, I entered. "Hi, honey! I'm home!"

A laugh came from the direction of the kitchen. "About damn time!"

I headed that way, where my aunt immediately enveloped me in as crushing a hug as she could give. Her unbound mane of frizzy blond hair completely obscured my face, but I didn't mind one little bit. I breathed in the faint scent of lavender touched with jasmine—calm and sweet, totally unlike her personality, yet still completely *her*.

"I've missed you!" she said after finally releasing me.

"I've missed you too," I replied with a smile. "Sorry I wasn't over sooner. Everything went crazy as soon as I got back."

She turned and began to run water into the kettle. She wore a flowing gauzy skirt paired with a clinging top of blue and purple gradients, and big dangly earrings that I knew would look absurd on me but suited her perfectly. "Dealing with crazy stuff get you crazy times," she said. "No doubt about that."

I pulled myself onto a stool at the counter and made a

sour face. "Yeah, and I'm in super mega-craziness right now." The kitchen itself felt as welcoming and familiar as my aunt—dark granite countertops, wallpaper with subtle patterns of climbing ivy, a deep dusty-rose tiled floor, and stainless steel appliances without a smudge or fingerprint in sight.

She set the kettle on the stove, turned the burner on, then took a seat on a stool opposite mine. "Tell me. What's going on now?"

"Well . . ." I had to think for a moment about where to begin. "When's the last time you talked to Katashi?"

Tessa's brow creased in thought. "It's been a while."

"Good," I said, relieved. At least I didn't need to tackle a problem in that arena. "Please let me know if you hear anything at all from his people. *Anything*."

"You told me Katashi caused some trouble for you." Her gaze sharpened. "Has something else happened with him?"

I spread my hands flat on the cool marble of the countertop. "You could say that." I proceeded to fill her in on the Idris situation and the craziness at the warehouse. Tessa listened carefully while I spoke, and when the teakettle began to whistle she got up to pour water into two mugs.

"Crazy stuff indeed," she said as she dunked teabags into each mug. "Idris. He must be pretty important."

"He's amazingly gifted, especially considering he's barely twenty." I smiled. "You'd like him. Super nice guy."

Tessa placed my tea before me, curled her hands around her own mug. "What was he doing in the demon realm in the first place?"

I shamelessly reached for the bowl of sugar cubes and dumped several into my tea. "Training with Mzatal. He was under agreement—it's sort of like a contract."

She took a sip, brow furrowed. "Is that what you have with Mzatal?"

"We did," I said. "We don't now. I mean, nothing official. He trains me, and we work together. We're partners."

Her eyes dropped to the ugly scar on my left forearm. "Is he the one who removed Rhyzkahl's mark?" she asked, tone abruptly sharp and biting.

I looked down at the ripple of scar tissue. "No. Rhyzkahl did that," I said, voice expressionless. Yet I hesitated before continuing with the rest, the details of *how* he'd sliced the mark from my flesh, and what else he'd done to me. I hadn't told her any of that yet, had simply left it at "Rhyzkahl betrayed me." I knew Tessa had seen my sigil scars when she summoned me back to Earth, but she had yet to ask about them, and I didn't want to push it. Last year, she'd been captured and used in a ritual that left her comatose, her essence lost in the void. After she returned to her body, she'd been fragile. Docile. Completely unlike the Aunt Tessa I knew. She even stopped summoning for months, and only resumed in order to rescue me from the demon realm. Carl had played a significant role in keeping her on track despite the oddity of their match, and I could only speculate that his near-emotionless manner helped to ground her and keep her focused.

Yet even though she'd come a long way in her recovery, a measure of fragility still clung to her. The hideous details of my torture would only upset her, and I saw no need to risk destabilizing her now.

I rubbed the scar, changed the subject. "Back when you studied with Katashi, did you learn the sigil technique called the pygah?" Mzatal had told me the pygah was part of the foundation for all other summoning work, yet Tessa had never even mentioned it.

She set her tea down, brow furrowed as though trying to remember. "Pygah," she murmured, then her face lit up. "Pygah. Yes, I did. I haven't thought about it in years. Not since . . ." She trailed off, staring past me with unfocused eyes.

Frowning, I laid my hand on her forearm. "Tessa? Not since when?"

She blinked, brought her gaze back to me. "Not since I found out I was pregnant. I remember clear as a bell doing a pygah then, but," she shrugged, "I haven't thought of it since."

Worry flared hot and bright. *How do you "forget" a major arcane tool?* I did a frickin' pygah of my own to help maintain a façade of calm.

"Why did you pygah when you found out you were pregnant?" I asked.

That earned me a raised eyebrow and a withering look. "Wouldn't you?"

Okay, she had a point there. "You were still with Katashi when you got pregnant?" I asked, oh-so-casually.

"With Katashi?" Confusion clouded her eyes. "It was a fling with an American living in Japan. He left before I knew I was pregnant so, when the baby was stillborn, I didn't call him."

Goosebumps shivered over my entire body. Those were almost the exact words she'd used the last time I'd asked, and again I had the disturbing feeling she wasn't so much remembering it as reciting a story. "Programmed" was the word that came to mind, and right behind that, "manipulated." Even though I didn't have a badge anymore, my cop-instinct still worked, and right now it tingled like crazy. I knew in my gut that baby didn't die. What I didn't know was *who* had made Tessa believe so and *why*?

"What was the father's name?" I kept a pleasant and casual smile on my face.

"I had a fling. He was American." Tessa waved a hand dismissively.

Yeah, well, she could dismissively gesture all she wanted, but I wanted some answers. "Back when you had the, ah, fling with the American," I pressed, "you were still in training with Katashi?"

A slight frown crossed her face. "I remember we summoned the reyza, Pyrenth," she murmured as though trying to dust off twenty-year-old memories. "But that was before I was pregnant."

"I met Pyrenth in the demon realm," I said. "At Rhyzkahl's. He was my escort at times." I leaned forward. "What else do you remember about your training back then?"

"I remember working on this, over and over." She traced her fingers through the air as though drawing a sigil, and her frown deepened. "What *is* that called?"

Sick worry tightened my chest. Tessa had a great memory for arcane structures. "It's called a *durik*, for ritual stabilization," I told her, lifting my hand to trace the sigil. "It's usually used in combination with a . . ." I trailed off. Not a mere sigil. The durik and its companion were floaters.

Icy coils of dread wrapped around me. The art of tracing floaters could only be learned in the demon realm, and Tessa had *never* mentioned or even implied she'd ever been there.

"*Durik*. Silly of me to forget that." Tessa stood and carried her mug back to the stove, topped it off with hot water even though she'd only taken a few sips from it.

My heart hammered at the implications. "It must have slipped your mind, like the pygah. No big deal." Except that it was. It was a huge fucking deal. "Tessa? Have you ever been to the demon realm?"

Her mug crashed to the floor, sending out a splatter of hot liquid and shards of stoneware.

"Shit!" I jumped up and came around the counter. "Are you okay?" I grabbed at a dishtowel and crouched to mop up the spreading pool of tea.

"A little clumsy, that's all," she murmured. She looked down at me, brow faintly furrowed, yet didn't stoop to help me clean up the mess, which was very unlike her.

I stood, dishtowel in my hand, raked my gaze over her to make sure she hadn't been cut or scalded. No visible blood or burns that I could see, but she looked pale as death. She pressed her hand over her solar plexus. "I feel strange," she said, voice thready.

I dropped the dishtowel back on the floor amidst the shards, took her gently by the arm and led her around the mess and into a chair at the kitchen table. My already high worry wound tighter as she went without protest. "Do you need some water?" I asked.

Tessa blinked, seemed to come back to herself a bit. "Some tea would be nice." Her eyes went to the mess on the kitchen floor, and she winced. "I'd better clean that up."

"I'll take care of it," I insisted. That was more normal for her at least. "Do you want me to call Carl? I'm sure he'll come right back."

"Oh no, sweetling. No need to worry him." She gave me a smile that only reassured me a little.

I quickly readied another mug of tea and set it in front of her, then finished cleaning up the spill and broken mug while I mentally replayed the incident. Once I finished the cleanup I sat at the table with her again. "Are you feeling any better?"

"I'll be right as rain as soon as I finish this cup," she said brightly. "Now what were you telling me about your agreement with Mzatal?"

What the fucking hell? Had she forgotten the last few minutes of our conversation? My anxiety clawed higher, and I had to take a long sip of my tea before I could keep my voice and expression composed enough to speak casually. "I said that we have an agreement based on mutual respect. We ditched the contractual one." I plastered on a smile. "I learn a lot from him . . . in the demon realm." I watched for any flicker of reaction and saw nothing but honest interest in her face. I hesitated, then jumped in with both feet. "Have you ever been to the demon realm?"

Again she pressed her hand to her solar plexus. Her eyes went wild for a second, then her face relaxed and brightened. "That water hot yet?"

My hands tightened around the mug. "Your tea is in front of you."

"Oh!" She looked down. "So it is." She smiled, lifted it, and took a sip.

This wasn't some sort of dementia, not with this odd *programmed* feel. It was something far more sinister, more deliberate. Mzatal would be able to get to the bottom of it but I had another day before I summoned him again.

I took a breath and calmed myself. This had been with her for twenty years. Another day wasn't going to harm her. "I'm summoning Mzatal again tomorrow," I told her. "I'd love for you to meet him."

Tessa's mouth tightened. "This one must be quite different from Rhyzkahl."

You can say that again! "Yes, he's very different," I said. "I care about him a great deal."

Worry shadowed her eyes. "I don't want you to get hurt," she said.

I reached to give her hand a light squeeze. "I know. It's why I'm training with him. I need to get really damn good at what I do so that I won't be as vulnerable."

She opened her mouth as though to speak then jerked her head up to look at the clock. "Crap! I need to go. I promised Melanie I'd close at the store tonight." My aunt owned a natural food store in downtown Beaulac, and after her hospital stay last year hired her ditzy nurse, Melanie, as a full time worker.

"That's cool. I'll call tomorrow." I stood as she did. "I want to bring Mzatal over to meet you, since I'm shacking up with him and all that." I faked a grin as I added silently, *And since it's obvious someone has messed with your head.*

"That'll be good," she said, belying the flicker of disapproval in her eyes. "I should meet him."

I kept the fixed smile on my face. "You mind if I use your bathroom before I go?"

"As if you need to ask?" Tessa rolled her eyes. "Go for it. I need to scoot. Lock up when you leave, please."

With that she hurried out and to her car. I surreptitiously peered out the front window, watched her drive off as anger and sorrow wound together in the pit of my stomach.

Someone had manipulated my aunt.

I intended to find out who and why.

Chapter 17

I quickly slipped into my aunt's bathroom, retrieved a handful of hair from her brush and dug a used tissue out of the waste basket, then left the house—making very sure to lock up behind me since I would *never* hear the end of it otherwise.

Eilahn dropped from an oak tree in the front yard, landing with impossibly graceful ease. I had to wonder what the neighbors thought of a beautiful woman shimmying up a tree but doubted Eilahn gave a crap about what they thought.

She moved to me, brow creased. "You are disturbed."

"My aunt. She's . . ." I drew a breath in a doomed effort to steady my voice. "She's either having a stroke or she's been manipulated."

Concern narrowed Eilahn's eyes. "If she is having a stroke, does she not require medical attention?"

Scowling, I sat down on the step. "She's not having a stroke. That would be easier to deal with." I gave her a quick recap of my conversation with Tessa and the associated weirdness.

Eilahn pursed her lips. "A manipulation to avoid focus on time in the demon realm as well as to fabricate the death of a child. This is indeed a grave matter."

"No shit!" I exclaimed. "But why the hell would she need to be manipulated about *that* and by who?"

"This I do not know."

Frustrated and worried, I returned to my car and retrieved a pre-addressed padded envelope from the back seat. I placed the used tissue in a plastic bag, then carefully selected about a dozen hairs with the root follicle still attached. I tucked those into another bag and slipped both into the envelope to join the others containing Idris's hair and his toothbrush.

One way or another, I'll know for sure.

I sealed the envelope and headed to the post office, where I nearly ended up in a knock-down-drag-out fight with Eilahn over our apparent need for several hundred stamps with pictures of kittens on them. I finally talked her down to a slightly more reasonable eighty stamps, which was still far more than I could possibly need, and would no doubt last me until the next century. I paid the too-cheerful postal employee for the stamps and the overnight shipping charge for the envelope, then quick-stepped back to my car with Eilahn while she made delighted noises at each and every stamp.

She abruptly cut off her rapt perusal, lifted her head, and went demon still.

Alarm crept in. "What's wrong?"

"Wards have triggered at the house," she told me, voice serious as she continued to assess. "Intruders at the perimeter near the fence line on the west side. Multiple people."

I surged toward my car. "Shit! Does Zack know?" Though as soon as I asked the question, I knew the answer. "Never mind. Of course he does." Zack had set the majority of the wards along the new fence line. If Eilahn felt the alarm wards trigger, Zack surely had as well. "Can the intruders get through?"

"Unless they have a demahnk or a qaztahl with them, they will not pass."

I stopped and wheeled to face her. "They don't, do they?!" The most likely culprits were Katashi and his summoners, which meant it was sickeningly possible they had one of the Mraztur with them.

"I can only sense presence, not the specifics," Eilahn replied, which did nothing to ease my anxiety. "Zack may know more. Is Ryan at the house?"

"I don't think so," I said as I yanked the car door open. "He had to go to the office." My phone rang. I snatched it from my pocket, checked the number. "Zack! You're at the house? Eilahn said someone's trying to get onto the property."

"I'm not at the house," he said, utterly calm. "I was calling to let you know about it. They've withdrawn now, but it was a serious, focused attempt."

"Do you know who it was?" I jammed my key into the ignition, cranked the engine.

"I wasn't there to see," he said. "I'm heading that way momentarily."

"Any sense that Rhyzkahl or one of the other assholes was there?"

"No. They definitely didn't have a qaztahl with them."

I exhaled in relief. "All right. I'm heading home now too."

"I'll see you there," he said and disconnected.

As I drove home my thoughts churned back and forth between Tessa's manipulation and the attempted intrusion. It was only when Eilahn reached and touched her cool hand to my shoulder that I realized I'd been muttering under my breath.

"All will be well," she said with such solid conviction that I found my anxiety slipping away.

"Thanks," I said and gave her a grateful smile. The syraza was a kickass bodyguard, but she also did a damn good job protecting my mental health.

I made the turn onto Serenity Road, a narrow two-laned affair with deep ditches on either side. My dad had died on this road—killed by a drunk driver when I was eleven—and I'd avoided it for close to a decade afterward even though the road offered a significant shortcut into town, shaving the travel time from forty minutes to the thirty it now took. When I became a cop I began to use it again, and the first time I drove it I couldn't even find the place my dad was killed. The tree he'd been crushed against had long since been cut down, and even the tight curve had been straightened and graded in the intervening years. I probably could have located the exact spot from the accident report, but what would have been the point? Sometimes the past was best left in the past.

"Kara!" Eilahn shouted, but I'd already seen the dark blue Lexus sedan swerve into our lane and had my foot jammed hard on the brakes. For an instant I weighed whether going into the ditch would be worse than hitting the car head on.

Then both options disappeared as the sedan screeched to a stop sideways, blocking the road.

"Shit!" I skidded to a rubber-burning stop, all the while aware that the other vehicle's move was intentional. Too precise to be anything else. And the location had obviously been carefully chosen. A quick glance in the rearview mirror revealed another car coming to a stop behind us.

"It's a trap," I snarled as I threw the car into park. "Bail out!" I hit my seat belt release and shoved the door open all in one motion, yanked my gun from its holster and prepared to dash to the trees beyond the ditch.

I made it two steps before I stuttered to an awkward stop, freezing at the sight of the MAC-10 submachine gun leveled at me. Heart thundering, I extended my hands out to the sides in as non-threatening a manner as possible and kept my gun lowered as I took in the details beyond the muzzle of the submachine gun. A red-and-grey-haired powerhouse of a man in a well-tailored black suit held the MAC-10 as he stood beside the open front passenger door of the Lexus. Out of the corner of my eye I saw Eilahn motionless on the other side of our car, though her stance told me she was poised to move. Ever since she'd been shot she habitually wove protective arcane shielding, but it wasn't infallible.

I heard car doors open behind me, but I didn't waste my focus looking. Eilahn could assess with far more ease and accuracy. Besides, MAC-10 guy hadn't shot us dead yet, which meant the trap had a different goal in mind.

The back door of the Lexus opened, and James Macklin Farouche stepped smoothly out. I'd never met the man in person, but the pictures I'd seen of him did nothing to convey the confidence with which he carried himself. Immaculately dressed in a perfectly-tailored dark suit, white shirt, and a blue and gold-patterned tie, his steely gaze penetrated, though his expression remained one of utter ease.

Slowly, I crouched and placed my gun on the ground, then straightened and gave a nod. "Mr. Farouche."

Farouche flicked a glance to my gun then to me as he began a slow approach. "Smart girl," he said with a confident smile, and I had to fight to control a scowl at the condescension. Not such a saint after all. "No one's going to get hurt as long as you remain smart," he continued. "I simply want to talk."

I lifted my shoulders in a casual shrug. "Then talk."

"You are holding my people, and I want them back." His voice reminded me oddly of Mzatal—not in tone, but in expectation of compliance. "Where are they?"

Paul and Thatcher. Now I understood. *Farouche* was behind the failed raid on my house. "You're mistaken," I told him. "I'm not holding your people."

He was only a few yards away now. "Where are they?" he asked again, voice cool and insistent in a way that wormed itself right into my core.

Tension knotted my back, and I pygahed. "Not on any property of mine," I answered.

"Indeed true," he said as though somehow discerning the veracity beyond the words. "Where then? Where are they?"

I sucked in a sharp breath as a sudden and pervasive fear engulfed me like a shroud of frost wrapping around my essence. Part of my mind wondered why I was so weirded out, while the rest of me freaked like a rabbit beneath the eagle's talons. "Not where you or I can go," I choked out.

Farouche lowered his head, gaze heavy upon me. "They are returning to you," he said, and I had the unnerving feeling he'd read it from me. "When?"

The sick fear increased as he took a step closer. I licked dry lips, but somehow managed to stand my ground. *How the hell can he read me?* "I'm not certain." It was almost true.

His smile turned predatory as though he knew he closed in on his goal. "They will return in three days?"

Cold sweat pricked my back and underarms, and my pulse slammed an unsteady tempo. "P-possibly."

Satisfaction lit his eyes. "Sooner, then. Excellent."

No, he wasn't reading me. Somehow he could interpret beyond my words, sift truth from lies with glimpses of more. Not that it fucking mattered at this point.

Eilahn let out a hiss, clearly disliking the turn of this conversation. An arcane tingle crackled over my skin as she extended her shielding to me, likely in preparation to make a move. A new rush of fear rolled through me at the thought. "Eilahn! No. It's . . . it's okay."

Farouche flicked a glance at Eilahn, then returned his sharper gaze to me. "You will call me when you have my people *on your property* again, yes?"

Protest rose within me, followed instantly by a paralyzing sliver of primal terror. I gave a shaky nod. "Yes." Immediately the terror faded. *Something is seriously wrong,* the thought whispered.

"Then we understand one another completely, do we not?" he asked, still holding the predatory smile.

Sweat rolled down my sides. "Yes," I said. And I meant it.

"Of course we do. I look forward to working with you in the future," he said with polished confidence. "Have a nice day, Ms. Gillian." He turned and strode back to his car, slid in and closed the door.

MAC-10 guy kept his eyes and weapon on me for another few seconds, then climbed into the front passenger seat. The car backed, turned and headed away, the crazy fear retreating with it. Sight, sound, and full awareness returned, though I hadn't realized they'd been diminished.

I glanced to Eilahn, noted her facing the car behind us. I turned, saw the two men with guns still pointed in our direction. One stocky and Caucasian, with an angled face and an expression as hard as the steel of his gun, the other Hispanic, of average height and build with a soft gaze and determined manner. At some unspoken signal they retreated into their car, then drove right past us in the wake of Farouche's vehicle. I didn't bother getting their plate number. There was no point. I knew who they were.

Eilahn came around the car, scooped my gun from the ground and put it in the console between the seats. "I will drive," she told me as she took me by the arm then walked me to the passenger side and stuffed me into the vehicle. "Bad," she muttered. "Very, very bad."

"What the hell was that?" I asked after she slid behind the wheel. "I said I was going to call him." I scowled, shook my head. "Like that would ever . . ." I trailed off as my chest tightened in vague panic. I knew the truth. "Eilahn," I gasped out, "I'll call him when they get back. If I even think about *not* calling him . . ." I clenched my teeth on a mewling whimper as a surge of terror left me shaking. It passed within seconds, leaving its mark like a trail of slime.

"You will *not* call him," she stated as she drove toward the house. "I will sit on you until Mzatal can assess what has happened." Her hands tightened on the wheel. "I also felt it, though it did not affect me."

I rubbed at my eyes, clung rigidly to the knowledge that my current mental state wasn't right, even though I knew in my gut that accepting the fear as normal would ease it. "Maybe Zack can fix this or . . ." Nausea roiled at the thought of fixing it. "Shit. This is vicious. No, call Ryan." The fist in my chest tightened, and I gasped. "No." I shook my head almost frantically. "No, I'm okay with it now. It's cool." The fist eased, the nausea retreated.

Fortunately, Eilahn didn't agree with me one tiny bit. Her face remained locked in a fierce scowl as she drove one-handed and called Ryan on my phone with the other.

"Come home," she said when he answered. "She needs you." I couldn't hear his response. She simply repeated, "She needs you," then hung up and drove like a hell-bound demon the rest of the way home.

I found myself comparing the bizarre incident to Elinor's influence, yet where her touch was subtle, Farouche's overwhelmed. I knew, *knew*, that if I stopped fighting his influence, relaxed into it, the unnatural fear would subside, but I'd lose all ability to maintain distance. It would become an ingrained part of me. I couldn't, *wouldn't* let that happen, and so I danced its dance without allowing it to take me home for the night.

The car crunched along the gravel of the drive. Eilahn looked over at me. "Ryan will be here in ten minutes."

"I told you I don't need Ryan. I'm cool," I insisted through clenched teeth.

"He is coming anyway," she insisted right back as she parked the car.

I managed a nod, flung open the car door and staggered out. I made it into the house and collapsed onto the living room sofa with a groan, ignoring the growl of Fuzzykins as I disturbed her gestational nap at the other end. In the background, I heard Eilahn on the phone with Zack.

"Zack is on the property adding warding to the perimeter," she told me. "He is coming in."

I didn't try to respond. I curled on my side, focused on telling myself over and over that this was wrong. I backed off when I felt the fear about to drown me and pushed more when it receded. I danced the dance.

A few minutes later, Zack crouched beside me. "Kara, I'm here. Ryan will be here in a minute."

"I'm fine," I insisted, shivering. "I'm cool."

"You are *sooo* fine, and the coolest," Zack said, light tone tinged with worry. "It's why Ryan is coming to see you."

I gave a nod. "Yeah. Sure," I said. "This is *wrong*." Terror flared, and I gasped out a whimper. I backed off and did my best to keep dancing.

I heard the door, then Ryan's voice. "What's wrong? What happened?"

Zack stood. "Kara ran into some trouble with Farouche," he told Ryan. "You know how you do the memory shift thing? I think she needs help like that. He's got some sort of fear compulsion bullshit going on with her. You up for giving it a try?"

My nails dug into my palms as I clenched my hands hard. "Hurry," I said, then hissed through my teeth and squeezed my eyes shut. This was nothing, *nothing*, compared to what Rhyzkahl had done to me. I silently repeated that over and over, still barely able to hold on against the rising tide of fear.

"Damn right I'll try." Ryan shoved the coffee table out of the way and helped me sit up, then crouched in front of me and took my head between his hands in a firm grip. "Hang in there, Kara," he said. His eyes locked on mine, and a heartbeat later his face went stony, and his jaw tightened. Ryan couldn't read minds—if he could, Zack wouldn't let him anywhere near me since he'd pick up the truth about Ryan/Szerain—but he could feel *into* a person and muddle recent memories. Ryan considered it a quirky talent. In reality it was a hint of Szerain's mind reading and manipulation ability that bled through. The hope intruded that Szerain could surface enough to actually neutralize this, yet terror followed close in its wake.

I gripped Ryan's wrists and gave a half-hearted tug. "I'm fine!"

"Hold still, damn it," he said, mouth tight in concentration. "This is . . . I don't know."

Sick fear rose, and I tried harder to pull his hands away. "No. I'm okay. Really."

Wasn't I?

Vertigo struck as a fragment of the dream flooded me. I threw my arms wide as my inner world tipped, and I lost my footing on the plain of glass.

Memory whispered like falling sand.

Rowan.

"Kara!" Zack said forcefully. "*Kara.* Be still." His voice cut through the fear and the dance and the dream and all of the bullshit. I dropped my hands to my sides, clenched them in the fabric of the couch.

Ryan shifted his grip. "You're not okay. This doesn't feel right. I don't understand what it is, but I'm going to try to make it feel like . . . you. Do your best to relax."

I unclenched my hands and tried to focus on something, *anything* besides fear or not-fear or the horrible sense of my Self sliding into oblivion. The cat hissed at me again. Fuzzykins. I could focus on our mutual-hate relationship. I closed my eyes, imagined a world without cats who wanted to claw my face off.

The next thing I knew, Ryan withdrew his hands from my head. "That feels better to me now," he said. I opened my eyes to see him peering at me critically. "How are you doing?"

I shook my head to clear it. The cat wasn't on the sofa anymore. "Wow. That was totally bizarre." Frowning, I rubbed my temples. "It's still there, but not at all like before."

Ryan sat beside me. "What the hell happened?"

I gave him the rundown about the roadblock and the conversation with Farouche. "Ryan, it was crazy. There was one time when it seemed as if he read my thoughts, but mostly it was like he could tell whether or not I was telling the truth, and he narrowed my answers down to what he wanted to know." I shook my head. "All that's bad enough, but he has this fear thing going on too. When he told me to call him when Thatcher and Paul got back, the mere *thought* of disobeying him was utterly terrifying." I rubbed at my temples. "It's still there, but muffled. I can handle it, at least for now."

"That sounds like what Paul and Mzatal told you about," he said. "I didn't really get it before, but damn, it really had you."

"Looks like Farouche's halo is pretty fucking tarnished," I said.

"He's very dangerous," Zack agreed. "Now that you're stable, I'm going to go back and finish my perimeter inspection."

"Thanks, Zack," I said. "I have some things I need to talk to you about. I'll check in with you in a bit."

He gave me a nod and disappeared out the door.

"Are you going to be all right?" Ryan asked, concern in his eyes.

I gave him a reassuring nod. "That shook me up, but I'm good now. I'll call if anything else comes up." I slanted a look over to Eilahn. "Or Eilahn will. She doesn't listen to me when I'm acting all crazy." The syraza returned the look with a smugly pleased one of her own.

Ryan snorted. "You mean most of the time then."

Laughing, I snatched up the sofa cushion and smacked him with it. "You'd better get back to work, fed boy."

"There are better ways to get attention you know," he said with a grin, then wisely fled the house before I could hurl the pillow at him.

Chapter 18

I took some time to take care of a few mundane household tasks, both to settle myself and to see if any weird feelings or sensations cropped up. All seemed fairly normal, and since I didn't feel a sudden burning need to betray anyone who depended on me, I went out to look for Zack.

I found him busily reworking wards by the back fence beyond the pond. Since I had three hot topics to pursue with him—the attempted raid, Farouche's assault on me, and Tessa's weird behavior—I decided to get the least disturbing out of the way first.

"Hey," I said as I sauntered up, "you find out anything more about how they tried to get in?"

Zack glanced back at me. "Not a lot. There were five of them, judging by the tracks outside the fence." His mouth tightened. "They managed to get within about ten feet which means they were determined enough to work through the aversions."

"It sucks ass to be under attack at my own house," I said with a scowl. I moved up to the fence and peered at the intricate ward. "Farouche isn't playing around. And meanwhile, Katashi has Idris who the hell knows where."

Zack continued to trace arcane sigils, fluidly weaving them into protective wards. "I have a bad feeling it'll get worse before everything settles down . . . oh, in a few hundred years or so."

I groaned. "I'm going to pretend you're kidding even if you aren't." The demonic lords and the demahnk were several thousand years old, which meant it was possible Zack was being completely serious. "It feels as if we've done nothing but chase leads and put out fires since I got back," I said. "I haven't had the chance to thank you for the fence and gate, and all the improvements in the house." I smiled wryly. "I admit, I had a moment where it bugged me, but I got over it. Anyway, I really appreciate it, and I know all this must have cost you a fortune."

Zack laughed and began another ward. "Yes, it did, but you don't need to worry about that. I have my ways. Not unlimited ways, but we're good for now."

Too weird. A demon masquerading as a human with a trust fund. "The fence is awesome," I said, "but I wish we'd been able to get a look at the intruders. What do you think about a camera surveillance system for the perimeter?"

"I think it's needed." He smiled. "And no, I don't mind footing the bill. I can handle it."

"Farouche is a confident, aggressive son of a bitch. I wouldn't put it past him to try again." A touch of fear whispered through me as I spoke of him. I breathed through it and used it as a segue to the second hot topic. "He didn't even touch me. How the hell could he affect me so heavily?"

Zack's hand stilled, sigil half traced. He looked back over his shoulder at me, shook his head slowly, lips pressed together. "Think of a qaztahl's aura, but specialized. With Farouche, if you can feel it, he can affect you. It's disturbing." He went quiet, but it was one of those pauses where I could tell he had more to say. "Kara, I'd like to encourage Jill to move in for a while. I have her house warded, but right now we all need to be together."

"I'm cool with that," I replied, "especially now that we know Farouche is an exceptionally dangerous asshole." Plus, Jill would have more time with Zack if she moved here, which might ease some of the tension between them. "But I have two questions for you. First, she's a pretty independent chick. You think she'd agree to it?"

"Nope. I've tried. For months," he said with undisguised frustration. "That's why I'm enlisting you."

"Gee, thanks." Changing Jill's mind wouldn't be a walk in the park. "Let's say, by some miracle, she does agree. My second question is where do you intend to *put* her?"

"For now I figured an RV—one of the really nice big ones—near the tree line on the east side of the house would work," he said as he finished another sigil. "She'd have some privacy, I'd ward the hell out of it, and, because it would be within the fence and these perimeter wards, it would be as safe as your house."

"The RV plan might work, but *privacy*?" I raised an eyebrow. "Puhleeease. It's still me, you, Ryan, and Eilahn next door. Plus Thatcher and Paul when they get back, for who knows how long. And Mzatal when he's here. Can't forget the demonic lord." I leveled a smirk at him. "If I were you, I wouldn't try to sell her on the privacy part."

He smirked right back at me. "Good. At least you know what *not* to use in your persuasive approach with her. I'm telling you. She won't hear it from me."

"Okay okay okay." I lifted my hands in surrender. "Since I think it's for a good cause, I'll try to convince her." I shook my head. "Not sure she'll listen to me any more than to you though."

Zack exhaled. "You'd be surprised. Anyway, thanks."

"No problem." Now for the last of the hot topics. "I have a new issue that's bothering me, and I hope you can help me get some perspective."

"Sure. What's up?"

"It's Tessa. I think she's been manipulated."

Zack stopped tracing a sigil, dispersed it with a sweep of his hand and turned to face me. "Why do you think that?"

"Because we talked, and every time it came around to one particular subject it was like it hit reset on a game, and she backtracked a minute." Frustration and helpless anger rose again. "Also, her memory of another event seems programmed. It's fucked up."

"That does sound like manipulation," he said, face serious but revealing nothing of his thoughts. "What was the topic?"

"Weirdly enough, the reset was when I asked her if she'd ever been to the demon realm." I folded my arms, watched him carefully for any reaction. "Which begs the question, why the hell would my aunt be manipulated about that if she hadn't been there?"

Zack cleared his throat. "Do you have any working theories?"

"One is that she was in the demon realm at the end of her time with Katashi and, for whatever reason, was then manipulated to forget all about it," I said. "But I'd really like another theory." My outrage at the violation of Tessa flared again. "I'll take anything that isn't 'someone fucked with my aunt's head.'"

"Your current theory is very sound." He said it with a disturbing contemplative calm.

Fucking shit. My blood pounded in my ears. "Has Tessa ever been in the demon realm?"

Zack shifted from one foot to the other and didn't answer. Anger seethed like a ball of fire in my chest, and I took a step toward him. "You *know*. Fucking tell me, Zack. *Now*. Has Tessa been in the demon realm?"

He gave a barely perceptible nod.

"With which lord?" I demanded. "Whose realm?" A horrible dread suddenly coiled through me. *What if he says Mzatal?* Katashi had been his sworn summoner, which meant it was more than possible. *No, Mzatal wouldn't hide that from me,* I thought, casting the worry aside. I knew that much.

Zack stood in infuriating silence, his eyes on mine as I moved to the next worst possibility. "Rhyzkahl?"

Another micro nod.

Rage clogged my throat for several seconds. "You've known this all along and you didn't *tell* me?" I shouted when I could finally speak. "What the fuck? You're supposed to be my friend." It hit me then, and I stared at him in sick horror. "You're *his* goddamn ptarl. Does ptarl trump friend? Or were you ever my friend at all?" I'd had a dozen lifetime's worth of betrayal from Rhyzkahl, but the very thought of the same from Zack was a knife in my gut. Like lord, like ptarl? "I guess that means you didn't tell me before so you could protect his sorry ass and won't fucking tell me now either!"

He drew a breath. "It's true. I can't tell you what happened."

"This is my aunt," I snarled. "You know what happened to her, but you won't tell me because you're still loyal to *him*."

"Kara." His eyes sought mine, but I was too distraught to read the emotion that burned within them. "I am here," he said. "Not there."

"It doesn't help that you're *here*, in my goddamn house,

if you're still loyal to that *chekkunden*." I bared my teeth. "Can I trust you? Or do you report everything you see and hear back to him? Will I wake one morning with a knife at my throat and enemies in the house? Is that why you refuse to free Szerain? Do you remain a good little jailer for your fucked up master?"

An aggrieved expression touched Zack's face. "I loosen Szerain's confinement as I can, offer him relief." He shook his head. "And I do not contact Rhyzkahl," he added.

"Whew! I feel better now," I said, with heavy sarcasm. "But you're not answering my goddamn question!" Yelling felt pretty damn good at the moment. "Where are your loyalties? To him? Or to us?"

His jaw tightened. "It is not as simple as that, not so black and white."

"Then explain," I said and threw my arms out wide. "I'm all ears! You know what he did to me. How can you have *any* loyalty to him and still pretend to be on my side?"

"Kara, there are ancient ties, ancient agreements, ancient oaths." His hand trembled, and he tightened it into a fist. "It does not mean that I act against you."

"Ancient ties!" I spat the words back at him. "Rhyzkahl tortured me! Carved me up! You *know* what he'd have done to me if it hadn't been for Mzatal and Idris." A sense of utter betrayal swept over me, and I clung to the anger like a lifeline. "If you still have any loyalty to him, if you can't tell me what I need to know, then you *are* acting against me."

Zack shifted his weight again. "No," he said, voice weirdly hollow. "I'm not acting against you. I am . . . not."

"Then tell me about my aunt and Rhyzkahl."

He remained silent for several heartbeats, tension holding his body rigid. "I *cannot*."

"You are completely full of shit," I sneered. "You stand back and convince yourself you're not doing any harm, that you're not a threat to us. You have all these 'ancient ties' to excuse your behavior." I firmed my mouth. "How about I clear some shit up for you right now. As long as you keep vital information back, you're not on our side, and I can't fucking trust you." A dim part of me knew I was overreacting, pulled at me to stop and breathe, but I couldn't stem the raging emotions. Instead I turned and fled down the trail and back to the house. I stormed through the kitchen, retreated to my room and slammed the door hard enough to rattle the windows.

Hands clenched in my lap, I sat on the edge of the bed and willed myself not to cry despite the near overwhelming need to do exactly that.

A moment later, Zack spoke softly from the other side of the door. "Kara."

"What."

"I'm sorry."

No way could I say "It's all right" or "I forgive you" or anything like that, because it wasn't and I didn't. But I didn't want to twist the knife further either. Zack had been oathbound long before he met me. Desperate worry about Tessa wound through my gut, along with the beginnings of a horrible suspicion about who Idris's daddy might be, yet the idea that I might lose the Zack I thought I knew added a nauseating veneer. "Look, I can't talk about this anymore," I said in a shaking voice. "I need to be alone."

Silence, then, "Would it be easier for you if I stay away from here?"

I didn't know what I wanted except for the sick ache to disappear. "No, you don't have to leave." Why did this shit have to hurt so much?

After a moment I heard a soft noise as though he'd lifted his hand from the door. "All right," he finally said. "I'm heading back to the office." When he spoke after another moment of silence, his voice held no luster. "Kara, I'm really sorry you're hurting."

I didn't answer, couldn't answer as I fought to hold back tears. When I heard the front door close I finally buried my face in my pillow and gave in.

Chapter 19

Eventually the hurt, betrayal, and worry coalesced into a more comfortable and familiar anger and general upset. I sat up and scrubbed my hand over my face. Enough unproductive bawling. I needed to get my ass up and move, lose myself in sweat and exhaustion. A perfect time to try out the obstacle course.

The fed-boys had done a good job with it, I decided with grudging respect. Without removing any living trees, they'd managed to create a clever and circuitous route through the woods, and had installed a dozen obstacles in existing natural clearings along it—walls of various heights, rope climbs, low crawls, wobbly log bridges, and more—all challenging without being ridiculous.

Forty-five minutes later and two rounds through the course, I stood bent over at the waist, hands on my knees, sick from the heat. Once hadn't been enough. Twice hadn't quite done the trick either, but I knew a third time would likely kill me. Besides, there were other tried and true ways to deal with emotional upheaval.

Once I could walk again without puking, I headed into the house to down a big glass of water. After that—and as soon as I knew my stomach wouldn't rebel—I grabbed a spoon and a gallon of chocolate fudge ice cream, then flopped, stinky and dirty, into a chair at the kitchen table. A shower could wait. I had more important things to do.

About four spoonfuls in, I heard the front door open. *Shit, don't let it be Zack, not yet*, I thought, then released my breath, relieved, when Ryan came into the kitchen. He pulled off his sunglasses and dropped them to the table with a clatter. I glanced at him, defiantly ate another spoonful.

"Sweat, stench, and ice cream," he said. "What's wrong?"

"Your partner," I said and barely remembered in time that I couldn't tell him the whole story since Ryan didn't know Zack was a demon. "He's a jerk."

He stiffened. "Surfer Boy *Zack* got you worked up enough to stink and shovel ice cream? That's my job. What did he do?"

"It's hard to explain. Anyway, I'd like to let it go now."

Ryan got an odd look on his face, as though he was trying to work through a complex problem while on good drugs. He looked at me, but I wasn't sure he saw me.

"Ryan? You okay?"

Without any indication he'd heard me, he stripped off his suit jacket and hung it on the back of a chair, then headed for the back door.

Something with Szerain? With the faintest of pouts, I stood and shoved the ice cream back in the freezer. *Can't even have a decent pity party around here.* I followed Ryan out and stopped on the porch, watching. He paced this way and that in the grass before settling cross-legged with his back to me. My skin prickled. That was the same place Mzatal had identified as a potency confluence, where he'd gone to recharge.

I slowly moved to sit facing him. Ryan stared down, his hands wound in the grass in clenched claws. I waited in tense silence, certain that Szerain sought to express, and I didn't want to disturb the process. A quick mental pygah helped me shed the distraction of the issues with Zack, and I hoped would also help Szerain.

A beetle trundled between the clenched blades of grass. An ant crawled over one knuckle and then down to the dirt again.

"Kara."

I watched in fascination as the ant found a seed and hoisted it. What a strong fellow it was!

"Kara."

I heard Szerain speaking, voice strained. "Kara," he repeated, as though testing his ability.

Speaking to *me*, I abruptly realized. I yanked my gaze up to him. "Here," I said quickly. "I'm here, Szerain."

A tremor started in his hands and quickly swept over the rest of his body. "As . . . am I."

"How? How can you be surfaced without Zack releasing you?" *Or Vsuhl drawing you out.*

"Practice. Focus. Confluence. Grate looser." He drew a deep shuddering breath and gave a moan that sounded like pleasure. I guess he'd learned not to take the simple things for granted. "What trouble with Zakaar?"

"I had a falling out with him. A humongous one." I exhaled as the memory and emotions returned. "I found out that my aunt has been manipulated to not know anything about being in the demon realm. I asked him if it was Rhyzkahl, which, after a lot of prodding, he confirmed. Then I asked him where his loyalties lay." I sighed. "I had to sweat and scarf down ice cream after that."

"Did not like the answer."

"No. No, I didn't. Rhyzkahl inflicted heinous torment on me." The sigils carved into my torso itched and tingled like thin lines of sunburn at the reminder. "I don't understand how Zakaar can maintain *any* connection to him."

"Ptarl," Szerain said as though it explained everything.

"Yeah, he's still that asshole's ptarl. Why?" I asked. The anger and frustration flared again. "How can he be my friend?" My jaw tightened. "Never mind, he can't be that. How can he be an *ally* and still be with Rhyzkahl?"

He lifted his head in a motion that took supreme effort judging by the increase in his tremors. He struggled to open his eyes. "Still ptarl. Always." Finally his gaze met mine, and enveloped me in ancient depths. "The bond." He paused, as though recovering from the ordeal of opening his eyes. "The bond is made."

"Yes, fine, he has a bond," I said, "but some things are deal breakers—or at least they should be."

Szerain recoiled from the words as though I'd spoken blackest heresy, though for the life of me I couldn't fathom why. His face contorted in a disturbing dance of pain and horror and fury, all overlaid with madness. His hands curled into fists, ripped up tufts of grass. "No! Cannot be. There *cannot* be deal breakers. Not with ptarl."

I seized one of his hands. "Szerain, it's okay. I didn't mean to upset you. Here, I'm pygahing. Feel it." I emphasized the command in my tone, hoping to penetrate the grip of what had set him off. *Deal breaking related to a ptarl*.

Shit. I'd forgotten Szerain was one of two lords separated from their ptarl. Kadir's simply didn't associate with him, but Szerain's ptarl was either in hiding or dead, though most thought it was the latter. From what I gathered now, separated didn't mean the bond was broken. Did being away from his ptarl add another degree of misery to the already tormented Szerain? At any rate, it was clearly a sore point I needed to avoid with him in such an unstable state.

Szerain drew a shaky breath and squeezed his eyes shut, but to my relief some of the tension left his body. His face eased back to normal. I unwound his fingers from the grass and held his hand securely. "I'm sorry. I didn't realize."

"You did not know." He opened his eyes again, focused on mine as though drawing support from me. And maybe he was. Moment by moment his speech improved. "Zakaar. You doubt him."

"I do," I admitted. "The thing with Tessa is pretty big to hide from me. And he hesitated back at the warehouse when I needed him to bring Mzatal." I scowled. "And shit, he didn't point blank warn me about Rhyzkahl before I ended up with a torso full of body art. As long as he's bound to Rhyzkahl, I don't see how I can trust him." I searched his face. "Am I being unreasonable?"

"Rhyzkahl's ptarl. Reasonable doubt."

A sliver of dismay went through me. I'd hoped for some brilliant rationalization of why it was okay to trust Zack despite all the shit. "That's the conclusion I came to," I said with a sigh. "I asked Ilana about him, and she said he opposed Rhyzkahl's actions and chose to guard you. And I was actually cool with that until I found out he knew about Tessa's manipulation." I leaned closer, looking into eyes that were Ryan's but not Ryan's. "Szerain, do *you* trust him?"

His face tightened as though a wave of pain swept through him. "Zakaar. Yes. With my essence."

I processed that. *With his essence*. Then again, Szerain didn't have much choice in the matter. Zakaar controlled his existence—very literally *held* his essence. If he didn't trust Zakaar, what did he have? I felt my mouth tighten as I mulled over the implications. So what if Zakaar rewarded him every once in a while by loosening the grate? It sure as hell didn't make up for keeping him submerged in the first place.

Yet to Szerain, those times would be precious gifts, conditioning him to dependence and attachment. The torturer lets up on the pain a little, offers mercy and brief kindness, and becomes the hero. A technique as old as pain itself.

A shudder crawled over me. Rhyzkahl had used that method when he carved the sigils in my flesh, and if not for Mzatal's intervention it would have worked. Throw in the fact that Szerain had been enduring this for *years*, and it was a full blown case of Stockholm syndrome.

Szerain's fingers spasmed on mine before his grip firmed. "Kara. No," he murmured, and I realized with a startled shock he'd read my thoughts. "So much more than that."

His quiet voice held such intensity and presence that I went still, focused on him. "Okay. Tell me."

"I am not insane."

"No, you're not," I acknowledged as I tried to figure out where he was going with this. He wasn't stable by any means, but he wasn't nuts either. "And that's pretty amazing. I wouldn't have lasted a week."

"Some times of madness. Despair. But I am still . . . here." He lifted his free hand, rubbed the fingers together as though to reassure himself he really was. "Because of Zakaar. *Only* because of Zakaar."

I considered that. "Because he occasionally eases the pressure?" I couldn't fathom how that would be enough to counter the effects of the submersion, especially long term.

"No. Yes, though that is only a small part." He trembled then extricated his hand from mine and placed both hands palm down on the ground. "Every night—*every* night for over fifteen years—he speaks to me while Ryan sleeps. For hours. Tells me stories. Reads to me. Keeps me focused. Passes glimmers of potency to me, palm to palm. Halts my certain descent into madness."

I stared at him as I tried to assimilate this new information into my perspective. "That's some pretty serious dedication."

"He does not have to do this. It is his choice." Another spasm of pain twisted his face. "He expends much potency in my care. He grows tired. He does not say it, but I know it is truth. This does not change what you experience with him, but it is unfair to include his treatment of me in your considerations unless it is weighted in his favor."

"Point taken," I said, subdued. I remained quiet for a moment as I rearranged my perception of Zakaar in my mind. "I heard this from Ilana," I finally said, "but I'd like to hear it from you. It'll help me—" I sought the right word to capture what I meant. "It'll help me reconcile everything. Did he really oppose Rhyzkahl and distance himself because of it?"

"This is truth," Szerain replied. "And distanced himself yet more by coming here with me since Helori was prepared to be my guardian." He closed his eyes as though gathering the strength to speak again.

I willed calm and focus for both of us as I considered his words. I had no trouble seeing the demahnk Helori as a guardian. It was Helori who nurtured me in the days immediately following Rhyzkahl's torture. Mzatal healed the physical damage, but without Helori's firm, gentle presence and imperturbable patience, I never would have recovered from the mental and emotional trauma.

Szerain drew a labored breath, opened his eyes and continued. "Though Zakaar stood against Rhyzkahl's actions on many levels, it was still a heavy blow to Rhyzkahl to lose contact with his . . ." Szerain's face went ashen. "To lose a ptarl. To lose . . ." His gaze sharpened, fierce and predatory. "Kara. Call Vsuhl. I *need* my blade." He reached, caught my wrist. "I cannot call it as I am. Diminished. Through you. *Through* you."

I tensed in shock at the instantaneous shift in his manner, but then a snarl curled my lip. No way was I calling the essence blade for him. Not now. Hell, not ever. I'd worked my ass off for it and damned near destroyed the demon realm to get it. Then I felt it—an insidious drawing sensation as he used our contact to call to Vsuhl through me.

"No!" I shouted. I yanked my wrist from his weak grasp, scrabbled back and lurched to my feet. Breathing hard, I watched him warily. "You *ever* try shit like that again, and I'll kick your motherfucking demonic ass."

His hands went limp in the grass, and his eyes grew wild and unfocused. An instant later he jerked heavily, collapsed to the side and went into convulsions.

My anger evaporated in an instant. "Shit! Szerain!" I threw myself to my knees beside him, caught movement out of the corner of my eye and glanced that way. "Zack!" Relief flooded through me as he loped quickly toward us. Of course the guard and guardian wouldn't be far away. "He tried to call Vsuhl."

Zack gave a nod, crouched on the other side of Szerain. He spoke in demon as he laid his hand on Szerain's forehead, and within seconds the convulsions stilled. "I will put Ryan into deep sleep and fog Szerain as much as I am able."

"It came out of nowhere," I told him, brow creased. "We were having a good conversation. Then he told me to call Vsuhl, and grabbed my wrist. When I broke away, he collapsed."

Zack lifted his eyes to me. "The blades have a strong hold."

"So I've noticed." I scowled. "He's obviously obsessed. When he tried to call the blade, it was like I suddenly didn't know him. Before that, even though it was Szerain without Ryan, he was familiar."

"You've held Vsuhl. You know a hint of its allure." His gaze penetrated me. "Not a day goes by that you don't think about the feel of it in your hand, even toy with the idea of calling it."

I opened my mouth to deny such an absurd notion, then realized he was right. "Sure, but that's no big deal," I said, feeling an obscure need to defend myself.

"I'm simply asking you to consider that you held the blade twice. He held it for millennia."

Feelings I couldn't identify tumbled through me. "Whatever the deal is, I don't want to go through that with him again," I said with a shake of my head. "Maybe you can, um, get him to chill." *Chill?* That was a pretty insensitive request, I realized with chagrin. Zack already worked his ass off to keep Szerain controlled and sane. "Crap. That was unfair of me. Forget I said that." I shifted, grimaced. "Szerain told me what you've done for him. Do for him." I gave him an apologetic wince. "I jumped your ass pretty hard earlier. You think we could call a truce?"

Relief I hadn't expected shone in his eyes, and a faint smile touched his mouth. "I'd like that."

"I can't say it doesn't still bug me—the whole Rhyzkahl's

ptarl thing, and you not spilling everything you know about Tessa," I said, "but we all need to stick together right now. There's too much at stake."

"You're right," Zack replied. "This isn't a time for division. I know you don't fully trust me, and may never again." He scooped Ryan into his arms and lifted him. "But I'm here," he went on. "And I don't intend to bring harm to you. My presence here is . . . complicated."

I stood and nodded. "Okay. Fair enough for now. If I actually stop and think about it instead of flying off the handle, I *can* see the difference in actively helping Rhyzkahl and keeping your mouth shut about things you can't—for whatever reason—share."

Zack gave me a relieved smile, then headed toward the house with me. I opened the back door and held it for him to pass. "Szerain acted like this ptarl bond thing was forever and irrevocable. Is that true?"

"The qaztahl have no memory of a time without the bond," he said as he passed through the kitchen, "and despite ptarl grievances, as with Rhyzkahl and Kadir, no bond has ever been broken."

I followed him in. "So, hypothetically, a ptarl bond *could* be broken?"

Zack glanced at me as he made his way down the hall and toward the basement door. "Hypothetically, theoretically, yes. Practically, realistically, no."

"Why?" I opened the basement door for him.

Zack stopped on the top of the stairs, turned to face me. "Unknown consequences. Disruption of the arcane flows. Potentially deadly effect on the qaztahl. Inconceivable loss. Ripples in all directions for many."

But if no one had ever done it, how did he know for sure? It wasn't that I didn't believe him. It was simply that it was so far away from anything I'd experienced, I had no reference. "If it was a little *more* practical and realistic," I pressed, "would you break the bond?"

A wave of agonized distress passed over his features. "I don't know."

I accepted that as a victory over a flat out No. "Go take care of Ryan," I said with a smile. "If you're lucky, I might even start dinner."

Zack let out a weak laugh. "I'm not sure I'd call that luck."

"My cooking isn't *that* bad." My mouth twisted. "Or maybe it is. I'll keep it simple."

"I'll be right back to supervise," he replied with a hint of mock-panic in his voice. Or possibly real panic.

"Maybe you can pick up some culinary secrets," I said sweetly, then closed the door behind them and headed for the kitchen to forage for something "simple." In other words, Kara-proof.

Szerain and Zack had given me a lot to think about on top of the Idris issue, Farouche, and Tessa's manipulation. *Oh yeah, and let's not forgot the evil demonic lords trying to take over the world.* On top of all that, I needed to talk to Jill and see if I could convince her to move into what was rapidly becoming a compound. *Kara's Kompound.* I muffled a laugh, then mulled over what I'd say to her while I tried to decide between frozen lasagna or waffles with bacon for dinner. Or bacon lasagna. Yum.

Zack returned with a stack of files and his laptop as I closed the oven door on the frozen lasagna. "I have Ryan sleeping. Szerain is in turmoil," he said. "I'll do some intense work with him tonight." He set the laptop on the kitchen table and passed over a file folder. "I made copies of all the Symbol Man case file notes for you, as well as everything we have for Amber's murder. Figured it couldn't hurt for you to have it all."

"You rock," I said and took the folder. "I'm going to grab a shower while the lasagna cooks. Twice through the obstacle course. I think I stink a little."

"More than a little. You're ripe."

"It's much more gentlemanly to deny my stench."

"Then you'd doubt it was me," he said with a low laugh.

"You got that right." The familiar banter was a relief and reminded me that, while the problems weren't gone, they were manageable. "I'll call Jill first and see if she wants to meet me tomorrow for a lovely early morning walk. Not only will it shock the hell out of her—me, exercise, morning—but I'll have her as a captive audience to sell her on the benefits of her potential new temporary home."

He grinned. "She won't be able to resist it, not with your smooth sell."

"Riiiiiight." I rolled my eyes dramatically. "Seriously though, I'll do my best. Too much shit going on right now to risk her."

"Thanks," he said fervently, and the worry and love for Jill in his eyes was another bit of reassurance for me. "I'll get to work on the deeper mysteries of my open cases," he said and headed for the living room.

I put the case files by the stack of Tracy Gordon journals, then made a quick call to Jill to invite her over for a persuasive sales pitch—disguised as a stroll around my property—for the next morning. I also gave her a summary of the harrowing roadblock incident with Farouche. I figured it couldn't hurt to prime the danger pump.

No new crises emerged during my shower, to my relief and delight. The lasagna smelled great, and I had chocolate fudge ice cream to spare in the fridge. What the hell? A quiet night kicked back at home?

Don't get cocky, I reminded myself. Best to take it minute by minute and not get my hopes up for the *whole* night.

Chapter 20

I opened my eyes to sun slanting through the blinds. No alarm clock. No phone call. The smell of something baking. I glanced at the clock, pleased to see that I'd slept over eight hours. I could get used to this.

I had about thirty minutes before Jill arrived for our walk and talk. When I wandered out to the kitchen, I found Ryan at the table, already dressed and with his laptop open.

"You made coffee," I observed. Plenty of time for coffee. Hell, I'd *make* time for coffee.

He looked up and gave me a smile. "I sure did. It shortens the Grumpy Kara time if it's ready to go when you wake up."

"I'm never grumpy," I protested unconvincingly. "Ever." I filled my cup and dumped in sugar and cream. "How are you feeling this morning?" I had no idea if Ryan felt any residuals of the convulsions Szerain had yesterday.

"I'm feeling fine," he said giving me a wary look. "Is there some reason I shouldn't be?"

I smiled sweetly. "No! Not at all. Can't a girl ask about your well-being?"

"You? Nope," he said with a grin, then gestured toward the oven. "I made some bacon-topped maple roll things. They're done, but I'm sure you're not hungry. Zack and I will manage to keep them from going to waste."

"Nice try." I pulled the oven door open, and the sight and smell of the rolls set my mouth watering. I grabbed a potholder and moved the baking sheet to the stovetop, transferred one of the delectables to a plate, then took a bite. "Holy shit. You've been keeping these secret all this time? I'll have to run the obstacle course three times, but it's worth it."

"My mom's recipe," he said. "I found it tucked away in a photo album. I don't remember her making them, but they sure are good."

I stopped chewing as my heart clenched with a fierce ache. Of course he didn't remember his mom making them. He wasn't really Ryan Kristoff. *How did all of that work*? I wondered as I resumed chewing. As far as I'd been able to determine, Szerain took over the real Ryan's life a decade and a half ago, and the Ryan I knew was actually Szerain with an arcanely altered face. Before then, Ryan Kristoff had a full life that included family and college and work. How had Szerain replaced him without raising suspicions? And what happened to the real Ryan?

I finished my bite. "These are damn good," I said. "Any other secret recipes hiding out?"

"A few. I'll let you taste test if you're a good girl."

My witty retort went unsaid as the gate control panel buzzed. I glanced over at the screen to see Jill's car pulling through the gate. "Crap! I'm not even dressed." I hurried to down the rest of the coffee.

Ryan grinned. "I'm so damn interesting you can't even think straight."

I set the cup in the sink and thwacked him on the shoulder as I passed by on the way to my bedroom. "Yeah, that's it. Had me all aflutter and hanging on every word. Since you're so interesting, you can entertain Jill until I get ready."

Ryan answered with a laugh.

After taking a few minutes to throw on clothes and shoes and take care of some other necessary business, I returned to the kitchen. "Hey, mama."

"Hey, yourself. I brought some fresh fruit cups from the market," Jill announced with a smile. "But I've ruined all of that and indulged in one of Ryan's evil rolls."

I laughed. "Yeah. You're weak like that. Me? I resisted."

She leveled a mom-worthy glare at me. "Kara Gillian. Number one, I know you better than that. Number two, you have maple drizzle on your chin."

Damn. I hurriedly swiped at the evidence.

Ryan tucked his laptop into its case and pulled on his

suit jacket. "I know this is going to be a blow to you both, but I can't stay. Court."

"Aw, man!" I said with a mock-pout. "And we were going to talk about female bodily fluids!"

Jill grinned evilly. "I've been learning all about post-pregnancy discharge."

Ryan made an agonized face. "I did not hear that. Did *not*." With that he gave us a wave and left.

I laughed. "Makes them squirm every time. You ready to go? The boys have been doing their best to turn my property into a theme park."

"I know. You can't even imagine the things I talked them out of."

I gave her a wary look as I opened the back door. "Like what?"

"For starters, a pool table in the living room. Can you believe it? In the *living room*."

"A pool table," I repeated in disbelief. "I guess I should be glad that the majority of my summoning chamber remained untouched." Amusement at the possibilities set me laughing again. "I'm picturing returning from the demon realm and landing in a hot tub." I stretched as we reached the bottom of the steps and started across the grass. "I can't complain about the kitchen though. And the yard looks better than it ever has."

"I contributed to the state of the yard by sitting on the porch and watching them work," Jill said with a grin.

"I think you get a free pass on yard work for a while," I said with a nod toward her enormous midsection as we walked toward one of the trails into the woods. "Good thing we got an early start. The day's gonna be a scorcher."

She peered up at the cloudless sky. "We're supposed to get a front through late afternoon. That'll cool things off." Her gaze returned to me. "You're summoning Mzatal back today?" she asked. "And the other two?"

I nodded. "Things are starting to get pretty complicated now. Too many bad guys to keep track of."

"Fortunately, most are in the demon realm, not here."

I glanced over at her. "Not anymore." We walked along in silence for several minutes. "Okay, I'm not going to try to be all devious or subtle," I finally said. "I told you what happened to me yesterday. You need to come live here."

Jill stopped and turned to face me, her lips pressed tightly together. "I *knew* there was more to this let's-exercise-in-the-morning thing. Zack put you up to this?"

I regarded her seriously. "Actually, we both came at it from different directions, but yes, I totally agree with him. It's safer here."

"It's safer in a maximum-security prison cell," she all but snarled, "but it doesn't mean I'm going to move into one." She raised a hand and took a step back from me, clearly indicating she'd already shut the door on this conversation. "I go to work every day without a bodyguard. That wouldn't change if I lived here. Zack has my house warded. Same here. You have a billion people here. I have my lovely, quiet house. I *need* my privacy."

"Look, the warding on your house is *nothing* compared to what we have here now," I stated. "And yes, we have a lot of people here, but there's a reason for that. It's fucking dangerous right now, and we're better off pooling resources and brainpower." Frustration edged my voice. "And, damn it, we care about you—Zack, Ryan, me. So, like it or not, when you're not here, we worry about you."

Indignation swept over her face. "Is that supposed to be some sort of guilt trip?"

"Not at all. I'm simply telling you the way it is," I replied. "And I'm sorry you're in the middle of a mess you didn't make, but you are. I have enemies who don't play around. You're close to me. You're a target."

"Great," she said, throwing her hands up. "You're telling me there are people who want to hurt or kidnap me? *Me*?"

"I don't know, but it's a big enough possibility for Zack and me to be riding your ass about it."

She shook her head in a definitive *No*. "I can't live like that. Afraid to move. No way. What's next? Quit my job?"

I drew a breath and sought calm. "You know the body in the semi-trailer? The one with the sigils carved all over her torso?" I wanted to add, *The one who was raped and sodomized?* but didn't. She knew. "That was done by the people who have Idris. The body had a trap on it, set for me. And let's not forget that Farouche had me at gunpoint for ten minutes yesterday." Her brow furrowed, and I could tell I was gaining ground. "These assholes mean business, and the people who love you want you and the bean to be as safe as possible." I softened my tone. "That's all. It wouldn't be for very long." I hoped that was true. "Surely you can sacrifice a little privacy for a month or two for peace of mind? At least until the bean is born?"

She took back the ground I'd gained and stared at me with new horror in her eyes. "A *month*? Or *two*?" she said, aghast. "Zack didn't say anything about *months*—not that we got that far."

I sighed and started down the trail again. "I don't understand. You're not shy. You're great with people. Why is this such a big deal?"

"Sure, when I want to be out among people." She paused as if to organize her thoughts. "It's just . . . I need alone time every day to chill. I couldn't even do a dorm in college. Being around people whether I want to or not?" She shook her head firmly. "No. Nuh uh. And, yes, Zack said he'd get an RV," she said with exasperation. "That's better than living in your house, but it would be cramped and— " Distress flickered in her eyes, but she pulled herself together in a flash, as though accustomed to suppressing whatever thought had triggered it. She took a breath and continued, "Here's the deal. I have a house I love that's five minutes away from work, not thirty. Zack has it armed to the teeth with wards. I need my space, and I don't do well with group living. Too much stress. It's nothing personal. I know you're trying to help."

I winced, exhaled. "All right, but the invitation is always out there." Jill tended to be practical, not stubborn, which told me that more lurked behind her aversion to living in a community than she chose to share. A traumatic event? Family drama? Zack and I would need some insight on the real issue and a sweeter offer than an RV if we wanted her to agree to move here. I'd have another chat with Zack later. "Let's forget about it for now. You okay with that?"

"Totally. I am so done with it," she said then flashed me a smile to signal we were complete.

Complete for now. But I went ahead and changed the subject. "I told you about Paul, right? I think you'll like him. He's a sweet kid." I shook my head. "No, not a kid. Twenty-ish, but he comes across with that youthful exuberance."

Jill laughed. "A kid to you. You *are* over thirty you know."

I held back a sigh. "I know. I sure missed spending that milestone with my best friends." It had passed unnoticed in the demon realm, with Mzatal holed up in the plexus for the days before, during, and after. By the time he came out it seemed silly to even mention it since I knew his focus had been on finding Idris. I couldn't even blame Mzatal for not making any sort of deal over it. What was thirty years to someone who'd seen thousands of them?

"Yeah, that kind of sucks. Maybe we can make up for it later," she said with a wink. "You told me Paul and the other guy are super close. Are they a couple?"

"Y'know, I get the feeling Paul is gay, but I'm pretty sure it's more like a big brother kind of thing between those two."

"That's cool," she said with approval. "With what he's been through with the kidnapping and everything, sounds like he could use that kind of support."

"Thatcher was pretty much unconscious the whole time he was here, so I don't know yet if he's a dick. However, I do know he took a bullet for Paul without hesitation." I replayed the scene in my mind. "Dude has some awesome reflexes. He jumped in front of Paul before that stupid security guard even squeezed the trigger."

"Could be he has Paul dependent on him," she said. Worry swept over her face. "Same thing that gets me worried about you and Mzatal, and yeah, I know—it's not like that."

I winced and shook my head as we headed across the lawn to the house. "Trust me, I've thought about it a lot. Stockholm syndrome, all of that." We walked a moment in silence. "But, I'm not dependent on Mzatal, and he does want the best for me. He dissolved our agreement because he said if we can't simply trust one another, the whole thing was pointless." I smiled a bit. "He loves me," I said, then smiled more. "And yeah, I love him too."

Jill put on her best fake-tough-girl face. "He hasn't earned the Jill seal of approval yet. When do I get to check out this so-called loverboy? I missed him last time he was here."

I laughed. "Come over this afternoon, and you can check him out all you want."

"I'll do that," she said. "I have to go to birthing class this morning, because y'know, she'll never come out if I don't have proper training." Her face fell.

"What's wrong, chick?" I asked.

"Zack's only made it to one of them," she said and sighed. "I told him I would change to evening classes, but he still didn't say, 'Oh yes dear, that will be wonderful! I can make it then.'"

"Sheesh. Men." I snorted "*Demon* men." I tilted my head. "Maybe it's simply that he already knows all the stuff and doesn't realize it's more for your support? I'll slap him and inform him, if you think it'll help."

Jill narrowed her eyes at me. "How would a demon know all about human childbirth?"

"I'm sure he's been around plenty of humans. There used to be a lot of back and forth between the two worlds up until sometime in the sixteen-hundreds."

She considered that. "So he's read a book or whatever. It's not the same thing—" She turned and stared at me. "Wait. *Wait.* You're telling me that Zack was around in the seventeenth century?"

Whoa. He hadn't told her news as big as *that* yet? "Umm, well . . . yeah," I said, shifting my weight a couple of times as if preparing to flee her impending wrath. "Plus a couple thousand years earlier, most likely."

Jill went super-calm scary. "I'm going to kill him."

The urge to flee grew. "I honestly thought he'd have told you this stuff by now."

She added narrowed eyes to her scariness. "What other 'stuff' is there?"

Where would I even start with something like that? "Let's back up." I summoned up a glare of my own. "Have you ever asked him to tell you about his demon-ness."

"Sure I have," she insisted. "But he didn't say he was around to witness the fall of Troy!"

"What did you ask him?"

She fidgeted and looked away "I don't remember!" she exclaimed. "Something about what it was like being a demon."

I knew Jill. She would never hesitate to ask all sorts of embarrassing questions if she wanted to know the answer. She'd been with Zack for a good while now, and she *might* have asked him a vague question about being a demon? Nope. That didn't cut it.

"It's scary, isn't it," I said gently.

"Scary? Zack?" She tried to laugh it off, shook her head.

"Yeah," I said. "It's pretty scary. All really weird and different. It's hard to think of Zack as a demon too, which probably doesn't help." Zack played his human role well. He blended, a surfer dude. Nice guy and tough fed. No one would have a clue he was anything but human. The only reason I did was because he'd shown superhuman strength and speed when picking me up to race me away from an attempted summoning. "Have you ever seen his demon form?"

Jill sobered and went a bit pale. "No."

I sighed. What the hell was Zack thinking keeping her in the dark like this? "Jill, you should. The demahnk are beautiful. You still care about him, right?"

"Yes. Sure I do," she said, but the look in her eyes reminded me of a rabbit ready to run.

Worry rose in me for both Jill and Zack. "Look, please, for your sake and your daughter's, please talk to him about this. Ask him about *him*."

"Okay. Yeah. Sure." She glanced at her watch. "I gotta go! Time to learn how to squirt this kid out."

Run rabbit run. "Okay." I gave her a hug along with the best smile I could manage. "You'll come by later, right?"

"Yep. After lunch and errands."

"Sounds good. Happy squirting!" I frowned. "That came out wrong."

Jill laughed. "It sure did! See you later. Make sure your honey is all spruced up for his inspection."

I grinned. "I think you'll like what you see."

Chapter 21

After Jill left, I took care of my morning ablutions, got myself all prettified again, then texted Zack an update.

J still says no. Find out real root issue why. Also RV too small. Mobile home instead?

That task completed, I headed down to the basement. There wasn't much to be done to prepare. Zack's assistance, with clearing the area and again topping off the storage diagram, had been invaluable. Yet another point in his favor.

An odd rhythm in the flows caught me briefly off balance as I began the summoning, like waves on a white-capped lake. Breathing deeply, I waited and watched for lulls, found as much of a pattern as I could, then made the call during a calmer period, like waiting for a pause in the rain to dash to one's car.

The arcane wind picked up and whipped my hair into my eyes. I added power to the flows and stabilized the perimeter of the portal, once again grateful to Zack for the additional power in the diagram. It would be poor form to lose any of the four I was bringing through, to say the least.

Finally the wind died, and I felt the rush of potency that told me the call was complete. I anchored the flows and settled the weird turbulence as much as I could before releasing the portal.

Mzatal knelt in the center of the diagram, head lowered. Bryce stood beside him, bent over at the waist with his hands on his knees. Paul lay sprawled on his back by Mzatal, breathing hard. Jekki, curled in a tight blue ball, lifted his head and gave me a chirrup, then raced upstairs as if the summoning had been a walk in the park.

"Whoa," Paul moaned. "That was a lot worse than going."

My attention remained on Mzatal, and I clung to the hope that he was truly rested and recovered. "Good to see you again, sweetheart," I said.

He lifted his head, opened his eyes, ancient gaze upon me. A smile touched the corners of his mouth. "I have missed you, beloved."

Potency radiated from him, and his eyes damn near glowed with strength and vitality. My smile widened. "You look good, Boss." I moved to him, crouched, slid my arms around him. A humming vibration passed through me. Hot damn, was he ever supercharged.

The vibration increased as he wrapped his arms around me, kissed me. Though I felt no threat, I had the sense he was so strong in this moment he could snap me in half with his arms if he chose to. I smiled into the kiss. What the hell had he been up to? Whatever it was, I liked it.

After a moment, he broke the kiss and released me. He laid a hand on the downed Paul's shoulder briefly, then stood in a smooth movement and held his hand out to me.

I took it, rose from the crouch then looked over Bryce who still stood doubled over beside us. "Thatcher, you look a lot better than the last time I saw you." I smiled. "I'm Kara Gillian."

With effort, he pushed himself upright. Medium build, lean and efficient, he wasn't an overly handsome man, but he was also far from unattractive. His hair was about the same color as mine—boring dull brown—but his hazel eyes held an interesting combination of *kind* and *dangerous*. "Ms. Gillian," he said, extending his right hand. "I owe you my life. And please, call me Bryce."

I took his hand, shook it. "Not a problem. I'm sure we'll figure out a fair trade." I grinned to signal that I wasn't serious.

Bryce gave me a smile. Nothing toothy but not as subtle as Mzatal's either. "I'll see what I can do about that."

Paul groaned and struggled up into a sitting position.

Bryce moved over to him. "Hey, kid, you okay?"

The young man staggered to his feet, swayed. "Sure," he said with a gasp that left me doubtful, though I knew Mzatal would address it if Paul had suffered any true harm.

Bryce caught his arm and studied him, a look of concern on his face. "No shitting me. Are you okay?"

Paul dragged in a deeper breath and straightened his shoulders. "Yeah. I'm good. I promise. A little shaky is all." He gave Bryce a convincingly reassuring smile. "Thanks."

"Go sit until you're not shaky anymore," Bryce ordered and herded Paul toward the futon.

Their interaction spoke volumes of true concern. I breathed a sigh of relief and allowed myself cautious optimism that their relationship was genuine.

Mzatal squeezed my hand, laid his fingers on my cheek. His eyes narrowed. "Beloved, what has happened to you?"

He felt the discord remaining from Farouche's influence. "I had a run in with Farouche and got zapped by the same sort of thing that affected Paul," I said, then continued with a summary of the road encounter, trusting he would read the details from me. "It was awful. Ryan cleared the worst of it, but I figure you can get rid of the rest."

He brought his other hand up in readiness to place on my head, paused, waiting for my consent. That was *huge* progress from our first days together when he did precisely what he wished whether I liked it or not.

I gave him a smile. "Please do what you can."

Mzatal cradled my head between his hands, and I felt the subtle whisper of his mental touch. "This is the same energy I cleared from Paul in the warehouse and from Bryce during his healing," he murmured. He went quiet for a moment, working, and I felt the release of the fear response like the *pop* of a soap bubble. As a test, I consciously considered kicking Farouche in the balls. Not even a hint of fear in reaction, when a few minutes earlier the thought would have elicited near panic.

I began to smile in relief, then realized that Mzatal remained utterly and impossibly still, even though the Farouche influence was clearly gone.

A wave of dread and worry came to me through the bond. Tensing, I reached up to grip one of his hands. "Boss?" I said, keeping my voice low to not draw the attention of the two men. "What's wrong?"

His eyes opened, and in them the dread was magnified a hundred-fold. "Rhyzkahl's virus, the implant in you—its containment was . . . cracked by the incident with Farouche," he said.

Sick fear threatened to swamp me, but deep breathing kept it at a low simmer. "All right," I said, rather pleased that I sounded calm. I sure as hell didn't feel it. "But you can re-contain it, right?"

Mzatal didn't answer for what was probably a full minute. An eternity of time, while he continued to assess and measure and consider. "I can," he finally replied. "Though it will require frequent reinforcement now, as it is . . . leaking." He stroked his thumb over my cheek, visibly holding his own dread in check. "Confusion, or feeling not yourself, would be signs that you are in need of care."

"Got it," I said, gave him a light smile I didn't feel one bit, not with *rakkuhr* contaminating me like radiation from a faulty nuclear power reactor. "We'll have to be joined at the hip then, won't we?" I took a deep breath and released it. "We'll find Idris, get back to your realm, and then fix this shit once and for all."

"We will find the means to counter it," he replied, voice still low yet filled with intensity. "It is still far from coalescing here," he touched my sternum, "for the final stage."

My mouth felt as dry as Death Valley. "And if it coalesces?" I knew I'd become Rowan, but would it be like turning on a switch? A gradual morph? Or would I change like a werewolf? *WereRowan*, I thought somewhat hysterically.

I felt his mental caress, his understanding that I needed to find any shred of humor I could to shield myself from the utter horror of what I faced. "The *rakkuhr* would crawl sigil to sigil in the order they were created," he murmured. He slid his hand to my chest, then down my side and to my back, "until it reaches Szerain's, to finalize with you lost to Rowan."

I realized I had a death grip on his other hand, and I forced myself to unclench my fingers. "All right," I said with a slight nod. "If shit starts to get bad, we go back to the demon realm, and you and Elofir can lock it down again." I didn't wait for him to confirm or deny that. I didn't want to dwell on it for an instant longer. "How about I get you caught up on what's been going on?" I said, and immediately proceeded to fill him in. Idris and the phone call. Everything he said, including the possible StarFire reference. His sister's death and his mother's probable role as hostage. Katashi on Earth. The "Rowan" bit at the end of the call, and I now wondered if that had contributed to the crack in the containment of the virus? During the entire summary I consciously remained mentally open to make it easy for Mzatal to read details and nuances. Sometimes that whole no-privacy-around-lords thing was convenient. "Oh, and my aunt—"

"Where is this Farouche?" Mzatal interrupted, his face dark and determined, and I felt his spike of focused anger through our connection. I didn't have to be a mind reader to know what he was thinking.

I fixed him with a determined look. "No! You canNOT go find the man and throttle him. Not with Idris's mom being held, and the chance Farouche is involved in that. We have to tread softly until we have more information and can make a definitive move." I needed another topic to break his dark mood. "There's more. Idris said, 'Tell Mzatal I still have his ring and haven't forgotten the *gheztak ru eehn*.'"

Mzatal closed his eyes, and I peered up at him. "Zack told me it translated roughly to 'the devastating failure,'" I went on. "I don't get the connection, but I'm thinking you have a clue."

Mzatal exhaled and looked down at me. "*Gheztak ru eehn* is how I designated my loss of you to Rhyzkahl," he said, voice hoarse with emotion. "It marked that moment and was the driving force for the two of us to work incessantly until we retrieved you from him."

Comprehension dawned like a flower blooming in high-speed photography. "I get it. By telling me he has your ring, he's letting us know he's still on our side. Then he acknowledged that he knows we won't stop until we get him back, otherwise there'd be no point in him saying that at all." With the full meaning unfolded, I felt as if Idris was with me now. "It's not just acknowledging, it's approving," I added. "Especially since he gave me the StarFire clue, which trumps everything he'd said earlier about not going after him. 'I'm still on your side. I know you'll find me. Here's some help with that.' Damn clever execution on Idris's part."

Mzatal smiled. "He is brilliant, and we will retrieve him." He drew a deep breath. "I have assessments to complete outside and have been overly long in the confines of this chamber."

I felt the anxiety building in him. "Go do what you need to do, lover. I'll get the guys settled in."

He gave me a lingering kiss, then departed the basement.

"C'mon upstairs," I said to Bryce and Paul. "Zack has a pot roast in the slow cooker, and I'd hate to see it go to waste." I led the way and gave the pair a basic rundown of the layout of the house, showed Bryce his room—the guest room where Zack had been staying. We stopped at the doorway of my so-called office/library. "I hope the futon in here will be okay for you, Paul. If you find it's too lumpy or uncomfortable, I'll get you an air mattress."

"I'm sure it'll be fine," he said, his eyes on my dinosaur of a computer, complete with the gigantic seventeen-inch CRT monitor that occupied most of the desk. "Thanks."

"You're welcome to dink around on my computer if you want," I told him. "It's ancient, but it does what I need it to do, albeit slowly." I gave him an apologetic smile. "Reeee-ally slowly."

He looked over at me with a huge grin as though I'd given him a pony for Christmas. "Thanks! You're the best."

"Maybe you should reserve judgment until you try it out," I said, then winced as he plopped down in the chair and nearly fell off as the seat tipped. "Sorry. You need to watch out for the chair. It has a mind of its own, but I tell myself it helps me improve my core strength."

"Gotcha." He carefully resettled on the wonky chair and pushed the computer's power button. It coughed, made a weird screeching whine, then finally settled to a vaguely unsteady whir. "This'll do great," he told me with a brilliant smile.

"That will keep him occupied for a while," Bryce said as we left Paul with the finicky machine and went on to the kitchen.

"Zack picked up some clothes for you and Paul," I said. "Let me know if you need anything else or if stuff doesn't fit."

"Thanks. It's been a pretty surreal couple of days," he confessed. "I seriously thought I was dead and in some bizarre afterlife."

"With equally bizarre food," I added with a laugh.

"No shit." He grinned. "But most of it was damn good, so I learned to get past appearance pretty quickly."

"Yep. The cat turds," I said and gave him a knowing nod. I got out plates and silverware. "You mind dishing up food? I need to make sure Mzatal has what he needs."

Bryce took the top off the slow cooker. "No problem."

"Thanks. I'll be right back." I went out back and stopped at the top of the porch stairs, watched Mzatal walk an expanding spiral around the point of confluence. I descended the steps and approached slowly, not wanting to interrupt him.

From the woods I heard a strange whooping call followed by a whistle. Eilahn. I'd once asked her what she did during all the time she spent in the woods when I was home. She'd given me a pitying look, as if I was mentally challenged, and told me, "I am with the trees, *of course*." Silly me.

Mzatal finished another loop of the spiral, then looked over to me. "I believe it is possible to develop the confluence into a convergence and subsequently create a rudimentary nexus."

I moved to him. "What does that mean in layman's terms?"

"If all transpires as intended, it will give me an anchor point of potency, which should considerably increase the length of time that I am able to remain on Earth." He stroked my cheek with his fingertips. "It will also be of use to you as a resource, though much greater once you have mastered the shikvihr."

A layer of my tension eased. "That's awesome," I said. Anything that allowed him to stay longer was good with me. "Do you want my help with any of it?"

Mzatal gave me a fond smile. "It would not be possible without your aid, zharkat." He shifted his attention to the sky as though considering something there. "In perhaps an hour we can begin."

"Got it." I glanced upward but saw nothing other than blue sky and a few clouds that heralded the approaching front. "I'm assuming Bryce checked out all right?" I had zero doubt that Mzatal had thoroughly assessed his potential to be a threat to us.

"He currently harbors no intention of causing harm to anyone within your household," he reassured me. "Elofir completed much of the physical healing, and we both cleared the fear-compulsion influence. It was ingrained far more deeply in him than in Paul, or in you."

"He'd been with Farouche for a long time," I pointed out.

"I am certain the influence was reinforced repeatedly over the years," Mzatal said with a slight nod. "However, I have placed blocks in the two men and in you to ensure that the influence cannot be re-established."

"Like being immune to a disease once you've survived it," I said with a grin. "I love it. And I'm glad we can trust Bryce."

"As much as any human," Mzatal replied. "Likely more at this point. He knows that sacrifices have been made for him, and he does not take it for granted."

I wrapped my arms around his neck, kissed him. "Thank you. That helps me a lot. You'll let me know when you're ready to do the superduper nexusy thing?"

He slid his hands down my sides, smiled. "I will, zharkat."

I returned to the house, smiling as I felt his gaze still on me like a warm embrace. In the kitchen I found that Jekki and Bryce had the table set and lunch ready to serve, though I noted only two plates on the table. "Isn't Paul going to eat?"

"Yes, ma'am," Bryce said. "I took a plate to him. He's already absorbed in your computer." He nodded toward the roast. "This sure smells good."

"Zack's a pretty awesome cook," I said. "I only found that out recently. Ryan's not bad either, for that matter." I laughed "I pretty much relax and do the eating." I sat, and Bryce followed suit. He'd deliberately waited for me to sit first before taking his own seat, and my good impression of him climbed even higher.

"That would be Zack Garner and Ryan Kristoff, right?" he asked. At my nod, he continued, "According to Paul, I owe them as well. I'm sorry we got you involved in our mess."

"We all did what was needed in the moment." This was my first opportunity to really speak to Bryce, and I was grateful for the opportunity. Paul obviously revered him, but for all I knew he could be a bona fide asshole in other areas.

"There were so many things I should've done differently

that day," he said, shaking his head. "But that *guard*. He should never have been carrying a gun."

"No shit!" I made a disgusted face. "Probably a wannabe cop who spent too much time watching action movies." Then I sobered. "You heard what I told Mzatal about my encounter with Farouche?"

Bryce's expression tightened. "Yes. And that he . . . affected you." He blew out his breath. "Lord Mzatal explained to Paul and me how Mr. Farouche's influence works. If I hadn't lived it, no way would I believe it."

I proceeded to give him the full story, including the mandate to call Farouche when he and Paul returned. I watched him as I spoke, noted a sheen of sweat on his forehead, and a tremor in the hand that held his fork. When I finished, I busied myself with eating in order to give him time to compose himself. Even though Mzatal had fixed him up, I figured it would take some time for Bryce to shed the residual effects of being influenced for so long.

After about a minute Bryce set his fork down. "The one with the MAC-10 is Mr. Farouche's personal bodyguard, Angus McDunn. He's been with Farouche for over twenty years. Ruthless. The other two were Charles Clancy and Sonny Hernandez. Mr. Farouche made a personal appearance in order to get you under his influence. He wouldn't trouble himself otherwise." Bryce exhaled. "He'll want me back dead or alive. He'll want Paul back alive."

"We won't let that happen" I said firmly.

"It *can't* happen to Paul. He deserves better."

I smiled. "I like him. Crap, this sounds insulting, but it's not meant to be at all: He's adorable."

Bryce laughed. "Don't let him hear you say that."

I grinned. "I'm sure he wouldn't take it well." I pushed back from the table. "Is there anything you need or want that will help you settle in? Anything Paul needs?"

Bryce exhaled, shook his head. "I honestly don't know yet. I feel like I'm in a different world. *Naked* in a different world."

My brow furrowed as I tried to figure that one out. "Naked?"

Bryce gave a weak laugh. "Figuratively speaking. I haven't been without my weapons in over a decade."

I blinked. "Oh! Hang on." I quickly retrieved the box

containing his cleaned gear and clothing from where I'd stashed it, returned to the kitchen, and placed it on the table. "There's .40 ammo in the cabinet over the dryer," I said as I unloaded his stuff from the box. "I cleaned the gun and got the blood off the rest, though I tossed your shirt since it was pretty trashed. Hope you weren't too attached to it."

Utterly shocked, Bryce looked from the plethora of lethality on the table to me and then back at his gear. "You're serious?"

"If you were a threat to us, Mzatal would know about it," I replied. "I want you as an ally, and you're more useful as such if you have your stuff."

"I understand," he said, face reflecting relief. "Thanks." He checked his guns and knives, then slipped various holsters and sheaths on and tucked his weapons away with smooth and practiced efficiency.

"Feel better?" I asked.

He made adjustments, straightened. "Do I ever." He smiled, shoulders and back relaxing as tension slipped away. "Any house rules I should know about?"

"Don't pee on the toilet seat."

He snorted. "Anything else?"

I shrugged. "Common sense. Um, you and Paul probably shouldn't leave the property or go to near the property edge for that matter." I abruptly realized how that sounded and hurried to clarify. "I mean, you're not prisoners or anything, but—"

Bryce salvaged my faux pas. "I get it. Even if Mr. Farouche knows we're here, it's better if we're not seen."

"Exactly," I said, relieved that he understood. "The fed boys have a game console in the living room that you're welcome to use."

"Excellent!" A grin split his face. "Paul set me up with one in our unit at Farouche's plantation. Helped keep me from going stir crazy while he did his computer stuff."

"You'll probably have some time on your hands here," I said with a slight grimace. "Sorry."

"No worries, Ms. Gillian. I have a master's degree in killing time."

"You stayed with Paul at the plantation? I gather he gets pretty deeply involved in what he does."

"Yep. Sinks right into it," he said. "I have to remind him to eat. He set up a number for Sonny and me to text if we need his attention. Anything else makes him lose his train of thought."

"I know he's valuable to Farouche and does computer stuff, but what exactly does he *do*?"

Bryce pursed his lips, tipped his head back in consideration. "He's a computer security expert and can do all sorts of white, grey, and black hat work," he explained. "He can get into just about anything—system, network, database, whatever's out there—but don't ask me to tell you exactly what he does or how he does it. It's beyond me." A corner of his mouth lifted in a fond smile. "I say 'work,' but for him it isn't. When Paul's in deep, he's having a blast exploring and uncovering information."

I straightened. "What kind of information?"

"Pretty much anything you could possibly think of. He knows how to delve, and he's fearless when it comes to infrastructure."

Somehow I managed to hold back the delighted chortle. "I have a project for him, if he's up for it."

"The bigger the challenge, the more he likes it."

Paul chose that moment to enter the kitchen, tablet tucked under one arm, empty plate in the other hand, and eyes red despite his smile. "Good lunch. Thanks. What's up?"

"I could ask you the same question," Bryce said, frowning. "What's bothering you?"

Paul scrubbed his free hand over his face and looked a little embarrassed. "I, uh, was listening in on a conversation."

Bryce folded his arms across his chest, narrowed his eyes. "Whose conversation upset you?"

"Sonny," Paul confessed. "I probably shouldn't have tapped in, but I was worried about him and wanted to make sure he was okay."

Sonny. One of the gunmen at the encounter with Farouche.

"Well, was he?" Bryce asked.

"He sounded a little stressed, but otherwise all right," Paul replied. "I was worried something bad might happen to him since he was my handler too."

There was no mistaking the relief on Bryce's face. "You did good, kid."

"Yeah? Thanks." He smiled. "Hearing him made me miss him more, that's all."

Bryce patted his shoulder. "I totally get it. Who was he talking to?"

"His sister. About how he'd be there for Christmas this year." Paul winced. "She didn't believe him, yelled at him, and hung up."

Surprise and disbelief flashed over Bryce's face. "Sonny called his sister?"

I frowned at the exchange. "Something wrong with that?"

"Not *wrong* exactly," Bryce said. "But it means he's on edge with Paul and me gone." Bryce rubbed the back of his neck, grimaced. "He hasn't talked to his family in over a decade. I mean, you don't *do* that around Mr. Farouche."

"That's right," Paul said with a serious nod. "B.M. doesn't play around."

"B.M.?" I asked, puzzled, then remembered that Paul's nickname for James Macklin Farouche was Big Mack. I let out a peal of laughter. "B.M. That's classic."

Paul grinned. "If the acronym fits . . ."

Bryce cocked an eyebrow at the young man. "Wasn't so hilarious when you accidentally called him that to his face. Anyway, Ms. Gillian wants to know—"

"*Please* call me Kara," I interrupted.

Bryce gave me a nod. "*Kara* wants to know if there's anything you need."

"No. She doesn't," he said with a wry smile. "I can *need* a whole lot of very expensive things."

"Okay," I said, smiling, "is there anything without which you can't do your work?"

He gave me a sly look. "I already ordered a laptop and some other stuff," he told me. "It'll all be here tomorrow." He paused, fidgeted. "I need a few local things today though, if it's not too much trouble. I can pay you back."

"Write it down, and I'll get the elves to take care of it," I told him.

A smile bloomed on his face. "Wow, thanks!" He shifted the tablet from under his arm and started tapping on it one-handed, so fast I had a hard time picturing him actually typing anything that made sense. "You want me to help with the Idris stuff?" he asked. "The lord told me about him. I figure I can do some work on that, right?"

My phone dinged, and I fished it from my pocket. "Um, yeah. Hang on." I checked the message, blinked. His shopping list—composed and sent to me in about ten seconds flat. I smothered a laugh. Chai tea, Krunch 'n Krackle snacks, and pistachios. All absolutely necessary for deep computer work, I was certain. I started to ask him how he knew my number, then decided against it. I had a feeling that would probably earn me a withering look.

I sent the message on to Zack, with a "please buy" added. "That's right," I told Paul. "We're looking for Idris Palatino. Anything you can find on him would rock." I spelled the name and gave him Idris's date of birth.

Paul tapped on the tablet. "What sort of info you want? Sightings? That sort of thing?"

"Anything you can get. Sightings, rumors, mentions, you name it, especially within the last week. We don't know where he is other than what you heard me tell Mzatal in the basement. He called me night before last from a stolen cell phone, heading northwest out of Austin. Farouche is involved, but we don't know to what degree. We know Isumo Katashi's organization is in on it. Tsuneo Oshiro. Tito—I don't remember his last name."

Paul looked up at me. "Tsuneo. That's the name of the guy who ran away at the warehouse?"

"That's right," I said. "And Tito was the one Mzatal killed."

"I'll see what I can find out," he said, then wandered down the hall, busily tapping on the tablet.

I waited until Paul was back in the office before I turned to Bryce. "Time to shift gears a bit," I said. "You in the mood from some mild interrogation?"

"As long as it doesn't involve beatings with rubber hoses, I'm game," he replied with an easy smile.

"No beatings," I said with a chuckle. "Not from me at least." I took a deep breath. "But I need to know if the name Tracy Gordon rings a bell. Or you might have known him as Raymond Bergeron."

A frown puckered his forehead. "I don't think I know either name. Why?"

"Tracy was a summoner, killed about six months ago," I told him. "Your name is in one of his journals along with a bunch of others."

"Why would a summoner have my name?" Bryce asked, perplexed. "And yes, I know that's precisely what you're asking me." He shook his head. "Sorry, but I don't have a clue."

So much for my fantasy of uncovering a simple explanation. I felt Mzatal's mental touch, and I put on hold any thoughts of other avenues to take with the journal information. "We'll figure it out later," I said with a tinge of regret. "I'm going out to do some work with Mzatal, and I don't know how long it will take. My best friend Jill may come by at some point." I smiled. "She's way pregnant. Can't miss her. Y'all help yourself to anything in the kitchen, and don't forget the game console."

"Got it covered," he said with a sharp nod.

I gave him a parting smile and headed toward the back.

Chapter 22

Mzatal stood on the sweet spot in the grass, hands behind his back and eyes closed in a familiar stance of focused concentration. He opened his eyes as I approached. "Zharkat. I am ready to begin."

"Tell me what I need to do."

He took my hand, drew me to him. Carefully and patiently, he explained the process and showed me the needed sigils for the diagram, and for the rest of the afternoon we prepared the unassuming patch of grass. For the first hour we did little else but clear residue and stabilize the power of the confluence, like pressure washing grease-encrusted drainage pipes. After that came the foundation anchors sunk deep, and meticulously woven flows. Then dozens upon dozens of rings of sigils, with every link checked and double-checked. Jekki kept us amply supplied with food and tunjen, and after more than four hours of work—and a quick potty break for me—we felt ourselves ready to begin the ritual itself.

Thunder rumbled in the distance as we returned to the confluence, and I glanced up at the sky. Clouds hid the sun, and little gusts of wind whipped high branches. As I lowered my gaze, I caught sight of Jill at the kitchen window, watching with avid curiosity though I doubted she could see any of the sigils. We probably looked rather weird as we walked around in seemingly random circles in my back yard.

Jill grinned and waved at me, but then pointed toward Mzatal and made a point of fanning herself. I grinned right back at her, ridiculously pleased that she'd made it over to see my mega-hot boyfriend. *Wait 'til she sees him up close*, I thought, chuckling low as I returned my attention to my work.

While I checked the sigils around the perimeter, Mzatal walked spirals, a slight frown on his face. Paul emerged from the house, tablet in hand, looked out to us then down at the tablet. Mzatal's frown deepened, and he stopped, eyes on the ground.

"What's wrong?" I asked.

"I am unable to locate the virtual center." Frustration rolled from him like a slow tumble of boulders. "All is shifting, and I need the precise alignment."

"One step back and one to the right," Paul said, eyes glued to the tablet as he crossed the grass toward us and stopped about ten feet away.

Mzatal lifted his head, regarded Paul, and then to my mild surprise took one step back and one to the right.

"Too much," Paul said with a shake of his head, face fixed in concentration. "Left again a little."

Mzatal moved as instructed, went still, and drew a deep breath. "Yes."

"Yes!" Paul exclaimed. He looked up with an exuberant grin, then his mouth dropped open as if he'd just realized what he'd done.

"Well done, Paul," Mzatal said. Paul flushed, to my amusement.

Mzatal took my hand again. "What was that all about?" I asked quietly.

A faint smile touched his lips. "He has an affinity for the flows," he told me. "In this world, he touches them through his devices, and it gives him unconventional access to information. Even in the demon realm he feels the flows." Rare delight lit his eyes. "He is innocent, and it is simply natural to him, a part of who he is. I find him fascinating."

I smiled. "You like him quite a bit."

"I do," he replied without hesitation. "He is . . . comfortable."

Thunder rumbled in the distance, and gusts of wind whooshed through the tops of the pines. "Time to get this show on the road," I said with a glance up at the cloudy sky. Hopefully this wouldn't take too long.

Together, we danced the first seven rings of the shikvihr; Mzatal traced floating sigils that I enhanced and amplified as I followed. When those seven rings were set, I remained in the center of the diagram as Mzatal finished the remaining four. That was a first for me, and with every ring I felt the increase in potency like a vibration inside of my bones.

Once the entire shikvihr was complete, he moved to the center with me. He ignited it in a burst of potency that made my head spin—in a good way—and left me feeling energized, as though fresh from a nap and a brisk walk all at the same time. Together we walked the perimeter and assessed for any anomalies in the sigils. The wind picked up, gusts stronger and more persistent, and carrying the scent of rain.

I took note of the dark, agitated clouds. "We need to finish soon, lover. A thunderstorm is headed this way."

Mzatal laughed. "It is indeed." He gave my hand a squeeze. "Glorious, is it not?"

Lightning flashed nearby, followed by a deep rumble of thunder. "Yeah, glorious," I said doubtfully. "Glorious to watch from the safety of a nice dry house."

"No, beloved," he said as he walked us back to the center of the diagram. "I am calling the storm."

I stopped dead in my tracks. "The fuck?"

Mzatal gave me a sideways look, and a smile crept over his face. "I am calling the lightning. We will use it to activate the nexus."

I felt my eyes stretch wide open. "*Lightning*?" I'd lived in Louisiana all my life and had a healthy respect for dangerous weather.

"Yes." An undercurrent of excitement rippled through his voice. "I work in great harmony with lightning."

Reluctantly, I moved to the center with him. "You do know that human bodies are kind of allergic to big jolts of electricity, right?"

"It will be an experience you will not forget, zharkat."

"For the remaining ten seconds of my life, you mean," I muttered, already sweating at the thought.

Mzatal turned to face me and laid his hands on my shoulders, expression serious. "Beloved, I will not allow harm to come to you," he assured me. "But I do not wish to bring you distress. The activation will be stronger with you here with me, but I will not mandate it."

The truth of it showed in his eyes. I exhaled softly, leaned in and kissed him. "I'll stay, but you'd best remember that if you fry me, I won't be much fun in the sack afterward."

Mzatal returned the kiss, trailed his fingers along my cheek and smiled. "Then I will most assuredly *not* fry you."

He moved behind me and dropped his left arm over my shoulder and across my chest, pulled me back against him. With this close connection, I *felt* him call the storm, felt the increasing charge in the air. He inhaled deeply, as if bringing in all of the energy from the diagram around us.

"Focus on the full pattern," he murmured. "See all of its parts as a single unit." He raised his free arm high above his head. "When the strike comes, send it to every aspect."

I swallowed. "Sure. Got it. I'm an old hand at this." Wind whipped around us and rushed through the nearby woods, as if we were the calm center of the storm. Movement caught my eye, and I looked up to see Jill and Bryce emerge from the house to watch us from the sensible shelter of the covered porch. Paul knelt in the grass halfway between the perimeter of the diagram and the house, rapt focus on us as he clutched his tablet to his chest.

"Paul!" Bryce called out. "Get under cover!"

Paul didn't move or even acknowledge him. Bryce scowled, said something I couldn't hear and pointed for Jill to stay against the wall of the house. He leapt off the porch and hurried toward Paul, staying low as leaves and large drops of rain lashed through the air. "Paul! Jesus, kid. You need to get out of here!"

Paul startled as Bryce put a hand on his shoulder. "What?" He jerked his eyes up to Bryce. "No. I'm okay."

Bryce shielded his face with his forearm. "Yeah?" he shouted over the wind. "You're giving *me* a heart attack."

Paul's face filled with sudden worry, then he scrambled to his feet and returned to the porch with a deeply relieved Bryce right behind him.

With one hand still held high, Mzatal tightened his arm around me. "*Now*, zharkat."

Lightning leaped to his hand, and a *CRACK* of thunder ripped the air. Power slammed through me, like a ten-foot-high wall of water crashing down, but without it crushing me or bowling me over. Even though I'd never been struck by lightning, I knew without a doubt this wasn't at all the same. Every particle of every atom in my body screamed in joyous furor, utterly painless yet with an intensity that threatened to overwhelm.

Almost as an afterthought, I remembered to shunt the power out to the pattern, filling every aspect and sigil and loop as it ignited in a glorious rush. I felt Mzatal's approving acknowledgement of completion as he released the strike.

Eyes wide, I breathed in shaky gasps. It felt like a roller coaster ride, the kind where you scream you want off while it's happening, then can't wait to do it again as soon as it's over. "Hot fucking damn," I managed, though I knew I had a crazy grin on my face. Every cell in my body seemed to vibrate on the verge between *uncomfortable* and *ecstatic pleasure.*

Mzatal lowered his hand, radiating strength and power as he dropped his head beside mine and nuzzled my neck. "Do you wish to remain for more, zharkat?" he asked, voice rich and intense. "The diagram is complete, but I am not."

I gave an unsteady laugh. "I can take it if you can." I leaned back into him, not wanting the moment to end. In my peripheral vision I saw Bryce shield Jill protectively on the porch, while Paul stared at us in utter awe.

Rain lashed around us, and the trees groaned under the onslaught of the wind, though we remained untouched in our arcane creation. Mzatal straightened, lifted his right hand again. "This one is for pleasure."

The second strike was as heart-stoppingly kickass awesome as the first—even more so as Mzatal held the power, reveled in it, and shared it with me, with no need to shunt it to the diagram. Our connection expanded and crystallized in near orgasmic ecstasy, and in those extraordinary seconds, I saw through his eyes, felt what he felt, knew what he knew. When he released the lightning, the intimate hyperawareness went with it, but the entire experience still left me breathless, amazed, and feeling somehow *more* than myself.

Mzatal, vibrant and *alive*, turned me and gathered me close. "Well done, zharkat," he murmured.

"That was wild," I said with a soft laugh. "And a little terrifying."

"It is exhilarating," he agreed. "And another means to enhance potency."

I smiled up at him, certain I was glowing. "Did it work?

Do we have a mini-nexus now?" I felt plenty of power around us, but I had no idea if it was from the lightning strikes, was generated by the diagram, or simply radiated from us.

"We do. It is perfect."

I grinned. "A bouncing baby nexus."

For a brief instant he tried to hold back the laugh, then gave up and let it out—a glorious rich sound. "Yes," he finally said, eyes still swimming with mirth. "And we its proud parents."

He cradled the back of my head in one hand, slid the other to the small of my back, pulled me close for a deep and smoldering kiss. I slid my arms around his neck and returned it eagerly. I clearly felt his *enhanced potency*, and I had some neat ideas for how to celebrate the addition of a mini-nexus to our magic family.

But not right here in full view of spectators. I broke the kiss and seized his hand. "Pond," I gasped, and then we were off at a run down the trail. I let him lead since I figured he could see better in the rainy gloom, and running smack into a pine would probably cool my ardor a teensy bit.

Lightning still lit the clouds as we emerged into the clearing, reflected in the pond like earth and sky joined in perfect synchrony. Dozens of sigils glowed around his little pavilion, adding their own color and sparkle to the surface of the water and casting soft light on the surroundings. Literally a magical setting, I thought as he drew me close again for another searing kiss. I moaned against his mouth as my hands worked the buttons on his shirt. Or tried to.

I pulled back with a curse of frustration. "Shitballs goddammit!" I snarled as the wet fabric defeated my attempts. "Are these stapled together?" Great. Magical setting overwhelmed by a ridiculously mundane issue.

He laughed, took my hand, and focused, and a heartbeat later power wrapped around us to pull the rainwater from our clothes and hair and vaporize it with a hiss.

"Show off," I teased, then made short work of divesting him of the now-dry shirt. The rest of his clothing quickly followed along with my own, and then he scooped me up in his arms, strode to the pavilion, and tumbled me to the mattress.

Laughing, I took hold of his braid and delighted in his

groan as I tugged him to me with it. The groan shifted to a growl of desire as he lowered his head to my breast and claimed a nipple. I let out a gasping cry as I arched up to his mouth, wrapped my arms around him, and savored the perfection of his body against mine.

He shifted lower, and I dropped my head back, grip tightening on his head and hair as he wrung incoherent noises from me. Hands and mouth and everything that was *him*, so familiar to me now yet still as exhilarating as our first time. I eagerly succumbed to it all, cried out and clenched and felt his satisfaction and delight mingle with my pleasure.

Mzatal lifted his head as I fought to catch my breath, his gaze filled with stunning joy and passion. "Zharkat," he murmured, then shifted forward.

"Not so fast," I said with a throaty laugh as I once again seized his braid, wrapped it around my hand. "My turn." Seizing control, I used the grip on his braid, shifted my weight and hooked a leg around his to reverse our positions. Mirthful delight danced in his eyes as he went to his back and I knelt astride him. We both knew he could have resisted easily, but where would be the fun in that? Yet the smile he turned on me was anything but indulgent. I claimed his mouth and tasted my own pleasure on his lips. A groan ripped from his throat, and the hands that rose to grip my hips shuddered with his own unslaked need.

I nipped and kissed along the sculptured landscape of his torso, toyed with sensitized nipples as he clenched his fists and throbbed against me. My fingers skimmed down his sides with a trail of goosebumps to mark their passage. Moving further down, I stroked and slid my flesh and mouth against him, loving upon him and giving back all he'd given me and more, until the clearing echoed with his own cries of need and pleasure and release.

His eyes met mine as our connection reverberated with all we were to each other, *for* each other. Shifting forward again, I indulged in a long and slow kiss until heat once again clutched at my belly, and he throbbed hard and urgent between us. As I moaned into the kiss, he slid a hand to my backside and brought the other up to tangle in my hair to hold me close. He rolled me to my back, and I went unresisting, opened to him and wrapped my legs around his hips as he slid inside me. My hands dug into his shoulders as he drove deeper, quickened the pace. Without words I urged him on, merged our desire and ecstasy.

With a strangled cry he plunged into me as I bucked against him, gripped him close, and greedily took all he had to offer. His eyes shone with wild need, and as we crested together, I dragged his head down, covered his mouth with mine, and joined my scream of release with his.

Chapter 23

I stroked his chest while I pillowed my head on his shoulder. "Do you do that lightning thing often?"

"Perhaps thrice a year," he replied. "Though I called it only two days past after returning home because of the severe depletion."

"You don't feel at all depleted now," I said, pressing close. "We should work on that some more."

His hand slid to my ass, and he chuckled low. "Ah, you will indeed deplete me, again and again."

I laughed. "Before any more depletion, I need to get something to eat," I told him. "Plus, my friend Jill is here. Y'all should meet."

"Yes, it is time to know Jill Faciane," he agreed.

We found our scattered clothing, quickly dressed, and returned to the house. Jill and Jekki sat at the kitchen table, heads bent together and apparently deep in conversation. She looked up as we entered, sly smile on her face in an I-know-what-you've-been-up-to expression, but then her eyes widened in obvious *Wow, Holy Shit!* appreciation as she took in the sight of Mzatal up close.

Yeah, my boyfriend was pretty impressive. Especially as radiantly vibrant and super-charged as he was right now.

"Hey, Jill," I said with a smile. "This is Mzatal. Mzatal, this is Jill."

She managed to scrounge together some composure, stood and offered Mzatal a hand, though she was clearly trying hard not to stare. "It's nice to meet you."

Mzatal took her hand in both of his. "Jill Faciane," he said with a small smile. "It is a pleasure to finally meet."

Jill's mouth dropped open, and I knew she felt the tingling vibration from super-charged Mzatal along with a good dose of his natural mojo.

She abruptly jerked and let out a small *Oof!* "Sorry," she said with a shaky laugh as she put her other hand on her belly. "She's a bit wiggly right now."

Mzatal's eyes dropped to Jill's belly, and an odd expression came over his face, fascinated and perplexed at the same time. He tilted his head slightly, kept hold of her hand, and placed his other hand on her belly. His expression grew even odder, as if struggling to remember a phrase or saying that was on the tip of his tongue.

Silent, I watched the curious exchange. Surely Mzatal had encountered a pregnant woman before? Jill remained motionless and didn't say a word about the somewhat rude business of touching her belly without permission, though I saw it in the slightly wary-but-baffled look in her eyes. Beneath their hands the baby kicked some more, to judge by Jill's occasional winces. I sensed him extend, mentally touch the baby.

Rare, naked curiosity lit Mzatal's face. His lips parted as he leaned closer, feeling the movement of the baby, and connecting on the non-physical level. He abruptly sucked in a gasping breath and straightened, face contorted in pain as he jerked his hands to his head and took a staggering step backward. I seized his arm to steady him.

"Mzatal!? What's wrong?" I demanded, worry flaring as I sensed his excruciating pain. He let out a low groan and took another step back. I shot a look at Jill as she backed away in confusion. "You okay?" I asked. She blinked and nodded, and I immediately shifted my full worry and attention to Mzatal.

I snaked an arm around his waist. "Outside," I said as I worked to maneuver him in that direction. "You do better outside. C'mon, Boss."

He didn't resist, but it took all of my effort to keep him steady. He nearly stumbled down the back steps, but grabbed onto the post in time to shift the fall into a heavy sit onto the steps.

Jekki ran up beside me, chittering in distress. Keeping a hand on Mzatal's arm, I shifted to crouch before him. "Mzatal? Boss? How can I help you? What do you need?"

Mzatal kept his eyes squeezed closed in a rictus of agony. "Ilana," he managed to choke out.

Shit. Couldn't ask for something simple, like Percocet. "She's not here," I said. "I can try to summon her." Could one of the demahnk even *be* summoned? I turned to the faas. "Jekki, is Zack here?"

"Dahn dahn dahn." His tail twisted in worry.

Yeah, that would have been too easy. "Can you get tunjen for Mzatal, please?"

The faas darted off, and I returned my attention to the lord. "Boss, talk to me," I urged. "What's going on?"

His breath hissed between his teeth, and a sheen of sweat covered his face. He gave a sudden cry that sounded more like frustration than pain. A shudder wracked his body, and a heartbeat later the rictus of agony faded from his expression. He opened his eyes, wiped an unsteady hand over his face.

"I do not know," he said, voice thready. Jekki ran up with the glass of tunjen and gently pressed it into his hand. Mzatal murmured a low thanks and sipped, color slowly returning to his face.

"It started when you connected with the baby. Was something wrong with her?"

He started to say No—I *felt* it—but then the pain spiked through him again, as if caused by the mere *thought* of extending to touch the baby. He drew a breath and remained quiet, and the tension in his face diminished.

My worry for his immediate well-being began to ease a bit now that he didn't look as if his head was going to explode, though I had plenty of concern beyond that. "Has this ever happened before?"

He drank more tunjen, then set the glass aside and reached for my hand. "Yes, many times," he said, fingers tightening on mine. "Not for almost a year though."

I moved to sit beside him on the step. "What triggered these other times?"

He took a long breath and released it. "No single trigger that I have found," he said. "It has happened when working deep in the plexus. Once when simply talking with Helori. Many times with . . . nightmares."

I brought his hand up to kiss his fingers. "I'll try to summon Ilana," I told him. "Maybe she can help."

But he shook his head. "The demahnk rarely answer a summons," he said. "I am unsettled, but the pain has receded. Do not worry, beloved."

"Yeah, like *that's* going to happen," I said with a roll of my eyes, then kissed him gently. *Rarely answer.* Did that mean they could resist at will? "You should go lie down."

"Yes, it would be wise," he agreed. "Yaghir tahn."

"No need for apology, love." I gave him a warm smile.

He finished the glass of tunjen, then stood, swaying slightly. "I will be by the pond."

I rose with him and slipped an arm around his waist. "How about I walk you there."

His arm encircled me as we started for the path. "I much prefer it that way."

We made it to his pavilion without incident. I got him onto the bed and made sure Jekki would monitor him. It was clear that Mzatal remained very unsettled, even if the pain had gone.

He rested a hand on the faas's head, his eyes on me. "Thank you, zharkat."

"I'll be back to check on you," I told him. I leaned over to kiss him. "I love you."

Mzatal laid his other hand against my cheek, the simple gesture like a caress of my essence. "I love you," he replied, then took a deep breath and closed his eyes.

I stayed a few more minutes to watch over him, then gave Jekki's head a scratch and returned to the house.

Jill sat at the kitchen table distractedly flipping through an old *Forensic Times* magazine. She snapped her gaze to me as I came in. "What the hell was that all about?"

"I don't know," I said. "And I don't think Mzatal does either." I slumped into a chair. "I felt him connect with the baby and then felt him wracked with blinding pain. No clue *why* though," I saw the worry in her eyes, and I hurried to reassure her, "but I honestly don't believe it was because something might be wrong with you or the bean."

"Okay. Good." She let out a breath and relaxed. "I want you to know, your boyfriend is seriously hot and seriously freaky."

"Yeah," I said, then grinned. "I think I like the freaky."

She snorted, laughed. "You have pine needles in your hair from whatever *freaky* things you two were doing in the woods." I opened my mouth to respond, and she jerked a hand up. "Do *not* tell me what they were." She paused, appeared to consider. "Not right now, at least."

"I'll save the sordid details for the next girls' night out."

"Make notes so you don't forget anything."

·I laughed and headed off to my room.

A quick shower and a change of clothing did a lot to restore my overall equilibrium. As I came into the living room, Bryce glanced up and paused the game he played, leaving a purple and green alien frozen in mid-splatter on the screen.

I flopped onto an empty space on the couch. "Is this day over yet?"

"Still a few hours until midnight," Bryce said as he set the controller aside. "A little lightning wear you out?"

"What, that?" I gave an exaggerated snort. "Pshaw. I have lightning strike through me *all* the time. Old hat!" I twisted my face into a comically freaked out expression.

"I'm not going to lie," Bryce said with a shake of his head. "That was unbelievable."

"Mzatal says it will help him remain here longer." I mentally crossed fingers for that. Even three or four days at a stretch would be nice. With Idris on Earth, there wasn't much Mzatal could do from the demon realm.

Bryce nodded. "He said as much back at his place." He let out a low whistle. "He worked with the lightning there, too—while standing on the balcony rail about a billion feet above the rocks. I've *never* seen anything like it."

I eyed him. "He was standing on the railing of the balcony?"

"Yep, barefooted and shirtless and calling in a storm," he said. "On the *railing*."

"I'll kill him," I said with a sweet smile.

Bryce's face abruptly twisted into the expression of a man who suddenly realized he'd told his buddy's girlfriend that said buddy had been at the strip club all night. "Uh, he didn't fall or anything," Bryce fumbled out as he struggled to retract his earlier statement. "I mean, he seemed to be in complete control of what he was doing."

I snorted. "I'm sure he knew what he was doing." Then again, it wasn't as if I could call Mzatal on it. He'd simply give me an implacable *look* and tell me he was always in control. Dating a demigod sure carried its own set of unique issues. "I'm glad I wasn't there to see it, though."

"I'm glad I *was*," Bryce said. "I'd only talked to him once, briefly, before witnessing the lightning-on-the-railing thing. I'm not likely to forget it." He shrugged. "And today's was impressive too, but something about there being nothing but sky beyond him, and the whole different world thing, it was beyond surreal."

Jill came into the room with a large bowl of something weird and gloppy half-resting on her belly. "Jekki made pickle peanut butter pretzels for me," she announced. "Anyone want some?"

"Oh, wow, gee, Jill." I made an exaggerated wince. "Y'know, I *just* had that for lunch, so I guess I'll have to pass." I shuddered.

"I'm not even going to pretend I want any," Bryce said, giving Jill the warmest smile I'd ever seen on the man. He nodded toward the bowl in her grasp. "That looks and sounds disgusting."

Jill returned the smile, chuckling softly as she lowered herself into the chair and rested the bowl atop the swell of her belly. "Says the man who likes spicy pickled cabbage."

I looked at the two of them. They'd sure gotten to know each other quickly. The alarm panel in the kitchen buzzed, indicating that someone authorized was coming through the gate. Either Zack or Ryan, since all the other chicks were at home to roost. I stood and moved to the window. "Zack's home," I remarked to nobody in particular. Nobody who was paying any attention to me, at least. I watched as Zack pulled into his usual spot and got out of the car, face grim. He closed the car door, then leaned back against it and looked up at the sky, expression somber and with an odd longing I couldn't quite parse.

"Yes, but there are other people who like and eat kimchee," Bryce was saying with a laugh. "I doubt *anyone* else eats that concoction."

Jill merely gave a serene smile. "Pregnant chicks all over the world would eat the hell out of this if they knew it existed."

Zack pushed off the car and headed up the steps, expression all surfer-dude Zack and not somber at all by the time he reached the porch. I stepped away from the window as he opened the door and entered.

He gave Bryce a broad smile, everything in his posture indicating customary good mood and joviality. I almost doubted that I'd seen the earlier gloom. "Welcome back to the land of the living, Mr. Thatcher," he said with a congenial air as Bryce hurried to stand.

"Bryce, this is Special Agent Zack Garner," I said to help him out.

"It's nice to meet you, sir," Bryce said to Zack, extending a hand. "Can't thank you enough for everything you've done for Paul and me."

Zack took his hand and shook it, and I noticed the faint flicker in Zack's eyes as he did. Assessing Bryce, I knew. Apparently he passed the quick assessment since Zack continued by saying, "Sure you can. You can lose to me—badly—in a game of *Alien Bloodbath* later."

Bryce chuckled. "I'll be sure to go out in an impressive blaze of glory."

"Of course you will," Zack said with a laugh. "I'm that good."

Jill snorted and rolled her eyes, but when Zack moved to her and leaned down to give her a kiss, she melted into it, then lifted a hand to his face and gave him a lovely, warm smile. "Hey, babe," she said. "How was your day?"

"Long. And not over yet." He sighed and dropped to sit beside her. "Waiting for Ryan to get home at this point."

I watched as her smile flickered, saw the thought plain upon her face: *He's bailing on me again.* And since she had no understanding of *why*, how could it feel like anything but rejection? Yet on the heels of her disappointment, I saw a shimmer of relief. If Zack bailed on her, then that was one more night where she wouldn't have to face the giant winged elephant in the room and ask him about his demon side.

"You're off again as soon as he gets here?" she asked gamely.

"We'll be working in the basement," Zack told her. He took her hand and kissed her knuckles. "It will probably only be an hour or two, sweetie. You'll still be here?"

Her shoulders lifted in a too casual shrug. "I don't know. It's getting late, and I have some stuff I need to do at my house."

I rolled my eyes so hard it hurt. "For fuck's sake." I

glanced at Bryce. "You'll have to excuse me, but there's something I need to take care of." I strode over to where Zack and Jill sat on the couch, removed the bowl of pretzel things from Jill's lap and set them aside, reached down and grabbed her hand, then Zack's. "You two are coming with me right now," I said with my expression and manner fiercely conveying, Do Not Even Think of Resisting Because OMG, You Two!

Jill looked suddenly terrified. "I have some things I need to do." Zack didn't resist, but he didn't stand either.

"No you don't." My fierce look grew fiercer. "We're doing this *now.*"

Zack sighed, stood. "I think she might be serious, sweetie."

"Damn straight," I said. I tugged Jill to her feet, waited for Zack to steady her, then hauled both of them into the guest room and kicked the door shut behind me.

I released their hands and pointed at the bed. "Sit."

Jill scowled at me, but obeyed. Zack simply shifted from foot to foot. I leveled a glare at him.

"You too, demon boy."

His eyes narrowed, but he went ahead and sat beside Jill. "Man. Demon *man*," he muttered.

"Then you need to start acting like one." I narrowed my eyes right back at him. "Zack, you've been keeping secrets from your beloved." I swung my attention to Jill. "And you've been too much of a weenie to ask Zack about his demon-ness."

"She doesn't want to know," he said, expression serious.

"Yeah?" I planted my hands on my hips. "And you've never even tried to push the issue a teensy bit? Never tried to gently introduce aspects of your not-human-ness to her, to gradually get her more interested and maybe not so scared to death of this *really big deal* that she found out only after you knocked her up?" I returned my glare to Jill. "And you! Get over it already! You're about to have a *kid* together."

Her scowl deepened, but I saw the chagrin in her eyes. She knew I was right. "I don't even know where to start," she said, with an almost apologetic look to Zack. "I don't know *what* to ask."

I took a deep breath. "Okay, then I'll start. First thing

then," I stepped back, "Zack, I think it's time for you to show the mother of your child, your best beloved, your demon form."

He winced. "I'm not certain that's the best *starting* place."

"Possibly not," I said with a shrug, "but at this point I think we need to dive right on into this. So, have at it."

Jill made a low noise and set a hand on her belly. "The bean just started kicking like crazy," she said, then glanced at Zack, worry tinged with panic in her eyes. I had a good idea I knew what she was thinking, what she was afraid of. The only demons she'd ever met were Kehlirik and Jekki. Would Zack be big and scary? Or small and furry?

Zack gave Jill a long look before glancing my way. "Under protest," he stated with the faintest of glowers. But he stood and removed his suit jacket, dropped it on the bed. His tie followed, then the shirt. His movements remained very deliberate, and for the first time I saw the lines of strain on his face.

Shit. Now I felt guilty. The grim face by the car had reflected his true state. He'd put on the smiles and congeniality for our benefit. Zack was already under a ton of stress, and my pushing the issue wasn't helping. But it was too late to turn back now. And hell, who knew how much longer Jill could have handled not knowing? The baby was only a month away, and these two were so stubborn the kid would be graduating from high school before they finally got around to talking this shit out.

Still, it behooved me to try and make it easier, if possible. "If there's anything I can do to support you," I told Zack quietly, "let me know."

He paused his movements. "A *jinig* and reverse *natulik*," he replied. "Trace and simply feed for a moment."

Hot damn, those were two I actually knew. Like wards, these didn't require the use of chalk, simply a surface on which to set them and weave the potency strands. I crouched and began to trace them on the floor, then realized he'd no doubt intentionally picked sigils I'd already learned.

Jill sucked in a breath and covered her belly with both hands. Her brow furrowed as she looked at Zack. "I think maybe she's excited?"

Zack toed his shoes off, unzipped his pants and dropped trou. He smiled. "Yes, she is."

Jill met his eyes, the fear in them beginning to fade. She even managed a small smile as she stroked her belly. Meanwhile, I did my best to be totally blasé about naked Zack's human-form junk right at my eye level.

Zack pulled off his socks, stood with his eyes closed and began to draw through the sigils I'd traced. I remained crouched and carefully fed power to the sigils as needed.

For almost a minute nothing happened. I remained perfectly still as I felt him draw power. Jill watched him with wide eyes. Even the bean went still, or at least I assumed so, since Jill had stopped making little noises of discomfort.

And then his form abruptly broke into a billion pieces that dissolved into amorphous sparkly multicolored light, so beautiful as to be nearly incomprehensible.

He remained thus for what felt like millennia though it was probably more like half a minute, then I felt the draw on my support sigils. In the span of a single heartbeat, the billion pieces coalesced into the form of a demahnk, half a head taller than any other I'd seen. I blinked, as if waking up from a dream, only now realizing how very different this had been from the transformation I witnessed with Eilahn or the smooth shift of Helori.

Jill's eyes filled with tears, and she gave Zack a weepy smile. "You're *gorgeous*."

Chiming softly, he stretched his delicate, iridescent white wings wide, then settled them close to his body. "Demahnk, sweetie."

Jill wiped at her eyes. "Okay, wow." She let out a weak laugh. "Wow."

I sat on the floor, relieved as all hell, while Jill stood and moved to him. Almost a foot taller in this form, he towered over her. She hesitated, then touched his chest—tentatively at first, then with her whole hand upon his pec. He caressed her cheek with two fingers of a three fingered hand, then lowered his head and touched his forehead to hers.

"You're still you," she breathed. She closed her eyes and slid her arms around him, belly bumping into him as he enfolded her in his wings.

"Yes, only a different form," he said, voice still very much Zack's but infinitely richer, and imbued with the chimey birdsong qualities of the demahnk. "All else is the same."

I climbed to my feet, insanely pleased that my intervention was working. So far, at least. "Perhaps you should go back to human for the rest of this," I suggested to Zack. "There's still some more explainin' that needs to happen."

He shook his head, chiming low. "I am yet unable."

"Sorry." I winced. "I don't know how all that works." I gestured to the wings and all of him to indicate the shape-change. "But I do think it's time you told her why you're here. With Ryan." I met his violet eyes. "She'll understand and accept that you need to spend so much time with him if she knows *why*."

Zack dipped his head slightly. "*I* cannot."

"Crap, that's right." Zack was still oathbound to not speak of Szerain's crime or his fate to any who didn't already know. "Will you be forced to intervene if *I* tell her?"

His lips parted in a small demahnk-smile. "No."

A frown began to tighten Jill's mouth. "Someone had better spill whatever this big secret is."

I debated telling her she should sit down, but then I realized that would only piss her off again. "Ryan is actually the exiled demonic lord, Szerain. Zack is his guardian, and he's pretty much been busting ass for the last fifteen or so years to make sure that Szerain remains sane in what's a truly brutal imprisonment. All those long periods of needing to do shit with Ryan? Most of those are spent helping Szerain."

To my private amusement, she sank to sit on the bed and stared at me in astonishment. Zack lowered himself into a sit-kneel.

"And your sweetie's demon name is Zakaar," I said, unable to resist adding one more level of *weird* to the whole thing.

She blinked, shook her head like a dog shedding water. "Wait. Ryan . . . *Ryan* is a demonic lord? Ryan?!"

"Weeelll, it's complicated." I grimaced and rubbed the back of my neck. "Ryan Kristoff is . . ." I had to swallow back a sudden wave of sadness. "He doesn't actually exist. There was a real Ryan Kristoff and, as far as I can tell, he died and his, um, life was taken over as a cover for the exile of Szerain." The grief clogged my throat briefly, and it was a few seconds before I could speak properly. "He's an overlay, basically. An identity with a real person's background, but he's an *aspect* of Szerain. He's not real."

"Ryan Kristoff died in my arms," Zack said.

I stared at him, unable to form any possible reply to that statement. I'd thought about it, rationally accepted the truth that the Ryan I knew and, yes, loved wasn't a real person. But hearing it like that—from someone who *knew*—seemed to wrench my whole world off its axis. "What happened?" My voice cracked. Since I already knew the basics, I hoped that Zack had enough freedom around his oaths to fill in the details I so desperately needed.

"I sought a candidate for Szerain, for his exile. Similar in body and face." He tipped his head back, inhaled deeply. "I was carefully watching many possible choices. Ryan Kristoff was the one to succumb in a circumstance that proved suitable. He and a friend went hiking in the Adirondack mountains. Ryan lost his footing and tumbled a hundred feet down a steep rocky slope." Zack lifted one long-fingered hand, tilted it to indicate a precipitous grade. "His friend went for help. I went to Ryan."

Grief swallowed me as I listened. I pygahed in an effort to maintain any sort of control. I'd wanted to know this. As hideous and painful as it was, I wanted to know the truth.

"He was close to death," Zack continued after a moment, voice a bit less rich. The memory affected him as well. "I eased him, removed the pain, held him, and spoke to him, in the moments he had remaining."

Tears slid down my cheeks, but I didn't wipe them away. I felt frozen in shock and sorrow, dimly aware that Jill also quietly wept, eyes on Zack as he spoke.

"What did you do with his body?" I finally asked.

"I incinerated him. Collected the ashes." Zack lowered his head.

"And then you created the overlay?" A part of me marveled that I was able to continue to question him so calmly.

"The Demahnk Council sent Szerain through to me," Zack said. "He had been submerged for some time already, but yes, I then formed the overlay, shifted his features, and—" He paused for a long moment, iridescence of his skin dulling. "And created injuries appropriate to such a fall, including head trauma to account for memory loss." He shifted, settled his wings and lifted his head. "When Ryan's friend returned, he found his hiking buddy injured but alive. The ultimate identity theft."

I stood in numb shock, pulse ringing in my ears as the strange and horrific savagery of the entire thing rolled over me. And what must it have been like for Zack to brutalize Szerain for the sake of a stable prison? "What happened to the ashes?"

"I still have them," he replied, words barely a ripple in the air.

Jill found her voice. "What happens now?"

Zack went still and pulled his wings in close. I felt a tug from the sigils and realized he'd recovered enough to make the shift back to human form. Carefully, I fed power into the sigils and observed his transformation. First the dissolution to sparkly-transparent, a pause, then finally to solid limbs and torso. The change from demahnk to human seemed easier for him, perhaps because he was so used to being in human form after all these years.

He drew a deep breath, then lifted his head and gave me a nod. "It is enough," he said in reference to the sigils. "Thank you." He gave Jill a weary smile. "Sorry, babe. I know it's weird."

I dispelled the sigils and sat on the floor. "You might want to tell her how old you are too."

Zack shot me a disgruntled look before he spoke to Jill. "Millennia," he told her.

I didn't miss that he kept it nice and vague.

Jill gave a breathless laugh. "Wow." She stroked a hand over her belly. Then she gulped, fear darkening her eyes again. "Will our baby look like, um, your winged form?" She'd seen a normal-looking ultrasound, but after witnessing Zack's transformation into Zakaar, I didn't blame her one bit for wanting more reassurance.

Zack laid a hand on the bed, used it to help him rise from the floor. "No," he said as he sat beside her. "She will be beautiful like you."

"God, you're a slick talker," Jill murmured as she leaned in for a kiss.

Zack returned the kiss. "You know it, sweetie."

And that's my cue to leave. They could handle it from here. I quietly departed and closed the door behind me.

A lovely heady scent filled the hallway, chocolate but *more*, and a bit of sniffing told me it originated in the kitchen. Paul and Bryce were there, chatting and relaxed, while Bryce stirred the contents of a saucepan.

"What am I smelling?" I asked as I moved forward, nose twitching like a bloodhound's.

"Bryce makes the *best* hot chocolate ever," Paul announced, grinning. "He's doing up a big batch."

I nosed my way in to peer at—and inhale the scent of—the contents of the saucepan, then shifted my gaze to his face. "I've always liked you, Bryce. You know that, right?"

Smiling, he snagged a mug from the cabinet. "As much as you've done for me, I think you're pretty much guaranteed a full serving." He ladled the thick, creamy liquid into the mug and passed it to me. I wrapped my hands around it, sipped.

"Marry me," I moaned.

Bryce laughed. "I'm flattered, but I don't think that would go over very well with the lord."

"Details!" I sat and spent some lovely minutes savoring the creamy drink. "If chocolate was a weapon, the Mraztur wouldn't stand a chance."

"Weaponized chocolate." Paul grinned. "Turn any bad guy good."

I grinned and sipped. "We have you two as allies. That's pretty hard core." It was nothing to sneeze at either, I knew. Paul could supposedly work miracles with computer and infrastructure, and I'd already had the chance to see Bryce in action. My posse was getting bigger and better.

I finished the hot chocolate and resisted the urge to shove my face into the mug to lick out as much as possible. My ring clinked softly against the ceramic as I set it down, and I dropped my gaze to the thin crack in the blue gem. Unique and beautiful—which gave me an idea. The summoner who'd received Idris on Earth had worn an unusual ring, red and black stones set in a gold filigree. "Paul, if you had a picture of a fairly unique ring, would you be able to track it down?"

Paul screwed up his face. "That all depends on how unique it is, photos, sales records, stuff like that. Sure, it *can* be done in some cases, but I can't make any promises until I get into it. What do you have for me to go on?"

"I'll, uh, get a sketch to you later," I said, tentatively. Crap. Good idea, shaky execution. My drawing skills sucked.

"Do that, and I'll do what I can," he said cheerily, then

grabbed another mug of hot chocolate and returned to the office. Bryce poured more for me, gave me a wink and then retreated to the living room.

A few minutes later I heard the guest room door open and close quietly. I looked down the hallway to see Zack.

"She's napping," he told me softly, then moved on to the basement door. Time for him to tend Ryan/Szerain.

I found paper and a pencil, then settled at the table to drink awesome hot chocolate and sketch the ring as best I could. The house wasn't exactly quiet—the sound of whatever game Bryce was playing mixed with the hum of the washing machine and the whirr of the air conditioner—but it all wound together into a comforting white noise of home and family. An odd family, to be sure.

After about half an hour I decided there wasn't much more I could do with my raggedy sketch of the ring. I quietly entered the office and slid it onto Paul's desk. He didn't even twitch in acknowledgment of my presence, eyes totally locked on the screen. I bit back a low laugh as I returned to the kitchen, then pulled my phone out and sent him a text to tell him the sketch was in front of him. A minute later I heard, "Got it!" from the office. Now to see what he could come up with.

Jill came out of the guest room and gave me a smile. "I hate to admit it, but you were right. I needed to know about Zack's demon-ness."

"Yes, you did," I agreed. "For the bean's sake as well." I gave her a smile. "Anyway, I'm glad that's over with. You staying for the night?"

She shook her head. "I don't have a change of clothes here, and I'd rather sleep in my own bed than wake up early to go home and get ready for work." She slung her purse over her shoulder and gave me an exaggerated mock scowl. "Also, Zack and I talked about the whole moving in thing again, and," she rolled her eyes and sighed, "I told him I'd *think* about it."

"Cool," I said. "I'll add you to the chore rotation list."

She snorted. "I knew you had an ulterior motive."

"Always. Give me a call tomorrow, okay?"

"If you're lucky," she said with a laugh, then departed..

Pleased, I returned to my seat at the kitchen table and busied myself with arcane homework—boring-but-necessary stuff that wasn't anywhere near as cool as tracing glowing sigils, but was essential in order to understand the fundamentals and theory and *why* certain strands linked only in certain ways, etc.

Sometime around midnight, Zack finally came up from the basement and closed the door quietly behind him. I looked up as he approached, but I didn't say anything. I still wasn't sure how he felt about what I'd done.

"A warning would have been preferable," he said, but gave me a smile as he dropped into the chair across from me.

Relieved, I returned his smile with a wry one of my own. "I was afraid that a warning would give either of you a chance to escape." I shrugged. "And I figured it was time."

"Time for Jill, perhaps," he said. "It was not ideal for me."

I angled my head, regarded him. "When *would* it have been ideal?"

He sighed, passed a hand over his face. "With warning, in a day or two. Still not ideal, but not detrimental. And yes," he said with a faint nod as if reading my thoughts, "I could have refused today, but then where would that have left Jill?" Regret flickered in his eyes. "Hurting more."

Spreading my hands on the table, I carefully mulled over his words. "I honestly didn't know how you'd react to my pushing the issue," I admitted. "You haven't allowed me into your thought processes and plans lately. And, at that point, I was more concerned about Jill." I took a deeper breath. "That said, I apologize for putting undue stress on you."

He regarded me in silence, for long enough that I began to conclude he wasn't going to respond at all. But then he laid a hand on top of mine. "You are right," he said quietly.

Until that moment, I hadn't realized how scared I was that he might reject me. I sucked in a ragged breath that was perilously close to a sob and turned my hand over to clasp his. "When you talked about Ryan, the real Ryan, something broke inside me," I said. "I see Szerain coming out more and more, and I tell myself I know Ryan's not *real*, that he's only an overlay, but I couldn't make myself believe that he'd be going away." My throat tightened. "But now I know he will. Someday, probably not too far off, Ryan will be gone. He'll really be dead." I felt tears slide down my face. "And I'm sitting here watching my best friend die, and he doesn't even *know* it." I was crying in earnest now as I looked up at Zack. "Promise me," I said almost desperately. "Promise me you'll let me say goodbye to him before . . . he's gone forever. Please." My voice cracked on the last word, and I fell silent.

"Yes, I promise." His fingers closed around mine. "I am deeply sorry," he said, sounding as if he was apologizing for more than the current topic.

I gripped his hand while I cried, feeling the full grief of the loss of Ryan for the first time. It wouldn't be the same with Szerain. It could never be the same. I struggled to get a hold of myself before Bryce heard me bawling and came to investigate, but it was a lost cause.

Keeping a firm hold on my hand, Zack stood, tugged me to my feet and led me out to the back porch. As soon as the door closed behind us, he wrapped his arms around me and pulled me close.

And then I couldn't hold it back anymore. I clung to him as I sobbed into his chest and let it all out. He held me, somehow giving me the comfort of being enfolded in wings even though he was most certainly in human form.

Gradually, I quieted to sniffles, though I kept my head leaned against him.

"It is unfair and unjust," he said gently. "And, from my perspective, the opposite."

"The opposite?" I tipped my head back to look into his face. "I don't understand."

"Ryan masks the one I know," he said. "The one I . . ." He exhaled, troubled sadness in his eyes. "The one I know."

"Oh, I see." It was, indeed, the opposite viewpoint of mine. "I don't understand why you can't be *his* ptarl."

He went eerily still, barely seemed to even breathe.

"Zack?" I said, worried. "Did I say something wrong?"

His eyes met mine. "No, Kara Gillian, you said something very right."

"You mean about becoming Szerain's ptarl? I mean, his ptarl is gone, and it seems like he could sure as hell use one."

"Yes, he could," he agreed, tension whispering across his face before he shook his head. "Though we both are bound elsewhere with bonds that serve none."

I fell silent for a moment, turning all of that over in my

head before speaking. "A bond—any bond—should be a benefit to both parties," I stated. "If it isn't, then one of the parties is a parasite."

He closed his eyes and lowered his head. I felt a tremor pass through his body. He was already stressed to the nines, and I wasn't exactly helping matters right now. Maybe time for me to ease up on the dude for a while.

I sniffled. "Sheesh, I'm all puffy-faced and red-nosed now." I gave him a squeeze, then pulled away. "Jill said she was considering moving in. You got through to her."

He smiled softly. "Like you said, there were some past issues she needed to face. I can't say they aren't a factor anymore, but I don't think they'll keep her from making the right decision. And she *almost* smiled at the idea of a double-wide mobile home rather than an RV."

"You know just how to charm her." I yawned and considered going out to the pond to snuggle with Mzatal, but when I extended I felt him sleeping. I didn't want to risk waking him when he needed the rest so badly. "I'm going to sneak to my bedroom and do my best to sleep the sleep of the righteous."

"Righteous," he echoed, faint smile on his mouth. "I suppose there are times when the word suits you."

"As long as it suits me with about eight hours of sleep." I gave him a quick kiss on the cheek, then returned inside to see how much righteous or unrighteous sleep I could manage.

Chapter 24

A weird tingling sensation rippled through me, jerking me out of a sound sleep. Fully awake, I assessed, realized it was wards I'd laid, triggering. I sat up and focused to determine which wards, dimly aware that it was still dark outside my bedroom window. A glance at my clock told me it was 4:13 a.m.

Another ripple. *Jill's place.* I threw off the covers and pelted down the hallway, burst into the kitchen to find Jekki burbling softly by the table and Zack standing stone still, a knife poised over mushrooms on the cutting board.

He had wards at Jill's house too, I remembered, and was no doubt assessing. I ducked into the utility room to grab jeans, t-shirt and sports bra out of the dryer, tugged them all on while I kept my eyes glued to Zack and waited for him to come out of it.

He finally exhaled, shoulders relaxing. "No immediate danger. No one's on the property now."

"What happened?" I demanded. "Do we need to go there? Or was it a new paperboy or something."

"I don't know what happened exactly," he said. "There were two men. It was quick and on the periphery. They're gone now."

"I'm going," I told him. "You coming with me?"

He gave a serious nod. "Give me a sec to get my gear. I'll meet you at my car."

I left him to get my own gear, found shoes, buckled on my gun and holster. I felt Mzatal awake and deep in his work with the mini-nexus, seeking Idris, and I asked Jekki to let him know what happened, and that I was going with

Zack to check on Jill. He scurried out the back, and I went out the front to pace by the car. A moment later Zack came down the porch steps, phone in hand and expression stone cold.

I headed around to the passenger side of the car. "You don't want her going out into something dangerous," I said. "You should call her and tell her to stay inside."

Zack slid smoothly into the driver's seat and passed the phone over to me after I got in. "Make the call?" he asked, starting the car.

I found Jill's number on his list, called and waited impatiently for her to answer.

"Zack?" she said muzzily.

"No, sugar muffin, it's Kara. Your sweetie and I are on our way over because something pinged the wards we have around your house. And if you go outside to check, I swear I'll string you up by your cute little ears. We'll be there in about—" I was going to say twenty minutes, then took Zack's demon-enhanced driving into account. "It'll be about ten minutes."

"Someone's on my property?" she asked with alarm, all sleepiness gone from her voice.

"Zack says not anymore, but we don't know if they left any surprises behind." I double-checked to make sure my seatbelt was securely buckled as Zack hit the gas. "Stay put."

"Shit. Okay, I'm getting dressed."

"Stay inside!" I insisted.

"Did I say get dressed and go *outside*? Nope."

I made a frantic grab for the oh-shit handle as Zack took a turn on two wheels. "Okay. Good. Call if you see or hear *anything* weird."

"You know I will," she said and hung up.

I closed my eyes for part of the drive. I trusted Zack's demon reflexes and senses, but that didn't mean I needed to *see* how close we came to obstacles, ditches, and other cars. I finally reopened them as we got near and kept a sharp eye out for anything unusual, but it was tough to see much.

Zack slowed, then pulled into her driveway. He cursed as the headlights passed over a suspicious lump on the lawn.

"That's not good," I muttered.

Zack backed up a bit and turned so the headlights lit the

front yard fully. I scanned the area with normal vision and othersight, then un-holstered my gun and stepped out, gun at the ready position.

Zack exited the car at a more sedate pace. I noted his eyes flicking here and there, likely picking up information from his wards.

"We clear?" I murmured.

"All clear."

I moved forward into the wash of the headlights, confirmed it was indeed a body on the lawn. White male, naked, probably in his early twenties, long and lean with little muscle tone. I stopped, shifted to othersight again and looked for any sign of arcane activity on the body. I remembered the near disaster with the arcane trap on the body of Idris's sister, and didn't want a repeat scenario.

Everything appeared normal, but that didn't reassure me. "Zack, you see anything on it?"

"Hold on." He moved up beside me and put a hand on my shoulder. An instant later a shimmer of blue and gold sprang up between us and the body, and with his free hand Zack lobbed a tightly coiled sigil. Upon contact with the victim it flashed in an expanding ring of light, then dissipated.

Zack exhaled, tension easing from him. "All clear. If there had been a trap, it would have triggered."

"Gotcha," I said. "Like throwing rocks into a minefield."

"The analogy fits." His hand dropped from my shoulder. "I didn't detect the trap on Amber's body, and I apologize for that. The *rakkuhr* is alien and devious."

"No apology needed, demon-man," I told him with a reassuring smile.

Still with my gun at the ready, I cautiously moved forward then crouched. The victim lay twisted on the grass, partially on his back, his limbs in a haphazard tangle. Something rested on his chest and I eased closer, peered at it.

Sick nausea knotted my gut. A security company patch had been cut from a shirt and nailed to his left pec. Apex Security, a lesser branch of the StarFire company, reserved for more menial security details. Last time I'd seen one of their guards was—

Shit. I shifted my gaze to his face, but it was too battered to be recognizable. Then I saw how weirdly long his arms were in proportion to the rest of his body. "Sonofafucking-bitch," I muttered. It was the security guard who'd shot Bryce.

I didn't touch anything, stood and looked back over my shoulder. "Zack, you need to call this in," I said, then shook my head. "No, Jill needs to call this in. That way we can say we're here for moral support." I glanced to the front window of the house, certain Jill was behind it, watching. I spread my pinky and thumb of my left hand, held it to my ear in the universal sign for making a phone call. With my right hand, I pointed to the body, held up three fingers then made a zero, confident she would know I meant a thirty, our area's law enforcement code for a murder.

Zack snorted, and I glanced over to find him watching me in amusement. "I could just go tell her."

I rolled my eyes. "And what would be the fun in that?"

"All righty then. Charades over?" he asked with a smile. "Looks like it worked. I can see her on the phone." He moved up beside me. "What do we have?"

I peered down at the corpse. Deep ligature marks on the wrists, flesh flayed in gruesome strips on abdomen and legs, bruising on the torso, various ugly blotches in different locations as though he had been struck repeatedly with a blunt object. "It's a goddamn message from Farouche," I said in a tight voice. "He's telling me this is what he can do, and that he knows where our friends are." I shook my head, teeth clenched. "I'm getting really sick of bodies being used as messages. Don't the fuckers have email?"

"Sure, but it doesn't have the same *uumph*."

Jill emerged from the front door, phone in hand. "What the hell?"

I moved to her. "It's the security guard who shot Bryce."

She stared at me. "Why would he be killed, and why would he be dumped *here*?" Her eyes went to the grotesque form on her lawn.

"Courtesy of J. M. Farouche," I said, glowering. "He wants his people back. He wants me to know what he's capable of, and that he knows where the people close to me live."

"Shit." She pressed close to Zack as he slid his arm around her. "Now what?"

I gave her a sweet smile "Now you move in with us willingly so that we don't have to go through the hassle of kidnapping you."

"Yep. That's what." Zack looked down at her, gave her a squeeze.

Jill drew a shaky breath, exhaled forcefully. "All right. All right. I get it."

I heard sirens in the distance. "Okay, chick, you need to deal with the cops. And best not to mention Farouche."

"What do I tell them?"

"Easy," Zack said. "And it's true, kind of. I couldn't sleep and called you, we were talking. You heard a noise out front, looked out the window and saw the body. We came over for moral support."

She eyed him dubiously, then shrugged. "Close enough. Let me at 'em," she said and headed down the drive toward the street to meet the arriving units.

I stayed put, looked over at Zack. "I had a thought. Because you *know* she won't want to stop working, despite how dangerous everything is now."

Zack folded his arms across his chest, his eyes on me. "What's your diabolical plan?"

"What if Jill had her own syraza bodyguard?"

Zack regarded me for a long moment. He drew breath and released it slowly. "It is certainly a possibility."

"I was thinking of either Zimmek or Steeev." Both syraza dwelt primarily in Mzatal's realm, and I had a friendship-type relationship with each.

"Neither has spent time on Earth," Zack noted. "Steeev is better suited. Far older."

I smiled. "He has a good sense of humor too. I think Jill would like him."

"Yes," Zack agreed, his eyes on Jill and the cops. "I think he'd be amenable."

"I should be able to do it sometime later today."

"You'll need to ask Mzatal about it first," he said. "Let me go be all moral supportive for Jill." He stepped off the porch and headed for Jill and the two cops.

I stared at his back, mildly unsettled by the instruction to ask Mzatal. Was it to ask his permission to summon the syraza? Or to give the syraza permission to come here? I shook my head. Best to wait and hear what Mzatal had to say before going too far down that path.

When the detective's car pulled up, I headed that way. Pellini emerged, surveyed the scene. He looked over to me as I approached. "This one weird?"

I dodged the "weird" question. "I'm not here on official business," I told him. "I came over to give Jill moral support." I gave him the basic information, but left out our suspicion that Farouche was behind it. Until we had a handle on the Idris situation, I didn't want anyone else stirring that hornet's nest.

It took a few hours for the cops to finish their investigation and clear out. I hung with Jill while she packed and fretted about leaving her house, though she did *finally* agree that it was for the best, especially with the baby. To my surprise she even called in sick. Hell, it wasn't every day you could use dead-body-on-the-lawn as an excuse. Zack disappeared for a while, but came back as the last unit pulled away.

Zack and I drove back in his car, and Jill followed behind, having pointed out that she'd eventually need her vehicle for work. As we pulled up to the house, my gaze went first to the two pickup trucks, then to the brand new double-wide mobile home and the workers busy around it, about fifty yards from the house on the east side.

"Um, Zack?" I said, dragging my eyes from the sight to him. "It's barely eight a.m. You had this ready and waiting, didn't you."

He glanced over, smiled innocently. "Did I?"

"Sneaky," I said chuckling. "Jill will figure it out."

"What's wrong with being prepared?" he asked, wide eyed. "It's not like I'd already moved it here or anything."

"Right," I said with a laugh. "That's why they're connecting plumbing and power that just happened to be running out by the woods."

"Uh, it was put in earlier this morning?" he offered with a sheepish grin as he climbed out of the car. "I planned on putting an RV there and had the pipes and lines installed a month ago. I bought the mobile home yesterday, then scrambled people this morning for the installation. They still have a few more hours work, but I knew she'd be happier if it was in progress when she got here." He paused. "Happi-er," he emphasized, "not necessarily happy."

"No," I agreed. "But she'll be okay. She knows the deal now, and if nothing else she'll do it for the bean."

"If that body had to be dumped, I'm not complaining about the location."

"That's the spirit!"

He snorted. "I'm going to go make sure everything's in order, then I have to get to *work*."

"Fun times." I looked over at the mobile home and the deck being assembled in front of it. "Looks like a nice one. You did good, Zack."

"With a little help from my friends." He gave me a wink and a smile, then strolled off to prepare the nest for his sweetie.

Chapter 25

I left Zack to show off the mobile home to Jill, and headed into the house with breakfast on my mind, drawn by the delicious smell of something Jekki had cooking. I caught a glimpse of Bryce in the utility room as I entered the kitchen, ducked into the doorway and saw him gazing at the panel of our conventional security system. "Everything okay?"

Bryce winced as though he'd been caught overstepping guest prerogative and glanced over at me. "Should have asked before coming in here. Sorry."

"It's cool. I know you're okay." I peered at the panel I had yet to learn how to operate. "You know about this stuff from your work with StarFire? Anything wrong with how it's configured?"

"Nope. Looks solid," he said. "And Zack said there are also magic, er, arcane protections."

"Around the whole perimeter and on the house."

He nodded. "Only thing I'd like would be visuals on the fence."

"We definitely want a surveillance system but haven't had time to make a solid plan." I tilted my head. "You interested in pulling together a concept for us?"

A broad smile lit his face, nicely breaking the tough-guy façade. "Sure! You have a budget?"

"How about you propose the best plan to adequately cover the property, and we'll work from there."

His brow creased. "You sure you're okay with me working on this?"

"If you meant us any harm at all, I'd know by now," I reassured him. "It's cool."

"Yeah," he said, smiling wryly. "Can't keep secrets around here, not with the lord."

I glanced out the window to where Mzatal ceaselessly traced sigils and worked the flows of the mini-nexus in his search for Idris. "Not a chance," I said with a low snort. "This will be a big help to us. Thanks. We need this place secure as possible."

Bryce cleared his throat, took a breath as if to say something, then didn't.

I frowned. "Something on your mind?"

"Yeah," he said. "There is. You have a minute?"

"Sure. How about we leave the luxury of the utility room and go out on the back porch." I headed for the door. "I have *chairs* there, plus I can keep an eye on Jill's new place in case she or the workers need anything." I could also intercept anyone who headed toward Mzatal, though I suspected he had aversion wards set. To those without the ability to see arcane flows, Mzatal would appear to be engaged in graceful movement akin to T'ai Chi.

Bryce followed me out, and we settled in the rocking chairs Ryan and Zack had assembled in my absence—after three years of the chairs' remaining boxed and untouched in my shed. The heat and humidity were already rising, but for now it was still bearable enough to be outside.

When I looked over at him, he seemed distant, troubled. "Hey, you okay?"

"Nope," he said, his face a grim mask. "Paul tracked what happened this morning. Did the body you find have prominent ligature marks on all limbs and neck, or only deep ones on wrists?"

I frowned. "Wrists only."

He nodded. "Probably heavy bruising along the ribs under the arms on both sides and, if they were serious, flaying." He delivered the description in an expressionless voice, eyes flat.

I regarded him. "You know who did this. I mean, specifically which one of Farouche's people."

"I've eaten lunch with him a hundred times."

I controlled a shiver of *ick*. Bryce met my eyes. "Kara, before any more time passes, I need to make sure you know exactly who you have in your house."

My brows lifted. "Did I miss a memo?"

He rubbed a hand across his forehead. "Yesterday, before the lightning show, I was in there talking to Jill, watched a movie with her and got a chance to feel her baby kick. Then it hit me." His throat worked. "She's a cop. If she knew what I am, she wouldn't be anywhere near me, especially with the baby. And Ryan, Zack, you. All cops. You did right by me, and you deserve to know who . . . *what* I am."

I shifted to face him more. Mzatal had been with him for two days in the demon realm, and I knew Bryce wouldn't be here now if he was any sort of a threat to us. But it was clear he needed to come clean, and I could totally respect that. "All right. Tell me who I have in my house."

He took a deep breath. "About fifteen years ago I started in security and bodyguard duty with StarFire. Three years of clean work. Nothing that crossed any lines." He looked away, then back to me, kept steady eye contact. "Twelve years ago I was . . . promoted. I've been over the line ever since."

I noted that he left out the leap from Veterinary Medicine to security. "You've killed people?" I asked, purposefully keeping my face as expressionless as his and my tone even.

Bryce gave a micro nod worthy of Zack.

"How many?"

"Twenty-seven."

"Any of them in self-defense or defense of another?" Though the number shocked me, I kept my voice neutral.

"Yes." He shifted his weight in the chair.

"Any of them straight up murder?"

He drew a breath and reverted from speech to the micro nod.

"Any of them outside of Farouche's orders?"

He blinked then answered with a strong, "No." Pain swept over his face, and he shook his head. "Shit. Yes. The first. An accidental shooting."

I gave a neutral nod of acknowledgement. The roommate and friend, the one with the rottweiler. "Tell me about this promotion of yours."

His eyes went barren, empty. "I went from StarFire to Mr. Farouche's inner circle. The rules changed. I never looked back. Couldn't look back."

I gave my head a slight shake. "No. Tell me about it. Tell

me how you were brought into his inner circle." I held his eyes. "Tell me how you went from bodyguard to hit man."

"I—" he began then stopped, drew back. His expression grew haunted as though recalling a nightmare.

Leaning closer, I softened my voice. "Bryce, take a deep breath and tell me."

He took a deep breath. "Kara, it was ugly, but it doesn't change anything."

"Tell me."

Bryce clenched and unclenched his hands, fell silent for several seconds, then nodded, as if encouraging himself to go on. "Mr. Farouche called three of us out to the plantation for a promotion interview," he began. "Me, Sonny—who wasn't much older than Paul is now—and Owen, a friend who I'd worked with on lots of assignments. We went to a room where Mr. Farouche and McDunn—the one with the MAC-10 on the road—waited. They had a coworker, Ben Freeman, strung up by the wrists and in bad shape. Farouche said Ben had screwed up in a big way, and it was the perfect opportunity for us to demonstrate our loyalty and take care of him."

I pygahed to remain impassive.

"The deal was for each of us to stab him, with me delivering the killing blow to the heart. McDunn held a knife out for Owen." Bryce paused and drew a shaky breath. "Owen went white as a sheet, said he didn't want a promotion. Before the rest of us could even blink, McDunn drew a Beretta 96 and shot him point blank in the forehead."

"Jesus," I breathed. I tried to imagine being a street cop called in to the chief's office along with some buddies and having one shot dead for refusing to murder a detective.

"Owen had barely hit the floor when McDunn turned to Sonny and offered the knife to him," Bryce continued, voice growing more strained. "Sonny was about to bolt. I could *feel* it. And I knew he was dead if he did. I put my hand on his shoulder." He looked away. "Damn it. I'm sorry. I can't."

"Go on," I said softly. I had a feeling he'd never told this to anyone before.

After a moment, he gave himself another nod, looked back to me. "I knew that no matter what we did, Ben wasn't walking out of there alive and, if we refused, neither were we. So I told Sonny to do it. I fucking told him to *do* it."

"And then you took your turn?"

"Yeah." His voice was bleak, and he didn't elaborate.

I sat back, regarding him, absolutely *dying* inside for what he'd gone through.

"In the space of about a minute," he continued, "I'd not only killed a man—a friend and co-worker—without even knowing why, but I'd also set Sonny up for an ugly life. I still wake up at night wondering if it would've been better for him to take a bullet quick and easy that day." He exhaled, shook his head. "But that's hindsight. In the moment, I thought we'd do what they wanted then find a way to get the hell away from Farouche. I had no idea that wasn't going to be a possibility."

"Because of his influence, the fear and compulsion," I said with an understanding nod. "I got a taste of that and was lucky enough to have friends to help clear it."

"Right. I didn't understand it either, not until Elofir and Mzatal fixed it," he said. "You felt it. Farouche has a *way* about him. He knows things he shouldn't, couldn't. Once he brings someone into the inner circle, any thought of crossing him in any way brings up unnatural, paralyzing fear. That's mainly the people who do or know about his wet work and other illicit activities. It's not like that for the rest of his employees and associates. Most of them absolutely fucking love the guy. I mean, totally devoted."

"Sounds like he can turn it both directions," I said with a frown. "Gets his loyalty with fear or love."

"Yeah, that sounds right. Shit." He scrubbed a hand over his face. "Now that his hold on me is gone, I look back and wonder how I could do what I did because of *fear*. I'm not afraid to die, but that motherfucker had me so terrified, I'd kill for him, *execute* for him."

I'd seen him take a bullet for Paul. He wasn't lying about not being afraid to die. "Sonny's been with you since the beginning of all this. You and Paul are close to him."

"Yeah." Pain and regret shone in his eyes. "It's hard on him. He's a decent guy. I'd give anything to get him out of there."

I had a feeling he'd lay down his life if it meant Sonny could be free of Farouche. He carried the responsibility for what Sonny was now. "After we get Idris, maybe we can help make that happen." I met his eyes. "Bryce, what you went through was utter shit. I have no problem with you being in this house. Do you have any problem being here?"

His face grew hard, and I saw the killer in him plain as day. "Not unless you have a problem with me having one more mark on my hit list."

"No problem at all." I knew exactly who he meant.

"That's dangerous thinking for a cop."

"I'm not a cop anymore." I pushed down the ache that rose at the reminder.

He gave me an oddly penetrating look. "Can you ever get away from being a cop, even if you aren't carrying the badge?"

Bryce sure as hell wasn't a meathead thug. "No, not really. Not having the badge is like losing a bit of me." I batted a mosquito away. "It's stupid, and I know I'll get over it, but being a cop was as much a part of me as the summoning." I paused, then shook my head. "No, it was more. A lot more. I belonged. I was part of something. I felt like I could make a difference as a cop." I blew out my breath. "The summoning was just a super cool thing I did. There wasn't any particular *reason* behind it. Not until last year. Then everything changed once Rhyzkahl made an appearance."

He digested all of that, nodded. He looked calmer now, as if a weight had lifted from him. "Thanks for everything. And as long as we're clear, I'm grateful to stay in your house." His voice held a slight hitch. A lot of emotion lay beneath the tough guy exterior.

"Glad that's settled." I slapped my hands on my thighs. "C'mon. Let's grab whatever Jekki has on the stove, fire up the game system, and kill some aliens."

"You're singing my tune," he said with a smile.

Chapter 26

Half an hour later I'd been made into mincemeat by aliens more times than I could remember, and Bryce was back to himself again.

Fuzzykins abruptly heaved her very pregnant butt onto the sofa and into Bryce's lap. She hissed at me, then looked up at him with a *Mrow?*

"Don't be shy about moving her," I said, narrowing my eyes at the feline. "She's a persistent pest with people she *likes.* I'm not one of those. She's Eilahn's."

"I'm okay with her on me." He scratched her head. "You don't like cats?"

"Cats don't like me. They were fine when I was young, but hated me when I got older." I shrugged, pushed down the bloom of regret. "Found out last year that it has something to do with being a summoner." I glared at her in mock menace. "No great loss, you mangy beast."

Bryce gave a laugh. "Looks like you're going to have a houseful soon."

I groaned at the thought, then felt Mzatal's touch and smiled. "I have something to take care of," I told him. "I'll leave you two to get acquainted and catch you a little later. Need to pick your brain a bit."

"Might be some slim pickings," he said with a smile. "I'll get started with some ideas for the camera system. It'll keep me out of trouble."

Mzatal knelt on the mini-nexus, head lowered and hands splayed in front of him as though sensing. A road atlas lay on the ground before him, open to a map of Texas. A faint tingle of potency flowed to him as he drew upon the resources of the convergence. I remained still and waited for him to complete whatever he was doing.

After about a minute he lifted his head, gave me a smile. "Zharkat."

I gestured to the map. "Did you find something?"

"Great disruption in the flows here," he said as he traced a wide circle around the Austin area. "Precipitated by an event that occurred the same day you arrived back on Earth."

"Idris was near Austin when he called me," I said, narrowing my eyes in speculation.

Mzatal nodded. "I sense an echo of his arcane signature amidst the tangle of flows, yet I have not yet located the cause or point of origin of the event." Frustration darkened his eyes, and I reached for his hand to give it an encouraging squeeze.

"It's still huge progress," I told him, then smiled. "You're too used to having the world at your fingertips in your plexus."

He exhaled, gave my hand a return squeeze. "Yes. Here, it is as if—" A whisper of amusement pierced the frustration. "It is as if I am forced to use a mere calculator after utilizing the full scope of the Internet."

I blinked at his use of such an Earth-centric analogy, then laughed. "*You* have been talking to Paul."

Mzatal's mouth twitched in a faint smile. "He sought me out during one of his breaks when no others were awake, and I spent a pleasant hour conversing with him."

"Sounds like you needed the break as well."

"I did, though I knew it not at the time." He touched the map before him. "Yet it was after I returned to my search that I found the trace that eventually led me to the disturbance."

"Excellent. I'm adding 'Make Mzatal Take a Break' to his job description."

The screech of a power tool had us both wincing. Mzatal glanced toward the mobile home and the workers then back to me. "Tell me of the events of the morning," he said, expression serious again.

"Farouche killed the trigger-happy security guard from the warehouse and dumped the body on Jill's lawn a little after four a.m.," I told him with a scowl. "He's letting me know how tough he is and that he knows where my people are." Anger swept through me again, but I didn't pygah. I wanted to be mad about this crap for a while. "On the plus side, Jill's finally agreed to move in." I gestured toward the mobile home. "Of course now I'm worried about Tessa. Shit!" I smacked my forehead. "It's been so crazy around here I totally forgot to tell you. I'm almost positive Tessa's been manipulated." I proceeded to fill him in on my odd visit with her and the way her responses felt programmed. His expression darkened as I spoke and was positively black by the time I reached the bit about Zack's micro-nod confirmation that Tessa had spent time in the demon realm with Rhyzkahl.

Though the anger on his face pretty much told me what I needed to know, I still had to ask. "Do you remember her being in the demon realm?"

"No," he replied. He stood, body stiff with tension. "However, with Katashi's associations at that time, she could have been brought in undisclosed."

In other words, Katashi had been betraying Mzatal for over twenty years, at the very least. It made a sick sense. The other lords wouldn't have been content to sit back and let Mzatal have full access to Katashi—the one summoner who pretty much controlled all the other summoners. Perhaps Katashi had been utterly loyal and well-intentioned at one time, but that wouldn't have stopped the Mraztur. They would have found his weakness, his price, and done everything possible to swing his loyalty and cooperation to them.

Not that it made a difference now, except to remind me that the Mraztur were playing a long game, and treachery could come from any direction.

"Will you assess her and help me figure out what the hell happened?" I asked him.

"Yes," he replied, muscle in his jaw twitching. "We must go to her."

I put a hand to his cheek, gave him a reassuring smile as I silently willed him calm. "I'll call her now." I pulled my phone from my pocket as I stepped a few feet away.

Tessa answered on the second ring. "Hello, sweetie!"

"Hello, yourself," I said, smiling at the buoyant sound of her voice. "Are you at home? I'd like to swing by for a bit."

"Nope," she said, sounding a bit breathless. "I'm at the airport boarding my plane."

Worry spiked. "Airport? Why? Where are you going?"

"Aspen with the old man for a few days," she told me. "He surprised me with a trip. It's been a whirlwind to get ready, but I'm not complaining!"

"Why Aspen?" I asked, baffled. "Ski season is over. And why didn't you call me?"

She laughed. "No skiing, sweetling. Perhaps some hiking instead. Aspen is beautiful this time of year. Hold on," she said followed by scuffling noises that sounded like her getting situated in her seat. "I haven't had a minute to call between packing and getting the staffing sorted out at the store. I was going to call as soon as I got to Colorado."

I silently cursed. "Will you still do that, please? I want to know you made it there safely."

"Are you okay?" she asked. "You sound frazzled."

"Yeah, I'm okay. Just a lot of shit going on. You don't need to worry." There was no point ruining her vacation. The manipulation had been around for twenty years. A few more days wouldn't make a difference. Besides, it was turning out to be a decent scenario. No way would I be able to convince her to move into the relative safety of my house any time soon, and she'd be safer in Aspen—away from home and the crap going down here in Louisiana. "Mzatal's here and I wanted you to meet him. When are you coming back?"

More scuffling around. "Next Sunday. Will he still be there?"

She asked it as casually as if he was a visitor from Miami rather than the demon realm. "I honestly don't know."

"I'll hope for the best. Gotta hang up now, sweetling."

"All right, be sure to call me when you get there." I made my goodbyes and hung up. "Crap," I muttered, then sighed and looked back at Mzatal. "At least she'll be out of town and away from Farouche."

"I would prefer her to be close, though it does indeed remove her from this area," he said. "When she returns, do you intend to insist that she move in here?"

I let out a bark of laughter. "Yeah, right. I don't think I could pry her out of her house with a—" I fumbled for a cool analogy and failed. "—a big frickin' lever. She's worse than Jill." I sighed, dug at the grass with the toe of my shoe. "With any luck all this crap will be over with by the time she gets back."

He reached and touched my cheek in a gesture of understanding. "Are there others for whom you worry?"

"Not really." I stopped and thought through my meager-yet-awesome circle of friends. "Jill, Zack, Ryan, Tessa. That's about it. A few people like Cory Crawford from the police department. Right now I'm mainly worried about Jill and the baby." I took a deeper breath. "Which brings me to another big question: Is it okay with you if I summon one of your syraza?"

"You need not ask this, beloved," he said, gentle understanding in his eyes. "Who do you have in mind?"

I smiled, relieved. "Steeev," I said. "Zack told me I should talk to you before summoning him." I angled my head, brow creasing. "I was kind of wondering why I needed your permission."

"You do not," he confirmed, though a questioning frown curved his mouth. "Why do you require Steeev?"

"Jill needs protection," I stated. "I already knew that but after the body showed up on her lawn, that need got a whole lot more urgent."

"Ah." His expression cleared, and he gave a nod of comprehension. "You intend to ask Steeev to remain for an extended period. That would be why Zakaar advised you to speak to me."

"How does that make a difference?" I asked, curious. I hadn't realized there were mechanics and protocols for this sort of thing.

"Because it requires potency support for a syraza to remain on Earth and would be a direct drain on me," he explained. "Do you consider Steeev's presence here to be necessary?"

I considered carefully before answering. "Zack is wearing himself out trying to keep Szerain stable while also keeping Jill safe—and who knows what else. It's like a domino effect. If something happens to Jill, then Zack will falter, then Szerain will crash and so on." I took a deep breath. "And Jill's very important to me." I frowned as a new concern arose. "No. Shit. You're already getting drained here. You don't need another burden."

"It is important to you, thus it is important to me, beloved," he said, inclining his head. "I agree to the arrangement and will adjust the mini-nexus to supply the potency for him while I am on Earth."

"Perfect." I gave him a grateful smile. "Thanks, Boss." My brow furrowed as another question occurred to me. "Wait. How can Eilahn be here? Isn't she associated with Rhyzkahl's realm?"

"It would be due to his agreement with her," he told me, "though I do not know the nature or extent of it. It is still in effect, or she would not be here."

Sudden worry gnawed at me, and I hated the implications. "Boss," I said quietly, "I can trust her, right?"

Mzatal moved to me, took my hands and kissed my forehead. "She is devoted to you," he said with quiet assurance. "Whatever agreement he made with her, this was not how he envisioned it. It is a constant drain for him."

Relief had me tightening my hands on his. "Whew. I love her so damn much. It would kill me if she was on team Rhyzkahl." And now I remembered Helori's explanation: Eilahn had been determined to go to me and had conspired with another syraza to put the idea in Rhyzkahl's head to make her my guardian.

Mzatal smiled. "You may delight that he forged a poor agreement, one with exploitable loopholes." He lowered his head to kiss me.

I returned the kiss. "Does it really drain him?" I laughed with vicious glee. "That's awesome!"

His eyes flashed with shared amusement. "Yes, it does. And I have no doubt it rankles him deeply."

"I love it!" I said, grinning. "Okay, lover, I have some errands to run, so I'd better go track down Eilahn." I gave him a quick hard kiss, with some added incidental groping, then left him to his search.

Before returning to the house, I made a quick detour to Jill's new digs to make sure she was getting settled in and had what she needed. A few workers still bustled around outside, but the deck was finished, making access easy. Jill assured me Zack was taking care of the few things she lacked, then granted me a quickie tour of the inside. It was definitely *cozy*, but then I remembered her own home wasn't very large either. Moreover, it was nicely furnished and had good quality appliances. *Zack done good*, I thought with pleased approval.

I also made *zero* mention of the possibility of a syraza bodyguard. I knew her too damn well, and it would be way too easy for her to say No to the whole thing before I summoned Steeev. Sure, I was being devious and underhanded, but Jill was too important to me to take any chances on her hormone-enhanced stubbornness.

I found Eilahn as she exited the front door, a big smile on her face.

"You seem awfully chipper," I noted somewhat warily. Eilahn could be delighted over the oddest things. "What's up?"

"I am certain that Paul will enjoy decorating for the Fourth of July celebration day," she announced. "We *must* plan to be on Earth! He is very enthusiastic."

I eyed her dubiously. "He told you this?"

"No, he did not need to," she said with a sly and knowing smile. "When I gave him the box from the delivery personage, he threw the bumpers into the air with such abandon that I recognized him instantly as a fellow Earth celebration enthusiast!"

Demon logic. No. *Eilahn's* logic. "Riiight," I said. "Probably had nothing to do with the laptop he ordered yesterday." I frowned. "Wait. What are bumpers?"

She held up a pink anti static packing peanut between her thumb and forefinger, as if it was a delicate treasure. "They are superbly suited for Valentine's Day, are they not?" She let out a wistful sigh. "We missed it this year. I will come to agreement with Paul on conservation and storage of the bumpers for the next occurrence."

"You do that," I said, unable to keep a smile off my face at her enthusiasm. Paul would have his hands full if she drafted him into her Excessive Decorations Committee, yet I found it awfully charming that she'd taken the young man under her wing.

Her expression became grave, and she laid her hand on my arm. "I have a deeply serious request."

Anxiety spiked. "What is it?"

"There are many items I require for the comfort of Fuzzykins in her gravid state," she told me. "I cannot leave you to acquire them. Will you accompany me to the pet supply store?"

The look of delight and hopeful pleading in her eyes shot down any possible argument I might have mustered. "Sure," I said with a sigh. "Why the hell not?"

"Excellent!" she all but squealed. "I will return at once so that we may depart!" With that, she ran off toward the woods, "bumper" in hand, and I abruptly had a weird vision of a secret hoard of Earth treasures in a hollow tree, and the bumper in a place of honor between a corncob holder and a losing lottery ticket.

"I need to shower first!" I called after her, but she was already lost amidst the trees. I shrugged and headed inside, doing my best to shut out the garish mental image of the porch festooned in red, white and blue.

Chapter 27

After half an hour in the pet store with Eilahn I began to look back fondly on my last visit to the dentist.

More toys. Treats. A special blanket. A cat bed—selected only after Eilahn poked, prodded, sniffed, and rubbed her face against every variety available. Brushes and combs— and I had to seize her arm to keep her from trying *them* out. By the time she trundled her shopping cart down the food aisle I was ready to snap.

"Eilahn, here's cat food," I said with a slightly manic smile as I grabbed the first bag available. "It's a big bag! We won't have to shop again for *ages*. It's even on sale!"

She looked over at me with a very serious expression. "I will get *organic* Kitty Cuisine Niblets for Fuzzykins," she informed me primly. "She is eating for seven and superior quality nutrition is critical."

"Seven?!" I released the bag and stared at her, aghast. "Wait, there'll be six copies of her running around, glaring and hissing at me?"

"Yes! Is it not wonderful?" she exclaimed, beaming. "I am still deciding on the names."

My horror increased. "Are you planning on keeping them *all*?" I shook my head frantically. "No no no. You have to find homes for them."

Her lovely brow furrowed. "I would not send them away if they do not want to go." She frowned. "That would be barbaric." Then she lifted her chin. "Whether they choose to go or remain, they need names."

"Call them all Fred," I suggested with a glower as we continued down the aisle.

"As they only have limited telepathic communication, that would be extremely confusing for them," she stated as if lecturing a three-year-old. "Names are special. Unique."

I groaned. "Telepathic . . ." I shook my head to rid it of the horrifying concept. "You're telling me that Fuzzykins is okay with being called Fuzzykins?"

"Certainly!" She gave me a *look* as if wondering whether I suffered from some form of mental disorder. "I would not speak a name for her that brought her distress."

I was saved from more talk of telepathic cats by the ringing of my phone. A Beaulac PD number. "Kara Gillian," I answered.

"Hey, Gillian, it's Marcel Boudreaux," the familiar nasal voice said. "You busy right now?"

"Nope, whatcha got?" I said. Eagerly. Malfunctioning stop light? Cockroach invasion? Crowd control at a 90%-off shoe sale? Anything to get out of this store.

"Got a detective here from St. Long sheriff's office with some questions about one of your old cases."

"Yeah, I can come by," I said. "I'm only about five minutes away."

"See you in five then," he replied and hung up.

"Okay, enough cat toys, Eilahn," I told her. "Need to go to the PD."

She balanced a large box atop the rest of her haul. "A fresh water fountain is not a *toy*," she lectured. "It is for optimal health, well-being, and happiness." She indicated the words on the box.

I felt a twitch forming in my left eye. "Fine. Let's get it and *go.*"

To my relief she headed for the check out. As soon as she was done I jogged to the car and popped the trunk open, while she proceeded at a more leisurely pace.

"You seem distressed," she said as she carefully tucked the fountain, cat bed, food, toys, and all the other paraphernalia into the trunk. "Do you want me to drive?" She closed the trunk and gave me a calm smile, though I caught the wicked humor in her eyes.

Yep, my demon bodyguard was a smartass.

I decided I wouldn't dignify that with a reply and climbed into the driver's seat. I was even nice and waited for her to get *in* the car before I drove off.

*   *   *

There was no street parking to be found, and the visitor's lot was full, so I finally cheated and found a place in the far corner of the detective's lot. To be safe, though, I quickly traced an aversion ward on the hood, just in case anyone decided to ticket or tow it.

Eilahn lingered in the foyer while I headed through the familiar Investigations door. A sharp twinge of nostalgia went through me as I walked down the hall with its stained tiles and cheap wood paneling and ever-present scent of burnt coffee.

My former sergeant, Cory Crawford, wasn't in his office. A vaguely familiar young man earnestly typed away at his laptop in the closet-sized room that used to be mine. He'd been a road cop, I realized as I passed by. Must have snagged the promotion when I left.

Yet as soon as I passed the open doorway I had to stop and take a several deep breaths. I wasn't a cop anymore. I'd *known* it before, but now the truth of it hit me hard in the gut. *Not a cop.* I wasn't really a consultant for the FBI either. What the hell was I now? A summoner? That didn't adequately describe it. Not anymore.

Squaring my shoulders, I continued on to Boudreaux's office. He was on his phone, but when he saw me he covered the mouthpiece and said, "Interview three," with a jerk of his head in the direction of the interview rooms.

I nodded and continued to the side corridor that housed the various interview rooms. The first two rooms were dark, their doors open. The third, at the end of the hall, was lit and the door ajar. I headed to it and peered in, even as a sudden hard shove in the middle of my back propelled me fully into the room.

I let out a startled yelp and stumbled forward as the door closed solidly behind me, but then I registered the other occupant of the room. Gritting my teeth, I recovered and tugged my jacket straight.

"Got all the cops under your thumb?" I asked Farouche with a tight smile.

Impeccably dressed in an obviously high quality steel-grey suit, dark shirt, and pale blue-patterned tie, he stood with the fingertips of one hand lightly resting on the table, silver cufflinks glinting at his wrist as he regarded me. "They are eager to accommodate me," he replied mildly.

"Must be boring to always have things go your way," I said with a mock-tragic sigh. "No surprises. No adventure."

He straightened and adjusted his cuffs, flicked a miniscule bit of dust from his lapel. An elegant band of gold and diamonds rested on the ring finger of his left hand, and I found myself weirdly surprised that he still wore his wedding ring. I knew about the cancer center and his dedication to the search for his abducted daughter, but this clear sign of devotion to his deceased wife struck me on a different level. A sentimental monster?

"How odd," he said as he took a step toward me. "I've always found it to be exhilarating." He took another step closer, but when I didn't flinch or back away his brows drew together, and a whisper of tension creased the skin around his eyes.

With a small impatient sigh, I folded my arms over my chest and gave him a bland look. "Is there something you wanted to say to me?"

A look of true bafflement came over his face, and I knew damn well it was because I wasn't sweating in fear and jumping to do his bidding.

"What have you done?" he murmured, eyes searching over me as if trying to find whatever hidden trick I was using.

Fiendish glee soared through me, but I widened my eyes and brought my hands to my mouth in mock dismay. "Oh no! Was I supposed to call *you*?" I exclaimed with great drama. "I've been sitting by my phone waiting for you to call *me!*" I fluttered my hands. "Oh my goodness, what a faux pas!" I gave him an innocent look even though fury roiled through me. He was pulling his shit on cops and friends, and *that* was way beyond the pale.

Yet he didn't seem to fully hear my words. Feet shifting ever so slightly, his expression flickered for a brief instant in a weird mix of confusion, worry, and anxiety.

A second later it hit me. *He's not in control. And that's completely unfamiliar territory. Payback's a bitch, motherfucker.*

"It was him . . . Mah zahtal," Farouche breathed, mispronouncing the name, though it didn't seem to be intentional. And the *Oh shit* in his eyes might as well have been written in neon.

I laughed low, and I sang a line from "My Boyfriend's Back."

Uncertain and shaken—though it was clear he fought to keep it hidden—he shot a look to the surveillance camera in the corner of the room and flicked his hand to the door. A few seconds later it opened, and he departed without another word.

Now that he was gone, my pulse hammered at the insanely close call. I counted to five then moved to the door and peered out, while keeping a *very* sharp eye out for any of Farouche's cronies.

Instead I saw Eilahn bound around the corner, consternation on her face that shifted to stark relief as she saw me in one piece.

Still she pulled me fully into the hallway, raked an assessing gaze over me then peered hard into my eyes before relaxing. "I saw the ginger one and *him* as they departed," she told me with a low growl beneath her words. "Forgive me. I did not expect a threat in this place."

"No reason for you to," I reassured her. "And you can't ride my ass everywhere. I figure you'd have known if I was in any real danger." I went on to relate everything that happened.

"You sang to him?" Her brow puckered. "Is this a traditional means of taunting?"

"Well, sort of." I paused to consider. "But it depends on the song. 'We Are the Champions' is certainly better than 'Muskrat Love.'" Then again, the latter would probably be more effective as torture. "Let's get the hell out of here," I said. "I'll educate you on the way home."

Before we left the station I stopped by Boudreaux's office to find out what he knew about Farouche and why he set me up to be in a room with the man. As much as Boudreaux and I failed to get along, I nevertheless *knew* in my gut that he wouldn't deliberately fuck me over. Had Farouche put the fear whammy on him?

Yet, if anything, it turned out to be the opposite. Farouche had wanted to surprise me with a job offer, Boudreaux told me, eyes near glowing with an eager desire to please Farouche. It hadn't occurred to him to question the scenario, because this was how Farouche had wanted to meet with me.

I extricated myself from the weird conversation and left the station with Eilahn. "Bryce was right. It's not just fear," I said after several minutes of brooding and driving. "He can also lay on the charisma and make people devoted and loyal." I shuddered. "I'm not sure which one scares me more."

"He is a very dangerous man," Eilahn muttered.

I continued on home in complete agreement.

Chapter 28

Mzatal was still deeply involved on the mini-nexus when we returned home, and I decided to have Eilahn tell him about my encounter with Farouche while I summoned Steeev.

Paul and Bryce weren't in the common areas when I returned to the house. I scrawled "do not disturb" on a sticky note and slapped it on the basement door, then poured a big glass of tunjen and headed down. It felt both weird and good to perform a summoning in the middle of the day with utter confidence. A year ago—hell, a few months ago—I would've balked at the mere idea due to the lack of lunar influence and the extra difficulty that posed. Training with Mzatal had stripped all that nonsense away, and I'd learned how to adapt and compensate for different summoning conditions.

I set the tunjen aside and got to work. The storage diagram was nicely topped off, and it took only about fifteen minutes to change the existing ritual diagram to the parameters for a syraza. I checked and rechecked the sigils, bindings, and power flows, tapped the storage diagram, and began.

I spoke the name "Steeev" as the invocation to call the syraza, confident and calm. I knew I had a successful summoning. It felt *right*. Only once did I encounter a shift in the currents of power as I formed the portal, but I smoothly adjusted the anchors and dealt with the shift with no further issues, and silently thanked the hundreds of hours of practice Mzatal had insisted I do.

The syraza arrived with a jolting pull in the potency flows. I grounded and anchored the power, then looked up to see him, kneeling and breathing hard, in the center of the diagram.

"Steeev," I said, "I apologize for summoning you without warning."

He lifted his head. "Is . . ." He paused as though testing his ability to speak. "Is there a problem with the qaztahl?"

"No!" I said quickly. "No, Mzatal is well." Of course that would be his first assumption, especially since, according to Zack, Steeev had never been summoned before. "I need a favor from you," I continued, "but I want to discuss it with you first since it's a big one. Would you like tunjen?"

Steeev blinked several times, still trying to get his bearings. "Tunjen. Yes." He attempted to rise then apparently thought better of it. "What favor, Kara Gillian?" he asked as he sank back into a kneel-sit. "When my body moves where my mind wills, perhaps I will be able to accommodate." He chimed in laughter. "Unless I am forever in the swirling state."

I retrieved the glass of tunjen I'd brought downstairs and pressed it into his hand. "It fades, I promise," I assured him with a smile, then crouched before him. "Here's the favor. I need protection for a dear friend of mine. She's Zakaar's lover too, and carries his child."

Steeev drained the cup then looked at me, head angled slightly to one side. "Jill Faciane. Zakaar does not protect her?"

"He does as much as he can, but he also has a duty to Szerain." I took a few minutes to explain our current situation, including the body dump and the threat to Jill. "I'd rather she be overprotected than have something happen to her."

Steeev stretched his wings wide, then folded them and stood. "Mzatal has agreed to this?" He put on a syraza version of a scowl, tucked his hands behind his back and lifted his chin in a surprisingly excellent mimicry of Mzatal. "Or does he protest?"

I laughed. "He has agreed to this."

The syraza let his Mzatal impression go, chimed softly. "For what span of time?" He took a deep breath, then stiffened and curled his lips back. "What is that *smell?*"

I let out a cough of laughter at his reaction. "The span of time would be at least until the baby is born. A month or two," I said. "The unpleasant smell is likely hydrocarbons, and the savory smell is gumbo. Crawfish gumbo. It's pretty good."

"It has been long since I have seen a human babe." He bared his teeth in a syraza smile, chiming with amusement. "Noisy and smelly and ear-pulling."

"They do grow out of that—most of the time." My amusement faded. Now came the tricky part. "Here's the deal," I said, all seriousness now. "I haven't yet talked to Jill about you, or about having a guardian at all. First, because I know her, and if I asked before she met you, it'd be too easy for her to say No." I paused, inclined my head to him. "And second, I didn't want to bring it up with her until I knew your decision."

"The decision cannot be made without her agreement," he stated. "That said, I am not opposed and, in not being opposed, am indeed willing—if she is willing—to accept guardianship." He tilted his head, peered at me. "On the condition that she is at least marginally pleasant."

"I'll let you be the judge of that," I said, relieved. I gestured grandly to the raggedy basement stairs. "Come upstairs and see my demesne."

"Lead on, Kara Gillian," he announced with a teeth-baring smile. "I will wobble and teeter along behind."

"You can lean on me if you wish," I offered.

He gave a snort-chime. "The great guardian arrives, leaning heavily upon the summoner. It does not serve. No, no. Not at all."

"Then you'd best stop your whining," I advised with a grin as I led the way.

Steeev followed, chime-muttering. Once upstairs, I gave him a quick rundown of the layout of the house and property. "Jill likes her privacy, so she's staying in a mobile home at the side of the house," I explained as we entered the kitchen.

Bryce was at the table—papers and notes in front of him that I figured were probably stuff for his surveillance camera proposal. He glanced up as we entered, blinked in surprise at the sight of a syraza.

Steeev chimed. "Fair greetings, Bryyyce."

Bryce's expression cleared, and he chuckled. "Steeev. You're the only one who drawls my name out like that. Good to see you again."

"Steeev will be sticking around for a while as Jill's guardian," I told Bryce. "That is, if we can get it through her stubborn head that she needs one."

Bryce looked from me to Steeev then back to me. "I get it. Like Eilahn." He nodded. "Jill needs that, especially now."

"We're about to let her know she's always wanted one," I said, then continued out to the back porch.

I caught a streak of blue near the woods out of the corner of my eye, accompanied by a shrill chirrup-whistle. Jekki. Beside me, Steeev returned the greeting with a melodic trumpeting, and an instant later I heard a piercing whoop that I recognized as Eilahn's. Good thing I didn't have any close neighbors. They'd be wondering about the weird wildlife.

I glanced back at Steeev as I stepped off the porch and started toward Jill's place. "Okay, here's the plan. You're going to be so charming, she can't refuse."

He bared his teeth. "I thought you said this would be a challenge."

I laughed. "Forgive me. I forgot who I was dealing with."

We crossed the grass and climbed the steps to the redwood deck. Zack had moved damn quickly to make the place as nice as possible. "Yo, chick!" I called out as I knocked on the door. "Got someone here I want you to meet."

A few seconds later Jill opened the door. "Who?" she asked, then her eyes widened as she looked past me. "Oh. That's who."

I stepped aside to give her a better view. "Jill, this is Steeev. He's a syraza, like Eilahn." I turned my attention to the demon. "Steeev, I would like you to meet my very dear friend, Jill."

Jill stepped out onto the deck. "Nice to meet you, Steve," she said with a polite smile paired with a questioning look in her eyes.

"It's Steeev," I corrected.

She gave me a slightly perplexed look. "Right, Steve."

I shook my head, thoroughly enjoying this. "No, y'gotta draw it out more. Steeev."

Jill's mouth thinned into a flat line as she swept a gaze over Steeev, then narrowed her eyes at me. "Is this some kind of insider summoner joke?"

"Nope," I said with a laugh. "But it is fun. His name is Steeev. There's a bit of an extra 'e' sound in there."

It was obvious she still didn't completely believe me. She regarded Steeev as he stood by the top of the steps, radiating as much innocence as a demon could. "Is this true?" she asked. "You're a demon named Steeev?" The dubious look on her face told me she was ready to receive the punch line.

Steeev bared his teeth in a syraza smile and took a step closer. "Unless my name has been changed in the space of the last few heartbeats, I am indeed a demon—a *syraza*—by the name of Steeev."

"I'll be damned," she said, then offered him a wry smile. "It's very nice to meet you, Steeeeeeev."

I burst out laughing. "Okay, babe. That's a bit of overkill on the *eeeeeee*."

She joined me in the laughter. "Make up your mind!"

And with that the two of us descended into ridiculous and hysterical laughter, no doubt fueled by the stress and weirdness and everything else going on. It took a few minutes for us to regain something akin to composure, not helped at all by the fact that whenever one of us started to find some control the other one would make a silly *eeeeeee* sound and we'd go off again—all while Steeev looked on in bemused tolerance. Or maybe he was trying to come up with some way to sneak back to the demon realm. Anything was possible.

When we finally got our breath back, I cleared my throat. "Jill, I summoned Steeev for a reason. It has to do with you, and I really hope you'll agree to it."

Realization immediately dawned in her eyes. My Jill wasn't a dumb chick by a long shot. But even as she opened her mouth to protest, Steeev stepped forward.

"She will," he said to me, then brought his gaze to Jill. "You will, will you not? Your Kara Gillian friend believes you need protection." He tilted his head. "Do you need protection? You seem quite capable to me, so I am certain I would need to do little more than watch, and most assuredly would not be a nuisance." He shook his head. "Not *much* of a nuisance."

He paused barely long enough for Jill to begin a response, then folded down onto one knee and took her hand between his. I watched in amusement and more than a little awe as he blinked up at her in the hitherto unheard of syraza equivalent of puppy dog eyes. "Jill Faciane, only you can prevent my return to the demon realm, utterly rejected, steeped in shame."

Jill gaped at him, but it took her only a second to pick up the humor. She fought to hold back a laugh, with only partial success. "I am seriously having the weirdest day ever," she muttered.

"As am I," Steeev said, still kneeling before her. "I was very inoffensively trouncing Safar in a game of *kessa*, and whoosh! Dragged to Earth."

"Dragged to Earth to be my bodyguard?" She turned an accusing glare on me.

I twisted the toe of my shoe on the deck and whistled innocently. "Only if you agree to it."

Steeev gazed up at her. "You do, do you not?"

A scowly-disgruntled expression began to form on her face, but then it shifted to a wince. She laid a hand on her belly, sighed. "Ah, jeez, bean."

I masked a smile. The bean wanted Steeev around. Yay, bean!

Jill narrowed her eyes at Steeev. "Please tell me you can do the changing-to-look-human thing like Eilahn and Zack."

His features scrunched. "It is possible, yes. Perhaps. I have not done so before, but I do not shy from a challenge."

Jill rolled her eyes, then gave a dramatic slump of defeat. "Okay, *fine*. If you can get human-looking, then I won't send you back an utter disgrace."

I silently sang the hallelujah chorus.

Steeev stood, her hand still clasped flat between his as he gazed down into her face. "Jill Faciane, this is not to be done under duress," he said, all joking gone from his voice and manner. "It is wholly your choice and my choice. I offer my service in my willingness to work with you. If you choose not to accept, then I depart with no ill will. This is between us now. It has nothing to do with what others want."

Jill stared up at him with a stunned look on her face as the sincerity of Steeev's proposal permeated the air around us. She took a shaky breath. "I've . . . suddenly realized I don't like being on edge all the time. So, yes, Steeev. I'd like it very much if you would stay and, um, be my bodyguard."

"Guardian," he gently corrected, then leaned down and touched his forehead to hers. "And so it is. I have Mzatal's support and will forge the tie that binds me here and to you. It may feel bizarre, but no harm will come of it."

She inhaled sharply, eyes widening in shock, but a few seconds later she relaxed into unfocused peace. Eilahn had connected to me like this, I remembered, though she'd told me that no words could have prepared me. Then again, Steeev's words seemed to have worked pretty well.

The pair remained still, forehead to forehead for several minutes, while I sat on the steps and amused myself by looking at clouds. Finally the palpable intensity faded to nothing. Steeev straightened, exhaled. "I am delighted *that* part is complete," he said with a baring of his teeth, his laughter like a cascade of bird song.

Jill swayed a bit and gave a weak laugh. "Oh my god. That was . . ." She trailed off, apparently deciding that words were inadequate or unnecessary. "What now, Steeev the Guardian Demon?"

"You require that I take on the form of a human, and so I shall," he replied.

"Do you need privacy?" she asked tentatively.

Steeev chimed softly. "No, I require assistance."

Jill shot me a baffled look heavily flavored with desperation, then fixed her gaze on Steeev. "What kind of assistance?"

"Mzatal already offers direct potency which will ease the transformation greatly," he explained. "However, I also require guidance from you."

"Wait," Jill said, "you want me to pick what you'll look like?"

He shifted his shoulders and wings in a shrug. "Not *precisely*. I will not choose a particular form as much as create a composite from what you bring forth. Guidance."

"Jeez, the pressure."

Steeev chimed in laughter. "As I have never adopted a human form, I would prefer to do it with your guidance so that I may not omit anything vital," he said. "It will be an adventure, Jill Faciane!"

Jill rolled her eyes and grinned. "Okay, bring it. We can't

risk having you run around here without all your bits and
pieces."

He guided her to sit on the top step. "As I have not done
this before, I know only what I have heard from others." He
knelt on the step below her feet. I cleared my throat to get
his attention.

"Steeev, transforming leaves Eilahn pretty shaky. You
might want to go down to the bottom of the steps." I gave
him a grin. "I'd hate for you to fall and mess up your new
body."

He inclined his head to me and moved to kneel on the
grass. "Thank you, Kara Gillian," he said, then looked up at
Jill. "Now, call forth a vision of your ideal guardian so that
I can feel it."

I stifled my laughter as I watched Jill's face contort in
concentration, no doubt desperately trying *not* to think of
Kevin Costner in *The Bodyguard*. A moment later she
sucked in a gasp as Steeev began to shimmer and slowly
change. As with Eilahn, it was nothing like the smooth CGI-
worthy morph the demahnk Helori had demonstrated in
the demon realm, but more as if reality flickered in and out.
I watched, curiosity tickling. Zack was demahnk, yet his
shift hadn't been at all like Helori's. Maybe it had to do with
Zack being on Earth?

The flickering faded. A naked man knelt at the base of
the steps, eyes squeezed shut and breath coming shakily.
Steeev. Jill still had an unfocused look about her, so I
ducked quickly inside, found a towel, and returned outside
as Jill began to come out of her fog.

Jill blinked, then grabbed the edge of the step with both
hands as if to keep from toppling over. "Whoa. That was . . .
I don't know what that was." She let out a breathless laugh,
then focused on Steeev. "Whoa. You look really good."

"I have all my bits and pieces?" he asked, eyes still
closed. His human voice was light, pleasant, and smooth.

She snorted. "Uh, yeah."

I descended the steps, wrapped the towel around
Steeev's waist. "I'll find some clothing for you."

He opened his eyes. Nice golden-brown eyes set in an
amiable, dark-skinned face. "I do *not* recall agreeing to
clothing," he said, his smile displaying even, white—but not
too white—teeth.

"You'd definitely distract any attackers," I said with a laugh. I returned to Jill, sat and wrapped my arm around her. "You okay, chick?"

She smiled. "Yeah. The bean's going crazy, and I'm dizzy, but that's it." Her smile grew into a grin. "Holy shit! I have a demon guardian named Steeeeeeeeeeev."

Chapter 29

As I returned to the house, I allowed myself a moment to bask in the success of the Jill and Steeev venture. Yet at the same time I knew how incredibly fucking lucky we'd all been. Farouche obviously didn't know how much Jill meant to me. He likely thought her a close friend at the most. I knew damn well that if he'd known how much I loved that stubborn woman he wouldn't have settled for a simple dump of a dead body on her lawn. His people would have grabbed her at the first opportunity to use as leverage to get Paul and Bryce back.

Mzatal was still on the mini-nexus, and as I passed I *felt* how much stronger the flows were than the previous day, coiled with potential energy like a compressed spring.

An exultant shout from the direction of the obstacle course drew my attention. I heard another shout, then the sound of Bryce cursing along with a musical peal of laughter. A few seconds later Bryce and Eilahn burst from the woods pelting neck and neck toward the house. At least I assumed it was Bryce. It was hard to be sure since he'd apparently done a face-first, full-body plant into mud somewhere along the course.

However, he didn't let what looked like an extra ten pounds of mud slow him down, and even though I knew damn well Eilahn could outrun any Olympian, and was certainly sandbagging a bit for his benefit, Bryce still managed a final kick to finish neck and neck with her.

Eilahn grinned widely as Bryce flopped to the ground. "You fight dirty," he managed, then let out a wheezing chuckle. "I love it."

"I should have warned you about her," I said as I approached them. "No such thing as a fair fight in her book."

Eilahn bared her teeth. "A fair fight is the one you survive."

"I'm with you, sister," Bryce said as he pushed up to sit. He swiped a hand over his face and flicked mud away. "Though I admit I didn't see eye to eye with you when you hooked my leg and shoved me into the mud."

"I wished to be certain of my victory," she stated.

"And stepped on my back."

"Very certain."

"You were already winning!" Bryce said in exasperation. "You stopped, waited for me to jump the log, and *then* tripped me."

Eilahn tilted her head. "I wished to be very certain of my victory. And it *was* most amusing."

Bryce lobbed a chunk of mud at her which she nimbly dodged. With a parting musical laugh she loped off into the woods.

I cocked an eyebrow at Bryce and smiled. "Do you want the hose?"

"I think that'll be a good start," he replied with a laugh.

He levered himself to his feet while I fetched the hose and turned the water on for him.

"I'll let you sluice yourself off," I said, handing him the hose. "But I'd like to pick your brain once you have the worst of the mud off."

"I'm all yours," he said with a smile as he began to rinse.

"I need to get something from the living room, and then I'll meet you on the back porch."

He nodded and held the hose over his head. Smiling, I headed inside. It took me a few minutes to find the journal I needed in the stack on the coffee table, and by the time I returned to the back porch Bryce had not only finished rinsing off but had even found a battered towel to dry himself. He'd also exchanged his wet and muddy clothing for battered-but-clean t-shirt and shorts, and his drying shoes sat in the sun on the steps.

"Ready for my brain picking," he said.

"I'll try and make it painless," I replied and sat in one of the rocking chairs, gestured for him to do so as well. "This is one of Tracy Gordon's journals—the one that has your name in it along with several others." I passed it over to him. "Do you know any of these other names?"

He read through the list, all humor fleeing from his expression. "Shit."

My gaze locked onto him. Finally, *something*. "You *do* know them? How?"

"I know about half of them." He looked up at me, perplexed. "What the hell?"

"Anything unusual about them? Any common link you can think of?"

"The ones I recognize work—or have worked—for Star-Fire or other companies Mr. Farouche owns." He frowned in thought as he drew a finger down the list. "But they do all sorts of things. I mean, they're not all—" Pain flashed briefly over his face before he could control it. "They're not all like me. Hanson is an accountant. Stevens is Mr. Farouche's in-house financial advisor. Sonny—he's listed here as Jesus Ramirez—is kind of like me. Aberdeen is the surveillance specialist for StarFire. And Henrietta—" He shrugged in bafflement. "Hennie is a damn *cook*."

I slumped in the chair. Great, so at least half of the people on the list worked for Farouche, but we still had zilcho idea why they were in Tracy's journal. "Any link apart from working for Farouche you can think of?"

Bryce considered for almost half a minute, then gave a shrug. "Nothing I can come up with."

"Did you all come on board at the same time?" I asked, frustration rising. "Are you all from the same area? Are you all allergic to Ethiopian peanuts?" I threw up my hands in desperation. "There has to be *something*."

"I'm sorry. I'm trying here." He shook his head, grimaced. "We weren't all hired at the same time. Hennie's been around longest. Otherwise it's spread out over a few years. Nothing in the past eight years though." He scrutinized the list again. "I think the theory of being from the same area is out. Hennie's from Vegas, and Sonny's from California. Not sure on the rest."

I blew out a sigh of disappointment. "Thanks anyway. I'll check with Paul to see if he can run the names. Maybe something will pop as a connection." I closed the journal and stood.

"Wait!" Bryce said. "Shit. I just realized—there *is* a connection."

I spun to face him. "There is? What?"

"There was this one time we all went down—passed out or got really sick and dizzy—all at the same time. Several at the compound, including Mr. Farouche and Paul and me. It didn't hit everyone, but every person I know on that list was somehow affected."

My skin tingled. This was it. "Tell me what happened."

"It was sudden, struck us all at once," he said, face intense with the memory. "Some people had a bit of nausea, headache, vertigo, that sort of thing. Others collapsed completely. Lasted about ten minutes. Seriously weird."

I felt my pulse quicken. "When was this? Date? Time?"

"No clue on the exact date. It was in November, late afternoon." He paused in thought, then gave a firm nod. "It was a Wednesday, because Wednesday was always sushi day for Paul, and we'd decided to go eat dinner at Auntie Mimi's Super Sashimi."

Hot damn. "I know what the link is to the people collapsing," I said with barely contained glee. "That's the same date and time an attempted gate to the demon realm got fucked up and nearly collapsed." I gave him a tight and triumphant smile. "It happened in that warehouse where you got shot, where you and Paul went chasing a wiggle."

He nodded, but his brow creased. "Why would a collapsing gate affect some people and not others?"

"That's what we have to find out," I told him. Could it be summoning ability? No, I decided. There was no way there were that many summoners or people with arcane aptitude running around. I frowned. Farouche and the essence-eating murderer I'd tracked down the year before were non-summoner humans with arcane abilities. *But what if it isn't something so blatant?* "When you think of each of those people, is there anything they do really well, or is unique?"

"You mean like arcane stuff?" He shook his head. "Paul and I are normal. I saw what the lord did in the demon realm, what you people did out here yesterday." He lifted his chin toward the back yard. "We can't do any of that."

I smiled slyly. "Actually, that's not true. Mzatal told me that Paul uses his computers and equipment to play with the arcane flows of Earth and can even sense them in the demon realm." I hadn't known Bryce long, but I'd seen him in action. "You ever get hunches? Feelings or intuition that seem to always pan out?"

Bryce shrugged. "Sometimes. Everybody does."

Not the way he did, I was willing to bet. I traced a sigil on the porch rail. "Do you see anything? Feel anything?"

"Nope, don't see anything." But then he frowned. "I, uh, feel something right here though," he said doubtfully, pressing a hand to his stomach. "Maybe. Probably my imagination."

I dispelled the sigil. "Now?"

His frown deepened. "It's gone." He peered at me. "What's the deal? I have stuff like that all the time."

"Bear with me." I pretended to trace another sigil. "What about now?"

"Nope, nothing. See? A coincidence."

I smiled. "Yeah, sure," I said and traced a complex warning sigil that pulsed and emitted a "loud" arcane broadcast.

"The back of my neck itches a little," he said with a shrug, though I saw him wince.

I grinned and dispelled the sigil, feeling *most* triumphant. "Ha! You are *so* sensitive. I didn't trace a sigil the second time."

He shook his head in obvious disbelief. "I don't know, Kara. That's pretty out there."

I gave him a withering look. "Excuse me. You spent two days on another world, were brought back from the brink of death by magic healing, and you say that butterflies in your tummy are Out There?"

Bryce gave a bark of laughter. "I mean for *me*. I'm just muscle."

"Yeah, suuuure." Brains too. He sure as hell didn't get into vet school on brawn. Tito, the man Mzatal killed in the warehouse, fit the bill of muscle with a little arcane sensitivity. I had a feeling Bryce had a splash of arcane-bolstered intuition thrown in as well. "How many times have hunches saved your or your boss's ass?"

He waved it off. "I have pretty good instincts in the field, and yeah, it's been handy."

"You're one of the best Farouche has, right?"

"*Had*," he clarified. "But yeah, I was one of his best."

"I think your former boss is trying to load his staff with people who are *really* good at what they do. Tell me," I said, tilting my head, "is there anything special about the cook?"

"Hennie?" A fond smile touched Bryce's mouth. "She's a great cook. Nothing exceptional though." He paused and considered. "Except maybe her red velvet cake," he added with a chuckle. Then his brows drew together in thought. "She's always on top of people's allergies and preferences. Like, she never forgets and serves Jerry peas, or lets different foods touch on Carter's plate. She cares, for sure." He looked up, shrugged. "But it's not a super power or anything. I will say she does make the best soup for a cold or flu though. Really does the trick."

"Bryce, let go of the notion that sensitive people need to be X-Men mutants."

He smiled wryly. "Gotcha. I guess that's the picture I had in my head."

"What about Sonny? What's special about him?"

Bryce exhaled. "That one I know. He has this way of calming people. Mild-mannered, unassuming, often overlooked or underestimated. He was the Hispanic one you saw on the road with Farouche."

"He didn't look so mild-mannered with a gun pointed at me," I said. "But I also know he's under Farouche's influence." I folded my arms across my chest. "I find it pretty interesting that your former boss is hiring freaks like you."

"Interesting for sure," he said. "You know the accountant on the list? You could ask him to do any sort of calculation, and he'd have the answer before you could type it into the calculator. He got sick of us testing him."

I pursed my lips, nodded. "Take a single aspect and super-charge it. Gives your former boss a lot of power. And not only does he hire people with talents, he somehow *finds* them in the first place."

Bryce rubbed a hand over his stubbled chin, frowning in thought. "Y'know, I think there's more to it than that."

"Such as?"

"Now you've got me thinking about it," he said, "and, well . . ." He grimaced. "I'm not sure how to explain it."

"Try me."

He remained silent for several seconds, very obviously gathering his thoughts. "The people who are 'talented' get better at whatever they're talented at after working for Mr. Farouche for a while," he finally said. "Like Paul. He was a damn good hacker before we snatched him, but after a month he was, well, you've seen him in action. It's like he leveled up. And I've seen the same sort of thing in several others, though I didn't really connect it all until now." He gave a self-conscious shrug. "Myself included. My instincts have always been good, but they got a *lot* better after I was recruited."

I let out a low whistle. "Not only does Farouche have a way to find talented people, but he *amplifies* their talent."

"Kara! Bryce!" Paul shouted from inside. "Come quick!"

Bryce and I hurried in and down the hall to my so-called office where Paul sat in front of his new laptop.

"What is it, Paul?" I asked.

"Is this him? Is this Idris?" he asked, practically bursting with excitement as he spun the chair to face us.

I hurried forward to peer at the grainy image on the screen. "Shit! Yes! Where is he? When was that?"

"Private jet at a small airport not far from Amarillo," Paul informed me proudly. "Morning of the day before yesterday. He came off the plane with—" He clicked, changed to an image of a sturdy red-haired woman.

"I've seen her before," I said, but the memory of where and when eluded me like a handful of smoke.

"Gina Hallsworth of Katashi's organization," Paul supplied after a few clicks in another window. "I ran searches for known associates of Katashi and have reference pics for most of those now."

That was all I needed to trigger the recall. "She's a summoner," I announced. I'd seen her a few times when I spent my miserable time at Katashi's.

Paul clicked again. "Bryce, this is who was at his elbow."

Bryce's arm brushed mine as he moved in closer. "Shit. Nigel Fox."

"One of Farouche's people?" I asked.

He grimaced. "A top man. Worked out of Austin. If he's babysitting Idris, Farouche is serious."

I let out some inventive curses. "Great. Farouche and Katashi's people are definitely working hand in hand," I muttered. "Muscle *and* summoners." And Farouche's controlling influence, I realized with dismay. Idris was brilliant and resourceful and his captors would want to be absolutely certain he was under control. If Farouche hadn't already put the fear-whammy on him, he'd surely do so at the first opportunity. *So why did he need Idris's sister and mother as insurance?* Farouche's influence was more than powerful enough to keep Idris under control.

Realization dawned an instant later. It was likely the same reason Rhyzkahl couldn't simply manipulate Idris to be compliant. That sort of mental adjustment interfered with summoning skills, and the same might very well hold true for Farouche's fear crap. Therefore, they needed backup leverage, i.e. his family. Damn it.

"Got anything else?" I asked.

"There were five, including Idris," Paul said. "Isumo Katashi right here."

"Shit."

"And then this guy," he said. "Last off the plane."

I peered at the distant image of the man, shook my head. "No clue." His hair was pulled back in a ponytail and he wore a poet type shirt, but I couldn't tell much else about him.

Bryce shifted beside me. "Mystery Man Twenty-two."

I gave him a baffled look.

"Some of Farouche's visitors remained anonymous," he said with a shrug. "We had nicknames to keep them straight." He leaned closer to the screen. "No doubt on that one. He's been in and out for years."

"I know the jet," Paul told us. "Belongs to Farouche. And they loaded into cars that belong to Farouche. No GPS though. They're being careful." He clicked back to one of his screens displaying incomprehensible streams of numbers and text. "The plane is back in Louisiana, and I'm keeping an eye on the flight plans for it and Farouche's other jets." He glanced back at me. "That's all I have for now."

"Don't suppose you found anything on that ring I drew?" I asked hopefully.

"Um." He flushed, grimaced. "No." He opened his mouth to speak, then closed it, grimace deepening. I gave Bryce a baffled look in the hopes he could translate.

Bryce chuckled under his breath. "What he's not saying is that the drawing sucks and there's not much he can do with it."

Paul smiled sheepishly. "Sorry, but yeah. That's pretty much it."

I gave him a reassuring smile. "It's cool. My talent sure as hell ain't art." I knew my crappy drawing had been a long shot, so I couldn't be *too* disappointed. "Awesome job with the pics, Paul," I added, totally impressed that he'd found the video. "Keep on it and let me know what you come up with." Like I needed to tell him to keep on it. He was already typing away, totally absorbed and probably no longer aware we were even in the room.

Bryce headed off to shower while I went out back to tell Mzatal what Paul had found. It didn't look to me as if Mzatal had moved since I last saw him, but the half-full glass of tunjen told me Jekki diligently tended to his needs.

I felt him acknowledge my presence, and a few seconds later his eyes opened. I quickly filled him in on the sighting.

"It's two days old, which means they could be anywhere by now," I said with a wince. "But it's more than we had before."

"The information is very useful," he assured me. "Knowing his location within the last few days will allow me to narrow my searches through the flows, much as if tracking footprints."

With a quick parting kiss, I left him to his work, and as I returned to the house I mulled over the various new information we'd gleaned over the past few days. Farouche was no saint, Katashi was busy on Earth, and now, thanks to Paul, we had confirmation of Idris's cryptic StarFire clue and knew for certain the two were working together.

I stopped dead. Facts shuffled and re-ordered. How could I have missed this possibility? If Farouche was involved in holding Idris, surely he had a hand in related matters as well.

I broke into a run, burst through the back door and raced down the hall to the living room. "Bryce!" I called out as I shuffled through folders on the coffee table, found the one I needed. "Bryce!"

He emerged from the bathroom holding a towel around his waist with one hand and a toilet plunger in the other. "Kara?" Shaving cream covered half his face, but he had a look in his eye that said he was ready to take down whatever threatened me. With a towel and a toilet plunger, apparently. "What's wrong?"

I winced. "Sorry. There's something I need you to look

at, but it can wait a few minutes," I said. "Can you meet me in the kitchen when you're finished?"

"No problem. Two minutes," he said and ducked back into the bathroom.

I flipped through the case file folder and chose photos. Less than two minutes later Bryce came in, fully dressed and freshly shaved, with a piece of toilet paper stuck to a nick on his jaw, probably caused by my bellow.

"Reporting as ordered," he said with a smile. "What's up?"

"I want to see if you recognize any of these people." I laid out a half dozen photos on the table.

He peered carefully at them, took his time with each one before moving to the next, then went through them all again.

"Only one of them," he finally said. "This one." He picked up a photo of a smiling woman in her late forties standing on a beach with the waves behind, and holding up a whole sand dollar. Laugh lines crinkled around hazel eyes set in an attractive face. Light brown hair with blond highlights waved to her shoulders.

It was the pic I'd hoped he would choose. "How do you know her?" I tried hard to keep my voice neutral, but Bryce was a sharp cookie and didn't miss the tension and excitement that leaked through.

"She's a detainee of Farouche's."

"Still? When did you last see her?"

"She was at the plantation on the morning of the day I was shot." His eyes met mine. "Who is she to you?"

Adrenaline surged through me as a floodgate of possibilities opened. "This is Idris's adoptive mother. We think she's being held as a hostage to assure his good behavior."

His expression went from curious to grim.

I pulled the wedding photo of Idris's sister from the folder, passed it over to him. "What about this one? Was she at the plantation too?"

After a brief look, he nodded. "Yep. Until about a week ago."

My pulse quickened. "Tell me everything you know about what happened to her."

Bryce dropped both photos back to the table. "I wasn't assigned so I don't know a whole lot, but Sonny was their handler after they arrived," he said. "They were brought in from out of state at the same time, but kept separately. Neither knew the other was there." He tapped Amber's photo. "I never talked to her. Jerry left with her about a week ago. He came back. She didn't. I don't know anything more."

"Jerry?"

"Yeah. Jerry Steiner. Like me." He shook his head, distaste curling his lip. "No, not like me. He never loses any sleep over the job. Gets off on it." He sighed out a breath. "She's dead?"

"Yeah, she is," I said grimly. I touched the photo of her smiling and beautiful on her wedding day, then tugged out a crime scene photo of the young woman—naked and displayed with the sigils all over her torso and legs.

His expression went flat and cold. "Raped?"

I nodded.

"Jerry would do that," he said tightly. He continued to examine the photo. "But the cuts? Jerry didn't do that. Not that he *wouldn't*, but those cuts are too careful. Controlled."

"That's specialty work with a big dose of the arcane," I told him. "But he probably brought her to whoever did it."

"What was her name?"

"Amber Palatino Gavin," I told him. "I would dearly love to nail her murderer to the wall, but right now I want to get Idris's mom to safety even more."

Bryce's expression remained dark, but I caught the flicker in his eyes. He wasn't Amber's killer, but twenty-seven other ghosts haunted him.

"The mom," he said after a moment. "She was a nice lady. And being kept as a five-star captive."

That much was a relief at least. "I can't imagine Idris's mom *not* being nice," I said. "You know Farouche. Do you think he'd move her?"

He folded his arms, considered. "It's not a black and white answer, unfortunately," he finally said. "If he thinks she's compromised in any way at the plantation, then yes, he'd move her. But he feels pretty invulnerable there. If I was to venture a guess, I'd say that she'll be there until needed elsewhere."

I carefully gathered up all the photos and printouts and tucked them back into the folder, then pulled out a photo of Idris, smiling at his high school graduation with his mortarboard precariously balanced atop his unruly mop of curly blond hair. "This is Idris around two years ago. He's had to grow up fast."

"Poor kid. He's in a bad spot."

I let out a soft sigh. "I'm not sure yet, but I think he may be my cousin."

Bryce stared at me for a moment then gave a sharp nod. "Kara, we'll get him back."

His voice held such conviction that I found myself wondering about his own family. What connections had he been forced to sever when he entered Farouche's inner circle? Before I could ask, I felt Mzatal's touch, and when the back door squeaked I looked up. "You got all that, Boss?"

Mzatal strode into the kitchen, his stance taut like a cat ready to spring. "Some, and the remainder now." His eyes locked on Bryce. "Where is Angela Palatino?"

Bryce stood firm though I wouldn't have blamed him one bit if he'd retreated a step. "On the Farouche plantation. About seventy miles from here."

"I will go for her," Mzatal stated. "I require transportation."

"You can't just *go* for her!" I blurted out.

He turned his gaze on me, darkly intense and questioning.

"She's a hostage," I explained, fully aware that he wouldn't know the Earth/human dynamics. "That means they'll kill her before you get to her."

"She's right," Bryce said. "I know the layout and operations of everything on the plantation." He lifted his chin, impressing the hell out of me that he could do so in the face of Mzatal's intensity. "Here's the deal. If I was still Farouche's man, as soon as I got wind that you were on or near the property, I'd hold a gun to the woman's head, get on the PA and tell you to retreat or I put a bullet in her skull." He shifted his weight and looked away, and I knew it was shame in the knowledge he'd have done exactly that. "Not to mention there'll be plenty of armed men to take shots at you."

"The projectiles are of little concern when I am prepared," Mzatal stated. He paused and his aura flared like heat from an oven. "Yet, the other perspective is valid." Anger born of frustration dropped his voice to quiet menace.

"We need a solid plan, Boss," I said gently. "We'll come up with a way to get her out of there."

Mzatal gave a stiff nod, turned and swept out of the house. I watched him go, extended to him, and felt his answering touch. Inaction killed him. I knew that feeling all too well.

"Holy Christ, I'm glad I'm not his enemy," Bryce breathed.

I snorted. "No shit."

Chapter 30

Bryce and I headed into the living room. He sank into the chair, face once again in its practiced tough-guy mask, while I flopped onto the sofa, and practiced looking worn out. I found it surprisingly easy to do so. Maybe because I'd been going hard all day on only four hours of sleep?

I snorted. *Nah. Too easy. That can't* possibly *be it!*

My phone rang, and apparently Santa thought I'd been a good girl this year because my phone was in my pocket instead of a million miles away, like in the kitchen or on the coffee table. I pulled it out and smiled at the caller ID. "Hi, Aunt Tessa. You get in to Aspen all right?"

"Hello, sweetling," Tessa said, voice perky and light. "We had a little confusion with the rental, but finally got it all straightened out. We only made it to the ski lodge a few minutes ago. The air up here is *amazing!*"

A few more knots of tension unwound. "That's good to hear. What lodge are you staying at?"

"Snowy Snake Ski Lodge. Ten thousand feet elevation!" She laughed. "I was ready to take a nap after climbing the stairs. The rooms are absolutely lovely. Everything going all right down there with you?"

The lilt of her happy chatter wound around me like a hug. "Everything's going great," I lied. No way was I going to put the slightest dent in her good mood, and up in the mountains was a nice, safe place for her. "Careful with the altitude. Drink lots of water and take naps."

"I'm chugging a bottle down right now. Oh, wait, I'm getting the signal that we're heading to dinner soon. I'll call you back as soon as I'm not altitude-fuddled."

I smiled. "Do that. And don't let the bears eat you."

"I'll eat them first."

Laughing, I made my goodbyes and hung up. Another member of my posse safe and sound. I liked that. Yet my thoughts now circled around the issue of Idris's mother and how to get *her* to safety. As much as I wanted to see Mzatal storm Farouche's plantation/compound and reduce it to smoking rubble, it simply wasn't a feasible plan. And the same went for any other infiltration or attack. First sign of trouble, and a gun would go to Angela Palatino's head.

Which meant that first we had to get her to safety, and *then* Mzatal could wring Idris's location from Farouche's scummy mind.

Zack could do it, the thought whispered. While on Earth, Eilahn and Steeev had limited ability to travel, or teleport, or whatever the hell the demons called it, and certainly couldn't do so with a human in tow, but Zack was demahnk and had none of those disadvantages. However, the warehouse incident along with our "discussion" regarding his loyalty had made it painfully clear that, for reasons I had yet to fathom, his demonic assistance was by no means a sure thing. I figured it was a heads-or-tails chance he'd agree to help, but if I never asked, I wouldn't even have those odds. I yawned and glanced at the clock on the wall. Six p.m. Zack would be home soon. I'd pounce on him then.

The second hand ticked its way around the clock face. Home. That meant something. I was sure of it. I dragged my gaze away from the hypnotic movement of the second hand, sat up and rolled my neck on my shoulders. The feline curled at the end of the sofa lifted her head and growled at me, low and throbbing and laden with menace.

I turned a feral smile on the creature as she stood, bristling. Her growl deepened, and she swiped bared claws toward me—

"Kara! Watch out!" Bryce scooped the cat up and away from me, and I jerked, blinked. "Did she get you?" His concerned gaze tracked over me in a search for claw marks as he expertly cradled her.

Kara? Oh, right. Of course I was Kara. "No, I'm good," I said, though I checked my arm for blood just to be sure. "Thanks for the save, though."

Fuzzykins abruptly ceased her growl, shifted to bump

her head against Bryce's chin. He gave a low chuckle and
scratched behind her ears. "You silly girl," he murmured,
then glanced to me. "Damn, she really does hate you. I
thought she was about to rip your face off." He shook his
head, shifted the cat in his arms then sat again and settled her on his lap. "She seems okay now though," he
said, regarding Fuzzykins with a puzzled frown, then he
rolled his eyes as she looked in my direction and gave a
bored hiss before snuggling into his lap with a loud purr.
"Or not."

I stuck my tongue out at Fuzzykins. Weird cat. I couldn't
think of anything I'd done to make her go off on me like
that. "So, wow, Paul's pretty amazing," I said, shifting to a
more comfortable subject. "Getting that airport vid was a
huge break for us."

Bryce smiled as he stroked the cat. "He's a good kid. Got
through to *me*." His smile faded, and he blew out his breath.
"I was the one who kidnapped him in Albuquerque. Sonny
and me."

I angled my head. "How'd you go from kidnapper to taking such good care of him?"

"I got assigned to him twenty-four/seven when we first
brought him in," Bryce said, then chuckled softly. "He grew
on me. Farouche saw we had a good rapport, and, since he
wanted to keep Paul happy and productive, he put me on as
his permanent bodyguard and advocate."

I smiled. "You two really care for each other. I mean, in
a bromance sort of way."

"Yeah. I think we're family," he replied with no trace of
embarrassment.

"Does anyone miss him back home?"

He winced, then shook his head. "No."

"What's the deal there?" *Please please*, I thought almost
desperately, *please don't tell me you killed them.*

"Paul's mom died when he was ten," Bryce began, then
his face hardened. "His dad, a cop, beat the shit out of him
about a year and a half ago. Almost killed him." Cold anger
rose in his eyes. "No siblings. Any other family is distant
with no contact or interest. He was on his own in a little
basement apartment when we took him."

"Damn," I breathed. "Paul told me his dad beat him up,

but that's all." I scowled. "Why? Paul seems like such a quiet guy."

He glanced back over his shoulder toward the hallway, spoke quietly. "His dad found out Paul was gay. Lost it. I mean, totally fucking nuts lost it. Whaled on him for a while, left him for an hour or two then went back for more."

My right hand tightened into a fist. "Where's his dad now?"

"He got killed," Bryce said after the barest of hesitations. "I drove Paul to the funeral about eight months ago."

I heard the edge to his tone. "Got killed *how*?" I asked, attention fully on him.

Bryce rubbed his eyes, sighed. "A hit. Farouche ordered it. Set up to look like an arrestee recently released from prison did it."

"You do it?"

"No." He jerked his eyes to mine, denial firm within them. "No," he repeated. "Jerry Steiner made that hit. Same guy who took Idris's sister to get murdered. Paul doesn't know, and I intend to keep it that way."

"Yeah." I gave a slow nod. "I can understand that." Hard to believe I almost sort of barely agreed in a mildly sociopathic way with Farouche on this particular issue. "He won't hear it from me."

"I'll be honest," Bryce said. "I'd have pulled the trigger on the motherfucker and not lost sleep." He let out a low snort. "That's one of the reasons the hit wasn't assigned to me. It would've been personal, and Farouche doesn't operate like that." He picked up the legal pad that had his security camera system proposal on it. "In retrospect, I'm glad I wasn't the trigger man."

"Keeps it a lot cleaner between you two." I gave him a sympathetic wince. "As clean as it can be given the situation."

The buzz of the gate alarm preceded the telltale crunch of gravel beneath tires. I shoved up from the sofa and tweaked the curtain aside to peer out. Zack's Impala.

"I need to talk to Zack for a few," I told Bryce and received a nod of acknowledgment. I headed out front and waited at the bottom of the steps as Zack parked.

He climbed out of the vehicle, keys and laptop case in hand, and quirked a smile at me. "Welcoming committee?"

"Yeah, it's a new Kara's Kompound perk," I said. "Oh, and everyone gets a pony too."

"I like it," he replied with a chuckle. "Except for the part about who has to clean up after the ponies."

I wrinkled my nose. "Okay, maybe no ponies. Anyway, you got a sec? I need to talk to you."

"I have a ton of case files to go through tonight, but I always have time for you," he said with a broad smile. "What's up?"

"The super ultra mega big news is that we know Farouche is holding Angela Palatino—Idris's mom—at his plantation." Excitement flickered, but I did my best to hold it in check.

He let out a low whistle. "That's definitely super ultra mega," he agreed.

"Right. If we can get her to safety, it takes away much of the Mraztur's hold over Idris." I put a hand on his arm. "I was hoping you could give us some *special* help."

Zack went still, tilted his head. "What sort of special help?"

"Special help as in going and getting her out." I gave him a hopeful smile. "Demahnk help."

In an instant his face slipped from open and relaxed to grim and haunted. "Kara, I can't."

My smile melted, and I slumped. Even though I'd known his cooperation wasn't a sure thing, the pang of disappointment remained sharp. "I don't understand."

He shook his head. "I know you don't. I'm sorry."

"Can you at least try to explain it to me?" I asked, baffled.

He looked away and remained silent.

My confusion increased. He'd helped us in so many ways before. Even though Zack had initially balked at bringing Mzatal to the warehouse, in the end he *had* done so. Why was this so different? "Zack, all you have to do is go get her and bring her back," I said. "What am I missing?"

"I can't," he repeated and met my eyes again. "It's complicated."

I gripped my head, certain it might explode from frustration. "Would you *please* stop doing that?" I snapped, far more harshly than I'd intended. Releasing my head, I smoothed down my hair, tried again. "Please stop evading me. Please stop giving give me lame shit like 'It's complicated.' I'm not a child, so could you grant me some basic courtesy and at least help me try to understand?"

I expected him to look defensive or chagrined, but instead his entire posture slumped into apparent weary sadness. "Even that crosses the line."

Time to regroup my thoughts. "All right, then let's take a step back," I proposed. "Tell me what the *line* is."

He regarded me for a second, then swept past me to his car. At first I thought he was walking away from the discussion, but instead he yanked the driver door open and dumped his laptop case onto the seat. He closed the door with a little more force than necessary, though his demeanor made me think it was more general frustration than anger at me. He jerked his head toward the back of the house, then briskly strode off.

I followed, though at a more ordinary pace. No way could I match that long-legged stride without running. As I rounded the corner of the house, I saw him heading toward the pond trail. Mzatal sat motionless on the mininexus as I passed, and I sensed him deeply involved in the flows. Sparrows twittered their business in the trees as though all was right with the world, and a crow announced its presence with a raucous triple caw. When I reached the pond a ripple of potency touched me, like a breeze through an open window. On the far side of the water, Zack crouched beside the valve and worked his hands over it in unfamiliar patterns. I felt shifts in the potency, but othersight revealed nothing more than transparent shimmers in the air above the coruscating blues and greens that marked the valve itself.

Puzzled, I slowly made my way around the pond. "What are you doing?" I asked quietly.

"Pulling some potency before I collapse," he told me with a low sigh that I realized was born of exhaustion. After a moment he looked up. "I created this branch valve. It's one of thirty-three off the valve trunk in the north of Rhyzkahl's realm." A sad, nostalgic smile touched his mouth. "The first full system in place after the cataclysm."

Zack had to have been in a near-constant state of damage control since that catastrophic event centuries ago, I realized. And now he had the care of Szerain on top of that?

No wonder fatigue seemed to permeate his every cell—far beyond any sort of normal tiredness.

He continued to work his hands over the valve. I sat cross-legged beside him, reminded of an orchestra conductor as I watched him move. After a time he brought his hands together, and the rippling potency breeze died away, as though he had closed the window.

He sighed softly, lifted his eyes to mine. "You asked what the line is," he said. "It's those ancient agreements, oaths, and decrees that frustrate the hell out of you."

Decrees. That implied an enforcer. I filed that away. "That's an understatement," I said with a wry smile. "I'd like to move beyond that."

He shifted from the crouch to a sit with one knee up. "You're right." He rested his forearm on his knee as he regarded me. "You're not a child. Not anymore. You've grown so much, through betrayal as well as love."

"I'm not the same person I was a year ago, that's for sure." My throat tightened. "Sometimes I'm not sure who I am anymore." I shook my head, scowled. "And not because of Rhyzkahl's stupid *rakkuhr* virus either."

Zack plucked a long and heavy-headed piece of grass and rolled the stem between his fingers. "No. And I know it's hard to find your footing." He let out a soft snort. "My being a confusing pain in your ass doesn't help."

"You're not." I did my best to smile, but I had a feeling it ended up more like a rictus of pain. "I don't understand what the rules are, so I feel like I'm trying to find the walls of the room with all the lights off, and I keep bumping into furniture and knocking shit over."

A dragonfly zipped and hovered around Zack's head like an iridescent green helicopter. Off to my right a frog croaked and entered the water with a *plop*. Further into the woods a squirrel chattered its displeasure at some other creature.

"I said earlier that any explanation crosses the line," Zack said quietly.

My mouth drew down into a scowl. "Right, so my dark room has no light switch."

To my surprise he shook his head. "The switch is there. But I keep moving it." He dropped the piece of grass and lifted his hand. The dragonfly alighted on his index finger as though he'd called it to him. "I've spent most of my existence walking that line and others, sticking my toes over." His eyes remained on the elegant insect. "In law enforcement terms, I'd have a rap sheet full of misdemeanors, a fistful of felonies, and be wanted by Interpol." He gave a light shrug. "I'm a troublemaker."

"No wonder I like you." This time a faint smile curved my lips. "How about we back up one more step. Can you explain why there's a line at all?"

"Explaining that would be like running across the line and shooting the bird at the ones who drew the line." He raised his dragonfly-free hand with middle finger extended and others folded to clarify that he didn't mean a sparrow. "I can't go there. Not now." He paused. "Not yet."

"Ones? Not Rhyzkahl?"

"No, not Rhyzkahl. The Demahnk Council," he paused, looked away. "And others." The last two words came out as a near breathless whisper.

My frustration degraded to something closer to despair. I could barely comprehend the oaths he had with Rhyzkahl. How was I supposed to understand more beyond that, of the Council and of others he wouldn't even name? "I don't know what to do, Zack," I said, brow furrowing. "Should I stop asking you for help?"

The dragonfly whirred away as Zack snapped his head toward me, gaze sharp. "No!" He drew in a breath. "No," he repeated a bit more calmly. "Let me see how I can put this." He closed his eyes, and I imagined him sifting through words to find the least incriminating ones. "It is so very complex. In the convoluted insanity of the agreements and decrees, some interventions—such as using the demahnk ability to travel—carry consequences in certain Earth situations." True distress creased his forehead. "I know a woman's life is at stake right now, but I *must* weigh the consequences against the benefits."

"What kind of consequences do you mean?" I asked, determined to get *some* sort of useful info. "Are we talking volcanoes and locusts? Or, you get in trouble and get put in time out?"

"Volcanoes and locusts if I went too far," he said, expression grave. "Extensive consequences. But every transgression carries personal consequences. Very personal." He retrieved the dropped stem of grass. "If I extract Angela Palatino, we win the battle, but I cripple myself for the greater war." He gripped his temples between his thumb and fingers, shook his head. "Kara, this is . . ."

I reached over, gently pulled his hand from his head, and wrapped my fingers around his. "I'm sorry," I said. "I'm sorry I'm stressing you out. I don't understand who has you boxed in like this, but I get that you are. That's more than I knew before, and it's enough for now." I peered at him, smiled. "So tell me how I can help *you*, other than not asking you to blip out and pick up my dry cleaning."

Relief eased his features. "You're doing it right now," he assured me, then tipped his head back "The other night you said that if a bond isn't mutually shared, symbiotic, then one party is a parasite." He cast the stem of grass away like a spear into the water, watched the ripples spread from it. "You're right," he continued. "The bond in question was never intended to be mutually beneficial. However the imbalance now is . . . intolerable."

I felt myself frown. "Whenever I mention breaking the ptarl bond to Mzatal or Szerain they kind of freak."

"Because it is inconceivable for them," he stated.

"It's inconceivable to them," I said, "but not to you. Why?"

He regarded me, eyes unveiled and ancient. "Any inferences that you make from that are yours, but I can't go there." He lifted his hand, middle finger extended, but I didn't take offense. This was his way to signal that the answer was too far over the line and into shooting-the-bird territory. "And in all fairness," he added, "it's almost inconceivable to me."

I mulled over what little I'd learned so far. Okay, so the bond between a lord and his demahnk ptarl was never intended to be mutually beneficial, but the demahnk clearly weren't at the beck and call of the lords. So what was the deal? "The demahnk initiated the bonds with the lords, not vice versa," I said after a moment of thought.

Zack offered no verbal or physical cues of affirmation or denial, and that on its own spoke volumes. "I don't know if I could do it, even if it is . . ." He trailed off, his voice thick with emotion.

"Even if it's right?" I asked. I shuffled the bits and pieces of clues into what I hoped was a logical order. "I guess you'd have to weigh the long-term effects of doing it," I assumed he meant breaking the bond with Rhyzkahl, "against the long-term effects of letting the parasite continue to feed."

"Plus the short-term effects, and medium-term effects. And if it is indeed 'right.'" He looked away, exhaled. "Throw on top of that a sincere desire to protect and cultivate the parasite, and it gets more twisted."

No kidding, I thought as I filed information away. Since Zack seemed to have more freedom saying parasite rather than Rhyzkahl, I stuck with the metaphor. "Parasites are funny things," I said conversationally. "They can be beneficial to their hosts, but the kicker is that it's only because it's beneficial for the parasite." I stood, chucked a stick into the water. "And sometimes there comes a point when it has no further need of its host." I slid a glance to him. "Then again, most parasites aren't with hosts who have friends who will stand right by them and pick them up when needed."

"Very, very true." He fought for a smile, but his eyes held a fear I'd never seen in him before. His throat bobbed in a noisy swallow. "I wonder what happens to the host when isolated from both the parasite and the other hosts?"

Tidbits of information filtered through his words. Other hosts. He'd expanded beyond himself. The other demahnk? "The other hosts would still be prisoners of their parasites," I said, then crouched before him. "The free host would be with others who are free."

He squeezed his eyes shut as though blocking physical sight would block a concept too traumatic to consider. "Not others of its own kind." He opened his eyes and repeated in a voice as empty as the void, "Not others of its own kind."

An ache of sympathy tightened my chest. How well would I be able to face a choice that meant isolation from all humans as one of its consequences? There was a reason why solitary confinement was a punishment. "I'm so sorry." I slipped my arm around him in a cradling hug. He leaned into me as though craving any form of comfort he could get.

"I'm so tired, Kara," he said. "So tired. I don't know if I

answered why I can't go get Angela." He paused. "No. That's not true. I can, but I won't."

"It was enough," I reassured him. "We'll find another way." And we would. Somehow. What good would it do to save Idris if we lost Zack?

He remained still and quiet for a moment. "Kara, this is the part where I'm supposed to strip from you everything that you've inferred, surmised, or heard."

I took a moment to process that. *Zack can do mind manipulation*, I realized. I'd harbored some suspicions about that due to the nature of his work with Szerain, but the demahnk in general certainly didn't advertise that they possessed that particular ability.

Has he been reading me, all of us, all this time? I suddenly wondered, then dismissed the worry. I didn't want to open another can of worms after finally getting the lid on the first one.

More importantly, I knew that if he chose to, he could strip it all from me right now and I'd never know the difference. I hated—*hated*—that aspect of manipulation.

I shifted to look into his face. "You're supposed to strip it, but you're not going to, are you?" I gave a cheeky smile. "Maybe it's because you know that if you do, I'll keep on annoying the crap out of you by asking you to do shit you're not allowed to do." I pursed my lips, raised an eyebrow at him. "But I don't think that's the case. You don't want others reading it from me, but you also don't want to strip the information. And, being the self-proclaimed rebel and troublemaker that you are, you figure you can get away with leaving it, probably by shielding it."

He regarded me soberly, though a hint of humor danced in his eyes. *Finally.* "You're on to me."

"I'm a smart bitch."

He gave a sharp laugh, but didn't argue. "Does this mean you agree to succumb to shielding?"

"I do." My brow furrowed. "Shielding me doesn't change the fact that you leapt across the line and shot the bird. How's that going to work for you?"

"Probably about as well as boiling spaghetti in gasoline," he said with trace of a smile and a resigned shrug.

I waited for him to lay his hand on my head, gave him an

expectant look when he didn't. "Aren't you going to do the shielding now?"

"It's already done."

I blinked. *Innnnnteresting.* Faster than a lord and without touch. Zack was continuing to feed me subtle information without telling me a damn thing directly.

"Slick," I said with a smile, though my worry remained. "What if Rhyzkahl reads it from you?"

He shook his head. "The qaztahl cannot read the demahnk."

Even more *innnnnteresting.* "Is there anything else you need from me?"

"How about a big posse breakfast-for-dinner at Lake o' Butter complete with bad jokes, bad table manners, and a crappy waitress?" He managed a comical facial expression filled with equal measures of hope and doubt.

I grinned and rolled my eyes, relieved that we'd moved beyond the tension. "That would go over great, except for the fact that we'd be sitting ducks for Farouche. But, damn it, now I want pancakes." I considered the alternatives, smiled. "I bet Jekki could make some, and between you, me, Bryce, and Paul, we have the bad jokes and table manners covered."

"Kara's Kafé! Beats Lake o' Butter by a carbohydrate landslide." Zack scrambled to his feet and shuddered like a dog shedding water. In the space of a few seconds he seemed to cast off all of the heaviness of the last half hour and was back to cheerful, casual, relaxed Zack again.

Except now I knew it was an illusion. It wasn't all fake, but there was a shitload more below the surface.

"Don't you have files to work on?" I asked as we headed for the house.

He draped a companionable arm over my shoulders. "Some things are worth the price you have to pay."

"Pancakes," I said, though I doubted he meant either dinner or work. "Pancakes are *always* worth it."

"Damn straight, Kara."

Kara's Kafé opened that night, with all eight of us crowded into the kitchen and none of us minding, not even Mzatal. Good company and bad jokes. Jekki's hysterically failed attempts to be a crappy waitress. Pancakes, bacon, and syrup, then wine, conversation, laughter, and companionable fellowship into the night.

The Mraztur had their schemes of world domination, but they'd underestimated the ultra-sappy and mega-cheesy power of love, friendship, and family.

No two ways about it. My posse rocked.

Chapter 31

"More cofffeeeeee, Kara Gillian!" Jekki announced as he deftly topped off my mug.

It had turned into something of a game between us this morning, where he could only refill my mug when it got below half full, but if I drank it past the three-quarters mark then I apparently "scored." Moreover, it was cheating if I chugged it, and if he was ready with the coffee pot I had to allow him to refill it. I wasn't quite sure how he managed to score. Maybe he got a point every time I had to get up to pee? Either way, he seemed to be enjoying it tremendously.

I also didn't mind being overdosed with coffee this morning. Weird dreams had awakened me a number of times during the night. Not exactly nightmares, but somehow worse, since they continued to hang around in jumbled bits and snatches. Idris was in them. And Tessa. And Tessa's fruity tea. A swimming pool full of it. And the damn ring I'd glimpsed as Idris was sent to Earth, the ring I couldn't sketch for shit—though, in the dream, it was more of a ring-shaped dirigible that hovered over my house.

The bizarre images floated through my head while I nursed the latest cup of coffee. Every ounce of intuition I possessed told me the ring was a key clue, a link to the specific person who had received Idris on Earth, which would then—hopefully—lead to a location.

Right now, however, we had it narrowed down to "someone working for Katashi and/or Farouche." Yeah, that was useful.

I needed an artist. An artist who could draw it from my description. *Like a police sketch artist,* I thought, then immediately dismissed the idea. Dinky little Beaulac PD didn't have one of those. For that matter, New Orleans was probably the closest place with a trained police sketch artist, and I'd have a hard time explaining why I needed their services to find a damn ring.

What about Ryan? Beneath the overlay of Ryan was Szerain—the sculptor, painter, and consummate artist, as demonstrated by the hundreds of works of his I saw while in the demon realm, all brilliant and evocative. I had yet to see Ryan show any sort of artistic ability, but I'd also never seen him try.

Frowning, I lowered my mug. There were two problems with asking Ryan to do it: The first was that I had no idea if Szerain's talent was accessible to Ryan. Second, he'd have to read me to get what the ring looked like, and I wasn't even certain he *could* read me as Ryan. I only knew he had the ability to shift memories around. And, if he *could* actually read me, it would be disastrous if he happened to pick up the whole, "Oh, by the way, you're also an exiled demonic lord." Of course, if Ryan *could* read that info, Zack never would have allowed him to do the memory-shift thing after my encounter with Farouche, which meant that, either way, Ryan was out of the running.

Jekki gave a delighted burble as he refilled my mug, then a trill of unparalleled glee as I took a quick break to "unget" coffee. One point for Jekki.

On my return to the kitchen, I took my musings on a different tack. *What about Szerain?* Perhaps he could sketch the ring from my memory if he was unsubmerged enough? He'd surfaced on the confluence before, so logically, he'd do even better on the mini-nexus—as long as I kept well away from any touchy subjects relating to ptarls or his essence blade.

"Jekki, have you seen Ryan?" I asked as I dug in the kitchen junk drawer for a pencil.

"Climb and run and jump," he burbled with a flick of one hand toward the back of the house. *The obstacle course.*

I found a partially chewed pencil with a bit of eraser left, then slugged down the rest of my coffee, thanked the faas and headed out back. I saw Ryan by the wall at the end of the course; he was smeared with mud and his t-shirt dark with sweat, but to my surprise Mzatal was there with him.

The two stood face to face, obviously having *words* of some sort to judge by the expressions on both faces.

I stepped off the porch to approach them, and as I did so Mzatal turned abruptly and strode off down the path that led to the pond.

What the hell was that all about? I moved towards Ryan. "Hey, everything okay?"

His body jerked, and he took a stagger step back. He turned and blinked at me, disoriented, and I realized with a start it had been *Szerain* having angry words with Mzatal.

"*Ryan,*" I said with force, hoping the name would help him get his mental balance. "You okay?" Sure, I wanted to talk to Szerain, but in a more controlled manner.

He squeezed his eyes shut for a second, then lifted a hand to wipe sweat from his face as he opened them and focused on me. "A little dizzy, that's all." He gave me a rueful smile that was very much Ryan. "Coffee, no breakfast, and a hard workout. I'm smart like that."

I laughed in response, though I didn't feel very amused. "Go shower and get some food, and then I need to use you."

He gave me a comical leer. "Your place or mine?"

Snorting, I smacked him in the shoulder. "You have no *place*. I'm the mean landlady in this scenario."

"Ooh, roleplay!" He laughed as he ducked my punch. "Yes, mean. Very mean. Okay, fine, I'll go clean up then meet you in the kitchen." He turned and jogged to the house.

A fierce ache bloomed in my chest as I watched him go. I was going to lose this. Ryan wasn't real, and I was going to lose this awesome friendship, this person I could joke around with and tease. And there wasn't a damn thing I could do about it but keep the smile fixed on my face while one of my best friends slowly disappeared forever.

I followed him inside and heard the water already running in the bathroom. A search of the fridge for leftovers revealed half a pan of lasagna, some sort of chicken salad, guacamole, and half a cheesecake. After a moment's hesitation, I pulled out the lasagna. Probably more calorific than the cheesecake, but I wouldn't have a sugar-rush crash half an hour later.

By the time Ryan returned, dressed in khakis and a black

t-shirt, I had two plates of lasagna heated up and on the table. He gave me a smile and dropped into one of the chairs. "For a mean landlady, you're pretty nice."

"I'm lulling you into a false sense of security," I told him as I sat, and we both fell silent for a few minutes while we downed the perfect combo of carbs and protein and fat.

"Damn, Zack can cook," Ryan finally said, scraping up the last bits. "Okay, what do you need to use me for?"

I stuffed the last bite into my mouth and gulped it down. "Can you come out to the mini-nexus with me? I need to know if you can sense something."

He leaned back, patted his stomach. "Sure, now that you've bribed me with food."

On our way outside I paused to grab the pad and pencil as well as a tarp so we wouldn't get wet butts from sitting on the ground. I spread the tarp over the mini-nexus and sat, then gestured for Ryan to sit in front of me. He gave me a questioning look but complied.

"Now, close your eyes and chill," I said. "I'm trying something."

He closed his eyes, frowned. "Trying what?"

"Chill!" I ordered. "Sheesh."

He snorted, but subsided. I pygahed, and after a few minutes his posture shifted subtly. He drew a deep breath, though his eyes remained closed.

"Here," Szerain said in a small, near breathless voice.

Relief swept through me. "We need a better drawing of the ring I saw when Idris was sent to Earth." My mouth twitched. "I've been told that my art skills are, ah, less than optimal. Can you help? I have paper and a pencil."

A faint smile curved his lips. "Yes, I've seen your drawings." But then his throat worked in a swallow. "I do not know if I can help."

"Would you please try?" I asked. "I know this is a big request."

He remained silent for long enough that I decided it was a refusal. I started to thank him and get up when he finally spoke in a soft voice.

"Show me."

Settling back down, I took his hand and placed it against my cheek, aware that physical contact improved reading ability. I closed my eyes and called up the memory of the ring. *Dual stones, dark red and onyx, set in intricate gold filigree.*

"It is enough," he said after a moment, though he still didn't move.

Uncertain, I lowered his hand and set the paper and pencil in his lap. "Do you need me to do anything?"

"Help me to grip the pencil," he said, voice wavering. "Difficult. Specific blocks are in place to deter. Will attempt."

A pang sliced through me at the cruelty upon cruelty. His prison had been fitted with a goddamn anti-art filter. For what purpose other than to twist the knife? I curled his fingers around the pencil, then placed the tip on the paper. Silently willing support, I reached to take his other hand. Yet he remained inhumanly still, his hand ice cold in mine. I extended, touched the mini-nexus and waited silently. This *had* to work.

An odd ripple went through my body, and I realized he was using me as a conduit to draw potency from the mini-nexus. Controlling the flare of uncertainty, I allowed it, though I kept a damn close watch for any sign of him using that potency for anything other than the task at hand.

The pencil jerked across the pad in shaky, short movements. I remained quiet, pygahing for him and supporting. My eyes dropped to the pad. Little more than scribble marks on it.

Sweat dripped from his face to splop onto the paper. "New . . . page," he said, voice intense and strained. I quickly turned to a clean sheet, and he began to draw again.

We repeated this process half a dozen more times, each sketch gradually improving on the one before, all while his other hand maintained a hard, ice cold grip on mine. Finally he began to move more fluidly, and he created a sketch of the ring far *far* better than my horrible rendition.

"Again," he croaked. I flipped the page, though I took more care with this one to avoid smearing it. He drew a deep breath. "Pygah. Please," he whispered in desperate determination.

Focusing, I mentally traced the calming, centering sigil, consciously facilitated the flow of potency to him. He sketched the ring one more time, then dropped the pencil. "All . . . I can do."

I pulled the pad to me and let out a delighted laugh. "Hot damn! Thank you! That's ten billion times better than mine."

Szerain jerked, and his head lolled for an instant before Ryan straightened and blinked. I quickly closed the pad to hide the drawing of the ring.

"Did it work?" he asked with a puzzled frown, completely Ryan in voice and manner. "Felt like I went out for a while."

"You did," I said and gave a low laugh. "You fell asleep."

He flexed his hands, puzzlement flickering in his eyes. "I'm freezing. In Louisiana. And sweating. Weird." He shook them out. "What did you do?"

"Oh, I tried to call up your past lives," I said with a casual wave of my hand.

Ryan laughed. "You are such a liar." He started to say more, but his face abruptly took on an *I'm gonna barf* look. I let out a curse as he rolled from cross-legged to hands and knees, and I shifted away barely in time to avoid the splatter of lasagna and who knew what else.

"Shit, Ryan." I moved to his side—avoiding the barf—as he subsided into dry heaves. I rubbed his back as he barfed again, though it was little more than bile at this point.

After about a minute he shakily wiped his mouth with the back of his hand, then grimaced and scrubbed the hand on the tarp before shifting away from the splatters to sit again. "Well," he croaked, "I'm not a fan of whatever you did."

"Sorry." I winced. "It was, um, an aversion, but it wasn't supposed to do that."

A streak of blue caught my eye, and a heartbeat later Jekki zipped up to Ryan with a tumbler of tunjen in his hand.

"You're the best, Jekki," I said fervently. "Drink that, Ryan. It'll help."

He took the tumbler and gave the contents a dubious sniff. "What is it? And yes, before you give me a smartass answer, I know it's fruit juice." He gave me a crooked grin. "Something exotic?"

"It's a demon realm version of the ultimate sports drink," I told him.

He took a careful sip, blinked. "That's good." He quickly drained the glass.

"Told you." I smiled, relieved to see his color return. "Better?"

"I feel fine now," he said, getting to his feet. "But you get to hose down the tarp."

"Only fair," I admitted. "It was my fault, after all."

"Glad my puke could be of service," he said, then gave me a weak grin and returned inside.

After I hosed down the tarp and set it out to dry, I took the sketch pad, went in search of Paul, and found him dozing on the couch with his tablet on his chest. Nearby, Bryce sat in the comfy chair and fervently vaporized aliens with the sound muted.

Paul looked so damn adorable it seemed a crime to wake him. "Hey, Bryce?" I said quietly. "You think Paul will be awake soon?"

Bryce paused the game. "Only to stumble to his futon." At my questioning look, he continued, "He keeps weird hours. Usually sleeps from about five or six in the morning until afternoon. He says that's what feels normal to him, and makes it easy for him to connect with his contacts on the other side of the world."

I controlled my disappointment with effort. A few more hours wouldn't make a difference, right?

Bryce saw right through it, and his eyes dropped to the pad. "If you have something for him, he'd want you to wake him up."

Well, Bryce knew him better than anyone, and I didn't need any more encouragement. "Hey, Paul?" I touched him on the shoulder.

He startled enough to send a wisp of guilt through me, then gave me a sleepy smile and stretched like a waking kitten. "Hey, Kara. You need the couch?"

Somehow I managed to control the *D'awwwwww, you're so darn cute* sappy smile. "No, but I do have something for the Idris hunt," I said. "Sorry to wake you, but Bryce said you'd want to see it."

Paul pushed himself up to sit, curiosity winning out over a desire for more sleep. "Yeah? Whatcha got?"

I opened the pad up to the final drawing of the ring, carefully tore out the page and handed it to him. "What about this? Can you do something with this?"

He set his tablet aside and took the sheet, eyes widening in surprise at the quality of the drawing. "Wow. I can totally work with this." He looked up at me, incredulous. "You did this?"

I laughed. "Are you kidding? No, someone else did, but it's best not to ask too many questions about that."

"That's cool," he said with a grin. "I'm used to not asking questions." He stood and started toward the office with page and tablet in hand. "I'll see what I can come up with."

"You're wonderful," I said fervently, then flopped down in the place he'd vacated. Jekki whooshed in and put a plate of mini-pancakes and bacon on the coffee table.

Bryce thanked him and tossed the second controller to me. "Bet you a dollar Paul will have something in ten minutes."

I took the controller, raised an eyebrow at him. "I'll take that bet. No one's that good."

Bryce opened his mouth for a comeback, but Jekki beat him too it. "No doubting the Paul-dude!" he exclaimed then zoomed back to the kitchen.

Bryce and I burst out laughing. He lifted his controller. "You heard Jekki. We only have ten minutes. Let's do this thing."

And we did. I sucked at video games in general, but even with my crappy skills, I still found something deeply satisfying in a recreation where I knew exactly who my enemies were and could then blast them into messy bits.

"Hey, Kara?" Paul shouted from the office a little later.

"What?" I hollered back, eyes still glued to the screen. These aliens weren't going to kill themselves.

"I think I have something on the ring!"

Bryce laughed and put out his hand. "Pay up!"

I paused the game, then gave a mock-scowl and made a show of looking at my watch. "Damn. That took him a whole six minutes," I muttered. "Freakin' geniuses."

"Never doubt the Paul-dude," Bryce said with a sage nod.

My brain and experience told me there was no way Paul had found anything of significance so quickly, but I unfolded my legs, stood, and proceeded to the office. Bryce followed and leaned against the doorframe.

"Show me," I said.

"I don't know if it's the same one," Paul said as he beckoned me over to where he sat at the desk, laptop with mouse in front of him, and my old monitor to the side displaying a screen full of rapidly changing numbers. "But it looks pretty close to the drawing."

Every possible doubt I had of his skill evaporated as I peered at the picture on his laptop screen. A faded color close-up photo of a woman in her early thirties or so seated at a picnic table and flanked by a smiling boy and girl about five or six years old. Twins perhaps? All appeared to be of middle-Eastern descent and each held up a paper cup as though for a toast. The trunk of a humongous redwood tree dominated the background. But the detail that drew my eye was the woman's right hand and the ring on her middle finger, clearly visible against the white of the cup.

"That sure looks like it," I murmured. I took in the features of the unusual ring and allowed myself a mental sigh of disappointment that we didn't instantly have our guy. The hand I'd seen had definitely been a man's. "Can you zoom in?" Paul clicked the mouse a few times, and the ring obligingly grew larger, though fuzzy.

"It's a scan of an older photo, which is why it's pixilated," he explained. "It was scanned about a decade ago, but I think the photo itself is about forty years old judging by the clothing style."

"I can see the ring well enough," I said. "Zoom back out, please?" He obliged. I tried to see if anyone in the picture looked familiar, but came up empty.

"It's either the same ring or one exactly like it," I said.

"This is the only image I felt," he told me, "which means that if there are more like it, it's unlikely there are pictures of them anywhere online."

I blinked. "That you *felt?*"

Paul ducked his head and hunched his shoulders. "Um, yeah." He fidgeted. "I didn't mean to say that."

"Mzatal told me you use the computers as a way to connect to the Earth flows." I gave him a reassuring smile. "Is that what you mean?"

His face brightened. "Yeah. I didn't know that's what it was until I met Lord Mzatal. I, um, don't usually talk about it." He glanced beyond me to Bryce as though for reassurance, then brought his gaze back to me.

"Trust me, this is a safe place for talking about weird shit," I said with a laugh. "Is that how you found an obscure photo of the ring so quickly?"

"Pretty much." Then he rolled his eyes. "If I'd used conventional methods alone it would have taken *ages*, or I might not have found it at all."

"And it's exactly what I was looking for." I lifted my chin toward the screen. "However, it wasn't on a female hand when I saw it. Can you find out who this woman is?"

Paul smiled. "Way ahead of you. It was easy to link to the photo. I'll show you the name. Better than me trying to pronounce it." He changed screens so I could read it for myself.

I straightened. "I know that name. She's a *summoner*." Rasha Hassan Jalal al-Khouri. This was the woman who'd summoned Jekki's partner, Faruk, during the Christmas celebration while I was in the demon realm. According to Mzatal, it was the first time she'd summoned in almost a decade. I looked back toward the door. "Jekki!"

Bryce smiled at Paul. "Good job, kid."

A streak of blue flashed past Bryce's legs. "Kara Gillian!"

I grinned at the demon's exuberance. "Jekki, we have a lead. Can you please go tell Mzatal I need him here?"

"Kri! Kri! Kri!" He spun and zipped out of the room, down the hall and out the back door like a little blue whirlwind.

Paul's face held a pleased smile. "It's probably the right ring then?"

"It's a really good possibility," I said, more than a little pleased myself. "You rock. I don't suppose you can get a current address on her?"

He let out a dismissive snort. "Seriously? Give me something *hard* to do." His screen shifted to something full of commands and code and who the hell knew what else, but Paul seemed utterly at home with it. His fingers flew across the keyboard, and about ten seconds later the printer hummed and spat out a sheet.

"That's her current address, along with her vital statistics," he informed us with a tilt of his head toward the printer. "Born in Egypt in 1934. Married in 1952 to a man named Sapar, who died October 31, 1956 in the Suez Crisis. She and her two children, twins born in 1955, emigrated to the U.S. in 1958. Has four grandchildren and two great grandchildren now as well." He changed screens again. "And here are some more recent pics." He leaned back to allow us to see better.

Several photos showed the same woman, looking quite hale in her sixties and perhaps seventies, but I didn't recognize anyone else in any of the pics.

I plucked the sheet from the printer, skimmed the info and the address. "Austin! Hot fucking damn."

Bryce gave me a questioning look.

"The phone call I got from Idris was made northwest of Austin on a phone stolen there," I explained. "Plus, Mzatal detected the aftereffects of an event from a few days ago that disrupted the flows in a wide area around Austin. He felt Idris's signature, but couldn't pinpoint the source. I don't think any of it's a coincidence, and now we have an address."

Bryce peered at the photos on the screen. "She's not exactly a spring chicken now. You suspect she's directly connected?"

I gave a humorless laugh. "I've learned that age is simply a matter of who you know. Katashi is over a hundred years old, and that bastard is going strong." I tapped the paper. "She's worn the ring, *and* she's in Austin. That's enough to keep her on my list of potential baddies until I find out otherwise."

"Guilty until proven innocent," Bryce said.

"When I'm dealing with the Mraztur and summoners, hell yeah."

Bryce let out a snort of agreement. His gaze returned to Paul's screen, then he frowned and jabbed a finger at one of the pics. "Paul, that one. I need to see that one bigger." Paul tapped a key and the thumbnail enlarged to show Rasha much older, with an utterly gorgeous young woman at her side. Perfectly styled long black hair, medium dark complexion, full lips with a deep rose color, and a voluptuous body.

"I know that girl," Bryce murmured. "I've seen her before."

"That's her granddaughter, Jade," Paul said. The printer hummed again.

"Where have you seen her, Bryce?" I asked.

"At the compound. The Farouche Plantation." He tapped his chin. "I *know* I've seen her there."

My eyes narrowed. "The granddaughter of a known summoner is associated with your ex-boss? Is she a summoner too? What was she doing there?"

A grimace flickered across his face. "No idea. I saw her in his wing of the house a few times this past year. She came and went with . . ." He trailed off, blinked. "Mystery Man Twenty-two. The guy who was last off the plane with Idris in Amarillo. Fucking hell, she came with Mystery Man Twenty-two!"

Paul made a frustrated noise. "Why did I give B.M. my secrets?" He spun the chair to face us. "I can't pull archive surveillance vid to show you, 'cause Big Mack followed my instructions and installed the firewall of doom on his servers plus took surveillance vids offline. I couldn't even leave a back door for myself because, well—"

"That's acting against his interests which triggers the fear," I said with a nod of understanding.

"Exactly." Paul scowled. "Trust me, I tried. Once."

I heard footsteps on the back porch. Bryce drew a sharp breath. "Damn," he murmured. "You can really feel when Mzatal gets close, can't you? Wasn't as noticeable in the demon realm, but here, wow."

"I've grown used to it," I confessed, though now that I focused on it I knew exactly what Bryce meant. Like an invisible pressure wave that grew more and more tangible as the demonic lord approached.

Mzatal stepped through the doorway. Instantly the feel of the office shifted from roomy to cramped broom closet. *Yep, he certainly does have the whammy*, I thought wryly.

He went still for the span of a heartbeat—reading and assessing the current status and the discovery of the ring's bearer—before leveling his full attention onto me.

"You believe Rasha consorts with Farouche," he stated.

"It's very possible," I said. "Her granddaughter certainly does. However, the ring wasn't on a woman's hand, so I want to find out who has it now and who Bryce saw with Jade."

"It is possible she passed the ring to her offspring, or a student," Mzatal pointed out.

"True. Either way, it's worth checking." I lifted the paper. "We have an address for her. In *Austin.*"

"Excellent," he said brusquely. "We will proceed there, and I will assess her." He announced it as though it was no more of a challenge than walking to the neighbor's house.

"I need to talk to you before we make any plans," I told him, taking his hand. After a quick *excuse us* to Bryce and Paul, I led Mzatal to the front porch and closed the door.

"You do realize that most of the means of travel in this world involve getting into a metal container of some sort for several hours?" I asked him. "Rasha lives in Austin. That's either an eight to nine hour drive, or a flight involving airports and security and lots of interaction with people. Which, pretty much means we have to drive. In a car."

Mzatal lifted my hand and kissed it. "It is as it is, zharkat," he murmured. "I will manage it."

I gave his hand a squeeze. He knew I worried about him. "Next question. Can you, um, turn down your mojo at all?"

"It is minimal now," he informed me. "What preparations must be made?"

Fine, I'd let him dodge the subject. For now. "First, we decide who's going," I said as we returned inside. "Zack and Ryan need to remain here to hold down the fort. They can handle any weird crises that come up, and help Steeev watch over Jill." I entered the office and considered Bryce and Paul. Both of them would be pretty damn useful. The only hitch would be finding a way to sneak them out of town without any of the bad guys knowing. "Y'all up for a road trip?" I asked them.

Paul drew in a pleased breath and flicked a hopeful glance to Bryce, face brightening as the older man gave a nod.

"Austin? Sure," Bryce said as Paul swiveled back to the computer to resume typing. "What do we need to do to prep?"

"We'll probably want an SUV so we aren't too cramped," I said. It would be hard enough for Mzatal to be enclosed in a vehicle for several hours, so might as well get something big. "Eilahn can follow on the motorcycle."

"I can help with the driving," Bryce pointed out, and I gave him a grateful nod.

"When will this SUV be acquired?" Mzatal asked.

"We'll rent one," I said, then shifted my attention to Paul. "Can you find a company that will deliver one here within the next few hours?"

A grin spread across his face. "I'm working on it. Unless I'm completely wrong—which I'm not—I can get an Escalade here in an hour and a half. Two hours at the outside. You guys gonna wager on whether or not I can set it all up in under five minutes?"

I shook my head, smiled. "One of these days I'll remember how good you really are. No way am I betting against you again."

Paul simply grinned.

"Wait," I said. "How are you going to pay for it?"

He gave me an unmistakably withering look while Bryce choked on a laugh.

I lifted my hands in surrender. "Forget I asked. Holy shit, but I'm glad you're on our side," I said, then a slow smile spread over my face as a plan came together in my head. "Hang on." I scribbled an address on a sticky note and gave it to Paul. "Have it delivered there instead of here."

I quickly laid out my clever, and actually quite simple, plan to sneak Bryce and Paul away. We'd have the SUV delivered to the back lot of an out-of-business furniture store, which was a five mile drive from my house via the highway, but only about a half mile trek through woods beyond the back fence of my property. I had no gate or driveway there, and the woods were heavy enough I figured the chances were exceedingly slim that Farouche would have people watching along the fence line.

Bryce listened carefully, then had Paul call up a satellite photo of the area. "You're right," he said as he noted the clever shortcut. "He wouldn't have people watching the middle of the woods. That should work." To my relief, no one else found any glaring problems with the ruse either.

Mzatal nodded, face serious and focused—in other words, utterly Mzatal-like—then exited the room. Bryce and I followed him out, though Mzatal continued on outside and to the mini-nexus, while we two humans stopped in the kitchen. Bryce's gaze followed him.

"I'm having a hard time seeing him in a car for eight or nine hours," he murmured with a frown.

I winced. "I imagine we'll be taking a lot of breaks." Crap, this road trip would probably end up taking closer to ten hours. "We'll be getting to Austin after dark. I'll get Eilahn up to speed and have her watch for anyone tailing us then hook up with us once we're clear."

"What do you need me to do?" he asked.

"Pack snacks," I replied. "Jekki can help you. And get all of Paul's stuff charged up."

He gave a crisp nod, smiled. "Munchies and power for Paul. I'm on it."

Chapter 32

The next hour turned into a flurry of activity as humans and demons scurried about to get everything ready, though I had a brief setback when I caught Eilahn by her motorcycle with an empty cat carrier, a colorful tangle of bungees in one hand, and duct tape in the other. For the next ten minutes I waged a grim war to convince her that Fuzzykins could *not* come with us. I made a little headway with the fact that Fuzzykins would be miserable cooped up for hours in the carrier on the back of the motorcycle. I lost ground on the alternative of the back of the SUV, then reclaimed some advantage with the assurance that Zack would take good care of Fuzzykins here, and *of course* Eilahn could call her as often as she wanted. Yet it wasn't until Fuzzykins stalked off the porch, wound around Eilahn's ankles and apparently told her, "No, I do not choose to go this day as I am certain the motion will upset my digestion," that Eilahn finally put away the duct tape and bungees.

Ludicrous as it was, in that one shining moment, I loved that stupid cat.

With the Fuzzykins crisis dealt with, I went back inside and ran through my mental checklist of things to do. Jill stepped through the front door, looking relatively well-rested after her night in her new place. "What's going on?" she asked after a few seconds of watching our frenetic activity.

"We got a hot lead," I told her as I threw stuff into a bag. "We're going to Austin to follow up on it."

She backed to the wall and put her hand over her belly as Jekki scurried by, rolled her eyes and smiled as he chittered to her in passing. "Looks like you're leaving any second now," she observed. "You already tell Ryan, or you want me to let him know when he gets home?"

"Crap." I grabbed for my phone. "I want both Zack and Ryan here to watch over you, and yes, I know you're tough and you have a demon guardian now," I said with a smile, "but I still want them here, 'cause you never know."

"I'm tough," Jill agreed with a steely glint in her eye. "But everything is different now because of the bean." She laid her hand on her belly and her expression softened. "I'm not taking any chances."

"Damn glad to hear it," I said, then quickly called Ryan, filled him in, and dutifully agreed to text him when we arrived and if we had any problems. Next, I called Zack and got his assurance that he'd keep an eye on the house, Jill, and Fuzzykins.

After I hung up, I grabbed a pile of Tracy's notebooks and journals, stuffed them into my bag and zipped it closed, then went outside to where Mzatal sat cross-legged on the mini-nexus. "Boss? We're hoping to get going pretty soon. You ready?"

He drew a deep breath. "It is far to travel from this place."

I knew he meant the tacit security of the mini-nexus. "I wish there was a faster way to get there and back that was feasible," I said with a small sigh. "But driving makes the most sense. We'll get there a little after dark and should be back by midday tomorrow at the latest." I didn't add *if all goes well.* Didn't want to jinx things.

"I am sufficiently prepared," he said.

I laid my hand against his cheek. "You've been on Earth a couple of days already. You sure you have the reserves to do this?"

He covered my hand with his. "I am faring well, zharkat," he told me. "I have used the mini-nexus to greatly slow my potency depletion, and without undue expenditure will be able to maintain perhaps another five days."

I peered at him, felt his reserves and smiled. "Excellent. I'll go finish getting our stuff together." I gave him a quick kiss, then made sure everything we needed was packed up and ready to go on the back porch.

Paul leaned out the back door, as excited as a kid going

to Disney World. "The Escalade will be there in about twenty minutes," he announced.

"Thanks for the update," I said. "We'll leave here in five."

He disappeared back inside as Bryce stepped out with a small duffel bag in one hand and a cup of coffee in the other.

"Will Paul be able to work on the road?" I asked him. "We need to check out Rasha and her connection to the ring, and see if she had anything to do with the flow-disturbing event, but also really need to keep digging into the rest. I hate the thought of waiting until we get back."

Bryce clucked his tongue at me. "Have you learned nothing about Paul? He can do pretty much anything as long as he can get a cell phone signal."

I held up my hands in surrender. "I will never doubt him again."

A few minutes later we assembled on the back porch, made a final headcount, then started out across my yard toward the back of my property, like a bunch of Sherpas about to tackle Everest. I heard a soft patter of feet behind me and glanced back to see Jekki eagerly trotting along in our wake. *Oh, damn.*

"Jekki." I grimaced in apology. "I'm so sorry, but you can't come with us."

He stopped, sat up on his two back feet and peered up at me, looked at Mzatal's retreating back and then to me again. "Why, Kara Gillian? Mzaaaatal walks."

Sighing, I crouched. "You're beautiful and colorful and very unique," I told him. "And if anyone beyond this property saw you, it would draw a lot of attention which could jeopardize everything. I'm very sorry."

He chittered in distress as Mzatal stepped onto the trail through the trees. "Dahn dahn dahn! Who tends Mzatal?"

Boss, I need your help here. "Eilahn and I will tend to him to the best of our ability."

Not at all mollified by my assurances, Jekki continued to chitter, then ran to Mzatal as the lord turned back. I stood and moved toward them, silently cursing myself. I should have foreseen that the devoted little faas would want to come along.

Mzatal crouched and stroked Jekki's head, spoke low in demon. Jekki's incessantly moving tail went almost completely still as he listened.

The lord stood as I reached them, though his hand remained on Jekki's head. "He will accompany us to the fence," he informed me. He gave Jekki one more gentle caress before tucking his arm through mine and continuing to the path.

"He is distressed yet," Mzatal continued softly as we reached the cool shade of the trees, "but I have asked him to tend Szerain, and he is better with that."

I had a silent moment of hilarity as I pictured the faas trying to ply Ryan with sliced fruit and fix his hair. "Thanks," I said, then gave his arm a squeeze. "I'll do my best to take care of you as well as he would."

The trip through the woods was utterly uneventful, which was totally okay with me. Jekki spoke with Mzatal again when we reached the fence, but remained on my property without protest as we all climbed over. I glanced back as we made a turn that would take us out of view in the dense trees and saw him, his little hands upon the sturdy wire fence, still as a statue and watching.

The silver Escalade was exactly where Paul had asked the agency to leave it, though we waited for Mzatal to assess the area before we exited the woods. Once we knew it was safe to proceed, Paul made himself comfortable in the back with his laptop and tablet, while Mzatal took the front passenger seat. I put the journals and notebooks in the middle of the backseat, on the off chance the mood struck me to continue grinding my way through the damn things.

"I'll drive until we get out of the area," I said to Bryce as we finished loading our stuff into the vehicle. "Once we're sure we're clear you and I can trade off."

"I *do* know how to drive," Paul piped up, though his eyes remained glued to his laptop.

"Do you *want* to take a turn driving?" Bryce asked Paul, eyebrow raised.

Paul looked up, frowned as he considered, then shook his head. "Nah. That would suck."

Bryce rolled his eyes. "Which is why we didn't ask you to drive. I know you pretty well by now."

I bit back a laugh. Those two were as bad as siblings.

With that settled, we headed out.

We stopped about every ninety minutes, or whenever Mzatal started looking a bit peaked or antsy, though it was actually more of a feel than a look. The pressure of his aura would take on an uncomfortable edge, and everyone *knew* it was time to stop.

By the third hour of driving we developed a smooth routine: feel the aura, find a suitable spot to stop, let the demonic lord out to breathe and chill for a few, check in with Eilahn, get back in and change drivers, keep going.

"What's the plan when we get to Austin? Go straight to this woman's house?" Bryce asked as he settled into the driver's seat for his turn at the wheel.

I winced. "Pretty much. Unfortunately we don't have any intel on what to expect when we get there."

"In other words, we're winging it?" He glanced in the rear view mirror and gave me a wry smile.

"You got a better plan?"

Bryce chuckled. "Nope. Luckily I'm pretty good at making it up as I go." He passed a slow-moving car then waited until he was clear and back in his lane before speaking again. "What about this woman? Is there anything personal about her that might help?"

I leaned forward. "Boss? You're the one who actually knows her."

Mzatal turned his head to look at me. "She is near eighty years of age. Other than the summoning of Faruk at Christmas, I have not known her to summon in recent years. I have not encountered her in person nor, to my knowledge, has she ever visited the demon realm. She is competent, having survived to this age."

"Was she ever involved with Katashi?" I asked.

"I am unaware of any current association," he said, "though she is one of his oldest living students."

I chewed on that. Katashi had performed his miraculous first summoning in about 1926, so he'd probably been summoning for twenty-five or thirty years before she became his student.

Was she summoning while she was married? I wondered. What did the normal family life of a summoner look like? I sure as hell wasn't an example, nor was Tessa. "I know you said she hasn't summoned much in a decade. Was she pretty good at it when she summoned regularly?"

He regarded me, inclined his head. "For her time, she excelled."

"I wonder why she summoned Faruk," I mused aloud as I settled back in my seat.

"To play chess," Mzatal replied.

I blinked. "Seriously? She went through all of that for a chess partner?"

"Faruk reported that Rasha was lonely," he said. "There may be more, but it seemed Faruk told all she knew." He exhaled. "And Faruk is a relatively simple summons."

A wash of pity for the old woman temporarily eclipsed her place on the possible bad guy list. I'd spent my summoning life isolated from other summoners except for Tessa and the few I met during my brief stint with Katashi. Hell, I'd grown up socially isolated as well, and pretty much without friends. "Lonely" and I were old and bitter pals.

Pushing the unsettling thoughts away, I stuck my headphones on and started the playback of Idris's call. I doubted that the two clues I'd found so far—StarFire hidden in *start a fire*, and the subtle implication of his family in his use of the word *people*—were the only ones he'd seeded into the conversation. Now I knew to listen for micro-pauses, inflections shifts, or emphasis, and during my second break from driving I finally got two more, one right after the other. Once I heard them, I couldn't believe I'd missed them.

I smiled, played it again.

At first I thought they were trying to. Plant a. Seed of doubt, wanting me to. Shun. My old associations. But there's FAR *more shit going on than I ever dreamed of. You think you have everything figured out, then* whOOSH! *the game changes.*

Micro-pauses around "plant a" and "shun." Plantation. Then he blatantly emphasized "far" and the end of "whoosh." Far oosh. Farouche. Clever dude to leave as many clues as possible. After another dozen listens without any more discoveries, I shut the recorder off and kicked back to watch the scenery for a while.

Even limiting the "breathe and chill" breaks to ten minutes, it was well after dark when we finally arrived in Austin.

Bryce followed the navigation commands of the GPS, focus sharpening as we neared the address. I remained silent until the nav system directed us to her street, then straightened and peered at house numbers. A retired sum-

moner living in a nice middle-class subdivision in Austin.
That was more than a little surreal.

"There's her house," I said. "The ranch style, second on
the right. Bryce can you circle the block? Everyone else,
keep your eyes peeled for anything that looks off or might
be a threat."

"Can do," he said as we drove past. Normal protection
wards flickered in my othersight, but a first glance didn't
reveal anything complex or serious. The area looked like a
solid middle class neighborhood that had hit its prime a
decade or two ago. Not shabby by a long shot, but in decline. Well-kept houses in a mix with those in varying states
of disrepair. One of the three streetlights on the block was
out, and pothole repair obviously wasn't high on the munic-
ipality's priority list.

Bryce drove around the block, then parked several
houses away from Rasha's while he kept up a constant scan.
"I don't see anything," he said. "Though I could easily miss
something in the dark."

"What do you want me to do?" Paul asked.

"You're coming with us," I told him as I unbelted. "Bring
your laptop." I climbed out of the Escalade and looked
around carefully as the others got out. Eilahn parked the
motorcycle behind us, climbed off, then stretched. She carefully placed her helmet on the seat and gave me an I'll-be-
nearby look before she disappeared into the shadows to
serve as our outside sentry. I took Mzatal's hand, then gave
Bryce a tilt of my head to indicate I needed to talk to the
lord for a minute. He apparently understood, and beckoned
to Paul.

"You stick close to me, kid," Bryce said as he walked
with Paul a short ways down the cracked sidewalk. "We're
going to be hanging back a bit."

Once they were out of earshot, I looked up at Mzatal.
"We're all upset and worried about Idris, but I need you to
please not scare the living hell out of this woman."

His mouth curved into a frown. "It is not my intention to
do so."

"Yes, I know it's not your intention," I said dryly. "But
you're a *wee* bit intimidating without even trying." I cocked
an eyebrow at him. "Probably better if we don't give her a
heart attack before we find out what we need to know. So,

could you be aware of it and try not to radiate your usual 'Ima gonna fuck you up' mojo?"

"It has served well," Mzatal stated as if reminding me.

"On Earth?" I asked, pursing my lips.

His frown lessened. "I do understand your meaning," he said. "I will not cause her undue distress."

"No looming, no glowering, and especially no scowling," I stated.

He narrowed his eyes down at me. "You are stripping me of my finest devices."

"You still have me," I informed him with a grin. "Maybe I should do the talking, and you can be my heavy."

A second passed before he smiled, no doubt needing the time to glean the mental imagery of what I meant. "I am willing to utilize this technique . . . once."

I chuckled, relieved. "Thanks, lover."

He slid his arms around and gave me a deep and luxurious kiss, then nuzzled my neck before releasing me. "I am now prepared to be heavy."

"Remind me to prepare you to be heavy more often," I said a bit breathlessly.

With that settled, we continued up the street toward her address, Bryce and Paul falling in behind us. Despite the slight decline of the neighborhood in general, Rasha's property seemed to be well-maintained and neat.

Mzatal approached the door, stripped the warding with a single gesture, as if brushing away cobwebs, then put his hand on the doorknob. It was locked, but he smoothly worked a strand of potency into the lock, and a second later he turned the knob and stepped in.

Exhaling a breath, I followed, listening and scanning carefully, though I knew Mzatal would inform us of any threats. Paul and Bryce entered quickly behind us and closed the door with barely a click. I heard a clink of dishes in the kitchen and put a hand on Mzatal's arm. *Let me lead*, I silently reminded him. The skin around his eyes tightened, but he allowed me to move in front of him.

With Mzatal's mojo like a roiling sun behind me, I stepped through an archway into a tidy kitchen. Rasha stood with her back to us, a delicate china cup in one arthritic hand as she placed a teakettle on a burner. A simple emerald green velour robe hung over her nightgown, above fake-jeweled slippers that managed to look elegant rather than gaudy. A thick braid of white-grey hair hung past her shoulder blades, and what I could see of her face revealed fine lines and graceful aging.

Mzatal's dark aura rolled over her. She turned and sucked in a breath, warm brown eyes widening in shock as the cup slipped from her bent, rigid fingers to shatter on the tile floor. She made a strangled noise and took a step back, fumbled for the cane that rested against the counter as her eyes went from me to the lord who loomed behind me—despite the no-looming warning. Crap, she might *still* have a heart attack.

"Rasha Hassan Jalal al-Khouri," I said as I stepped forward. "I am Kara Gillian, and this is Lord Mzatal." I didn't bother to specify which of the three men behind me was the lord since it was fucking obvious. "We must speak with you."

Her lips silently formed my name as she backed into the counter. "I didn't know," she said, shaking voice holding a mere whisper of accent. "I . . . I couldn't stop it. I should have warned you."

Wait, what? I had a demonic lord at my back and it was *my* name she triggered on? I knew Mzatal delved for the reason even now, but I didn't have that nifty advantage. I had zero clue what she "couldn't stop," but there was no need to let her know that.

"How could you not know?" I asked, keeping my question nice and vague.

"They didn't bring the poor child in until after we summoned Isumo." Grief clouded with anger touched her voice. "I agreed to assist Aaron and the others with the summoning, not with what they did *after*."

Something I needed to be warned about? An act related to me she wanted to stop, but couldn't? *The poor child . . . Isumo . . .* I stared in numb shock as the disjointed fragments lit a spark to illuminate a hideous picture. The *rakkuhr* trap in the semi-trailer. Isumo Katashi. And Idris's murdered sister, Amber. It had to be.

Mzatal's already-heavy aura rose in a choking wave, backed by an ominous growl unlike anything I'd ever heard from him before. Rasha paled and clutched weakly at the counter as she swayed. I caught her arm, then shot Mzatal a warning glare. *Stop! She's about to fucking drop dead!*

With seething anger barely contained, Mzatal turned and strode away down the hall. I felt his deep turmoil and knew he distanced himself from her now for her benefit as well as his own. Extending, I touched him with what little reassurance I could offer. He'd read something terrible from her, but I'd find out soon enough what that was. For now I returned my attention to the shaking woman beside me.

She inhaled, and her trembling eased. I felt the flicker of calm like a soothing touch and realized she'd pygahed.

"Rasha, tell me who Aaron is."

Her fear evaporated into anger. "Aaron Asher." She spoke his name with such contempt that I half-expected her to spit on the floor. "An arrogant, disrespectful son of a bitch. Once a colleague and student of mine."

My eyes narrowed. "Brown hair pulled back in a pony-tail? Dresses in stupid flowy poet shirts?"

At her nod, more of the terrible picture lit up. Aaron Asher was Mystery Man Twenty-two, who at times brought Rasha's granddaughter, Jade, along with him to Farouche's plantation. Moreover, we'd seen him with Idris in the video clip from the airport near Amarillo.

I reviewed Rasha's words and filled in the gaps. Rasha had assisted Asher and "others" with the summoning of Katashi, after which Amber had been brutalized and murdered and rigged with the *rakkuhr* trap. Which meant Katashi had to have brought the *rakkuhr* with him, direct from the Mraztur, prepped and ready to place on the young woman as a trap for me.

"When did Asher come here?" I asked. "When did you help him summon Katashi?"

"Almost a week ago," she told me. "Monday. Yes, it was Monday, mid-afternoon."

Only a few hours before I arrived on Earth, and within the same time frame as the disruption in the flows that Mzatal had pinpointed—a disruption based in Austin and with hints of Idris's signature. "Who else was with Asher?" I asked, well aware that my voice had gone hard. "Who else helped you summon Katashi?"

Fear shone in her eyes again, but it wasn't the perfectly natural fear of imminent destruction by a demonic lord. This was a more subtle, more insidious fear, and one with which I was all too familiar.

Son of a bitch. Farouche. Like a "getting warmer" clue in the game of Hot or Cold, the fear in her eyes told me my question prodded uncomfortably at Farouche's interests.

I leaned close. "Was the other summoner a young man with curly blond hair?"

She trembled in my grasp and swayed again. *Hot, blazing hot! Nailed it first try.* She opened her mouth and fought to answer, but her trembling only increased.

"It's all right," I said, voice softening. "You don't have to tell me." Her reaction told me all I needed to know. Idris had indeed been here with the others.

Her shaking subsided, but cold sweat dotted her upper lip. I glanced back at the two silent and watchful men.

"Could y'all please take Rasha to the living room so she can get off her feet?" I asked, then gave the woman a smile as Bryce and Paul came forward and gently took her in hand. "I'll be back in a few minutes," I told her. "Everything's going to be all right."

It wasn't until they left the kitchen with Rasha that I allowed myself to look upon the full horror of all that happened here.

My chest tightened, and I had to remind myself to breathe. Amber Palatino Gavin had been murdered here in this house, with her brother, Idris, present.

Chapter 33

I went in search of Mzatal and found him in the room at the end of the hall—Rasha's summoning chamber. A permanent base diagram had been beautifully etched in the clay tile of the floor, and Mzatal stood atop it now, head lowered, hands in fists at his sides, and black fury roiling through his aura.

"Did he see it?" I asked, *had* to ask, though my voice quavered. "Did Idris have to watch his sister's rape and murder?"

Teeth clenched, Mzatal lifted his head. His eyes met mine, and within the rage and pain and guilt that burned in them lay my answer.

"Show me," I whispered hoarsely. He looked away, and I moved to him, seized his hand. "Boss, show me. I need to know what you read from her."

He didn't move for another several heartbeats, then finally laid his fingers against my temple.

Images and impressions from Rasha's memories tumbled through my mind, and I fought the urge to pull back from the disorienting wave. A heartbeat later I felt him focus, and the influx eased and resolved.

My hand remained clenched on his as I processed the flood of visions and sounds and emotions, slipped into the flow of the woman's memories.

Idris leads us in the summoning ritual. Tsuneo and Aaron assist while I anchor. It is kind of the boy to leave that aspect to me. So very difficult to work the potency strands with hands stiff with pain. Talented and adept as well as kind. The summoning is smooth and perfect . . .

Isumo arrives, his face contorted in agony. He carries a sigil like nothing I've ever seen. Red and chaotic and twisted. It feels wrong, but my questions and protests are ignored. Isumo calls for "the girl," and my confusion rises as two men enter with a bound and gagged young woman . . .

Idris is horrified. Amber, he shouts, and while Isumo and Aaron place the girl within the diagram, Idris struggles wildly against the men who brought her. Now I learn it is a death ritual, to be used to entrap one called Kara Gillian. I protest and refuse to assist, beg Isumo to reconsider. I do not understand why he would follow such a terrible path, yet he orders me removed from the chamber—my chamber. Tsuneo and Aaron take me out, and I see one of the other men look toward the girl with an ugly smile. He straightens and unfastens his belt . . .

I sit in the living room. Isumo calls for the sigil to be placed in her. Rakkuhr, he calls it, and even the word feels unclean. I hear her weep and Idris beg mercy for her. Then cries and screams punctuated by sadistic grunts of pleasure. Then there are only screams and whimpers. For hours I listen and despise myself for not interfering, for doing nothing while they abuse her . . .

Finally, silence, save for a low murmur of voices. After a few minutes the door to my chamber opens, and Tsuneo and the one with the ugly smile come out carrying a black body bag . . .

What can I do? Terror fills me at the mere thought of calling the police. I am a foolish and useless old woman, and the girl's blood lies on my hands as heavily as any of them. The men leave through the garage with the body bag and do not return . . .

Idris is led out, shoved forward to sit on the couch. He does so, numbly, as if he has no fight left. "We were following node emissions," he murmurs, stricken. "I was cooperating. They didn't have to do that." His voice is so hollow and lost, yet I think perhaps he has much fight yet within him, more than they can imagine. Isumo and Aaron finish in my summoning chamber, and then they all leave . . .

The wave of memories receded, and I found myself with my forehead resting on Mzatal's chest and his arms around me. Rasha didn't have a name for the man with the ugly smile, the one who'd raped Amber, but I did: Jerry Steiner. He'd taken her from the plantation, brought her here, and helped ensure her end was not an easy one. Shuddering, I held Mzatal close as we shared the pain and found balance within each other.

"They don't know him," I murmured and lifted my head to look into Mzatal's face. "They don't know Idris, and they made a huge mistake." The Mraztur and their Earth accomplices could have ensured themselves a long-term and highly useful tool, simply with a touch of Farouche's disturbing fear-influence and members of Idris's family held as hostages. But instead they chose to defile and murder his sister before his eyes, when an unrelated person would have served as well for their gruesome death ritual. And certainly no need for Idris to witness it. I'd seen Idris's face through Rasha's eyes. They'd destroyed their tool along with his innocence and forged a true enemy.

"They have indeed erred, to our advantage," Mzatal said, though his voice still held a growl.

"Idris told Rasha they were following node emissions. Like the geyser effect at the warehouse? Why?"

"There is potency to be harnessed through the emissions, as Tracy Gordon attempted with the gate at the warehouse node." He shook his head. "Though I do not know the Mraztur's plan, that it involves the nodes is both enlightening and disturbing. It is unwise to tamper with such, and it disturbs me that Idris is involved."

"We're going to bring him home."

"Soon," he replied with utter conviction, and in the ancient depths of his eyes lay grim resolve and the promise of vengeance.

"Then let's get started," I said. "Rasha is under Farouche's influence. Probably best to take care of that first." The teakettle began a plaintive wail from the kitchen. "I'll make some tea for her. She could probably use it."

Mzatal gave a slight nod, then exited the chamber to tend to Rasha while I returned to the kitchen. Paul was there, in the process of removing the kettle from the heat. A broom leaned against the counter, and I saw the shards of china in a neat pile.

He gave me a tentative smile. "I figured I'd make myself useful."

"Like that's *ever* a problem with you," I said. "How's Rasha?"

"Freaked *out*." He plucked a cup from the cabinet, dropped a tea bag into it. "Bryce is doing pretty good keeping her calm though."

"She has the Farouche juju on her," I told him. "Mzatal's clearing that right now."

He poured the hot water into the cup, then retreated to his laptop on the table. "You'll want to see this," he said as he typed. "Check this out." He turned the screen toward me to reveal a photo of a lovely dark-haired woman in an evening dress, in her fifties or so and with a Middle Eastern look about her, posing with the governor of Louisiana. "I recognized her from photos in the living room and pulled this up for you. It's Big Mack's first wife," he told me. "Rasha's daughter, Aria *Farouche*."

"Fucking shit," I breathed. "This is one hell of a tangled mess." Farouche had divorced this woman seventeen years ago, a couple of years after their five year old daughter—who I now knew to be Rasha's granddaughter—had been abducted. "Where is she now?"

"Living happily in New Orleans with plenty of cash from B.M.," he said. "They apparently still get along pretty well. She came to the plantation several times last year for holidays and stuff."

"How cozy," I said. "Is she Jade's mother?"

He shook his head. "Her aunt. Jade's parents died in a house fire when she was eight. Jade survived but had some bad burns on her legs."

I let all that sink in as I took the teabag from the cup and set it aside. "Anything else?"

"Not yet. That's all I had time for."

"You rock," I stated. "Let's go see what other surprises she has for us." I picked up the cup of tea and turned toward the living room then stopped and stared at the notepad beside the phone on the kitchen counter. My name and number were written on it in awkward, shaky writing. She'd wanted to call me, to warn me, but hadn't. Or couldn't because of Farouche's influence. Poor woman.

As I moved down the two steps into the sunken living room, I quickly took in the surroundings. A worn sofa, chaise lounge, and two wingback chairs. A fireplace, coffee table, and various shelves holding a host of framed photos. Everything neat and clean, with only a modicum of dust.

Face dreamy, Rasha sat in one of the chairs with Mzatal behind her, his hands on her head. It was clearly her usual spot to judge by the tissues, eyeglasses case, and books on the table beside it. Two framed photos rested by the books: one of teenaged Jade dressed in a blue and white cheerleading outfit, and one of a laughing girl about five.

I placed the cup on her table, then settled on the chaise lounge and waited for Mzatal to finish his work. Bryce maintained a watchful position by the arch that led to the entryway, and Paul settled onto the step beside him.

After a few minutes Mzatal lifted his hands from her head and moved to a position beside me, expression as unreadable as ever, though now he merely loomed instead of *LOOMED*.

Rasha's eyes filled with tears as she looked from Mzatal to me. "Macklin was behind this? He came for a visit before. He seemed so concerned about me. So normal."

Mzatal had apparently given her some basic halo-tarnishing information on James Macklin Farouche once he'd cleared the bastard's influence.

"Yes, he was," I said, not surprised by the visit. To lay the fear, no doubt. "At least for some of what's occurred on Earth. I'm sorry."

Grief deepened the lines in her face. "He changed after Madeleine was abducted. My beautiful granddaughter." Her hand trembled as she touched the picture of the little girl on the side table. "But I never imagined he would go this far. I never saw that in him."

"He's hurt a lot of people," I told her. "It has to stop."

She drew a shaky breath. "I am deeply sorry for my part in this."

"Rasha, we know you didn't condone what happened." I kept my voice gentle. She was like one of her china teacups—elegant and beautiful, aged and fragile. "I saw my number by your phone," I continued. "I know you would have warned me if at all possible." I pulled the sketch of the ring out of my bag. Though I suspected I knew whose hand I'd seen wearing it, we needed to be absolutely certain. "We're still looking for Idris, and you might be able to help." I showed her the drawing. "Where is this ring now?"

Rasha's mouth thinned, and her eyes hardened. "Aaron has it," she said, vehemence thick and sharp in her voice. "I saw it on his hand when he was here. I gave it to Jade on her sixteenth birthday. *He* says she gave it to him last year."

"What did he do to her?" I asked as I tucked the sketch away again.

"When she was nearly seventeen, he came here to train her and also to learn what I had to offer." She leaned forward, mouth twisting into a sneer. "He thought he knew so much. I had been summoning for more than thirty years when he was still a babe at his mother's tit. *Thirty years*, back when it was dangerous and the flows more capricious." She sat back, shook her head. "When Jade was barely eighteen, she and Aaron announced that they were together and assumed I would simply accept it."

Great. The young, nubile Jade was a summoner too, and her boyfriend, who grandma didn't approve of, was also a summoner except he was sort of evil. I'd seen soap operas with less drama. *As the Portal Turns?*

"But you didn't accept it," I said.

"How could I and still have a conscience?" She drew herself up proudly. "He was and is an insufferable ass who lacked respect and restraint."

I wasn't about to argue that point. "She didn't come with Asher last Monday?"

Sorrow clouded her eyes, and her shoulders slumped. "Five years ago I tried to talk sense into her, told her Aaron was no good, and I wouldn't tolerate him in my house for training or otherwise." She looked away. "She walked out with him and never returned," she said, voice breaking.

"I'm sorry." It was a story as old as time, and Rasha had played the role of disapproving elder with fervor. And even though her intent had been noble—to protect her lovely granddaughter from an untrustworthy man—she paid the price with crushing loneliness so deep she'd risked injury or death to summon Faruk, simply to play chess with her last . . . *Christmas.* My chest squeezed tight. She'd been completely alone for Christmas.

And how many Christmases have I spent with only my aunt? I pushed the unpleasant question away. I didn't want to think about that right now.

Mzatal abruptly stepped forward. "Rasha Hassan Jalal al-Khouri."

Rasha looked up at him, eyes wide, but with caution now instead of fear. "Lord Mzatal."

He dropped into a crouch before her. "You carry heavy burdens, old and new," he said, voice rich. "Aaron Asher has committed a great offense against me, and he has used you. I will find him, and I will extinguish him."

Her mouth curved into a fierce smile. "I am in your debt, my lord."

Mzatal gently took her gnarled hands in his, lifted them to touch his forehead before returning them to her lap. "No, honored summoner. You have served well for more than half a century. It is a gift." He folded her hands between his. "As is this." He glanced to me. "Beloved, will you assist me?"

I smiled, deeply pleased as I felt his intent. "You got it, Boss." The rhythm of the healing patterns felt familiar now after working with him on Bryce, and I slipped into our connection effortlessly.

Mzatal shifted his hold and worked the stiffness in her joints. "You will soon find it easier to summon again."

Rasha inhaled sharply as healing warmth suffused her hands, and understanding dawned in her eyes an instant later. "Oh my," she murmured, then closed her eyes and sat quiet and still while we worked.

A few minutes later she opened them again, brow puckered. Mzatal's lips twitched in a smile as we continued to work the healing. "Speak, Rasha."

A whisper of fear crossed her face as she realized he could read her thoughts. "My lord, I meant no offense."

"Speak," he repeated.

She took a careful breath. "You call her beloved," she said quietly, no doubt embarrassed I could hear, but unwilling to defy the lord's command.

He moved his hands to her wrists, and his smile grew fond. "Yes. I only speak the truth."

"Yet she calls you *Boss*, my lord?" she asked, clearly perplexed and probably wondering why he tolerated such disrespect. I studiously kept my eyes slightly unfocused as if I wasn't paying any attention and carefully suppressed a smile.

"She does indeed name me such," he agreed. "Frequently." Mzatal's smile kicked up another degree. "It is the energy behind the word, not the word itself," he explained. "Have you not heard a human speak a term of endearment, yet put such harsh intent behind it that it could as easily have been a knife to the essence?"

The old summoner let out a dry chuckle. "Ah, yes, of course." Then she gave a wistful sigh. "My Sapar, he would call me his third doughnut. Odd, to be sure, but he meant it sweetly. I miss him still." Her forehead creased, as if struggling to recall those days with her long dead husband.

"You have lived long alone," he murmured.

She looked into the distance, smile trembling. "I had my granddaughter Jade for many years after my son and his wife died," she said, then sighed. "Such a joy she was, despite all she'd endured. So beautiful."

Mzatal gently released her hands, then brushed his fingers along her temple. Her expression cleared, and joy replaced the confusion as if Mzatal had dusted off those old memories.

"Oh . . . my lord." She lifted her hands, opened and closed her fingers, eyes brimming with tears. "You have given me a great gift."

"One richly deserved," he replied.

"Rasha, you have my number by your phone," I said. "Call me if anyone threatens or pressures you, and *especially* if anyone tries to hurt you."

She nodded grateful assent.

"Now you must rest," Mzatal said and sent her into sleep before she could either protest or thank him. With a tenderness that few, other than I, had ever witnessed, he lifted the aged summoner and settled her on the couch. His hand remained on her shoulder for several more heartbeats before he straightened and drew a light blanket over her.

"I have eased her memory of the ritual," he told me quietly. "She is able to remember it, but only with focus and intent. It will no longer haunt her."

"You're such a softy," I said with a low laugh, and planted a not-soft kiss on his mouth. He'd expended a good portion of his reserves with the healing, and I resolved to get him home to the mini-nexus as soon as possible.

Bryce and Paul and I finished cleaning up the kitchen and the broken porcelain, while Mzatal restored the wards in her house and beefed them up to demonic lord levels. At long last we departed, leaving Rasha sleeping peacefully on the sofa.

Eilahn emerged from a clump of brush on the other side of the street, smiled and readied the motorcycle. I kept my hand in Mzatal's as we walked back to the SUV. "I'm proud of you." I slid a glance his way.

He gave me a sidelong look in return. "My heaviness met your expectation?"

"Well, you did a fair bit of *looming* for the first part of the visit," I pointed out.

His brows drew together. "I was simply *heavy*." Before I could reply, he moved swiftly behind me, aura shifting to black menace as he pressed close against my back. I felt his breath on my neck as he spoke with dark and sinister horror. "*This* is looming."

I sucked in a gasping breath and had to bite back a cry of terror. Ahead of me, Bryce staggered and clutched at the SUV, face paling. Clenching my teeth, I drove an elbow back into Mzatal's gut.

He grunted at the blow, then let out an actual laugh, horrific aura dissipating to his normal "heavy" mojo in an instant. Bryce and Paul turned to stare at the lord, both apparently finding the laughter almost more disturbing then the menace.

I couldn't help but laugh as well. It felt good. "Holy shit, she'd have keeled over dead if you'd done that to her." Throwing my arms around his neck, I planted a kiss on him, and didn't mind at all when he wrapped his arms around me and returned it with a fervor that was possibly illegal on the streets of Austin, Texas.

Reluctantly, and only because Bryce and Paul were doing their best to look anywhere but at us, I broke the kiss. "Let's get back home," I said. "And if we run into Asher or Jerry or Katashi or Farouche, you can *loooooom* all you want."

Chapter 34

I waited until we were at least an hour out of Austin and then took an exit onto a small dark highway with a closed diner and one lone gas station. Four pumps. Grimy windows. Probably had the bathroom key attached to a hub cap. Only one car, which was likely the clerk's since it was parked near the back of the building. It was the kind of station that no female traveling alone—especially in the middle of the night—would *ever* patronize except in a dire emergency.

It was perfect.

"Paul, any cameras?" I glanced in the rear view mirror as I drove past the station and saw him already typing away on his laptop.

"Hang on." He muttered to himself for another few seconds, then looked up in triumph. "Got it. It's an old system, so best I can do is shut it off. Should work okay."

"You're a god, Paul."

He blushed and grinned. I turned around then pulled in at the front pump and shut off the engine. "I'll go get snacks and stuff," he announced, undoing his seat belt.

Bryce snorted. "You just want to see if they have Krunch 'n Krackle."

Paul laughed. "I'm addicted." To my surprise he then looked at Mzatal. "Lord Mzatal, you wanna come with me?"

My surprise increased when a smile touched the lord's face. "I do, Paul."

Bemused, I watched as the pair exited the SUV and headed toward the station, Paul chattering companionably about how awesome Krunch 'n Krackle was, and Mzatal apparently listening closely and murmuring responses. *He likes Paul*, I thought, pleased and weirdly relieved. Mzatal's incredible capacity for affection and love had gone untapped and unused for far too long. Millennia. He needed friends.

I could relate, though on a much smaller scale. It was only in the past year that I'd developed an honest-to-god circle of friends. My posse. Even when things were at their shittiest, knowing these people had me in their thoughts made all the difference in the world.

I climbed out as Eilahn stopped at the pump behind us. She parked the bike, swung her leg over and shook her hair out of her helmet, then stood and preened a bit. I couldn't blame her. If I looked that damn good on a motorcycle I'd likely do the same thing. She still rode Tessa's bike, which I realized now probably wasn't cut out for long highway road trips. Eilahn needed something more powerful—something fast. A sleek crotch-rocket or a model equally dangerous to mere humans. I smiled at the thought. Maybe when the FBI paid me.

Bryce came around the back of the SUV, eyes going to Eilahn for long enough to prove he was a healthy heterosexual male, but not so long as to be pervy. "I'll pump," he told me with an easy smile.

"I'll watch and pay," I replied and swiped my card on the pump, maintaining faith in Paul's assertion that it couldn't be tracked. My gaze went to the sight of Mzatal and Paul within the store. What would the super powerful demonic lord make of a back-country gas station? Did it have a big jar of pickled pigs feet on the counter? Or a container of boiled eggs suspended in an odd red liquid? In my entire lifetime of living in the South, I'd never been brave enough to try either staple of southern culture. I'd stick to M&Ms, thank you very much.

My musings came to a sharp halt as a vehicle pulled off the highway, and my gut did a nasty lurch at the sight of the light bar on top of the Crown Victoria.

"Shit," Bryce murmured from beside me.

I kept the pleasant smile on my face as the cop pulled up and parked along the side of the station. Sheriff's deputy. A sergeant, I noted as he exited his vehicle. Late thirties, tan shirt over brown trousers. Service weapon and a deceptively casual air. No gut. Fit and trim.

He gave me a polite nod and smile, then did a once-over assessment of Bryce, the SUV, and Eilahn, in a way that let me know he was more than some local yokel. This was a cop with a good eye who took his job seriously and probably had some damn good instincts. I loved his type, but damn, it was inconvenient for him to show up right now. *Hell, he probably pulled in* because *there's a carload of people and a motorcycle here in the middle of the night*, I decided. That's what a good cop would do, especially at a place right off the highway in the middle of nowhere with only one clerk working.

The deputy finished his assessment, gave us all another nod-smile then turned and headed toward the front door of the station.

"Shit," I muttered. "Bryce, hang tight. I'm going to check on our two."

His jaw tightened. "Damn it. I shouldn't have let Paul out of my sight."

"I'll get them," I said. "It's all good." I headed toward the door, trying to hurry without actually looking as if I was hurrying. Easy, right? Mzatal and Paul were still visible through the window. Paul was describing something, using animated gestures to emphasize his point. Mzatal actually smiled at whatever he said, and it wasn't a polite, indulgent smile either. Mzatal didn't do those.

A bell dinged as the deputy opened the door "Hey, Georgie," I heard him say as he gave a nod to the clerk. "Anything happening?"

"Hey, Frank! Didja hear that Joe Johnson wrecked his—" Whatever Joe Johnson wrecked was cut off as the door closed behind the deputy. As I approached the entrance I could see Frank perfectly well, watched him do a scan-sweep of the store as he spoke to the clerk and checked the mirrors. His focus sharpened on Mzatal. And his face changed.

Mzatal abruptly lifted his gaze from Paul to the deputy, and his entire bearing transformed from the relaxed ease to Demonic Lord. The cop's right hand went to the butt of his gun in what I knew was a purely instinctive reaction to a perceived threat.

"Lemme see your hands!" Frank shouted, eyes wide. I knew what he felt—power and menace held in tight control.

And if he was even the slightest bit sensitive, Mzatal's mojo would hit him that much harder. I barely managed to restrain myself from yanking the door open and barreling in. In this scenario, that would be a good way to get myself shot.

Paul let out a yelp and dropped the bags of Krunch 'n Krackle in his hands, but Mzatal's aura only grew heavier at the shouted order. The deputy's breath quickened, and he drew his gun. His face showed his confusion as he sensed danger, even though there was nothing identifiable as a threat. I carefully pulled the door open, distantly noting that the clerk had wisely chosen to take refuge somewhere out of sight behind the counter.

Damn it. I knew the demonic lords weren't the type to obey meekly, but surely every now and then they could unbend and cooperate a teensy bit?

Lift your hands and show him they're empty! I mentally "shouted" at Mzatal while I kept my eyes on Frank and my own hands in very plain sight. To my undying relief Mzatal slowly lifted his hands, though he still radiated power like a nuclear reactor.

"Deputy, he's not armed," I said, pitching my voice low and calm but clear enough to carry. *Can you please pull your damn aura in some?* I thought furiously at Mzatal. "It's okay. We're not causing any trouble."

Frank heard me. I knew that much by the battle between logic and gut instinct that played out on his face. His gun was out, but he hadn't yet raised it to point at Mzatal. Thank everything for that, because I could imagine all too well what the lord's response might have been if he'd felt threatened.

I risked a quick glance to Mzatal. "Boss . . . rein it in." It wasn't exactly an order. More like a *Holy fucking christ, if you love me at all will you please do this tiny little goddamn thing for me?* Then again, he too was operating on instinct, reacting in patterns carved by millennia of interactions with humans and other lords. "There's no trouble here," I repeated to the deputy. "No one is causing any problems or creating a threat. You know that, right?"

Frank's gaze remained locked with Mzatal's. The deputy licked his lips, drew a shaky breath. "I . . . don't know what I know."

Mzatal ended the stare-down and turned his eyes to me as he slowly lowered his hands and pygahed. Immediately the intense, smothering pressure of his aura diminished to its typical I-can-kill-you-anytime-I-want-and-don't-you-forget-it level. He inclined his head slightly in my direction, and I knew he'd toned it down and stepped back from the confrontation as a concession to me.

As Mzatal looked away, Frank blinked and gave his head a slight shake. He swallowed hard, then looked down at the gun in his hand. His face paled as he hurriedly shoved it into his holster. "Jesus," he muttered, voice cracking.

I damn near wilted in relief and went ahead and put a hand on the beef jerky display to steady myself. "Paul, go back to the car, please," I managed. "I'll buy your snacks."

He gulped and obeyed with alacrity. The bell on the door dinged behind him as he did a fast-walk to the SUV.

Mzatal was not so pliant and moved toward the deputy instead of toward me and the door and the highway and *away* from this place and this whole situation. Shit.

"Deputy, he won't hurt you," I told the man, watching the struggle on his face to *not* step back, to *not* draw his gun as Mzatal closed the distance between them. This was instinct again, a big Alpha Dog putting a little yappy thing in its place, holding teeth around its neck until it shut up. "He won't hurt you," I repeated while I silently cursed ingrained patterns of behavior. "I swear it."

Mzatal paused barely within Frank's personal space, face utterly unreadable, which was a scary-as-hell expression in its own right. He gazed down at the man for half a dozen heartbeats while the cop firmed his jaw and struggled to maintain control.

Finally Mzatal moved past the deputy, past me, and out the door.

Frank let out a ragged breath as the bell dinged behind Mzatal. His stress showed as he clenched and unclenched his hands, but he didn't make a move to stop Mzatal from leaving. I hurried to the snack aisle, grabbed a handful of the Krunch 'n Krackle, then ran back to the front and threw a twenty dollar bill on the counter.

"Keep the change!" I called to the still cowering clerk, then hit the door at a run. "Fucking hell," I muttered. This whole incident stood as a stark reminder that none of the lords were tame or culturally socialized. Even with Mzatal on super-best behavior, this had been a near-disaster. It chilled me to think of an unscrupulous lord loose on Earth.

I yanked the driver's door of the SUV open, then stopped dead. Everyone was in the vehicle and belted in, even Mzatal. Except that Mzatal was in the *driver's* seat.

I spluttered something that was probably best left unsaid, then took a deep breath. "Boss? What are you doing?"

He gave me an implacable look. "Waiting for you to get into the vehicle so that we may depart."

I shot Bryce a horrified glance. He shrugged in response and gave me a slightly pained look that clearly said, *How the fuck was I supposed to stop him?*

"You all need rest," Mzatal stated. "I will drive."

Scowling, I shut the door, ran around, and climbed into the front passenger seat. "Fine. Whatever. Let's get the hell out of here." I tossed the bags into the back seat for Paul, and remained tense as Mzatal started the engine and pulled away from the pump.

"Paul said the cop freaked out," Bryce said, lingering tension in his voice. "What happened?"

"Yeah, he did!" Paul exclaimed, already typing furiously on his laptop. "We were just looking at the snacks and all of a sudden the deputy was like—" he dropped his voice to be more cop-like, "—'lemme see your hands!'" He blew out a breath. "No reports so far. No pings." He looked up. "What did he say after I left? Did he ID us or what?"

I shook my head. "Not that I know of unless he ran the tags. The SUV would come back to the rental, but Eilahn's motorcycle is registered to my aunt." I paused, giving a hard look up and down the highway as Mzatal pulled onto it and headed toward the interstate. "The cop must be sensitive," I continued. "He *really* felt Mzatal's aura."

"Yes, he is, and he did," Mzatal stated.

Bryce muttered something foul under his breath then glanced over at Paul. "Anything ping yet? Did he run us?"

"My connection sucks. I'm still checking."

"Just let us know if we need to watch for anyone coming after us," I said. Then again, what the hell could the deputy do? He'd pulled his gun for no apparent reason. He might go ahead and run the tags out of curiosity, but I couldn't fathom him pursuing us. And unless he jotted down the tag numbers as we were leaving, he'd be out of luck since Paul had hacked the gas station's security.

Still, I continued to check the rear view mirror obsessively. After several minutes of no blue and red flashing lights behind us, I finally turned to Mzatal.

"You're sure you know how to drive, know the rules of the road, and what route to follow?"

"I have observed carefully." Calm confidence radiated from him.

Rolling my eyes, I shrugged. "Eh, what's the worst that can happen. I mean, other than death in a fiery crash."

His mouth twitched into a smile. "Trust me."

Apparently I didn't have much choice. I tried to put out of my head the scene from the movie *Starman*, where the alien is driving and thinks that a yellow light means Go Very Fast, since he'd seen the human woman speed through a yellow.

"You do know that a yellow light means it's about to turn red, and you have to stop, right?" I asked, just to be sure.

His only response was a low chuckle.

I allowed myself to relax as we made it to the interstate without any sign of police vehicles following us, and without any crashes, fiery or not. After about ten miles I had to admit that Mzatal knew as much about the operation of a motor vehicle and the rules of the road as the average human, and he certainly had better instincts and reflexes.

Since I still had too much adrenaline pumping through me to sleep, I snagged up one of Tracy's spiral notebooks from the stack on the back seat and pulled a flashlight out of my bag, propped my feet on the dashboard and began to flip through. It was the notebook with no cover that had all the date and time info for the warehouse node. I'd never actually finished going through this one, since Eilahn and I had raced to the warehouse the instant we realized the "event" was that same day.

Then again, it didn't look as if I'd missed much. More ritual configurations, some of which looked completely wrong to me. A doodle of an elephant beside another one of the weird tree sketches. A convoluted twisting sigil that didn't seem to have any logical structure.

I began to toss it back to the stack, then stopped, flipped

it open to the page that had all the dates and times for the warehouse node. My pulse did a stutter-step.

"Fucking shit!" I dropped my feet and wheeled back toward the stack. "I need the leather journal with the blue cover."

Bryce quickly fished the correct one out of the pile and handed it to me. "What's going on?"

"Node emissions." I flipped through the fragile pages of the old journal as quickly as I dared. "Idris told Rasha he was following node emissions," I said. "Tracy tracked the one at the warehouse, which is why we were there when you got shot."

After a few seconds I found the pages I needed. "Here." I held the journal and flashlight so they could see. "Six more lists in a *really* similar format to the warehouse one, so I think those might be for tracking node emissions too. Tracy's grandparents started these lists, and then Tracy continued and added to them."

Bryce and Paul leaned forward to peer at the odd lists. Paul frowned and opened his mouth to speak, and I jerked up a hand to stop him.

"Yes, I *know* there are no fucking locations for any of these," I said. "All we have are the number series from grandma with dates from her time period, and then Tracy's cryptic Peter-Piper-picked-a-peck-of-pickled-peppers shit along with the dates he filled in."

Bryce's eyes skimmed over the numbers and odd phrases and dates. "If he was tracking so meticulously, then it stands to reason the location is encoded in all of this somehow. He wouldn't want to get mixed up and put a date and time on the wrong list."

"Right, and he kept it coded because he didn't want to risk anyone else finding the nodes and blocking his use." I tapped the page. "We figure it out, and we *might* know where they're going next with Idris." *Might* being the operative word, I thought with a grimace. We had no way of knowing if Idris was tracking any of the same locations. Still, we had to try.

I looked back at Paul and put on an encouraging and confident smile to hide my fear that we were chasing shadows. "Okay, Wonder Boy, you up for the challenge?"

"You got numbers, I got answers," he replied with a

bright smile. "Well, y'know, probably," he added. "I'll do my best."

"Your best is pretty damn awesome," I reassured him as I handed over the journal.

Paul took it and settled in to work. I reached over and stroked Mzatal's hair. He hadn't said a word during all of this, but I'd felt his tension and hope for the possibilities rise right along with mine. *We're getting closer, Boss.* Yes, we were chasing shadows, but they were beginning to take on more substance.

Mzatal slid a brief look to me, gave me a soft smile along with a mental caress that seemed to lift the anxiety from both of us. I closed my eyes, willed myself to relax.

Sleep slowly slides, I thought with a silent snort. Tracy didn't have *that* one in any of his weird lists. Hell, I could play that silly game too. Maybe *gas guzzles green* for how much it cost to fill the damn tank of the SUV, and *deputy debates demon* for the mega-tense encounter at the gas station.

My eyes popped open. Tracy didn't have G or D or SL alliterative sounds in any of his three-word phrases. I swung around in my seat. "Paul! The three word phrases—what letters do they start with?"

He jerked his head up. "Uh . . ." He blinked, frowned, and dropped his eyes to the journal. "Sick sirens sink, thick thread thrives, old over out, every eaglet ejects—"

Excited, I waved at him to stop. "The lists have one long phrase at the top—five or six words or so—but then how many three-word phrases are there in each one?"

Brow creased in bafflement, he quickly tallied. "Three of them have fourteen and three have fifteen."

A giggle bubbled out of me. "And let me guess, there's a phrase in the middle and at the end that start with N, S, E, or W, right?"

The bafflement on his face deepened to comical proportions. "Only N's and W's. One of each in each list. Naughty Nantucket nuns, Nancy needs nookie, woman weeds wagon—"

"It's coordinates!" I crowed. "Latitude and longitude! The first letters of the words correspond to the first letters in the word for a number. Like 'sick sirens sink' is six. The exceptions are the phrases for North and West!" For longitude and latitude, the letters for direction always followed the numbers. I did a giddy little dance in my seat. "Oh, yeah, I'm awesome. Uh huh, I'm awesome. Go, Kara! Go, Kara!"

Paul's eyes widened. "Degrees, minutes, seconds." His face split into a grin, and then his fingers flew over his keyboard. "The first list, the one with 'Cowboy creek crevice creates confusion' at the top . . ." His eyes flicked between the journal and the laptop. "Thirsty thieves thrive, forlorn foxes fold, finicky fire fizzles, sick sirens sink, zygote zucchini zings, eat ears early, night noise nears. So that would be thirty-four degrees, fifty-six minutes, zero-eight seconds, North."

"Well?" I demanded. "Where is it?"

He shot me a withering look. "Hang on, lemme get the longitude." He mumbled to himself while I jiggled impatiently, and Bryce looked on in bemusement.

"Got it," Paul finally announced. "'Cowboy creek crevice creates confusion' is a location near the town of Rock Creek in the Texas panhandle."

A smug smile spread across my face. "The titles are clues and hints for Tracy so he knew which list was for which node without having to look up the coordinates each time he tracked an emission, but the cryptic phrases kept it from being obvious to anyone who didn't know the code." A thought abruptly speared its way to the surface, and I sucked in a sharp breath. "What about the dates? Was there something at that Cowboy Creek node in the last few days?"

Paul nodded. "A couple of days ago."

I bit down on a shriek of delight. "That's when we had video of him getting off a plane not far from Amarillo in the goddamn Texas panhandle!"

Bryce straightened. "Hot fucking damn," he murmured. "We might be able to anticipate where they're going next."

"Right, though now we have to hope to hell that Tracy knew about the same nodes that Katashi and his crew are checking." I wagged my hands at Paul and the journal. "Work, Wonder Boy. Work!"

Paul grinned and quickly sank into processing the data. I faced forward again and tried to chill while he worked, but could only fidget.

"Whoa," he said a few minutes later.

I twisted around in the seat. "What is it?"

"Here's what we have." He tapped a few more times. "The 'Mountains mean multiple mergers' one works out to near Basalt, Colorado. 'Ashes are always around' is about seventy-five miles outside of Austin. And 'Wet wilderness wonder waxes' is in Oregon. 'Weird wondrous wares waver wildly' is the warehouse. But the last one . . ." He blew out a breath. "'Boss-boy breaks boss's balls,' is smack dab in the middle of the Farouche Plantation."

Adrenaline surged through me even as Mzatal's aura flared. "Let me see the journal," I said and practically snatched it as Paul held it out. I quickly skimmed the dates. There were only three—one from over a year ago and one more than a year away. But the third set my heart pounding. "There's one in three days." I heard the tremble in my voice and didn't care. "Idris will be there. I *know* he'll be there."

"And we will retrieve him." Mzatal stated with dark determination. He'd made the same claim about me once and followed through against impossible odds.

"Damn straight," I said. We had yet to come up with even the slightest inkling of a plan, but I had the ultimate faith that we would.

With the rush of excitement over, we fell into a comfortable silence. I mentally brainstormed various plans with myself, each more outlandish than the last, and finally decided to stop before I thought too seriously about the one where we all swooped in on hang-gliders.

I glanced toward a low snore to see Bryce with his head tipped back and his mouth open. Paul remained head down, his entire focus on his laptop, face weirdly lit by the screen. I relaxed in my seat and finally let myself think about the encounter with Rasha. The visit had unsettled me on numerous levels, and not all related to Idris and Amber. Rasha had been summoning for almost fifty years, living a life of careful isolation to keep it secret. Paul's information showed that she'd married at eighteen and had a set of twins a few years later. Her husband had been killed in the Suez crisis, and at some point in all of that she'd become a summoner. And for what? To end up old and alone, used by others who sought power? She barely even saw her family. The most she could do was surround herself with pictures of them.

Propping my feet on the dashboard again, I watched the moon flicker through the trees that lined the interstate. I understood being so lonely that summoning a demon for a game of chess was a reasonable choice. I'd been there before. I wasn't there anymore, but what about in thirty years? Fifty?

Mzatal reached over and took my hand. "I will not abandon you, beloved," he said softly.

Tears pricked my eyes. I gave his hand a light squeeze. "Thanks, Boss."

I drifted off to sleep with my hand in his.

Chapter 35

When I woke the sky ahead of us glowed with the pinks and blues of sunrise. I sat up, rolled my head on my shoulders to get the crick out of my neck. Mzatal looked over from where he still sat in the driver's seat and gave me a fond smile.

"Hey, Boss," I said as I rubbed the gunk out of my eyes. "How long have I been asleep?"

"Six hours and twenty-two minutes," he replied.

A glance at the backseat showed the other two men still sleeping. "Have you been driving this whole time?" I asked him.

"Yes."

I groaned. Damn it, the last thing I wanted was for him to wear himself out again. "You're majorly stubborn, you know that, right?"

"Zharkat, it is much less confining this way," he reassured me. "I am well."

I peered at him and had to admit he did look much less stressed than on the trip to Austin.

"All right." I ran fingers through my hair and tried unsuccessfully to bite back a yawn. "You want me to drive for a bit now, or are you good?"

"I will continue," he said. "Have you need to stop elsewhere before journey's end?"

I shook my head. "I just want to get home."

"Not long now," he said. "Sleep more."

And I did.

* * *

The abrupt silence of the engine woke me the second time, and I opened my eyes to see trees bordering a parking lot. "Are we home?" I asked.

"We have but the short walk through the woods," Mzatal replied. "And you are more rested."

Bryce roused and prodded Paul awake and out of the SUV. We made quick work of unloading our stuff, then tromped through the woods, over the fence, and back to the house, where a bouncing and burbling Jekki greeted us with delight. After reassuring the faas he was indeed well, Mzatal went straight to the mini-nexus. Bryce bundled the still sleepy Paul off to bed, then headed to the kitchen to scrounge breakfast while I went to join Mzatal.

We sat quietly for a while, facing each other in the center of the mini-nexus, the potency tickling like the nibble of minnows as we listened to the chirp of sparrows and drone of insects.

"Boss," I said after some time, "we need to do something about your aura. If you're going to function here on Earth without causing chaos, we need to figure out how to tone it down. A lot."

He grew contemplative, reading the implications behind the words. "It is a marked problem while among humans," he admitted.

"Perhaps Szerain could help," I ventured. "No one feels his aura."

Mzatal's frown deepened. "He is submerged. I cannot mimic that."

"Yes, I know. But I've been around him unsubmerged, as well as when he's expressing way more through Ryan. It's as if he's able to keep a lid on his aura projection. Maybe you could talk to him about it and see how he does it?"

I felt the resistance in him. He frowned, as if looking for any other alternative, and it was a long moment before he spoke. "It is the best and most expedient solution," he said, though his tone was certainly *grudging*. "I will speak to him."

There was something going on between those two, but I didn't have time to deal with it now. At least he'd agreed to talk to Szerain.

I yawned, still tired. Even though I'd slept quite a while

in the car it wasn't the same as sleeping in a proper bed. I frowned. Why had I been in the car for so long?

"Kara!" Mzatal said sharply.

I jerked and blinked at him. "Shit." My pulse lurched. "The implant containment."

He laid one hand on my shoulder and the other against my cheek. "We are joined at the hip, beloved, as you have noted," he said, calm and placid. "I will reinforce it again."

He went still and quiet for only a few minutes, but it was enough time for me to go through plenty of worry. "I need to get some real sleep for a couple of hours," I told him. "Could you give me a little of your magic sleeping mojo?"

He smiled and kissed me. "It is done. Be in your bed in five minutes or you will find yourself napping on the floor."

I laughed, kissed him back, and headed inside. Yet as I passed the dining room I had to stop and do a double take. The elves had been at work expanding Kara's Kafé while we were in Austin.

The dining room hadn't been an actual room for *dining* in the entire time I'd lived in the house as an adult. But now, storage boxes, miscellaneous items, and cobwebs had been cleared away, and a simple but lovely eight chair dining table occupied the middle of the hardwood floor. Nostalgia tugged hard as memory filled my senses of the last Thanksgiving before my dad died: family and friends and food.

I smiled. I still had family and friends, and they were helping me turn my house back into a home.

I continued to my room, crawled into bed, and fell asleep with a smile on my face.

Three hours later I stretched awake with no remembered dreams and no sense of time having passed. After a quick shower and a cup of coffee, I felt more than ready to get back into the hunt.

My first move was to transfer case files and Tracy's journals from the living room to the dining table. I doubted the guys had meant for me to christen the new table with work, but it was loads better than the sofa or kitchen table for spreading out.

I worked and munched on Jekki-made finger sandwiches while I tried to glean more useful information from Tracy's notes. After about an hour my eyes started glazing over, and I pushed back from the table with a groan. Out in the living room I heard Bryce and Jekki talking.

"Hey, Bryce," I called out. "You busy with anything right now?"

Bryce came in through the kitchen, looking sharp and dangerous in his polo shirt and shoulder holster. "Nope. Paul's up and working, and there's no more I can do on the camera system until we get those quotes back. Whatcha need?"

"I need another set of eyes," I told him. "I'd like to know if there are any more references to locations in these journals. Anything is good, but particularly Texas and the Southeast."

"I can handle that." He pulled out a chair and sat. "Slide the pile this way."

I shoved one of the stacks toward him, a miscellany of notes, case files, journals and photos. "Go wild."

We worked in silence for a while, each absorbed in our own world, neither of us announcing any great discoveries. I finally sat back and pressed the heels of my hands into my eyes. "Damn it. This shit gives me a headache."

Bryce tossed the journal in his hand aside and picked up the next one, then put it down again. Frowning, he tugged an overflowing photo folder from mid-stack and slid an eight by ten from it. "Shit," he murmured.

I glanced over. "Got something?"

"Maybe. I don't know," he said, his brow furrowed. "What are these drawings?"

I took a closer look at what he held: a crime scene photo from over a year ago of the office of murdered Greg Cerise, with sketches of people, demons, and other-worldly settings plastering the walls. "Greg Cerise drew all of those," I told him. "He had a knack for finding people who were arcanely gifted." I pulled out some photos that had better views of the sketches. "I think he either visited the demon realm at some point or he was awfully damned prescient, because his drawings are dead on." I made a face. "His dad, Peter Cerise, turned out to be the Symbol Man and used Greg's drawings to find his victims."

"Like Farouche finds talent," Bryce observed.

"Yeah, I guess it's something like that." I lifted my chin toward the photo in his hand. "Why did that one grab your attention?"

"You have any better photos of this sketch here?" He tapped one of the drawings in the photo, and a chill went through me. Rhyzkahl.

"Sure. Hold on." I did my best to keep my face neutral, pulled three comics from another pile. *Shattered Realm*, the graphic novel written and drawn by Greg Cerise. I found a page with a good representation and dropped it on the table in front of Bryce.

He stared at the page—a full-color of Rhyzkahl in armor looking out over the battlements of a castle. He sat back in the chair. "Jesus. Mega-Fabio."

"Bryce, spill," I ordered.

"He's a goddamn demonic lord, isn't he."

I stood. "That's Rhyzkahl," I said, my voice flat and hard. "Tell me how you know him."

Bryce shoved up from the table. "I've seen him several times, once as close to him as I am to you. He's in with Farouche. Big time."

My heart pounded unevenly. "How? When? When did you see him?"

"Shit, I don't know the exact dates," he said with a shake of his head. "Now it makes sense. He doesn't feel at all like Mzatal or Elofir, but he has his own aura just as strong. Shit! I should've realized it sooner."

"It's okay. Just tell me *when*," I said, unable to hide the urgency in my voice. "Ball park. Anything."

His mouth firmed. "The first time was in the spring last year. Not sure exactly when. He showed up at the compound gates at about three a.m., demanded to see Farouche, and *did*. That's unheard of."

Cold sweat pricked the small of my back. "Spring. You said it was night. Do you remember anything in particular about it?"

He frowned. "Not much. It was pleasant and clear, and there was a big full moon hanging low over the house."

Shit. Shit! Ice formed in my gut. That was the first night I'd summoned Rhyzkahl—completely by accident. I'd been trying to summon a luhrek named Rysehl, and the demonic lord had hijacked my summoning to escape the Symbol Man's attempt to summon and bind him. He'd seduced me that night and had apparently then gone straight to Farouche when he was done.

"That fucker. That . . . *fucker*." My nails cut into the palms of my hands as I clenched my fists. "How many times? Was it always late at night?"

"I saw him six, maybe seven times," Bryce told me. "He'd always arrive late, and usually stay until around noon the next day, sometimes a little later."

Stupid stupid stupid! I railed at myself. Of course he wouldn't waste all of that lovely access to Earth I so generously gave him. *But how? How did he get from my house to Farouche?* Every time he left me, he disappeared—I assumed to return to the demon realm. Sick anger spread through my chest and gut. *Easy enough to manipulate me to believe that's what happened,* I realized. Manipulate me, stroll outside, and call a syraza to him to give him a lift.

"Oh god," Bryce breathed. I jerked my attention to him to see a look of deep dismay on his face.

"What?" I managed to ask.

Bryce drew in a ragged breath. "That's where the abductees must've gone, to the demon realm. I don't know whether that's good or bad, but I don't feel very good about it."

I moved around the table, eyes on him. "Abductees?"

"Farouche acquired people for him," he told me, voice pained. "Mostly women. Mega-Fabio would take one or two back with him every time he visited. Sonny was the pickup man and handler for all of them, except for one. Not a woman. A StarFire inner circle guy who'd pissed off Farouche and was already in his custody." He gripped the back of a chair. "God almighty, Sonny hates those assignments."

My mind raced, and I forced myself to think past the horror of human trafficking. Sonny. Maybe he was the key. Of all the people Bryce and Paul had left behind, Sonny was the one they truly missed and worried about. *And he's still on the inside.*

"You consider Sonny to be a decent guy, don't you?" I asked.

Bryce exhaled. "Sonny hates what he does, but he does it. Then again, with jobs for Farouche, we all do—did— them. Some get off on it, some consider it nothing more than a job and get plenty of sleep at night, and some get ulcers." He tugged fingers through his hair. "He's done a few hits, but only as the second man. He's lead for . . ." He hesitated, then sighed before continuing. "He's often lead for pickups—abductions—because he can really keep people calm. That talent we talked about. But despite all that, yeah, he's a decent guy."

Murder, kidnapping, and who knew what else. Farouche was definitely a Grade-A piece of shit. But a few days ago Paul had tapped into a conversation between Sonny and his estranged sister, and discovered that Bryce's disappearance had shaken up Sonny's world. That sounded like a man desperate for a change. "Do you think he'd be a mole for us and help get Idris's mom out?"

Bryce began to shake his head, then stopped and frowned. "I was about to say no way in hell—not with Farouche's influence. But it's Sonny. I don't think he would've made it if I hadn't pretty much held him together for the past twelve years. He has a soft streak that's perfect for," he grimaced, "his specialty, abduction, so Farouche tolerated him." He rubbed a hand over his jaw, expression thoughtful. "I guess it's possible," he finally admitted.

"I know you want to get him out of there," I said. "Let's see if he can help us help him. This could be a parting shot."

"I do want to get him out," Bryce said slowly. "But I don't want him to get fucked up in the process, y'know?"

"I understand," I said, "and we'll do our damndest to keep it safe for him. But if we don't help him, he'll *never* get out."

"You're right," Bryce said, voice hollow, then sighed and straightened his shoulders. "Here's the deal. Making that call to his sister was out of bounds. Against Mr. Farouche's rules. That tells me he's desperate, and somehow managing to push through the fear. That's the *only* reason I think there's a chance he won't run straight to Farouche if we contact him."

"Maybe it has something to do with his talent," I suggested. "Perhaps the super-calm somehow helps him override the fear?"

Bryce stared at me. "Y'know, that could be it. He's never been pushed like this without me there." He nodded. "We'll need to feel him out. A text from Paul."

"Right, and if we like what we get, we set up a meeting. I'll trust your judgment on how to proceed with that."

"He should be able to receive a message and avoid trouble." Bryce mused, clearly warming to the plan. "And if we're right about his state of mind, I don't think he'd go straight to the boss."

"It's possible he might set us up," I said, "but we'll be able to sniff out a trap." I considered the various aspects, then nodded. "If he agrees to meet with us, we grab him and Mzatal will clear Farouche's influence from him. If he then agrees to be a mole, that's awesome for us, but even if he doesn't, he'll be free."

"Oh, god," Bryce said, voice thick. "It'd be wonderful to get him the hell away from there." Years of pain and doubt swam in his eyes.

I ached for him. He'd saved Sonny's life, and then had to carry the heavy guilt of what Sonny became. "Let's get Paul to text him and go from there."

We found Paul yawning on his futon, and quickly filled him in on our desire to get Sonny away from Farouche and use him as a mole, if he was willing.

Paul's face brightened instantly. "Awesome! What's the plan?"

"Let's start with a simple text that says 'Hey' and see what we get back," I suggested.

Paul tapped at his tablet. "There, sent." About twenty seconds later, he grinned. "He texted back 'You OK? Bryce?'"

I smiled. It was a good start. "Um, tell him you're both okay, and you miss him."

He did so. It felt like ages for the response to come in, though it was probably more like thirty seconds.

Really miss you two. Hard without you.

I pumped my fist into the air. "Perfect! We know he's freaking out a bit without you and Bryce there. Now tell him you'd like to meet with him, only him, to see him again. Oh, and don't let on that we're going to keep him."

Paul rolled his eyes. "Yeah, I was going to finish it off with, 'Hey, Sonny. We're totally *not* going to kidnap you, okay? TTFN!'"

I maintained a serious expression. "Wow, then it's a good thing I warned you!" I snorted, grinned. "Smart ass."

Paul laughed and sent, *Bryce needs to talk to you, and we both want to see you. We want to meet.*

Another eternity of waiting, this one far longer than

thirty seconds. Or even a few minutes. Bryce began to look a little antsy, and I struggled not to fidget. Paul finally looked up at Bryce, his face worried and sad.

"Give him a little more time," Bryce told Paul. "This is a big deal." Through the tension in his voice I heard the acknowledgement of the other possibility—that Sonny was informing Farouche.

The instant the words left his mouth the tablet pinged, and Paul lit up again. "Where? When?"

I heaved a big sigh of relief. It didn't mean he *hadn't* warned Farouche, but at least he was still communicating. "Bryce, they probably track the cars, right?" At his nod, I continued, "Where's someplace he usually goes that wouldn't raise suspicions?"

"The Beaulac Nature Center," he said without hesitation. "He goes there to chill and spend time alone."

It took several more texts to sort the details out since we had to consider what time would be best for Sonny and to arouse the least suspicion on his end. Moreover, we needed time to prepare.

At long last the plans were set—a nice casual meeting between good friends at the remote Nature Center at four p.m. Nice and friendly. No pressure. Only one slightly dastardly plan to kidnap him.

"Let's hope he comes through for us," I said and glanced at my watch. Two hours until the meeting.

Time to start moving our pieces into place.

Chapter 36

Once again our trek through the back woods and over the fence went without a hitch, though this time instead of a rental SUV, the fed boys waited for us in their Impalas. Eilahn muttered something in demon that included kiraknikahl as she passed Ryan's car on her way to Zack's, but at least she didn't snarl. That was progress.

Zack greeted me with a brilliant smile that felt just as much Zakaar's. "Well, sheriff," he said in an accent worthy of an old Western movie, "I reckon we better git the posse saddled up and hit the trail."

I grinned. "At least you made me the sheriff."

He winked, then slid behind the wheel of his car. "I considered you for the saloon girl part, but you can be a bit *bristly* at times."

"Bristly?" I laughed. "Is that what you call it?"

"When I'm being polite," he replied, and with that we loaded up the two cars and made our way to the rendezvous with Sonny.

Thunder rumbled in the distance, as we pulled into the Nature Center's empty parking lot. The air held the heavy feel of impending rain, lending an ominous atmosphere to our surroundings as we exited the cars and did a careful look-around. Even on the best of days the Beaulac Nature Center—also known as the Crappy Trail Through Mosquito-Infested Swamp and Woods—wasn't a big draw, but the hot, muggy afternoon coupled with the promise of a thunderstorm added an extra layer of deterrent.

Worked for me. The last thing we wanted was bystanders, though I hoped the rain would hold off until we were finished here.

Eilahn slipped into the woods and was out of view within seconds. Mzatal stood motionless, assessing, then gave me a nod. "No other humans or demons are near," he assured me.

"Awesome." I turned and gave Zack and Ryan a thumbs-up.

"Text when you're done," Ryan called through the open window, then he and Zack drove off.

I swept my gaze over the Plexiglas-covered map of the trails and the weathered shack that made up the Center. The last time I'd been here was to work the murder scene of one of Tracy Gordon's victims, sacrificed as a crude means for him to locate a valve in the area. And only a few days later Mzatal and Idris finally managed to summon me to the demon realm.

I've changed a teensy bit since then.

I checked my watch. "Forty-five minutes 'til showtime," I said.

Bryce shook his head. "Sonny'll be here early. Best to get in position." He didn't wait for me to give assent or comment and headed down the trail in long strides.

Paul chuckled under his breath. "He'll never admit it," he murmured to me as we followed Bryce, "but he actually really enjoys the planning and tactics side of things." He smiled at the older man's back. "I think it's like a puzzle for him. It tweaks that logic center in his brain."

"And I'm damn glad to let him plan his little heart out," I replied with a smile.

About a hundred yards in, the trail opened into a clearing with a few decrepit tables and moss-covered concrete barbeque pits. Beyond, the trail continued to an equally poorly kept deck over the swamp.

Bryce and Paul settled at a table they proclaimed to be Sonny's favorite, while Mzatal strode directly to the valve near the edge of the clearing and crouched, frowning. I moved to stand behind him as he worked his hands in slow, precise arcs over the valve. Othersight revealed an odd fraying of the twisted potency strands that formed the perimeter of the valve, like braids of rope that had been overstressed.

I set my hand on his shoulder. "What's up?"

Mzatal's frown deepened as he continued to work, and I noted the frays smoothing. "Tampering," he said. "The primary node has been touched from the demon realm side."

"Touched?" My eyes narrowed. "You mean something's been pushed through it?"

"Nothing has come through this one recently," he told me. "I feel Rhyzkahl's resonance, and there is a distortion I do not understand. You see the damage. There has been stress on the structure." He passed his hands over the valve once more then stood and took my hand. "The man approaches." He paused, his eyes distant. "He is alone."

Mzatal and I quickly moved into the underbrush to crouch not far off the trail. Though Mzatal's initial proposal had been to simply net Sonny in potency at the first sign of resistance, I'd managed to argue the lord down to a somewhat less traumatic option, in which we would simply block Sonny's retreat, leaving potency-netting as an absolute last resort.

Within minutes, I heard the whisper of shoes on damp pine needles, and I peered between the leaves toward the sound. A Hispanic-featured man about five-foot-ten of medium build made his way down the path toward us. I recognized him as one of Farouche's gunmen, though instead of a suit he had on jeans and a navy blue t-shirt. If I hadn't known what to look for, I'd have missed the slight bulge of his shirt where an inside-the-waistband holster held his gun.

His face broke into a cautious smile as he came within sight of Bryce and Paul, but as he came abreast of us he faltered and stopped. His eyes flicked left and right in wary alarm, and he slipped his hand under his shirt to rest on his gun.

Mzatal's aura, I realized with a silent curse. Sonny *felt* something was off.

Bryce stood. "Sonny, it's okay. I promise," he said with quiet but firm assurance. "Please, we need to talk."

At Bryce's words, a wild fear lit Sonny's eyes—Farouche's influence, I knew all too well. He shook his head and took a step back. "I . . . can't," he said, voice tight and strained, even as crushing disappointment twisted his features. "I'm sorry," he gasped out and spun to leave.

In two quick strides I crashed through the brush and

onto the trail to block his retreat. "Wait. Please." I held my hands out to show they were empty. "We're here with Bryce and Paul to help you."

Sonny stopped, hand still on his gun, though he didn't make a move to draw it. I remained still, secure in the faith that Eilahn and Mzatal were poised and ready in case Sonny tried to do anything foolish. He puffed out quick, adrenaline-fueled breaths, and I didn't need to be a mind reader to understand his distress at being lured into a trap, especially one contrary to Farouche's interests. Sonny shifted, eyes flicking from me to Bryce and then widening on Mzatal as he stepped onto the path.

Bryce moved toward us slowly. "Sonny, it's okay. We're going to help you. I swear."

"Bryce, goddammit," Sonny said, voice hoarse with a barely controlled panic. "You know I gotta get out of here. You *know* it. Fuck! You set me up." Pain overshadowed the fear on his last words. "How could you do that?"

"It's not what you think," Bryce said, voice and manner calm and cool. "Look, we can get you out, get you away from Mr. Farouche. Lord Mzatal helped me and Paul, and he's agreed to help you, too."

Hope flared on Sonny's face for a blinding instant before the fear eclipsed it again. A choking sob welled in his throat even as his hand twitched on his gun.

Shit. This was going to require a lot more than talk. Sonny had been driving under the influence of Farouche for a long damn time.

Even as I thought it, Mzatal moved toward him. Sonny drew his gun but fumbled it under the crush of Mzatal's full-on aura. He staggered back as the lord advanced, caught his foot on a root and fell hard, then crab-scuttled backwards a few feet until brought up short by the trunk of a pine.

He stared up at Mzatal, eyes wild and panicked. Mzatal crouched smoothly and clamped his hands around Sonny's head, and in the next instant Sonny's mouth dropped open, and he went completely still.

"I will clear enough of the fear for him to productively interact," Mzatal told me, then focused his full attention on the man in his grasp.

Step one accomplished, and no one got shot, I thought

with relief as I picked up the dropped gun and handed it off to Bryce. He checked it, tucked it into his waistband and stood silently, watching Mzatal work. Paul stood near the table, naked worry on his face, his tablet clutched to his chest like a security blanket. I kept an eye on the trail toward the parking lot in case any nature lovers decided to wander our way. This would be an interesting tableau to explain.

Mzatal finally straightened and stepped back. Sonny remained pressed back against the tree like a trapped animal, but the crazed and unnatural fear no longer filled his eyes.

"Come on, Sonny," I said as I held my hand down to him. "Let's talk."

He blinked, looked from me to Bryce, then back to my hand. After a moment's hesitation, he took it and stood. "What the hell?"

I gave him a reassuring smile. "Lord Mzatal cleared some of the abnormal fear Farouche instilled in you," I told him. "I'm Kara Gillian. It's good to finally meet you."

"She's not kidding," Bryce added. "I'm free of him. Really free. You can be, too."

"I don't get it," Sonny said, doubt paired with unmistakable hope in his voice. "How?"

I hooked a thumb toward the picnic table. "How about we sit down and talk. There's a lot we need to cover."

"Talk. Yeah. Okay." He moved toward the table with me as though in a weird dream, gave a flickering smile to Paul. "Hey, kid. Ugly as ever."

Paul grinned, joy and relief bright in his eyes. "Hey, Sonny. Still a total pain in the ass."

Bryce followed. "All I'm asking is that you listen to what Kara has to say," he said to Sonny. "You make your own decisions after that."

Sonny regarded Bryce for a long moment, then gave a nod and sank onto the bench. I sat opposite him and, with Bryce's help to fill in the gaps, quickly offered a thumbnail of who we were and why Mzatal was there, then moved on to how Farouche was holding people who we wanted back. When I finished, I took a deep breath and spread my hands out on the rough surface of the picnic table. "The bottom line is, do you want our help to get away from Farouche?"

Sonny swallowed, nodded. "I want out. I gotta get out."

"Then we'll make that happen," I assured him. "First, Lord Mzatal has to finish clearing the hold that Farouche has on you. Once that's done, we can talk more."

A flicker of fear touched Sonny's eyes, and Bryce reached across the table and put a hand on his arm. "Sonny, look at me," he said firmly. "Look at Paul. You know damn well I couldn't have set up something like this while under Farouche's influence." He let that sink in for a few seconds. "It works. We're really free of him."

"It's true," Paul confirmed with an emphatic nod.

Sonny rubbed a hand over his face as if checking to make sure he wasn't daydreaming. "Uh, sure." He looked around, glassy-eyed. "All right. What do I need to do?"

"Just relax," I said.

Mzatal moved behind Sonny, laid his hands on his head. Sonny's face went slack except for a crooked smile, as if he was enjoying some great painkillers. Paul gravely lifted his tablet and took a picture of his expression, and Bryce laughed.

"Blackmail," Paul told me with a wink.

I smiled, even more pleased about the decision to get Sonny out. These men were obviously friends as well as co-workers, and now I saw that another layer of tension had peeled away from Bryce and Paul. *Leave no man behind,* I thought with satisfaction.

After another few minutes, Mzatal stepped back, and Sonny lost the good-drugs look.

"How do you feel?" I asked as Mzatal returned to his position behind me.

"Okay, I guess," Sonny said, though he didn't seem very certain of it.

"Now think about leaving Farouche's employment."

Fear flickered in his eyes for an instant in pure ingrained reflex, then his mouth dropped open. "That's . . . impossible."

"It's *normal*," I corrected.

"You'll get used to it," Bryce added.

"Now for part two," I said. "And I'm sorry to forge ahead so quickly, but we're hoping you can help us." I gave him a second to acknowledge with a nod. "Bryce says you're taking care of Angela Palatino."

"I am. She's at the plantation." He flinched, as if expecting lightning to strike him for saying something so directly against Farouche's interests then visibly forced himself to relax.

"She's the mother of Idris Palatino, a friend of ours," I told him, "and she's being held as hostage to help ensure his cooperation."

His mouth twisted. "I had a feeling it was something like that. Orders were to treat her well and tell her nothing."

I leaned forward. "Here's the kicker," I said. "We have reason to believe Idris will be brought to the plantation within the next two days. Do you know anything about that?"

Sonny pursed his lips, then tipped his wrist to check his watch. "Nigel Fox and Mystery Man Twenty-two were supposed to land about half an hour ago at a private strip not far from the plantation." He glanced back up. "Escorting a package. That could be your Idris."

"Holy shit," I breathed as Mzatal's intensity flared behind me like summer heat off pavement. *And Mystery Man Twenty-two is Aaron Asher.* My pulse thudded in a mixture of shock, excitement, and victory. *It's not a victory yet,* I reminded myself. Not even close. We didn't even know if the package was really Idris.

I forced myself to chill. "That leads right in to what I have to ask you. However, I want to be totally clear right up front: You can absolutely say no. We won't coerce or guilt trip you."

The skin around Sonny's eyes tightened. "Say no to what?"

"We have a couple of plans," I said. "One of them," *and the best one*, I added silently, "needs someone on the inside to help us." I watched him carefully. I was basically asking him to walk into a dragon's lair and punch the dragon in the balls.

He went still, barely breathing. For a good ten seconds he let that sink in before he stood up, eyes on Bryce and gave a head jerk away from the table. Bryce slid a glance to me then retreated about twenty feet away with Sonny. Paul seemed oblivious to their departure, his attention fully on his tablet, earbuds in, and his eyes with the familiar distant and glazed look that said he was in deep.

Mzatal shifted behind me and murmured, "Sonny Ortiz can be manipulated to cooperate fully."

I actually considered it for about two seconds. It would be so damn *easy*. "No, Boss. He can't." I sighed and glanced back at him. "We'd be no different than Farouche. If Sonny doesn't agree to do it, we'll find another way." I understood why he proposed it. Manipulation was a tool at his disposal, one that would bring him closer to Idris, but I made sure my views and feelings about this were easy for him to read. And, to his credit, I felt Mzatal receive my input and accept it. Good enough for now.

Yet I had to control a shiver at the reminder of how dangerous the lords could be to humans. An instant later, I felt Mzatal's hand on my shoulder. He was willing to resist those ingrained patterns of demonic lord behavior, at least in this moment. I covered his hand with my own, deeply appreciating that he made the effort.

"It's him!" Paul looked up from the tablet and gave a triumphant smile. "Sonny's right. Idris came in with Fox and Asher. Both of Big Mack's jets are in their hangars, so I broadened the scope. Found a Gulfstream G650 belonging to a business associate of B.M.'s that landed at the private strip half an hour ago. No video, but I caught Idris's name in a phone call. He's at the plantation."

I stared for a second, processing not only the confirmation of our suspicion, but the magnitude of Paul's talent. "You have successfully kicked all the ass," I said. "Hot damn. That seals it."

Paul grinned, then glanced over at Bryce and Sonny as they returned to the table. Sonny still looked dazed, but there was a determined set to his mouth. Bryce met my eyes and gave a slight nod.

The two sat again, and Sonny cleared his throat. "Yeah," he said. "I can do it. I *need* to do it."

I drew breath to respond, even as Paul whooped and shot to his feet.

"You're the *best,* Sonny!" he exclaimed, eyes bright with excitement. "All you have to do is go to the server room by the security station and disconnect my firewall of doom from behind the third rack of servers and plug in a dongle I have all ready to go. Then I can run all sorts of interference, kill their comms, and totally rule the plantation so Lord Mzatal can come in blazing!"

I fought back a grin at Paul's enthusiasm. "Yeah, what he said."

But Sonny's expression grew more serious. "There's something weird with that room since yesterday," he said with a slow shake of his head. "The door's closed, and I get queasy if I look at it too long."

My brief euphoria slipped away. "Shit," I muttered. "It's been warded. Sonny, you won't be able to get in there." I drummed my fingers on the table as I considered our plans and the giant gaping holes that now appeared in them. "As it stands now, Mzatal can't go in because the alarm would be raised and Angela would get a gun to her head, but if Paul can get his doogle—"

"Dongle," he corrected.

I snorted. "If Paul can get his *dongle* to the server room, then he can shut their comms and alarm down and all sorts of other good stuff. But it looks like only someone with the ability to remove wards can get into the server room." I smiled tightly. "I think that leaves me."

Sonny grimaced. "Easier said than done. First you have to get onto the plantation grounds, which isn't even remotely easy. Fenced perimeter, surveillance, the works. And even if you manage that, then you need to look as if you're supposed to be there for long enough to do the thing to the server room. Problem is, it's in the main house, and *everyone* knows everyone else. Not like you can pretend to be a new hire or something." He shook his head. "Don't get me wrong—I'm all for taking Mr. Farouche down, but—"

"Paul tracked your car today," Bryce interrupted, eyes bright and expression determined. "You made a forty-three minute stop at the residence of Amaryllis Castlebrook and then staked out her workplace. You prepping for a grab?"

I swung my attention to Bryce, surprised and thoroughly impressed by the tidbit of information and follow-through. Though Mzatal said nothing, I felt his focus intensify as he read the two men's nuances faster and with greater clarity than they could speak.

"It's scheduled for tonight," Sonny said, then comprehension dawned on his face only an instant behind my own.

"You take me instead," I breathed. Damn I loved my posse.

"Everything's easier now," Bryce said, voice rich with satisfaction.

Sonny looked off into the distance, no doubt running through the possibilities. "Yeah," he said after a moment. "It could work."

An ugly thought wormed into my mind. "Sonny, is Rhyzkahl at the compound now? Or has he been there since yesterday?" I couldn't unwind the wards if he'd set them.

At Sonny's puzzled look, Bryce clarified, "Mega-Fabio."

"No," he said. "He hasn't been around for a few months. But I suspect he's coming back." Anger deepened the lines in his face. "Rumor has it that's who this pickup is for."

My mouth curved into a tight and cold smile. "Even more perfect. When are you supposed to grab her?"

"Tonight, between nine and ten as she leaves a cocktail party at Bimini Bay restaurant in Villafleur—about an hour from here," he said. "First night of a corporate training seminar being held at the hotel down the street." He shrugged, then exhaled. "Take her tonight, and she won't be missed for two days."

Bryce glanced at me. "Abductees are *always* brought in at night," he explained.

Sonny nodded in agreement. "And any bad shit happens indoors, away from prying satellite eyes."

"Nice to know Farouche has a solid business plan," I said with a snort. "We'll ask Ryan and Zack to collect Amaryllis before the party and get her to a safe house."

"Sonny, who's with you?" Bryce asked.

Distaste touched his mouth. "Jerry."

Jerry. The one Bryce said loved his job and didn't lose sleep at night over it. The one who brought Amber to be raped and murdered. "Does Jerry or anyone else know what Amaryllis looks like?" I asked. "It'll be pointless to try and sub for her if it's obvious I'm not the mark."

Sonny peered at me. "Jerry's expecting a blond twenty-something," he said. "With a good wig you'd pass for her well enough. Plus, I'd bring you in hooded, and no one will check since *no one* crosses Mr. Farouche." He paused, then shifted, his face coloring slightly. "But, ah, the other girl is more, um . . ." His flush deepened as he gestured vaguely with both hands.

"Endowed?" I offered, hiding my amusement at his discomfort.

"Yeah. Curvy." He winced. "Sorry."

"It's cool." I grinned. "In fact it's perfect. Now I have a place to hide my weapons."

Chapter 37

Plans and preparations for the infiltration and raid on the plantation could have easily turned into pure chaos and been doomed to failure from the start, but Bryce took firm charge with an uncompromising hand. Even Mzatal deferred to his judgment, to my surprise and relief. Within two hours of leaving the Nature Center, and with the help of Paul, Ryan, and Zack, we had maps and satellite imagery, a communication system, and all sorts of other gear that I never would have thought we'd need but suddenly realized that yes, we most certainly did.

And, most of all, we had a *plan*. Sonny and I: infiltrate and get me to the server room for the dongle-thing. Paul: take down comms and security. Mzatal: strip the wards and burn through the fence. Sonny and Bryce: Rescue Angela Palatino and get her through the fence and off the property. Zack and Ryan: watch our backs. Everyone: Do whatever is needed to Acquire Idris.

At about seven p.m. Zack arrived at the house bearing a wig, dress, shoes, and appropriate padding for my role as Amaryllis. I immediately fell in love with the dress, and silently promised myself that after all of this was over I'd have it tailored to fit my normal not-as-curvy figure. Alluring without being slutty, it had a gathered bodice and a side-slit skirt—both of which would allow me plenty of freedom of movement. Most importantly, it came with a sheer and clinging black lace top that slipped over the dress and covered every inch of the sigil scars without reducing the *allure* level one bit. I didn't even mind that the sleeves of the lace top were a bit too small. *Muscles*, I thought with a grin. *I gots 'em.*

It took me damn near a half an hour to get the dress and my pseudo-curves adjusted properly to accommodate and hide my little Keltec .32 in a slim thigh holster, but I eventually achieved concealment, along with a voluptuous look I doubted I'd ever be able to achieve by natural means. That accomplished, Paul, Zack, and Eilahn continued to load me up with other necessary equipment. My watch doubled as a GPS tracker, I had a backup tracker shoved somewhere around my right boob, and beneath the left was Paul's dongle. And yes, I giggled every time I thought about Paul's dongle. Finally, Eilahn and Zack double-teamed me to get the wig and makeup just right, then stepped back so I could see the result in the full-length mirror on the back of my bedroom door.

"Wow," I said. Then said it again. "Wow."

I didn't look *anything* like me. The woman in the mirror was sweet and curvy and harmless, with an almost-shy smile on rosebud lips, and honey-blond hair that somehow gave her grey eyes an interesting hazel tinge.

"Kara," Eilahn said, eyes on me. I jerked my gaze away from the reflection and stepped away so I couldn't see it anymore.

"Yes." *I'm Kara.* It was a reflection. Black dress and lace sleeves, wig and shoes and all. The woman in the mirror wore a ring with a cracked stone—

I shook my head sharply. No, Kara wore that ring. *I* wore that ring. I looked down at it on my hand. Amaryllis would never wear a ring like this. Too bold, too unique. But Kara would. Cracked stone and all, because the ring and the stone and the crack held a meaning that couldn't possibly be conveyed in mere words.

I looked back up at them. "I'm ready."

Eilahn exchanged a quick glance with Zack, then returned her attention to me. "No, you are not," she said firmly, gripped my upper arm, and walked me to the back of the house.

"What the hell?" I asked, baffled.

Mzatal stepped onto the porch as Eilahn escorted me through the back door. "The containment," she stated, which was apparently all the information Mzatal required.

"Oh," I said, voice small. Shit. I hadn't even realized.

"Zharkat," he murmured as he lifted a hand to my cheek. I felt the conflict within him, felt him waver in his willingness to risk me for the sake of Idris.

"Boss." I squared my shoulders and shoved aside the gnawing worry. "It's my choice to go do this. Idris is my family." Whether by blood or not, the truth of it remained. "I couldn't live with myself if I didn't even try. You can reinforce the containment, right?"

He exhaled. "I can." His thumb stroked across my cheek. "And now I have."

I smiled, took his hand and laid a kiss in his palm. "Then we're all good. As soon as we have Idris, we'll take our asses back to the demon realm, and you and Elofir can fix this shit right up."

"So we shall." He kissed me, eyes remaining warm on mine for a moment more. Finally, he gave a nod to Eilahn, then turned and strode to the mini-nexus, hands clasped behind his back.

I returned to my bedroom with Eilahn and allowed her to fuss over my wig and makeup one more time, and after a few minutes she nodded, satisfied. "It is time to depart," she said and took my hands. "Is there aught else you require?"

I gave her a reassuring smile. "Can't think of a thing."

"I will never be far from you," she stated with such fierce loyalty that I felt tears come to my eyes. "Dahn!" She pulled her hands from mine and snatched a tissue from a box on the dresser to dab at my eyes. "You will smear your cosmetics if you weep!" She wore such a look of asperity on her face that I couldn't help but laugh.

"Okay, okay! I won't mess up the makeup."

Eilahn finished dabbing, stepped back and eyed me critically before giving me a satisfied nod. "Kara Gillian, you will indeed kick all the ass."

"Damn straight," I said fervently. "I was taught by the best."

This is not ass-kicking. This is hell.

"Who the hell knew telecommunications analysts could be so rowdy?" I muttered as I narrowly dodged a slosh of wine from the giggling woman beside me. I edged away from her, turned down yet another slurred offer that I assumed was sexual in nature, and finally found a place to put my back against the wall. I'd been "mingling" in the crowded bar area for the past thirty minutes while I waited for everyone to get into position, and had fended off more passes in that time than I'd received in my entire life. I was damn near ready to trace an aversion ward on my ass.

"It's considered one of the most boring jobs to have, Kara," Paul told me in an amused voice through the tiny receiver tucked into my ear. "Can you blame them for letting loose when they have the chance?"

"Yeah, well, the guy whose hand 'let loose' up my skirt is sporting some cracked metatarsals now," I said. My *stomp* reaction had been swift and instinctive, and I'd slipped away through the press of the crowd while the assailant whined in pain. He probably never even realized the sweet blond thing had a bite. Okay, maybe there was a little ass-kicking.

Luckily I didn't have to worry about breaking character until I got outside. Nobody in here would ever think I was pretending to be Amaryllis Castlebrook—if any of them even knew her in the first place. To them I was simply another partying teleco-whatever on the first night of what was probably a deathly dull training seminar.

"Serves the jerk right, Kara," Paul said, then added, "It's the dress. Even *I* think you look smokin' hot. And you look really good with blond hair."

I hid a grin and pretended to take a sip of my drink. Paul was right—the dress rocked, even if I did have to pad the curves a bit. "Maybe I'll try blond highlights once all this is done," I said, carefully avoiding eye contact with anyone and everyone, since I'd learned it was interpreted as an invitation to come annoy me. "I'm ready to ditch the wig, though. It itches. And I think one of the bobby pins has worked its way through my skull."

Paul chuckled. "I'll get you a purple heart, Kara."

"Hey, Paul? What's with the sudden obsession with my name?"

He cleared his throat. "Orders from above," he said a bit sheepishly. "Eilahn and Zack and Mzatal want me to keep, er, reminding you who you are."

A warm fuzzy glow started somewhere in my middle, and I felt a silly grin spread across my face. "Y'all are so fucking awesome it's stupid."

"It's a posse thing, *Kara*," he said with a laugh. I heard some soft beeps in the background, and when he spoke again he was all business. "Got the ping from Ryan. Amaryllis is safe and away, and all's clear." Earlier the two FBI agents had gently scooped up Ms. Castlebrook as she stepped out of her hotel room, leaving me to be her doppelganger at the cocktail party.

"And now I have Sonny's signal," he continued. "He's on the corner half a block down, waiting for you." He paused. "Good luck, Kara."

"Thanks, Paul," I murmured. I glanced at my watch. Nine p.m. Amaryllis was going to make an early night of it. "Here goes everything." I set my drink on a side table and slipped through the crowd to the door, my little Keltec a comforting weight in the thigh holster. Having Paul in my ear was another major comfort. He was coordinating the entire operation from his tablet for portability, and he'd rigged up everyone with nifty communicators like mine. All except for Mzatal, since he received annoying bursts of static any time he manipulated potency. The plan was for Paul to stay pretty much glued to Mzatal's side for this thing, so it hopefully wouldn't make any difference that the Boss wasn't wired up.

Exiting the restaurant, I faked a slight stumble on the bottom step as if I was a little intoxicated—after first making sure no one nearby was looking my way. Last thing I wanted was for someone to offer to walk me back to the hotel, either out of kindness or with more insidious intent in mind. Either way, they'd no doubt end up hurt. My performance was for the two men waiting down the street. They were watching, I knew, even if I couldn't see them yet.

The hotel was around the corner and half a block down. I looped my purse over my shoulder, headed down the sidewalk, and did my best to act relaxed and oblivious.

"Sonny's ahead and to your right, Kara," Paul told me, no doubt watching my progress through hacked security and traffic cameras in addition to monitoring my location via my GPS trackers.

"Got it," I murmured. I stepped off the curb to cross a well-lit corner parking lot, bordered by manicured bushes and colorful flower beds. Just the sort of place a naïve girl would let her guard down. Moreover, it made perfect sense for a woman wearing heels to cut through the lot. Sonny sure as hell knew his business.

Sonny, appearing utterly harmless and seeming to pay absolutely no attention to me, stood near the exit to the street, looking at nothing in particular as he spoke on his phone. As I made my way across the mostly empty lot, I noted his approach in my peripheral vision, but only because I was totally expecting it.

"Hey, hon'?" he said in a voice pitched with concern. I feigned a startle and an appropriately wary look, but the gentle smile he turned on me would have disarmed a Navy SEAL. "You'd better be careful. Looks like you've had too much to drink." He took a step closer. "Where's your car? I'll help you."

In the shadows by the building a lanky man in a dark suit leaned against a white Lexus SUV, and I only noticed him because I knew he'd be there. Jerry Steiner, the man who'd brutally raped Amber before Katashi murdered her.

I kept my gaze away from him though, and stayed in my role. "Um, I'm fine thanks," I said, adding in a shy little bite of my lower lip. "My hotel's right down the street." I let out a girlish titter, then had to clamp down on a scowl as Paul snorted in laughter. I turned away and continued walking through the lot, more than a little curious about how Sonny expected to pull off a quiet abduction in a place that was still somewhat public.

"You sure you're okay to walk that far?" Sonny fell into step beside me and touched my arm, and not in a skeevy way. In fact, a sensation of calm flowed over me. I felt relaxed, not at all nervous or worried or feeling any need to be cautious. *Ohhhhh, now, that's damn interesting.*

"I only had one glass of wine," I told Sonny, utterly fascinated by his effect. The dude was like a walking pygah. It wasn't something that lulled me into somnolence or fogged my thinking, either. I still had no problem assessing my situation and locating threats. If anything, my focus was sharper, simply because I was so calm.

But *I* knew exactly what was going on here. Turn that pygah-mojo on an unsuspecting mark, and they wouldn't stand a chance. *And Farouche's merchandise arrives in good condition and not completely freaked out.*

Sonny caught my elbow. "I think you had more than

one," he said, maintaining the same calm tone. He too was playing a role. He had to follow the typical mode of operation to the letter to keep Jerry from getting suspicious. *In other words*, I thought, *this is exactly how he grabbed all of those other women.*

He leaned close and lowered his voice, though I knew there was a chance his partner could still hear. "Listen to me," he said. "I'm not going to hurt you unless you give me trouble. Even think about making a sound, and I'll drop you." He shifted his other hand to show the stun gun in it. "You're going to get in the backseat of my car, nice and quiet."

You stun gun me and I will kick your ASS, I thought, but I widened my eyes in shock and got into the role. "Wh- what? No . . . no!"

The calm flowed over me. "I don't want to hurt you," he said, and with the words came a sense that he truly meant it. He didn't *want* to hurt me. Everything would be *alllll* right if I simply did as he asked. "But I will if I have to," he continued, and I *beliieeeeved* that as well.

Utterly amazed and truly impressed, I didn't resist as he walked me quickly to the car. Jerry pulled the back door open, and when Sonny told me to slide on in, I complied. Beige leather seats and side windows tinted to near black. They didn't want anyone seeing what happened in the back of this vehicle. *That explains the choice of an SUV*, the ex-cop part of me considered. Legally, back side windows of a sedan were required to allow twenty-five percent light in. No such law for vans and SUVs.

Not that it mattered at this point.

Jerry got behind the wheel, looked back at me with hard hazel eyes in a craggy face beneath receding brown hair. His gaze traveled to my chest and stopped there in a brazen leer, and I didn't have to fake my slight recoil.

Sonny slid in beside me and made sure I was buckled, then nodded to Jerry, who gave me a nasty smirk before he turned to face front again. As soon as the car moved out, Sonny zip-tied my wrists together in front of me then tapped my wrist twice, face impassive. I dropped a quick glance down, relieved to see the notch he'd made in the plastic. If things went to shit I could snap it without too much injury to myself.

"Where are you taking me?" I remembered to ask in a quavering voice, carefully balancing how calm I felt with what I figured a normal kidnapped woman would feel in this situation.

"To a place you're going to stay a while." Pain and guilt flashed in his eyes for a sliver of an instant before he shuttered it. If I hadn't been looking right at him—and known what it was—I'd have missed it. He hated this. Hated who he'd become.

A place I'm going to stay a while. I twisted my face into an I-might-cry expression to mask the fury that swept through me. All of those girls, yanked out of their lives to be sold to the lords. I hadn't thought it was possible to hate Rhyzkahl any more, but that hatred flared supernova hot now. And Farouche. I fully intended to make absolutely sure that motherfucker went down in flames.

I pygahed, since even Sonny's talent couldn't fully tamp down the spike of fury, and did my best to look scared and not like a fucking pissed off bitch. "I don't understand. Who are you people?"

"My name's Sonny and that's Jerry," he told me. "That's pretty much all you need to know right now." He reached to the front seat and retrieved a black cloth bag. "Time for you to wear this," he said, holding it up. Not a bag. A hood. "You gotta trust me," he added, with another touch of calm. "I'm not going to hurt you."

I'd been prepared for this, so I faked a tremble and allowed him to slip it over my head. Pygahing again, I extended all senses and listened as Paul murmured location updates in my ear, for which I was surprisingly grateful. Sure, Sonny was on our side now, and Mzatal would have detected any hesitation or duplicity on his part, but I was still going undercover into a snake's den. Paul's running commentary was a reminder that I had a significant safety net.

But more importantly, Paul's periodic murmur of my name in my ear helped me maintain my Self against the role I played. *I'm Kara,* I repeated silently. *No one else but Kara.*

After about an hour I heard gravel crunching beneath the tires. A few more turns, and the car slowed to a stop, then I heard the hum of the driver's window going down.

"Any problems?" A man's gruff voice from outside the car.

"Smooth as silk." That was Jerry.

"That's the best way. Unit twenty-three is prepped."

The window went back up, and the car started forward again. My skin prickled and arcane flickers abruptly appeared in my othersight. We'd gone through a security gate, I realized as I peered at the wards, smiling within the hood that I could do so without *seeing*. The warding was good, but even the quick glance was enough to tell me they weren't demonic lord good.

Sonny placed a hand on my wrist, interrupting my musings about warding. "Here's what's going to happen, Amaryllis," he said. "Once we park. I'm going to get out. You're going to stay right here in the car with Jerry. I'll be back in a few minutes, then I'll open your door and walk you to the place where you'll be staying. You understand?" He delivered it all in a smooth recitation that told me he'd said this many times before.

I did the scared gulp-thing. "And th-then what?"

"I'll get you settled in for the night. You'll be staying here for a while."

"A while" being less than an hour, I thought grimly, but I made the sort of shocked-scared sound a different girl might make at the terrifying vagueness of his statement.

Jerry drove for a few more minutes before pulling to a stop. "Sit tight," Sonny told me. "I'll be back in a couple." With that he opened the door and departed, taking the palpable sense of calm with him. Damn, that was a hell of a skill.

Jerry certainly didn't exude calm of any sort. Out of curiosity, I let out a low whimper to see how the hard-faced man would respond.

I heard him shift in his seat. "You got it good, honey," he said with a low snort of rude amusement.

Sucking in a sharp breath, I stiffened. "What do you mean?"

Fabric slid across leather and, judging from the sounds, I figured he'd turned and laid his arm across the back of the seat to look at me. "Because if you'd been my mark, I'd be having some fun pretty soon," he said, ugly smile in his voice. "Can't say the same for you though."

Shrinking back, I took a few seconds to control the fury.

Had he taunted Amber like this during the trip to Austin?
"D-don't you dare touch me!"

He let out a dry chuckle. "You get turned over to me, and
I'll touch you all right. You'll be begging me to stop, but I
won't."

Teeth clenched, I seethed but let out another whimper to
stay in character. The rape of Amber had been part of his
goddamn *job*. How many other women had he been allowed to use simply because they were available? Even one
was too many, and I knew damn well the number was far
higher.

"Oh, yeah," he drawled. "I'll have some fun with you
when they're done playing around."

"Kara," Paul murmured in my ear. "Please wait until *after* you do your thing in the server room to feed this asshole
his balls."

I smothered a laugh and had to quickly turn it into something that sounded like a frightened sob. *But if Sonny
doesn't return soon I probably* will *blow my cover and commit violence against this worthless piece of shit.*

As if my thoughts summoned him, the door beside me
opened. "Come on out," Sonny said. I did so, weirdly relieved as the calm descended again and hideously glad to
get away from Jerry. Sonny took my arm, then paused.
"Goddammit, Jerry," he said, voice tight with anger. "I'll
deal with you later."

Interesting, I thought as he led me away. He'd sensed that
Jerry had fucked with me. Jaw tight, I moved where Sonny
guided me: gravel and then a sidewalk beneath my feet. I
actively sank into the ease he projected, using it to center
myself.

He paused long enough to open a door, then led me inside, closed it behind us, then pulled my hood off. "No surveillance in here unless I turn it on," he told me, fatigue and
stress coloring his voice. He took a folding knife from his
pocket and sliced the zip tie on my wrists.

"Jerry's a real prince," I said. "I intend to castrate him
with a dull knife, first chance I have."

A muscle in his jaw leaped, and he nodded. "We need to
wait about fifteen minutes before going to the house," he
told me. "It'll be quieter then."

"Not a problem," I said. "I trust your judgment." I looked around. We were in an open-plan room with kitchen area, table with two chairs, sofa, bookshelves, TV, bed, and a door to a bathroom. All nicely appointed, like one would find in a decent hotel. "How long do the women you bring in for Rhyzkahl usually stay here?"

"Anywhere from a few days to seven or eight weeks," he said. "And not only women. Three men so far. Ones the boss said deserved harsh punishment."

I was pretty sure that if the men were sent for punishment, they were going to Kadir. The men were dead or worse by now, but the women were far more likely to still be alive. "Are there any others being held here now for Rhyzkahl?"

He shook his head. "Amaryllis was to be the first of two," he told me, then looked away. "The ones for him weren't the only ones—not the only grabs I've done."

The heart-wrenching despondency in his words took me aback. I'd focused exclusively on the handful of recent abductions related to Rhyzkahl. Yet Sonny had been at this for a dozen years. How many more had he taken for reasons other than to be given to the qaztahl? Men and women wanted by Farouche for any number of nefarious purposes. "Sonny. I'm so sorry. No more."

He looked back to me, face and eyes haunted. "I couldn't even kill myself to make it stop," he said, voice thick. "I tried. I *tried*, but Mr. Farouche . . ." He shook his head.

Though I hadn't thought it possible, my loathing of Farouche ratcheted up another notch. Sonny paid for his crimes with his soul every waking moment, and I was willing to bet his dreams weren't full of rainbows and unicorns. *Let's hope suicide isn't still on Sonny's agenda*, I thought grimly.

Sonny returned his focus to me. "What happened to the ones who went with Mega-Fabio?"

"Most likely used for sex," I told him frankly, doing my best to keep my voice level even though the topic induced white-hot rage in me. I forced calm and sifted back through my memory of snippets of information and conversations that made more sense now. "They'd be traded to other lords for favors, I'd imagine." I angled a look at him. "If it helps, I believe that most of the lords would treat a woman well." I grimaced sourly. "Even Rhyzkahl would take good care of a woman he desired." I highly doubted Amkir would, and I didn't think Jesral would be the picture of loving kindness either. And Kadir seemed pretty damn asexual. *He got those men,* I thought. *And not for sex.*

Sonny looked relieved. "I pretty much knew sex would be the purpose. Rhyzkahl seemed to like Janice a lot. He said he'd chosen her to live with him. It's good to hear they'll be okay."

I clamped down hard on the *No, they won't be okay!* response that leapt to my lips. This was human trafficking, plain and simple. But saying that wouldn't accomplish anything and would only distress Sonny more. He knew what he'd done, and right now he scrambled for any shred of comfort he could find. Now wasn't the time to yank that away from him.

"What's your usual routine with a new acquisition?" I asked in a sharp change of subject. "I don't want anyone wondering what's going on if you're supposed to be somewhere else."

He shook his head. "With the women, I usually spend some time to get them comfortable, anything up to an hour or so, depending on what they need." Guilt clawed across his face again.

"You did your best for them," I said gently. "You weren't simply taking care of the merchandise. You did everything you could to make a horrible situation a little less horrible. And the very fact that you came *back* here to help us proves you're a decent person and a fucking brave one at that."

"It has to stop. Not only for me. For everyone."

"We'll stop it," I promised, then bared my teeth in a hard smile. "It will rain fire, and we'll kick all the ass."

He let out a dry laugh, then glanced at his watch. "Let's do this. Carter will be on the desk. I'll walk you in as if I'm taking you to see the boss. I'll get you inside, then I'll get him away to give you time to get into the server room."

"Got it." I went to the mirror, adjusted the wig to make certain no stray brown hairs poked out, and dabbed away a bit of smeared makeup under my eyes. Amaryllis had pretty eyes. My reflection gave a shy smile—

I jerked my eyes from the mirror. "Paul," I muttered.

Somehow he *knew.* "Kara," he replied, firm and certain. "You're Kara."

Kara. I'm Kara. I moved to the kitchen area and filled a tumbler with water, gulped half of it down through a mouth dry as sand. Kara.

"Kara," Paul echoed.

I focused on deep and regular breaths until I felt like myself again. "Thanks, Paul," I said quietly. "Y'all ready?"

"Ready," Paul replied.

I turned and gave Sonny a nod. "Let's go."

He took my elbow. "Last time I'll ever lead a woman into that house."

"Last time *anyone* will."

Chapter 38

Sonny didn't put the hood back on me, probably because once a "permanent" abductee was here, it didn't matter what they saw. He kept hold of my arm and walked me along a curving brick sidewalk toward the lovely three-story Farouche Plantation house.

Farouche. A self-serving southern gentleman crime boss allied with demonic lords while masquerading as a philanthropic businessman. Too weird.

Numerous graceful wrought iron lamps cast soft, warm light on the grounds and brought out the color in gorgeous well-tended flower beds. To my left a small lake glimmered, and I picked out a dock with a flatboat moored to it. Off to my right stood several larger buildings, all either converted from original plantation structures or built in the same style. I remembered them from the satellite photo as the gym, pool, and shooting range.

I noted the barest shift in the shadowy leaves of an oak by the lake; Eilahn, letting me know she was in place. Paul continued to say my name into my ear about once every minute. Props to him for remembering my implanted *rakkuhr* virus on top of everything else he was tracking.

As we continued on, I marveled at the lovely gazebo that stood between the lake and the main house. Tiny white fairy lights wrapped pale marble columns and created the illusion of a star field on the underside of its domed slate roof. A ripple like a mirage distorted the lights for a fraction of a second.

I blinked. Had I actually seen it ripple? Then I felt it, an arcane touch like the whisper of silk against my skin. I tugged Sonny toward the gazebo, but he tugged right back.

"Can't go there," he told me, voice low. "It would draw instant attention."

I pursed my lips. "Surely no rule about fixing my shoe." I bent and pretended to adjust a strap while I snuck a better look at the gazebo with othersight. Blues and greens coiled sluggishly in the center of the marble platform, arcane vapor rising and falling above it like the breath of a giant. No mistaking that.

"Paul, the node is at the gazebo," I muttered. The latitude and longitude from Tracy Gordon's journal had only narrowed the location of the node to the back lawn of the plantation. "And it's, uh, breathing."

"Okay. Got it, Kara," Paul replied. "I'll let Mzatal know."

I counted columns, then quickly counted again. Shit. "Tell him it has *eleven* columns. He'll understand."

"We need to move," Sonny said with an edge of anxiety in his voice.

I stood and made a show of testing the shoe, then continued toward the house. "Sorry," I said quietly. "I had to check that out. We didn't know exactly where it was."

The more I saw of the house and grounds, the more the place felt like a pleasant resort. Yet I knew that not far from my room, a building designed for torture and murder hunkered beyond a screen of shrubbery and a security fence. Some resort.

A whisper of droplets pattered briefly across the walkway. Far off to the west, lightning lit clouds in a soundless dance. We'd have rain before the night was over. I intended for us to be long gone by then.

"When we get inside we're going to pass a man at a desk," Sonny murmured. "Behind that desk is the door to the server room you're looking for. I'll take you down the hall and around a corner, supposedly to have you wait in the holding room until Mr. Farouche or one of his cronies sends for you. No one will question it."

I nodded. No one ever did anything against Farouche's orders, which meant no one would suspect that Sonny was stabbing him in the back. This was where Farouche's controlled loyalty would bite him in the ass.

The house rose above us in stately splendor, a true antebellum gem. Left and right, a pair of broad curving stair-cases led up to the second story, and lights winked beyond sheer curtains in many of the tall windows.

"Don't forget to look scared," Sonny reminded me as we approached.

Good thing he did since I was in full observe-and-assess mode. I quickly schooled my features into "shocked, freaked, and terrified." Sonny gave a short nod of approval, so apparently I wasn't overdoing it—which immediately pissed me off. *No woman should have to feel that vulnerable and scared*, I silently raged, then made myself focus on the calm Sonny projected to keep from appearing as angry as I was.

He escorted me to a ground level door situated between the two staircases. Probably a servant's entrance at one time, I decided. He kept hold of my arm as he led me inside to a cramped foyer and hallway beyond with plain décor and low ceiling, compared to what I'd glimpsed of the rest of the house through the broad windows.

About ten feet inside, a middle-aged black man with close-cropped hair and keen eyes sat behind a desk. As the entrance door closed, his focus shifted from his computer screen to us. A huge map of the compound, and a dozen flatscreens displaying various surveillance camera views, flanked the door directly behind him. That was my target. Plain and uninteresting to ordinary eyes, the door rippled with wards in my othersight.

The eyes of the man at the desk tracked over me, assessing, noting my appearance, and no doubt my demeanor. Unlike Jerry, though, his gaze was purely to catalog. All business, this one.

"Carter," Sonny said with a short nod without breaking stride.

"Sonny," the man replied with a similar gesture as we passed, then he returned his attention to his computer screen.

We continued down the hall and around the corner, my heels clicking on the tiled floor. I could only imagine how the sound must have felt for the other women—like seconds of life ticking off. Sonny looked up and down the hall before opening a door.

"Here you go, Amaryllis," he said in a voice pitched normally for Carter's benefit. "Just relax in here for a bit, all right? Everything's going to be fine."

"Kara," Paul stated right after the "Amaryllis."

I quickly slipped my heels off and set them inside the door of the small room. Sonny pulled a pair of flat slippers from his jacket pocket and handed them over, then closed the door with us both still in the hall. He took a deep breath, readying himself. I touched his arm, gave him an encouraging smile.

"You got this," I whispered as I tugged on the slippers. Too bad I couldn't give him the same calm he gave to others. And also too bad the adorable lace top was about a size too tight. Another hour of wearing it, and I wouldn't be able to feel my fingers.

Sonny exhaled, met my eyes and nodded, then headed back toward the entrance. I followed to the corner and waited, listening.

"Any problems?" I heard Carter ask.

"Not with the mark," Sonny replied.

"With who then?"

"Jerry." In the name was a wealth of animosity and contempt. "He fucked with my mark when I checked in."

A low curse from Carter. Either his opinion of Jerry was similar, or he didn't like the fact that Jerry was messing with Farouche's "merchandise." *Or both*, I reminded myself, remembering Bryce's words about the people who worked for Farouche. Of those who did the dirty work, all were influenced, but there was evidently a wide spectrum of how much people enjoyed the job.

"You know as well as I do this isn't the first time he's done this," Sonny continued with unmasked vehemence, "but I'll deal with him later."

"Did he touch her?"

"Not this time. Scared the shit out of her though," Sonny told him. I had no problem imagining how terrifying Jerry's talk would be to a recently kidnapped woman.

Carter muttered a curse. "Fucking moron. Someday he's going to mess with the wrong chick, and Mr. Farouche will fry him."

"He sure as hell wasn't hired for his brains," Sonny replied. "Anyway, I spotted an issue with the surveillance camera array by the Ops building when I walked her in. Can you come out for a minute so I can show you?"

"Sure. Let me log off here," Carter replied, obviously never imagining for an instant that Sonny would be up to no good. I heard a few clicks of a mouse, and then the footfalls of both men heading away followed by the opening and closing of the door.

I did a cautious peek around the corner, verified that the foyer was indeed empty, then flew on my slippered feet toward the warded door. A quick assessment revealed decently constructed wards that lacked the quality of demon-laid ones. Perhaps Tsuneo's work?

And he *hasn't been training in the demon realm,* I thought smugly as I unwound the protections. At least I didn't think he had, especially since it took me only about a minute to disarm his work. Either way, my seventh ring shikvihr trumped his sorry ass. After a final check, I slipped through the door and quietly closed it behind me.

"I'm in," I said softly, though I wasn't sure Paul would hear me over the whir and hum of the machines. A desk, chair, and computer workstation sat not far from the door. Two long rows of computer stuff, that I assumed were servers, occupied the rest of the floor space, with neatly bundled blue wires *everywhere.*

"Good deal, Kara," Paul said, then quickly gave me easy-to-follow instructions on which cables to disconnect, which ones to switch, and where to plug in his dongle—which looked like an ordinary USB drive to me, but what the hell did I know?

"That's it?" I asked as it slid into place.

"Hang on." A pause. "Aw, hell yeah! I'm in, babeee!" I grinned at the triumph in his voice. A second later the lights dimmed, then came back on.

"Please tell me that was you," I said.

"Sure was," he replied cheerfully. "I'm driving the bus now, and just uploaded my first little present for Big Mack. Not so clever *now,* asswipe!"

I had to press the heel of my hand to my mouth to keep from bursting out laughing. He'd told me earlier that his first "present" was a virus that by morning would send copies of Farouche's confidential files and emails to the feds—

after wiping all electronic references to himself, Bryce, Sonny, and a few others who Bryce said were also coerced.

"All right, Baby Bear," I said with a grin, "are you and Papa Bear in position?"

"Yep. We're outside the fence waiting to hear from Sonny," he told me. "I'm setting up everything I need to wreak havoc, and once we know Sonny has Idris's mom, Papa Bear will take down the wards. I'll let you know the instant it's a go."

While I waited, I divested myself of the the wig, padding beneath the dress along with, to my regret, the increasingly uncomfortable lace top. It was lovely, but I needed to be able to *move*, and it was no longer vital that I hide the sigil scars.

A few minutes later Paul spoke again. "We're solid, Kara," he announced. "Sonny's heading out with Idris's mom. Mzatal's through the wards and is burning a hole in the fence right now, and then Bryce will rendezvous with Sonny outside the fence to get Mom safely across the bayou."

I felt Mzatal clearly now, like a sun on the edge of my peripheral vision. Raised voices and running footsteps passed by the door. "I think they know you're here," I said as I cautiously peeked out.

"I'm sowing chaos," Paul replied with glee. "Their surveillance and comms are completely down. Plus, I terminated all of Big Mack's cell phone accounts. Failure to pay! Ha! They're running deaf and blind."

"I love it." I retrieved my gun from the thigh holster. "I'm on my way out to join up with y'all."

"Sounds good, Kara. See you soon. We're through the fence now."

After another careful look and listen, I eased out, then ran to the door and outside, keeping a sharp eye out for potential trouble. I slunk out past the big staircases, but made it only a few steps down the sidewalk before flood lights abruptly snapped on to turn night into day. I bit back a curse and dove for cover in a nearby cluster of azaleas. The sound of quick bootsteps came from the direction of the Ops building, and I flattened myself onto cypress mulch while I prayed the black dress would conceal me enough.

"Report any sign of the intruders directly and in person to Ops," I heard someone shout, then the boot-wearers were past, and I could cautiously peek up again.

Though he was still distant, I sensed Mzatal off to my right. I'd no sooner maneuvered my way to the back side of the azaleas when two figures abruptly burst out of the door I'd just exited. Heart pounding, I ducked into the deep shadow between the nearest staircase and a huge gardenia bush, and nearly went sprawling as I tripped on a wiggling bundle. I peered into the gloom, then realized it was Carter, gagged and trussed in what looked like a *very* secure hogtie.

I gave him a sweet smile and a shrug of apology, then shifted my attention to the two men as they took off at a jog toward the gazebo—and the node, I realized. One of the men, mid-thirties and average height with pony-tailed shoulder length wavy brown hair, repeatedly looked at his cell phone as though it would miraculously start working. *Mystery Man Twenty-two,* I thought. *A.K.A. Aaron Asher.* The other, tall, athletic, with a mop of unruly blond curls, followed with his face set in determination.

"I see Idris," I murmured, keeping my voice low and controlled with effort. "Asher's with him." Cautiously, I eased out from behind the stairs as the two went up onto the broad platform of the gazebo and crouched in the center. "They're doing something arcane with the node," I said. "Can't tell what though."

Idris straightened after a moment, and I got a good look at his face for the first time. He looked older, tired. He'd lost the boyish innocence, and even from this distance I could see the lines of stress in his face.

Not just stress, I realized. Fear. Grief. And anger.

His gaze swept around the area, passed over me, then returned. He gave me a slight nod then tensed, a flicker of indecision in his eyes. I recognized the look. He struggled to resist the Farouche-induced compulsion to tell Asher he'd seen me. My pulse thudded unevenly as I waited for the outcome, then I exhaled in relief as he gave me another little nod. That confirmed my suspicion that Farouche's influence on him was light. Perhaps Rhyzkahl had let Farouche know he'd rip the man's head off if he ruined Idris with his fear-whammy.

I gave Idris an exaggerated What-the-Hell shrug and motioned toward the gazebo. *What are you doing?* I mouthed.

To my bafflement, he lifted his hand to his head in the universal sign for telephone, then tilted his head slightly toward where Asher crouched.

Phone call? Then my gut lurched. Was he saying they had a way to use the node to communicate with the demon realm? If anyone could figure out a way to use them for communication, it'd be Idris. *Damn it.* That gave the other side one hell of an advantage.

"Tell Mzatal I think Asher and Idris are sending a message through the node," I said softly to Paul as I watched.

"Hold on," Paul replied after a few seconds. "Mzatal just scowled and said something in demon that I'm pretty sure is a bad word."

"Yeah, I'm saying a few myself."

Asher stood, and I ducked back into the shadows as the two headed to the house again. Asher maintained a slight lead, his mouth curved in a supercilious sneer. "We have to tell Mr. Farouche they want the area kept clear of humans and that there's to be no interference from anyone," he said over his shoulder to Idris. "And don't forget, the *savinths* must be held so the node doesn't collapse when they come through," he added with a pompous air.

A look of annoyed disgust swept over Idris's face. "I know," he shot back. "I'm the one who taught you how to do it."

I suppressed a rude snort at Asher's ego. Idris had trained with Mzatal for over half a year and another four months with the Mraztur after his kidnapping, and had mastered nine rings of the shikvihr. Asher had solid skills, but I *highly* doubted he knew even half of what Idris knew.

Indignation flashed across Asher's face. "Just do what you're supposed to do," he snarled. "I've got the node at the warehouse aligned, so it will anchor enough, in any case."

"No, you *don't*," Idris said through clenched teeth. "And no, it *won't*." His eyes flicked toward my hiding place then ahead again as they passed me.

They returned inside, and the meaning of the exchange abruptly clicked. Were the Mraztur going to try and come through the node? How was that even possible? I quickly relayed the entire conversation to Paul.

"We're still a couple hundred yards away," Paul told me in a breathless voice as if running. Or trying to keep up with Mzatal's long strides. I knew that pain. "Mzatal's not happy," he added, "at *all*. Says they'll cause a node incident which will be catastrophic at worst and disruptive at best. He scowled more and said a lot of bad demon words too. You need to get away from there and come toward us."

"I will as soon as it's clear," I replied, keeping my voice low as more men ran past. "You stick like glue to Mzatal, you hear me? I keep overhearing chatter about everyone being told to pull back and clear the lawn. Something big is about to happen."

"Don't you worry," he replied. "He moves fast, but I'm right on him."

"Good deal." I peered out and confirmed I was in the clear, then scooched out of my hiding place, gun in hand. Eilahn started toward me in a graceful run near the perimeter of the lawn, keeping to the shadows of trees. Fortunately, bright light made for really dark shadows.

A weird trilling call set the hair on the back of my head on end, and brought Eilahn to a stop. She crouched in a defensive stance, teeth bared as a lanky dark-skinned man loped out toward her. He didn't stop or slow, and when he was only a few paces away, she sprang to engage him. The two met in a beautiful and terrible mid-air collision, immediately shifting to grapple and claw and fight with deadly and perfect skill.

Another syraza! I realized and had barely finished the thought when the pair suddenly winked out.

I stared in horror at the empty space. "Paul! Eilahn's gone!" I blurted out. "Another syraza came out, and they started fighting, and then they blipped out. Where is she?!"

"Hang on. Shit." He mumbled to himself for a moment. "Shit. She's in New Orleans East."

I cursed. Eilahn couldn't travel more than about a dozen feet on Earth, which meant the other syraza had initiated it. And not only could I not do a damn thing to help her, this also meant she was out of the fight. Even if she kicked the other syraza's ass immediately, it would take her a couple of hours by car or taxi to get back to me. Hell, that was probably the other syraza's intent all along.

Staying low, I started a nerve-wracking dash from concealment to concealment as I worked my way toward the east side of the compound. The good news was that I didn't see anyone out and about anymore. Bad news was that I was pretty damn positive the lawn was being watched. *And possibly watched through the scope of a rifle,* I thought grimly.

"Kara, I don't know what just happened," Paul's agitated voice cut off my pleasant musings about snipers. "Ryan and Zack were at the fence line as planned. I let them know about what you saw with the node, and then Ryan said he looked over and Zack was *gone*. I don't have anything on where he might be. No GPS. His link is dead."

My heart clenched. *Zack knows the lords might come through.* Was he getting the hell away from here to avoid violating agreements and crossing The Line? Or was he preparing for a confrontation with Rhyzkahl? "What's Ryan doing?"

"He moved inside the fence about a hundred yards," Paul told me. "He's behind the apartment units right now. He's a little, um, tense." A pause. "Bryce just met up with Sonny and Idris's mom. They're heading out now."

With Zack gone without explanation, Ryan was probably starting to reflect an agitated Szerain. "Once Mom and the boys are clear we can move on to grabbing Idris and kicking ass," I said. *And hopefully get the hell away from here before any of the lords come through.* I edged around a dense clump of ornamental trees, doing my best to stay out of sight of any windows in either the main house or the Ops building. Maybe I was being too paranoid, but I was feeling kind of risk-averse at the moment. What if being in Rhyzkahl's presence made it even harder for me to resist the *rakkuhr* virus? I didn't know, and I didn't want to find out. Yet at the same time, I doubted Mzatal would leave here and allow the lords unchallenged access to Earth.

A stiff breeze swirled across the lawn, picking up a few stray leaves to toss onto the lake. It brushed the water to form tiny waves, then shifted to bring the scent of rain my way.

Mzatal abruptly strode out onto the illuminated lawn,

his essence blade Khatur in hand, and Paul only a few steps behind him. The protections around them flared and crackled in my othersight. No worries about either of them getting shot if someone got stupid. As I watched, Mzatal stopped about a fifty yards from the gazebo, lowered his head in a stance to carefully assess. A few heartbeats later he took three steps back, then began to dance the shikvihr.

Too late to stop the Mraztur from coming through, he prepared instead to face them.

Chapter 39

The staff door of the house opened, and once again Asher and Idris came out and jogged toward the gazebo. Idris appeared stressed and disturbed, while Asher looked triumphant. *Idris knows how fucked up this is*, I thought, feeling equally grim.

Idris's gaze flicked briefly to Mzatal, while Asher eyed the demonic lord with a great deal of wariness. I looked around carefully. If there were any snipers who could get me, they'd have to be hiding in the cattails surrounding the lake.

Rising slightly from my crouch, I shouted, *"IDRIS! YOUR MOM IS SAFE!"* If he only had a light dose of Farouche's influence, that knowledge would hopefully give him much greater freedom of action.

Idris's head snapped around at my shout, and relief bloomed on his face. Asher looked over at me as I ducked into the bushes again, but Idris didn't give him any chance to speak or act. Without hesitating an instant, Idris seized Asher by the upper arm, swung him around and delivered a hard punch to his face. Idris was stronger and in much better shape than Asher, and it showed. Asher staggered and collapsed even as Idris dropped down to slug him again with his entire bodyweight behind the blow.

I held back an exultant cheer. Yep, that was definitely some freedom of action going on right there.

Idris stood and shook his hand out, face hard. He glanced my way, gave a slight nod, then turned and ran to the gazebo.

What the hell?

A low rumble rattled my bones, then waves—part arcane, part physical—spread out from the gazebo like ripples from a rock thrown into a pond. I staggered to keep my footing as they passed under me, then pressed my hand to my stomach as nausea hit. We didn't exactly get a lot of earthquakes in southern Louisiana. This had to be instability caused by the node, and it wasn't even open yet. Not good.

Another low rumble, and then the ground shook as if a giant jackhammer slammed into it about a hundred times a minute. I lost my balance and went sprawling. Idris fell in the gazebo but immediately scrambled to his knees and began to weave potency around the node. Not to open it for the Mraztur, I realized with relief, but to stabilize it.

Windows shattered with *pops* and *cracks* that sliced across the lawn. To my left, a statue toppled over and tumbled down the far set of steps. Asher staggered to his feet, blood streaming from his nose and mouth, and managed two steps toward the gazebo before falling again.

There didn't seem to be any point in trying to get up with the ground still shaking, though Mzatal continued to dance the shikvihr as if nothing was amiss. Even if I hadn't been able to see him, I'd have known he was there. His aura pulsed and flared like heat from an active volcano. Paul knelt a few feet behind him, his focus on his tablet. Mzatal completed the final sigil and ignited the full ritual, and I sucked in a breath as its power filled me in a delicious torrent through our connection.

"Kara!" Paul's voice crackled in my ear, excited and nervous. "Sonny and Bryce are clear. Mama's out the back fence, across the bayou, and away. Still no sign of Zack. Ryan's going to wait where he is in case Zack comes back, and Bryce will be heading our way momentarily."

"Got it," I replied.

The jackhammer feel suddenly stopped, only to be replaced by the madly uncomfortable sensation of too much pressure, as if I was a hundred feet underwater. I dug my fingers into the grass, and a heartbeat later the pressure seemed to reverse, and I felt as if I was going to float away while my eardrums threatened to burst. Mzatal called to me, touched me through our connection, and I returned the touch, assuring him I was okay.

"Node is open!" Paul cried out, tinny and distant. "Node is open!"

I gripped the grass hard as I looked up and over at the gazebo. Tendrils of potency like vines of shimmering blue light flowed out of the center, twining up and over the structure until the whole thing glowed. It flared in an arcane blaze, and in the next breath a concussive blast ripped the gazebo apart and sent debris flying in all directions. I yelped and ducked my head down, glad that I was already prone. Rubble from the columns and shards of slate rained down around me, but the force of the blast left nothing big enough to cause me any significant damage.

"Paul! Idris!" I yelled, though my voice sounded distant to my own hearing. I swallowed to pop my ears and tried again. "Paul!" Peeking up, I tried to assess. No gazebo anymore, only bases of the columns like jagged teeth on the stone platform, and rubble scattered like gravel far across the lawn. Ice clutched at my chest. Idris. He'd been right there in the middle of that huge blast. "Paul! Are y'all okay? Answer me!"

Mzatal got to his feet, expression hard, and his shikvihr still intact and glowing brightly in othersight. Static buzzed in my ears. "Yeah." Paul's voice crackled and popped through a suddenly horrible connection. "I think. Yeah." Now I saw him about five feet behind Mzatal, struggling upright, his tablet clutched to his chest.

"Stay down, Paul," I ordered, relieved to see him comply. The comms were in bad shape, but at least they hadn't been knocked out entirely. My gaze swept the area and finally rested on the sprawled form of Idris about halfway between my position and the node. "I see Idris," I said, voice shaky with relief. "He's down, but breathing, and I don't see any blood." Though the blast had been a fierce combination of physical and arcane power, I stubbornly clung to the hope that he was merely stunned. After a few more seconds of searching, I located Asher lying face down on the bank of the lake, lower legs in the water. Maybe the lake had leeches. That would be cool.

Though a good half of the floodlights were dying in impressive showers of sparks, I caught sight of Farouche standing on the veranda above the steps with his bodyguard, Angus McDunn, right beside him. McDunn touched

Farouche's arm, spoke to him, and Farouche responded with a tight nod. I imagined it was something like, *We need to get off the veranda while weird and dangerous shit is happening*, since Farouche turned, and the two disappeared into the house.

I returned my full attention to the node. No longer a low, compact arcane weave, it rose a dozen feet above the platform, a disturbing column of potency that oscillated from blinding rainbow light to the utter blackness of the void. The ground shuddered and an eerie whine issued from the node. In the next heartbeat the whine crescendoed and then died as Rhyzkahl stepped out of that column of power, shoulders rising and falling with heavy breath, though appearing collected and confident otherwise.

My eyes went to Xhan in his right hand. The lurid red of *rakkuhr* wrapped around the essence blade and up Rhyzkahl's forearm. My lips pulled back from my teeth as I dug my fingers hard into the ground and tried to clench my hands into fists. "Rhyzkahl's here. Paul, stay down and behind Mzatal."

"Mzatal says—I don't know what he means," Paul said, and I heard the stress in his voice even through the static. "Says no rules here and no way to contain Rhyzkahl? Shit!" Static filled the connection for several seconds as the node flared. "Says must incapacitate. Engaging."

Cursing, I pushed up to hands and knees, easier now that the ground wasn't shaking and nothing was blowing up. "As soon as Rhyzkahl is occupied, I'm going to get Idris and drag him over your way." Mzatal needed me by him for combat support and so that his attention wouldn't be split. In my peripheral vision, I saw Rhyzkahl tracing protections as he stepped off the gazebo platform and toward Mzatal.

I made it to my feet and began a slightly unsteady dash toward the sluggishly moving Idris. A heartbeat later a reyza appeared beside Rhyzkahl, spread his wings and bellowed. Not quite as large as Gestamar but formidable none the less.

"He called Pyrenth through!" I steadied my legs, but almost stumbled as the node whined. Another lord stepped from it, fierce smile and aura like a jungle cat on the hunt. "Jesral."

"Oh, shit," Paul breathed through the static. "Got it."

Jesral took a step, staggered a bit, then shook his head as if to clear it and get his bearings. Had the sly lord ever been to Earth before? If not, I was ready to welcome him with a good hard kick in the balls.

I took a second to make sure Jesral's attention was on Mzatal rather than me, then sprinted to Idris and did a super-quick injury check to make sure I wasn't going to damage him irreparably by moving him. He was breathing easily, and I didn't see gushing blood or protruding bones—though he had a glassy-eyed look of shock and a shitload of little blisters, likely an arcane affect of the blast. I flinched as the first potency strike of the battle burst with an ear-splitting *crack*. Heart thudding, I seized the back of Idris's collar and began hauling him toward Mzatal and Paul. Easier said than done. Idris was a solid chunk of muscle, which made for a lot of dead weight. I sure as hell wouldn't think of him as a kid ever again.

He let out a low groan, then began to thrash, disoriented. He was still too out of it to get free of me, but it made dragging him about ten times as hard. "Stop struggling, Idris!" I panted, holding on with both hands as I backed toward friendly lines. "Holy shit, how much do you fucking weigh?"

Pyrenth bellowed again, then bounded in my direction. Adrenaline dumped hard into my system as two things became crystal clear: Pyrenth would reach me in about five seconds and, unless I did something quick and decisive, he was going to recapture both Idris *and* me for Rhyzkahl.

I'll never be me again! The terrifying thought surged through me in a flash. The *rakkuhr* virus held that potential. Rhyzkahl was a certainty. No time for my gun, and it wouldn't be enough to stop the reyza anyway. In the instant I had to react, I realized I had only one possible course of action. I released my grip on Idris's collar, jerked my hand up into the air and called Vsuhl to me.

In the next heartbeat Pyrenth was on me, clawed hand reaching to grasp and hold. But I'd practiced with Gestamar in all sorts of close-quarter fighting, and knew the balance points and the weak spots. As the blade coalesced in my hand, I snapped out a side kick into his hip, throwing him off balance enough for me to evade his grab. Moreover, it shifted his unprotected chest toward my right. Letting out a guttural cry, I took advantage of the instant of vulnerability, surged forward and buried Vsuhl to the hilt in Pyrenth's chest.

He let out an agonized bellow and staggered back. The blade's approval whispered through my mind as it made its insidious presence known. The hilt wrenched from my hand even though my grip on it was solid, almost as if it clung to Pyrenth's flesh. Breathing hard in triumph, I watched him go to his knees and scrabble at the hilt. I'd taken one opponent out of the game, and dying on Earth simply meant he'd most likely return to the demon realm.

Except . . . this didn't look like the other times I'd seen demons die here. There was no light spilling through the wound, no ripping *crack* or the smell of ozone and sulfur.

Pyrenth was *bleeding*.

Sick horror formed a knot in my gut. I moved forward and seized Vsuhl's hilt. The blade howled in protest as I yanked it free, and it seemed to require ten times the effort it should have. Yet then I could only stare for several eternal seconds at the blood that spilled down Pyrenth's broad chest.

"I don't understand," I croaked out. I dropped my eyes to the blade in my hand, felt and heard it urge *more more more*, then returned my gaze to Pyrenth. He sagged to his side, his expression calm, relaxed. He might have looked peaceful if not for the blood that bubbled from his mouth and darkened his fangs.

"Well . . . played," Pyrenth breathed.

The fighting continued around me as I struggled to understand. I felt Mzatal's focus on me, his insistence that I banish Vsuhl. Felt him take a strike for his distraction. I dimly noted that another concussion rocked the lawn, though not as severe as the first. Paul was shouting something in my earpiece, and it took me several seconds to comprehend the words.

"Kara! Mzatal says to send the blade away! Send the blade away! Jesral!"

I jerked my gaze up and saw Jesral's eyes locked on the blade and me. Quickly, I banished the blade, and briefly reveled in the look of rage that came over him before I returned my attention to Pyrenth.

"I don't understand," I repeated, almost desperately. "I only meant to send you back to the demon realm!"

His lips pulled back from his teeth in a reyza smile. "Vsuhl. Takes all. Gives no mercy," he rumbled, so low I doubted anyone else could hear him.

"Yaghir tahn," I said, throat clogging. "I'm sorry. I didn't mean to . . ."

"*Kahl dar*," he said. "*Juntek lakuna jaik. Srah lorvahlo. Haakir.*"

I understood him. Or at least the basic meaning—perhaps because of the whisper of the grove I felt through the open node. *All is well. I finished with honor. Well played.* Then he drew a deeper breath, let it out, and was still.

Guilt and sorrow clawed at me, sharpened by a scalding wash of Rhyzkahl's anger over the death of his reyza. This was not at all how I wanted revenge against Rhyzkahl. Never like this. I dragged a hand over my face, and it came away wet with tears.

"Kara!" Paul shouted though the earpiece.

I forced myself back to the present. Rhyzkahl and Mzatal were deeply engaged in arcane battle. Jesral took a step toward me, then staggered back as Mzatal cast a heavy strike his way.

The ground shook again. I spun to see Idris stagger to his feet, swaying, eyes still seeming somewhat unfocused. Baring my teeth, I channeled my guilt into rage that I'd been forced into murdering Pyrenth. Yet with the rage came hurt and disappointment with Mzatal. *Why didn't he warn me? If he'd given me any training with the blade, like I'd asked him to, this wouldn't have happened.*

I seized the front of Idris's shirt. "Come *on!*" I snarled, then had to yank him off balance as he resisted, disoriented enough that even Farouche's mild influence had him fighting me. "Idris. It's me, Kara. We're going to Mzatal."

He took a ragged breath and stopped pulling at my hand. "Kara! I'm . . . okay," he gasped even though clearly he wasn't. Wild confusion filled his eyes, and he shook from the arcane and physical damage from the blast.

"Sure you are, big guy," I said, gritted my teeth, and ran-dragged him back toward Mzatal. Yet my thoughts kept circling back to Pyrenth. I'd killed a sentient creature. All these years of being a cop, and this was my first true kill.

But I had no choice, I realized with sick certainty. Training with the blade wouldn't have changed my choice in that instant. No way could I have reached my gun quickly enough, and the chances of stopping him with a .32 were slim. *If I hadn't used Vsuhl on Pyrenth, Idris and I would be prisoners of the Mraztur again.* Yet knowing it was justified didn't ease the guilt one bit.

The node whined. "Three lords, Kara! Another just came through!" Paul's voice, shot through with static and agitation.

"Three!" *Shit.* "Black hair or blond?" I snapped, too focused on keeping Idris upright and moving to look for myself.

"Black."

"That's Amkir," I replied through gritted teeth as Idris began to balk again. "The King of the Assholes."

"Gotcha, Kara. Bryce is near the Ops building and moving your way to help you."

Idris abruptly gave a low cry and yanked back hard against my grasp. Cursing, I swept his leg and dumped him to the ground, then dropped down with a knee on his chest. He gave a whoosh of expelled air as I'd intended, and as he gasped for new breath I seized his arm and rolled him face down then held him in an arm-lock as I looked for Bryce.

To my relief, he was almost to me. He quickly closed the distance, scanning for threats as he pulled zip-ties from his belt and efficiently bound Idris's wrists and ankles. A potency-burn marked the left side of Bryce's face—an angry stripe of raw flesh from his temple to his jaw line. Othersight revealed a vicious little coil of potency clinging like napalm to his cheek.

"Hold still," I ordered, then unwound and dispelled the thing.

"Thanks. Caught the edge of a blast," he said. "Was wondering why it still burned. I'll get Idris behind our lines," he continued, clipped and efficient. "Mzatal needs you now. His attention is divided with you out here."

I knew it to be true. Leaving Idris to Bryce's care, I sprinted to a spot about ten feet behind and to the left of Mzatal. His braid swung in a rhythmic pattern as he engaged all three enemy lords, essence blade in hand—shielding, striking, and deflecting in a beautiful and deadly dance. Paul knelt on the ground to his right, fingers dancing over the tablet, eyes unfocused. I didn't see Ryan or Zack anywhere, and could only hope they were okay.

A strike from Rhyzkahl rocked Mzatal's shielding, and its residue peppered me like wind-blown sand. Turning to face the enemy, I sought to tap into Mzatal's pattern. Yet the link that had been as easy as taking his hand evaded me now, with his movement and weaving of flows seeming more like a random jumble of sigils and potency.

I shook my head sharply. Pyrenth's death had me badly rattled. *I'll angst later,* I railed at myself, then pygahed, inhaled deeply, and once more tried to focus. What was I trying to focus on? I looked around, confused.

"Kara!"

I jerked as Paul shouted from nearby, his voice also cutting through the static in the earpiece.

Shit. The virus. "Kara," I confirmed through gritted teeth. Now I sank into the link, echoing and amplifying Mzatal's dance with my own. I felt a deep touch from him—reassurance and stability. I returned it with one of my own and used his support and confidence to solidify my center.

The Earth flows seemed to bend toward us, enabling Mzatal to merely extend slightly in order to tap them. Curious, I tried to see why, then nearly fell over in shock as I found the answer: Paul. Somehow, he was nudging and adjusting the flows to give us that slight advantage. Hell, more than *slight*. I doubted Jesral and Amkir had any experience tapping the relatively weak Earth flows, so for Paul to divert what little was available to them would be like replacing their bullets with paint balls.

A smile curved my mouth as I wove my touches into our offense. No wonder Mzatal liked Paul so much.

Bryce loped behind our lines with the zip-tied Idris over his shoulders in a fireman's carry, then carefully deposited him on the ground. I continued to enhance Mzatal's patterns, yet even with my support and Paul's, I felt him weakening.

Mzatal deflected a hard strike, though the edges of it licked within his protections. He shifted, stepped back, and in that instant of movement Rhyzkahl lunged forward and sent a hammering blow into Mzatal's shields. The shock of it slammed through us both. Mzatal stumbled back another step before recovering, breathing hard while Rhyzkahl smiled in triumph.

"Fuck this," I muttered, then yanked my gun out of the

thigh holster and fired three shots at Rhyzkahl. I knew he was shielded, but maybe it would distract him a little. Plus, it felt good to shoot at him.

As expected, the bullets stopped an arms length from him, then dropped to the grass in molten puddles of lead. His gaze snapped to me, and if anything his expression grew *more* triumphant. "Rowan."

I stiffened as the name struck me like a fist, drove through my mind. I felt as though the earth tipped, lost my footing. *Rowan?*

"Kara!" Paul shouted in my ear as Mzatal spoke the name to my essence.

I sucked in a breath. *Kara.* Lifting my chin, I shook off the horrible feeling. *I'm Kara, and he's a parasite.* I shoved the gun into its holster and continued to work Mzatal's pattern.

He took another hard strike from Amkir, but riposted with a barrage of arcane spears, so quickly that I knew he'd allowed the strike. I understood Mzatal's purpose, that he preyed upon the inexperience the others had with the Earth flows. Amkir let out a choked cry and stumbled back to fall sprawled on the grass. Immediately, Mzatal blanketed him in potency, pinning him to the ground and effectively taking him out of the fight, at least for the moment.

Without a pause in his flow, Mzatal deflected two strikes from Rhyzkahl, then blasted Jesral off balance and cast a constricting net of potency around him.

Another small concussion rippled across the lawn, joined by a rumble of thunder. I jerked my attention to the node.

"Ah shit," I breathed.

The last of the Mraztur to make an appearance, Kadir swayed heavily as he stepped through the node, his expression an odd mix of anger and panic before he smoothed it. Though not completely smoothed away, I noted, even as I fought down my own panic at the idea of four lords against one. Anger still tightened his mouth and the skin around his beautiful eyes. I'd never seen Lord Creepshow display any sort of strong emotion. *He must be* seriously *pissed,* I thought. But at who? Or what? Not that it made a fucking bit of difference at this point. We were totally screwed.

Rhyzkahl's expression grew even *more* triumphant with Kadir's arrival, though I hadn't thought it possible. Baring teeth, he flung another hard strike at Mzatal and followed it with two lesser bursts in quick succession. Mzatal deflected all, but I felt him reach deep into his reserves, and knew he didn't have much more in him. Right now he had Amkir pinned and Jesral struggling with the net, but it took effort to hold them, and he had nothing left for any sort of offense against Rhyzkahl. Hell, he barely had enough to maintain his defenses.

Kadir swept his cold gaze around, then crouched beside the node, began working over it. *He's trying to stabilize it,* I realized in shock. It was difficult to tell from this distance, but his work looked like an amalgam of what Mzatal did at the Nature Center valve and what Zack did at my pond.

A louder roll of thunder swept over us, and I suddenly understood the subtle undercurrent I'd felt. Mzatal knew he had no way to contain all of the Mraztur. His only hope—our only hope—was to incapacitate them. He'd been calling the storm to us. But would even lightning be enough?

Movement near the lake drew my eye, and I saw Asher doing a low-crawl toward a cluster of bushes. But then my gaze went to a figure standing a few feet beyond the remains of the gazebo: Zack.

His expression might have been carved in stone, and I felt the tension in him even at this distance. He wanted to end his bond with Rhyzkahl. I knew that. Logic—at least, my human logic—weighed heavily in favor of his doing so. Yet logic didn't factor in the terrible price he'd pay.

What would I do in his place? I tried to imagine a life of complete isolation from my kind—never enjoying another silly meal with friends at Lake o' Butter, never being able to even talk to another human. I'd felt the ache of it during the months with Mzatal, with only demons and lords for company. Yet even that had been tempered for a while by Idris's presence, and after that the notes and letters exchanged with my aunt, Jill, Zack, and Ryan had been a solid reminder that, even though I wasn't with them, I was always welcome back.

I watched Zack, waiting to see what he would do. In front of him, Kadir stepped off the gazebo platform and strode toward Asher.

Mzatal's touch stroked the edge of my awareness, and I shifted more focus to him though I kept my eyes on Zack. *I have no more,* his meaning came through. *I will call light-ning.*

"Call, but don't strike yet," I murmured as Zack took a step forward, and then another. Rhyzkahl shot a quick glance over his shoulder, and victory shone in his eyes as he faced us again. I felt Mzatal's cautious acknowledgment of my request as he continued to call the storm to him. My focus remained locked on Zack as he moved toward us. I walked forward, then paused at our implied line of scrim-mage, and looked over at Mzatal. I'd be beyond his protec-tions if I continued, and I felt the worry in him, sensed his distraction through the shudder in our defenses.

"Boss," I murmured. "Trust me."

He gave me a single nod. "*Eturnahl,*" he replied softly in demon and sent a confirmation of it through our bond. *Eternally.* I smiled, returned the touch with a loving one of my own, then turned to watch Zack again.

Zack continued forward and up to Rhyzkahl's right, laid a hand on his shoulder. Rhyzkahl smiled and lowered his hands, confident. With his demahnk ptarl at his side, he knew he held victory and apparently wished to savor the moment.

"Parasite," I muttered under my breath, but otherwise remained utterly still, watching Zack. *I trust you,* I thought to him. I had no idea if he could read my thoughts from a distance, but I sent the assurance out to him anyway. *I know you won't betray us. I'm here for you, no matter what your decision or the outcome.* Then I murmured, "Tah agahl lahn, eturnahl, Zakaar." Agahl—the love of friends.

He inclined his head very slightly to me in acknowledg-ment, whether to my words or my thoughts, I didn't know, nor did it matter right now. Either way, he knew where I stood.

Zack continued past Rhyzkahl into the space between the combatants and turned a slow circle. Amkir lay pinned on the ground, utter hate in his glare. Jesral stood immobile on the other flank, eyes narrowed impatiently as if wishing Zakaar would get on with whatever he was doing so that the Mraztur could go ahead and claim victory. Kadir siezed Asher by the hair then stood and watched the tableau.

Mzatal spread his hands to his sides to show his lack of aggression in the moment, though he made no move to release either of the restrained lords. Rhyzkahl observed all with an air of utter confidence. I watched the dynamics with wary amazement. Clearly a demahnk held a shitload of clout to be able to bring everything to a halt like this, and as the lords couldn't read a demahnk, none knew his purpose. Though, for that matter, neither did I, not for certain.

Zack . . . *Zakaar* came to a stop barely on our side of the halfway point between Mzatal and Rhyzkahl, then turned and faced the latter. As Zakaar's eyes passed over me, his gaze lingered for the barest fraction of a heartbeat—long enough for me to *feel* his need and desire for support.

In the lull of the cease fire, I moved forward. Zakaar's gaze went from Rhyzkahl to the node and then back to him. "What have you done?" he asked Rhyzkahl, voice as mild as if inquiring whether the milk had expired. He spoke in demon, but the whisper of grove touch through the node was enough to let me comprehend meaning, and I had a feeling Zakaar was boosting my ability to understand as well.

Guilt flickered for a bare instant in Rhyzkahl's eyes. Although Zakaar and the other demahnk had created the valves and nodes, Rhyzkahl obviously hadn't expected a need to defend his actions. "We have joined the worlds," he answered, also in demon, recovering his aplomb. "Now we take what is ours." His gaze lingered on me before returning to Zakaar. "Come, ptarl. Let us finish this."

I moved up to stand beside Zakaar. He set a gentle hand on my shoulder, then pulled the neckline of my dress aside and set the sigils on my body aglow with the red wash of the *rakkuhr*. I drew a shuddering breath and lifted my chin.

"What have you done?" Zakaar repeated, and this time there was no mistaking the vehemence and disappointment and anguish in the words.

Rhyzkahl narrowed his eyes. "I have forged a tool for the good of us all," he stated. "What does it matter what means I use?"

"I made no secret of my view on the use of *rakkuhr* for any reason," Zakaar said, voice carrying far. "For this reason," he nudged his head toward me, "using this means, I am *vehemently* opposed." He released the neckline of my dress and quenched the glow of the sigils, then laid his arm across my shoulders. "I have counseled you before not to take this path. Now I simply say," he lifted his head and fixed his gaze upon Rhyzkahl, "*turn from this path.*"

A muscle flexed in Rhyzkahl's jaw. "Your counsel is unreasonable and needlessly conservative," he retorted. "This *means*," he flicked a hand toward me in an impatient gesture, "is viable and brings Earth into our grasp with minimal conflict."

"It is . . . unacceptable," Zakaar replied, voice low but with an intensity that carried it far. He hesitated, and I felt a tremble go through him. This was the moment of decision: continue as Rhyzkahl's ptarl or stand ground and face possibly unbearable consequences.

I slipped my arm around his waist. *I'm here for you.*

Rhyzkahl sneered at my gesture, then he gave a slight nod. "Your opinion is duly noted, Zakaar. Perhaps it is time for you to leave your duties here and return to my realm." He looked pointedly at my arm around Zakaar's waist. "I fear you have formed unwise attachments that have warped your perspective."

Zakaar tightened his arm around my shoulders, needing a support that went far beyond the physical. "I will gladly return to your realm if you turn from this path," he announced, then extended his hand. "Take my hand, and we will go together."

A low wind swirled around us, lifting Rhyzkahl's white blond hair and setting the cattails on the lake swaying. The lord remained silent for nearly a full minute while he looked at Zakaar as if not quite certain who he was. The delay told me that Zakaar's offer at least had him considering. More than I expected. "Zakaar, you have lost your direction," he finally said. "It is you who must turn away, abandon these," he waved a hand to encompass all that was Earth and humanity, "mayflies."

Zakaar lowered his extended hand. Another bone-deep tremble went through him. "I am . . . so very sorry, Rhyzkahl," he said, voice thick with pain.

If Rhyzkahl noticed Zakaar's anguish, it didn't affect him. "As am I," he replied, mouth tight. "It is time to finish my business here. Step aside, ptarl." He paused, smiled. "And bring Rowan to my side where she belongs."

A burst of static had me wincing. "Kara!" Paul all but shouted in my ear. "Your name is *Kara.*"

I masked a smile and kept my arm firm around Zakaar's waist. My posse was *awesome*. And Rhyzkahl was a parasite.

Off to my right I saw Kadir throw Asher to the ground hard. He planted a booted foot in Asher's back then stared at Zakaar and Rhyzkahl with a look of combined horror and fascination on his face. Kadir was acting almost *human*, which was really starting to weird me out.

"No, Rhyzkahl," Zakaar said. "I cannot, *will* not continue to be party to your machinations. I . . ." He paused, shaking, though it was only apparent to me because of my physical contact. When he spoke again his voice was strong and clear. "I renounce the ptarl bond."

I wrapped both arms around Zakaar and held him firmly, letting him know I was here, would always be here for him. This was Rhyzkahl's last opportunity to capitulate, and Zakaar's last to back out.

But Rhyzkahl could only stare blankly, as uncomprehending as if Zakaar had suddenly announced he was a goldfish. "I do not understand."

"I am breaking the bond," Zakaar said, his trembles slowly easing. "Breaking the oath."

Horror spread over Rhyzkahl's face. "You cannot!" He shook his head in denial at the very idea. "The bond is inviolate," he practically sputtered. "Zakaar, your time on Earth has driven you mad."

Off to my right, Kadir reached down without ever shifting his eyes from us, gripped Asher by the hair at the back of his head then expertly slammed his forehead into the ground to leave the summoner stunned and limp. That done, he straightened, stepped over Asher and moved several feet closer to—as far as I could tell—get a better view. It reminded me oddly of tying up a pet dog to make sure it doesn't run off while the owner steps away to look at something interesting.

Paul's voice crackled in my ear. "Oh, man, the feeds are nuts! They totally shifted when you went up by Zack." I flicked a quick glance over to Kadir as I realized it was the feeds—the potency flows—that had him so fascinated.

Zakaar slowly shook his head, eyes never leaving Rhyzkahl. "No, my time on Earth has brought me a breath of sanity." He closed his eyes, and his focus grew palpable. Undoing the strands that held a several-thousand year old bond wouldn't be an easy task, much like picking the lock of long-rusted prison chains, but I knew Zakaar was determined to find a way. I pygahed for both of us, supporting him physically and emotionally.

"Whoa, coooool," Paul breathed. "Now things are coiling and going all over the place."

Kadir took another step forward. Rhyzkahl jerked as if stung. "Zakaar!" For the first time fear flickered in his eyes. "Cease!"

"There is no stopping now," Zakaar said in a voice full of sorrow. Uncertainty flooded to me from Mzatal, as if echoing Rhyzkahl's experience. I touched him, sought to soothe him.

A weird non-physical vibration went through me, and Rhyzkahl jerked again, harder. Kadir's eyes narrowed, head swiveling this way and that as he tried to assess the shifting flows. I caught a hint of movement behind me and to my right, and I glanced back to see Paul on his feet, lips slightly parted as he focused on his tablet, a bizarro mirror of Lord Creepshow's fascination.

Abruptly, Kadir spun and moved back to Asher, seized him by the hair and dragged him to the node, then literally threw him in. The summoner disappeared with a weird *pop*, but Kadir remained and turned back to watch, having put the pet dog in the kennel.

Rhyzkahl dropped to his knees, face a mask of anguish and loss. "No. No! Come back to me," he pleaded, voice breaking. "Zakaar!"

A sliver of pity wormed its way in, and I allowed it to remain for now. None of the lords had ever been without a ptarl. *Ever.* I couldn't even think of a human parallel. Divorce? Not even close. Losing a limb? Horrible, but not unthinkable. Losing a loved one? A tragic part of existence, but an accepted one.

Zakaar's arm tightened around me as I *felt* him reach for the last strand. One final cut to sever an unbreakable bond. "*Tah si firkh.* I'm here for you," I said softly, held him to me.

His breath came in short gasps as he remained poised above that last strand. Then he tensed, every muscle rigid as iron, and made the final cut to free himself.

Rhyzkahl let out a strangled cry and fell to his hands and

knees. His blade, Xhan, tumbled out of his grasp as he stared at nothing, face stricken with unimaginable loss. "Zakaar," he pleaded.

The tension abruptly fled Zakaar, and his knees buckled. Taken off guard, I managed to lower him to the ground with a bit of control, then knelt beside him and cradled him to me while I murmured *I am here, I love you* over and over.

Zakaar, his face twisted in tormented sadness, jerked heavily, much as Rhyzkahl had done, as a low anguished noise issued from his throat. A wave of desolate despair swept over me from him. Eyes still on Rhyzkahl, he gave me a brief mental touch, like the brush of a phantom's fingers, then vanished.

Chapter 40

Unbalanced by Zack's abrupt departure, I barely caught myself before going sprawling and struggled quickly back to my feet. Worry for Zack swept through me, followed by a wave of frustration. He'd sacrificed himself and now he needed support more than ever. An agonized cry broke through my thoughts, snapped me back to the here and now.

Rhyzkahl crumpled to his side then rolled to his back, eyes wide as he began to puke. With a stunned look on his face, Kadir stepped smoothly forward and rolled Rhyzkahl to his side, then set a foot on his shoulder to hold him there so he wouldn't drown in vomit. His eyes came to me, and I felt his slicing regard. Did he fear that his own ptarl, Helori, would follow Zakaar's example? Or did he hope for it, estranged as they were?

"Kara," I heard Mzatal say from behind me, plea in his voice. "Come back."

I returned to Mzatal's side, and guilt stabbed me at the shock in his face, his unsteady breath, his uncertainty. *I should have warned him somehow.* "I'm here, Boss."

"Kara. Zharkat." I watched him visibly fight for focus. Now that the unthinkable had happened to Rhyzkahl, the other lords knew it was possible and could conceivably happen to them. "They are not done," he said. "Jesral and Amkir."

"Hold it together, Boss," I told him, centering for us both. "Focus on the now. It's all good." A peal of thunder startled me, and a moment later rain pattered down in hard and fierce drops for several seconds then stopped again.

Jesral abruptly threw off the potency net that had held him. He looked just as shaken and freaked as Mzatal, but his focus returned as he concentrated on the situation at hand. Three quick strides brought him to where the blade, Xhan, lay on the ground between him and Rhyzkahl. He stooped to pick it up, then dropped it with a curse and shook his hand as if it had burned him. Jaw set, he pulled a cloth from an inside pocket of his jacket, doubled it, then carefully retrieved the blade and tucked it away. With that accomplished his attention shifted to Amkir, who still lay pinned on the ground. The two lords' eyes met. Jesral gave a slight nod. Amkir returned it.

Those two are up to something, I thought—and had no time to do anything more.

Jesral's head swiveled toward me, and he lifted a hand, even as Amkir gestured to where Idris lay bound behind Mzatal. In the next heartbeat I let out a hoarse scream as the sigils on my body flared in hideous reminder of the agony that had formed them. Distantly, I heard Idris cry out, and I realized Amkir must have activated a recall implant in Idris. Like an arcane homing device, the recall was intended to return its subject to the one who placed it. But because Idris was still behind Mzatal's protections, it could only pull; like tying a rope around someone's middle and then attempting to yank them through a chain link fence. Pull the rope hard enough and something has to give.

Jesral twisted his hand, and instantly my agony ratcheted up and flashed in quick sequence through each of the eleven sigil scars of the lords, before settling into a steady white-hot burn. My vision went grey, and I staggered, saved from falling as Mzatal threw an arm out and pulled me back against him. The agony abated very slightly with the contact, but behind me Idris gave another pain-filled cry.

A primal scream of fury and frustration burst from Mzatal. His resources were exhausted, and I sensed his awareness that he could perhaps save either Idris or me, but not both. And then even that awareness burned away in the fury that seethed within him.

Jesral closed his fingers, and a pinpoint of searing heat like a tiny sun burned over my sternum. Red tinged my vision, and I shuddered then looked down at the arm around my waist. Why was Mzatal holding me? I began to struggle against the hold. No. I needed to return to Jesral, to Rhyz-kahl.

"Kara! Kara!" Paul's voice yanked me back to myself.

Breathing raggedly, I ceased my struggles. The sigils still throbbed, but I knew who I was. I tried to touch Mzatal through our connection, but his focus was fully on the storm as he called it closer, pulled the lightning and power to him.

Amkir snarled and tightened his hand. Idris screamed again as though being ripped apart, even as thunder pounded across the lawn. Jesral exuded cold, calm focus, a vulpine smile curving his mouth as he twisted his hand again. I jerked in Mzatal's hold, screamed, "*KARA,*" through a closing veil of *rakkuhr* red. Mzatal raised his arm, and I *felt* him bring the lightning through Khatur. The strike came to the blade in a blinding flash that drove all hint of the red haze from me, and in the next instant the lightning split to slam into the two enemy lords. Jesral flew back nearly a dozen feet and landed in a crumpled, smoking heap not far from Rhyzkahl. But Amkir took the strike solidly, pinned down as he was, and barely had time to utter a choked scream as it seared over and through him.

The pain in the sigils stopped as suddenly as if a switch had been thrown. I dragged in a breath and leaned heavily on Mzatal as I fought to get my equilibrium back. Instead of the exhilaration of the lightning I'd experienced on the mini-nexus, this ripped through me with near-sentient wrath, disturbing and familiar. *The essence blade.*

I heard Paul give an unsteady laugh, and when I looked over I saw him curled on the ground a few feet away with one arm over his head and the other holding his tablet tightly to his chest. He lifted his head, gave me a wavering grin. "That was so cool," he breathed.

I gave him a weak smile in response. Easy to enjoy the light show when one was in a Mzatal-made protective cocoon. A dozen or so feet beyond him, Bryce knelt with a hand on Idris's shoulder, expression tight as Idris's body twitched.

I looked back at the lords who'd started this bullshit. Both Jesral and Amkir lay moaning, heavily burned, and clearly not an immediate threat, though Jesral struggled to get up. Mzatal's arm remained an iron band around my middle, and I felt his rage couple with the sentience of the blade and go even darker.

"Boss. It's done." I pulled vainly at his arm. "It's cool now," I said, but he didn't seem to hear me. I twisted to see his face, deep dread rising at the wrath that contorted his features. "Mzatal?" I sought to touch him, but a wall of anger blocked all else.

Once again he called the lightning to him. I bit back a shriek, covered my head with my arms as thunder slammed into us, and Mzatal danced the searing power over Jesral and Amkir. The two jerked and writhed beneath the assault for at least a dozen heartbeats, then Mzatal pulled it all into himself, restoring exhausted resources and supercharging.

"Stop!" I yelled at him as soon as he released the strike, but before I could take a breath to say anything more he called it again, this time enhancing it with potency and feeding it through Khatur. Blue-tinged blasts smashed into Farouche's mansion and the Ops building, fully orchestrated by Mzatal. His breath hissed between his teeth as he raked the potency-fueled lightning over the house. Screams and shouts sounded from within as flames leapt in the lightning's wake, and in seconds people began to boil out, fleeing like rats from a sinking ship.

I screamed at him to stop, pummeled him with my fists, but he remained utterly distant, lost in his fury and vengeance. His lips pulled back from his teeth, and I felt the power within him build like a charging capacitor. "No, Boss. Mzatal! *No!*"

I squeezed my eyes shut in pure protective instinct, and in the next instant a flash of potency burst from him. Heat seared over me, though dampened by Mzatal's own aura and shields, but I heard a scream of agony, quickly cut off. *Paul. That was Paul!*

Heart pounding, I lifted my head. Everything within a ten foot radius was incinerated to powdered ash—all save the crumpled heap that was Paul. Most of his clothing was gone or seared and stuck to the raw and smoking burns covering his body. His hair had burned away, and one ear was missing. He lay curled on his side, arms crossed over his chest to protect the melted slag that was all that remained of his tablet.

Nausea rose in my throat. Paul's shielding had saved him from being cremated alive, but hadn't been enough to fully protect him. It had been meant for bullets and arcane strikes, not a mini-armageddon.

I looked past him to see Bryce and Idris several feet outside the circle of destruction. Bryce had thrown himself over Idris to shield him, but he looked up now. Naked horror filled his eyes. "Paul! Oh god, no . . . Paul!" He lurched to his feet, then dropped to cover Idris again as Mzatal called the lightning and connected upward. The clouds took on a blue glow as multiple thin lightning streaks hissed and crackled incessantly over the entire area like electrified serpents. Rain whipped down, sizzling through the power to land with stinging force.

Bryce found an opening, stumbled up and managed to run-stagger to Paul. "No. *NO!*" he cried out in wrenching anguish as he dropped to his knees by the crumpled form, desperately searching for any sign of life. "Paul!" He dragged the molten remains of the tablet from Paul's chest, then recoiled as a layer of ruined flesh came with it, leaving a gruesome wound of exposed ribs and sternum.

Seizing Mzatal's head, I fought to touch him, to reach him, only to find a maelstrom of rage and grief. Desperate, I struck him hard with closed fists. "No!" I screamed over the unending thunder. "Stop! You're hurting people!" I pried my hand beneath his fingers, twisted with moves learned from Gestamar. Mzatal's grip loosened, and I stumbled free of his grasp, yet I didn't think he was even aware I'd done so.

Singed hair lay wet and slick against Kadir's skull as he limped toward me, and a vicious and twisted burn marked a forked path from face to thigh down his left side. He staggered as a random strike hit a few feet from him, but continued inexorably forward, teeth bared as he looked beyond me. I yanked my gaze around to see Ryan standing several feet behind Mzatal, a few inches within the blasted circle.

Light and sound and heat and rain pummeled me from all directions, but I ruthlessly shut it out, stood before Mzatal and focused solely on him. Glowing with raging power, he planted his feet and raised Khatur high. The bizarre lightning stopped and the thunder ceased, but I knew Mzatal wasn't finished. Deep terror filled me as I sensed him draw power. The burst that so grievously injured Paul would be a mere spark compared to what he sought to do now.

"Ryan!" I shouted, desperate. "I can't reach him. Help me reach him!" I swiveled to Kadir. "Both of you! Do something to help me!" Lord Creepshow wasn't an ally by any stretch of the imagination, but right now we were *all* at risk of obliteration.

In answer, Kadir lowered his head and began to trace. Ryan gave a guttural cry, his features shifting weirdly as he called potency between his hands into a crude ball. I returned my full focus to Mzatal and called to him with everything I had. *Zharkat. Zharkat. You will slay me. Cease, my love. I beg you. You will slay me.*

A flicker, a whisper of response, the barest brush of awareness of me. He still drew power, still raged, yet it was a needed chink in the otherwise impenetrable wall.

Rain lashed down, plastering the dress against my body and blinding me. I reached again, called to him, shut out all but Mzatal. Distantly, I felt Kadir and Szerain prepare, then bit back my scream as they struck—Szerain with a crude hammer blow of potency in Mzatal's back, and Kadir with a superbly elegant burst that covered Mzatal's skin in a network of azure neon like freakish varicose veins.

Please. You must stop. You will kill us all.

The potency burned over Mzatal. It got his attention, but it was my presence and touch that riveted him. He breathed heavily through bared and clenched teeth, held the strike.

"Zharkat," I said, weeping. "Boss. Please stop."

His eyes found mine. He was lost—in the grief and anger and *power*, and in the need to vent all of it. His body trembled with the effort of keeping it in check.

I threw my arms around him as if I could help him hold the strike back. My focus widened, and now I took in everything happening around us.

Bryce knelt by Paul, performing CPR with desperate efficiency, exposed bone beneath his hands. *"C'mon, kid, God damn it, come on!"* Ryan had collapsed to his back, features completely his. Kadir watched with cautious intensity as he prepared another strike. Idris lay curled on his side, eyes wide and staring, jaw slack.

Mzatal felt it *all* through me—the destruction, the pain, the fear, the death—and his control of the fury wavered.

"Mzatal. Send Khatur away," I ordered, using every means of communication I had with him. "Send the blade away. NOW!"

His eyes locked on mine, as hard as silver-grey flint—

unyielding, uncompromising, but still holding the catastrophic potency at bay.

Boss. Zharkat. Beloved, I called to him. *Feel me. Remember yourself. Be right here. Right now. With me.*

Breath hissing through his teeth, Mzatal shifted his grip on the blade. For a horrific second I thought he intended to drive it through me, but then he let out a harsh growling cry and slashed the blade down across his forearm to open a deep gash. Luminescent blood sizzled and vaporized on the blade, and I staggered, nausea rising, as I *felt* Khatur take the offering. In the next heartbeat, the blade disappeared from Mzatal's hand, banished.

Mzatal shook with the intensity of the gathered potency, the cumulation of black anger I couldn't fathom. He still maintained enough control to keep it leashed, but not for much longer. Even now it ripped at him. I felt the pressure build—a sealed volcano, poised to explode, and when it did Mzatal would stand alone in the middle of a blasted crater.

"Down. Down!" I urged him. "Ground it into the earth and to the lake."

He let out a tortured cry, dropped to his knees, and flattened his palms on the ground. I went with him, kept my arms around him, called to him.

The lake, I told him. *Send it to the lake.* The world trembled. A narrow fissure split the ground between us and the water, a crack of earthen lightning. An instant later the lake erupted into a boiling cauldron.

Holding Mzatal, I helped him channel the power as it poured out of him. Steam rose in a massive, seething cloud. The shaking in the earth eased. The worst of the steam dissipated, leaving behind a fetid stench.

Breathing hard, Mzatal knelt with hands still flat on the ground, regret and frustration echoing through him in discordant rhythm along with a headache that sliced at him, much like the one he'd had at my house.

I slowly released him, stood unsteadily, and looked around. Kadir, intently watchful, gave a slight nod then limped to the burned and moaning forms of Amkir and Jesral, seized each by the collar and dragged them toward the node. Flames licked from the roof of the plantation house, tempered, but not quenched by the heavy rain. Half of the Ops building lay in ruins, and potency residue still writhed over it like fine arcs of electricity. People moved, shouted, and screamed in the flickering light, but all seemed too caught up in their own nightmare to bother with the intruders who'd just nuked the place. No doubt someone had called nine-one-one by now but, as isolated as the plantation was, it would be a good fifteen minutes before significant response arrived.

"Mzatal," I said, sickened. "Paul . . . Paul needs you."

He pushed up to kneel without meeting my eyes. As he stood, I felt him consciously withdraw from me and close me off as he went to crouch by Paul. For a moment I could only stare as our connection thinned until it felt like the vacuum of space, cold and silent. What was he doing? I mentally extended, found a wall and no entry. "Mzatal?"

I dimly heard Bryce shouting. "*You fix him, goddammit! You did this to him! You goddamn bring him back!*"

Mzatal ignored him, ignored me, as he straightened and moved to Idris. Bryce cursed and resumed CPR on Paul. In othersight I saw Mzatal unwind the arcane hooks that would have killed Idris in a few more minutes. That was good. A wave of vertigo came and went. I liked Idris. Clever and talented, that one.

I frowned. Did I know Idris that well? The rain eased from a torrent to a gentle fall, and I turned in a slow circle, taking it all in. Kadir shoved Amkir and Jesral through the node portal, then turned and surveyed the area with narrowed eyes as he approached Rhyzkahl's motionless form. Mzatal carried the unconscious Idris back to set him down near Paul, then knelt and placed his hands on the horribly burned young man and went still. Bryce shifted back, jaw set and eyes on Mzatal, but he didn't say anything as the lord worked on Paul.

I lifted my hand to the silent receiver in my ear, unable to escape the feeling that someone was supposed to be telling me something. Reminding me of something. Vertigo flickered over me once more. My hand dropped, and I fought to hold onto a slick plain of never-ending glass, tilting me toward oblivion—

"*Kara.*"

I spun toward the voice, toward Ryan as he climbed to his feet. Dream fragments merged with reality, dispersed to reveal firm ground beneath me. *Kara.* "Here," I gasped.

"I'm here. Kara." The grove. I still felt the grove through the open node. That's what I needed to focus on right now. I was Kara, and Kara could do cool shit with the grove.

"Kara," Ryan repeated as he moved to me. "Kara."

I took a deep breath, tasted the boiled lake in the air. "Ryan, I killed Pyrenth," I said, voice cracking. "And Jesral almost had me, and Mzatal, he . . ." I trailed off, unable to voice it.

"Kara," he murmured as he gathered me close. "Be right here, right now. You have to focus. Too much is going on."

I clung to him, fought my way back up and dug in. "Right. Right. I'm here."

"Kara." That was Mzatal, voice tight and mega-controlled. "Kara," he said again, yet the connection remained silent and empty. I released Ryan and moved toward Mzatal. The ground seemed to pitch and roll beneath my feet, but I couldn't tell if it was the aftermath of all the tremors, like trying to walk on land after a long boat trip, or if it was simply my own tenuous grasp on my reality because of the *rakkuhr* virus.

Idris let out a low groan from where he lay beside Paul. Paul didn't groan. I wasn't even sure Paul was breathing beneath Mzatal's hands. At the edge of my vision I saw Kadir carry Rhyzkahl onto the gazebo platform, push him through the node then stride away in the direction of the burning mansion. My hatred of Rhyzkahl remained unchanged, but for now I banked the fires of my rage. He suffered terribly with the loss of his ptarl, and it was enough for me in this moment.

"Kara," Mzatal said, and I returned my focus to him. "Call Vsuhl." His words came sharply, bitten out to slice the air, and I didn't know if it was because he had everything focused on Paul or if he'd closed off even basic warmth from me.

Yet I did as he asked. Perhaps he needed my help to save Paul? The blade coalesced in my hand, edge catching the glare of the remaining floodlights and the fires. None of Pyrenth's blood on it. *A self-cleaning blade,* I thought with an edge of hysteria. How fucking handy was that?

Mzatal jerked his hand out toward me. "Give it to me."

I didn't move. Behind me I heard a weird cough-gasp that I knew was Szerain fighting his way up through Ryan.

Mzatal demanded Vsuhl back with no regard for what I'd gone through, no regard for what he'd so recently wrought through his own blade, through Khatur, no regard for . . . anything?

"No." I said it softly, but I knew he heard me.

Mzatal gathered up Paul in his arms, teeth gritted against the headache that I could see still plagued him. "Kara, no time for this," he said, flat and harsh. "Give me the blade."

The silence in our connection beat at me at me like nightmare wings. "No." I took a slow step back, and my gaze dropped to Paul. "You need to go."

I wanted to feel some sort of reaction to my denial of him, but there was nothing. No flicker, no clench of the jaw or distress in his features. Mzatal's gaze merely flicked past me to Szerain, and I felt the exiled lord's desire for Vsuhl like that of a starving wolf for a doe. "Then send it *away*," Mzatal said, tone curt and blunt as he brought his gaze back to me. He placed his foot gently on Idris. "Kara," he said, yet there was nothing there but the word. None of *him* came with it. "Kara," he repeated, more softly.

I banished Vsuhl without protest. I wanted to understand what happened. I wanted to scream *WHY*. But I didn't. There wasn't time for *me*. "Go," I told him, the silence between us a heart-wrenching void. "You need to go and save Paul." Bryce took a step toward Mzatal. He intended to go with Paul, I knew.

Mzatal's expression, already stony, went to the lord-unreadable mask. His eyes came to me, then rested on Bryce. In another heartbeat he was gone with Paul and Idris.

Bryce gaped at the empty patch of sodden ash. "No. No! He left without me!"

I wanted to collapse and hug myself and cry, but I didn't have the fucking luxury to do so. "Ryan," I said with as much resolve and conviction as I could muster. "I need you to go to Sonny and get Ms. Palatino away from here and to safety."

He nodded. "Can do. After that I have to find Zack."

"I'll take care of it," I assured him. Focus on the job now. I could do that. "I'll find Zack. I promise."

Ryan hesitated then gave another nod and loped off toward the hole in the fence.

"Bryce, I need you with me," I said.

He still stared in shock at where they'd been. "What the fuck?"

"*Bryce*," I snapped out like a whip. "I need you with me."

His shoulders jerked back as he focused. "Right," he said, still shaky. "Right," he repeated, more firmly this time. Paul was gone and there wasn't a fucking thing he could do about it. I knew more about that feeling than I wanted to.

He bent and picked up Paul's fried tablet with its bits of charred flesh as though it was nothing more than a piece of litter. Looking my way, he opened his mouth to speak then shut it, gaze going behind me.

I turned to see Kadir approaching, limping heavily from the massive burn that charred his thigh. Deep burns also distorted the left side of his face and torso. His eyes stayed riveted on me as he led a gasping and stumbling Farouche by a noose of potency around the man's neck. I watched their approach warily. As much as it rocked my world to see Farouche in such a position, I wasn't in the mood for Kadir's weird-and-creepy shit right now.

He stopped two paces away from me, drew Farouche up to stand beside him before releasing the potency noose. Farouche drew in a ragged breath, a combination of fury and fear burning in his eyes. Yet he lifted his chin and put on a fierce smile in an attempt to regain some composure.

I offered Farouche a deliberately bland look before I shifted my attention to Kadir, doing my best to give the impression I was dismissing the man as uninteresting and unimportant.

Expression tight with what had to be unbearable agony, Kadir regarded me. "Kara Gillian," he rasped. "in the agreements and protocols of this world, is this one," he gestured toward Farouche, "considered deserving of punishment?"

I knew exactly why Kadir would ask me this, especially after finding out about the men who'd been sent because they "deserved punishment." I'd been warned by more than one lord about how dangerous Kadir was, and how he liked to . . . hunt. Hell, even Rhyzkahl had warned me about him.

But Kadir had simply asked me a question. And so, I simply answered.

"Deserving of punishment?" I nodded. "Yes. Without question."

Farouche's smile shifted to a smirk. "You're judge, jury,

and executioner now, Ms. Gillian?" he drawled. "I believe this is better decided in a proper court of law."

I readied a retort, but before I could speak, Kadir turned to him, aura shifting to *cold as fuck*.

"No, James Macklin Farouche," he said in a voice that set my own bowels clenching even though it wasn't directed at me. "*I* am judge. Jury. Executioner." He punctuated each word with potency. "Kara Gillian confirms what I had already drawn from here." He traced a burned finger slowly down the man's temple.

Sweat beaded on Farouche's upper lip as he paled. "I'm a businessman," he said, no longer smirking. "That's all. Sometimes business gets a little ugly."

"He wouldn't get the justice he deserves here in this world," I said somewhat dully, part of me hating that I was sending Farouche to what was surely a fate worse than death, with another part of me knowing how fucking evil the man was and how many lives he'd utterly destroyed. If anyone deserved a fate worse than death, it was this bastard. "He'd easily be able to influence the jury and witnesses," I continued, sick despite it all. "I doubt he'd spend a single day in prison."

Kadir snaked the loop of potency around Farouche's neck again. "The *businessman* will spend time with me."

"No," Bryce said, interrupting Farouche's gabbled protest. He dropped Paul's fried tablet. "He's mine."

Farouche's head snapped around as Bryce stepped forward, and relief filled his eyes. I didn't have to read minds to know the thoughts going through his head: A little of the old fear-whammy and Bryce would be his dog again. *Oh, dude*, I thought with a whisper of bitter amusement. *You have* no *idea.*

I took a slight step back to defer to Bryce as Kadir turned a penetrating gaze on him. A chilling smile curved Kadir's lips as he no doubt read Bryce's claim and his intention. Kadir glanced to Farouche, gave the potency leash a brief tug. "Are you indeed his?"

Ignoring the leash as best he could, Farouche smiled, smugly confident. "Yes. Justice demands that Thatcher have custody of me. We have a long history."

Bryce's expression didn't so much as flicker from the impassive mask as he regarded his former boss. "Yes, we have a long history." He met Kadir's eyes. "He's mine," he repeated.

I took another step back. Kadir narrowed his gaze at Bryce. "I understand he is yours," he said through clenched teeth. "I acknowledge he is yours." He reached to grip Farouche's wrist in a tight grasp, and by the pain that flashed over the man's face I knew it was *just* on the verge of bone-breaking. "But in *this* moment he is mine for facilitating this." He gestured toward the unstable node, and I suddenly understood Kadir's anger. He was *OMG* crazy and dangerous and unpredictable, but at the same time an order-and-rules freak—which was probably how he managed to function at all. The screwed up node was not only likely rule-breaking of the highest order but was also messy and threatened to fuck up the order of things in both worlds. His first action upon arrival had been to stabilize the node portal, and was probably the only reason he broke the rules and came through at all.

And *now* I realized why Kadir hadn't joined the attack on Mzatal here, or accompanied the other Mraztur four months ago at Szerain's palace when I performed the ritual to call Vsuhl. It was against the rules for the lords to engage in anything but one-on-one combat.

"In another moment he will be yours," Kadir continued, then drew Farouche's hand to his mouth in a smooth and powerful motion. Before Farouche had time to react, Kadir sunk his teeth into the flesh at the base of the man's thumb and ripped a chunk free.

Farouche let out a hoarse scream as Kadir spat the gobbet at Bryce's feet. Bryce didn't shift away or react and kept his face utterly smooth and expressionless as Kadir tightened his grip on Farouche's wrist with an audible *crack* of bones. Farouche screamed again, knees buckling as Kadir viciously wrenched his hand and then, merely by touching the man's temple, roused him from a near faint to full awareness.

"Such a brief time, a moment," Kadir murmured as he allowed the trembling Farouche to go to his knees, "yet so much can transpire." He crouched, hissing low as the crisped flesh of his thigh crackled grotesquely, then reached and gripped Farouche's balls, wringing another—higher—scream from Farouche as he squeezed and twisted hard.

Kadir held the man in this agonizing position, one hand squeezing the broken wrist and the other tightening on his nuts, until Farouche's eyes rolled back in his head. Only then did Kadir release him, though immediately gripped him by his hair to again touch his temple and rouse him to full consciousness. But he wasn't finished. He ripped Farouche's shirt open, and as though reading from Farouche the torments he had inflicted on others, Kadir used potency to create four parallel slices in the man's chest. Methodically, he ripped away the strips of flesh, wringing screams of agony from Farouche. He dropped the bloody strips to the ground, licked his fingers, and potency burned the remainder of the blood from them. He stood, hauling the gibbering Farouche upright, then shoved him to crumple at Bryce's feet.

"And now the moment is yours," Kadir stated and wiped the blood on his mouth away with the back of his hand. I kept my teeth clenched, pygahed desperately, and prayed I wouldn't upchuck.

Bryce gave a slight nod, face still betraying absolutely nothing, which impressed the hell out of me considering my own reaction. "You're finished with him?" he asked.

"I am."

Bryce dropped his gaze to Farouche. "Mr. Farouche? Can you look at me please?"

Breathing in pained whimpers and cradling his arm to his chest, Farouche turned his head to look up at Bryce. His face shifted subtly, and I knew he was attempting to exert his influence, get Bryce back under his thumb—or what was left of it, I thought with a silent snigger.

Bryce met Farouche's eyes, then drew his gun and shot him in the head.

I jerked, even though I'd known it was coming, but I managed not to startle when Bryce put a second round into the man's skull.

Bryce exhaled softly and holstered his weapon again, tension slipping from his stance. He'd never intended to taunt Farouche or torture him, I realized. For Bryce, killing Farouche hadn't been revenge. He'd killed the man to make sure no one else ever died on his order or suffered the way he and Sonny and Paul and countless others had.

Kadir's gaze went from Bryce to me, then he spoke to

me in demon. "Kara Gillian, *shik-natahr*, zharkat of Mzatal. There is no other but you to seal the node when I depart."

I had no idea what "shik-natahr" meant. The tenuous grove connection hadn't provided that meaning, but a glance at the node told me that leaving it unsealed was *not* a viable option.

"Tell me what to do," I said.

He lifted his hand toward my temple, paused as I tensed. A faint smile of dry amusement touched his mouth. "I honor my agreement with Mzatal concerning you," he stated. "I only wish to transfer that which you require in order to seal the node."

Right. He wouldn't fuck around with agreements *or* the condition of the node. I gave him a slight nod and controlled the automatic urge to pull back as he touched my temple. My vision flickered for the barest instant, and then he pulled away, turned, and limped off without another word. I waited a few seconds before following, instructions clear in my head for what to do. Kadir crouched, made a few adjustments to the flows surrounding the node, then stepped through and was gone. I crossed the rubble-littered ground to the gazebo platform and stood before the node portal. I shivered at the feel of the energy—as if the portal sought to pull me through from the inside out. I couldn't even imagine how miserable traveling through one would be. I pygahed to ensure utmost focus, then quickly sketched the needed sigils and made the adjustments as if I'd been born knowing them. Three heartbeats later the portal aspect of the node narrowed, then closed with little more than a sub-audible *pop*.

I turned to Bryce. "Let's get out of here."

Chapter 41

Somewhere in the numb void left by Mzatal, I found enough focus to keep going. We weren't out of this yet, and the hint of distant sirens only emphasized that point. Bryce pulled a flashlight with a red filter from his pocket and lit our way as we double-timed it across Farouche's property and to the hole Mzatal had melted in the tall and formidable metal fence. I felt Mzatal's arcane signature as we passed through, like catching a whiff of cologne on a shirt. My chest tightened, and I slowed, but Bryce caught my elbow and urged me onward, over a rise and through a thick stand of bamboo to where an inflatable raft waited on the bank of the bayou that paralleled the fence line.

The rain was barely a light mist now, and stars glimmered to the west, peeking out from behind the retreating storm clouds. After we paddled our way across the sluggish bayou, Bryce pulled a knife and made three long gashes in the vinyl of the raft. Working quickly, we found several decent-sized rocks, rolled the shredded raft around them, then tossed it into the middle of the water to disappear beneath the mud-brown surface. Ryan would have done the same with the raft that had carried him, Sonny, and Angela across. No need to leave them on the shore and make it obvious that people had crossed.

I began to climb up the levee, but Bryce paused, still facing the water. Twitching with impatience, I watched as he unholstered his pistol and disassembled it in about three seconds flat. His expression remained utterly stoic as he chucked the slide and magazine into the water, then he pulled a slim toolkit from a pocket and removed a rasp from it. In a practiced move, he scraped the rasp through the barrel several times, hammered it against the firing pin, then tossed the rest of the gun pieces into the water.

He replaced the little rasp in his toolkit, slipped it back into his pocket, then turned to me. "Let's go." The whole process had taken perhaps thirty seconds.

Professional hit man, making sure the gun can't be traced to the two bullets in Farouche's skull. But I didn't comment aloud, and together we scrambled up the levee and made our way to the vehicles.

Ryan paced an anxious line in front of his car. Sonny leaned against it with his arms folded casually, though his fingers drummed a nervous staccato on his bicep. The back door of the car was open, and as we hurried up a woman I recognized from her picture as Angela Palatino stepped out.

I wanted nothing more than to get the hell out of there and start looking for Zack, but I knew I couldn't *not* take a few minutes to deal with her. I owed that much to Idris.

The tight grip she held on the top of the car door betrayed the level of her tension, and obvious signs of weeping marred her lovely face. I shot Sonny a questioning glance. Misery filled his expression, and then he briefly put his arms in a baby-holding position.

Baby? I thought, baffled, but then it clicked. Her daughter. Angela had no doubt asked Sonny where Amber was, and he'd been forced to tell her the brutal truth.

"Is Idris all right?" she asked, eyes flicking briefly past me as if expecting him to come over the levee at any moment.

"Yes, ma'am," I said, only lying a little. Idris was a mess the last time I saw him, but I knew Mzatal would call in every favor he had to *make* him all right. "He went with one of our other operatives for debriefing," I continued, lying a *lot* this time, then shoved down my impatience to get out of there. "I'm very sorry about your daughter."

Grief clouded her face. "Thank you." I saw the questions forming in her eyes—*Why did all this happen? Why was Idris's cooperation so necessary? Why did my daughter have to die?*—and I quickly spoke to forestall them, since I hadn't the faintest fucking idea how to answer.

"Agent Kristoff is going to take you to the rest of your

family," I said, gesturing to Ryan. "I'm sorry, but there's not much more I can tell you at the moment since the investigation is ongoing."

"But I *will* get answers?" she asked.

"As soon as we have them," I lied yet again. Her scrutiny remained on me for several more excruciating seconds, and I had the gut-twisting feeling she knew damn well I was feeding her a pile of bullshit. She finally gave a nod, sat back within the car, and closed the door, though I had the definite sense she wasn't done with me or any of this. She'd merely given me a reprieve.

It was enough for now. I moved to Ryan. "Can you handle getting her to the safe house on your own?" I asked. "I need Sonny."

Ryan gave me a nod. "Yeah. I got it."

I glanced to Sonny. "You okay with that?"

He had a deer-in-headlights look about him, but he gave a nod of assent. "Sure. Whatever you need." A tug of sympathy went through me. Sonny was suddenly in a different world with different rules—a world without Farouche and his influence—and it was clear he didn't have the faintest clue of how to deal with it. Luckily, I had an idea.

Ryan leveled a stern look at me. "You be careful."

"Always," I said.

Sonny slid into the backseat of Zack's car. Bryce stood by the open passenger door but didn't get in, and it took me a second to realize he was holding it open for me. "I can drive," I insisted.

"I know you can." He smiled, but there was steel behind it. "But I'll drive."

My protest died away. He was acutely aware of my identity issues, and intuitive enough to recognize that Mzatal's behavior and cold distance had left me even more distracted. No doubt he preferred not to be a passenger with a muddled-me driving. I met his eyes with silent gratitude and climbed in.

Bryce settled behind the wheel and cranked the ignition. "Where to, chief?"

"We're looking for Zack." Where the hell would a distraught demahnk go in the middle of the night? "Let's try the Nature Center. There's a valve there. Gotta start somewhere."

As Bryce pulled out, I found my phone and called Zack. Voicemail picked up after half a dozen rings.

"Zack, it's me," I said. "We're looking for you. Hang in there. I'll keep calling." I disconnected and glanced over to Bryce. "Well, it didn't go straight to voicemail, which means he still has it on."

"That's good." A frown puckered his mouth. "What the hell *happened* with Zack? All I know is that he somehow took out Rhyzkahl, then vanished."

I did a mental head-smack. Of course Bryce was clueless. The exchange had been entirely in demon and he didn't have the benefit of the universal grove translator.

"It's really complicated," I said with an apologetic wince. "You can't breathe a word of this to Ryan." Bryce gave me a nod, and I glanced in the back seat and got Sonny's as well.

Of course now I had to figure out what to say. "You remember Ilana?" I asked Bryce. I knew Sonny would be clueless, but no way could I explain the whole demon realm dynamic right now.

When Bryce nodded, I continued. "She's Mzatal's demahnk advisor, his ptarl. And Zack is . . . was . . . Rhyzkahl's ptarl. What you saw was him breaking that bond." I paused for emphasis. "That's never *ever* been done before."

Bryce maintained his bland expression, but there was a hint of *holy shit* in his eyes when he glanced my way. "That sounds pretty big. What happened to Zack?"

"I wish I knew," I said. "But we have to find him. When he left he looked shattered." *And how long will Ryan remain stable without him?*

Yet we didn't find him at the Nature Center or the next two places we looked, and though I called his phone several times, it continued to ring then go to voicemail.

"One more try," I said after a frustrating hour of searching and calling. "If he doesn't pick up this time, I'll have to enlist Ryan to trace Zack's cell." I *really* didn't want to involve Ryan in the search, nor did I want to deal with whatever official channels would be necessary for such a thing, but we were running out of options.

"You gotta do what you gotta do," Bryce noted with pragmatic calm.

Once again I called Zack and waited through five rings.

But this time, it stopped ringing without going to voicemail, and my heart rate spiked. I couldn't hear anything on the other end, but I knew Zack had answered. I willed calm into my voice. "Hey, Zack. I'm out looking for you, dude."

Silence for a good ten seconds. "Kara," he said, voice thick and hoarse. "I'm okay."

"You're such a liar. Where are you?"

"By the lake." Each word came through as though a huge challenge to speak. "Park in the Worms and Perms lot," he managed. "West about a hundred yards, then walk in toward the lake. I . . . can't come to you."

I looked over at Bryce. "We're heading for the bait shop on Lakeshore Drive. You know the one?" He nodded and I returned my attention to Zack. "We'll be there in five minutes, and no, I'm not hanging up."

The line remained silent, and I had the distinct impression that Zack was gathering enough energy simply to speak. "What happened after I left?" he asked after about half a minute. "I know . . . the qaztahl are all gone, but I can't sense like I should."

I did my best to fill him in as we headed his way. The conversation remained fairly one-sided, but I had the sense it helped him simply to hear me talk. I caught him up on the various details, and did my best to ease his deep concern for Szerain/Ryan by relating my theory that he'd used the node to stabilize himself.

The car lurched as Bryce pulled into the empty rutted gravel lot of *Bubba and Barb's Worms and Perms*, a mom and pop beauty salon and bait shop that had been a lake fixture for almost forty years. It had been rebuilt after Hurricane Katrina, but already had a dilapidated air about it. A single floodlight illuminated the shabby, faded blue building with BEAUTY SUPPLIES, LIVE BAIT and GET WORMS HERE painted on the side. I wasn't too sure about the selling point of the last one, or the whole concept for that matter, but the place did a thriving business so what the hell did I know?

Bryce parked in the shadow of the building. I climbed out of the car and wrinkled my nose at the smell of the minnow tanks inside and ripe fish guts in the trash. "Zack told me he was a hundred yards that way then straight in toward the lake," I said. "Bryce, stay with the car and keep your phone handy, please. Sonny, I need you with me."

Sonny gave me a perplexed look. "Anything you say, but why me?"

"He sounded pretty strung out on the phone," I told him, then smiled. "I think your 'chill out' knack might be handy."

Comprehension bloomed on his face, along with gratification. I wondered how long it had been since he'd been able to use his ability for good.

"Also," I continued, "he said he's not sure if he can walk or not, and I sure as hell don't want to try and carry him."

Sonny let out a soft laugh. "I can handle that."

We left Bryce and made our way through tall grass, swarms of mosquitos, and questionable footing. "Couldn't he have blipped to a place with a trail?" I grumbled, then lifted the phone to my ear. "Hey, Zack? We should be getting close. Do you hear a herd of elephants nearby?"

"Rhinos," he replied. "Definitely . . . rhinos, and they need to bear right . . . make their way around the curve."

We continued to follow his directions and finally found him on a flat spit of stone that extended into the water. He lay curled on his side, his phone on speaker beside him.

I tucked my own phone away. The clouds were gone and the rising moon cast everything in soft light. A fat toad hopped across my path as I moved to Zack and knelt beside him. "I'm here, *ghastuk*," I said softly, the demon word for friend coming up naturally.

"You're right, I lied," he said. "I'm a wreck." He made what I suspected to be an attempt to sit up but ended up as little more than a body jerk.

I laid my hand on Zack's shoulder, caught Sonny's eye, and silently beckoned him to us. "No shit. But it's going to be all right."

Sonny moved in quickly, helped me get Zack sitting cross-legged, then withdrew a few feet, watchful. Zack scrabbled for my hand, found it, and hung on.

"It's not all right," he said. "It's *not*." The desolation in his voice matched the despair in his eyes. "There is only silence. *Silence*," he said in a heart-wrenching whisper.

"We're going to help you," I told him. "That's something you can hang on to." The reminder of Mzatal's silence and imposed distance twisted like a knife in my heart, but I swallowed the temptation to sink into my own pain and focused on Zack. I kept hold of his hand and wrapped my other arm around his shoulders. "Tell me what's going on with you so I know how to help."

"Isolated." His voice lurched as though the word forced its way through suffocating grief. "Crippled."

I gestured Sonny closer. He moved forward until he was only about a foot away. Zack took a deeper breath and eased his grip on my hand, and I hoped that meant Sonny was having a positive effect on him.

"All right, you're isolated from the other demahnk," I said, doing my best to understand. "It's some sort of telepathic link that's silent now?"

"From Rhyzkahl as well," Zack said, expression bleak, but then he shook his head. "Not telepathic. Different. You . . . understand."

I frowned, puzzled. "I do? How?" I thought for a moment. "You mean with Mzatal?"

"Similar."

"Oh." Now I had a far better understanding of the magnitude of his loss. Mzatal had built a wall but he hadn't cut our connection. When I followed the silence, he was still there. Not so for Zack. And it hadn't been just one connection. He'd lost them all simultaneously. Pain sliced through me in sympathy.

"How are you crippled?" I asked. Maybe knowing the specifics would help me help him.

"Cannot sense properly," Zack said. "Cannot feel. Cannot travel. I managed to get here, but no more." His voice broke, and he trembled softly. "Cannot flow. Cannot extend. Bound to human flesh."

I had no idea what flowing or extending meant, but now wasn't the time to ask. Wrapping my arms around him, I held him close. He clung to me like a drowning man to a life preserver, and then gave in to his sorrow. He wept in big shuddering sobs that shook us both, and grief and loss as powerful as the aura of a qaztahl washed over me. I wept with him, held him, and did as much as I could to let him know I was there for him.

After a time, he eased and went still in my arms. I continued to cradle his head to my shoulder and stroke his hair.

Sonny knelt on one knee behind Zack, face serious and focused and full of genuine concern. Zack sucked in a shaky breath and pushed himself to sit straight again, lifted his hand, and brushed my cheek with his fingertips in a gesture of gratitude far deeper than words.

"Do you need Jill?" I asked softly.

He drew in a sharp breath and stiffened, eyes reflecting panic. "No! No, I can't," he said emphatically. "It's not her. I just *can't*."

"It's okay. I understand," I hurried to assure him, then considered the situation. "You need time. You need to feel safe. And you don't need to be alone. But you need to be with someone . . . neutral."

"Yes. I'm so sorry." The words came out in a pained whisper, and the veil slid from another level of understanding. Zack was accustomed to being the caretaker and guardian, the elder and advisor. He was the one with vision and understanding. Yet, for the moment, he couldn't serve in any of those roles, and instead was the one who needed care. The whole mess surely made for a confusing and heavy burden.

"No need to be sorry, Zack," I said. "You went through a major trauma. I needed a few days away from it all not too long ago." If Helori hadn't accompanied me to the wilds of the demon realm for a timeout after Rhyzkahl tortured me, I never would have recovered. "How about Jill's house?" I suggested. "It's already warded, and she's at our place with Steeev which means you'd have it to yourself."

A flicker of relief passed through his eyes. "Yes." He swallowed, gave an unsteady nod. "Yes, that's good."

"After we get you settled, I'll call her and let her know what's going on. She'll understand." I had faith in my friend. "I also think Sonny should stay with you."

Zack looked at me with naked hope in his eyes. "Will he?"

That response alone told me I'd made a good call. I looked over at Sonny. "Zack could use your company for a little while. You cool with that?"

Pleased relief lit his face. "Sure thing. Whatever you need."

"Great. It'll be good for you as well," I said. "In fact, it's probably best for both of you to simply trust me, go along with everything I say, and not argue."

Zack managed a weak smile. "Opportunistic dictatress."

"That's Stubborn Opinionated Bitch," I corrected. "Come on. Let's get out of here. The mosquitoes are vicious."

Zack made a failed attempt to stand. "I don't know that I can walk."

Sonny moved close, drew Zack's arm across his shoulders, pulled Zack up with him as he straightened. "You don't have to, Agent Garner. I've got you."

I ducked under Zack's other arm and wrapped my arm around his waist. Getting back to the car was a lot harder than going in, but we eventually got Zack tucked into the backseat with Sonny.

I quickly filled Bryce in and told him where to go. Zack slumped against the door with his eyes closed, while Sonny fidgeted and exuded calm all at the same time. Bryce brooded in silence, no doubt worried about Paul, and I remained quiet as well, thoughts and questions about Mzatal, Vsuhl, Pyrenth, and my own identity issues whirling and colliding within me.

Trampled grass in Jill's yard remained the only indication there'd been a crime scene only a few days ago. Bryce pulled into the driveway and parked, then Sonny helped Zack into the house to get him settled on the sofa. Bryce got out of the car, leaned on the hood and looked up at the sky. I started to ask him if he was okay but caught myself before the dumb question slipped out. Instead, I laid my hand on his arm, gave it a squeeze, then turned and headed into the house.

I checked the kitchen for supplies, relieved to find plenty of food in the pantry and fridge. Sonny quickly explored the small house to get a feel for the layout. Zack sat hunched on the sofa with a pillow hugged to his chest, looking confused and lost. I'd promised him everything would be all right, but what if I was wrong? *Could* he recover from such a deep trauma?

I knew a little about trauma, and I remembered how awesome it felt to wade into the sea after my torture ordeal. Though a bath was a far cry from the ocean, it held plenty of merits of its own. I went into the bathroom and cranked the water on full in the tub, then hunted in Jill's closet and found Zack a set of his own sweats. A scrounge under the bathroom sink turned up some simple herbal sea salt, and I tossed a handful into the steaming bath, glad that Jill had something not too perfumey.

I returned to the living room, stooped, and slid Zack's arm over my shoulder. "C'mon, demon-dude. I have something for you."

He didn't resist as I helped him to his feet, and we made it to the bathroom without either of us falling over. Zack looked at the filling tub as he steadied himself with a hand on the counter. "That bad, huh?" he asked with a flicker of a smile.

I smiled. "You have grass in your hair, and you've been downwind from a bait shop. Now strip and get in."

He pulled his clothing off and let it drop to the floor. Once he was in the tub, I shut the water off, knelt on the bathroom rug, and proceeded to gently bathe him, as if caring for a child. I had the unshakable sense he needed simple nurturing and physical contact. And judging by the way he relaxed into it, my sense seemed to be right on target.

Zack closed his eyes, leaned back. I took my time, often simply soaking the sponge, then squeezing the water out over his torso. Once I'd cleaned all the decent parts, I set the sponge on the side of the tub. "I'm gonna let *you* scrub your balls, 'kay?"

"You're such a chicken," he murmured and cracked one eye open at me.

"Cluck cluck," I shot back with a smile. "There's a big fluffy towel and your sweats right here. Soak for a bit and then holler if you need help getting out."

He opened his eyes fully, found mine. I felt a whisper of his mental touch, and then a gentle caress of my essence along with a flood of love and gratitude.

My throat clogged, and I had to wipe tears from my eyes. I laid my hand on his forearm, squeezed lightly. "Take your time," I said, voice rough. "We're here for you."

I left him in the bath and returned to the living room. After about ten minutes he emerged under his own power—which was an improvement—though he remained unsteady on his feet and disturbingly pale.

Hiding my worry as much as possible, I guided him to the sofa, sat beside him. "I'll let Jill know the gist of what's going on with you," I told him. "We'll all take care of Szerain and make sure he spends time on the mini-nexus until you come home. Sonny will call if you need me for anything, all right?"

A smile struggled to his lips. "Yeah. Thanks."

I gave him a hug. "I'm so sorry it turned out like this for you."

He held me close, then surprised me by gently kissing my cheek. "Some things are worth the price you have to pay."

I returned the gesture then left him with Sonny. Deep resolve formed in my gut as I returned to the car and Bryce. Zack had sacrificed himself to save us all in a moment of crisis—and possibly in the greater battle as well.

I intended to extract a *price* from the ones who'd made it necessary.

Chapter 42

As soon as Bryce and I were on the road again, I left a message on Ryan's phone to let him know we'd found Zack but that he needed time alone and was staying at Jill's. The next call was tougher since the first thing Jill wanted to do was go to Zack. It took a bit of finesse and a lot of stubborn bitchiness to convince her, but she finally gave in and grudgingly accepted it as some sort of demon thing.

With that done, I let my gaze drift out the window. The moon floated high in a sky empty of clouds. I rubbed at my eyes as the fatigue I'd held at bay with adrenaline-charged action wormed its way in. Hard to believe that first meeting with Sonny had been less than twelve hours earlier. And then I'd become Amaryllis for a while, and then . . .

I rubbed my eyes again. Who had I been after Amaryllis?

"Kara!" Bryce said sharply.

I jerked and swallowed. Remembered. "Thanks."

"You're exhausted," he said, voice laden with worry. "You should catch a nap while I drive."

He was probably right, but I wasn't ready. "Not yet." I rolled my neck on my shoulders, felt things pop. "I can't call it quits until Ryan's home, or I've at least heard from him. Gotta account for everyone in the posse, y'know?"

Bryce frowned but nodded, then drove in silence for a time before speaking again. "I don't think he was breathing."

It took me a few seconds to figure out what he meant. "Mzatal wouldn't have taken Paul to the demon realm if there was no hope," I told him. "And you know better than anyone that he can work healing miracles."

A subtle layer of tension eased in his face. "Right. Sure, that makes sense."

"It's going to be all right," I reassured him, while I tried to convince myself as well. My phone rang with Ryan's caller ID, and I quickly answered. "Hey, you."

"I got your message, and I'm on my way home," Ryan said. "Everything's taken care of with Angela Palatino. Where are you now?"

"Turning off Serenity Road. Should be home in less than a minute."

"About ten for me. You doing okay?"

"Yeah," I lied. "Good as can be expected. You?"

"I feel a little weird, like my brain is too big for my head," he said, "but otherwise I'm good."

"We can chill together when you get home. We're at the driveway now."

"Deal," he said. "See you in a bit."

I stuffed my phone into my pocket as Bryce parked, climbed out of the car, and then stopped and looked at the house. The new floodlights under the eaves cast warm pools of amber while also throwing odd shadows onto the porch. The swing creaked gently in the soft breeze, and water dripped from the gutter spouts. Light shone through the front windows, and I wondered if the owners were home.

My hands clenched at my sides. *No, it's my house. MY house.* I fought my way back up the slippery slope. *Kara's house. And I'm Kara.* It only seemed unfamiliar because of all the changes. *But can it change so much and still be mine?* I found myself wondering.

"Kara." Bryce touched my arm, and I startled, blinked. Concern puckered his forehead. "Kara, you really need to get to bed," he said. "Like, right now."

"Sure," I said. Yet I wasn't convinced sleep could fix it. Who would I wake up as?

I walked up the steps, hesitated before opening the door. Gritting my teeth, I silenced the voice that told me I should knock first, then turned the knob and entered. I dropped my stuff on the table by the door—because it was my house, and I could do that—went to my bedroom and flipped on the light.

Fuzzykins lay curled on my bed. Blinking in the sudden light, she lifted her head and hissed at me. I started to hiss right back at her, then saw the little squiggling lumps. *In the middle of my bed.*

"You . . . you horrible beast!" I yelled. Bryce burst in behind me, clearly ready to deal with a demon or something worse.

He followed my gaze, then exhaled in relief. "Shit, it's just Fuzzykins,"

"It's my *bed,*" I gritted out. "She had her damn kittens in my bed! Eilahn bought her a ridiculously expensive cat bed, but no, she had to drop her spawn on my comforter!"

Bryce moved forward to peer at the lumps. "She sure did." A smile spread across his face as the cat *mrowr*ed up at him, but he wiped it away when he looked back at me. "Want to crash in the guest room for now, and I'll, uh, move them or something?"

"Shit." I sighed. "No, they're newborns. Better not to move them." I scowled at the cat. "She knew that too, the little bitch."

"Actually the proper term for a female cat is a queen, not a bitch . . ." He trailed off at the look on my face. "And you don't care about that." He cleared his throat. "Anyway, you still should crash in the guest room—"

Eilahn burst in and shouldered her way past us, cutting him off. "Fuzzykins! You good girl!"

"Yeah, what a good girl," I muttered. "More creatures in the house who hate me." A weird and miserable pang went through me at the thought. It bugged the hell out of me that this cat—*all* cats—despised me simply because I was a summoner. The unfairness of it gnawed at me, though I knew my current exhaustion exacerbated my reaction.

Eilahn continued to coo and ah over the kittens, clearly oblivious to the fact that she sported a black eye and ripped, bloodstained clothing. "Oh, you wonderful girl!" she gushed to Fuzzykins. "There is Bumper and Squig and Granger and Fillion and Dire and Cake!"

Bryce touched my arm and gave me a reassuring smile. I realized he'd likely picked up on my mood. "Maybe in a couple of days," he said softly, "after they've settled in, and you've had some rest, you could see what would happen if you got to know one early on. From the beginning."

"Maybe," I said. "I don't know. All cats hate me." I rubbed my gritty eyes. "I'm going to go crash on the couch or something."

"Kara, use the guest room," he insisted. "You need some quiet."

I watched Eilahn fuss over the kittens, unsettled by the weird feeling that I'd lost her, too. I knew it wasn't true at all, but right now everything felt *off*. Why hadn't I even tried to call her? "Yeah, okay." I turned and left my bedroom, walked down the hall, and into the guest room. Then stood in the middle of the floor and looked around, confused. I'd thought I was home, but no. Guest rooms were for guests. That made sense. I shook my head at my lapse.

I heard Bryce curse and pivoted to look questioningly at him. He stood in the hallway outside the door with his phone to his ear. His critical gaze raked through me as though finding me lacking, and it left me unsettled, shaken.

An overwhelming sense that I'd forgotten something vital slithered through me, something barely beyond my reach. My mind scrambled to figure out what was missing, and the sensation increased, as if once again I stood on a tilting plain of smooth glass with nothing to hang on to. "Bryce?" I choked out, struggled to dig in, grab on to *anything*. This was wrong. *Une. Due . . . Due . . .*

Or maybe I was just tired? Tired and imagining things. Yes, that was it. Simply tired. I looked over at the inviting bed. Everything would be better once I slept. I'd feel like a new person.

"Kristoff? Thatcher here," Bryce said tersely into his phone, eyes never leaving me. "How far away are you? Kara's slipping. I've never seen it this bad."

Who was he talking about? *Should I be worried about her?* I wondered distantly.

He shoved his phone into his pocket, moved in and gripped me by my shoulders. "Kara!" he shouted at me and gave me a sharp shake. "Your name is Kara!"

I sucked in a breath, surfaced. Kara? A flare of sick dread gave me something to hang on to, though it too threatened to melt away. "R-right. Kara." I reached up to cling to his upper arms, looked into his face, my eyes wide in panicked desperation. "Bryce, this is bad. Don't let me go. Please."

"I have you," he said with fierce reassurance, and comprehension suddenly bloomed on his face. "That's why

Mzatal left me behind," he murmured to himself, so low I barely caught it. He shook himself and returned his entire focus to me. "*Kara*. Mzatal is going to take care of Paul, and I'm going to take care of you. Kara." He shifted to grip me by the upper arm, then led me out and toward the living room.

I didn't resist. "Yes . . . yes. He'll take care of Paul. And I'm Kara." That was right. Wasn't it? I felt my eyes squinch in doubt, looked up at him as we walked. "You're sure?"

"I'm damn sure," he told me. "Rhyzkahl did this to you. You're Kara Gillian. Summoner. You have Mzatal who loves you. You have good friends: Zack, Jill, and Ryan who'll be here in less than a minute. You're *Kara*." He sat me on the sofa, dropped down beside me, and kept hold of my arm. "You have an aunt, uh, Tessa, and a demon guard Eilahn. You rescued Idris a little while ago. *You are Kara*."

I gave him a jerky nod. "Sure. Okay." I looked around the living room. Eilahn crouched a few feet away, eyes on me. Why was she tracing sigils, and why did she look pissed and intense? "Kara," I echoed, but the name felt strange on my lips, and the familiar room didn't seem as inviting as it had a moment ago. "I don't feel right."

"I know, Kara." Bryce shifted to face me more, shook me a bit. "It's the sigils, the scars. It's Rhyzkahl and his fucking implanted virus." His gaze flicked to the door then back to me. "I hear Ryan's car. We're going to take care of you."

I clung to his words. "I trust you," I said and held his arm in a death grip. "You'll take care of me."

Ryan burst through the front door. "Kara!"

Distress spiked as I heard the name. I released Bryce, twisted to face my friend. Yes. Ryan was my friend. "Ryan! Something's wrong." He would help. That much I knew. "I don't know what, but it . . . it *is*."

Ryan moved to crouch in front of me, face a mask of worry. "Shit," he breathed. "Kara. Kara!"

My brow furrowed at the shout. Was that *my* name? It didn't seem right.

Bryce scrutinized us, jaw tight. "You two are going out back," he commanded, then stood and pulled me to my feet. "Let's go." He jerked his head at Ryan. "Now."

I offered him a tremulous smile. I trusted these two men,

and that absolute certainty helped ease the churning disquiet. Obviously distressed, Ryan led the way down the hall to the back.

"This is a nice house," I murmured as we passed through the kitchen. Ryan shot a startled look back at me, and Bryce's hand tightened on my arm.

"It's *your* house, Kara," he insisted. "Your house."

Fear twisted my gut as I struggled to process that. I looked around for anything that clicked as personal, as *mine*, but found nothing. How could this be mine? None of this made sense.

Ryan took my other arm as we stepped off the back porch, and together the two men quick-walked me to the mini-nexus. As soon as we crossed the boundary of the power focus I dragged in a shuddering breath, feeling as if the curtain obscuring my *Self* reopened a crack. I clawed my way up, clung with everything I had to that slim awareness. "Kara," I gasped out, tasted it, fought to reclaim my name. "Ryan. Bryce. I'm Kara." I wrestled against the uncertainty and panic that threatened my tenuous hold. But how long could I do so? For now I held fast to the sloping plain of glass, but if it tipped more . . .

The converged potency of the mini-nexus seeped through me, threw the curtains wide and added power to my grip. Yet I knew it could only delay my descent. The instant I lost the potency, I'd be gone. *Kara* would be gone. Forever.

Fuck no. Not while I have breath in my body.

I drew from the mini-nexus, called up all of my internal reserves. "I know who I am. I know what I am," I said through clenched teeth. "The instant I leave the nexus I'll lose it, but I'm not fucking giving up yet. I'm going to beat this shit," I looked from one to the other. "*We're* going to beat this shit."

"You're goddamn right," Bryce said fiercely. Ryan gave an equally determined nod. Eilahn crouched a foot beyond the perimeter of the mini-nexus, still tracing sigils, teeth bared and eyes glowing with relentless focus. They had my back. Always had. My posse.

Kara's posse.

The scars on my torso abruptly flared white hot, then

quickly subsided to a billion tiny ant bites of prickling heat. Shit. No way was that a good sign. I drew measured breaths—in through my nose and out through my mouth, with a silent "*Kara*" each time.

Ryan released his hold on my arm, shifted to face me, expression intense. Without warning or preamble, he seized my dress at the neckline and ripped it from me, leaving me in nothing but bra and panties. I knew why he'd done so, but Bryce jerked in surprise.

"Shit! What the hell?" He lifted his free hand to intervene, then paused as comprehension lit his eyes. "The sigils," he murmured.

Ryan yanked my bra free and cast it aside to fully reveal all of the patterned scars. I focused on his face. No. Same hair, same eyes as Ryan, but now with subtle differences in the features. Not full-fledged Szerain, but headed that way. And far more stable than ever before, perhaps because of the potency from the node at the plantation combined with that of the mini-nexus.

A pinpoint of heat ignited over my sternum, much the same as when Jesral attacked me earlier. An instant later, it diffused and Mzatal's sigil crawled with fire. I sucked in a gasping breath. "They're waking up." I swallowed hard. "Not good. Last phase." In through the nose, out through the mouth. *Kara*.

Szerain squeezed his eyes shut. "Zakaar," he breathed. He needed Zakaar, needed his support. I now saw that the breaking of the ptarl bond had shaken Szerain as deeply as the other lords, and was made even worse by Zack's absence.

"No!" I put every bit of power I could into the word. "Zakaar can't be here," I snapped out. "It's only us four, and it won't even be *me* much longer if you don't pull yourself together." I leaned closer. "Szerain! Right here. Right now. I *need* you."

His eyes flew open, the uncertainty of a moment before replaced by fixed intensity. In a slow, deliberate move, he laid his fingers on my sternum where the invisible arcane fire crept upward. "Mzatal," he pronounced. The first to be carved by Rhyzkahl, the sigil sucked away the heat then writhed like ice beneath my skin. A wave of vertigo hit me,

and I swayed, yet Bryce's firm grip on my arm kept me upright. A soft buzzing drone set my teeth on edge, as though
a dozen voices hummed out of tune.

Szerain slid his hand up to rest beneath my collar bone.
"Rhyzkahl." Then to my side. "Kadir."

With each name, ice twisted beneath his fingers, and the
hum grew clearer as though a voice found a harmonious
note. *Mzatal. Rhyzkahl. Kadir.* The exact order Rhyzkahl
had carved their symbols into my flesh.

Heart pounding, I seized Szerain's wrist. "You're activating the series. *Why*?"

Bryce shifted his grip on my arm. A quick glance at him
revealed a shimmer of doubt in his eyes, though his face
revealed nothing. Eilahn stopped tracing sigils and stood,
watching us intently.

Szerain twisted from my grasp. "Rhyzkahl began the
process when he struck you with the virus," he told me, almost growling the words. "Jesral completed it when he drew
the *rakkuhr* to your chest earlier. Now the series activates,
as was Rhyzkahl's intent, and I can't stop it. But I *can* complete the circuit before the virus does." He leaned closer,
face intense. "Kara, I don't have a backup plan."

I took that in. "You complete it, and then what?"

"I keep you from losing yourself." He said it with calm
assurance, but the droplet of sweat that slid down his cheek
betrayed his tension.

A feather touch of heat brushed my chest through the
ice, and the hum wavered—Rhyzkahl's activation breaking
through while we stood debating.

"Do it," I said quickly, pulse slamming. If I thought about
it any longer I'd lose my nerve. And myself.

Szerain touched his hand to my belly. "Jesral." Ice answered him, and the hum steadied. He moved around me.
"Seretis." One by one he activated the sigils.

"Vahl."

"Vrizaar."

"Rayst."

"Elofir."

With each, the harmony steadied and the cold fire increased, like ice encapsulating the heat of *rakkuhr*. His
hand rested on my tailbone. "Amkir," he said with particular vehemence.

Only one sigil remained. A single note of the hum whined out of harmony like an insane mosquito. The horrible icy ache penetrated to my bones. Szerain laid his hand flat against the sigil on my upper back, and I closed my eyes, braced myself for the next level.

I felt a tremble go through him, yet he said nothing.

"Szerain." I named the sigil for him, my voice tight and hoarse. "*Szerain*."

A sob choked from him. "Szerain," he echoed. The searing ice receded, leaving only phantom echoes. The hum shifted to soft harmonious tones, eerily familiar.

He slid his hand to the small of my back, rested it on the twelfth sigil—the one meant to unite the other eleven, but never ignited. The scar blossomed with heat under Szerain's hand, and I jerked in shock. I'd *never* felt anything in that sigil. The tones cut off and the world abruptly dipped and swayed. Only Bryce's hold on my arm kept me from falling.

"What's going on? Szerain?" Blood pounded in my ears. "What did you do? That's never been anything but a scar!"

He drew his fingers over the sigil in swirling patterns laced with fire. "Kara, it has *never* been a mere scar. A scar can be resolved to unblemished skin."

Mouth dry, I fought to balance the rising apprehension with my trust of him, of Ryan. "What are you doing to it?"

"I am using it to stop what Rhyzkahl started," he told me. "Now I need Vsuhl."

Numb shock seeped through me. "No, Szerain," I said, voice shaky. "I can't do that."

"Yes, you can. And you *will*." He wrapped his arm around me and pulled me back against him. "I have activated the unifier. I need Vsuhl. Without it, I can't finish what I've begun, and the sigil is nothing more than a detonator." He spoke close to my ear, confident, uncompromising. "When the virus reaches it, you don't lose yourself—you die. I *need* Vsuhl. *Now*."

Eilahn gave a cry of anger even as Bryce's grip tightened to pull me away.

With a sweep of his free arm, Szerain raised a transparent barrier of shimmering blue along the perimeter of the nexus to block Eilahn. In the same motion, he slammed Bryce away from me with a hammer fist of potency, snaked arcane bindings from the ground to hold him fast where he stood.

Fear wound together with fury to rip through me. "You fucking piece of shit." I said through clenched teeth. "You turned me into a ticking time bomb to make sure I didn't have a goddamn choice." And I didn't. I had no fucking choice. I held my hand down at my side, focused, called the blade to me.

"You would have made the wrong choice otherwise." He held me tighter, his arm locked around my waist. "Kara, give it to me. Now," he commanded, voice fierce.

Eilahn railed at him in demon, screamed *kiraknikahl*, oathbreaker, over and over along with a few other words. In my peripheral vision, Bryce cursed and struggled against the bonds, jaw clenched and eyes riveted on me.

Vsuhl coalesced against my palm, whispered. *Rakkuhr* heat crawled up my chest and down to my side, igniting Kadir's sigil. Szerain had no reason to save me once he had what he wanted, I realized, hating the feel of him against my back. With grim resolution, I connected to Vsuhl, *felt* it and wondered what an essence blade would do buried in the heart of a lord.

Teeth bared, I shifted my grip on the hilt, slammed my foot onto Szerain's instep, and twisted in his unwelcome embrace. "Take it, *chekkunden!*"

Vsuhl sang as it bit into him, low on his side, but Szerain caught my wrist and wrenched it hard. I lost my grip on the hilt, and the world tipped crazily as Vsuhl tumbled to the ground.

With a harsh cry, Szerain wrapped his hand in my hair and threw me face down on the grass. Air whooshed from my lungs as he planted his knee over my shoulder blades. As he reached and claimed Vsuhl his aura smothered me, subtly powerful, covert, and tinged with chaos.

Breathing heavily, Szerain spoke in demon, the cadence like an invocation. I struggled for air, scrabbled for purchase in the grass to throw him off. A line of thin fire lashed through the twelfth sigil. Vsuhl, drawing my blood, tasting me. Three more swift cuts, and then Szerain shifted to straddle my thighs and pressed both hands against the small of my back.

I sucked in a desperate breath, felt the flare of the re-structured sigil.

"*Vdat koh akiri qaztehl*," he pronounced with precise clarity while I struggled vainly beneath him.

The *rakkuhr* answered him like a dog called by a beloved master. Where it had crawled through the first three sigils, it now raced across my body, igniting one after another. It paused at my upper back, in Szerain's sigil, coalesced in a fiery mass of red heat, then dove down my spine to the twelfth beneath his hands.

Silence like the void engulfed us.

Szerain stroked my back, trailed his fingers over the sigil and wove the *rakkuhr* with disturbingly familiar ease. Into the silence he spoke a word that made all else pale.

"Rowan."

"No!" I screamed. "Szerain! What have you *done*?" My foundation tilted, and I again found myself on a glassy plain with nothing between me and oblivion. "I can't hold on!" I cried out in horror as I began an inexorable slide into the void. "I'm Kara!" *I'm . . . Kara?*

Eilahn let out an inhuman shriek and dove at the barrier, crashed against it. Bryce fought the arcane bonds, shouted my name.

Szerain moved off of me, gripped me by the arm, and dragged me to my feet. He shifted his grasp to the hair at the back of my head, leaned close, his face a hard mask.

"No," he snarled. "You are *Rowan*."

The name ripped through me like a mass of spinning razor blades, severing me from my *Self*. I mentally clawed for stability, but this time there was nothing—*nothing*—to cling to. My *Self* fell away until it was little more than a tiny, distant pinprick of light in the void.

As if through a fog, I saw Bryce jerk against the bindings. "You *fix* this!" he shouted at Szerain. "I swear to god, if you don't, I'll fucking kill you!"

Doubtful, little man, I thought as the fog cleared. The identity of whom the prisoner spoke slipped away like sand through my fingers, unimportant.

Szerain released my head and stepped back, his always-keen eyes on me. A slice in his dark t-shirt revealed a hint of skin and faintly luminous blood.

I rolled my head on my shoulders, looked down at my body, at the glorious scars given to me by my lord Rhyzkahl.

I ran my hands over my face, my throat, my breasts, *my* body, then raised my eyes to Szerain in triumph. I watched his features shift into fuller lips and higher cheekbones as he embraced the reconnection with Vsuhl. Yes. This was the Szerain I knew so well.

He drew a deeper breath, lowered his head slightly to regard me. Behind me, the bound captive cursed. That one would be a choice prize for Lord Kadir or Lord Amkir.

"Szerain," I said, smiling calmly as I inclined my head. A greeting of sorts, I supposed.

"Rowan," he replied.

My smile widened. "You know me."

"I called you," he said mildly as he took a half-step closer, blade down at his side. "And yes, I do know you. Very well. You should not be here."

"But *you* called me here." Amused, I swept my gaze around before returning it to him. "And this place will serve as well as any other." I let out a low laugh. "Better than any other. I have this." I gestured to the mini-nexus below us. Ah, yes, my lord Rhyzkahl would be most pleased to have control of a converged confluence on Earth.

Szerain's grip shifted on the blade. Nervous? Satisfaction coiled through me. *He should be.* I'd have Vsuhl back from his diminished grasp soon enough, ready to hand over to Lord Jesral in triumph. Another few minutes of integration and my metamorphosis would be complete, my power beyond the imagination of any mere summoner.

"*You* do not have anything, Rowan," Szerain stated. "You are owned." A sneer touched his mouth, though his eyes remained hard upon me, assessing. "Nothing but a tool."

I lifted my hands, looked at them, then looked beyond them to Szerain. I frowned. Why did that bother me? I was the tool of *gods*. In the void, a pinprick of light flickered distractingly.

"Aren't we all?" I asked him, lips curving into a smile.

"Some more than others," the lord replied, low and resonant.

I fixed my gaze on the repulsive ring, on the cracked stone. Unworthy of one such as I. My lord Rhyzkahl would offer me true treasures, not the dross given by a lesser qaztahl. I slipped the ring from my finger, held it up before me.

Delicious potency answered my call, flowed easily to me from the nexus. I focused it on the gem, delighted in the discordant vibration that rose within it. A heartbeat later it shattered in a magnificent shower of crimson sparks. "And I revel in the knowledge that I am owned by my lord Rhyzkahl."

"No," Szerain said through clenched teeth, stepped closer. "You, Rowan, are owned by *me*."

I let the ring with its empty, twisted prongs drop to the grass, swung my gaze to him. "In that, Lord Szerain, you are mistaken—"

—The syraza shrieked and dashed herself against the barrier. The prisoner shouted a word, a name, *her* name—

—as Szerain buried the blade in my chest.

I managed one brief gurgled gasp before white hot agony seared through me. I vaguely heard the captive yelling, cursing as he fought against the bonds of potency that restrained him. The syraza too screamed in rage, clawing at the arcane shield as I clutched at Szerain's hand and arm.

Blood filled my mouth, and I pulled my eyes up to Szerain's. His mouth twisted in a merciless snarl, one hand locked in the hair at the back of my head as he twisted the blade, shoved it sideways. My knees buckled, but Szerain's hold on the blade and my hair kept me upright. I coughed, and blood spilled over my chest and his hand.

His eyes remained hot and intense upon mine, and once again he twisted the blade. Agony ripped through my entire body, as if Vsuhl excised life from every cell.

Impossible. I am Rowan. I am . . . invincible.

I tried to scream but had no breath, could only stare at Szerain in horror as my vision dimmed and the blood pounded in my ears. *Kara . . . Kara . . . Kara . . .*

The captive. Still shouting her name. Face contorted in distress. So much like another who'd called to me. To me? Who was I?

Vsuhl whispered. *You are mine. I will keep you. I will hold you. Mine.*

Szerain cried out, screamed a word in demon, savagely twisted the blade once more and then banished it even as it remained buried in my chest. It dragged barbed hooks through me as it left, arcane pain more terrible than when Rhyzkahl sliced the mark from her arm. Kara's arm?

Kara . . . Kara . . . Kara . . . Elinor!

Bryce. Mzatal. Calling. Giovanni. Calling.

Elinor! Kara!

I collapsed to my side. No breath. No pulse. No pain. Grey mist filled my vision.

Szerain shoved me to my back, pressed his hands to my chest.

Kara . . . Kara . . . Kara . . .

Bryce. Calling. Calling my name. Mzatal. Calling . . . my name.

My name.

Kara.

My name is Kara.

Kara. I *knew*. Then a black wind swept in, and I knew nothing more.

Chapter 43

I woke on the sofa in my living room beneath a faded quilt. Sunlight beamed through a window, throwing a pattern of squares onto the rug. *Not squares*, I thought. *No right angles.* I struggled for a few seconds to come up with the right word. *Quadrilaterals.* Yeah, that was it. Still had my third grade math skills. That was cool.

Someone stepped in the quadrilaterals, turned and stepped through them again. I lifted my focus a few feet. Bryce, pacing back and forth in front of the fireplace, stark worry twisting his features. Bryce. He'd called to me, shouted my name.

Kara.

I sucked in a gasp and jerked upright as memory crashed over me. Both hands flew to my chest, clawed at a blade that wasn't there.

Bryce whirled to face me. "Kara?"

My pulse thundered as I fumbled at my chest. "Bryce?" I croaked. "I—" *Pulse. Heart beating.* I stilled my shaking hands and pressed them hard over my sternum. Felt the reassuring thud beneath it.

A shift of movement near the door pulled my attention. Eilahn, eyes on me and a smile whispering across her face as she sat with one knee up and the other leg tucked beneath her. Bryce crouched before me and took hold of my shoulders, his features battered by uncertainty and fatigue as he searched my face. "Kara?" he asked. *Asked.* He wasn't sure, couldn't be sure who I was.

But *I* knew exactly who I was, and that knowledge steadied with each beat of my heart. "Yeah, I'm Kara," I said, rewarded by relief that shone in his eyes. "I'm Kara," I repeated, and would have said it a third time except something sharp jabbed at the palm of my left hand, distracting me.

I pulled my hands from my chest to see what poked me, went cold and still at the sight of the twisted gold and silver prongs that thrust up from the empty setting of my ring like imploring hands. Sick grief wound through me. *She* had destroyed the stone. The cracked and perfect stone of the ring Mzatal had given me.

Bryce released my shoulders, let out a low sigh. "He put it back on your finger," he said in a low voice and touched a finger gently to the prongs. "After he brought you back, that is." A whisper of pain and horror threaded through the words, and I looked up sharply. Shadows huddled beneath bloodshot eyes, and stubble marked an uneven path along his jawline.

"You look like hell," I blurted.

He let out a wheezing laugh. "You're one to fucking talk!"

I struggled to laugh along with him, but it was a pitiful effort. Bryce sensed it and let his own die away, then shifted from the crouch to sit on the coffee table before me.

"He told me he had to . . . summon her, summon Rowan in order to get her out of you." Bryce shook his head. "I'm not explaining it very well. Sorry. I was kind of yelling at him a lot and probably missed some of what he said."

"It's all right," I murmured, then took a deeper breath. "I'm me again, and the virus is gone." Of that I was certain. Szerain knew the *rakkuhr* with terrifying intimacy, knew Vsuhl's hunger, and had used one nightmare to defeat another.

And I didn't know how to feel about any of it.

"What happened after he," I gestured vaguely at my sternum, "did that?" I had on a t-shirt, I suddenly realized. And running shorts. Eilahn's work, no doubt. I gave her a nod of gratitude, for far more than the clothing. She inclined her head in response, relief stark on her features. She'd had no way to divine Szerain's true intent and, like Bryce, had surely thought the worst.

Bryce's mouth twisted into a smile. "You mean after you joined the 'Devastating Chest Wound' club?" He thumped his own chest in mock-solidarity, and this time my laugh was more genuine. "Jesus, Kara," he breathed. "When he stabbed you and twisted the blade, I thought that was *it*." Remembered shock and horror flickered over his face. "But then the knife vanished. He dropped to his knees beside you and slapped his hand over the wound, started working the healing." He blew out a breath. "I don't think he was sure he'd be able to save you. He was sweating it, hard."

I touched my chest again. "Yeah," I said, voice quavering only a little. "I doubt that kind of damage to the heart by an *essence blade* is a walk in the park to fix."

He shoved a hand through his hair. "Well, I don't *ever* want to do that again."

"I'm with you there," I said fervently. "I am one hundred percent cool with never getting stabbed in the chest again."

"So." Bryce cleared his throat. "Agent Kristoff is a demonic lord. Did *not* see that coming."

I smiled weakly. "Surprise?"

He let out a short, sharp laugh. "Understatement of the year."

My fingers moved over my sternum, and I felt the sigil scar beneath the shirt, a gap in its lines where Vsuhl had cut and Szerain had healed. And Szerain had done something to the twelfth sigil, changed it. *But to what?*

"So, uh, where's Ryan?" And wasn't *that* ever a loaded question, I realized after I asked it. My last memory of him was as a completely unsubmerged Szerain in full possession of his essence blade. I had no idea what sort of state he'd be in now.

"I don't know," Bryce said with a slow shake of his head. "He left this morning and said he'd be back tonight."

"Did he look like . . . Ryan when he left?" I asked somewhat hesitantly. I had a sudden image of an unsubmerged, Vsuhl-wielding Szerain out in the world. I couldn't help but worry about, well, *consequences*.

"Yeah, he did," Bryce said to my relief. "While you were busy getting pesky holes in your chest, Sonny left about a billion messages on my phone telling me Zack wanted to talk to Ryan—I mean, Szerain." He grimaced. "Szerain went down to the basement to return Zack's call, and when he came back up a little after sunrise he was all Ryan. Looks, mannerisms, everything."

Zack had sensed it all—the blade, Szerain unsubmerging. That must have freaked him out pretty hard. *But how did Szerain get to be Ryan again?* As far as I knew, the act of submersion—including making him *look* like Ryan—was inflicted on him by another. Had Zack recovered enough to blip over and do it? I found that improbable; he'd been a total mess when I left him. Could he have done it over the phone somehow?

Or did another enforcer come to take Zack's place? My mouth went dry at the thought. I doubted any other would show Szerain the mercies that had kept him sane for all these years.

I shoved the thought away. I couldn't deal with that right now. "Anything to eat around here?"

"There should be leftovers," he said. "Plus sandwich stuff. Hang tight, and I'll check." He stood and headed for the kitchen.

Not so easy to hang tight with a bladder about to burst. I made my way to the bathroom, did my business, then flopped back on the sofa and promptly fell asleep again.

I woke to find a ham and cheese sandwich with chips on the coffee table, and Bryce dozing in the comfy chair with his head cocked to the side in a way that would likely leave him with an aching neck. A half-eaten sandwich rested forgotten on his thigh. I got up, gingerly retrieved his sandwich and returned it to a plate on the side table, adjusted his head to a more comfortable position then grabbed my food and headed for the kitchen.

I ate slowly, savoring the sandwich, the feel of my kitchen, the scent of gardenias from the bush outside the window. But mostly I took the time to appreciate being *me*. Who I was had nothing to do with being a cop or a summoner or with who my friends were. It was far more intrinsic than any set of externals.

Tunjen and a handful of grapes finished off the meal. I felt *good*, definitely better than I had since Rhyzkahl hit me with the *rakkuhr* virus. The ache to share with Mzatal threatened to take over, and I pushed it down, sealed it away. No point in going there.

It worked. A bit.

After I tucked my plate into the dishwasher, I realized I

had no idea what to do next. There were plenty of things that needed to be dealt with, but nothing immediate and in my face.

Get clean, I decided. *When in doubt, shower.*

Once in the bathroom, I stripped, gazed at my reflection in the mirror. A patch of smooth skin between the ribs to the left of my sternum marked the place where Vsuhl had pierced. Technically, it wasn't a scar at all, but rather a lack of one within the other scars. Yet it felt like one as it marred the lines of Mzatal's sigil, left a gap in the flowing curves of his signature mark. I touched the spot, reflexively reached for him. I sensed him, even though he was in the demon realm, but what would have been a faint, tingling hum before was now rigid, cold silence. *Why, Mzatal? It shouldn't end like this. Not without a word.*

With a shuddering breath, I pushed away thoughts of what I couldn't change right now, ran my hands over the other scars. Still the same.

Except for one.

I turned slowly away from the mirror, looked back over my shoulder at the reflection of the twelfth sigil, the one Szerain had altered. Then stared. I'd felt four cuts, nothing more, but he hadn't simply added to the existing scar. He'd changed it completely. How was that possible? The angular rigidity of the original had been replaced by artistic curves and flourishes that spoke of delicate strength. But even that wasn't enough for my World of Weirdness. It wasn't even a scar anymore. It was more like an arcane tattoo—beautiful, captivating, and *glowing* sapphire in othersight.

I twisted while I looked over my shoulder in the mirror and reached awkwardly for the altered scar—or whatever it was now. Smooth skin, a nearly imperceptible tingle. It didn't feel *wrong*, arcanely or otherwise. But still—

"Eilahn!" In a heartbeat she came through the door. "What did Szerain do?" I asked her, my voice shaking in a blend of anger tinged with fear. "Did he fucking *mark* me?"

She laid her hand on the sigil. "I would not be here in peace had the kiraknikahl placed his mark upon you."

No, she wouldn't. I allowed myself a bit of relief. "What then? Why is it a live sigil rather than a scar?" But the answer hit me before she could respond. "Because Szerain completed the process," I breathed. "If Rhyzkahl had finished his torture ritual, all of the sigils would be like this, and I would be the Rowan bitch with arcanely glowing body art."

"You are correct. And Szerain saved you with this," she said, lightly patting the sigil. "I do not know its full purpose, but without it, Kara Gillian would be no more."

And with that cheerful thought, she left me to my shower.

Half an hour later I was clean, Bryce was snoring in the chair, and I was still at loose ends. Fine then. *When clean and in doubt, surf the Internet.*

I spent about an hour checking news sites and watching reports online, then shut the computer down and returned to the kitchen.

Bryce shuffled in from the living room as I pondered the menu for the Kara's Kafe dinner special of the day. I cocked an eyebrow at him. "Dude, you look worse than you did before you napped," I noted helpfully. "You should go crash for real."

"Yeah. I will in a bit," he said, rubbing at his eyes. "I need a shower and some food first."

"You've been through a lot of shit," I said. "Always feels good to wash it off. And I speak from vast experience." I gave him a smile. "I'll get the food part handled. Go shower."

The dryer buzzed in the laundry room, and I headed that way. Mundane tasks. Dishes. Dinner. Laundry. Boring and comfortable. I knew the normalcy of it was an illusion, but I intended to cling to it while I could.

I dumped the dryer contents into a basket, hefted it, and returned to the kitchen. I could fold while I figured out what to cook. Yet when I returned I saw Bryce staring out the window, still unshowered, and with a troubled expression on his face.

A glance out the window showed nothing but my backyard in the late evening light. I plunked the basket onto the table. "Bryce? You okay?"

He turned, leaned back against the counter. "Did you

see what they're saying on the news about the plantation incident?" he asked. "Or rather, what they're *not* saying."

I nodded. "The official line is that it was a big fire with several suspected dead, and that a body resembling James Macklin Farouche was found at the scene although ID has not yet been confirmed." I pulled out a towel and started folding. "Investigations are already ramping up, but I doubt you'll be seeing any stories on the ten o'clock news about a wizard calling lightning, especially since the eyewitnesses have so many conflicting stories." I shrugged. "People always find a way to explain weird shit and make it something rational. And with everything from 'alien invasion' to 'secret government experiment conspiracies' popping up on the Internet, anyone who tells the truth about what happened will be labeled a nutjob and dismissed."

He gave a slow nod of agreement. "Makes sense." He picked up a shirt, flipped it right-side out then folded it in a crisp series of moves. "I saw Lon Harris get electrocuted when a power line fell at the compound," he said as he set the folded shirt down and picked up another. "He's the one who tortured and killed Dickey, the security guard who shot me at the warehouse."

"Remind me to send flowers to his funeral," I said, sticking to the towels since Bryce's folding skills were vastly superior to mine. "Dead ones."

"Jerry made it out though," Bryce continued, muscle twitching in his jaw. "I caught him on some news footage coming out of the hospital with his arm in a sling." He snapped a shirt out with a sharp *crack*. "Too bad he didn't go down."

"With the investigations in full swing, he will, one way or another," I reassured him.

Bryce gave me a predatory smile. "Yeah, he will," he said, and I knew he'd make sure of it if the official channels failed.

I started on the dishtowels. "There's more bothering you," I said. "Spill."

He exhaled. "Paul wiped all digital evidence that he, Sonny, and I had ever been involved with Farouche." He stacked the folded shirt with the others, grimaced and looked up at me.

"But you're still worried," I finished for him. "Paper and off-line records are still out there, and will lead investigators right to you."

"That pretty much sums it up."

I met his eyes. "What if there was a way for you to have a clean slate?"

He began to pair socks, adroitly avoiding several pairs of undies. "I've done some really bad shit, killed a lot of people in cold blood. But I'm *not* that man anymore. Could I still kill? Would I still kill? Yeah." Sadness whispered through his voice. "But not like that. Never again. I won't do someone else's dirty work." He neatly tucked two socks together in a ball. "That said, I don't want to rot in prison. I don't want to stop doing what I can against the Mraztur. I don't want to leave Paul or Sonny. They're my family. If I can get a clean slate, I'll take it."

"I've already been thinking about it," I told him, "and I have some ideas on how to pull it off. Once Zack is back in the swing of things, he can help get new identities for you three." *If Zack is ever back in the swing of things.*

Bryce dropped the socks to the table. "That's . . ." he trailed off, shaking his head. "'Thanks' doesn't cut it."

I handed him the stack of dishtowels to put in the drawer. "If it wasn't for you and Sonny and Paul, we wouldn't have Idris back, and the Mraztur would be full steam ahead with their dangerous node-gate bullshit."

He tucked the towels away. "I sure as hell want to do more. I'm in the game."

"Good, then we're stuck with you," I said and thrust a bath towel at him. "And there's a no-stench rule for my posse. Go. Shower."

He smiled, took the towel, and turned toward the bathroom. "Kara's Kavalry?"

"No!" I shouted at his back. "*Posse.*"

Still smiling, I put the rest of the laundry away. I was putting the empty basket in the laundry room when I heard the front door open. Ryan.

My heart pounded. It was *only* Ryan. At least that's what I tried to tell myself. I returned to the kitchen and peered down the hall, wanting to see and *feel* for myself who he was before he reached me. I didn't want to misstep and say something I shouldn't.

He approached with a smile, completely Ryan-like in looks and manner and walk. "You look better than you did when I left," he said.

Well, shit. That didn't give me a clue. "Um, how did I look?"

"Laid out on the sofa. Wasted after the ordeal." He took off his suit jacket and laid it over the back of a kitchen chair.

"Uh huh," I said, watching his every move. "The, um, ordeal of the stuff at the plantation?"

"That and what happened out there last night." He nodded toward the backyard. "It's okay. You can talk about it."

My stomach did weird flip flops as I tried to shove the ragged clues into something that made sense. "How is it okay . . . Ryan?"

He still smiled, but a touch of sadness colored it now. "Because I *know*," he said quietly. "I know what I am, and I know that I stabbed you last night and healed you. I *don't* know all the whys of it here on the surface," he tapped his temple with a finger, "because I'm taking it one step at a time. This is pretty stressful."

"Oh," I said in a small voice. "So you're . . ." I nodded and struggled to smile. Was Ryan—*my* Ryan—gone?

"Szerain?" he finished for me. His brow furrowed. "I guess. It's a little confusing for me. Shit, a lot confusing. I'm sorry. I don't want to freak you out."

I moved hesitantly to him, took his hand and peered into his face. It was Ryan's yet more than Ryan's, though I knew I'd never be able to explain it. My head told me it was time to grieve, told me this wasn't Ryan anymore, but how could I grieve when he was still *here?*

"It's really weird that you know about Szerain," I said tentatively.

"You ought to try it from in here," he said with what seemed a genuine Ryan smile. "You're one tough chick, you know that?"

I let out a weak laugh. "Stubborn Bitch. Sheesh. Get the term right."

"Oh, yeah. I keep forgetting." He squeezed my hand, then blew out a breath. "So, what's next?"

I had a feeling he meant in the grand scheme of conflict and crisis, but I didn't have it in me to go there right now. Instead, I shrugged. "Dinner?"

He regarded me for a moment, relief in those green-gold

eyes that reflected both Ryan and Szerain. "Yeah. That's nice and normal. Let's fix dinner."

"Normal. Me cooking. Right," I said, laughing a little. He craved the illusion of a normal life right now as much as I did.

"More me cooking and you," he paused, "assisting," he suggested. "I think that's a better plan."

"Safer for everyone."

"Safety first." He turned and opened the fridge, scanned the contents. "How about BLTs and french fries?"

"With double bacon, I'm in."

Bryce and Jill joined us about halfway through the prep, and soon the kitchen echoed with jokes and banter and laughter. Each of us and all of us faced challenges and bore burdens unimaginable to ninety-nine point nine percent of the population, but for this evening we ruthlessly pushed them aside and gorged on food and friendship.

Chapter 44

The ringing of my phone jarred me from an oddly logical dream about encyclopedias and babies and ladders. I peered at the name on the caller ID and instantly shot directly to wide awake.

"Zack?"

"Hey, babe." He didn't sound as strained as a day and a half ago but didn't sound at all animated either. "Caught you sleeping, huh?"

I glanced at the clock. A little after eight a.m. "Yeah, working consultant hours is kind of cool. How are you doing?"

"I've been lots better," he said. "I'm not ready to leave here yet. I . . . can't." He went quiet for a moment. "I just wanted to talk."

I felt the subtle desperation behind the words. "I'm here for you," I assured him. "Eturnahl."

"Kara," he said in a voice so thick with emotion it brought a lump to my throat. "You're okay? Are you?"

"I am," I said, smiling softly at his concern. "I promise. I'm really okay." But then I sighed out a breath. "I'm sorry if giving Vsuhl to Szerain made things harder for you."

He echoed my sigh. "It's so convoluted," he said, as if the implications carried eons of pain. "I can't process all of the possible complications yet. What I do know is that if you hadn't given Vsuhl to him, you wouldn't be here, wouldn't be Kara. And that's all that means anything right now."

A warm glow went through me. It *mattered* to him that I was still me. "And you're still Zakaar. Even more than you were before."

He remained silent for several seconds. "How is Ryan?" he finally asked.

How could I explain it? "He seems all right. We had a pretty normal evening." Grimacing, I sat up. "Zack, he *knows* about Szerain, but he looks like Ryan. I don't understand. Did you partially resubmerge him or something from a distance?"

"No," he said as though pronouncing a death warrant. "He did that. On his own. With Vsuhl, he freed himself, and is using it to give him a measure of stability." He made a sound like a half-sob. "But he isn't ready."

My worry spiked. "Zack? What's wrong?"

"I can't do this," he said in a broken voice. "Szerain is in danger, and he's dangerous. I can't protect him or others. I can't deal with it."

"I'm not sure you have to," I said carefully. "Not the way you did before. He may not be ready, but there's nothing we can do about that now, and I know he's not going to abandon you. Neither will the rest of us. Once in the posse, always in the posse." I wanted to reach through the phone and give him a hug. "It's going to be all right."

"I can't see it," he said weakly. "But I'll believe you."

"You'd better," I told him.

I heard him clear his throat softly, take a breath, release it, then take another. "Kara, have you ever killed anyone in the line of duty before?"

The abrupt change of subject had me blinking in confusion. "No, I've never even been in a position to . . ." I suddenly understood where he was going with this: *Pyrenth.* That night, when I found Zack and brought him to Jill's house, he had no doubt sensed my pain over the reyza's death.

"Pyrenth was the first," I said, throat tight. "No, wait." An uncomfortable realization struck me. "He's the first I knew for sure. I Earth-killed a kehza and a graa, but, at the time, I assumed any demon killed on Earth made it back through the void to the demon realm." Now I knew that, while there was a good chance a demon could return, it was by no means a certainty.

"And if they'd died before on Earth and returned—"

"Then the good chance drops to crappy," I finished for him. A second death on Earth for a demon usually meant death for real. Eilahn had died on Earth once already, and so I worried doubly for her.

"Pyrenth had traversed the void once before."

The implications of that simple statement left me mentally scrambling and ripped a new wound in my pain over his death. I took a moment to put it all together. Zack waited in patient silence on the other end of the line.

"When I made the decision to use deadly force to stop Pyrenth from taking Idris," I finally said, "I was playing the odds that he'd make it through the void and back to the demon realm. My intention was to stop him, to kill him if that's what it took, with a secondary consideration that he'd have a chance of making it home. But it was a gamble." I closed my eyes and let out a long slow breath. "I thought his odds were better than they were, but it was *always* a gamble." Explaining it, actually *speaking* the words out loud, helped. My respect and gratitude for Zack climbed even higher. He was going through ten tons of shit and yet he still took the time and thought and energy to help me get through this.

"I chose the blade over a bullet because it had a better chance of taking him out of the game," I went on. "I didn't know there were no 'odds' with Vsuhl, that a kill was final."

"Pyrenth gambled too," Zack said gently. "Rhyzkahl couldn't force him to come to Earth. Pyrenth knew the danger and chose to come. You killed him in the line of duty, and he died in the line of duty."

Tears pricked my eyes. Those were hard terms though ones I could understand. It still gnawed that Mzatal hadn't warned me that dead by the blade meant Really Dead, but the heavy guilt around Pyrenth's death abated somewhat.

"Thanks, Zack," I said.

"*Sihn*," he replied, and I heard a whisper of smile in his voice.

"You doing okay with Sonny?" I asked, ready for a change in subject.

"He's a blessing. I'm not sure I'd have made it this far without him."

At least that much was working out well. "I figured it'd be good for both of you. He needed to help someone."

"I read him," he said. "He's a mess. Good pairing."

I laughed softly. "My whole posse is fucked up. It's perfect."

*   *   *

After reassuring Zack that Jill was doing well and Steeev was taking good care of her, I hung up, found some shorts, and then followed the smell of coffee. Ryan leaned against the kitchen counter, arms folded across his chest, and eyes unfocused as though lost in thought. I continued toward the coffee pot as it made its last gurgles.

"Morning, sunshine," I said with a bright smile. Yeah, let's just keep pretending everything's nice and normal.

He startled a bit, then smiled. "Morning, sleepyhead."

"It's not *that* late," I pointed out. "You're not exactly an early bird yourself today unless this is the second pot of coffee." I retrieved two mugs from the cabinet, filled them.

"Nope. I'm running late."

I placed the mugs on the table and sat. Okay, I was awake, and I had coffee. What the hell was I supposed to do now?

Ryan pulled out the chair opposite mine and dropped into it. "Now what?" he asked in an eerie echo of my thoughts.

I started to say I didn't have a clue, then shook my head. "We can't keep on pretending everything's normal," I said. "We both know it's not." He gave a grim nod, and I continued. "I need training still. I need to find out if Paul is all right. And I need to talk to Mzatal."

"Sounds like you have a plan." Ryan picked up the mug nearest him, took a sip, then made a that-doesn't-taste-right face.

I winced a little. "I guess I do."

"That's half the battle." He stood and moved to the spice rack.

I dumped sugar and cream into my coffee. "And what's the other half?"

"Perseverance and follow-through," he told me. "A lot of people have *plans*. They're useless unless you do something with them."

I gave him a wry smile. "Time to get my ass in gear then."

"Drink your coffee first," he said, then returned to the table to put a scant spoon of sugar and a shake of cinnamon into his cup.

I quickly lifted my mug to my mouth to hide my mild shock. *Ryan* always drank his coffee black. Was this whole Ryan-appearance simply a pretense to make it easier on me, or did Szerain need to keep it like this? A pang of loss went through me. Was there any of *my* Ryan left? I sipped my coffee and, for a moment, wished that I could go back to that beach in the demon realm where I'd gone with Helori, and simply be away from everyone and everything for a while. And just as quickly pushed the whiny self-pity down. This wasn't about me, and I wasn't going to run away from my problems. Too many others depended on me.

"What about Zack?" I left the question wide open to see where he'd go with it. I'd assured Zack that Szerain wouldn't abandon him as all the others had, but it was an assumption.

He set his cup on the table, swallowed. A weird ripple passed over his face as though he'd almost lost the Ryan features. "He's broken," he said in a strained voice. "I'll take care of him. I know broken."

I exhaled softly. "Yeah, I guess you do. Thanks."

He nodded. "When are you planning to follow through with your plan?"

"After I get caffeinated I'll go down and top off the storage diagram." Luckily I maintained a habit of keeping it as full as possible at all times. I sighed, rubbed a hand over my face. "And then I'll summon a little after noon, I guess."

"You're reluctant to do this," he observed.

"No, I'm not *reluctant*." I grimaced. "It's sort of a weird nervous-dread-anxious-resigned hybrid emotion."

"Well, that narrowed it down," he said with a twitch of his lips. "Caused by?"

I set my mug down, leaned back in my chair. "Caused by the fact that my demonic lord lover brought down the fires of heaven and would have killed me and everyone else if you and Kadir hadn't helped me stop him."

Ryan winced. "That would do it. He lost control."

"And then he closed me out," I said, then sighed and rubbed at my temples. "Weirdly, that was the worst part."

He looked at me sharply. "Closed you out?"

The ache tightened my chest again. "We have this *connection,* and he . . . went totally silent." I couldn't think of any other way to describe it. "Like he didn't hang up the phone, but wasn't talking on the other end of the line."

He breathed a curse—in demon, I noted with another weird pang. "I understand the hybrid emotion now."

"I guess I get to see if he'll still train me." I pressed my fingers to my eyes. "I don't even know what to expect." I dropped my hands and grimaced. "And he might be pretty pissed off I didn't give him Vsuhl when he asked for it."

"You're a good student. He'll teach you," he assured me. "And if you'd given him Vsuhl, you would now be Rowan, anchoring the mini-nexus for Jesral and Rhyzkahl."

A shiver ran over me as the memory of those bizarre few minutes as Rowan surfaced. Szerain had saved me, as had Bryce. I rubbed my arms, found myself smiling at Bryce's fierce loyalty. He'd called to me, had never stopped. *Kara . . . Kara . . . Kara . . .*

Like Giovanni called to Elinor.

"Shit!" Ryan surged up from the chair. "I'm late and I have a meeting." He quickly came around the table, pulled me to my feet and gave me a hard hug. "Summon Mzatal. If you don't think you can train with him, don't go with him. And if you do go, we'll hold down the fort here."

With that he kissed my cheek, grabbed his briefcase, jogged to the front door, and was gone before I could even form a reply.

Blinking, I stared after him. A disguised demonic lord in a meeting with federal agents. That was fun to wrap my head around. Then I scowled. A disguised demonic lord who'd left before I could ask him about Elinor. Or the twelfth sigil. Or anything else.

"You win this round, Szerain," I muttered. "But just you wait."

With the decision made to summon Mzatal, the rest of the morning turned into a frenzy of activity: I topped off the storage diagram, woke Bryce up and told him to pack since I knew he'd want to come with me to be with Paul, did my own packing, had a quick talk with Jill and confirmed everything was okay with the bean and that Zack had called her that morning—all the while forming, discarding, and reforming arguments to use with Mzatal for why he shouldn't shut me out and why I needed to be able to train with him and why I'd kept Vsuhl and then given it to Szerain. It was sure to be an entertaining discussion, one way or the other.

As soon as everything was ready, prepped, and packed, I called Tessa and wasn't surprised when it went to voicemail.

She was still in Aspen and wasn't the sort to be glued to her phone when out having fun.

"Hi, Aunt Tessa," I said into the recording. "Looks like I'm going back to the 'retreat' for a while. I'll, uh, write as soon as I can. Love you."

I hung up. It felt oddly unfinished to leave without speaking to her, but we'd been successfully sending messages and letters back and forth for months now. Everything would be fine.

The thought of messages reminded me to do a final check of my email. There was only one item in my inbox, and I realized that Paul had probably worked some of his magic to get rid of my mountains of spam. My pulse gave an uneven lurch as I noted the sender. I opened it, read the attached DNA test results, then read them again.

"Welcome to the family, cousin Idris," I murmured, pulse thudding weirdly. I'd suspected for a while, but having it confirmed raised even more questions. Or rather, one question in particular. One I dreaded asking.

I called Zack, held my breath as it rang. I'd made him promise not to answer the phone if he wasn't up for a call, but voicemail wouldn't cut it for what I needed to say and ask.

"Hey, Kara."

"Hey, Zack," I replied, relieved, though it quickly shifted to apprehension about the pending question. I stalled and took a moment to fill him in on my decision to return to training unless everything went pear-shaped between Mzatal and me.

"I'll miss you for sure," he said when I finished, "but it's what you need to do. I'll talk to Ryan tonight. We'll keep things together here."

I heard the unspoken "somehow," yet I still thought he sounded a bit better. He seemed to be holding it together at least.

"Zack, I had a DNA test done on samples from Idris and Tessa," I said in a rush. "He's my cousin."

Zack went super quiet.

I forged ahead. "Rhyzkahl's the daddy, isn't he." It was more statement than question. With the timing of Tessa in the demon realm, it made sick sense.

Zack cleared his throat. "I'm flipping you the bird right

now," he said, letting me know I'd crossed into territory where he couldn't or wouldn't stray. The mandates, agreements, and oaths that bound him originated with the Demahnk Council and those he named only as "the others." From what I could tell, the bond with Rhyzkahl was a subset of those oaths. Not that I truly understood how any of that worked.

But flipping the bird was answer enough. "Well, how about that," I said with a sour smile. "That asshole made something awesome." It also meant he'd had sex with me, all the while knowing he'd had sex with my *aunt*. Gah!

Shuddering, I hurriedly pushed the mental images away. "Does Rhyzkahl know about Idris?"

"He does not. I mean, hypothetically, if there was something to know." Strain laced his voice as he desperately sought the balance of telling me without *telling* me.

I had more questions, but the interrogation could wait until I saw Zack in person. I had plenty to mull over, and he sure as hell didn't need more stress right now. "You'd better write while I'm away at demon school," I said lightly.

"You know it," he said, sounding a bit more relaxed now. "On pink paper."

"Perfumed, or it doesn't count."

Chapter 45

I hung up with him, and then could put it off no longer. Eilahn had Fuzzykins and her squirming little spawn in a giant pet carrier in the living room, and as Bryce paced anxious circles around it, I went down to the basement and began the summoning.

I spun the power out from the storage diagram in brilliant strands of potency, interlocked and coiled them together to create the portal. I made the call, held the strands—felt through them as the summoning found Mzatal and took hold.

Yet when I pulled, nothing happened. Baffled, I felt down the strand. It definitely had the demonic lord, but instead of coming through smoothly like every other summoning, it was as if he'd dug his heels in. Breath hissing through my teeth, I fed more power into the strands, tugged and felt the resistance, like a fish on a line. Except that I had Jaws on the other end of my Ronco Pocket Fisherman.

The hold on him fractured and dissipated, and the portal spiraled closed with an uncomfortable *pop*.

Chest heaving, I released the portal strands and stared at the empty diagram. He wasn't going to even answer my call? Bleak dismay clutched at my gut, but a growing outrage quickly kicked that aside.

Oh, *hell* no. On the social etiquette scale, refusal to answer a summons from your lover ranked several steps below breaking up by text message. He could show his lordly ass up here and tell me to my face we were over, but no fucking way was I going to slink off and give up at this point.

I shot a quick look to the storage diagram. A little less than half-full, which meant I was going to have to pull some serious magic out of my ass to make this work. Teeth clenched, I cleared the diagram of the residual energies, retraced the sigils, and started over. Having that seventh ring of the shikvihr made a big difference now. No way would I have been able to attempt two summonings in a row six months ago, much less of a *demonic lord*.

Once again I cast the arcane strands out to form the portal, but I paused before I made the call again, assessing. The base wasn't strong enough, and if he resisted again, I risked a backlash on both ends, like losing hold of the fishing pole and falling on your ass.

I picked up the knife that lay with my other implements and made a quick sharp slice in my left forearm. As the blood welled, I traced over the anchoring sigils, grimly pleased as the strands amplified.

"Mzatal!" I shouted the name and once again felt the summoning find its mark. Arcane wind whipped from the portal and through the basement as I seized the strands and pulled. Yet unlike the first attempt, this time I felt the resistance yield. I sent out more strands, like vines wrapping around a branch, and continued to pull, breath hissing. There was no way I could draw an unwilling lord through, but I sure as hell wasn't going to make it easy on him to refuse. It felt like dragging an anchor across sand, but at long last the vortex portal formed, deposited my target and subsided.

Shaking from the effort, I grounded the strands and stabilized the energies. Black dots swarmed my vision, and I blinked them away, fought to stay upright. He was there in the circle, on one knee and facing away from me with the intricate rope of his braid marking a dark line down the center of his back.

Blood tickled my forearm in slow rivulets, slithering down to drop off the tips of my fingers. I felt into him, sick ache growing as I found the wall and the silence once again—not as profound as it was before I told him to leave, but with barely a whisper of more.

"Mzatal," I croaked, cleared my throat and tried again. "Mzatal."

He stood and turned to me, eyes betraying . . . uncertainty? Indecision? Either were totally out of place on him. He tipped his head back and inhaled deeply, and when he lowered it again his gaze held resolution.

"Zharkat," he said with tangible pain. "Beloved. Yaghir tahn."

"Open to me, Mzatal," I said, voice trembling slightly. Damn it. "I can't forgive you if you continue to do what wounded me most."

Our connection might have been mute, but his expression was not. Regret and desolation carved deep lines into his face as he moved to me and took my hand, ran his fingers over the empty prongs of the ring. "It is not so simple," he said. "Will you tolerate me thus until we speak at length?"

I gave him a short tight nod, though as soon as I made the controlled gesture I realized that I too was afraid to reveal too much of myself. Yes, he could read everything from me anyway. *But that's why the loss of our union hurts as much as it does.* The sudden clarity left me mentally groping for several seconds. The ever-present wordless communication and *knowing* made that drastic imbalance tolerable and acceptable. How else could anyone have a relationship with someone who could read their every thought?

"Yes, we do need to talk," I told him, relieved that he would, at least, still talk to me.

He lifted one hand to my cheek and, even though muted, I felt his awareness that he was face to face with losing me, felt the anguish behind that knowledge. "I do not want to lose you," he said, voice laden with the grief of that possibility. "Cannot."

I covered his hand in mine, leaned into the gesture. "Then let's work this out."

Mzatal exhaled in deep relief, leaned down, touched his forehead to mine and closed his eyes as I pulled him close. We sure as hell had some major serious *holyfuckOMG* looming Issues to deal with, but this was a *huge* start. But another big-ass elephant lurked in the room, and I had to ask about it.

"How is Paul?"

The color drained from his face, and he straightened and looked away. Cold gripped me. "Mzatal, is he dead?" I asked, grief already rising for the good-humored and brilliant young man.

"No!" He snapped his eyes back to mine, and I watched him pygah, as if he couldn't bear to even *think* of such an outcome. "No," he said again, less sharply. "He lives. The critical physical damage has been healed."

My worry grew for both Paul and Mzatal. "He'll get better though, right?"

He shook his head slowly. "I do not know," he said in a voice utterly devoid of luster. A heartbeat later he straightened, looked over my head with unfocused eyes and let out a low curse. "I left Elofir overwhelmed in the plexus and must return," he said, attention returning to me. "There is much disruption from the Mraztur's abuse of the nodes."

A coil of worry abruptly unwound within me as comprehension dawned. *He was deeply engaged in the plexus. That's why he resisted the summoning.* "What about Idris?"

"He will recover fully." The hint of a smile that accompanied the words flickered and faded. "Though he bears the burden of his sister's ordeal."

"Will you let me come back with you?" I asked, making the decision. "And Bryce as well?"

A smile brushed across his mouth, seeming foreign among the lines of worry and stress. "It is your home, zharkat," he said, like a promise.

I nodded, then turned toward the stairs and hollered, *"BRYCE! EILAHN! GET YOUR ASSES DOWN HERE! WE'RE GOING!"*

I looked back at Mzatal barely in time to see the wince, quickly masked, though it came with a trace of amusement. The basement door flew open, and Bryce came down three steps at a time, duffel slung over his shoulder. Eilahn followed more slowly, primarily because of the large cat carrier that already emitted ominous growls.

"Paul's alive," I hurried to tell Bryce, since I knew that was foremost in his mind. "He has some more recovery to go, but he's on his way." Guilt twinged at the truth-bending, but the relief on Bryce's face assuaged some of it.

"What of Szerain?" Mzatal asked. "He is not here."

"Um, no, he's at work," I said, realizing how bizarre that sounded as soon as the words were out of my mouth.

Mzatal's brows drew together. "I require use of your phone," he stated, then waited while I fetched it from the nightstand by the futon and returned. I dialed Ryan's number and handed the phone to him.

Mzatal held it to his ear with thumb and middle finger, and I was close enough to hear the *Hey, babe! What's up?* as Ryan answered. I muffled a snort of laughter at the annoyed look on Mzatal's face.

"I am not your *babe*," he began, eyes narrowed, and then continued in demon which I couldn't follow without the grove. There was a brief pause, no doubt to give Ryan/Szerain time to get away from other people, and then more conversation, some of it heated. Finally Mzatal touched the end call button and handed it back to me.

I replaced it on the nightstand, sobering as I returned to him. There was no mistaking that part of their conversation had held anger. "Boss, he saved me," I said quietly. "Him and Bryce both."

His expression softened some as he met my eyes. "I know, and I expressed my gratitude for such."

Of course he'd known. He'd likely read the details of the event from me the instant he arrived.

Mzatal shifted his attention to Bryce. "I am in your debt, Bryce Thatcher," he said, "for this and because I violated our agreement concerning Paul."

Agreement? I wondered, then realized that even a simple "I'll keep Paul safe," from Mzatal to Bryce would count as such.

Face like stone, Bryce simply gave a micro-nod, while I wondered if any other human had ever heard those words from him.

Mzatal took my hand. "Then let us depart."

Chapter 46

While Fuzzykins yowled her evil lungs out, Mzatal draped his arm over my shoulders and pulled me close. The feline protests cut off as he made the transfer, then started right back up again the instant we arrived in Mzatal's plexus. In front of us, Elofir startled visibly at our sudden caterwaul-enhanced appearance and nearly fumbled the iridescent potency strands he had woven into a stabilizing coil. Beautiful but complex and difficult as well, to judge by the sweat that plastered his shirt to his torso.

He quickly recovered his composure and anchored the strands, flicked his gaze to me along with a smile thick with relief. There'd obviously been discussion of me in the past day.

I returned the smile. "Lord Elofir. Good to see you again."

"Kara Gillian. Welcome back," he said warmly even as he returned his attention to the complicated stabilizer.

"Where's Paul?" Bryce asked Mzatal tersely, clearly in no mood for chit chat.

Mzatal said something to Elofir in demon with a rough meaning of *I'll be right back to help with this mess*, then gave Bryce his full attention.

"This way," he said and swept from the room with Bryce right on his heels. I followed a few steps behind, while Eilahn removed the cat carrier from the plexus. The sound of growl-hiss-screeched complaints gradually faded as they moved away.

We didn't have far to go. About thirty feet down the hall from the plexus, Mzatal gestured to a doorless arch that led into a room I remembered as empty when I was last here. Now its glass wall, which normally looked out over sky and sea, was covered with a makeshift heavy curtain, and a bed had been moved in. Instead of bright natural light, a soft amber glow from sigils placed in the corners of the room gave the space a homey, comfortable feel. Nurturing. Even without monitors and wires and IVs, it felt like a place of healing, a refuge for someone ill or injured. Like a hospital room *should* be.

Paul lay on the bed, eyes closed, pale, and looking weirdly delicate, as if the slightest touch would shatter him. To my surprise, Seretis sat on the other side of the bed with one hand on Paul's shoulder and the other on his thigh. Healing him, I knew, and in another heartbeat of consideration, I realized that Mzatal had either called in favors or incurred debt to help restore Paul.

Though I didn't know much about how the debt game worked among the lords, I had a feeling that Mzatal was far more accustomed to holding a debt than owing one. That he would do so for a human—not even a summoner human— told me a great deal about his affection for Paul. And his guilt.

Gone were the hideous burns that had covered most of Paul's body. No scars replaced them, nor even healing flesh. His skin was smooth and unmarred, as if the terrible injury had never happened, and a shadow of peach-fuzz new hair growth covered his scalp. To look at him there on the bed, he appeared perfectly fine, simply resting.

Yet he *felt* profoundly damaged, a weird, uncomfortable non-physical sensation, almost as if he didn't belong in his body. Though I couldn't identify the cause, it was clear Bryce sensed it as well. I stopped in the doorway while Bryce continued in to crouch by the bed, his eyes never leaving Paul's face as he oh-so-gently took Paul's hand.

"Hey, kid," he said, voice cracking, and I wasn't at all surprised to see tears on the man's face.

Paul smiled—a barely-there movement that seemed to boost his vitality despite its faintness. "Bryce," he breathed, not even a whisper, but it seemed to be an ocean of reassurance for Bryce.

I backed out of the doorway to give them privacy, even as Seretis rose silently and moved to exit, no doubt with the same thought in mind.

Seretis gave me a warm yet weary smile, then surprised me by leaning to brush his lips across my cheek. "Welcome back, Kara Gillian," he murmured. He then turned to Mzatal, met his eyes and put a hand on his forearm. Neither said a word, simply locked gazes for well over half a minute, but when Seretis finally turned and walked away, I sensed that Mzatal's tension was ever so slightly less than before.

He took a deeper breath then looked to me and laid his hand alongside my face. "I must work in the plexus for a time, beloved," he said softly. "The Mraztur's actions with the valve have had numerous repercussions in the flows. I must relieve Elofir, but I will be complete at sunset."

I kissed him lightly, nodded. "We'll talk then."

Mzatal held my gaze for a heartbeat before inclining his head to me. He proceeded to the plexus while I went the other direction and made my way to Idris's room on the level below.

I paused in the doorway as a faint hint of nostalgia settled over me. Not much had changed since he'd last occupied it several months ago. Though I'd been in the process of recovering from Rhyzkahl's torture, it had been a simpler time. The room suited Idris. Spacious and airy with a window wall overlooking the sea, and furnishings in varying shades of blue accented with silver. A scatter of books and papers topped his worktable, undisturbed since he'd been taken.

He lay on his back atop the covers of his bed, left arm thrown over his eyes, and right knee cocked to the side. He wasn't asleep though. The fingers of his right hand tapped on the bed in an uneven tempo, but I couldn't tell if it was in frustration or impatience or something else entirely.

I knocked lightly on the door frame. "Hey, dude."

He pulled his arm away from his eyes, looked toward the door. "Kara?" he asked, voice hoarse and raw.

Moving into the room, I gave him a smile. "Yeah, it's me. How you feeling?"

He let out a humorless snort. "Like my insides are scrambled, and my head's exploding." One corner of his mouth twitched up. "Y'know . . . not too bad."

I sat on the edge of the bed and peered at him. He looked like he'd been dragged through hell—which he had, now that I thought about it—but to my relief he didn't have any of the *damaged* feel Paul radiated.

"Well, Mzatal says you're going to be fine," I told him firmly. "You'll be running the stairs in no time." I smiled. "And I know you don't want me to catch up to you in the shikvihr, right?"

He gave a wry and somewhat pained smile. "Not much chance of that. Look." He traced an unsteady sigil that fizzled out in about two seconds.

I lightly smacked the back of his hand. "Then stop *doing* that. You need to rest. It'll come back." But then I rested my hand on his and sobered. "Idris . . . I'm so very sorry about your sister. The rest of your family is safe, though. We got your mom out, and she's fine."

His hand clenched in the covers, and tension surged through him. "They didn't have to do that," he said, each word infused with a rage I'd never seen in him before. "They didn't have to *DO* that."

"No, they didn't," I said, voice choked. "Idris, I'm so sorry."

Filled with pain and fury, his eyes went to mine. "Where is Aaron Asher?" he demanded, voice still hoarse but with a razor edge I'd never heard in him before. "Aaron Asher and Jerry Steiner." His neck corded as he snarled the names out. "Do you know where they are?"

"Kadir has Asher," I told him. "Farouche is dead. Bryce killed him." My eyes dropped to my hand resting on his fist. "There were a number of casualties and injured, but we spotted Jerry on a news clip." I lifted my gaze to his pain-wracked face. "I swear to you, I'll make sure you get him."

The black rage spilled away from him like water from a torn balloon. He let out his breath in a long and shaking exhalation, then he unclenched his hand and turned it over to take mine. "Thanks," he murmured. He simply looked exhausted now, and in that moment I wanted nothing more than to find some way to wipe away the dark circles beneath his eyes and smooth away the lines of grief and fear and anger. "Kadir won't damage Asher," he said after a moment, words beginning to slur. "Need summoners."

"Maybe he'll just hurt him a lot," I offered and got a short breathless laugh back. His eyelids were starting to lose the battle against gravity, though. "You should get some sleep," I said, then smiled softly. "Glad to have you back." *Cousin*, I added silently.

"Yeah . . . good . . . back . . . home," he mumbled as his eyes drifted closed.

So many questions I had for him. About his work with the Mraztur, about what he did in Texas with Asher, and so much more. All on hold for a while. The same way I felt on hold until Mzatal and I could talk about our own issues.

I sat with Idris for a few more minutes, until his breathing deepened and lines of stress in his face eased, then gently pulled my hand from his and crept from the room.

After that, I felt a need to move my body. I briefly debated going for a run, but a sluggish rain changed my mind. There were times I enjoyed running in the rain, but today wasn't one of them.

I finally settled on a long, steady swim in the glorious indoor natural rock pool. Once my muscles were the consistency of limp noodles, I sank into the hot springs basin beside it, traced a triple pygah to float above, and set it spinning. Sometimes I came here to think. This time I came to *not* think. I focused on breathing, the rush of the river falls below, and the melodic chattering hiss of the small waterfall that fed the pool. And it worked. I lost track of time and emerged feeling *cleaner*.

Hair still damp, and dressed in a comfortable demon realm version of designer sweats, I made my way to one of Mzatal's favorite places, the roof terrace. As always, when I stepped from the stairway into the spacious glassed conservatory, I felt as though I stood on top of the world. Two levels above that of the plexus, it commanded a three-hundred-and-sixty-degree view of the surrounding area. Plants filled the space, none over chest high so as not to obstruct the view, and the soft, sweet scent of a variety of flowers filled the air.

Rain slid down the glass in graceful rivulets, but a slash of blue sky to the west, far out over the sea, told me it would end soon. I made my way to the luxurious sitting area, intending to simply relax until sunset, a rare luxury these days.

A brush of sound alerted me, and I turned to see Elofir step from the stairs. He no longer wore the sweat-soaked shirt, but it was still clear the past few hours in the plexus hadn't been a walk in the park for him.

Faruk darted up the stairs and held out a towel and a glass of tunjen for him. Elofir thanked the faas, took a long drink of the tunjen, mopped the sweat from his throat and neck, then gave me a smile.

"Is the plexus all properly plexusy?" I asked with a return smile.

He dropped into a broad chair so cushiony that it seemed he sank a foot into its embrace. "It is far from stable," he said with a light grimace, "but Mzatal will work it until sunset, and then I will go back."

"Back to the plexus? Or your realm?"

"The plexus," he clarified. His gaze drifted toward the vibrant amethyst and emerald canopy of the grove to the south, and he looked briefly wistful. "It will likely be days before we return to my realm, though Michelle is more than ready. The node incident caused much instability."

I sat on a settee near him, tucked one leg underneath me. "Kadir looked *pissed* when he came through the node."

Elofir returned his attention to me, nodded. "Kadir is still . . . pissed," he said. "He was here earlier. He seeks Mzatal when he is distressed."

"Mzatal hurt him when he called the lightning," I said after a moment.

But Elofir merely shook his head. "That injury was as nothing to him," he told me. "Kadir bore no ill will over that. It is the node instability and disruption of the potency flows that has him angry and agitated. He is very . . . fastidious and exacting about the flows."

I considered these recently discovered aspects of Kadir the Creepy. None of them made him seem any less creepy, but they sure made it hard to get an honest feel for him. Capable of doling out unspeakable torment. Honorable to the point of rigidity concerning agreements—though I had no doubt he would seek and exploit a loophole in a heartbeat. Some sort of wizardly genius with the flows and rituals. Champion of maintaining arcane stability of the demon realm. Loved by *Fuzzykins*, for fuck's sake. Freaky-weird about pain. And the memory of the sight and sound of his burned thigh cracking when he crouched still gave me the heebie jeebies.

"Mzatal almost killed Paul." The words tumbled from me even though I'd intended to work up to the topic more gradually. "Almost killed all of us." It was the first time I'd said it aloud.

All trace of lightness drained from Elofir's face. "Yes, he told me," he said quietly. He wiped his face and neck one more time then set the towel aside. "He does not want it to happen again."

I dropped both feet to the floor and leaned forward. "Then how can I help him make *sure* it never happens again?"

Elofir's expression turned grim, and when he spoke, his words carried a foreboding resonance. "He will tell you he can prevent it. And it will be true." He stood and moved to the southern glass doors, opened them and stepped out onto the expansive open terrace despite the persistent weak drizzle. "He can build impenetrable walls," he continued. "Nothing gets through them. In or out."

I stood and followed him, frowned at his back. "Like when he shut me out? That's how he controls it?" I asked with growing dismay. "By shutting everyone out?"

"Yes. Being open means being open to the anger as well as all else. He chose to withdraw eons ago when he could no longer control it." He turned back to me. A deep sadness filled his eyes. "He lived thus for a very long time. Formidable, uncompromising, devious, though never speaking an untruth. Never wantonly cruel, but hard. Cold."

"Why did he change?" I asked, though I was pretty sure I knew the answer.

Elofir gave a slight nod as he read it from me. "Idris. You." He exhaled, wiped a hand over his eyes, flicked rain away. "The two of you found a hairline crack in his wall, broke him open. Kara, it has been over two thousand years since he and I have had any cooperative undertakings outside of the Conclave or anomaly control."

Two thousand years. Closed off and *alone* for all that time? I couldn't comprehend it.

I walked out to the terrace, looked out at the churning sea, then brought my gaze to the grove. Two thousand years meant nothing to it. A week, a day, an eon—none of it mattered. It was the grove. It existed. It simply *was*.

Turning, I focused on the tapering flat-topped pillar of

polished basalt atop a rise on the inland side of the palace. To culminate all eleven rings of a full shikvihr atop the pillar was the rare crowning glory of accomplishment for a summoner. That column represented *why* I was in the demon realm at all. To train. To complete the shikvihr. To become strong enough and competent enough to protect myself and everyone I loved.

But if Mzatal kept me walled out, could I remain here as his student?

I pivoted back to Elofir. "Do you think he can learn to control it without having to close everyone out?"

He crouched and brushed his palm across a cluster of azure flowers, set them toning like delicate wind chimes. "He carries a deep anger, always has," he said. "Long ago it would flash and then pass." He glanced to me. "We were close then. But after he created the blades, it would flash . . . and not pass." He shook his head. "It was as if the blades would not allow him to bury the anger again. He would not consider relinquishing them, nor would he live without control, and so he chose the terrible alternative."

"To close off and shut everything in and everyone out," I supplied, inwardly reeling.

And yet, if he remained open to me—was that what Rhyzkahl meant when he told Mzatal I would be his downfall? I lifted my hand to one of the floating sigils that glimmered above the enclosing basalt parapet, felt its meaning and purpose. *Sentinel.*

"I can't train with him if he keeps me shut out," I said, voice catching. I knew that in my essence. And it wasn't because of some lovesick longing. I wouldn't be able to train with him because I'd be grieving the loss of *Mzatal.* He wouldn't be him anymore.

I dropped my hand to my side. "But he said we'd discuss it."

Elofir nodded. "That in itself is unprecedented." He paused, face shadowing. "He is close to withdrawing fully, because of Paul and the rest of it. So close." He met my eyes. "But he has not."

"He's part of the posse now," I told him with a slight smile. "Not sure we'd let him withdraw."

It took him a second to read the meaning behind "posse," but then he smiled. "For selfish reasons, I do hope that is the case."

"Selfish reasons?"

He let out a sigh. "I lose him as well when he withdraws," he told me. "Even after several months I am still shocked when he names me ghastuk—friend—as he did long ago. I do not want to lose that again."

The simple admission touched me—that a demonic lord could crave and treasure a simple thing like friendship.

"You won't lose him," I stated. "I'll make sure of it." My gaze went to the grove. "Lord Elofir, would you excuse me? I have some thinking to do."

He leaned in and kissed my forehead. "Go."

With a parting smile, I hurried down the stairs.

Chapter 47

I found Eilahn in the central atrium below the mezzanines along with Gestamar, Faruk, Wuki, Dakdak, and a half dozen other demons, all crouched around an elaborate arrangement of blankets and bedding. A kittenless Fuzzykins held court from atop the pile like a proud and fierce queen, unruffled while demons cuddled and fussed over her newborns. Surely it was too soon to handle the babies? But what did I know.

Gestamar held one of the tiny kittens cradled oh-so-very gently in his clawed hand while he crooned softly to it. The two ilius coiled around another—apparently not feeding on its essence or anything of that nature, since I rather imagined Eilahn would protest.

Faruk zipped up to me, thrust a soft, warm ball of fluff into my hands before I could protest. "Fillion," she said, then returned to do homage to Fuzzykins.

I stared down at the tiny wriggling kitten in my hands, a feline that wasn't hissing, growling, scratching, or hating me. Not that it had much to work with, eyes closed and barely able to scrabble. I cupped it in my palm, gently stroked its orange and white fur with a finger. Maybe Bryce's suggestion of handling a kitten from early on really would work. Such a trivial consideration in the grand scheme of things, but it felt monumental to me in that moment.

My grove-sense tingled with an activation—Kadir, I noted as I nuzzled the kitten and made goofy noises at it. He was headed to the Little Waterfall, I had no doubt. Yet a couple of minutes later a ripple of movement went through the demons, as if they'd all heard something strange, and within the span of about five seconds every demon with a kitten settled it beside Fuzzykins and scattered, leaving only Eilahn and me. Even big and scary Gestamar quickly and soundlessly retreated down a corridor.

Kadir strode in a heartbeat later, which explained the sudden exodus. I quickly set Fillion with the others as I pulled a trickle of grove power to shield my thoughts. I stood and opened my mouth to demand what he was doing, then closed it. No way would Kadir enter any part of Mzatal's realm without explicit permission. Which means Mzatal invited him here. Which also meant the need was surely dire.

Fuzzykins *mrowed* at him, like a *Hey! Good to see you!* Crazy cat.

The androgynous Kadir glanced my way, then paused and scrutinized the air slightly to the right of me, nostrils flaring. He angled his head, lips parted, in an expression I finally concluded to be burning curiosity. "The *rakkuhr*, How did you clear—" he began, then looked sharply toward the stairs, turned and bounded up.

I followed quickly, though not to the point of running, caught up to him as he stood waiting at the entrance to Mzatal's level. There was no physical barrier between the stairs and the corridor, but demonic lord protocol backed by a number of potent wards served even better.

I took a perverse joy in stepping around him just as Mzatal exited Paul's room, his face unreadable and lined with stress. Without a glance, Mzatal swept past me to engage in a hasty, tension-filled exchange with Kadir. Terms of agreement, I gathered, but so quickly set that even with the grove as translator I could only get the bare gist. *Assessment. Heal if at all possible. Do no harm.* I had no idea what the payment terms were.

Kadir sauntered past me and to Paul's room while Mzatal remained where he was, back to me, hands in fists at his sides.

"Paul is dying," Mzatal said, his voice resonant and remarkably controlled.

Sick fear tightened my chest. Not Paul. Not that sweet, brilliant man. Tears sprang to my eyes at the thought of never hearing his quick laugh again.

I moved to face Mzatal, seized his head in my hands, and

forced him to look at me. "No! Paul needs you, needs to feel you *here*." My heart ached for Mzatal, and I understood the desire, the *need* to separate himself from it all, but I couldn't allow it. I stroked a thumb over his cheek, much the same as he often did to me. "*I* need you, beloved," I said, voice gentling a bit. "You must not close us out."

His face like stone, he reached up and gripped my wrists. I didn't need a mental link to know he fully intended to move my hands and turn away. But instead he met my eyes and went still.

"Mzatal," I murmured as I pushed through the shrouded connection to touch him. *I can help you. Pain shared is pain halved.* "I need you, too."

He closed his eyes and drew a long slow breath. As he exhaled, I felt him, as though he'd opened a crack in his impenetrable wall. He released my wrists, gathered me to him and tucked his head close beside mine. "Zharkat."

"Boss," I said quietly.

He cradled me close for several heartbeats, then straightened and laid his hand against my cheek. "Go to Paul," he told me. "I must attend Elofir in the plexus, then I will join you." He paused. "When Paul is stable, we will talk. Deeply."

I hoped for all our sakes that moment came soon. "Absolutely," I said, then kissed him quickly and hurried into Paul's room.

Bryce sat on the far side of the bed, looking stricken and pissed and grieving all at the same time as he held Paul's limp hand. The covers had been stripped back, and the young man's chest laid bare. I'd seen a lot of corpses, and if Mzatal hadn't told me Paul still lived, I'd have sworn I was looking at one. A discordant chartreuse sigil like tangled neon yarn drifted a handspan above Paul's heart and pulsed a deathly slow cadence.

Already deep into his process, Kadir leaned close to Paul's face and inhaled deeply. *Scenting.* He'd done the same creepy thing to me before, but now I realized it formed an integral—though odd—part of his assessment.

I moved to sit beside a wary and watchful Bryce, put an arm around his shoulders. "Kadir is going to help," I murmured, weirdly convinced it was true.

Bryce's managed a tight nod, his eyes locked on Paul. Kadir added erratic extensions to the tangled sigil over

Paul's chest. Its pulse took on a chaotic and disturbing rhythm—disintegration struggling to fuse with normality. Bryce and I both recoiled, but then a profound familiarity sang through me. I leaned forward in horrified fascination, eyes and arcane sense keenly focused. I laid my hand over my side, over Kadir's convoluted sign etched in my flesh. Like the other scars, it had burned or itched many times, but now it felt cool and . . . alive. *A by-product of Szerain's activation?*

The bizarre sigil continued to flutter and pulse but no longer seemed so irrational. I called to the grove, felt its warm response like the caress of a summer breeze. Kadir traced and enlarged the sigil to create a peculiar mat of neon strands the size of a sheet of paper above Paul, then pushed it down onto him like a bandage. The scar beneath my hand began to pulse, matching the slow death beat of the sigil. I drew more grove energy, then more still as I pressed my hand to Kadir's sigil scar and connected with the . . . chaos.

Kadir froze, snapped his gaze to me as if truly *seeing* me for the first time. His eyes slid down to where my hand covered his mark, deep curiosity in his expression again, along with a trace of shock.

"Don't stop now," I snapped. "He's *dying*. I can help you. I understand it." And I did. No way could I *explain* it, but between the grove and the activated sigil under my palm, I felt the creative genius of the healing sigil, the potential order in the chaos, and I knew how to assist. "Keep tracing."

Yet Kadir didn't move. "Show me, Kara Gillian," he said, the words intense though barely audible. He settled his hands in an *I'm-not-doing-shit* position on his thighs, his violet eyes hungry and burning with curiosity. "Then we bring this one back from the fringe of the void."

Annoyance at his power-play flared, but I understood now what he wanted, what he'd always wanted from me. The beat of the sigil slowed as Paul's life ebbed away, a grim reminder that we didn't have time to waste. I considered arguing that Kadir had an agreement with Mzatal, but figured he'd easily outmaneuver me on that one. Instead, I bared my teeth, reached across with my free hand and gripped a handful of golden hair hard and close to his scalp and gave him what he wanted.

"Here," I growled and opened a flood of grove energy. He'd challenged me at Rhyzkahl's, goaded me in Mzatal's grove. The bastard wanted to experience the enigmatic grove flows through me, but wouldn't simply *ask*. Well, now he had his chance.

The energy of the scar blasted through my body and to his with holy-crap-what-have-I-done intensity. I dragged in a breath, sought balance. Kadir's lips parted, eyes closing as his face took on a disturbingly orgasmic look. In the next breath, chaos poured from him and through me to unite with the scar.

I'd gone too far. Drowning in a sea of madness, I called to the grove, clung to its strong presence as I dragged myself above the chaos. In a flash, I felt a tsunami wave swamp Kadir's tiny island of order and relative sanity.

He jerked against my hand, and his eyes flew open, wild and unfocused, while his aura radiated chaos like a solar storm. Breathing hard, I forced my fingers to unclench from his hair. Kadir fell to his knees, hands white-knuckled on the edge of the bed.

Distantly, I heard Bryce call my name, but couldn't spare him a glance. The healing sigil sputtered with weak flickers. "Kadir!" I shouted. "We have to finish healing Paul or . . ." Or what? "Or you'll violate your agreement with Mzatal." It was a long shot but it worked. He clawed through the chaos to refocus on Paul. But slowly. Too slowly.

I gripped his wrist and placed his hand atop the contorted sigil on Paul's chest. Kadir straightened and spread his fingers, but his attempt to call the needed strands together failed with a shower of arcane sparks. I reached *through* Kadir—just as Szerain had reached through me on the mini-nexus to try to call Vsuhl—used the understanding and bizarre connection to adjust and ignite the sigil. It flashed bright green then shifted into precise and ordered curves. Grove energy still coursing through me, I stared at the pattern of the new sigil, at the order from the chaos. A torrent of information like a million minds connecting at once bombarded me, even as the sigil subsided to a faint glow on Paul's skin.

I jerked my hand from Kadir's wrist, then sat frozen in shock, struggling to suppress the impressions I'd received without losing them. I didn't want to *think* yet. Not here.

Not now. I didn't dare delve into what I'd experienced in that last heartbeat of connection.

Paul drew in a noisy breath, then another.

"Paul!" Bryce leaned in close, called his name over and over. Paul still felt damaged to me, but far less than before.

Radiating chaos, Kadir pushed himself to his feet, looking deeply shaken. With a hissing breath, he drew his nails down his cheek, deeply enough to draw blood. Helori appeared beyond him. Kadir's estranged ptarl. I had no trouble seeing why the two didn't mesh well.

Helori moved in close to Kadir. "Allow me to take you, qaztahl," he said quietly.

Kadir turned on him. "No," he snarled. "No!" He swept from the room without another glance in our direction, taking the suffocating blanket of chaos with him.

A look of profound sadness came over Helori's face, then he moved to the bedside, his eyes on Paul.

Somehow I managed to stand, mundane senses unbalanced while I held the chaos impressions in check. I sensed Mzatal deeply engaged in the plexus and didn't dare extend to even touch him for fear of shattering my balance, losing the hold on the Kadir experience.

"B-Bryce?" Paul opened his eyes blearily.

Joy and relief suffused Bryce's face. "Right here, kid," he said, gathering Paul's hand in his again. "You're going to be okay. Everything's going to be okay."

Helori moved to my side. "Do you want to go to a grove?"

I gave the barest of nods, certain that if I moved too much the seal holding in the impressions and sensations would break.

He took my hand, fingers warm and strong against mine, and in the next breath we were in a grove.

Not just any grove. Warm, salty air, the gentle crash and rush of the sea, the sweet trill of a tropical bird. This was where he'd taken me to recover from Rhyzkahl's treachery.

"Perfect," I whispered, easing very slightly as I soaked in the comfort of it all. Helori touched his forehead to mine, then straightened with a soft smile, turned, and walked up the tree tunnel to leave me in peace. I stayed where I was for several more minutes, until I felt stable enough to sift through the chaos, then followed him out.

A cloudy sky did nothing to detract from the beauty of the turquoise sea as it rolled onto the pristine beach. Helori crouched nearby, in human form now, barefoot and eyes on me. I ran my fingers over the twisted, empty prongs of my ring as I walked toward the water, not caring about the sand that filled my shoes. I didn't slow when I reached the edge of the surf, allowed the sea to surge and retreat around my legs in a comforting caress. I stopped before the water reached my knees, laid my hand over Kadir's still active sigil, and finally allowed the seal to crack.

I staggered from the force of the overwhelming chaos, but I caught myself, called the grove energy to mute the madness.

How can Kadir live like this? I reached deeper, beyond consciousness and into the chaos, into the impressions from the fringe of his essence. Like bubbles in a thick, simmering stew, bursts of *knowing* surfaced and dissolved in the crazy jumble. Not visions. Not words. Flashes of understanding. So much. Too much. *Enough.* With a gasp, I yanked my hand from the sigil.

Helori came up beside me, slid his arm around my waist. I couldn't process and hold it all. Most of it came and slipped away, like the waves around my ankles. But I clung to one understanding with stubborn tenacity.

"Kadir's mother was human," I stated. "He was cut from her—on *Earth*—premature, before his—" I struggled to find words for the alien concept. "—before his arcane nervous system fully formed." I kept my gaze on the water, watched the silver flicker of a school of fish beneath the surface. I didn't need Helori to acknowledge or deny. I *knew.*

And though I didn't *know* in the same way, my gut and logic told me Kadir wasn't an outlier. Every single one of the demonic lords had started his life on Earth, with a human parent.

Helori's breath shuddered out, and he held me a little closer. "They are not ready to know," he said, millennia of pain thick in his voice. "They *cannot* yet know."

I leaned my head against his shoulder. "Please don't take this from me." It would be so easy for him to wipe away this knowledge, this pesky little factoid from my memory. Though even as I said it, I realized he wouldn't have brought me out here to process the knowledge if he'd intended to remove it.

"It is dangerous for you to carry," he replied, voice barely above a whisper, "but I will block it only."

I gave a small nod of thanks, put my arm around his waist and leaned in to his comforting strength. Everything was dangerous, and nowhere was safe.

And nobody was truly who they appeared to be.

Diana Rowland

The Kara Gillian Novels

"Rowland's hot streak continues as she gives her fans another big helping of urban fantasy goodness! The plot twists are plentiful and the action is hard-edged. Another great entry in this compelling series." —*RT Book Review*

"Rowland's world of arcane magic and demons is fresh and original [and her] characters are well-developed and distinct.... Dark, fast-paced, and gripping." —*SciFiChick*

Secrets of the Demon
978-0-7564-0652-3

Sins of the Demon
978-0-7564-0705-6

Touch of the Demon
978-0-7564-0775-9

Fury of the Demon
978-0-7564-0830-5

To Order Call: 1-800-788-6262
www.dawbooks.com

DAW 176

C.S. Friedman
Dreamwalker

All her life Jessica Drake has dreamed of other worlds, some of them similar to her own, others disturbingly alien. She never shares the details with anyone, save her younger brother Tommy. But now someone is asking about those dreams...and about her. A strange woman has been seen watching her house. A visitor to her school attempts to take possession of her dream-inspired artwork.

Why?

As she begins to search for answers it becomes clear that whoever is watching her does not want her to learn the truth. One night her house catches on fire, and when the smoke clears she discovers that her brother has been kidnapped. She must figure out what is going on, and quickly, if she and her family are to be safe.

Following clues left behind on Tommy's computer, determined to find her brother and bring him home safely, Jessica and two of her friends are about to embark on a journey that will test their spirits and their courage to the breaking point, as they must leave their own world behind and confront the source of Earth's darkest legends—as well as the terrifying truth of their own secret heritage.

Available in hardcover February 2014
978-0-7564-0888-6

To Order Call: 1-800-788-6262
www.dawbooks.com

Laura Resnick

The Esther Diamond Novels

"Esther Diamond is the Stephanie Plum of urban
fantasy! Unplug the phone and settle down for a
fast and funny read!"　　—Mary Jo Putney

DISAPPEARING NIGHTLY
978-0-7564-0766-7

DOPPELGANGSTER
978-0-7564-0595-3

UNSYMPATHETIC MAGIC
978-0-7564-0635-6

VAMPARAZZI
978-0-7564-0687-5

POLTERHEIST
978-0-7564-0733-9

THE MISFORTUNE COOKIE
978-0-7564-0847-3

To Order Call: 1-800-788-6262
www.dawbooks.com

Necromancer is such an ugly word
...but it's a title Eric Carter is stuck with.

He sees ghosts, talks to the dead. He's turned it into a lucrative career putting troublesome spirits to rest, sometimes taking on even more dangerous things. For a fee, of course.

When he left L.A. fifteen years ago he thought he'd never go back. Too many bad memories. Too many people trying to kill him.

But now his sister's been brutally murdered and Carter wants to find out why.

Was it the gangster looking to settle a score? The ghost of a mage he killed the night he left town? Maybe it's the patron saint of violent death herself, Santa Muerte, who's taken an unusually keen interest in him.

Carter's going to find out who did it and he's going to make them pay.

As long as they don't kill him first.

Dead Things
by Stephen Blackmoore
978-0-7564-774-2

DAW 210

Seanan McGuire

The InCryptid Novels

"McGuire kicks off a new series with a smart-mouthed, engaging heroine and a city full of fantastical creatures. This may seem like familiar ground to McGuire fans, but she makes New York her own, twisting the city and its residents into curious shapes that will leave you wanting more. Verity's voice is strong and sure as McGuire hints at a deeper history, one that future volumes will hopefully explore."

—*RT Book Reviews*

DISCOUNT ARMAGEDDON
978-0-7564-0713-1

MIDNIGHT BLUE-LIGHT SPECIAL
978-0-7564-0792-6

HALF-OFF RAGNAROK
978-0-7564-0811-4
(Available March 2014)

"The only thing more fun than an October Daye book is an InCryptid book. Swift narrative, charm, great world-building . . . all the McGuire trademarks."

—Charlaine Harris

To Order Call: 1-800-788-6262
www.dawbooks.com

DAW 143

Diana Rowland

"Rowland's delightful novel jumps genre lines with a little something for everyone—mystery, horror, humor, and even a smattering of romance. Not to be missed—all that's required is a high tolerance for gray matter. For true zombiephiles, of course, that's a no brainer."

—*Library Journal*

"An intriguing mystery and a hilarious mix of the horrific and mundane...Humor and gore are balanced by surprisingly touching moments as Angel tries to turn her (un)life around."

—*Publishers Weekly*

My Life as a White Trash Zombie
978-0-7564-0675-2

Even White Trash Zombies
Get the Blues
978-0-7564-0750-6

White Trash Zombie Apocalypse
978-0-7564-0803-9

To Order Call: 1-800-788-6262
www.dawbooks.com

DAW 201